Trisha Telep was the romance and fantasy book buyer at Murder One, the UK's premier crime and romance bookstore. She has recently re-launched this classic bookshop online at www.murderone.co.uk. Originally from Vancouver, Canada, she completed the Master of Publishing program at Simon Fraser University before moving to London. She lives in Hackney with her boyfriend, filmmaker Christopher Joseph.

Also available

The Mammoth Book of 20th Century Science Fiction
The Mammoth Book of Best British Crime
The Mammoth Book of Best Crime Comics
The Mammoth Book of Best Horror Comics
The Mammoth Book of Best of Best New SF
The Mammoth Book of Best New Erotica 8
The Mammoth Book of Best New Horror 19
The Mammoth Book of Best New Manga 3
The Mammoth Book of Best New SF 21
The Mammoth Book of Best War Comics
The Mammoth Book of Bikers
The Mammoth Book of Boys' Own Stuff
The Mammoth Book of Brain Workouts
The Mammoth Book of Celebrity Murders
The Mammoth Book of Comic Fantasy
The Mammoth Book of Comic Quotes
The Mammoth Book of Cover-Ups
The Mammoth Book of CSI
The Mammoth Book of the Deep
The Mammoth Book of Dickensian Whodunnits
The Mammoth Book of Dirty, Sick, X-Rated & Politically Incorrect Jokes
The Mammoth Book of Egyptian Whodunnits
The Mammoth Book of Erotic Online Diaries
The Mammoth Book of Erotic Women
The Mammoth Book of Extreme Fantasy
The Mammoth Book of Funniest Cartoons of All Time
The Mammoth Book of Hard Men
The Mammoth Book of Historical Whodunnits
The Mammoth Book of Illustrated True Crime
The Mammoth Book of Inside the Elite Forces
The Mammoth Book of International Erotica
The Mammoth Book of Jack the Ripper
The Mammoth Book of Jacobean Whodunnits
The Mammoth Book of the Kama Sutra
The Mammoth Book of Killers at Large
The Mammoth Book of King Arthur
The Mammoth Book of Lesbian Erotica
The Mammoth Book of Limericks
The Mammoth Book of Maneaters
The Mammoth Book of Modern Ghost Stories
The Mammoth Book of Modern Battles
The Mammoth Book of Monsters
The Mammoth Book of Mountain Disasters
The Mammoth Book of New Gay Erotica
The Mammoth Book of New Terror
The Mammoth Book of On the Edge
The Mammoth Book of On the Road
The Mammoth Book of Pirates
The Mammoth Book of Poker
The Mammoth Book of Paranormal Romance
The Mammoth Book of Prophecies
The Mammoth Book of Roaring Twenties Whodunnits
The Mammoth Book of Sex, Drugs and Rock 'N' Roll
The Mammoth Book of Short Spy Novels
The Mammoth Book of Sorcerers' Tales
The Mammoth Book of The Beatles
The Mammoth Book of The Mafia
The Mammoth Book of Time Travel Romance
The Mammoth Book of True Crime
The Mammoth Book of True Hauntings
The Mammoth Book of True War Stories
The Mammoth Book of Unsolved Crimes
The Mammoth Book of Vampire Romance
The Mammoth Book of Vintage Whodunnits
The Mammoth Book of Women Who Kill
The Mammoth Book of Zombie Comics

The Mammoth Book of Irish Romance

Edited and with an Introduction
by Trisha Telep

Running Press
Philadelphia · London

Constable & Robinson Ltd
3 The Lanchesters
162 Fulham Palace Road
London W6 9ER
www.constablerobinson.com

First published in the UK by Robinson,
an imprint of Constable & Robinson, 2010

A copy of the British Library Cataloguing in Publication
Data is available from the British Library

UK ISBN 978-1-84901-112-9

1 3 5 7 9 10 8 6 4 2

First published in the United States in 2010 by Running Press Book Publishers

9 8 7 6 5 4 3 2 1
Digit on the right indicates the number of this printing

US Library of Congress number: 2009938217
US ISBN 978-0-7624-3831-0

Running Press Book Publishers
2300 Chestnut Street
Philadelphia, PA 19103-4371

Visit us on the web!

www.runningpress.com

Printed and bound in the EU

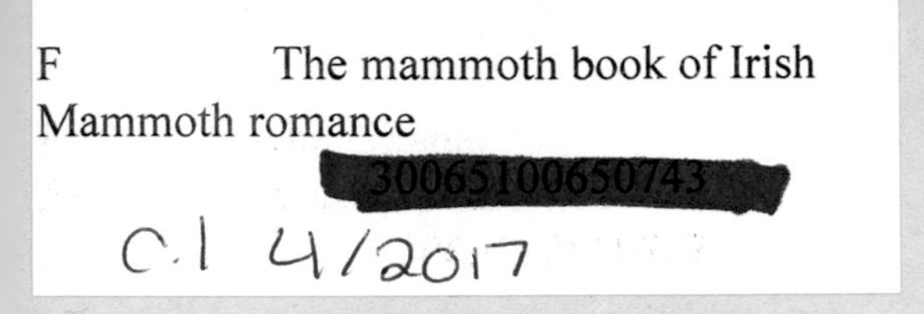

Contents

Acknowledgments

"The Blue Pebble" © by Shirley Kennedy. First publication, original to this anthology. Printed by permission of the author.

"The Ballad of Rosamunde" © by Claire Delacroix, Inc. First publication, original to this anthology. Printed by permission of the author.

"Oracle" © by Margo Maguire. First publication, original to this anthology. Printed by permission of the author.

"The Trials of Bryan Murphy" © by C.T. Adams and Cathy Clamp. First publication, original to this anthology. Printed by permission of the author.

"Nia and the Beast of Killarney Wood" © by Cindy Miles. First publication, original to this anthology. Printed by permission of the author.

"Beyond the Veil" © by Rice Enterprises. First publication, original to this anthology. Printed by permission of the author.

"Shifter Made" © by Jennifer Ashley. First publication, original to this anthology. Printed by permission of the author.

"Daughter of the Sea" © by Kathleen Givens. First publication, original to this anthology. Printed by permission of the author.

"The Warrior" © by Jenna Maclaine. First publication, original to this anthology. Printed by permission of the author.

"Eternal Strife" © by Dara England. First publication, original to this anthology. Printed by permission of the author.

"Quicksilver" © by Cindy Holby. First publication, original to this anthology. Printed by permission of the author.

"The Feast of Beauty" © by Helen Scott Taylor. First publication, original to this anthology. Printed by permission of the author.

"Compeer" © by Roberta Gellis. First publication, original to this anthology. Printed by permission of the author.

"On Inishmore" © by Ciar Cullen. First publication, original to this anthology. Printed by permission of the author.

"The Morrígan's Daughter" © by Susan Krinard. First publication, original to this anthology. Printed by permission of the author.

"Tara's Find" © by Nadia Williams. First publication, original to this anthology. Printed by permission of the author.

"The Skrying Glass" © by Penelope Neri. First publication, original to this anthology. Printed by permission of the author.

"The Houndmaster" © by Sandra L. Patrick. First publication, original to this anthology. Printed by permission of the author.

"The Seventh Sister" © by Sue-Ellen Welfonder. First publication, original to this anthology. Printed by permission of the author.

"By the Light of My Heart" © by Patricia Shagoury. First publication, original to this anthology. Printed by permission of the author.

Introduction

Ireland is a land of romance. Pure and simple. And you don't have to be an expert in Irish lore to appreciate the fantastic opportunities that Ireland offers romance writers: its tumultuous, battle-rife history of clans, territories and kingdoms; its pantheon of heroes, goddesses, saints and magic to rival Rome's, and its legends of the most fantastical beasts and magical creatures ever recorded. You don't need, either, to know everything about the *Tuatha Dė Danann* to appreciate these ancient gods of *eire* with their beauty, immense strength, and immortality. Irish legend and mythology are full of the ultimate heroes and the most romantic of stories. It is to a great extent in these Celtic cycles, tales and myths that romances – full of heroes, chivalry, courtly love and adventure – were originally born. No wonder popular writers from Tolkein to J.K. Rowling to George Lucas have been seized and inspired by the history of Ireland.

Because Ireland's history was an oral history until it was recorded by Christian monks in the Middle Ages, you can clearly see where problems might have arisen with an accurate portrayal of Ireland's wild pagan past! The ancient tribal Ireland of druids and high kings, therefore, is always ripe for reinterpretation. This is why such tales and folklore are constantly rewoven and rewritten; they are always a work in progress, a vibrant recollection of the past, still vital and alive today. It's also why you'll find many different interpretations, many different names and dispositions for similar characters.

Here are stories that weave a fiction from existing legend, stories that explore existing myth in greater depth, and yet more stories that stray from established lore entirely with a healthy dose of poetic licence, using Ireland's constellation of magical creatures in new, exciting ways. And then, of course, here are stories that are simply pure, unabashed, unashamed romance.

And the faery folk seem to have their fingers in most of the trouble and adventure that occurs. Love affairs between mortals and the faery host are put to the test, while the High King of the *Daoine* Sidhe, Finvarra's insatiable appetite for mortal women is legendary. Fairy interference – er, help – in mortal life in general is definitely a recurring theme in this collection. But you'll also be confronted with remnants of Ireland's Viking past, its legendary warriors, battles fought and won, and the mysterious sea god Lir and his mermaids.

Jenna Maclaine brings Morrigan, the goddess of war, and legendary warrior, Cuchulainn to life as erotic, constantly battling, immortals. And as always we have a few stories that reach out to the wider world of an author's current series (see, for instance, Margo Maguire's world of the Druzai). I am also proud to announce the brilliant debut of a brand-new series with a story from Jennifer Ashley presenting her exciting Shifters!

A tumult of styles and themes then, this is a refresher course in Irish history, with a nod to the behemoth that is paranormal romance. Here are some writers with the power to really take you on a ride through a Celtic mythological past, who can definitely hold their own amongst all the vampires, werewolves, shape-shifters and ghosts populating the bestseller lists today.

So why not allow these Irish paranormals – these *gancanaghs* (ethereal lovers who seduce young women then disappear), *alp-luachras* (evil, greedy fairies) and Irish High Kings of lore – a little room of their own? Let these writers take you into the lush, romantic, and above all magical heart of an Ireland that is, was and might-have-been.

Trisha Telep

The Blue Pebble

Shirley Kennedy

England – 1814

Passengers on the Royal Mail coach to London were surprised when the coach came to a jangling stop on the road not far from the town of Shrewsbury. No houses around. Only a winding driveway could be seen leading up through a heavy growth of trees to an immense Tudor-style mansion that nestled atop a low hill.

"This here's Chatfield Court, miss," the coachman shouted. "I'll toss your luggage down."

"Thank you kindly, sir."

While the pretty young woman in her twenties climbed from the coach, the other passengers looked at each other askance. Surely the girl should not have to carry that large portmanteau up the hill by herself. One of the gentlemen passengers stuck his head out the window and called up, "I say, coachman, can't you take her up the driveway to the entrance? We don't mind the extra time."

"Can't do it, sir. Against the rules."

"That's quite all right," the young woman assured him in a rich Irish brogue. She squared her shoulders. "This isn't the first heavy load I've carried in my life. I'll be fine." She picked up the battered portmanteau, smiled, waved a quick goodbye and started trudging up the hill.

The coach started up again, the remaining passengers making clicking noises and shaking their heads. That they were concerned about a passenger they'd known only hours was surprising. She had not uttered more than a few pleasantries, only briefly mentioning she'd been a schoolteacher in Ireland, as had her mother who had recently passed away. Mostly she sat silently gazing out the window; yet despite the paucity of her words, they all recognized an agreeable quality about her and wished her well.

"I liked that girl," one gentlemen said. "Don't know exactly why, but she had a certain . . . I guess you could say, serenity about her."

"More than that. It was like a special aura that surrounded her," one of the ladies chimed in. "It was almost as if I felt calmer in her presence."

"She had a magical quality," said another.

The gentleman laughed. "Magic? Well, I don't know as I'd go that far."

The lady nodded emphatically. "Magic. I felt it. I don't know what it was, but that girl had a special gift which we all felt, and don't you tell me otherwise."

Halfway up the driveway, Evleen O'Fallon had to stop and catch her breath. The heat of the summer day, plus the weight of the heavy portmanteau had done her in. As she rested and wiped her brow, she looked up the hill towards the dark stone mansion called Chatfield Court.

"I'm sure you will like it," her mother had said on her deathbed. "Lord Beaumont assured me you would."

Mother's gone. A tear rolled down Evleen's cheek. *I miss her so. What will I do without her?*

At the end, even through her suffering, Mama had thought of Evleen. "All your brothers and sisters have a place to stay, except you. As you know, I have sold the cottage, so you cannot stay here." She clutched a letter in her fingers, one she had received only the day before. "Some time ago, when I knew I would never leave this bed, I wrote to Lord Beaumont in England."

"But why?" Evleen was astounded.

"You are aware that Lord Beaumont's late wife was a cousin of ours. So I wrote and asked if he would take you in." She'd handed the letter to Evleen. "Here is his reply. Read for yourself."

With reluctant fingers, Evleen took the letter and began to read.

My Dear Cousin,

I am sorry for your illness and trust you will soon regain your health. In the sad event you do not, rest assured I shall be happy to give a home to your oldest daughter, Evleen. If she's as gifted as you say, perhaps she can help with the education of my son, Peter, who is seven. Since his mother passed away, he's been quite precocious and needs a firm hand.

I look forward to meeting Evleen. Rest assured, she will be treated not as a servant but one of the family.

Beaumont

When she finished, Evleen let the letter fall to her lap in dismay. "Leave Ireland? Never! How can I go and live with strange people in a strange land?"

"You will because you must," Mama answered firmly. "But one warning I must give you."

"And what is that?" Evleen asked, still numb with shock.

"You must never use the blue pebble in England. In fact, it would be best if you threw it away."

Evleen touched a small, bright blue pebble, strung by a leather thong around her neck. "But why?"

Mama looked deep into her eyes. "Because the English would never believe a poor girl from Ireland is possessed with magical powers. They would laugh at you – make your life a misery if you even suggested such a thing."

"All right, I promise," Evleen readily agreed. "I suspect the pebble would be useless in England anyway. I certainly don't expect Merlin to follow me."

"You had best throw it in the creek right now."

Somehow the thought of throwing the pebble away did not appeal to her. “Perhaps I shall take it along – just as a kind of souvenir.”

“Suit yourself.” Mama reached for her hand and clasped it tight. “Whatever happens, always hold your head high. You must never forget you are an Irish princess, that your father was Ian O’Fallon, son of the Duke of Connaught, who was a direct descendant of one of Ireland’s ancient kings who reigned over one of the earliest Celtic kingdoms.”

“I shall never forget, Mama.”

And she wouldn’t. Now, with a determined nod, Evleen picked up the portmanteau and resumed her trek up the driveway. No, she would never forget, but what good would being an Irish princess do her here in this strange land? Ah well, no matter. Only the future counted now.

I shall be brave. I shall make Mama proud.

“So, Miss O’Fallon, you are from Ireland?”

Seated on a silk upholstered sofa in the grand salon of Chatfield Court, Evleen hid her disappointment. Lord Beaumont had not been there to greet her, although he was expected back from London at any moment. She gazed into the cold grey eyes of Lady Beaumont, Lord Beaumont’s mother. “Indeed I am from Ireland. County Tipperary to be exact. I lived there all my life.”

Lady Beaumont, a stout woman with a large face and snow-white hair, cast an amused glance at the two other occupants of the room: Lydia, her daughter, and a giddy young woman named Bettina, soon to become her daughter-in-law. “Fancy that! I don’t know much about Ireland although I understand they are all quite poor.”

“Don’t they raise sheep and live mainly in hovels?” asked Lydia, a plain young woman in her twenties who appeared to wear a permanent sneer on her lips.

Of the two young women, Bettina, a slender girl of twenty or so, was the prettiest, with creamy white skin and a circle of bouncy blonde ringlets around her forehead. In a giggly voice she asked Evleen, "Isn't Ireland where the fairies live? And the elves and leprechauns?"

Yes, it is, Evleen thought, but wisely didn't say. "Not all Irish are poor," she evenly replied. "As for elves, fairies and leprechauns, I cannot say."

She'd been invited to the grand salon for tea by these three ladies, who obviously seemed to think she had just arrived from the moon. She knew they were laughing at her. In fact, since the moment she set foot into this huge room with its marble fireplace and plush furnishings, she'd felt acutely uncomfortable. It didn't help that the outfit she wore – plain wool skirt, wool jacket, simple brimmed hat and high top boots – was acceptable fashion for Ireland, but compared to the elaborate dresses these ladies wore, she might as well be dressed in a gunny sack. And these were just their morning gowns! Already they'd discussed their afternoon gowns, strolling gowns, evening gowns and who-knew-what-else kinds of gowns. Evleen took a sip of tea from her fine china cup, gripping the fragile handle uncomfortably. So different from home, where she drank her tea from a chipped mug and stirred it with a tin spoon.

Lydia was speaking. "So what did you do in Ireland? Is there a ton? Do you have seasons?"

"I taught school until my mother took ill, " Evleen earnestly replied. "This past year I stayed home to take care of her. And yes, we have seasons – winter, spring, summer and autumn, just as you have here."

For some reason, her reply set up gales of laughter from all three women. "Lydia doesn't mean that kind of season," Lady Beaumont explained in a lofty tone. "She means a social season, such as when we go down to London for the parties and balls."

"Oh, I see." Evleen could not prevent the blush she felt spreading up her neck and over her cheeks. Such a gaffe she'd made! And she hadn't been here an hour yet. She would never fit in with these people, nor them with her. *I want to go home.*

The door opened. A tall, powerfully built man in his early thirties entered, followed by a slender, fair-haired boy of seven or so. "Hello, everyone," he said in a deep commanding voice. He caught sight of Evleen. "I see our cousin from Ireland has arrived."

Evleen hadn't known what she'd expected, but certainly not this devilishly handsome man who stood before her. What gorgeous blue eyes! What a beautiful head of hair, dark, with a slight wave and an unruly lock falling over his forehead. She arose and dipped an unsteady curtsy, hoping she didn't look too much like a country bumpkin. "I am pleased to meet you, Lord Beaumont."

Beaumont bowed in return. "Delighted to meet you, Miss O'Fallon. Welcome to England." He placed a firm hand on the boy's shoulder. "This is my son, Peter. He's without a governess right now and I was hoping you might see to his education, at least temporarily. Not as a governess, you understand. I consider you one of the family."

"That's very kind of you, sir. I'll be happy to help any way I can."

"Very good then," Beaumont answered. Evleen noted he had yet to smile. She caught an air of unhappiness about him, a certain remoteness. Perhaps he was still grieving over the death of his first wife, Millicent. But still, she noted, he wasn't grieving so much that he wasn't planning to marry again.

Bettina arose from her chair and went to greet him, thrusting her arm possessively through his. "Richard, darling, so lovely to have you back." She cast a quick, unfriendly glance at Evleen, as if she resented his wasting even one moment of time on his poor cousin-by-marriage from Ireland. "Your dear mother and sister have been helping with our wedding plans."

"How very nice," Beaumont answered absent-mindedly. Evleen caught a certain indifference in his voice. He ignored Bettina and continued, "We must get you settled in, Miss O'Fallon. There's a bedchamber on the third floor next to my sister's. I thought it might please you."

Lady Beaumont uttered an audible gasp. "Are you sure, Richard? I had thought—"

"Thought what, Mama?"

"A room on the fourth floor would be much more suitable." Lady Beaumont's lips had pursed into a tight, disapproving line.

"The servants' floor? I think not," Beaumont answered firmly. "Evleen is Millicent's cousin's child. As such, she's a member of the family and will be treated accordingly."

"But of course," his mother answered with ill-concealed irritation. She cast stone-cold eyes at Evleen. "We're so happy to have you, Miss O'Fallon. I trust you'll be happy here. Dinner is at eight."

Evleen nodded a thank you and sent a small smile in return. Except for Lord Beaumont himself, she felt as welcome as the plague.

What a beautiful room, Evleen thought when she stepped into her bedchamber. Never had she seen such luxury. With its fine furnishings and lovely view of the rear gardens it was a far cry from the tiny room off the kitchen she had shared with two sisters. Ordinarily, she'd be thrilled, but the chilly reception she'd received in the drawing room made for a heavy heart. She sank to a chair by the window and gazed at the sculptured gardens that lay behind Chatfield Court. Ah, what wouldn't she give to be home right now! She closed her eyes and pictured her family's cottage. Built of stone, with lime-washed walls, it nestled in one of County Tipperary's lush green valleys. The forested slopes of the Galtees, Ireland's highest mountain range, lay not far beyond.

Next to the cottage were the scattered ruins of Tualetha, an ancient monastery, spread over several acres. As a child, Evleen often visited the ruins. She and her brothers and sisters liked to play hide-and-seek amidst the crumbled remains of stone buildings and huge tombstones, decorated with faded Celtic carvings, which towered over their heads.

Adrift in her memories, Evleen reached to touch the blue pebble that still hung around her neck. Despite her mother's advice, she could not bear to part with it, although now she always hid it beneath her clothing and had vowed never to use it. As they had countless times before, her thoughts drifted to the day, when she was just eight years old, that she visited the ruins alone. She had brought a book along and was sitting on a flat rock next to an ancient cairn when the persistent cawing of a bird caught her attention. Looking up from her book, she was surprised to see a huge black raven sitting on the low branch of an oak tree. It seemed to be staring at her. Suddenly the bird spread its wings and flew away. As it did so, a small black feather fell from its wing to the ground.

Evleen shut her book, slid off the rock, and went to retrieve the feather. As she bent to pick it up, she saw it had fallen next to a curious looking pebble of bright azure blue. How odd. Never had she seen a pebble of such a colour. While she examined it, she heard the cawing of the raven again. It had flown a short distance away and was now perched on another tree limb, staring at her and flapping its wings. Did it want her to follow him? It would certainly seem so.

Holding the feather and the pebble, Evleen followed the raven to where it sat in the tree. Just as she arrived, it again flew away, heading towards the dense woods close by. When again the bird alighted on a branch and stared at her, she knew for certain it wanted her to follow.

Her curiosity aroused, Evleen followed the raven on a path that led deep into the woods. The bird continued to lead, then stop to wait for her, until she realized she had gone into the woods deeper than she ever had before. She felt no fear, though, and followed the path up the side of a gently sloping mountain to the entrance of a cave with a yawning mouth. Still unafraid, she entered the cave. Finding herself in near-total darkness, she felt her way along the walls of a short, narrow chamber until she emerged into a room with smooth stone walls that shone like crystal. In the centre of the room, an old man with a long white beard, wearing a white robe, stood behind a steaming cauldron. The room was lit, the light seeming to come from everywhere. Finally she realized it emanated from the crystalline walls. At last a shiver of fear ran through her. She turned to run, but before she could, the old man spoke. "I have been waiting for you."

Astounded, she asked, "Who are you?"

He ignored her and instead waved his hands over the cauldron and intoned, "I call today on the strength of Heaven, Light of the Sun, Radiance of the Moon, Splendour of Fire, Speed of Lightning, Depth of the Sea."

She stood frozen during his incantation. When he finished, he addressed her again. "I am Merlin the Magician. Surely you have heard of me, Evleen."

"But how did you know my name?"

The old man smiled. "I have followed your progress since the day you were born."

"But why?" she asked, her voice trembling.

"You are a direct descendant of Queen Maeve, who reigned as Queen of Ireland back in the days of the Druids. She was a warrior whom I admired tremendously. Maeve was one of the great female figures of Ireland, a most splendid woman. Originally she was a goddess and only later became the queen of mortal men, although she always kept her magical powers." Merlin sighed. "I would tell you more, but you're a little girl and can only understand so much. But it's time you knew that you, too, have been endowed with magical powers."

Evleen gasped in astonishment. "Me? I cannot believe it!"

"Rub the blue pebble and make a wish."

She thought for a moment, searching her mind for something simple to request. Where had the raven gone? Rubbing the blue pebble, she said, "I wish to see the raven again."

In a twinkling, Merlin vanished and the black raven appeared, sitting on a nearby perch glaring at her with its beady bright eyes. "It can't be!" she cried in alarm.

In another instant, the bird had disappeared and Merlin stood before her again. "Over the years you will find I take many forms and shapes. The raven is only one."

"Over the years?" she asked

"This is only the beginning. My child, it is time you became aware of your magic powers. You must learn to use them wisely."

"But how will I always know what is wise?"

"I shall always be there to help." In another instant, Merlin had disappeared again, replaced by the raven that, in a great show of cawing and flapping of its wings, left her standing there and flew from the cave.

Evleen found her way from the cave and ran home. When she reached her cottage, she burst through the door, crying, "Mama, Mama, wait 'til you hear!" When she finished relating her story about the raven, the cave and Merlin, her mother seemed not the least surprised.

"I have always known there was something special about you, Evleen. Now I know what it is. Bear in mind, you must always use your powers wisely."

"Just what Merlin said."

"Then you have been warned. You must never take your powers lightly."

And Evleen never did. While she grew up, Merlin paid her many visits. Sometimes he taught her such things as the Druidic Symbols of Mastery, or a lesson from the Druid's Book of the Pherylit. Other times, he let her try out her magic powers. She used them judiciously, casting a spell to heal an animal that was sick, or for a lost item that was soon found.

Only once did Merlin refuse her request. When her mother lay dying, Evleen pleaded, "Please, can't we heal her?"

In reply, Merlin drew a perfect circle on the ground before her. "Within the perfect symmetry of a circle is held the essential nature of the universe. Strive to learn from it . . . to reflect that order."

She understood immediately. She could not interrupt life's cycle. Even Merlin's magic had its limits.

Now, in her new bedchamber, Evleen put thoughts of home behind her, turning them instead to her pitiful wardrobe. How she wished she could use her magic powers to replace every shabby piece of clothing she owned. Lady Beaumont had told her dinner was at eight. She must appear suitably dressed, but what could she wear? Nothing she had brought could begin to match the gorgeous gowns she knew the ladies would be wearing.

Just then, a knock sounded on the door. Evleen opened it to find a middle-aged, prim-faced woman dressed in a maid's uniform, with a white satin gown draped over one arm. In a French accent, she announced, "I am Yvette, Lady Beaumont's lady's maid. Lord Beaumont sent me. He thought I could be of assistance in dressing you for dinner tonight." She held up the gown. "This was his wife's, poor thing. She hardly wore it before the typhoid struck her down. You seem about the same size."

Yvette proved to be a godsend and, when eight o'clock arrived, Evleen took one final, incredulous look at herself in the mirror. The high-waisted gown fitted perfectly over her slender figure. But it was so low cut! Never in Ireland had so much of her bosom been exposed. "Think nothing of it, miss," Yvette assured her. "You will find it is quite modest by today's standards."

Evleen regarded her thick, dark auburn hair, which Yvette had piled atop her head in a becoming style with soft curls and fastened with a set of pearl combs. Pearl earrings dangled from her ears, matched by a luminous pearl necklace. The result? Never in her life had Evleen looked so . . . so . . . the word was *beautiful*, but modesty prevented her from saying so, or even thinking it to herself. Instead, she exclaimed, "Yvette, you have a wonderful way with both clothes and hair."

"And here is your fan, miss." Yvette produced a delicate ivory and white lace fan, which Evleen took reluctantly. Never had she owned such an accessory. A fan was not necessary in Ireland, she thought amusedly, especially when she was scrubbing clothes or cutting peat from the bogs and dragging it home.

"So what do I do with the fan, Yvette?"

"You flutter it, miss, and you flirt with it. The fan has a language all its own. You'll soon learn it if you're here long enough."

When Evleen hurried down the stairs to dinner, she was grateful she looked her best, yet dreaded another confrontation with the hostile ladies who no doubt would have preferred she eat with the servants. She found Lord Beaumont already seated at the head of the table, unsmiling as usual. His eyes opened wide when she sailed, head held high, into the dining room in her lovely gown, daintily holding her fan. "Good evening, Miss O'Fallon," he said, surprise in his voice. "You look quite lovely this evening."

"Isn't that one of Millicent's old gowns?" Lady Beaumont asked, none too kindly.

Beaumont replied, "There's no reason why Miss O'Fallon can't make use of it."

In a voice edged with sarcasm, his sister, Lydia, said, "How charitable of you, Richard, always lending the poor a helping hand."

Beaumont replied, "As a matter of fact, I'm sending for a seamstress to refresh Miss O'Fallon's wardrobe." Then he nodded towards a balding, thick-lipped man sitting to his right before addressing Evleen. "I don't believe you have met our cousin, Mr Algernon Kent, who's just come up from London to stay with us a while."

A feeling of dislike overtook Evleen but she nodded politely at Beaumont's cousin. Something about him was repulsive. Maybe it was the lecherous look in his near-lashless eyes when he gazed pointedly at her exposed bosom. She resisted the impulse to tug up the bodice of her gown.

Lord Beaumont spent much of the dinner discussing his son. "You will find he's extremely bright and never stops asking questions. By the way, Miss O'Fallon, the nursery and classroom are a bit cramped. While the weather is warm, you might find the gazebo at the bottom of the garden more accommodating for the teaching of lessons."

Evleen gladly thanked him, always happy for the opportunity to be outdoors. Later, after dinner, she became acquainted with a quaint English custom she'd never heard of in Ireland: the women adjourned to the drawing room while the men stayed at the dining table drinking brandy and smoking their cigars.

"Do you play cards, Miss O'Fallon?" Lady Beaumont asked as the ladies settled in the drawing room. Evleen shook her head. Beaumont's mother feigned a disappointed sigh. "What a pity. Well, I suppose you could stay here and read while we play, but of course if you're tired you might wish to retire for the night."

Lady Beaumont so obviously wanted rid of her, Evleen instantly said she was tired and left for her bedchamber. On her way out, she overheard Bettina and Lydia discussing Cousin Algernon.

"I cannot stand that loathsome man," said Bettina. "He's such a toad."

Lydia laughed. "Perhaps we could match him up with our little peasant from Ireland."

"If we could get rid of her, I'm all for it," Bettina replied with a giggle.

Evleen quickened her step. She did not want to hear the rest. She'd had quite enough of hurtful remarks for one day. Not that tomorrow would be any better, she sadly realized.

"Tell me about Ireland," said Peter. "I want to hear."

Evleen and Peter, both early risers, had eaten an early breakfast before the rest of the house was awake, then found their way to the gazebo at the bottom of the rear gardens. They were accompanied by Peter's beloved dog, Cromwell, a lively brown and white Border collie who followed Peter wherever he went.

What a lovely spot, Evleen reflected as she gazed at lush green lawns, clipped hedges and bright flowers. She was grateful the friendly little boy had taken to her instantly. She would start his lessons tomorrow, but today they would talk and get acquainted. Cromwell lay down next to his master and went to sleep while she began. "Let's start at the beginning. Ireland's earliest dwellers were the Celts, who lived many thousands of years ago. They had many gods and the Druids were their priests . . ."

Peter listened intently while she went on to tell more of Ireland's history. Finally the child pointed to the blue pebble that hung from her neck. "What is that?" he asked.

Somehow the pebble had slipped from beneath her jacket. She hastened to conceal it. "It's a magic pebble," she replied, knowing one could be perfectly honest with a child of seven who would take such information in his stride. "But you mustn't tell anyone."

Peter nodded vigorously. "Oh, I won't, I promise. But you must show me how it works."

"It only works when I'm in Ireland, but I'll show you how it's done." Evleen pulled out the pebble and rubbed it with her finger. "It's as simple as this. Now if I were in Ireland, a raven would appear and then—"

"But there is a raven," Peter interrupted.

She started to tell him there could not be any such thing when she heard a loud caw from behind her. Surely not! Her heart leaped.

Peter pointed. "It's behind you on that limb."

Slowly, reluctantly, she turned her head. The raven gazed down at her – she could swear – with triumphant eyes.

"Dear God in heaven!" She leaped to her feet and called frantically to the bird, "Go away! You are not supposed to be here!"

The raven sat silently, its sharp eyes watching her every move.

"Here comes my father," Peter said.

Oh, no! In dismay, Evleen spied Lord Beaumont striding through the garden. In seconds he would be here. She turned to the raven. "Please. The English don't believe in magic. You must go."

To her relief, the bird cawed softly one time then flew away. By the time Lord Beaumont arrived, Evleen had somewhat composed herself, although her heart still hammered in her chest. "Lord Beaumont." She dipped a curtsy, fighting to control the tremor in her voice.

Beaumont stepped into the gazebo and seated himself in a wicker chair across from hers. "Do sit down, Miss O'Fallon.

I came to see how you were doing." He glanced fondly at his son. "It appears he's taken to you."

"He's a fine little boy, and very bright. We shall get along fine."

He spoke to Peter. "Go feed your rabbits, son. I wish to speak to Miss O'Fallon alone."

After the boy left, followed by the faithful Cromwell, Evleen regarded Beaumont with questioning eyes. "I trust I have not done something wrong."

"Of course not." Beaumont leaned back in his chair and casually stretched his long legs in front of him. How handsome he looked, so different from the men she had known in Ireland, whose Sunday best attire could not hold a candle to Beaumont's elegant cutaway frock coat, perfectly tied cravat, breeches that fitted revealingly tight over his well-muscled calves. And those polished Hessian boots! So very masculine, so very appealing . . .

Uh-oh, he's been talking and I haven't been listening.

He took a long moment to gaze at her. His lip quirked, as if he were amused, but she didn't know why. "I find you an interesting woman, Miss O'Fallon."

"Call me Evleen. We're not nearly so formal at home."

"In that case, call me Richard."

She asked, "So why do you find me interesting when I'm only your poor Irish relative?"

"Because there's something about you . . ." His forehead creased in a frown. "You surprise me."

"In what way?"

"I would have thought a woman as attractive as you would be married by now."

"We Irish don't marry as young as you do in England." Modesty prevented her from recounting the number of proposals she'd received over the years, all rejected. "When I do marry, if I ever do, it will be to someone with whom I have fallen madly, passionately in love."

"So you've never been in love?"

"Not yet." She tipped her head quizzically. "Didn't you marry for love?"

"No, of course not." At her look of surprise, he continued, "Many marriages are arranged in England, as was mine. Rank . . . family background . . . the size of the dowry are more important considerations than whether one has been struck by Cupid's arrow. Actually . . ." He paused, weighing his next words. "I became most fond of my first wife. Millicent was a fine woman whom I greatly admired and respected."

"What about Bettina?"

She feared she'd asked too bold a question, but he readily answered. "Bettina is the youngest daughter of the Duchess of Derbyshire. Vast fortune. One of England's oldest families. Extremely generous dowry, of course. My mother's cup runneth over."

"But you don't love her either?"

A half-smile crossed his face. "I was raised to believe honour and duty come first. Thus, for me, love has never been an option."

How very sad, she thought, but decided not to say. They continued to chat, Beaumont showing no desire to leave. When his son returned, he arose reluctantly. "I have enjoyed our conversation. If you don't mind, I shall come back from time to time in order to check on Peter's progress."

"I wouldn't mind at all." And she wouldn't. Watching him stride away, she found herself admiring his broad shoulders and the easy grace with which he moved. Bettina was a lucky woman. Very lucky indeed.

In the days that followed, Evleen fell into a comfortable routine with Peter. She conducted his lessons in the classroom or, weather permitting, in the gazebo. Either way, Beaumont often joined them. Sometimes he sat quietly and listened; other times he joined in the discussions with a lively give-and-take of English history, or whatever was the topic, helping to answer his inquisitive son's endless questions. Best of all, she discovered he had a deliciously subtle sense of humour, often revealed when the corners of his mouth quirked into an irresistible little grin.

She welcomed his visits, even looked forward to them with increasing anticipation. But the trouble was, Beaumont's new-found attention to his son's education did not go unnoticed by the ladies of the house. Evleen had hoped that in time she could make friends, but now their enmity was even more evident. She overheard Lady Beaumont and Lydia again one day as she stood outside the drawing room.

"There is something very strange about her," Lady Beaumont was saying. "In fact, poor, dear Millicent once mentioned her Irish side of the family possessed certain mystical powers. At the time, I thought she had taken leave of her senses, but now I'm beginning to wonder."

Lydia replied, "There's something unpleasantly mysterious about all the Irish, what with their Celtic culture and those ancient Druids who, I understand, practised all sorts of strange, unholy rites – all quite unacceptable."

"I cannot imagine why Richard spends so much time with her," Lady Beaumont went on. "He claims he's only interested in Peter's lessons, but quite frankly I don't trust the woman. What if she casts some sort of spell over him? Well, she had best be careful. If she dares show the least sign of any so-called magical powers, I shall send her packing, and I don't care what Richard says."

"At least he'll be married soon," replied Lydia. "That should ease our minds."

"And Bettina's, too," Lady Beaumont answered with a caustic laugh.

Evleen's heart sank as she listened. How unfair! What had she done to deserve such hatred? Her behaviour with Beaumont had been completely beyond reproach. Not only that, she had taken great pains to be pleasant and civil to these difficult women who were bound and determined to dislike her. As for her magic, she stood by her promise. Such a promise wasn't easy, for often, when she was teaching Peter his lessons in the gazebo, she saw the black raven sitting on a nearby branch. It would stare down at her with a beckoning look in its eye, as if it were telling her that Merlin could hardly wait to reveal himself before her. So tempting! But she had refrained from rubbing the blue pebble. Mama had been very wise indeed to make her promise never to use her magic powers in disbelieving England.

But as much as she missed Merlin and his magic, a deeper sorrow lay heavy on her mind. For the first time in her life, she had fallen madly, passionately in love. Each night, she lay in her bed staring into the darkness, her anguished heart keeping her from sleep. She could see no way out of her constant misery, for the man she had fallen in love with was Lord Beaumont – a man she could never marry; a man hopelessly beyond her reach.

Late one afternoon, after Peter had left, Evleen remained in the gazebo to tidy up. She was pleased with the way the day had gone. Peter continued to be a delightful pupil who absorbed knowledge like a sponge. Also, on a personal note, she was wearing a new gown just completed by the seamstress. Made of a soft blue batiste, it had three satin bands of a darker blue circling the skirt and delicate white lace frills decorating the bodice and sleeves. Never had she owned such a beautiful gown. With her auburn hair contrasting with the blue, she knew she looked her best.

She had almost finished putting the lesson books away when Beaumont appeared. "How did the lessons go today?"

"Very well," she answered, her heart quickening at sight of him. She searched for something safe to say. "Have you noticed the sunset? It's quite beautiful."

He came to stand beside her. Together they watched the setting sun paint puffy clouds with gorgeous streaks of pink and gold. Finally he remarked with a sigh, "It won't be long now."

"Your wedding?"

"My wedding," he replied in a voice totally devoid of enthusiasm.

"You must be very happy." What else could she say?

"Happy?" he responded sharply. "How can I be happy when I—?" Abruptly he turned to face her. His hands gripped her shoulders, causing her to gasp in surprise. "Ah, Evleen, Evleen . . . the very thought of marrying Bettina is repugnant to me, not when I . . ." He drew a deep breath, seeming to attempt to control his emotions. "Do you know how beautiful you look in that blue dress?"

Taken aback by his intensity, she sought to make light of it. "The seamstress did rather a good job, I thought. She—"

He gripped her shoulders even tighter. "I love you, Evleen," he burst out, his voice breaking with emotion. "With all my heart I have fallen in love with you." He swung her into the circle of his arms, claiming her lips as he crushed her to him. Stunned, her knees weak, she returned his kiss with a pent-up hunger that spoke of the endless nights she had lain awake imagining herself in his arms. Finally, raising his mouth from hers, he gazed into her eyes. "I want to make love to you, my beautiful Evleen," he said, his breath coming hard. "I want to spend the rest of my life with you. Day and night my thoughts are full of you – your charming smile, your wit, your lovely Irish laugh, everything about you . . . Oh, God, I want you so much I—"

He seemed to catch himself. With an oath he thrust her away and strode to the other side of the gazebo. For a time, he stood with his back to her, hands clasped behind him, staring out at the garden. She could hear his breathing return to normal as he slowly composed himself. Finally he turned. "You must forgive me. I had no right to touch you."

"But I wanted you to," she replied. "I, too—"

"No! Don't say any more." He regarded her with anguished eyes. "I am betrothed. Do you know what that means in England? It means the moment I asked for Bettina's hand in marriage, my fate was sealed. I cannot simply change my mind. If I did, my family would be in complete disgrace. I, myself, would receive the cut direct."

"What is that?"

"Just like it sounds. People would not speak to me. If they saw me coming, they would turn their backs."

"How cruel."

"Yes, it's cruel, but that's the way of it in our society. I could endure it if I had to, but I cannot have my family disgraced. More than that, it's a matter of honour." He laughed bitterly. "Oh, yes, I am a man of honour, if nothing else. I shall keep my word. Forget this ever happened, Evleen. It will never happen again." With an expression of grief, mixed with self-reproach, he abruptly left the gazebo and strode back to the mansion with determined steps.

Evleen sank into a chair, her knees so weak she could not stand. Her thoughts swirled between joy and sorrow. Joy because he loved her. Sorrow because theirs was a love that was utterly hopeless. What should she do now? She could go away, but where? She could never return to Ireland – the cottage had been sold, nothing was left for her there. She could seek a position as a governess somewhere. She hated the thought of it. Horror stories abounded concerning the abysmal treatment of governesses in some of the great mansions.

Worst of all, if she left, what would happen to Peter? The boy had been lagging in his studies before she came, no doubt still grieving for his mother. But since her arrival, he had blossomed, showing a brilliance that must not be allowed to lie fallow again.

That settled it. She would stay even if she must suffer the pain of constantly seeing Richard together with his new bride. For Peter's sake, she would endure it.

"Ah, Miss O'Fallon, there you are!"

Algernon. A shudder of dislike ran through her. Cousin Algernon had remained at Chatfield Court the whole time she'd been there. Nobody could stand the man. The maids fled at the sight of him. Rumour had it that Lord Beaumont had chastised his cousin more than once, warning him to stop annoying the ladies as well as the female servants. Obviously Algernon had ignored all admonitions. Evleen noted that the spark of lust still gleamed in his eye, and the disgusting I-am-God's-gift-to-women expression remained on his pasty face.

She scrambled to her feet and began collecting books and papers. "Yes, here I am," she answered, hardly bothering to conceal the dislike in her voice.

"Here, let me help you." Algernon reached for the books in her arms, his hand "accidentally" brushing across her bosom.

She abruptly backed away. "I can manage for myself," she snapped. "I'm not finished here. You had best go back to the house."

"What a pity," he replied in his oily voice. "I had thought we might go for a stroll. It's time we got better acquainted."

Fury almost choked her. "I am much too busy for a stroll."

"Perhaps another time then." Totally unfazed, Algernon bowed and walked away.

To calm herself, Evleen stood for a while looking out over the garden. It wasn't long before she spied the raven, staring down at her from its perch in the nearby tree. *Merlin.* She longed to talk to him, especially after a day like this. Well, why not? She wasn't going to perform any magic, only talk to the magician who had been her mentor since she was eight years old.

She reached to rub the blue pebble hidden beneath her bodice. Instantly the bearded old man appeared before her, his clasped hands nearly concealed by the flowing sleeves. "Why haven't you called for me?" he asked.

"I have missed you but I must never use my magic in England," she answered frankly. "They would never understand."

"What is troubling you, child?" asked Merlin. "I see unhappiness in your eyes."

"It's that odious Algernon," she quickly replied. "I cannot stand the sight of him."

Merlin slowly shook his head. "It is true the man is odious, but you are quite capable of keeping him in his place. No, the cause of your unhappiness is not Algeron Kent, it's Lord Beaumont with whom you've fallen in love."

She knew better than to argue. "I should have known you knew. Then you are aware our love is hopeless."

Merlin pondered a moment. "I could easily cast a spell over your Lord Beaumont, one that would make him decide to end his betrothal to Bettina and marry you."

"No," Evleen cried. "Richard is an honourable man. He would never forgive me if I resorted to such a cheap, shoddy trick. And besides, he would be an outcast and would receive the cut direct. I love him too much to put him through such a disgrace. You must promise you won't."

"As you wish," Merlin replied. "Since you're so insistent, I give you my promise that I shall never cast a spell over Richard Beaumont. Does that satisfy you?"

"Yes, it does," she replied, greatly relieved.

"But you must call if you need me."

"I won't be needing you," she said. "No magic can help me now."

"We shall see." Merlin gave her a nod goodbye. Then, like a puff of dust, he vanished from her sight.

The next morning, when Evleen came down for breakfast, she discovered that Lord Beaumont had left for London at the crack of dawn. He would remain in London for the opening of Parliament and not return until the eve of his wedding, one month hence. Despite her disappointment, Evleen knew his departure was for the best. Having to see him now would be pure torture. She hated the thought of having to witness Beaumont's wedding to Bettina, but for Peter's sake, she would.

That afternoon, Peter came to the gazebo alone, without Cromwell. "My dog is sick," he said, his pale face strained. "He's awfully sick and I don't know what to do."

"Let's go see him," said Evleen. Together they walked to the kennel where she found the Border collie lying limp on the ground, panting heavily. Obviously the dog was in great distress. She suspected it did not have long to live.

Peter sank beside him, tears streaming down his cheeks. "Please don't die, Cromwell," he cried in a voice that nearly broke her heart. He gazed with pleading eyes at Evleen. "Isn't there something you can do to save him?"

She thought long and hard. Yes, of course there was something she could do, but she had promised never to use her magic again.

But on the other hand . . .

What would Peter do without his faithful friend who followed him wherever he went and offered nothing but boundless loyalty and love? The poor little boy had suffered a great loss when his mother died. Now Cromwell, too?

Evleen took the boy's hand. "Come along, Peter, there's someone I would like you to meet."

Peter stood next to her in the gazebo. When she rubbed the blue pebble, Merlin appeared before them. "I see you brought the boy," he said to Evleen.

Peter gazed in wonder. One moment he'd seen a black raven sitting on a tree limb. The next, a bearded old man seemed to have appeared out of nowhere. "Are you the wizard Merlin who advised King Arthur?" he asked in an awed tone.

"Indeed, I am, son," Merlin answered. "But I have been around long before King Arthur and his court."

"Evleen says you can help me." Peter told the magician how much he loved his dog, Cromwell, and would do anything to save him. When he finished, Merlin smiled down at the boy. "Go back to the kennel, son, and see how Cromwell is faring."

Evleen watched Peter dart eagerly away. "You have my deepest thanks," she said to Merlin.

"I am happy to oblige, but do you think it wise to break your promise?"

"It's never wise to break a promise, nor is it wise to allow a child to suffer needlessly."

Merlin shook his head in sympathy. "You're a compassionate woman, Evleen, not deserving of the fate that's been handed you. Why don't you allow me to—?"

"No! I broke my promise once, but it's not likely I shall do it again. As for casting a spell over Lord Beaumont, I absolutely forbid it. I hope you understand."

"Of course." The image of Merlin began to fade. "Until we meet again." The next instant, a black raven spread its wings and silently glided towards the sky.

Evleen heard both a sudden cry and a gasp behind her. Dreading what she would find, she turned. There stood Lydia and Bettina, both staring at her with wide-eyed horror.

With a shaking hand, Bettina pointed to the spot where Merlin had stood. "He . . . he's gone! Just disappeared . . . and the raven was there. I don't know where he went. It was like magic."

"It was magic." Both triumph and scorn blazed in Lydia's eyes as she addressed Evleen. "You're a sorceress, just as I suspected all along. Now I have proof of it."

Evleen stood mute. How could she defend herself when, in essence, what Lydia said was true? Finally she spread her palms wide. "For Peter's sake, couldn't you forget what you saw? It will never happen again, I assure you."

"Absolutely not! As far I am concerned, you will never see Peter again. Come, Bettina." Lydia took her future sister-in-law's arm. "We must go tell Mama immediately that my brother has allowed a sorceress to live in our home."

As they left, a joyous Peter came running through the garden, Cromwell bounding along behind him. It was worth it. Evleen knelt to put her arms around her happy young pupil and receive a lick on the face from an ecstatic Cromwell.

Alone in the drawing room with Lady Beaumont, Evleen sat stiff and straight in her chair, expecting the worst. Her ladyship sat across, lips compressed, nose quivering with suppressed rage. "I am appalled," she began. "Both Lydia and Bettina saw you engaging in your black magic, or whatever you call it. Were they wrong? What do you have to say for yourself?"

"Not exactly wrong, your ladyship. But you see, I—"

"I shall not tolerate a sorceress in my home!" Lady Beaumont's anger had turned into scalding fury. She leaped from her chair and started pacing. "I shall wait for my son's return. He must make the final decision. Meantime, you are relieved of your governess duties."

Her heart sank. "Not teach Peter? But he's been making such good progress and I—"

"I don't want you anywhere near my grandson. To that end, I am moving you to the servants' floor. You will no longer be welcome in our dining room. You will take your meals in your room. I don't want to lay eyes on you until Richard returns for his wedding, at which time I shall request he throw you out of this house, which you well deserve." She pulled herself up, one quivering mass of indignation. "I never wanted you here in the first place. And don't expect my son will side with you. In this matter he will do as I say."

Any further explanation would have been useless. Evleen arose from her chair, determined to maintain her dignity if nothing else. "As you wish, Lady Beaumont." She left the room, head held high, thankful she'd been able to choke back her tears.

In the days before the return of Lord Beaumont, Evleen spent most of her time in her tiny room on the fourth floor. With its lumpy bed, battered chest and cold, bare floor, the room in no way compared with the luxurious bedchamber she'd been forced to vacate. But in her despair she hardly noticed. She spent her time reading, or trying to. How could she concentrate on a book when thoughts of Beaumont's passionate kiss constantly crept into her mind, when she was full of concern about Peter, who she knew must miss her terribly, just as she missed him? Was he keeping up with his lessons? Had they found a new governess? The servants kept their distance. Not one member of the family talked to her any more, so she had no way of knowing.

As Beaumont's wedding day approached, the sounds of an increasingly busy household getting ready reached her ears. The wedding itself would take place in the nearby village church. The reception, a glittering affair with 200 expected guests, was to be held at Chatfield Court.

One sound made her cringe: Bettina's giddy laughter often wafted up to the fourth floor, reminding Evleen that the featherbrained young woman would soon become Beaumont's bride.

Lord Beaumont returned the day before the wedding. In her tiny room, Evleen was miserably wondering if she would even be allowed to speak to him again when a knock sounded on her door. She thought it must be one of the servants, but to her astonishment, Beaumont stood before her. She drew in her breath. "What are you doing here? I'm sure your mother would not approve."

"I am not concerned with what Mama thinks," he answered gruffly, shoving his way past her. "I must talk to you."

He sat on the room's one rickety wooden chair. She sat on the bed. "There's nothing more to say," she said. "I'm sure your mother has informed you of all you need to know."

Amusement flickered in his eyes. "Is it true? Are you indeed a sorceress?"

She thought a moment. If she told him the truth, he would doubtless be appalled, as well as angry, thinking she'd deceived him. But her forthright nature decreed she could not do otherwise than be completely honest. She looked him in the eye. "I don't think of myself as a sorceress, but yes, I have certain magic powers. I have only used them once while here in England and wasn't planning to use them again. But—"

To her surprise, Richard burst into laughter. "You know magic? But that's priceless!"

In amazement she asked, "But aren't you angry? Aren't you frightened I might cast some sort of evil spell on you?"

"Would you?"

"No, of course not."

"Well, then, I have nothing to worry about."

She protested, "But your mother is horrified, and very angry. She can hardly wait to get rid of me."

Beaumont's laughter died. He gazed around the tiny room and frowned. "You have been treated abominably. I shall see you are moved immediately."

"Stop," she said with a raise of her hand. "Your mother is right. It's best I leave Chatfield Court as soon as possible. Better for both of us."

A look of anguish crossed his face. "I love you, Evleen. Those days I spent in London made clear to me how empty my life will be without you." He stood, pulled her to her feet and wrapped her in his arms. "You don't have to find another position," he whispered in her ear. "I could set you up in London. You would never have to want for anything. You could—"

"I will not be a kept woman!" She pushed away from him.

"Of course." He swallowed hard. "I am so sorry, Evleen. I should have known you would never allow your reputation to be compromised. It's just . . . I love you so much. The thought of spending the rest of my life without you is an agony."

"I feel the same, but what can we do?"

"Nothing. Honour binds us both." Beaumont took up her hand and pressed a gentle kiss to the back of it. "Goodbye, my love, my dearest love. I shall remember you always."

He left then, leaving her to sit in her room and contemplate the lonely years that lay ahead. She knew they'd be lonely because she would never find another man like Richard Beaumont, and she would never settle for less.

The next morning, two piercing screams awoke Evleen from her sleep. They were screams so loud, so terrorizing, she leaped from her bed. Was the house on fire? Had someone been murdered? She flung her robe over her nightgown. Joining the alarmed-looking servants who had also heard the screams, she rushed downstairs to discover bewildered wedding guests, still in their night clothes, milling about, all looking for the source of the curdling shrieks.

When someone said they appeared to have come from the drawing room, Evleen, along with guests and servants, crowded inside, where she saw a strange sight indeed. Bettina's mother, the renowned Duchess of Derbyshire, lay in a swoon on the sofa, a letter clutched in her hand. A maid held smelling salts under the Duchess' nose. Lydia knelt beside her, waving a fan. Lady Beaumont looked on, her face so white and drawn Evleen thought she, too, might swoon at any moment.

"What is going on here?" Lord Beaumont, half dressed in breeches and a white shirt open at the throat, entered the room. "Mama, you don't look well. You had better sit down and tell me what's happening."

"What's going on is beyond belief," Lady Beaumont said in a voice that rose to near hysteria. She plucked the letter from the Duchess' fingers and handed it to her son. "It's a letter from Bettina. Read it."

With a curious frown Beaumont took the letter and began to read aloud.

Dearest Mama,

It is with deep regret I am cancelling my wedding to Lord Beaumont. I cannot marry him under any circumstances because I have fallen madly, passionately in love with Algernon Kent. Please don't follow me. By the time you receive this, my dearest Algernon and I will be well on our way to Gretna Green, Scotland, to be married.

Know that I deeply regret the sorrow this must cause you, as well as Lord Beaumont—

Bettina

"Oh, dear God!" Lady Beaumont's legs buckled. Her son caught her and helped her into a chair. "There won't be a wedding?" the distraught woman cried. "I cannot believe this is happening!"

"It would appear that it is," Beaumont equitably replied. He looked over at the Duchess whose eyelids were fluttering. "I shall go after them, of course. Perhaps it's not too late."

"Don't bother. That ungrateful girl!" The Duchess sat up straight, waving the smelling salts away. "The butler told me they left last night. There is no way in the world you could catch them now, nor would I wish you to. Algernon Kent? I cannot believe it!" She exchanged incredulous glances with

Lady Beaumont and Lydia. "How could my Bettina fall in love with the most loathsome man in the world? I apologize for my fickle daughter, Lord Beaumont. You must be devastated! Heartbroken!"

Evleen watched, secretly amused, as Beaumont placed a properly sombre expression on his face and make a gracious little bow. "Love works in mysterious ways, your grace. I shall do my best to contain my sorrow. Meanwhile, I want you to know that despite Bettina's shocking defection, I forgive her and wish her all the happiness in the world." He caught Evleen's eye from across the room. In the fleeting moment their eyes met, he sent a message that contained a mixture of astonishment, vast relief, and, best of all, his undying love and joy that at last they could be together.

Her heart full of gratitude, Evleen turned and left. Life was wonderful again! With joyous steps, she climbed the stairs to her room. Richard was not going to marry Bettina. Such a miracle! But how in the world could the silly girl possibly have fallen in love with the likes of Algernon Kent? Hadn't she said she loathed him?

An astounding thought struck her. Could Merlin possibly have had a hand in this? But no, it wasn't possible. The wise old wizard had promised he would not cast a spell.

When she stepped into her room, she stopped and gasped. A black feather lay on her pillow. From Merlin? Who else could it be from? Why the feather? What message did it convey?

She picked up the feather and went to her window. For a long time, she stood clutching it in her hand. Finally, as she knew it would, the message came clear. Of course! Merlin had promised he would not cast a spell on Lord Beaumont. And he hadn't. He had kept his promise. But he had not promised to refrain from putting a spell on poor Bettina.

"Why, Merlin, you old rascal," she said aloud and started to laugh. "What kind of spell did you use to make a woman fall in love with Algernon? I'd wager it was the strongest spell you had."

She touched the blue pebble. No more magic from now on. Absolutely not. Tomorrow she would throw the pebble into the nearby creek.

But then again . . . perhaps she should think about it first. No need to rush.

The Ballad of Rosamunde

Claire Delacroix

Galway, Ireland – April, 1422

The hour was late and the tavern was crowded. Padraig sat near the hearth, watching the firelight play over the faces of the men gathered there. The ale launched a warm hum within him, the closest he was ever likely to be to the heat of the Mediterranean sun again.

He should have gone south, as Rosamunde had bidden him to do. He should have sold her ship and its contents, as she had instructed him. Galway was as far as he had managed to sail from Kinfairlie – and he had only come this far because his crew had compelled him to leave the site of disaster.

Where Rosamunde had been lost forever.

Instead he returned home, to his mother's grave and the tavern run by his sister.

Padraig enjoyed music, always had, and song was the only solace he found in the absence of Rosamunde's company. He found his foot tapping and his cares lifting as a local man sang of adventure.

"A song!" someone cried when one rollicking tune came to an end. "Who else has a song?"

"Padraig!" shouted his sister. She was a pretty woman, albeit one who tolerated no nonsense. Padraig suspected there were those more afraid of her than her husband. "Sing the sad one you began the other night," she entreated.

"There are others of better voice," Padraig protested.

The company roared a protest in unison, and so he acquiesced. Padraig sipped his ale then pushed to his feet to sing the ballad of his own composition.

> *"Rosamunde was a pirate queen*
> *With hair red gold and eyes of green.*
> *A trade in relics did she pursue,*
> *Plus perfume and silks of every hue.*
> *Her ship's hoard was a rich treasury,*
> *Of prizes gathered on every sea.*
> *But the fairest gem in all the hold*
> *Was Rosamunde, beauteous and bold.*
> *Her blade was quick, her foresight sharp,*
> *She conquered hearts in every port."*

"Ah!" sighed the older man across the table from Padraig. "There be a woman worth the loss of one's heart."

The company nodded approval and leaned closer for the next verse. Even his sister stopped serving and leaned against the largest keg in the tavern, smiling as she watched Padraig.

> *"She vanquished foes on every sea*
> *But lost her heart to a man esteemed.*
> *Surrender was not her nature true*
> *But bow to his desires, she did do.*
> *She left the sea to become his bride,*
> *But in her lover's home, Rosamunde died.*
> *The man she loved was not her worth . . ."*

Padraig faltered. His compatriots in the tavern waited expectantly, but he could not think of a suitable rhyme. He remembered the sight of Ravenmuirs' cliffs and caverns collapsing, his men holding him back so he wouldn't risk his life to save Rosamunde. He put down his tankard with dissatisfaction, singing the last line again softly. It made no difference. He had composed a hundred rhymes, if not a thousand, but this particular tale caught in his throat like none other.

"*Her absence was to all a dearth*," his sister suggested.

Her husband snorted. "You've no music in your veins, woman, that much is for certain."

"*The son she bore him died at birth*," the old man across the table suggested.

Padraig shook his head and frowned. "There was no child."

"There could be," the old man insisted. "'Tis only a tale, after all." The others laughed.

But this was not only a tale. It was the truth. Rosamunde had existed, she had been a pirate queen, she had been both beauteous and bold.

And she had been lost forever, thanks to the faithlessness of the man to whom she had surrendered everything.

Padraig mourned that truth every day and night of his life.

He cursed Tynan Lammergeier, the man who had cost him the company of Rosamunde, and he hated that they two might be together forever in some afterlife. It was wrong that a man who had not been able to accept Rosamunde for her true nature should win her company for all eternity.

Because Padraig had loved her truly. His mother had warned him that he would be smitten once and his heart lost forever.

But he had held his tongue. He had spoken of friendship in his parting with Rosamunde, not the fullness of his heart.

Now he would never have the chance to remedy his error. It had been almost six months since Rosamunde had gone into the caverns beneath Ravensmuir, Tynan's ancestral keep on the coast of Scotland, six months since those caves had collapsed and Rosamunde had been lost forever, and still Padraig's wound was raw.

He doubted it would ever heal.

He knew he'd never meet the like of her again.

Padraig sat down and drank deeply of his ale. "Let another sing," he said. "I am too besotted to compose the verse."

"Another tale!" shouted the keeper. "Come, Liam, sing that one of the Faerie host." The company stamped their feet and applauded, as Liam was clearly a local favourite, and Padraig saw a lanky man rise to his feet on the far side of the room.

He, however, had lost his taste for tales. He abandoned the rest of his ale, left a coin on the board, and headed for the door.

"We will miss your custom this evening," his sister said softly as he passed her. Her dark eyes shone brightly in the shadowed tavern, and he doubted that she missed any detail.

"A man should be valued for more than the volume of ale he can drink," Padraig replied, blaming himself for what he had become. His sister flushed and turned away as if he had chided her.

He could do nothing right.

Not without Rosamunde.

Was her loss to be the shadow over all his days and nights?

Far beneath the hills to the north of Galway, Finvarra, High King of the Daoine Sidhe, templed his fingers together and considered the chessboard. It was a beautiful chessboard, with pieces of alabaster and obsidian, the board itself fashioned of agate and ebony with fine enamel work around the perimeter. When he touched a piece, it came to life, moving across the board at his unspoken will. His entire fey court gathered around the game, watching with bright eyes.

Finvarra was tall and slim, finely wrought even for the fey, who were uncommonly handsome. His eyes were as dark as a midnight sky, his long hair the deep blue black of the sea in darkness, his skin as fair as moonlight, his tread as light as wind in the grass. He was possessed of both kindness and resolve, and ruled the fey well.

His hall at Knockma was under the hill, and as lavish a court as could be found. The ladies wore glistening gowns of finest silk, their gossamer wings painted with a thousand colours. The courtiers were armed in silver finery, their manners both fierce and gallant, their eyes glinting with humour. The horses of Finvarra's court were spirited and fleet of foot, gleaming and beauteous in their rich trappings hung with silver bells. He had steeds of every colour: red stallions and white mares, black stallions and mahogany mares with ivory socks. Each and every one was caparisoned in finery to show its hue and strength to advantage. The mead was sweet and golden in Finvarra's hall, and the cups at the board filled themselves with more when no one was looking.

But all the fairy court was silent, clustered around their king's favoured chessboard. They watched, knowing that more than victory at a game hung in the balance.

As usual.

Finvarra did not care for low stakes.

Finvarra played to win.

The spriggan, Darg, sat opposite the King and fidgeted. Recently of Scotland, the small thieving fairy had travelled to Ireland in the hold of the ship of Padraig Deane, a blue-eyed and handsome pirate possessed of a broken heart. Caught trespassing in Finvarra's *sid*, a crime punishable by death, the spriggan played for its life.

Finvarra, in truth, tired of the game. The spoils were not so remarkable and the spriggan was a mediocre opponent. The splendour of the board, indeed, he felt was wasted upon the rough little creature. Certainly, his skill was.

Then Finvarra heard the distant lilt of human song.

> *"Rosamunde was a pirate queen*
> *With hair red gold and eyes of green . . ."*

As was common with Finvarra, the mention of a beauteous mortal woman piqued his interest. He turned his head to listen, just as the spriggan interrupted with a hiss.

"A laughing trickster Rosamunde did be, but she did not have the best of me."

"You knew this mortal?"

Darg raised a fist. "Stole from me! That she dared, but I did steal her from her laird. She would be dead but for me; now she owes me her fealty." The spriggan cackled then moved a pawn with care. It was a poor choice. "Not dead but enchanted she doth be, while I choose what my vengeance shall be."

Intrigued, Finvarra snapped his fingers and his wife, Una, brought his silver mirror to his hand. She knew him well. She caressed his hand as she passed the mirror to him, but Finvarra ignored her gesture of affection.

He didn't imagine her sniff of displeasure, but Una's pleasure was not his current concern. Not when there was a beauteous woman to be possessed. He murmured to the mirror and its surface swirled before his eyes, the image of this Rosamunde appearing so suddenly that Finvarra caught his breath.

Then his blood quickened.

Una, always able to read his response, spun on her heel. She strode from the hall, her ladies scurrying after her like so many sparrows. Finvarra was oblivious to his wife's mood.

This Rosamunde was not just beautiful but spirited.

Finvarra had to know more. He touched the queen, his favoured piece, sliding his finger up her carved back. She strolled across the board in perfect understanding of his intent, halted on the desired spot and tucked her hands into her sleeves meekly.

If only all queens might be so biddable.

"Check," he murmured with a smile.

"No! I shall not die, not by your whim!" The spriggan erupted from its place in fury, jumping across the board and kicking pieces left and right. "I demand we play the game again!"

Finvarra shook his head.

The spriggan scattered the pieces onto the earthen floor, then lunged at Finvarra. There was no contest between them, the spriggan being only as tall as the King's golden chalice. Finvarra struck the ill-tempered creature with the back of his hand, sending it sprawling across the floor.

The elegantly attired fey stepped away from the spriggan, whispering at its poor manners. It hissed at all of them, then made to run. Two elfin knights seized it, holding tightly while it bit and struggled.

"I have no interest in your life," Finvarra said with soft authority. The spriggan froze, staring at him in confusion. It was a crafty creature and Finvarra deliberately stated his terms so that there could be no deception. "I would trade your life for a specific treasure in your possession."

Darg's eyes narrowed into hostile slits. "No gem do I see fit to spare—"

"The woman," Finvarra decreed, interrupting what would likely be an impolite diatribe. "I trade your life for that of your captive, Rosamunde."

The spriggan regarded him warily. "I fear you make a jest of me, and would be freed 'fore I agree."

Finvarra rose and clapped his hands. "There is no jest. When Rosamunde graces my court, you shall be free to leave." He reached forwards and snatched at the spriggan, holding it so surely in his grip that it paled. He lowered his face to its sharp features, glaring into its eyes. Darg squirmed. "Deceive me, though, and I will have your life as well as the woman."

Darg's eyes gleamed and Finvarra knew the creature would willingly deceive him. He beckoned to his armourer, who produced a fine red thread at his master's bidding. Finvarra knotted that thread securely around the spriggan's waist. It appeared to be made of silk but was strong beyond measure and it held the spriggan to Finvarra's command. The small fairy struggled and fought against the bond, grimacing where it touched the skin.

"It burns, it does, the knot too tight," Darg snarled. "You cheat when I would do what's right!"

"Only I can unbind this thread, and I will only do so when you have fulfilled our bargain."

Darg continued to pluck at the thread, its displeasure clear. It cast a glance over the company, then its lips tightened. It straightened and addressed Finvarra with surprising hauteur. "As you command, so shall it be. You shall see that Darg lives honestly."

Finvarra smothered a laugh. He didn't doubt that the creature would try to break both cord and vow, but he knew such efforts were doomed to failure. "Tomorrow sunset," he decreed. "I would have her by my side for the Beltane ride two nights hence."

The spriggan grimaced at the time constraint, but before it could argue, Finvarra made a dismissive gesture. "It is enough time. Should it not be . . ." He raised a brow and the thread bound around the spriggan's waist tightened an increment. Darg screamed, swore agreement, then scampered across the court, muttering. Three elven knights followed it at a discreet distance, ensuring that it left the hall upon its mission.

Finvarra eyed the path Una had taken, heard the distant sound of her sobs, and decided to remain in his hall a bit longer. He clapped and called for music, for he was feeling as celebratory as Una was not.

After all, soon he would have a new prize to savour.

Rosamunde dreamed.

If she had been asked, she would have said that her expectation was to dream of Tynan through all eternity. But her dream took her further into the past, to an abbey on the coast of Ireland.

She had been summoned there by the bishop, anxious to increase the revenue of his remote diocese with the acquisition of a holy relic. One of the bishop's men had eyes of brilliant blue and a steady gaze. She strove to ignore him.

The bishop purchased a perfumed braid said to have come from Mary, daughter of Lazarus. They negotiated the price, the coin was counted and then deposited in Rosamunde's purse. She sensed that the man with the blue gaze thought the bishop intended to cheat her.

Outside, Rosamunde was glad to see her ship. She emitted a high whistle, a signal to Thomas waiting in the dingy out of sight. She was not prepared to find Thomas dead, bleeding in the bottom of the boat. She was not prepared to have a man assault her in the darkness – the purse ripped from her belt, her blade snatched.

And she certainly was not expecting the blue-eyed man to leap out of the shadows behind her attacker, slicing him from gullet to groin and kicking his carcase into the sea.

"I sicken of his thievery," he said softly, his voice as steady as his gaze.

"I thank you for your aid."

"You are most welcome, I fear I have lost my employ this night. Have you need of another man of your ship?"

Rosamunde found herself liking this man a great deal. "I always have need of men with stout hearts and quick blades. Have you a name?"

Padraig Deane."

Rosamunde shook his hand, liking the heat of his skin, the firmness of his grip.

"Welcome, Padraig. There is no better compliment than knowing a man can be trusted with one's own life.

She watched the moonlight play on his muscles as he rowed them back to the ship. He was determined, stalwart, and unafraid. Rosamunde wondered how she had failed to see the full merit of Padraig in all the years he had served her.

What lifted the scales from her eyes now?

Padraig wandered the streets of Galway, paying no attention to his course until he reached the gate in the Norman wall. He glanced back towards the harbour, then ahead to the hills cloaked in starlight and shadow. He chose to pass through the gate and walk out of town, knowing that the way was not without risk. He was but half-Irish, half of town and half of country, though there were those who would have little interest in the details.

He did not care about his fate as much as he once had.

And he had no taste for human company on this night.

He walked as the moon rose ever higher in the sky. He walked as the church bells sounded far behind him. He walked as the stars glinted overhead.

He heard the rustle of small animals in the underbrush and the tinkle of running water. He felt the ale loosen its hold upon his body and grief well in his heart.

He paused in the middle of the road, hours after his departure, and cast a glance back towards the sleeping town. His feet ached and he knew he should turn back.

Padraig just made to do so when he heard a woman singing, singing more beautifully than ever he had heard anyone singing. It could have been an angel he heard, and he was drawn to the sound.

He could not hear the words, and hastened closer.

"Una was the Faerie Queen
Fairest woman ever seen
Wed centuries to her King
Love meant more to her than his ring."

The ground rose ahead of Padraig in a mound, a low hill covered with grass. A circle of large stones surrounded the crest of the hill, like a crown upon it, and a hawthorn tree grew outside the circle of stones.

The hair prickled on the back of his neck for he had learned at his mother's knee to be cautious in the presence of the fey. If nothing else, this was the kind of place they favoured.

He could barely discern the silhouette of a woman atop the hill. She was sitting on a stone in the midst of the circle, combing her long hair, and he knew she was the one who sang. Two women sat at her feet, one with a lyre the like of which Padraig had never seen, the other humming along with her lady. They were all lovely, ethereal in the moonlight.

Her voice had a lovely lilt and Padraig wished to hear more of her song. He walked closer, trying to move silently as he didn't want to startle the women.

To his astonishment, as soon as he stepped within the circle of stones, the lady with the comb turned to confront him. She smiled, her hand falling to her lap as she sang directly to him.

With proximity, he could see more than her silhouette. Her hair was golden, as bright as sunlight, her eyes as blue as a southern sea. Padraig walked closer, awed by her loveliness.

"But Finvarra had an appetite,
For mortal women, both dark and light.
He vowed he'd have the pirate queen,
Held captive by the spriggan's greed.
One glimpse of the fair Rosamunde
Had left him filled with lust and love.
And so his wife did come to dread
Her spouse taking Rosamunde to his bed."

Padraig blinked. Surely she could not be singing of his Rosamunde?

The woman stood up, revealing that she was tall and slender. She wore a dress that was fitted to her curves and swept to her ankles; it was as blue as her eyes, rich with golden embroidery and gems encrusting the hem and cuffs. It seemed to Padraig that her slippers were made of silk the colour of moonlight.

Or perhaps she was wrought of moonlight. She seemed insubstantial as she walked towards him, both of this world and not. Was he dreaming? The hem of her skirt seemed to dance with a will of its own, and lights glinted around the perimeter of the stone circle. He remembered will-o'-the-wisp from his childhood and knew that he had strayed into the realm of the fey.

Only when the woman was directly before him did he see the numerous small courtiers holding the hem. They could not have stood as high as his knee, not a one of them, and were dressed in green livery. Their faces were sharp, their eyes narrow, and their hair caught with twigs.

Padraig remembered her own words and knew who he encountered.

The Faerie Queen, Una.

"Greetings, Padraig, sailor of the many seas," she said, her voice as melodious in speech as in song.

"Greetings, beauteous queen." Padraig bowed deeply, knowing well the price of insulting one of the fey.

"Perhaps you have guessed that I have summoned you here. I heard your song and knew that our goals could be as one."

"Heard my song?" Padraig glanced over his shoulder, unable to glimpse the lights of the town. "But that was miles away. You could not possibly have heard . . ."

Una laid a fingertip across his lips to silence him. Her touch was as cold as ice, as smooth as silken velvet.

She smiled. "She is not dead, your Rosamunde." Her lips tightened and she averted her gaze. "And now my husband, casting his glance over all of Faerie, with the aid of his treacherous mirror, has glimpsed the slumbering Rosamunde. He means to make her his own on Beltane."

"I mean no offence, my lady, but Rosamunde is dead." Padraig spoke with care. He knew of the fey inclination to trick mortals. "I saw the fallen rock, I tried to retrieve her from the destroyed caverns. She cannot have survived in any way."

Una smiled. "The spriggan Darg took her captive when she might have died."

"Darg!" Padraig exclaimed. He recalled the deceitful spriggan well, and its determination to have vengeance upon Rosamunde.

Una watched him carefully. "You know this creature."

"Indeed, I do, my lady, although I believed the spriggan to be yet at Ravensmuir."

Una's smile faded. "No. It came in your ship."

Padraig frowned. There had been items disappear on their last voyage, including the ale that he knew the spriggan liked so well. It was possible that Una spoke the truth.

"It trespassed in our *sid*. It has wagered with my husband and lost, so it will bring Rosamunde to him tomorrow. You must steal her from him."

"My lady! A man who steals from the Faerie king will not live to tell the tale of it!"

Una smiled. "With my aid, you will not be detected." She pressed a golden ring into his hand. "Wear this and you shall pass unseen in any company."

The ring was cold, as cold as the tomb. Even having it in his hand filled Padraig with dread. He was not afraid to risk his life for Rosamunde, not even of inciting the wrath of the fey king, but there was one more thing he needed to know.

"With respect, my lady, I would be certain of the desire of Rosamunde. It seems to me that it would be most fine to live at the Faerie court. She might not wish to leave."

Una laughed but not because of his compliment. "You must have heard the old riddle, the one with truth at its heart."

"Which is that, my lady?"

Her eyes glinted with humour. "What gift is it that a woman wishes most from a man?"

Padraig shrugged, not knowing the answer. Riches? Comfort?

Love? There were so many possible answers that he could not choose. He suspected the answer depended upon the woman.

Una leaned closer. "To have her own way." Her eyes shone with brilliant light as her courtiers giggled around her hem. "I suspect you are a worthy lover, Padraig Deane, and in tribute to your love, I give you a gift."

"You have already been too kind . . ."

Before Padraig could finish, the Faerie Queen framed his face in her hands. She leaned closer, her cold breath caressing his skin, then she kissed him full on the lips. He tasted death and loss, a chill that shook him to his marrow.

And Padraig swooned.

Rosamunde dreamed of another day from her past.

The sky was pink, a sure sign of trouble in the morning, and the dark clouds racing overhead made no better forecast. All the same, Rosamunde's heart leaped at the familiar cliffs that rose before her, the cliffs surmounted by the keep she knew as well as the lines of her own hand.

Ravensmuir.

Governed by Tynan, stern but fair, the man who had taken her to his bed, the man who had vowed subsequently never to wed her. The man who had chosen this pile of stones over her.

Twice.

In her dream, she was certain she would relive that last encounter, that final fatal rejection. But she did not. She dreamed again of Padraig.

Rosamunde stood on the deck of her ship, staring up as the land rose closer, her heart pounding with trepidation that Tynan would see her approach, that he would meet her in the caverns below the keep. She was in the moment of approach, felt her own hope and anticipation, yet at the same time, knew what had happened subsequently in those caverns. She felt the twinge of dread that she had felt that morning and knew it had been a warning. Although Tynan had apologised to her, he had once again chosen his holding over her.

And he had died.

Had she not died, as well?

Padraig came to stand beside her on the deck, but this time when Rosamunde turned to her most trusted friend, she saw him with clear eyes. He was tall and hale, was Padraig, experience tempering his expression and his choices. His dark hair was touched with silver at the temples, she noted, and there were lines from laughter etched around his eyes. His tan made his eyes look more vividly blue, and she was struck by his vitality.

By his masculinity.

With the clarity of hindsight, she saw what she had missed day after day in his company. Padraig was of an age with her, and they had shared a thousand adventures. He was unafraid of her truth, much less of her temper. He was quick to laughter; he was clever; he dared to challenge her when he believed her to be wrong. He was deeply loyal and she had always been able to rely upon him.

Her heart began to pound at the magnitude of her error, at her own blind folly.

"I will go into the caverns alone," she said, feeling the words she had once uttered as they crossed her tongue in this dream. Her quest had been the retrieval of a silver ring, once given to her by Tynan, demanded by the spriggan Darg as the price of its assistance, but returned by her to Tynan after his rejection. It had not been hers to take, but on this day she had returned to steal it to ensure the future of her niece.

"I will accompany you," Padraig said, determination in his tone. They shared this resolve to protect those they loved, Rosamunde realized, this ability to stride into the shadows so others would not be compelled to do so.

She and Padraig had walked the periphery of society together, daring all as they challenged convention.

At each other's backs.

While Tynan had upheld convention. He had found Rosamunde useful, he had accepted her favours abed, but he had never respected her or intended to honour her. It was no surprise in hindsight to realize that Tynan could never have loved her in truth.

"No, not this time," she argued in her dream, just as she had argued on that fateful morning.

She saw Padraig for what he was. She saw the ardour in his eyes. She saw his fear for her. She saw his valour and his loyalty, and she guessed the secret of his heart.

And Rosamunde regretted that she had surrendered her love to the wrong man.

She had suspected as much on that day. The ghost of the realization had teased at her thoughts, urged her to choose otherwise, made her words tumble forth with uncharacteristic haste. "Take the ship," she told him, in this dream as she had then. "See me ashore, then take the ship and sail south to Sicily."

It had been their jest, all those years, that they would one day sell everything and live out their lives in Sicily. They had both preferred the sun's sultry heat there to the chill of the north.

"But what of the contents?" Padraig's displeasure was clear.

"Sell them, sell them wherever you can fetch a fair price for them, and keep the proceeds for your own."

"But . . ."

"I owe you no less for all your years of faithful service." It was a facile lie and they both had known it, even then.

"But the ship?"

"Sell it as well, or keep it for your own. I do not care, Padraig." Rosamunde uttered that heartfelt sigh, acknowledging the shadow of dread that touched her heart. "I have had wealth and I have had love. Love is better."

It was a lie. She had never had Tynan's love. She had had the illusion of his love, and had been seduced by that. She had had no more than the physical expression of his love, and that was a paltry offering.

On the other hand, Rosamunde saw in her dream that Padraig's love had been before her, awaiting her invitation, for years.

"You will fare well enough," she said in her dream, and the

declaration of her gift of foresight struck her as ironic. "I have seen it and we know that whatsoever I see will be true."

"What do you see for yourself?" Padraig asked softly, his survey of her so searching that Rosamunde could scarce hold his gaze. He frowned and looked away. "I always said that you saw farther than most, but could not see what was before your own eyes."

There was a truth in his claim that she had missed on that red-stained morning. She declared her destiny to be at Ravensmuir, seeing in her dream how the notion displeased Padraig.

How could she have missed such an offering?

How could she have overlooked the affection of one who knew her better than she knew herself? She had been a fool and lost her life because of it. If only she had another chance, she would seize the opportunity Padraig presented to her.

"Farewell, Padraig," she heard herself say. "May the wind always fill your sails when you have need of it."

And Padraig embraced her, catching her close. She could feel the muscled strength of him, the resolve of him, the power he oft held in check. In her dream, she closed her eyes and savoured what she had lost through her own folly.

His voice was husky when he spoke. "We have fought back to back a hundred times, Rosamunde, and always I will consider you to be my friend." His blue eyes filled with heat as he regarded her. "You have been my only friend, but a friend of such merit that I had need of no other."

"No soul ever had a friend more loyal than I found in you," she said, her heart aching at her own folly.

"I did," Padraig said, his words fierce. His gaze bored into hers, then he turned away, staring at the cliffs of Ravensmuir. "I did," he added softly.

And in her dream, Rosamunde did what she should have done on that day. She reached out. She touched Padraig's shoulder. She saw his surprise when he turned towards her. Then she caught him close, hearing the thunder of her pulse in her own ears, and kissed him.

It was a sweet, hot kiss, a kiss that sent a torrent of longing through her. It was a kiss tinged with regret, filled with love, a kiss of yearning and potency. It left her dizzy. It left her hot.

It left Rosamunde wide awake and blinking at a ceiling she could not place.

Was she not dead?

It appeared not. She was simply alone. She touched her lips, caught her breath, and dared to wish.

Padraig awoke abruptly, his heart racing and his breath coming in quick spurts. He was hot and tight, the taste of Rosamunde upon his lips.

He had also slept, apparently, in the field.

The sun was rising in the east, gilding the hills and setting the dewdrops ablaze. He stared around himself. He was alone. He was cold and his clothing was damp with dew. The stone circle was a dozen steps away, silent in its secrets. The women were gone, if indeed they had ever existed, and there was no music echoing in his ears. No lyre, no small faeries, no footsteps in the grass.

Padraig heard a man shout at a cow as he drove her along the road to town.

He ran his fingers through his hair and his tongue across his lips. He tasted the kiss of Rosamunde again, closing his eyes at the rush of pleasure he'd felt beneath her touch.

Rosamunde had never kissed him.

Except in his dream.

He had indulged too much the night before. It was the ale, confounding him, feeding his desire and leading him astray.

Padraig shoved to his feet, grimacing at the distance he had to walk back to town. His feet were still sore and his head ached. He made to brush himself down, removing the twigs strewn across his clothes, and realized there was something in his hand.

It was a stone. The stone was round with a hole in the middle of it. It was the colour of gold. Was this the golden ring he believed the Faerie Queen had given him?

Padraig smiled at his own foolish dream. He had been in

his cups. Still, a stone of such a shape was unusual. It might be lucky. He was possessed of all of the superstitions of a seafaring man and a few more besides, courtesy of his mother's upbringing in these hills and her respect for the fey. If nothing else, it would be an error to cast the gift aside where the donor might witness his rudeness.

Padraig pushed the stone into his pocket and strode through the damp grass. And as he walked back to his accommodations in Galway, he savoured the memory of Rosamunde's kiss.

Even in a dream, it had been a sweet prize and was enough to put a spring in his step.

But Rosamunde, she had not died
In truth she breathed still.
She was a captive of the fey
And lost beneath the hill.
Such marvels she did see while there
Such beauty, wondrous still
Still Rosamunde did not wish to be
Captive beneath the hill.

The spriggan Darg was not a creature Rosamunde was glad to see.

Solitude was better than the company of this *thing*.

That the small fairy had a red cord knotted around its waist was curious, and surely did not improve the creature's mood. It hissed and spat, pinching her to wake her up then nipping at her heels to hurry her along.

"Make haste, make haste, the King is not inclined to wait."

"Where are we going? I thought Faerie was like limbo."

Darg chattered unintelligibly, as was its tendency when it was annoyed. The creature led her more deeply into the caverns beneath Ravensmuir and Rosamunde was glad to leave her past behind.

It wasn't truly the caverns beneath Ravensmuir, though. Those caves and their pathways were well known to Rosamunde, having been her secret passage to the keep for decades. As a child, she had played in them, learning their labyrinth, delighting in their secret corners. But they were dank and made of grey stone, dark and filled with the distant tinkle of running water.

She did not know the passageways that Darg followed. Rosamunde had never spied that entry lit with golden light until the collapse of the cavern and the death of Tynan. She suspected that Darg had opened a portal for her, but knew not where it truly was.

This cavern could not be fairly called a cave or even a labyrinth. Indeed, Rosamunde did not feel as if she were underground at all. There was brilliant golden sunlight, the light that had spilled from that unexpected portal. The sky arched high, clear and blue, over verdant fields. The air was filled with music and fine singing, and every soul she saw was beautiful.

It took Rosamunde a while to realize that she only saw nobility. There were aristocrats riding and hunting, borne by finely draped steeds so majestic in stature that the beasts rivalled the famed destriers of Ravensmuir. The women were dressed in silk and samite, their garb of every hue, their long hair flowing over their shoulders or braided into plaits. They wore coronets of flowers, and gems were plentiful on their clothing, even wound into their hair. Many played instruments as they rode. Golden flutes and silver lyres abounded in this strange country. The women's laughter sounded like music as well.

The men were just as well wrought, tall and slim, muscular. There was a glint of mischief in every eye. Their armour shone as if it was made of silver, their banners were beautifully embroidered and their steeds galloped with proudly arched necks. Silver bells hung from every bridle.

The land itself was bountiful, the trees lush with fruit and flowers blooming on every side. Rosamunde thought she saw fruit of gold and silver, and flowers wrought of precious jewels, but Darg did not delay their passage so she could look more closely. Birds sang from every tree, their song blending so beautifully with the ladies' tunes that Rosamunde felt they made music together.

Just passing through the beauty of this realm, even at

Darg's killing pace, lightened Rosamunde's heart. It healed her wounds and made her believe that she might live on, even without love. It made her think of the future with an optimism that she had believed lost.

It made her wonder where Padraig was.

It made her wonder how she might get from here to there.

"Where are we?" she shouted to Darg, who hastened ahead of her, muttering all the while.

"A foolish mortal you must be, to not know the land of Faerie."

Faerie. Rosamunde was a pragmatic woman, one who had never believed in matters unseen or places to which she could not navigate. Was she dreaming?

A butterfly lit on her shoulder, its wings fairly dripping with colour, its beauty far beyond that of any earthly insect.

Rosamunde realized with a start that it was a tiny winged woman. The fairy laughed at her surprise, a sound like tinkling bells, then darted away, disappearing into the blue of the sky with a glimmer.

"And why do we not linger in this magical realm?" Rosamunde asked Darg.

"Late we are, late we must not be! Finvarra waits impatiently." The spriggan tugged again at the red cord knotted around its waist. It spat in the grass with displeasure, then snatched at Rosamunde. "Hasten, hasten, by the moon's rise, we must be safely at his side."

"Who is Finvarra? And why do we go to him?"

"Questions, questions, instead of haste! Your queries do the daylight waste! We have far to go without rest: Finvarra will accept no less."

They crossed a bridge; the river running beneath looked to be made of mead. Rosamunde caught a whiff of its honeyed sweetness and saw a cluster of bees hovering at the shore. A beautifully dressed suitor offered a golden chalice of the liquid to his lady, who flushed, fluttered both wings and lashes, then accepted his tribute.

"But why do we go to this Finvarra? Who is he and what hold has he over you?"

The spriggan spun round abruptly, facing Rosamunde with fury in its eyes. "A match I lost, the price my life. His demand was you as his new wife. High King of Faerie is his task, a man whose patience does not last." Darg wrestled with the red cord, then released it with disgust. "This bond he knots, it burns me true; 'til you are his, this pain my due."

"You traded me to the Faerie King?" Rosamunde demanded, bracing her hands upon her hips. "What if I have no desire to be his toy? Or that of any other man, for that matter? I will not go complacent to his court, no matter what you have promised."

"I pledged my word, I swore my life; Finvarra will have you as his wife!"

"I think not." Rosamunde turned her back on her vile captor, having no inclination to make such a submission easier. She surveyed the beautiful countryside and spied a man tending a pair of horses that were drinking mead on the bank. He was handsome, and his gaze was bright upon her.

His hair was as dark as midnight, and if she narrowed her eyes, he could have been mistaken for Padraig.

Save that Padraig had neither wings nor pointed ears.

Perhaps he could aid her in finding Padraig.

When the Faerie knight smiled, Rosamunde found herself smiling in return. "I will take my heart's ease here instead," she said to Darg and turned her back upon the creature.

"No!" the spriggan screamed, as once it had screamed before in Rosamunde's presence. She glanced back warily, then ran when she saw that the spriggan had become a large and menacing black cloud. When enraged it could change shape with frightening speed – the last such eruption had led to Tynan's death after it had shattered the caverns.

"I saved your life, it's mine to give," Darg shouted. "I trade it now so I shall live!"

Rosamunde ran as quickly as she could, feeling the other faeries watching her with bemusement. She could not outrun Darg's fury, however. Her heart sank as the dark cloud enveloped her, surrounding her with fog as black as night.

Then she was snatched from the ground, as helpless as a butterfly caught in a tempest, and carried away. She thought she heard someone cry out, but Darg did not slow down.

Finvarra's wife. King or not, Rosamunde had no interest in his attentions. The very fact that he would trade a faerie's life for a woman, with no consideration of any desire beyond his own, was no good endorsement. She struggled and fought, knowing it was futile, and she wished again for a loyal friend to fight at her back.

Padraig. How could she have been so blind?

Padraig fondled the strange stone in his pocket as he returned to the tavern that night. It was falling dark, the sun blazing orange just before it slipped beneath the horizon.

He could not dispel his dream of kissing Rosamunde and, in truth, he did not want to do so. The dream had lifted the shadow from his heart, made him feel that there might be some purpose to his life even without his partner by his side.

"You are fair pleased with yourself tonight," his sister said as she set an ale before him. She smiled and propped her hands on her hips to regard him. "A conquest was it then?"

Padraig laughed for the first time in a long time. "Naught but a dream, but 'twas a fine one."

"I wager it must have been," she said, her smile teasing. "You dreamed then of a lady?"

"None other than the Faerie Queen," Padraig agreed amiably. "And she gave to me a token."

His sister sobered. "Did she then?" Her wariness reminded Padraig of their mother.

"A ring with the power to make a man invisible to others." Padraig chuckled at the whimsy of it all, then reached into his pocket to show her the stone. He thought she would be amused by the evidence of his drunken dream, but when he pulled the gift from his pocket, it had become a golden ring again.

Padraig stared at it on his palm and blinked in wonder. "But a moment ago, it was a stone," he whispered.

His sister caught her breath and took a step back. "A Faerie gem." She crossed herself quickly. "Mind your step, Padraig. A man does not easily elude the favour of the Faerie Queen."

Padraig barely heard her warning. He knew all the tales of the fey, courtesy of his mother. He simply could not believe that the ring had changed twice.

But then, if it *was* fey, the charm upon it would hold for the night and not the day. He stood and, leaving his ale, looked out of the door of the tavern. Sure enough, the sun had set completely and twilight, that time so potent for the fey, had fallen.

He gazed at the circle of gold. What if his dream had been true? What if this ring truly did have the power Una had stated? What if he could reclaim Rosamunde from the realm of the fey?

What if his dream of that kiss had answered his question – what was Rosamunde's honest desire? Did she wish for him as well as for freedom?

But before he dared to enter the Faerie mound, before he dared to abduct a women destined for the High King of Faerie's bed, Padraig would be sure of the ring's powers.

He left a coin for the ale, having no taste for it any longer. He strode out into the streets of Galway, slipped down an alleyway, then donned the ring.

To his astonishment, when he stepped back into the crowded thoroughfare, a man walked right into him, frowning at the obstacle he could feel but not see.

Padraig spent an hour testing the ring's abilities, but it was clear that no human eye could discern his presence.

Next he would check it among the fey. He borrowed a horse and rode like a madman to the stone circle where he had heard Una sing the night before.

Thus Rosamunde's lover true
Did meet the Faerie Queen.
Thus he gained the magical ring
That let him pass unseen.
And so it was that he did choose
To witness his lady's plight.

He held his breath and donned the ring
At the Faerie sid *that night.*
He saw his lady Rosamunde
All garbed in white and gold.
Her hair was braided thick with jewels,
A star was on her brow.
Her girdle was of finest silk,
Her shoes of purple leather.
So radiant was her countenance
He'd never seen her measure.

Rosamunde was displeased.

To be sure, the court was fine enough, and the hospitality was generous. She had been assigned some two-dozen ladies in waiting who cared more for the careful plaiting of her hair than she ever could have done. She liked the splendid fabrics, the jewels and the evident wealth.

She did not like that she had been unable to escape Darg, much less the creature's hoot of triumph when Finvarra had removed the red cord. The spriggan had disappeared so quickly that it might not have ever been.

She did not miss the vile creature.

Finvarra was a handsome man, confident in his appeal. His eyes were strange, or at least they did not seem to match his countenance. He looked to have seen no more than thirty summers, his body young and strong, his face unlined and handsome. But his eyes . . . his eyes were filled with the shadows of experience. There was the memory of sadness there, of joy, of triumph and defeat. Had it been her choice to meet him, had she met him when both were unencumbered, Rosamunde might have been intrigued by the Faerie King.

As it was, she saw that his fascination with her was no more than lust. She would be a conquest, a mistress, a frippery to be tossed aside when he became bored with her charms.

Rosamunde had never been so little and had no desire to be as much now.

Indeed, his interest reminded her of Tynan's *supposed* love, and she would spurn it as she had failed to spurn it previously. If nothing else, Rosamunde would learn from her error.

Then there was the matter of Finvarra's wife, Una, who had retreated to the far side of the hall. Una, no small beauty herself, had gathered her ladies about her and they clustered there, whispering and pointing.

Finvarra ignored his wife so deliberately that Rosamunde guessed she was but a pawn in some ongoing match between King and wife.

It was far less than what she wanted of her life.

She had tried to escape, without success. These maidens purportedly assigned to ensure her pleasure were also charged with keeping her captive. Their hearing was sharp, their sight sharper, their vigil complete.

Rosamunde folded her arms across her chest, smiled thinly and refused to participate in the festivities. If Finvarra's interest waned, perhaps she would be cast out of the realm sooner.

It seemed an unlikely prospect, given the gleam in his eye when he glanced her way, but Rosamunde had precious few options.

She disliked this role of a woman pampered. She disliked having no choice over her direction, having no ability to shape her own fate. It was utterly at odds with the way she had led her life, and Rosamunde fairly itched to return to what she knew.

First, somehow, she had to escape this court.

The music was intoxicating, so loud and sweet and melodious. The fey danced with a vigour that was astounding, seeming never to tire. The bounty of food on display was enticing, all manner of sweets and confections offered for the pleasure of the company. The mead smelled wonderful indeed, but Rosamunde feared the loss of her wits should she drink it. She simply stood and watched, and the hours drew long.

It was hours later when the faeries began a vivacious dance. It was clear that Rosamunde's maidens were captivated by the music, their eyes dancing and their toes tapping. Rosamunde encouraged them, one after the other, to take the floor, until finally she felt unobserved.

It would not last, but she would savour the interval.

No sooner was she alone than a man's hands closed over her shoulders. He stood close behind her, whoever he was, his breath in her hair and his chest at her back. Rosamunde jumped, then felt her eyes widen at a familiar murmur.

"At your back, as always," Padraig said. Thc feel of his breath on her neck made her tingle. "Say nothing, but listen."

Rosamunde felt her heart skip and feared her maidens would hear its tumult. She tried to quiet her response, but she felt the strength of Padraig's fingers on her shoulders, the warmth of him against her back. She glanced down but could not see his hands.

"An enchantment," he murmured and she heard the familiar humour touch his tone. "I know not how long 'twill last."

Rosamunde's mouth went dry. She didn't doubt that Padraig would be at risk if they realized there was an intruder in their midst. She scanned the hall, endeavouring to be casual in the survey, and realized that none could see Padraig. None even guessed his presence.

Then Rosamunde felt Una's gaze land upon her and saw the woman smile slightly.

Could Una see him?

Or was she simply gladdened that Rosamunde did not enjoy the celebrations?

"I do not know how much you know," Padraig said in quick whisper. "You are in the *sid* of the High King of the Faeries, Finvarra, and he means to make you his mistress."

Rosamunde nodded ever so slightly.

"Choose, Rosamunde, choose whether you would remain in this place or whether you would have me aid your escape." Padraig's voice dropped low and his grip tightened slightly. "I am not without my own expectation, you should be warned. I should have confessed my love for you years ago. I would love you. I would be with you. I would endeavour to make you happy."

Indeed, the man could not fail at that task. Rosamunde closed her eyes, overcome with joy at his words.

"My right hand if you would stay here," he murmured. "My left, if you would be mine."

Without hesitation, Rosamunde raised her hand, as if to straighten her hair, and brushed her fingertips across Padraig's left hand. She felt him catch his breath.

Una's smile broadened, turning smug, then she plucked a sweet from a proffered tray. The Faerie Queen's eyes gleamed and Rosamunde feared her deception.

"Eat nothing," Padraig warned. "Drink nothing. If you consume so much as one morsel, you will be captive here forever."

Rosamunde touched his fingertips to indicate her understanding. She was fiercely glad that she had not taken a bite since her arrival.

"Tomorrow night, the fey will ride out in procession for Beltane. You must go with the company. You must ride as close to the perimeter of the group as you can. I will come for you."

Rosamunde felt the burn of his lips against her nape. She did not doubt that Padraig would face a challenge in gaining her freedom. She closed her eyes, wanting to turn into his embrace, her chest tight with the gift of his presence.

Then Padraig was gone, like a shadow swallowed by the night.

And there was only the glitter of Una's knowing gaze locked upon her.

What treachery had the Faerie Queen planned?

And so the pair did plot their scheme;
So did they plan to keep their dream.
But the ring's charm did not hide all:
Una saw the mortal in her hall.

The Faerie Queen had no good intent;
Loyalty to her spouse had been spent.
None could have joy while she did not;
And so Una schemed her own plot.
Padraig might capture his love lost,
But Una ensured too high a cost.

It was Beltane, and Padraig was enough of his mother's son to know that anything was possible on this night of nights.

On this night and on Samhain, the fey were at their most potent.

He made his preparations, fully aware of that.

He bought the horse that he had borrowed and the ostler was pleased to be rid of the beast, given that it had gone missing the night before. Padraig got the steed for a better price than he might have otherwise. He prepared it with care, ensuring that there was no iron in its harness, less the fey realize it was not one of theirs.

It was a fine stallion, a high-stepping black horse with a proud gait. Its mane was long and dark, its eyes lit with a fire that made Padraig wonder whether it knew more of the fey than he. It was said that the faeries bred the best horses, and there was majesty in this one's lineage.

It had not even shied at the *sid*, but waited calmly for him at the hawthorn tree.

He declared his intent to sail with the morning tide, had his ship provisioned for the journey, and kissed his sister goodbye. He cleared space in the hold to create a stable for the horse, for he had no inclination to leave it behind.

He paid his debts and tried to sleep, that he might be at his best when night fell.

When the darkness slipped over the land, when the Beltane fires were lit in the hills, Padraig walked his horse to the old Norman gate. His heart in his mouth, he mounted and rode out into the night, slipping the ring on to his finger when he left the road.

His steed was proud, as black as night
He donned the ring, was lost to sight.
The steed ran on, proud and bold,
His hooves thundered on the road.
The lover knew he faced his test;
Without his lady, he'd know no rest.
Lit by the fires on ev'ry hill,
The heat of his ardour knew no chill.
Padraig rode for his lady heart,
Would the fey queen keep them apart?

Padraig reached the stone circle, but found only silence within it. The wind was still, the ground dark. He feared he had come too late, that the host had already ridden out – or that perhaps they had guessed his intent and chosen to forgo tradition to keep the prize of Rosamunde.

There was much he would forgo to keep her by his side.

Then the wind rustled in the branches of the hawthorn that grew to one side of the stone circle. His stallion snorted and tossed his head, then Padraig heard the clarion call of a distant trumpet.

The single note was clear, as clear as a mountain stream, as lovely as a summer morning. The sound melted his heart, dissolved his inhibitions, filled his veins with starlight and resolve.

The earth in the middle of the mound cracked; it gaped wide. A portal opened in the ground, one wide enough for four horses to ride abreast. Padraig glimpsed the hall beneath that he had visited the night before and his grip tightened on the reins.

Golden light spilled from the hidden court into the night's darkness and the Faerie host rode forth. Music accompanied them, the tinkle of ten thousand silver bells mounted on a thousand harnesses. Their steeds pranced with pride, confident of their splendour and beauty. The Beltane fires on the adjacent hills burned higher as if in tribute, their flames stretching to the stars.

And the fey laughed.

Padraig stared in awe at their magnificent display.

Then lo, he saw the Faerie host,
Their company more beautiful than most.
He saw the silver and the gold;
He saw the Faerie knights so bold;
He saw the maidens garbed so fine;
He heard the music, saw the wine.

The will-o'-the-wisp danced on the hill
Fey light glimmering and never still
The stars seemed to have come to earth

As the Faerie host rode in mirth.
And so it was he glimpsed his lady,
On the left of the King of Faerie.

There were horses in the company without riders, or perhaps their riders were too small to be seen. Padraig would have eased his steed to join the company, but the beast seemed to know his expectation – it marched alongside, as if it had done as much a dozen times before.

The Faerie host flowed over the hills, eased down to the valley and ascended the next hill. Small Faeries darted towards the occasional cottage, claiming whatever gifts had been left for them. They shared the milk and ale with their fellows, lapped the porridge and cast gold coins in their wake. Each Beltane fire they passed snapped and crackled in acknowledgment of their passage, and Finvarra laughed at the sight. His wife, riding on his right, smiled but there was no joy in her eyes.

Neither was there joy in the steady gaze of Rosamunde.

Padraig eased his horse closer to the royalty, stroking its neck to encourage it to pass between the other beasts. The stallion needed little encouragement, and Padraig considered the possibility that horses felt a natural attraction to the Faerie King.

Just as the Beltane flames acknowledged his presence.

Padraig did not know how long they rode, nor how far. He thought solely of getting closer to Rosamunde without attracting attention, and he made consistent progress in that goal. They crossed a vale and ascended another hill. When they reached the top, the shining dark water of Lough Carrib was visible, gleaming at the foot of the hills. There were more stars on this night than he had ever seen and the moon rose high in pearly splendour.

When they began to descend the hill, Padraig's horse eased so close that he could touch the hem of Rosamunde's dress.

It was time.

He spurred his horse, he galloped near
He seized the lady he loved so dear.
He stole her from the Faerie host

Claimed she Finvarra desired most.
The fey did scream, the horse did run,
Finvarra shouted 'twould not be done.
"Hold fast, hold fast," Rosamunde cried.
"For she would steal you from my side."
And so he held with all his might
Even as Una unleashed her spite.

The company jostled for position as they began the descent. The fey were celebratory, and less disciplined than when they had first left the hill. Their laughter was louder and their songs more merry.

Padraig lunged through the company with purpose. He dug his heels into the stallion's side, and the horse leaped with power. Padraig snatched Rosamunde from her steed, his arm locked around her waist, and placed her on the saddle before him.

Then he fled.

As the stallion raced down the hill, the golden ring upon Padraig's finger cracked in half. It fell from his hand and was trampled beneath the horses' hooves, leaving him revealed to the fey.

"Impostor!" they cried. "Thief!"

"Fetch my mistress!" bellowed Finvarra.

Padraig gave the horse his heels. The steed raced down the hill ahead of the Faerie host, running so quickly that the ground was a blur beneath their feet.

"Faster," Rosamunde urged, glancing back. "Faster!"

Padraig heard Una's song rise sweetly in the distance, but did not trust her ode.

"Padraig!" Rosamunde said, locking her arms around his neck. "She means to make you spurn me. Be not deceived."

Padraig guessed the test he would face a heartbeat before it began.

"They will turn me to an ancient crone
A woman wrought of sinew and bone.

A cold, rotted body from the grave
Hold fast, my love, you must be brave."

In his embrace, Rosamunde turned to a hag, appearing to have endured a thousand years of hardship. Her skin was wrinkled like ancient leather, her eyes yellow and her teeth missing.

She cackled at him, this apparition, and looked fit to devour him. Padraig could see the bones of her skull beneath the loose flesh of her face, he could smell the fetid stench of decay, and he felt the clutch of her skeletal fingers on his neck. Everything within him was repulsed and his urge was to cast her aside with all speed.

Padraig told himself it was but a spell and held fast.

"Next I'll be a writhing snake
With a toxic bite your life to take.
I will be as slipp'ry as an adder
My release lies solely in your power."

Rosamunde changed then to an enormous snake, green and slippery in Padraig's grasp. The snake bared its fangs and malice lit its eyes as it reared back to strike. He had no doubt its bite was poisonous, but he did not release it.

There were, after all, no snakes in Ireland. Padraig knew that this, too, was but a fey trick.

He heard Una's song, realized it was growing in volume, and knew there would be worse to come. Three tests there would be, he guessed as much, and they would become more fierce. He held fast to the writhing green snake and hoped he could keep hold of Rosamunde. The horse ran, outdistancing the shouting host at its heels.

The snake twisted in his grip, as elusive as a fish, but Padraig held tightly. The water of the lake drew ever more near and he wondered what the horse would do. He thought to direct it around the body of water, then Rosamunde changed shape again.

"And last I will become a flame,
As hot and fierce as ever came.
A Beltane fire, orange and hot
My love, my love, release me not."

In the blink of an eye, Rosamunde became a fire in his embrace. The brilliant light of the flames nearly blinded Padraig and surprise almost loosened his grip.

He cried out and tightened his grasp upon her. The fire burned his skin, the flames licking at his flesh. He closed his eyes to the sight of his own body burning, to the smell of his destruction. He held fast to the column of flame, even as he feared he could not have the strength to endure against the fey.

Padraig thought of the way Rosamunde's hair looked in the sunlight.

He recalled her bold stance on the ship as they sailed to adventure. He remembered the light in her eyes when they had first met. He thought of her determination, even when the spriggan Darg had stolen her charts and trapped the ship in a calm.

He recalled her pride in her nieces and her joy in seeing them well wed. He thought of her passion and her pride and he fortified himself with the truth of why he loved this woman with all his heart. Padraig squeezed his eyes shut as the pain built to a crescendo.

He could not lose his love.

He recited the paternoster, on impulse, recalling his mother's counsel. Tears stung his cheeks as he said the familiar prayer. *Our Father . . .*

The horse halted abruptly, reared, then it ducked its head. Padraig was thrown over its neck and gasped aloud when he landed in the lake with a splash.

He sank low, still holding fast to Rosamunde, and the cold dark water of the lake embraced them. He felt the flame in his arms turn to a woman again.

A naked woman.

A naked woman he loved more than life itself.

And Padraig knew he had triumphed. They broke the

surface together, Rosamunde's smile enough to light Padraig's nights forevermore.

When they might have spoken each to the other, a man cleared his throat at close proximity.

Finvarra stood on the shore, holding the bridle of the stamping black stallion. "And so the contest goes to you," the High King of the Faerie said. He stroked the horse's nose with affection and the beast nuzzled him. Finvarra smiled and his eyes glinted. "I shall take this horse into my care, seeing as it was once stolen from us and is rightfully returned."

Padraig understood why the horse had not been startled by the fey, why it had been so at ease joining the host. Recognition was possibly why it had been allowed to join the company in the first place.

He understood then why it had thrown him and saved Rosamunde. Padraig fancied that the horse had intended to reward him for bringing it back to Finvarra.

"You are a man of more cunning than most." Finvarra smiled. "I should have liked to have played chess with you."

"With respect, my lord, I have little to my name and nothing I would choose to lose." Padraig kept his arm around Rosamunde, noting how the King's gaze flicked between the two of them.

"Should his devotion falter," Finvarra said to Rosamunde, "you are always welcome at my court."

"I thank you, my lord, and thank you also for your hospitality," Rosamunde said with a bow.

"You and your fellows will always find welcome at our home," Padraig added with a bow of his own.

Finvarra smiled, his gaze trailing to his wife, who remained upon her steed and at a distance. "It is no crime to covet a beauteous gem," he said softly, "but a rare triumph to possess one. I salute you, Padraig. May your love never be tarnished."

With that Finvarra turned and led the prancing horse back to the company. Padraig felt the chill of the night air on his wet skin as he stood with Rosamunde fast at his side, but he could not tear his gaze away from the departing company. He doubted he would ever see them again. They rode forth, passing over the hills like a vision, leaving only the echo of their silvery laughter behind.

And Rosamunde.

"Thank you," she said, smiling up at him.

"You are welcome. I am glad to see you hale again." Padraig stared down at her, knowing his desire but afraid to speak of it too soon.

Rosamunde, as was typical of her, showed no such restraint. She twined her arms around his neck, sliding her fingers into his hair. "I am sorry, Padraig, that I erred so badly. I love you. I think I have always loved you, but I wish I had seen the truth of it sooner."

Padraig bent to touch his lips to hers, his heart swelling that his dream should be his own. "I know that I have always loved you," he murmured against her mouth.

Rosamunde laughed. "Then I shall have to spend the rest of our lives atoning for my error."

"I do not think it will be so onerous."

"Nor do I!"

Padraig laughed at the prospect, then he sobered. Rosamunde's eyes were the richest green, filled with a conviction that stole his breath away. "Marry me, Rosamunde. Marry me and seal our bond for all to see. I have little to offer you but myself."

"Your ship."

"*Your* ship, and the contents yours as well. I have only myself."

"And it is more than enough. I will wed you, Padraig Deane, and I will honour your love every day and night of my life."

It was everything he had ever wanted, and yet more.

Rosamunde's kiss sent a welcome heat through Padraig, a heat that her presence would never fail to kindle. Padraig knew that whatever he had suffered had been worthwhile, for he had gained his heart's desire.

When he lifted his head, her eyes were sparkling and her cheeks were flushed. She glanced about herself and shivered. "Tell me, though, that we can sail to warmer climes."

"I thought Sicily," Padraig said, smiling as pleasure lit her expression. "With the morning tide. All is prepared."

Rosamunde laughed. "A man of confidence, and one in pursuit of my own heart."

"I thought I possessed that prize already," he teased, loving the sound of her answering laughter.

"You do, you do." Then Rosamunde raised a hand to his cheek, as solemn as he had ever seen her. Her voice dropped to a fervent whisper. "Oh, Padraig, never doubt that I am yours." A tear glistened in her eye, a tear that he knew was rare for this bold woman. "I may have been late to see the truth, but I shall never forget it now."

"I shall never let you forget it," he retorted then winked. Rosamunde smiled and he swung her into his arms then strode from the lake. He had an idea of how they might warm themselves before the walk back to town.

One glance at his lady told him that their thoughts were as one. Yet again, they would challenge convention. Yet again they would follow their hearts. But from this day forth, they would do so together.

It was as close to heaven as Padraig Deane ever expected to be.

Padraig gained his lady's heart,
She vowed they'd never be apart.
Rosamunde was a pirate queen
With hair red gold and eyes of green.
Her lover true did hold her fast,
Showed all the fey his love would last.
They ne'er forgot those of Faerie,
And lived out their days most happily.

Oracle

Margo Maguire

One

The Isle of Coruain – 938 AD

Ana Mac Lochlainn came awake suddenly, her heart pounding, her mouth dry. She felt confused by the sights and sounds of destruction that were so real, so horrifying.

She opened her eyes and had trouble discerning her surroundings. At length, her vision cleared, and she saw that she was still in the Oracle's cave, sitting comfortably on the Seer's divan where she'd lain no more than a quarter-hour before.

"What is it, lass?" asked the màistreàs, the prime Oracle, the Seer to whom Ana would soon make her Oracle's vows. She had felt ready to make the commitment – to hold her virginity sacred, and keep a vigilant watch over her people, the magical Druzai – for weeks, but the màistreàs had said it was not yet time.

"The vision . . ." said Ana. "It was more vivid than any I've ever had."

The old Oracle nodded. "I've had inklings of it, myself. What did you see?"

"The people," she looked up at the old woman, "Our Druids, a king . . ." She shook her head in confusion. She was drawn to this king, to this *human* whose rugged features were more compelling than that of any Druzai she'd ever met. "They are under attack."

The old Oracle frowned. "By what? Could you *see*?"

Ana swallowed. "Not enough." But what she *had* seen was horrifying. Dark, malicious creatures – little demon ollphéists – near Lough Gur, creating discord and aggression among the clans of southern Ireland. The màistreàs would never believe it, for the Druzai chieftain had banished those destructive beings from the Tuath lands ages ago. And yet there had clearly been ollphéists in Ana's vision.

And they were being directed by some stronger power.

"I must go." She started for the entrance of the Oracle's cave, but the màistreàs reached for her arm, restraining her.

"'Tis too dangerous, my lady. There is much that a Druzai princess can do from the safety of our shores. Besides, you know very well 'tis forbidden for Druzai to intrude upon the Tuath."

"No. The vision . . . I am part of it." She touched a hand to her head. She did not know what would be required of her, but she'd never felt so strongly about any of her visions. The King – Rohrke Ó Scannláin – compelled her in a way that was entirely unfamiliar. Her heart clenched in her chest at the thought of his peril. "I must go."

The Oracle frowned fiercely. "'Tis against Druzai law. We removed ourselves from Tuath centuries ago, when—"

"Aye. I know our history. Druzai magic makes it far too tempting for one of us to try to enslave the Tuath, in spite of all the protections we've taught the Druids."

"They are merely wise men, my lady."

True, yet some were more than merely wise. Druzai had mingled with Tuath, giving some humans magical abilities.

Ana had to go to Ireland, to Ballygur near the sacred Lough Gur. She had to do what she could to find and destroy the creature that guided the vicious ollphéists.

And yet she knew that her cousins, the Druzai high chieftain and his brother, would object to her intervening in earthly affairs – which made it imperative that she act quickly and quietly before Merrick and Brogan learned what she was up to. They would forbid her to leave their enchanted isle, perhaps thinking they could manage the disastrous happenings in Ireland themselves.

But Ana had *seen* the visions. She knew it was her destiny to go.

"But your vows, my lady," said the Oracle.

Ana pulled on her cloak and started for the entrance of the Oracle's cave. "My commitment will have to wait, Màistreàs. There is trouble in the earthly lands."

Two

Lough Gur, Ireland – 322 AD

Rohrke Ó Scannláin paced through the tall grass near Lough Gur where the standing stones would draw everyone in the kingdom on the morrow for the summer solstice festivities. It would be the perfect opportunity for Teague Ó Fionn's men to execute their attack.

The situation was grave. Rohrke did not know if he could risk offending Áine, the sun goddess, by suspending her midsummer celebration. There was more than a fair chance that the Scannláin crops would fail, and the cattle would be barren in the coming season. And yet he could not allow the festival to go forward, not with Teague threatening their borders.

Rohrke needed a powerful ally. And he would have one as soon as he wed the daughter of King Maitias Mac Murchada.

He should never have hesitated with the marriage. Sláine Mac Murchada was a comely lass in possession of a generous dowry, and Rohrke should have wed her the day Maitias made his offer.

And yet naught burned between them when their eyes met. No shock of awareness sizzled through Rohrke when he looked upon Sláine's lithe form. She would never be the woman of his heart. Not that such a thing was crucial in a royal marriage. But he'd hoped to wed a woman he could look upon as something other than a sister.

Rohrke's Druid, Sedric, had advised him to marry Sláine anyway. Her father's alliance was far too important to cast aside such an offer.

Rohrke scratched the back of his neck. His clan had ruled this fine corner of Ireland for centuries, and there was no better land to be found in all the country. 'Twas no wonder Teague wanted it. But he would never have it.

Teague Ó Fionn's aggression was entirely unforeseen. Only a year ago, Rohrke had allied with him against the King of Uisnech, together defeating him soundly. Rohrke did not know what had happened to ruin their friendship. This antagonism of Teague's felt very strange. He could think of no reason for it.

Rohrke felt the air cooling, and saw that Áine had nearly made her journey across the sky, and would soon lie down to sleep in the west. In the meantime, a mist formed over the grass and tall shadows fell on the land, turning Rohrke towards home – the village of Ballygur.

The wind arose suddenly, and he felt the chill of night skittering down the back of his neck. A moment later, a wizened old woman touched his sleeve, causing him to jump.

"What are you about, crone?" he barked.

"Lost my way," she croaked.

Rohrke jabbed his fingers through his hair. His agitation did no one any good. He needed to get back to the village and begin preparations for war. "Where are you going?" he asked the old woman.

"To Clynabroga."

She lost her footing, and when he took her arm to steady her, he felt an odd sensation rush through his hand and up his arm. He released her abruptly. No doubt 'twas merely due to his nerves over Teague. "Ach, woman. Clynabroga is a fair day's walk." He looked at her bent body. "Two, maybe three days for the likes o' you."

"Which direction?" she asked, as though he would allow an old woman to begin such a long walk at that hour. Alone.

"You'll come with me." He turned to glance north-east, in

the direction of Clynabroga. "I'll find someone to take you there on the morrow."

But when he looked back to her, she was gone. He searched in every direction, but she'd disappeared in the mist. Rohrke muttered a small curse and took to the trail back to Ballygur. There was naught he could do about the woman now, but he hoped no one would find her corpse on the morrow. Not only would it bother his conscience for the rest of his life, it would be the worst omen possible. He needed only favourable portents as he embarked on war with Teague Ó Fionn.

"Ah! There you are," said Geileis Riaghan, approaching him on the footpath. She was a dark-haired, dark-eyed beauty who'd appeared with her servant, Peadar, in Ballygur a few weeks before. Rohrke wondered about her, but every time he started to ask questions about who she was and from whence she'd come, he lost track of his thoughts. *But not this time.* He was determined to keep his wits about him as they talked.

She took his arm and walked beside him. He felt potent and mighty when she stood alongside him, and he knew anything was possible. "Did you see an old woman walking this way?"

"Old woman?" Geileis laughed. "Who would be out at this time of night? Surely Áine does not walk these hills at twilight."

Rohrke masked his surprise. The thought of Áine had not come to him, but in times of old, the goddess had been known to show herself as an old woman at Lough Gur or Cnoc Áine. He hoped the crone was not the deity he would have to bed in order to become Munster's legitimate high king.

"Teague's men are gathering beyond the lake," said Geileis, and Rohrke forgot about the old lady.

"How do you know?"

"Peadar saw them when he went out to hunt."

Then war was truly imminent. His men must commence sharpening their spears and arrows right away, and he needed to order everyone to stay inside Ballygur's walls. Áine would just have to understand the unusual circumstances this year.

He considered the terrain near the lake as they walked,

and thought about battle plans. He wondered what Teague's strategy would be. How many men on horseback would he muster? How many swords and spears? His anger grew with every step, and he hoped for nothing more than to spit Teague on his own spear. He was so preoccupied with his fury that he barely heard Geileis' low chatter beside him.

When they reached the walls of Ballygur, it was almost full dark, and Rohrke could smell the hearth fires that burned in every house. Sedric drew him away from Geileis, and the anger that had burned inside him during the walk home seemed to recede gradually, as did his hazy thoughts.

Something was very odd, but Rohrke could not quite place what it was. He narrowed his eyes as Geileis' henchman came, took her arm and strode away with her, glancing back at him with a vacant grin. He knew little of the woman and her servant – but when they were together, he never had the wherewithal to question her.

She was beautiful, with hair and eyes as black as the bottom of a well. Her lashes were as dark as soot, and her skin shimmered like alabaster. But she did not stir him, which was just as well, for Sláine Mac Murchada was meant to be his wife.

"My lord, we must talk," said the Druid.

"Not now, Sedric," Rohrke walked towards his stone fortress. "There is much to be done."

"Aye, but we must try to understand what has happened and what Teague hopes to accomplish."

"He wants our lands. Our cattle."

"How do *you* know what he wants?" Sedric demanded, his frustration bleeding through his words. "Neither side has attempted to talk. We've always been on reasonably friendly terms with Teague. What's happened to change that?"

Rohrke blew out a deep breath. He wasn't sure. Except that his blood boiled every time he thought of Teague's grin. He wanted to bash the man's teeth in.

"Something evil works among us, my king," the Druid continued. "Something dark and terrible."

"Do not speak to me of elusive evils, Sedric," Rohrke said.

"What we face is real. 'Tis solid and well armed. We must prepare ourselves – see to our weapons and our horses."

"Aye." Sedric dipped his head in a slight bow.

"I don't know what's happened to destroy our relations with Teague. I will wed Sláine Mac Murchada tonight, and then we'll have the forces we need to defeat him."

"But, my lord," Sedric said gravely, "you must first bed the goddess."

Rohrke clenched his teeth. There were many myths and legends surrounding the Scannláin kings, and he knew some of them to be true. But there was far too much at stake now to be thinking about goddesses and solstice celebrations.

"Then I will wait. If my bedding Áine is meant to be, then it will occur upon the morrow, when the goddess comes to Cnoc Áine to partake of our celebrations."

He only hoped Teague would not attack before then. Rohrke kept moving towards his stone fortress as Sedric talked. "My lord, would you consider sending an emissary to Ó Fionn? There might be a way to end these hostilities peacefully."

"Why would you think—" Rohrke stopped short at the sight of a young woman approaching from the east end of the village. She looked vaguely familiar, and yet he knew he'd never seen her before. A ripple of pure male awareness surged through him when he looked upon her, but something far deeper touched him when his gaze met hers. "Who is that?"

"I don't know, my lord," said Sedric. "She is not of our clan."

"First Geileis. And now . . ." He was able to see her clearly in the fading light, perhaps because she was so fair, and clad in a shimmering robe of white. The gown hugged her curves and, when she pushed back her hood, he saw that her hair was as smooth and light as flax, and her eyes the green of a Druid's flame.

A sharp pang of arousal shot through him, and when she'd finally come to stand before him, Rohrke had to restrain himself from stepping closer, from touching her, from tossing her over his shoulder and carrying her to his private chamber in the keep.

He caught her elusive scent, a fragrance that was entirely unfamiliar – perhaps 'twas even bewitching, for he'd never felt such an intense attraction for any other woman. He wanted her under him, felt desperate to be inside her.

Everything within him shuddered with need that went far beyond his body's desires. He was not sure he understood it, and he knew he needed to maintain supreme control. Too much was going on in Ballygur – from his imminent marriage, to Teague's threats, and Geileis' presence – for him to lose his head in a whirlwind of lust. For that was all it could be. She was the most comely lass he'd ever encountered, and he wanted her.

But he could control himself.

"My lord." Her voice was low and seductive. She tipped her head in respect, but not obeisance. Somehow, he'd known she would not bow to him. "I am Ana Mac Lochlainn, a traveller in need of shelter."

Three

Ana paid extreme attention to her footing this time, for the solid, powerful presence of Rohrke Ó Scannláin had a surprisingly potent effect upon her. It was puzzling, for she knew any number of mighty Druzai sorcerers, and yet this Tuath man seemed to be the only one who possessed the power to cause her to trip over her own two feet.

She'd encountered him at Cnoc Áine, of course, while in the guise of the old woman. And even then, she'd needed to absent herself quickly, for the heat of his body and the strength of his touch had made her yearn for something other – something more? – than the Oracle's cave and the vows she would soon take.

Perhaps it was just because she'd never been away from Coruain, her island home. Her clan of warrior-sorcerers had left Ireland many millennia ago, so Ana had never encountered a Tuath human before. She couldn't have known they possessed a kind of energy that would skitter up her spine and make her yearn . . .

No. *Any diversion could not be*. Ana had been born to the most powerful Druzai clan, and had trained to become a formidable seer on Coruain. She'd been groomed from infancy to take her place as the next Oracle, and was deeply immersed in the process of preparing her body and mind for the grave responsibilities that faced her.

"You are a stranger to Ballygur," Rohrke said, and his voice seemed to rumble through her. She wondered if he had Druzai blood, for there was surely some kind of magic in him.

"Aye," she replied. "From . . . the north."

He frowned, scrutinizing her carefully. "You come from King Lochlainn Mac Cailein's realm?"

Ana nodded in spite of the lie, startled when he repeated the name Lochlainn. The Druzai high chieftains had certainly left their mark here in Ireland.

"Why have you come?"

She'd anticipated this question, but was unsure how to answer it. Clearly, she could not tell Rohrke she was a Druzai seer who'd foreseen troubles between the Irish clans with vile ollphéists in their midst. She could put a spell upon him, making him accept her as a mere traveller to Ballygur. But such tactics were unscrupulous, and Ana abhorred trickery.

However, a few small lies in the interest of preventing the carnage she'd seen would not be amiss. It was Midsummer's Eve. Surely there were many visitors to Cnoc Áine. "I've come to pay respects to the sun goddess." Her voice sounded strange to her own ears, soft and vulnerable.

"Aye, the solstice," said the Druid, but Ana had not been able to turn her attention from King Rohrke. He maintained her gaze with dark, piercing eyes that held no trust, no belief in her sincerity. He stood close, and she could almost feel his breath upon her face. His intensity shook her.

Somehow, she managed to answer the Druid with a non-committal shrug. She did not need Rohrke's approval or his assistance. She alone would discover how the monsters were coming to his realm and deal with them. And she would do it quickly, she hoped. She had no interest in staying away from

Coruain and her training longer than absolutely necessary. "I've long held Áine sacred, and wanted to come to Lough Gur."

"You've chosen an inopportune year for your visit," said Rohrke, and Ana heard the tension in his voice. "There is trouble on our borders. Did you not see an army amassing beyond the lake?"

"I did not come from that direction."

She saw no ollphéists in the village. Nor did Rohrke or the Druid seem as unnerved or as hostile as they should have been, had the little demons before influencing them. Ana did not think Rohrke's clan could be immune. And yet she knew the demons were present somewhere nearby. There was no mistaking what she'd seen in her vision.

"We are about to go to battle, lass. Perhaps 'twould be best if you returned to . . . wherever it is you've come from."

Before Ana could respond, Rohrke made a gruff sound and strode away towards the stone stronghold.

Ana remained standing beside the Druid, though she found herself drawn to watch the powerful man who walked away so purposefully. He was as tall as her cousins, with broad shoulders, narrow hips and the most powerful legs she'd ever seen.

But Ana was not one to ogle men, not even the handsome Druzai warriors of Coruain. She would soon make her vow of perpetual chastity, and then even the vaguest thoughts of pairing with any man would be moot.

A pesky *sìthean* – a small black, leathery creature that had been banished from Tuath many centuries ago – darted into Rohrke's path. Ana nearly shot it away from him with a burst of magic, but Rohrke sidestepped it as though he'd seen it. Or at least, *sensed* it.

The man could not be any more puzzling to her. As harsh and unfriendly as he seemed, she could not help but remember his kindness to the old woman she'd pretended to be at Cnoc Áine. Her heart warmed with the awareness that Rohrke would not have allowed her to walk all the way to Clynabroga alone.

She forced herself to turn to the Druid. Perhaps he had the information she sought. "What is the trouble at your border?"

"A neighbouring king," he replied. "Teague Ó Fionn has made threats of war."

"For what reason?"

The Druid shook his head. "'Tis unknown. Our clans were friends not too long ago, but all that has changed. And if King Rohrke does not soon wed Sláine Mac Murchada, we will not have the allies we need to defeat Teague."

'Twas just as she'd seen. The silent menace of the ollphéists was pushing the two clans towards battle, and each king would engage more and more allies until the whole of Ireland was locked in a bloody, devastating war. Men, women and children would be killed. Crops and livestock would die and finally the entire isle would be engulfed in famine.

Ana had to find out who controlled the monsters and how they were coming to Ireland from the dim netherworld where they had been banished so long ago. Someone, or something, had freed them, clearly intending to use them to maximize the carnage here.

She did not feel any hint of the malicious creatures now, nor was there any obvious portal for their entrance to the Tuath world. But Rohrke's presence seemed to have clouded her vision. She took a deep breath and centred her concentration.

The Druid looked at her strangely, and Ana feared he sensed she was not of his world. "Please, my lady, go with him, see if you can talk to him . . ."

Ana complied. If there was anyone who could change the course of the impending war, it was Rohrke Ó Scannláin.

Four

The attraction Rohrke felt for the beautiful stranger was entirely compelling. And completely unwelcome. He needed all his wits when he faced Maitias Mac Murchada and his daughter, Sláine, for he needed to negotiate the best possible terms for their alliance.

And the marriage.

Rohrke did not wish to see Sláine now. If circumstances were different, he would never consider marrying the lass, not when he'd felt such a sudden and intense desire for Ana Mac Lochlainn. He'd never reacted so strongly to a woman before, his body sensing her presence without even seeing her, touching her.

He'd left her as quickly as possible, before his body could betray him and cause irreparable damage to his alliance with Mac Murchada. He needed a few moments alone to prepare himself to meet the old King and settle the marriage pact.

A prickle of awareness crept up his spine, a feeling that nearly stopped him from his purpose. 'Twas Ana right behind him – he could feel her without even seeing or hearing her.

Rohrke stopped at the door to his great hall, then turned to face her.

She stood a few paces away, her bearing as regal as a queen's. Her skin seemed to shimmer in the firelight, and Rohrke took a step towards her. He could not keep himself from touching her.

Ana held her ground, but he saw her throat move as she swallowed tightly. She was no more anxious to be swept up in this untimely attraction than he was, but it was a force they seemed unable to control. "My lord, I must speak to you."

"Aye," he said, but in truth, he was in no mood for talk. He reached for her, touching her arm. When she placed her hand on his, he felt her tremble. "Come with me."

Rohrke led her to an isolated passageway inside, and settled her back against a cold stone wall. He touched her cheek then cupped her jaw with his hand. "You have not said who you are."

"But I have," she whispered, and he saw his own longing mirrored in her eyes. "I am Ana—"

He dipped his head and brushed her lips with his mouth. She clasped both his arms tightly and he felt her entire body shudder. By the goddess, he wanted her.

"Aye. Ana Mac Lochlainn." He withdrew slightly. "Why have you come now, lass, when disaster looms about us in every direction?"

She pushed away from him and clasped her hands together. "I know something of your difficulties. I . . . I believe I can help."

"How?" he asked. She might be small and feminine, but he sensed a deep strength within her. Perhaps she *could* help him avert war.

"I can say naught of my abilities, my lord. You will have to trust me."

"Trust you?" Oddly enough, he did.

"Aye."

"What do you need from me?"

"I need to look round Ballygur. And it would help if your people spoke freely to me, put their trust in me."

Rohrke scrubbed a hand across his face. "There has been a great deal of mistrust and antagonism among my people in recent days. 'Tis as though we've all been sleeping in beds of stinging nettles."

"'Tis because there are forces that—"

"Now you sound like Sedric. I've only one enemy, and his name is Teague Ó Fionn."

Five

The tingling frustration Ana had felt a moment before increased a hundredfold. Her body felt strange – hot and far more aware than ever before. And it wasn't entirely due to the presence of ollphéists near Ballygur. Rohrke unnerved her. "No. You cannot possibly understand all that threatens you."

She needed to get out and about among the people, and see if she could sense the demons were surely roaming among them. And she needed to put some distance between herself and King Rohrke. It would not do to fall under a sensual enchantment with him.

Ana reminded herself that she had the ability to resist him. To resist any man. She might be young, but she had become a powerful sorceress, tested by one of the most dangerous sorcerers the Druzai had ever encountered. And she was prepared to become her clan's Oracle, interpreting signs and divining events that would come to pass.

"Are you Druid?" Rohrke asked.

Ana inclined her head slightly. "Of a sort."

"You are a seer."

She nodded, unable to lie. "Aye."

"Where do we need to go? I'll come with you," he said.

"No!" Ana gasped, in spite of her desire to remain composed. She was having difficulty keeping her gaze from those chiselled lips that had barely touched hers. She hadn't known how soft and warm a man's mouth could be. Or the amazing sensations a mere kiss could cause.

Rohrke came very close, but did not touch her. "I *will* be coming with you, Lady Ana. These are my people, and I'll have no strange Druid walking among them."

"Suit yourself, my lord."

"As I am wont to do."

It was warm, so Ana removed her cloak and handed it to Rohrke. He tossed it over a railing and came alongside her. "Where will you go first?"

She was unsure. "I came because I saw . . . I'm not sure where to start. There is an evil presence that I hope I'll be able to sense as I walk through Ballygur. If I can determine how they're coming in . . ."

She hoped the ollphéists' entry point would be obvious once she stood close to it. The portal would likely be on the perimeter of the village, or in the very heart of it.

"We'll start here," she said, leading Rohrke from the great hall out to the standing stones that circled the central point of the village. Torches burned at the top of each stone, and a circular, cobbled pavement rounded the very centre in an elaborate pattern that reminded her of the beautiful stone mosaics at home.

It looked like the perfect place for a portal, but when Ana reached it, closing her eyes and touching the stones, there was no sense of any malignant beings. In fact, her sensations in the circle felt surprisingly familiar. She opened her eyes to see Rohrke gazing at her intently.

Ana swallowed and stepped away. His presence was distracting. And now the villagers had taken notice of her, and were starting to follow her movements. They did not look happy or content, and she could feel the ollphéists' influence among them.

The underlying hostility was disturbing, though it wasn't overpowering. Still, Ana could not let any of them distract her from her task. Ignoring their dark whispers, she walked the perimeter of the village opening her senses and her *sight* for anything that was out of the ordinary.

Her concentration was fierce, and she nearly stumbled once, but Rohrke caught her before she fell. She suppressed her immediate reaction to his touch and resumed her search for the portal. She examined every crevice and cranny in Ballygur's walls, as well as the wells and every other uneven lump in the ground. And still, she found naught.

"I need a quiet place to . . . to think," she said, noticing for the first time that the entire village had gathered and were following her, whispering quietly among themselves.

Rohrke took her arm and started back towards the keep, but Ana stopped abruptly. "What are they saying? They think I'm—"

"Áine? Yes. They believe you're the sun goddess."

Ana clenched her teeth and proceeded to the keep. She would have to disabuse them of such an outrageous misconception. "'Tis not true, you know. I am merely Ana Mac Lochlainn, and I—"

"*Merely*?" Rohrke said, his voice low. He took her arm again. "I would hardly use such a dismissive word when speaking of you, Lady Ana."

His words excited her in a strange way. It was a compliment unlike any she'd ever received before. Her cousins called her a brilliant sorceress. Her teachers said she was a gifted seer. Compliments had always been about her talents. Never about *her*.

Ana looked at him surreptitiously, and a purely feminine thrill went through her at the sight of the strong line of his jaw and his straight, narrow nose. His long, thick lashes caused a river of intense heat to shoot through her bones. Her palms started to sweat.

"I . . . I should be alone for this."

"Not a chance," he said. "But I won't intrude on your peace."

Ana sincerely doubted that was possible, but she went along with him to the keep, glancing behind her as the villagers dispersed. Rohrke led her into the stone fortress, up a staircase and onto the second level. They went into a spacious bedchamber with windows overlooking the standing stones in the centre of the village. 'Twas a warm night, so the hearth was cold, but small torches burned in sconces on each wall. Ana felt comfortable, in spite of the large bed that dominated the room, with a pure white linen sheet covering it.

Rohrke gestured towards it. "You are likely tired after your travels and all your searching. Please make use of my bed."

"Where will you be?" she asked.

He sat down in a large, stuffed chair. "Here. 'Tis quite comfortable, I assure you."

"I was not particularly concerned with your comfort, my lord, but my own privacy."

Six

By the goddess, she was beautiful—lush and golden. Rohrke could almost believe she was Áine, come down to see what was amiss in the world.

If only it were true. He would have no qualms about bedding Ana Mac Lochlainn. He did not know where Sláine and her father were, but they would surely not be pleased at the attention he was paying to Ana. Not when they expected him to make Sláine his wife.

He shook off his cheerless thoughts of them and watched Ana remove her shoes and lie down.

Her feet were small and delicate, reaching nowhere near the end of the bed. Rohrke could easily imagine sliding one of his own feet between hers as he pressed her into the soft mattress. He'd barely touched her lips with his, and he wanted more. Wanted to know her taste and the feel of her naked skin sliding against his.

She closed her eyes and expelled a long breath. She seemed completely relaxed, with her hands extended at her sides, her palms up. Her gown was soft and the colour of butter, or perhaps sunshine. And it lay perfectly arranged about her. There was nothing about her dress or her bearing that should arouse him, and yet . . .

He rubbed a hand across his face and closed his eyes. It was not wise to allow himself to think such suggestive thoughts about Lady Ana, a stranger whose purpose he did not really understand. Perhaps he should give further thought to what she and Sedric had said. That there was evil about.

He did not know what it could be. Or how it could such infuse him – and Teague – with such animosity towards each other. Nor could he understand what its purpose would be.

He stood and looked down at Ana, who lay perfectly still, hardly breathing. There seemed to be no colour in her lips or her cheeks, but her knew naught was wrong with her. Soothsayers had their own ways, ones he was not privy to.

Rohrke went to the window and looked down at the standing stones in the circle. Geileis was there, standing just outside its centre . . . waiting, it seemed. He scratched his head. Hadn't he seen her do this before? His memory was cloudy, as was his recollection of the time they'd spent together that afternoon. Or any other time. It was not like him to be so vague.

He derived no satisfaction from Geileis' company and, in fact, wondered why he did not know where she and her servant had come from. He could not quite remember how she'd arrived, either . . . on foot or horseback?

Ana was in her seer's trance. Rohrke was reluctant to leave her, but he was not a man to hover. He left her to her deep contemplations, and departed the room in search of Geileis. He hurried down to the village circle, determined to ask the woman some questions and gain some answers this time.

But when he arrived at the centre of the village, Geileis was not there. Rohrke glanced around and caught sight of some movement near the gate. Staying in the shadows, he hurried in the same direction, certain it must be the dark-haired woman and her servant.

He could not imagine where they were going so late at night, unless their purpose was illicit. They carried no torches, and managed to slip past the guards that had been posted at the gate.

With that troubling sign, Rohrke realized that Sedric and Ana had been correct. Something evil was present at Ballygur, and now he knew what it was – *Geileis.* She'd used some kind of magic on him, duped him and dulled his senses when he was near her.

He would not allow it to happen again.

Without making a sound, he came to the guards and motioned them to remain silent and to follow him. They took up their spears and fell in behind him as he followed Geileis, who was headed towards Lough Gur.

Seven

The sensation of Rohrke's kisses was nearly overpowering. Ana knew his seduction was only a vision, but she could actually *feel* the rasp of his whiskers on her cheek, then her neck. Her breasts tightened at his touch, and her legs trembled with anticipation.

The sensations were unlike anything Ana had ever experienced inside a vision or out. She wondered if this was what had compelled her to come to Ireland.

The acute awareness of Rohrke went on, his tender embrace, his gentle caress. Ana felt more alive in his arms than she'd ever felt before, and when they became one, she knew *sòlas,* the deep connection that was felt only by souls meant to be together. The revelation was deeply disturbing, and yet Ana could not dispute its veracity. Her visions were never wrong. They could be altered, however.

The vision changed sharply, and Ana suddenly *saw* Rohrke, beaten and bound in some dark, nasty place. Her heart lurched at the sight of his injured body, and she knew he'd been hurt by the evil ollphéists with their long claws and sharp teeth. When she finally saw them, they were coming out of water – a lake – rising out of it to meet a beautiful woman with black hair and white skin who changed during the vision to her true form. She became a hag with grey skin, colourless eyes, and hair that dripped ice about her face.

Cailleach!

Ana sat up suddenly, her visions completely gone. She'd recognized Cailleach, the goddess of death, at once.

The evil goddess' presence troubled Ana. Centuries ago, the Druzai had made it impossible for Cailleach to plague the human lands with her horrors. Yet somehow, she'd discovered a way to circumvent the powerful Druzai spells that kept her away. She was here. And she'd captured Rohrke, who was powerless to protect himself against her.

There was no time to waste. Ana would not allow the powerful goddess to harm the man who . . . *who possessed her heart*. The vision had shown her what was meant to be – she and Rohrke were destined mates. And she had no wish to alter that. Ana could not become the virgin Oracle, not after seeing the bond that she and Rohrke shared. She'd felt it as well, with all her heart and soul.

She recognized the lake in her vision. It was near Cnoc Áine, where she'd first met Rohrke as the old woman. Ana knew now that she'd fallen in love with him then. And yet she had not foreseen it.

She hurried down the steps and out of the keep, then ran to the gate, where she was surprised to see no sentries standing guard. It was an ominous sign, but in the absence of any threat at the walls, Ana left the village. The moon was nearly full, so she had no difficulty running across the barren plains that surrounded the walls. She hoped no enemy lurked in the forest beyond. But she felt no threat. Not here.

Cailleach would be at the lake, bringing monsters through to Tuath. And Rohrke would be somewhere near, tied and imprisoned. Ana had to find him quickly, before the goddess made her escape, taking him with her.

Ana did not use any sorcery to speed her trek to the lake, in case Cailleach could sense it. Many other creatures were able to see Druzai magic, and Ana knew she had to be cautious. The element of surprise must work in her favour when she confronted the goddess and her minions.

Desperate in her hurry to find Rohrke, Ana forced herself to slow her pace as she reached the trees close to Lough Gur. There were strange, furtive sounds in the distance, sounds that were not of this world. They were the gruff snuffles of the ollphéists, and Ana realized she was closing in on them.

She stopped to get her bearings, and to listen. Mostly for Rohrke's voice. She hoped she'd arrived before Cailleach could hurt him.

There was a slight rustle of leaves and a quiet splashing of water. Underneath those natural sounds, Ana heard furtive voices, and she sensed that another group of ollphéists was entering Tuath from their shadowy netherworld. They were not visible to a human's eye, but they could move about and make vile insinuations in people's ears. They were brutal, disgusting beings that thrived on discord.

And yet Rohrke seemed immune to their abhorrent suggestions. His people were vaguely hostile, but not as hateful as they should have been, had the monsters held sway over them. Something about the Ó Scannláin clan was different. Ana did not understand why they were not susceptible.

There was no time to puzzle over it now. She closed her eyes and focused her attention on finding Cailleach and making herself ready for battle. The goddess had a great deal of power, and Ana knew she could not act precipitously. She had to make sure Rohrke was unharmed, and that Cailleach could not take him back to her harsh world of black winds and sharp cold. She could take naught for granted.

Ana moved from one hiding place to another in the hope

of locating Rohrke while keeping out of Cailleach's sight. The goddess was cold and heartless, her only purpose to cause death and destruction. She thrived on plague and pestilence, and existed only to acquire victims to take with her to her terrible abode. Hence her plot to use ollphéists to destroy Ireland.

Standing at the water's edge, a number of the small creatures surrounded Cailleach, slavering before her. The goddess seemed to be giving silent instructions, and then they quickly began to scatter.

Ana had to allow them to go, but only for now. As soon as she found Rohrke, she would be able to protect him and use her Druzai magic to keep him safe while she sent Cailleach back to her Druzai prison.

The lapping of the water masked her movements and, when she'd gone far enough to be out of Cailleach's sight, she heard a low hum in the hillock that arose from the water's edge.

The sound grew louder as she climbed, and she soon found the gate guards from Ballygur, unconscious and tied together next to a deep hole in the ground. Dropping to her knees to climb down inside it, she discovered Rohrke fighting against a powerful vortex that was trying to draw him inside. His face was bruised, and he was bound by a thick brown vine that seemed to twist and grow around his limbs as he fought it.

"Let me help you!" Ana cried quietly.

Eight

The attack had come so suddenly and so viciously that Rohrke had not been able to defend himself. Hoards of partly hidden assailants had pummelled him, bringing him to his knees as they bound him with some charmed twine that twisted and lashed him every time he moved. They shoved him into a small, ominous space that seemed to be a gateway to some swirling black hole that was trying to suck him in. He struggled against it, but his bindings tightened and restricted his every move.

Desperate to escape the hole, he managed to push his feet against the walls to keep from being pulled in, but he could not hold on forever. One foot slipped, and he was sure it would only be another moment before he was pulled down. And then suddenly the ropes loosened and he could move.

He shoved away from the hole and, as he turned to pull himself out of the cramped space, he saw Ana Mac Lochlainn, reaching for him. He could barely see her, but he did not need his vision to know who it was. He'd felt her before she'd even touched him. It had never occurred to Rohrke that Ana would follow him to the lake. But he was very glad to see her.

"Come! We must get you away from here!" she said with a quiet urgency in her voice.

"'Tis Geileis," he rasped. "I've got to stop her!"

"Geileis? No. You do not know who you're dealing with."

He got out of the small space and felt Ana's hands upon his face. "Aye, I do. She is the one causing the trouble between our clans."

"True, but Geileis is only her human name."

His face no longer felt swollen and painful. Somehow, Ana healed his injuries with the touch of her hands. She had more skill than any Druid he knew.

"Where else are you hurt?"

He grabbed her hand. "You are a healer too, Ana Mac Lochlainn?"

"Among other things. Quickly, Rohrke. There is no time for explanations. Let me heal you so that you can get safely away."

"And leave you here? No."

"Please. I—"

He drew her into his arms and kissed her, not a gentle brushing of mouths, but a full possession of lips, tongues and teeth. It was what he'd wanted to do from the moment he'd seen her, approaching him as he stood with Sedric.

He felt as though they were part of the same whole, and wanted to show her . . . possess her . . .

She broke the kiss, and he heard a breathless catch in her

voice. "Aye, Rohrke. I feel it, too. But we must take action now, against the evil that walks among the clans. 'Tis Cailleach and her minions."

"The goddess of death?" Rohrke said, aghast. "What does she want with us?"

"What she always wants. Suffering and illness. War and death. My forebears locked her away aeons ago, but . . ."

"Who are your forebears, Ana? Are you Druzai?"

She took in a sharp breath of surprise. "You know of the Druzai?"

"The Ó Scannláin Druids have kept Druzai teachings alive for centuries. They have not allowed us to forget who you are." He turned towards the lake. "If 'tis Cailleach then we must act quickly."

"'Tis too dangerous," she said. "Stay here and I'll—"

"Ana, I am High King of all of the south. Druzai or no, I have no intention of allowing you to face Cailleach alone. Tell me how I can help you."

She took his hand and led him away from the vortex that had nearly swallowed him. Her hand was small, but it fitted perfectly in his, and when they'd gone only a few feet under the cover of the trees, she released him. "I am wary of involving you any further, Rohrke. My confrontation with Cailleach and her ollphéists will be dangerous. It could turn into a battle . . ."

"Ollphéists?"

"Aye. Creatures of the dark. Unseen demons that prey upon humans minds."

"And set us against one another?"

"Aye. They are vicious beings, and willing servants of the dark deities."

"How will you approach Cailleach?"

"Now that I know you are safe, I can use magic to send her back to her prison cairn."

"You have that much power?"

He saw her nod in the dim light.

"But Cailleach is powerful too," she said. "Your help might

give me an advantage. If you will walk towards her from here, I will circle around and attack from the east. Wait until you hear my word before you speak to her. I will need only a moment's distraction."

He grinned and pulled her to him. "I will do that and more for you, Ana Mac Lochlainn."

A moment later, she was gone. Rohrke remained standing where she had left him, and slid his hands across his ribs and down his thighs where he'd been beaten. There was no pain now, not even the slightest soreness. Ana had healed him completely.

He had not been entirely truthful with Ana. He'd known about the Druzai because the Ó Scannláin clan was descended from the sorcerer race. Its full history had been lost in the ages since, but every member of his clan knew the legends. It was why he saw and sensed things that were not perceptible to others.

"Rohrke." She whispered his name in his ear, as though she were standing right beside him. "Now."

He left the cover of the woods and ran along the edge of the lake. When Cailleach came into view, he shouted her name. She turned to face him and, almost instantly, there was a silent blast of blue lightning that hit the cold, cruel goddess, and knocked her off her feet. Before she was able to move and retaliate, Ana's lightning changed to become softer and more diffuse, and cocooned Cailleach inside a tight shell. No part of the Geileis-Cailleach creature was left in sight.

But then something began to strike Rohrke from all sides, and he decided it must be the ollphéists that Ana spoke of. The demons were without a leader now, and they were striking out at him – their perceived enemy.

He felt the same surge of strength that had always protected him in battle, and he used it to shield himself from their blows. And when Ana arrived, another gush of blue light destroyed his attackers.

With apparent ease, Ana used her magic to lift Cailleach's

cocoon from the ground. Again, she used the impossible bands of blue lightning to gather and imprison the hoards of monsters that Cailleach had brought forth. Rohrke guessed she was herding them away from the lake. He watched as she lifted both her arms and, in one quick movement of her hands, sent them all away, to some invisible realm far away.

Ana turned to him then. "They can do no more harm."

Nine

Rohrke was Druzai. Untrained and undeveloped, but Druzai. The knowledge of it warmed Ana's heart.

She might have sensed it earlier, but it had been so far beyond any expectation, she'd ignored the tingling recognition of his connection to her race.

"Will Teague relent now?" he asked, so tall and handsome, her heart clenched in her chest. Was this the way a virgin Druzai Oracle should react to a man – any man?

She nodded, her awareness of him so intense, she could barely find her voice. "The aggression of his clan will disperse within hours. He will feel naught but puzzlement at his actions of late."

He touched her face and she closed her eyes, swimming in sensation. She remembered his every caress from her vision, and wanted to experience it in reality. She hoped to feel his hands and mouth on her. She wanted to touch him and feel his shudder of pleasure. She wished to meld with her mate and experience *sòlas* as other Druzai couples did.

And Ana knew she could not be the virgin Oracle.

He kissed her then, and she relaxed as he slid his arms around her, pulling her against his body. Ana reached up to his shoulders and then slipped her fingers into the hair at his nape. She had not realized how incomplete she'd felt before. Or why she'd delayed taking her vows so many times.

"There is much to do in Ballygur," she said when he broke their kiss.

"Aye. I have a wedding to cancel. I'll have no bride but you, Ana Mac Lochlainn. I love you, lass."

Ana felt her heart swell in her chest. She'd never planned to wed, and yet her Druzai mate had found her in a way that she'd never expected. A very poor, but happy, Oracle she was, indeed.

The Trials of Bryan Murphy

Cat Adams

One

The 9th of October was drawing to a close, the last rays of sunset tinting the sky with shades of red and purple as the first stars twinkled. The temperature had dropped enough that the air was crisp, with just enough of a breeze to send the fallen leaves skittering across the ground. The security lights at the construction site flared to life, basking the parking lot in a flat, orange glow. *There'll be frost tonight.*

Bryan zipped up his leather motorcycle jacket. He bent down and picked up a pair of stray nails. They were old, very old, not at all what they were using on this project. The heavy rust that encrusted them and their square heads told him they must have been dug up when laying the foundations. He tucked them into his jacket pocket. It wouldn't do to leave them on the ground in the parking area. Someone would be sure to be getting a puncture.

Pulling on his helmet, he sent a thought to his wife. *"I'm headed home. Get ready. Remember the party is tonight, we're due at the pub."*

He heard her mental snort like a caress of air across his mind. *"As if I'd forget. Just get you home in one piece. I'll be ready when you arrive."*

Smiling, he climbed on to his old bike and kicked the starter. There was a time he didn't believe in magic – couldn't imagine he could share his innermost thoughts with one person. But then he'd met Bridget and everything changed. With a twist of his wrist the engine roared and he was headed home.

It wasn't a long drive, only a few minutes if he obeyed the speed limits. But when he was halfway home he felt something . . . *wrong.* His heart lurched, and he fed more gasoline to the engine. *"Bridget . . . Bridey?"* He called to her in his head, but her voice, the voice that had always been so clear, was the barest echo.

"NO! I won't! I don't want to go! NO! BRYAN!!!"

Panic raced through him as coarse hands grabbed his wife and tugged her out of their cottage. Their *home. "I'm COMING!"* He opened the throttle full out, and the bike leaped forwards. The powerful engine roared, in defiance he drove with blurring speed, avoiding every pothole in the road from memory, his body crouched over the bulk of the bike to cut wind resistance. The scenery blurred, and still he tried to make it go faster.

Their house was ahead, and in the distance he saw the faint outline of tall, pale, horsemen, seemingly in ancient armour of light and shadow. There were humans thrown across each saddle like so much luggage, men and women, seemingly oblivious to their undignified position. Only one fought, struggled against her captor, her red hair seeming to blaze with her fury under the yellow light from the lamps.

Bridget!

She heard his thought, and her head turned. Her captor followed her abrupt gaze. Eyes flashing ruby red beneath his helm. His long white hair seeming to flare and float in response to his agitation. Bryan could see his lips move. In response, the raid of the fae, for that had to be what it was, leaped into the air. Their horses' manes flickered and sizzled with energy as they flew home towards their sithen mound.

The motorcycle was a street bike. It had never been designed for trails, but it didn't matter to Bryan. He had to catch up to them. If they got to the mound, took Bridget inside, she'd be lost to him for ever. He couldn't, *wouldn't,* let that happen. Sheer desperation made him reckless. If the ride killed him, so be it. He'd rather be dead than live without her.

Branches slapped at him, tore at his jacket, the bike bucking and jarring beneath him as he wove through the underbrush. It would be trashed after this, he knew it. But whatever. Just let it get him there, and in time. He didn't dare look up, couldn't take his eyes off the path he was weaving through the darkening woods, but he could *feel* her, still fighting – and her struggle was slowing the horse, so that her captor's fellows rode faster, passing him by until he was the last in the line.

Up ahead there was a clearing. Through the leaves he saw pale figures and horses descend, moving down and through the seemingly solid wall of the mound in single file.

Bridey's rider was last in line to enter the sithen, but as Bryan's bike broke through the brush near the mound her captor finally passed through.

"NO!" Bryan roared his defiance, opening the throttle full out, forcing the damaged machine into one last charge, aiming for the narrowing crack that had served as the sithen entrance. He didn't even hesitate, hitting it hard and fast. He'd either catch the last of the magic or be killed trying.

Pain, and more than pain, a lurching *wrongness* as if space and time itself shifted, and he was through, and on to pavement as smooth as glass.

He didn't correct quickly enough from rough to smooth and the bike skittered then slid out from beneath him as he lost control. He let go as he went down, not even noticing as his body slammed hard against unforgiving stone. His jacket took the brunt of the damage, but he still saw stars. The screaming shriek of metal scraping over stone filled his senses as a shower of sparks erupted. The motorcycle crashed into the mound with a sickening crunch of metal that made the roaring engine sputter and die.

Bryan staggered to his feet, bloodied but unbowed he turned to face the crowd of armed Fae and their captives. Bridget broke loose with a fierce yank that forced her captor to his knees. She threw her arms around Bryan – weeping, but proud. *So proud*. He could feel it in his mind, in his very veins. "Oh, Bryan. Love, you're hurt. And you shouldn't have. But oh-thank-God you did!"

"Nay, you shouldna. She's right in that." A tall man, otherworldly in gleaming armour formed of light itself, stepped forward. He drew a sword from its scabbard, and if his armour was light, then the blade was darkness itself. "And you shall pay for the insult."

A harsh laugh bubbled out of Bryan before he could stop it. "You speak of *insult*? A common thief, ye are – stealing a wife as you might fruit from a tree. You've no honour to be damaged." Bryan shoved his wife behind him. He had no weapon, but he'd protect her with his body to his last breath.

The eyes of the swordsman began to glow with red-hot anger, so bright it tinted his hair. The fae advanced, blade forwards in a thrust position. There was nowhere to run that wouldn't endanger Bridget, so Bryan held his ground stubbornly. Perhaps being run through with a sword in the fairy world wouldn't hurt as bad.

The fae raider's arm moved back to strike, the finely honed bicep readying for the blow. A light trembling took over in Bryan's muscles, a product of his flight instinct being overwhelmed by his need to protect his wife.

He thought back to just a week before, when he'd found her crying quietly at the stove, dripping salty tears into the cabbage stew. He touched her face, wiping away tears in those beautiful polished-copper eyes and smiled. "Aye, and what's troubling you, lass?"

Her voice was so sad when she spoke that it nearly broke his heart to hear the sound. "Promise you won't forget me when I'm gone."

"*Pshaw.* And what makes you think you'll be going anywhere? Or that I'd let you leave me?"

She had shaken her head, and the tears fell anew. "They'll come, and I'll go. But promise you won't forget."

"As if I could," he remembered saying, and kissed her on

the tip of her freckled nose, and on those perfect lips, before carrying her down the hall to make the tears disappear altogether. She quieted after their lovemaking, but he knew she didn't believe him.

Now her hand tightened on his arm, a warning. *Be still, Bry. Say not a word. You hear me? You just keep still.*

"Halt." A woman's voice barked the order, but even that one harsh word was beautiful.

The crowd of warriors parted, heads bowing as the fae woman approached.

"What have we here?" The whisper slithering through the stone hallway like a frigid wind. She was beautiful, unearthly beautiful, with hair of winter white flowing in waves nearly to her ankles, skin like poured milk and eyes the colour of a midnight sky flecked with the cold sparkle of stars. Her dress was midnight as well, clinging to every delicate curve to pool on the floor, sparkling with crystal beads that glittered and made musical sounds as she moved.

It was Bridey's turn to protect him. Bridey, with her hair of fire and earthy warmth pulled him away and protected him, bringing him to himself. Because, Lord help him, he'd been moving towards the woman and her frigid beauty, without so much as knowing he was doing it.

"What have we? True love, betwixt our own blood and a wayward human? How . . . touching." The woman's voice was harsh now, like the cracking of ice on a night empty of warmth or stars. Actual frost began forming on the stones around them, and Bryan could see his breath misting in the air.

"He invaded our sithen, dared to bring cold metal into our midst." The one with the sword had not sheathed it, and would have raised it.

But again the cold beauty stopped him. "I told ye *halt.*" She snarled and did something Bryan could feel, but not see. The fae horseman struggled against the power, but it held him fast. Turning her back on him dismissively, she stepped in front of Bryan and Bridey.

Her voice was calm, reasonable – as she would speak to a

child. "She is his. This raider found her, and took her. You could go. An' should I release you, none here could gainsay it."

Go? *Go* . . . to leave his love with these . . . creatures? He found his voice, even as Bridget gasped and dug in her perfect nails. His utterance was cracked and full of fear, but there was no other answer to give. "No. We go together, or not at all."

The fae woman smiled. The beauty of it took his breath away, but it was a cold, harsh, beauty – the beauty of the ice storm that glitters and sparkles like diamonds as it freezes the very blood in your veins.

He repeated it, so none would be confused. "Bridget is my *wife*, bonded by blood and flesh. She alone is my queen, and she stays with *me*."

His words were not casual. The Queen, for that's what the fae woman must be to hold warriors back in such a manner, paced forward. Bridget had talked about her fae heritage – the time spent at court with the other halfling children while her fate had been decided. She'd been ejected from the sithen and had come to live among the humans.

The Queen's eyes raked Bridget in frank appraisal, from the tangled mess of red curls, to the bleeding soles of her feet. For just an instant Bryan saw his wife as the fae Queen saw her – so pathetic . . . so human. *Of the blood*, but not blood. Worthy to be nothing but a slave.

Bridget saw his thoughts, and tears filled her bright eyes to trace silver tracks down her cheeks. She started to pull away, her features pained and defeated. But it was that pain, those tears that reached him, breaking through the delicate magic that had ensorcelled him without him even guessing it.

Bryan pulled her close so that they stood together once again. "*She* is my queen. No other."

The Queen hissed with displeasure, and a frigid wind hit the pair of them like a blow, stealing the breath from their lungs. Bridey's hair flew back like a snapping banner, her body shivered against Bryan's from a bitter cold that should like to freeze them both.

"An' what would you do to save this fae halfling of yours? Would you face the trials?"

Another gasp from Bridget, but any words of warning dissolved in her delicate throat as she stopped mid-word. He turned to look at her lovely face, saw the expression of fear, frozen in place as surely as an insect in amber. He understood her worry. No, he was not so tall as some and was built slender and wiry. He was a head and a half shorter than the smallest of the fae raiders. But he was tough, born of ancient warrior stock. And while there were a few foolish enough to start trouble with him, they only did so once. He nodded, and saw pride flicker in her golden eyes. "Aye. If I must."

"So must it be."

Two

"Three trials is our tradition. An' he has faced two already." If the Queen was ice and darkness, her king was fire and light. He stood tall and proud, three handspans taller than Bryan. His hair was a red that put Bridey's to shame, lit with sparks that looked like molten gold, a perfect match for the colour of his eyes. His clothing was the blinding yellow-white of noonday sunlight, his magic was the heat that could make skin scorch at a whim.

The Queen's head snapped around as she turned to face her consort. "Two? No. How so, milord?"

He stood, pacing a slow circle around Bryan, who lay bound hand and foot in the stone dining hall.

"The sithen was closing, turning to stone before him. The first trial was when he faced his death, rushing forwards, refusing to turn back and let us have her."

The Queen acknowledged that by a glance at the ruined motorcycle, already knee deep under fragrant flowered vines. The King squatted down beside them, bound as captives on a long banquet table where the other fae ate and made merry. Bryan was forced to close his eyes against the glare. The stone beneath his cheek began warming, until it was almost painfully hot.

"The second trial, my love—" his voice seemed to crackle at his displeasure with the sound of flames "—was when ye used thy magic to ensorcell him. He left her not, came to *ye* not. Have ye lost thy . . . touch?"

Her blue eyes turned from diamond to lava at the insult. "I put no effort behind the sorcery. I was merely toying, not actively trying to bewitch him."

The King laughed, and his lady frowned. "When I took ye to my side, thy *least* effort would charm the birds from the trees to become as cold as death in thy hand. Yet ye would have us believe ye used less magic on an interesting human who braved the fury of the fae with naught but two tiny bits of iron, than on a *bird*?"

She didn't respond for a long moment – just tapped one pale finger on her dark gown. The other fae watched the interaction with interest. So much so that they stopped their meal to stare with wide, sparkling eyes. Bryan didn't understand the politics and Bridey was lost to him for comment. She remained immobile under her bonds, and he could not feel the touch of her mind on his. He was alone, as solitary in his own head as the day before he met her.

"Then, what shall his third trial be?" the Queen asked coldly. "I assume you've come up with something suitable?"

"I believe I have." He leaned back into the soft leaves of the tree that had woven itself to be a throne. The branches caressed him lightly, brushed the tangles from his hair and gently massaged his shoulders as he regarded them both. With a wave of his hand, Bryan felt the bonds on his ankles and wrists release.

Always show respect before the court, but not fealty. Never let them own you by your own acts. Bridget's words came back to him. He hoped beyond reason that the many stories she'd told while cradled in his arms in their bed would serve him well. Bryan swung his legs off the table and stood. He dusted off the bits of food that the fae had carelessly tossed at him, before approaching the throne. He dropped to one knee but kept his head unbowed and his eyes steady on the King's golden ones as he waited for the next words.

It raised more than just the King's brows. Murmuring started behind him, in a language he didn't recognize. It made him understand that the discussion between the King and the Queen was *meant* for his ears. Interesting.

"What is thy name, human? What shall we call ye?"

Such a simple question. But Bridget's words again whispered in his memory. *Words have power . . . such awful power, among the fae, Bry. Names had to be held close, dear to one's heart.* What power might they hold over him if they knew his given name? He felt a smile try to escape, but he put out words to ease the flow of lips over teeth. "I answer to many things, Highness. But *human* will do as well as any other. I wear the badge of my kind proudly and hold the word dear in my heart not as insult but as high compliment. I wish to be called *Human.*"

"We insist on your name!" The Queen sounded petulant, a small child denied a toy. But the King merely nodded, amused at his response.

"I asked what he wished to be *called.* He has answered. Very well, Human. I offer ye the opportunity to take a third and final trial. Understand that if ye accept, ye *must* complete the trial, or die trying. If ye refuse, ye may leave, but your woman canna. What say ye?"

What *could* he say? The only answer that existed in his mind and heart was: "I accept."

"Without even knowing what the trial *is*?" The question was leading, but how many times had Bridget cautioned him to make his word his bond, and the truth his word?

He rested one arm on his knee and raised his head up even more proudly, not caring to push away the unruly dark curls that spilled over his brow. "The manner of the trial matters not, Highness. The queen of my heart is worth any price, no matter how difficult or high." Now he let a small smile curl up one corner of his mouth. "I must presume that a noble of your obvious intelligence and integrity would make the trial at least *possible* for one of my kind to achieve."

The fae are proud creatures. Compliments to them are like sugar water to a hummingbird. Many are addicted and come to expect them after a long life. Bryan watched as the words had the expected reaction. The King puffed and straightened his shoulders while his queen let out a small growl of annoyance. "Of course it is *possible*. But hear this, Human. Pretty words will not help ye in thy quest. Only courage, wits and strength of will and body." He raised a hand. "Elwich, come forth."

The fae of the long hair and armour of light stepped to the throne and bowed his head. "Aye, milord?"

"I have decided ye will race Human. His dispute is mostly with ye and the prize ye claimed in the outside world."

Bryan felt air on his tongue as his jaw dropped. How exactly was a race possible against a fae? The raider smiled slyly. "To where shall we run, milord?"

But now the King settled back in his seat and laced fingers over his flowered vest. "'Twill not be a race on foot, but on steeds." He flicked his eyes Bryan's way. "'Tis *possible*, aye? Much depends on your selection. Ye will each choose a horse from among all we possess. Human will carry his heart's queen to the cave at the top of the nearest peak, where the crown stars grow." Now the blazing eyes moved to the fae, who was likewise shocked. "Elwich, *ye* will carry my wife and consort, Hermetia. The goal is simple. The first one to reach the cave and crown their queen wins. The loser . . . dies."

Queen Hermetia chuckled low and Bryan finally felt fear in his heart. How could he hope to defeat a fae warrior and the Queen of all the fairies in their home world? But at least he had Bridget. She knew this world and their ways.

The Queen stood and started towards the horses confidently. But she hadn't taken two steps before she completely froze in place. She pitched forwards and had not Elwich leaped up to grab her, she would have hit the ground face first. The fae warrior looked up at the King, stunned as both his and the queen's armour dissolved into so much dust.

"But this is a test of more than just horsemanship, as I said. If Human has no magic, then neither shall ye. When my fair lady queen awakes, she will be powerless and voiceless, as will Human's fiery halfling. But each woman has a personal knowledge and ye must watch and listen to learn what they can teach. I've found that true love can often be a . . . *burden* on those who are possessed by it. It robs one of common sense, and magic ability." The King glared at the white-haired fae and ice painted his words as surely as if he was born of winter. "Isn't that correct, Elrich?" The King raised an arm and he and the other fae disappeared into a puff of smoke, but his words continued to fill the air. "Have a care, warriors. Let no harm befall your beloveds or face my wrath. I will be watching thy progress and will tolerate no trickery."

Beloveds? Was the King claiming his consort was loved by another – not true to him? But no matter. That was a matter of politics and none of his concern. Bryan raced to Bridget's side to find her bonds were loose. She was pliant and could move her face to smile and mouth the words he'd heard so many times – *I love you*. The look on her face said more than words ever could, though, and he was warmed and made certain of his purpose.

But she could utter no sound and seemed terribly weak. "Ah, Bridey. Queen of me heart," he said softly, meaning every word. "I told you I would never let them take you. We'll be at home before the stew has finished boiling."

He picked her up easily and she lifted her arms to wrap around his neck. They raced to the horses that were tethered nearby, and he found it strange they were first to the steeds.

The horses tossed their fiery manes as Bryan and Bridget approached. The closer they got, the more agitated the horses became. First backing and pulling on their reins, and then rearing up to kick with their stone hooves hard enough to raise sparks. Bryan stepped away, baffled. How was he to ride one of these beasts?

But then he felt Bridget's hand on his shoulder. When he looked, she was shaking her head. She lifted her arm and pointed past the horses. But there was only dense undergrowth ahead. Was she suggesting they forgo the horses? "No horse?"

Her mouth moved and he concentrated to understand the words she was saying. "Iffer orz?" She shook her head, not so much angry as frustrated. She slowed down her movements and he mocked the motions with his own lips. "Ifferent . . . Oh! *Different horse!* Not one of these?" She smiled. Well, the King had said *any horses we possess*, so he presumed they weren't limited to the ones at the tether. She raised her arm again, and it gave him an idea. He lifted her hand to support her arm and he pointed one of her fingers, moving it slowly until she nodded.

Yes, just through the lush flowers, he could see a building. Without a second thought, he raced into the distance hand in hand with Bridget. From behind him, he could hear Elwich reach the horse line. The warrior's laugh taunted him as he left the horses behind. "Fool! Ye have no chance now."

Sure enough, he turned and discovered that the horses were disappearing into smoke. All except the massive black stallion with a sparkling blue mane that Elwich and his queen rode. Although it could hardly be said the Queen *rode*. Elwich had thrown her indignantly across the saddle, as he had with Bridget. The steed reared back in displeasure at the two passengers, but leaped into the air with a rush of wind that nearly pushed Bryan and Bridget to the ground. Bryan turned his worried face to meet his wife's eyes, but she only smiled and raised her arm again.

Had Bridget ever talked of horses? Wait! Yes, she had! *I called him Neverwhere, because he was never where he was supposed to be and wouldn't do as he was told. He would just suddenly appear and want to be ridden, already saddled. His hair was whiter than snow, with a coppery mane that was the same colour as mine. He allowed no other rider than me, and none could abide that – for a halfling to own the heart of the fastest of stallions. So deadly was he that they kept him away from the others for fear of breeding his stubbornness by accident.*

But if he allowed no other . . . no, he wouldn't consider that. He trusted Bridget, at whatever cost.

The paddock was quiet as they approached, but then a wind pushed them forwards. An eerie sound began from within the building: it was part scream and part battle cry. Bryan's blood chilled in his veins and every hair on his body stood at attention. Yet Bridey was smiling with a child's trust and love and he couldn't help but be strengthened by her reaction.

As they approached the building, she began to look around. He stopped and waited, happy to abide her desire, and frankly fearing getting closer. She pointed towards a hawthorn bush nearby. Was he to cut a branch? They were sacred, not to be harmed. Surely she wouldn't suggest such a thing. Then she mouthed, *Under*, and he looked down. He set her carefully on the ground near the bush. She began to snap off thick toadstools and motioned for him to do the same. That's right! He remembered the story now. *He loved me best because I knew how much he loved the mushrooms. They locked him up so he couldn't eat them because they made him tipsy, like drinking butter beer. But he did love them and would do anything I asked for even a wee piece.*

He started snapping off the thick mushrooms until she motioned for him to stop. He stuffed them in his pockets and followed where she led. As they approached the door, he could hear the maddened screams turn to snorts and then snuffles before being finally replaced by an excited snicker. It was no small trick to open the heavy paddock door but with her help the hinges gave way.

The steed was amazing to behold. It was easily half again larger than the other horses, of a white so bright it made him squint. "He's a fine one, he is. Just as you described him, love." Bridget smiled at him and then held out her arms to the horse. The beast came as far as the massive iron bars would allow, stretching its neck so she could run her wrist along his nose. But then the horse's attention was drawn to Bryan. The eyes flashed with a copper glow and it bared teeth unlike he'd seen in the mouth of a grass-eater. They were the teeth of a shark, rows of curved and vicious incisors that could easily cut flesh to ribbons. It lunged forwards, and would have taken a chunk from his arm if he hadn't moved quickly enough. Instead of reacting with fear, Bridget actually reached out and *slapped* the beast with the side of her hand.

It reacted more with surprise than anger, but cocked its

head like a curious dog when she reached her arms around Bryan and held him tight. She kissed his face over and over, tiny touches of her lips that made him weak-kneed. Then she smiled at the horse and patted his jacket.

"Oh! That's right. I have a treat for you, Neverwhere." Bridget beamed that Bryan had remembered the horse's name and even the steed looked interested. He pulled out a few mushrooms and placed them on her upturned palm.

Oh, how that tail flipped with joy! It sent sparks dancing into the room. Neverwhere ate them one at a time, savouring them like the finest delicacy. His mane shook and his whole body shuddered in pleasure before taking another with the same gentle action. After the third mushroom he licked her hand to get the last taste, making her giggle wordlessly. Seeing the two friends together – Bridget and her horse – made him realize how very hard it must have been for her to be rejected from this life, this world. There were things here he couldn't give her in the outside world. The intelligence in the eyes of this animal said it was more than a mere beast of burden. He was a pet, a friend, and possibly more. Bryan had no idea whether Fae steeds were sentient, but he wouldn't be at all surprised if Neverwhere started spouting poetry for Bridget's pleasure.

Bridget motioned for him to offer more of the mushrooms to the horse. If he really did get tipsy, he didn't want to give the animal *too* many, but it was a fairly large horse, so it should be able to manage a few more. He reached into his pocket and pulled out another of the tiny, fragrant treats. "Would you like another, Neverwhere?"

Bryan reached his arm forwards slowly, his hand still closed into a fist. He liked his fingers a little too well not to be cautious. The horse eyed his closed fist with distrust but looked back to Bridget who nodded and smiled. The horse snuffled the fist, the breath feeling as hot as the air from a furnace. Then it started moving its lips, trying to get the fist to open. The tail was moving again, showering Bryan in golden sparkles that made him laugh. Finally he opened his hand and the horse ate the mushrooms, just as carefully as it had with Bridget.

As he pulled back his hand, the bright eyes of the horse followed, hoping for another taste. Bryan was quite sure that Neverwhere would have leaped forwards and torn the jacket from his body if he thought there were more mushrooms hidden. He heard a thumping sound and realized Bridget was trying to get his attention. She was mouthing a single word, and he was having a difficult time understanding. It was short, just one syllable, but didn't match any word he could think of. She seemed to realize that and spoke more words, glancing from him to the horse and back.

Oh! She wanted him to *ask* the horse if it would take them. Frankly, he was fairly certain they'd already lost the race. How could Elwich and the Queen not have already arrived by now? This had taken too long, but it was hard to deny Bridget any delay she wished.

But there was no harm in asking, nor in trying to complete the quest. He faced the horse and, just in case it could be insulted as other fae could, he offered a short bow of his head as an introduction. "Neverwhere, would you be so kind as to carry Bridget and I to the cave where the crown stars grow? We would gladly share more mushrooms as a reward."

Bryan glanced at his wife and she gave him a tiny nod with a smile that said he'd asked well. The horse stepped back from the fence and seemed to contemplate the question. It looked from Bridget to Bryan and back again before nodding its head three times and letting out a shrieking whinny.

But before Bryan could open the gate, the horse disappeared in a puff of smoke – just as the other horses had. Was it a trick? Were they being punished for rejecting the horses offered? Fear filled the pit of his stomach and even Bridget looked worried. Her eyes filled with tears and she mouthed, *I'm sorry*, over and over.

"'Twasn't your fault, lass," he said quietly, and pulled her into his arms. "We'll just have to do our best." Perhaps they were meant to walk after all. If they died, then so be it. They'd do so together.

She buried her face in his neck. He could feel her cool tears wet his shirt as her body shook with soundless sobs. "No matter, love. Don't you think on it at all. If I must carry you the whole way, then I will, and to the devil with their rules and their contest."

Three

Let no food nor water pass your lips or they will own your soul.

The sun beat down on them like noon in the desert. Bryan's tongue felt three times the size and he could barely swallow from the effort and the heat. Did her warning mean *only* in the sithen? On foot, they would die without water. It could be days before they reached the cave at the peak of the mountain. "Can we drink nothing at all, Bridey? We won't make it without moisture of some kind."

She chewed at her lip, like she always did when she thought, and looked around the lush greenery. Suddenly her eyes lit up and she motioned him to the left. He went where she bid and came to the edge of a large red and green fern. The leaves were broader than his chest. *Nail* was the word she mouthed and he pulled one of the two nails he'd kept from the construction site from his jacket pocket. He was surprised he'd been left with them, but perhaps this was all part of the King's plan. Slow them, and then help them. He wondered if Elwich and the Queen were enduring the same sort of trials. Did their horse disappear from under them in mid-flight? He would have imagined they should already be there and have won if their horse was still able to travel.

Bridget broke off one of the thick fern fronds then indicated that he should use the rusty nail to puncture the leaf so they could drink from the plant.

The moment he stabbed the end of the nail into the frond it began to leak green fluid. After a few moments, the fluid changed to the clearest water and Bridget opened her mouth for a drink. Bryan couldn't have imagined it possible to love her more, but every moment that passed she proved she was smart and capable, all wrapped in a package of such beauty he could weep each time he saw her.

The flow of water seemed to go on far longer than it should have considering the size of the frond, but she seemed satisfied and he felt no odd sensation that he might be falling under a spell. He carefully plucked the nail from the plant and the water immediately stopped. It withered and died in mere seconds.

As he took Bridge's hand again, they heard the thunder of hooves. It seemed to come from everywhere at once and he couldn't decide where to move to get out of the way of the herd of animals that sounded ready to trample them.

Neverwhere appeared in a burst of tawny light. He bore a saddle made for two on his back. Bryan eagerly stepped towards the horse, but just as he reached for the reins, they were jerked from his grasp and the stallion disappeared again. Bridey's coppery eyes flashed with the same anger he felt. "So, he hopes to taunt us, does he?" He raised his face to the cloudless blue sky. "You'll not humiliate us, Highness. We require no animal to win this contest and your efforts only embolden us more."

Bridget nodded firmly, echoing his statement with her movements. But they hadn't taken more than a handful of steps before Neverwhere appeared once more. This time, it was clear the horse would not disappear so easily. It fought against whatever magic tried to snatch it away, kicking and thrashing as its reins were pulled into a sparkle of gold-white magic. But with a final throw of his massive head, it roared in anger and landed on the ground with such force that two trees were torn from the ground, narrowly missing Bryan and Bridget. If they hadn't moved quickly, the contest would likely have ended at that moment.

The horse shook his head, eyes flashing with the same fire that flew from his mane and tail. He looked around suspiciously, as though expecting to be pulled from them once again, but remained in place. Finally, he snorted, flipped his head in a very self-satisfied manner and trotted over to where Bryan and Bridget were standing. Neverwhere snickered softly and nuzzled Bryan's jacket pocket. He couldn't help but smile. "You really *can't* get enough of these, can you?"

Two mushrooms disappeared into the horse's mouth before an audible sigh and a bluster of lips. When the horse's eyes opened again, he turned to the side and offered the saddle to them. While Bryan was leery and feared the horse being taken from them again, the King had promised they could ride. He would have to take him at his word, for woe be to the fae, even the King, that went back on his word.

After making certain Bridget was secure in the saddle, he threw a leg over the steed and commanded firmly, "To the cave of the crown stars, Neverwhere. Be off with ye."

The world dissolved into light and motion such that he'd never experienced before. He loved to ride fast on his motorcycle, but nothing could compare to the stomach-churning roller coaster that was a fae flying steed.

"Isn't it wonderful? Can you see why I love this horse?" Bridey's voice from behind him made him turn so suddenly he was dizzy.

"You can talk!"

She smiled and then laughed. "Why do you think I insisted on Neverwhere? He's nearly completely resistant to magic. It's why he's untrainable."

The landscape slipped by, but Bridget seemed completely at ease with it, even though the back of the motorcycle had always made her nauseous. She nudged him with her chin and motioned down. The ground was so far down and moving so fast that his stomach lurched with vertigo. "Look, Deathknell is below, with loose reins and no rider. I was surprised Elwich chose him. He's fast, but never did like the Queen. I'll wager he threw them." Sure enough, a black horse with fiery blue mane was pawing the air below them, headed back to where they started.

"Of course, he could simply have dropped them off at the cave which means they're about to win."

Bridget slipped her hands around his waist and hugged him tight, resting her cheek against his back. "Elwich is a strong warrior, but has little patience with man or beast. He couldn't even grasp the idea of *asking* a steed to bear them, any more than he could ask a woman to accompany him back to the sithen."

He should know the answer, but doubt had filtered in at her ease in this world. "Would you have gone? If he had *asked*?"

Outrage painted her voice when she shouted over the rush of the wind in his ear. "Bryan Patrick Murphy! How dare ye even *think* that."

He could only helplessly shrug. "But how could you not love it here? The food and drink, the animals that love you, the beauty all around? Why wouldn't you stay, given the chance?"

She dug her legs into the side of the horse and it responded by leaping even faster into the wind, so quick now that it stole the breath from his lungs and made his eyes sting. "Endless song and wine grows old, as does the politics, Bry. I dinna lie when I said I grew tired, even before I was told to leave. It was likely the *reason* they chose to exile me." Their angle changed so rapidly she had to hurriedly hang on to the saddle. "Whoops. Hold on now, ye hear? Neverwhere's landings are a little abrupt."

She wasn't funning with him. The horse fell like a rock towards the hard ground and landed with a thud that shuddered the earth and made Bryan's jaws clamp together painfully. Neverwhere trotted forwards for a few steps as a thick mist began to roll out of the cave mouth. The cavern yawned menacingly, glowing an eerie green through the mist. But Neverwhere pranced forwards confidently. At least for the first few steps. Then it reared back with the same abruptness as an earthly horse happening upon a snake. They nearly lost their seating as he reared and backed away in a panic. It was only when the mist faded that he stopped prancing and settled.

But Bryan had seen what was in the fog, and it made him afraid. "Doxies, Bridey. I saw their tiny claws in the fog."

Her voice turned small and soft. "But we have to get inside. How—"

He nodded once and felt the warrior blood begin to boil in his veins. "We'll go forwards the same way as we planned . . .

on foot. I've boots on, thick ones for the road. It'll take time for them to claw their way through. I'll carry you so they can't touch you. It's just a little way and then we'll be done."

Bridget shook her head, even as he was slipping out of the saddle. "No, Bry. I canna let ye. One fang, even a single claw and you could *die*. Ye don't understand. The legends blurred them over the centuries, made them sound like a lesser threat than other creatures. But they're far worse than anything else in our world. The stuff of nightmares."

"But they're short. Aye? Can they reach above me boots if we move quickly?"

"How can ye move *quickly* while carrying me? Leave me here with Neverwhere and then ye can get inside."

As good as it sounded, he knew it wouldn't satisfy the King. "No. The King had to know the doxies were here. He planned this, as surely as the sun rises. He said true love could be a burden on a man, and this is where I prove to him that there's no burden too great for love." He reached out his arms and gathered her to him. "The King said we needed our wits as well as our strength. There were few things more satisfying than staring into her copper flame eyes. He kissed her slow and easy, feeling her lips move against his. His stomach warmed and he felt himself respond to her as he always did, at the least touch. He pulled her tight against him, kissing her until she was breathless and gasping.

When he finally pulled away, her eyes were glazed with need. He winked. "Had to do that once more, just in case it's our last kiss."

Finally she smiled. "It won't be. I have faith in ye, Bryan Murphy. There's no trial too difficult that ye can't prevail."

"Hope you're right, lass. I truly do." He lowered himself so she could climb on his back, hands around his neck. "I plan to wear my burden as a backpack, milady, so my hands and feet are free to fight, if needed."

"Fight!" Her eyes lit up. "You *can* fight doxies, Bryan. The nails. If we can make them into—"

"Spears!" he completed and began to look around for a

long stick. But there were none to be found. It was as though they'd all disappeared, and he didn't doubt that's exactly what happened – the same way the horses faded into smoke.

They finally settled on a compromise. He used a rock to pound one nail through the front of his boot so he could kick the doxies out of the way. The risk was it would throw him off balance. The other nail he held in his fist. They couldn't afford to fall into the mist where the poisoned teeth and claws could cut their skin.

A gong sounded from inside the cave. Had they already lost? Elwich and the Queen were nowhere to be seen. But there was no use stopping now. Bridget gave him a pained, but proud, look. "Remember I won't be able to warn you of anything. Once I leave the protection of Neverwhere's magic, I'll be mute again."

He nodded. He knew it was all on his shoulders. But that was often the way of love. One had to carry while the other was unable to cope. How many times had she carried him when he was so dead tired from work that all he could do was collapse inside the door? How many times had she bathed him, spoon-fed him when he was sick, washed and scrubbed the clothes and their home? This trial was nothing, by comparison. He'd be long dead if she hadn't found him, convinced him to give up the whiskey that was destroying him, and turned his life, and his heart, around. "You'll never be mute, my queen. You speak into me heart every day. I can hear you as clear as a bell with every breath you draw."

She tightened her thighs around his waist, clinging to his back. "Best of luck to ye, fair steed," Bryan whispered on the way past. The horse responded by pounding a hoof once against the stone.

"I hope you're ready, my queen. 'Tis time you had a crown befitting your beauty." With a primal yell, he bounded into the mist, keeping his back bent for balance and using his left boot like a dagger for anything that lay ahead.

The hands attacked him almost instantly, pulling and tugging at him so strongly that it slowed him from a run to a walk that was like wading through ankle-deep mud. But the satisfying tiny screams and poofs of blue dust said the nail was doing its work, and occasionally he would swipe down with the other bit of iron to get a claw off the top of his boot. Their tiny faces were long and lean, the faces of predators who knew they would win in the end. The claws were sharp, and worried at the leather so quickly that he feared he wouldn't reach the safety of the cave – if the cave were any safer.

But the fog had hidden more than the tiny creatures. It hid the sharp incline. He hit the edge of the ramp like a bull against a tree and went down, barely catching himself before Bridget tumbled off his back. But the damage was done. When he rose from his knees, there were bloody scratches through his pants, and tiny bite marks deep in his wrist and hand. He could feel the poison hitting his system even as Bridget urged him soundlessly forwards. His feet were going numb and he knew the King must be laughing at the foolish Human, a mere mortal who dared to oppose them.

"Sorry, lass," he choked out as he stumbled again. "But I swore to protect you, and I'll keep that vow." He swung to face her. "Know that I love ye, lass. Know that I wouldn't give in until ye were safe."

As she screamed soundlessly, he used his last ounce of strength to pick her up and throw her through the mouth of the cave. She struck the wall hard enough that, as he fell into the mist and felt the painful claws and teeth rip through his flesh, a single crystal fell from the roof of the cavern to land on her beautiful red hair. It lit up like a star and made him smile, and he suddenly didn't care that he would die here. *So beautiful. Lord, how I love that girl.*

He couldn't quite process it when she stood on her own feet and raced towards him, yelling like a banshee and slapping doxies with the strength of a dozen warrior fae. "Oh, no, Bryan Murphy. Dinna ye think you can slip away from me that easy." She grabbed under his arms and pulled backwards. He tried to help as much as he could, but everything was going numb and cold.

It took long minutes, but she finally managed to pull him back inside the mouth of the cave. She collapsed, breathing hard and sobbing, while he rested his face on her soft legs. He couldn't quite get his lips to work, so he spoke into her mind. *Don't cry, Bridey. Never cry for me. I did what I did by choice. I did it to save* you, *not me.*

She touched his hair, petted him and rocked. Tears dropped from her face to land on his cheek. After a moment, her face went cold and her eyes flashed and she called out a challenge that echoed through the cave. "Show yourself, false King! Mane shee who claims to be *fair* and worthy of your throne. Come face a halfling and defend yourself in battle! Unless you're a coward as well!"

A long moment passed and then a bolt of lightning broke the stillness. "You dare call me a *coward?!*" The King's roar of anger was like lava on Bryan's skin, but his fierce Bridey didn't flinch a bit.

Her voice was calm, but cold. "I do."

"I could strike you dead with a wave of one finger." Thunder rolled around the words, so loud the very air was painful against his eardrums.

Her brogue, which she tried to keep under control in the outside world, flared to full life. "Aye? And then ye'd best do it, afore the rest see thee for the coward ye are." He couldn't even move his head, and could only see her movements as flitting shadows in the growing darkness. "Ye swore on oath that the winner would go free. I dinna see your champion and your lady here afore us. Or is it *his* lady? Is that what this has been about, *milord*? To make the lady queen suffer the humiliation of being treated as a lowly human . . . to teach her a lesson?" Her words were sharp enough to cut stone and if Bryan could have only smiled, he surely would have. "I call thee coward for involving a mortal trying merely to protect one of the blood. Thrice I name thee coward, and prove otherwise soon, or suffer the wrath of the brethren who would take away thy crown for being unfit to wear it."

Was that thunder again, or . . . no, could it be *laughter*?

"Ah, Bridget Greenleaf, you're much as your mother was, daughter of mine."

Daughter? His beautiful Bridey was daughter of the King of the fae?

"You're right, this was a lesson to the Queen, and to an upstart warrior who would hope to usurp my throne by bedding her. When it didn't work, he tried to take ye to blackmail me."

Now Bridget softened her voice. "Aye. But he didn't count on the strength of will and wit of my Bry, father."

"I know now why you've remained in the mortal world, Bridget. You've a warrior true, and you've earned thy prize. Take Human home and nurse him well. It will be many days before the doxie poison leaves his system and I can offer only the crown star crystal to aid in thy fight and protect thy home. The burden now shifts from him to thee. Do ye accept this trial, daughter of mine, without even knowing the nature of it?"

Sound began to fade in Bryan's ears, even as he felt himself being loaded again on the broad back of the loyal steed that would carry them home. To *their* home, in an emerald grove where he could rest and recover.

But he did hear one last thing before the world slipped into darkness and it warmed his heart. "I accept, Highness. The nature of the trial matters not. There is no burden so great that I cannot bear it for love."

Nia and the Beast of Killarney Wood

Cindy Miles

County Kerry, Ireland – 1817

Nia of Clare cracked open first one eye, then the other, and peered over the edge of the blanket she had clutched to her chin. The damp cold stung her cheeks, but she cared not.

Tonight was the night.

Only the smouldering embers from the camp's fire gave off any light to speak of; the moon's absence would certainly be a hindrance. It would slow her down, aye, but 'twould no' stop her. As she vaguely made out the silhouette of one of her six guardsmen, her eyes narrowed, and anger simmered beneath her skin. Her da may think her unfit for a husband, but to her idea, she need no' have one at all. From what she'd learned of husbands, they were bothersome, bossy twits she wanted no part of anyway. Yet here she was packed up and guarded like some prized swine, being sent to the cloisters to live the rest of her days at a secluded abbey filled with grumpy old women.

Nia had other notions.

With a slow gaze she took in what little she could see of the camp. She knew where each of the guardsmen stood – rather, slumped. The buffoons took turns dozing, and it would only take a few moments for her to slither off into the darkness.

She'd stuffed her blanket with all her spare clothes. Rather lumpy, but still – from their drunken eyes, they'd ne'er notice till dawn. Besides, in the shadows of darkness it did sort of look like her slumbering body.

One could only hope.

Now!

Ever so slowly, Nia inched backwards on her belly, head down, cheek to the soil and matted leaves. The heady, earthy smell urged her on; it was freedom in her eyes. She made not a single sound as she eased away from her blankets, and she kept her gaze trained on the sentry about her. No one noticed!

At the edge of the campfire's ring of light, she slithered back just enough, until finally, shadows engulfed her. Holding her breath, she rose, patted the pouch at her waist containing her coin, pulled the cowl of her cloak down, and moved into the night.

Minutes later, the bark of the guardsmen's hound shot through the air.

Without another thought, Nia fled. Running blindly into the wood, her heart thumped as the guards shouted, booted feet pounded behind her, dogs howled with excitement, and her moment of freedom narrowed. Through the foliage she ran as fast as her legs could pump. Thorny vines slapped her face and ripped her flesh, but she didn't care. What harm could they do? With the air in her lungs burning, she swiped at branches, jumped over rocks and a fallen tree, until finally, the shouts behind her grew softer. Distant.

Still, she ran. The guardsmen wouldna follow her – that much she knew. Not into *this* forest. For deep within Killarney Wood lived a beast of legend. One with a savage thirst for human blood. One without mercy.

One she didna give a frog's fat figgy arse about!

Nia no more believed in such gory fairy tales than she did in fancy ones where knights on white steeds rescued their maiden fair. Neither existed. Both were ridiculous.

What did exist, though, 'twas her pending capture, so with that thought in mind she continued to run blindly through the shadowy wood. The night air chilled straight through her woollen cloak to her bones, but she didna care a whit—

Suddenly, Nia stopped dead in her tracks. Although she could barely see past her own nose, white puffs of warm air billowed out before her with every breath. Her ears tuned in to the verra noise that stopped her.

Footsteps. Moving through the brush. Faster. Heavy. *Closer*.

Her heart slamming into her ribs, Nia took off, the frosty air biting her cheeks. She didna look back to see which o' the guards neared – she merely ran. The muscles in her thighs burned as she made her way deeper into the wood and, just when she thought her predator had given up, a weight of steel crushed her to the ground, the air in her lungs whooshing out in one big breath. A large hand slipped over her mouth and, even though the breath had been knocked clean out o' her, she shivered at the strange, deep voice whispering in her ear.

"Dunna move."

Nia didna. She couldna breathe, much less move.

Then, at once, the ground beneath her belly shifted, and an odd cracking sound split the air. Before the next second, the earth gave way, the heavy body atop her swore in a language unfamiliar to her ears, and then they were both falling, tumbling downwards in a passage too small for their bodies. Sharp roots snagged Nia's cloak, rocks, pebbles and dirt scattered, until she fell no more. With a heavy thud, she landed, the steely body still wrapped about her. Pain shot to her shoulder as she heard a small pop. What air was left in her lungs was crushed out and little lights flickered behind the lids of her eyes like fireflies.

Then everything went pitch black.

When Nia cracked open her eyes, everything *remained* pitch black. Where was she? She couldna see a thing. The pungent smell of earth and peat permeated the cave. And the moment she pushed up on her elbow, she cringed and bit back a yelp as pain shot to her shoulder. No doubt she'd dislodged it again. Amidst the hurt, she managed to sit upright. Whoever had fallen with her may still be about. She drew a deep breath, and let it out slowly. "Hello?" A wave of nausea washed over her. She needed to fix her shoulder. 'Twould be difficult to do alone, but she'd managed before. "Is someone there?"

"Who are you?"

Nia jumped as the verra same deep voice from before now sounded at her ear. It was a harsh, unfriendly tone – more like a wild animal growling – and she shuddered. The movement jostled her shoulder, and she winced from the jolt, her heart pounding. She held her arm close to her body, stilling the shoulder. "I am . . . Nia Donovan . . . of Clare."

Silence. Then, "What is wrong with you?"

At first, that annoying fear which niggled at times gripped her. Had the stranger seen her horrid face? How could he have? The wood had been nearly as dark as the place they now were in, and she'd had her cloak pulled tightly about her. Once again, she noticed his voice – cold, angry, threatening and barely under control. Nia couldna decipher why, and it somewhat angered her, as well. "You fell on me, sir," she said. "And my shoulder is dislodged." Scooting her booted feet beneath her bottom, she tried to rise without the use of her arms. Before she could manage it, the stranger's hands were there, intimately on her hips, steadying her until she was standing. Strong, heavy hands remained against her, and Nia was shocked at how her skin flamed beneath her cloak and linens where he touched.

"Which shoulder?"

She could barely speak, so intense was the throbbing. "Right."

His hands left her hips, only to find her right arm, which hung limp by her side. Rough calluses skimmed her skin as the man felt upwards, until he had her shoulder clasped in his palms.

"'Twill hurt," he said, his breath brushing her cheek.

"I know," Nia whispered, and squeezed her eyes shut. A fierce wave of pain ripped through her as he pressed hard, and just that fast her shoulder popped into place.

Nia drew several deep breaths to keep the tears away. When the nausea passed, she rotated her shoulder several times. "Thank you," she said to the darkness. "Can I know your name, sir?" It seemed strange, being in such close contact with a stranger – a *man* – without knowing who he was, or even what he looked like. 'Twas a mite unnerving to say the least.

"Cyric."

His voice, not quite as hostile as before, ran of an accent unfamiliar to Nia. "Thank you again, Cyric."

"Aye."

Nia felt a shift in the air as Cyric moved away from her. "Is there a way out?" she asked.

"Nay."

This Cyric answered just as calmly as he had her other questions, and she now felt the first niggles of irritability settling in. Running away from her tyrant father's controlling grasp was one thing; dying of starvation in a pitch-blackened cave was quite another.

Her stomach growled loudly, and Nia placed a hand over it.

"When was the last time you ate?"

In the darkness, Nia felt her cheeks grow warm. "It has been a while."

Air in the cave shifted once again as Cyric silently moved about. How could he see? She held a hand up, a mere breath from her own nose, and wiggled her fingers. She saw nothing but blackness.

"Give me your hand," Cyric instructed.

Nia stilled. "Why?" What was this strange man about? Did he plan to rape her, mayhap kill her?

"I could do both, but will do neither."

Anger rushed through Nia's veins. She'd endured a lot in her twenty-two years, and threats from a stranger weren't going to rankle her. Small in stature, she would indeed be easy prey – but she'd put up a fight for sure. "Your attempts to frighten me are useless," Nia said, wondering how she'd managed to say her thoughts aloud.

Silence, then, "Give me your hand. I have food."

"Oh." Nia held out her hand.

"Dried meat. 'Tis all I have."

Well, now she felt like a fool. "Thank you. Again."

With a sigh, she lowered to the ground and sat. The

coolness seeped through the woollen trousers she'd stolen from the guardsmen and now wore, but she couldn't just continue to stand in the darkness. She ate in silence, grateful to have something in her belly. She only prayed it wasn't smoked rat. It was well cooked, and salty, so she wouldna complain.

"You were running away." Cyric's deep, steady voice reverberated within the cave's walls.

"I was, aye," Nia replied. She finished her meat and pulled her cloak tightly about her. "I willna go back, no matter what you do or say. I'd rather die in this cave."

"That may verra well happen," Cyric said in a low voice.

Nia ignored the threat. "Why did you jump on me?"

"To keep you from falling into this pit." His voice was closer now. "Who are you running from?"

Somehow, it caused a shiver to course through her. She wasna sure if 'twas the closeness of his voice, or the fact that she was trapped in a pit. "I'm no sure if my personal matters need be discussed. I dunna know you."

"You may no' ever leave this dark place alive, Nia of Clare. But suit yourself."

"There is no way out?" Nia asked.

A sigh escaped Cyric. "Aye, but 'twill take time."

The thought of dying didn't exactly appeal to Nia, but somehow, she wasna fearful. And she wondered briefly why he referred to *her* dying, yet no' himself. "Who are you, Cyric? Do you live close by?"

Silence filled the cave for several moments – so verra long that Nia thought the man wouldna answer. Then, he did.

"I've lived in Killarney Wood the whole of my life."

Nia pondered that. Certainly he didna mean *in* the wood. "Then you must have heard of the legend, then? Of the Beast?"

A low laugh – more like a growl – escaped Cyric. "Aye. I have."

"Have you e'er seen him?"

All at once, the warmth from Cyric's body grew intimately

close, crowding Nia in the already small enclosure. His breath grazed her neck as he whispered in her ear. "I *am* him."

Another shiver coursed through her. "I am no' amused, sir, nor scared."

Cyric gave another low laugh. "You should be, girl. And I dunna mean to amuse. But we are trapped here for now. I am confessing a secret to you, Nia of Clare, and you are the only soul I've e'er told." Silence, then, "I am what they call the Beast of Killarney Wood. And wi' good reason, I suppose."

Nia's heart quickened. "The Beast I've heard tales of skinned men alive and ate their innards. It craves human flesh and fights with a fierce rage," she said softly.

Cyric laughed. "Aye, and the Beast rips the heart out of a man wi' its bare clawed hand as well."

"Aye," muttered Nia. "That too."

Silence filled the darkened cave, only their joined breathing made any sound at all. What if his claim was true? She'd never believed in such childish lore before, even when it was used to frighten her as a small girl.

"Nia," Cyric said, his voice low, even, "do you think me a beast?"

"Give me your hand," Nia said. The air moved beside her, and she reached out. Her fingers grazed Cyric's arm, and she slid her hand down until she grasped his hand in hers; she inspected it with her fingertips. Large, strong, with long fingers, she gently searched. "No claws," she said as she touched his blunt nails, and ran her fingers over his palm. "Calluses I see," she said, and examined the back of his hand. With her middle finger she found a plump vein, pressed it and noted its spring, and then traced it up his arm. "You seem rather strong like a beast," she confided. "But I am no' easily convinced of fairy-tale creatures." She let his hand drop. "Or of brave knights who would die for the woman they loved, for that silly matter. Neither exists to my notion. Nay, methinks you are merely a man o' the wood."

Only then did Nia notice how Cyric's breathing had quickened, and how verra close he sat to her. She was aware of his body and, somehow, she wanted more than anything to feel his touch. It surprised her to know she was fiercely attracted to him, without even laying eyes on him. Heat flamed her cheeks at the thought of it, and she smothered a smile.

"Why do you wish my touch?"

Nia's mouth slacked open. Had she said the like aloud? *Again?* "If we weren't in a life or death state o' affairs, Cyric the Beast of Killarney Wood, I would die right here of mortification. Why must you sit so close that you hear my whispered words?"

Again, Cyric gave a light laugh. "I heard no' a whisper – 'twas in your head that I heard your confession. What else might you wish to tell me?"

Nia blinked in the darkness, speechless. Slowly, she placed her fingers over her lips and pinched them shut – just to make sure she didna speak aloud. Then, she thought, If you can hear me, Beast of Killarney, then tap the top o' my head.

A chuckle, then a single, solitary tap to the top of her head.

Nia jumped where she sat. "Oh! How did you do that?" He could hear her thoughts? He'd certainly just given her proof 'twas true. She'd have to be much more careful now.

"I dunna crave the innards of men," said Cyric, his tone grave, "but I am no' an average man. I do have a beast within me."

Nia found she wasna fearful of this. She instead fancied his voice. It sounded young, vibrant – and ancient at the same time. Odd. "That much I can see. What are you, then? And cease entering my thoughts. 'Tis rude."

"Why do you accept such witchery so fast?" he asked. "Most would either run away screaming, or no' believe me at all."

Nia sighed. "I see no reason no' to believe. You've already proven you can read my thoughts. Besides, what grown man would make up such nonsense to a complete stranger if it weren't true? Now, tell me your story."

Cyric grunted. "Aye, 'tis so." Silence, then, he said softly, "I am the last of my kind. And cursed to the wood for eternity."

Nia kept quiet, waiting breathlessly to hear the rest.

"The English called us 'berserkers'. Your ancestors called our blood-frenzy *ríastrad.* Our bloodlust becomes as such that we recognize neither friend nor foe. We just fight. Fight to kill."

Well. That certainly was something. Hardly believable, but something indeed. She couldna imagine this gentle man, who'd cautiously popped her shoulder into place turning into a bloodthirsty beast. "So with all that, you canna get us out of the cave?"

Cyric laughed. "Nay. I've ne'er been able to control my strength. It seems only to become useful whilst I am in battle." He seemed to think for a moment. "We were from the painted warriors. The Picts. And wi' all that strength and fury, nay, I canna get us out of the cave."

Nia pondered that. 'Twas nigh unto inconceivable, the thought o' it. She'd heard of the Picts. An ancient Celtic race of fierce males. "I remember stories of the Beast of Killarney from childhood," she said. She leaned back against the cave wall and rested her head. "Do you have markings of indigo upon your skin?"

"Nay," Cyric said. "Black."

"I see. Have you been here long?" She rubbed her arms vigorously. 'Twas getting colder in the cave and she began to shiver.

The sound of earth and pebbles grinding met her ears as Cyric moved next to her. Immediately, his warmth comforted her. "Centuries." He moved closer still, and his hand found hers and stilled it. "Your skin is like ice."

Nia ceased rubbing her arms. "Centuries? How is that possible?" She couldna fathom it. "You've . . . no one?"

"Nay."

That admission saddened Nia to the bone. Didna matter that she, too, had been alone most o' her life. Especially since her mother died . . .

Nia began shivering again, and this time her body shook uncontrollably. Then Cyric slid behind her, pulling her body against his, and he wrapped his arms about her. She let him.

"I will keep you warm," he said, his deep voice against her ear. "Rest, Nia o' Clare."

Never had Nia been so intimately close with a man the whole of her life, and yet with ease she settled against Cyric's chest, soaking in his warmth. She could tell he was quite powerful, as hardened muscles pushed against her own softness. Steel arms wrapped about her, and powerful thighs held her in place. If he was centuries old, he must look like an old man indeed; yet he felt very strong, vibrant, and she cared not about his looks. He was kind to her, and now sat trying to keep her warm. But would they truly just sit in the dark until death claimed them? Rather, claimed *her*?

She wondered briefly if he'd continue, should he know the truth of her own face.

With nothing but the sound of their joined breathing, and a faraway *drip-drip-drip* of water, Nia closed her eyes as slumber overtook her.

The verra last thing she remembered before drifting off to sleep was Cyric's fingers entwining with her own. She discovered not only did she like it, but that it felt completely natural . . .

Cyric dared not move; he didna wish to disturb the wee sprite sleeping in his arms. While the cold cave didna bother him, he knew she would freeze without his warmth. Yet the feel of her soft body against his was something he hadna prepared himself for.

How long had it been since he'd held a woman close? Nearly as long as he'd been cursed to Killarney Wood. How had the Elders ever suspected he'd find his Intended whilst banned from roamin' his beloved Ireland? No one ventured into the wood except vagrants, thieves and gypsies. He'd made little contact with mortals over the years, but still they'd turned his mere presence into a legend of terror. *The Beast of Killarney Wood.* Aye, if enraged, he truly was a beast; he remembered naught when he slipped into anger, and many times in the past he'd awakened with blood on his hands and body.

He truly was a beast. A berserker. And Nia's life was in more danger than she knew.

He didna feel like a beast, though, with Nia snuggled against his chest. So trusting and unafraid, he wondered, if she survived, what she would think of his appearance? Never before had he wondered that, but he did now. He discovered he wished powerfully to touch her. With only the slightest hesitation, he lifted a hand and found a lock of Nia's hair. He rubbed the long strands between his fingers and thumb, and was amazed at its softness. He wished he could see it in truth. Lifting the long strand to his nose, he inhaled. It smelled clean, sweet and fragrant, like the clover honey he stole from the hives in the wood. Then, he found her face in the pitch-darkness. But the moment his fingers grazed her cheek, she jumped.

"What are you doing?" Nia asked, scooting away.

"I didna mean to frighten you," Cyric said. "I wanted to comfort you. Or, myself. Mayhap both."

"Oh," she replied, her voice calmer. "I . . . dunna like people touching my face."

Cyric thought that to be odd. Did a woman not appreciate the stroke of a man's hand on their skin? Then again, what did he know? He wasna even a man in truth. He was a beast. He'd been merely acting on instinct, the desire strong enough to urge his hand to seek Nia's skin. The attraction was that powerful between them, and, aye, he could feel that Nia felt it, as well. A voice as sweet as hers surely had a face to match. "Why is that?" he asked. "You allowed me to touch your hand."

"Well," she began, "'tis an intimate gesture meant for lovers, the touching of one's face. Aye?"

The thought was more than curious to Cyric, and whilst he was confessing to a mortal who probably would no' survive, he continued. "I've never had one."

The silence stretched between them for several moments. Then Nia said, "You've . . . never had a lover? Ever?"

The surprise in her voice shamed him. "I've known nothing but blood, battle and war," he said quietly. "You have had lovers, then?"

Nia gave a soft laugh. "I was betrothed once, but . . . no, Cyric. I've never had a lover."

Somehow, that soothed him. He knew no' why, but it did. And for some odd reason, he wished to tell her. "That . . . pleases me," he confessed. "Tell me more about yourself, Nia of Clare. What of your mother and father?"

She was silent for several moments. "My mother died in a horrible fire when I was very young," she said. "I . . . barely escaped death myself. I believe my father resented me from then on, as he loved my mother fiercely. To lose her completely crushed him."

In the darkness, Cyric's mouth slacked open. "Was he no' gracious that you had survived?" He couldna fathom a father blaming a child for her mother's death. Although he could well imagine the sorrow of losing a woman he loved.

A slight sigh broke the darkness, and Nia shifted where she sat. "I'm sure he was simply overly distraught."

Overly distraught? He frowned, although he knew she couldna see it. "You're verra protective of a man who has mistreated you. 'Tis why you were running away. From him."

"You've no idea why," she said quietly. "And I no longer wish to discuss my family matters."

Anger seeped deep into Cyric's bones, and he had no clue why it affected him so much. Mayhap he was being irrational? Who was he anyway? An immortal beast who couldna control his fury. He was no better than her da. He reached for Nia's hand. "I am . . . sorry. I feel powerfully protective over you."

In the darkness, Cyric heard Nia's breathing ease, although she said nothing. He entwined his fingers with hers, marvelling at the slight bones in them, the softness of her skin. He stroked her wrist and slid his thumb over the quickened rhythm that matched her heart. He could hear it in the darkness, her heartbeat. The more he touched her skin, the more it raced.

His did, as well. 'Twas a feeling he wasna used to at all.

Then, Nia did something he didna expect. She slid closer, her hand resting on his arm. "Can I touch your face?" she asked quietly. "I'd like to know what you look like, sir."

Cyric blinked in surprise. "Did you no' say 'twas a gesture meant for lovers?" he said, truly surprised his centuries-old voice didna squeak like a young boy. His own heart quickened pace.

"Aye, I did indeed say that," she answered, her slight hand inching upwards over the linen tunic he'd stolen from a gypsy.

Her hand burned his skin, and he was shocked at the feeling it caused in the pit of his stomach. He dared no' move.

"But I suddenly feel overpoweringly compelled to touch you," she said on a shaky whisper. "I know that sounds wicked, but . . . may I?"

So close was Nia that her sweet breath slipped over his throat. "Aye," he answered, completely entranced.

The moment Nia's fingertips grazed his jaw, Cyric closed his eyes and exhaled. Ne'er had a woman touched him intimately, and without scorn or hatred. He didna know how much he craved it . . . until now.

Nia's insides shook as she slowly explored Cyric's face in the dark. The contact of her fingertips against the scruff of his jaw excited her, and 'twas a feeling she'd ne'er experienced in her entire life. She had no idea what compelled her, but nothing felt more . . . right. She let her fingers move over his cheekbones, his temples, the bridge of his nose, all while Cyric sat motionless. She fingered the long column of his throat, his ears. Only their rapid breathing sounded in the cave.

When her fingers gently caressed first his chin, then his lips, a low groan sounded from somewhere deep within Cyric. Full lips, perfectly shaped, and the sudden urge to taste those lips overcame her.

In the next instant, Cyric captured Nia's exploring hand with his own. He held her hand still. "Is that what you wish, Nia?" he whispered, his mouth close to her ear. "Shall I kiss you?"

"Yes," she whispered back, her voice shaky, excited. "Kiss me."

Cyric's warmth enveloped Nia as he grew close in the darkness and gently pressed his lips to hers. Softly they melded together, and they sat verra still for seconds. Nia's heart raced wildly, and then Cyric leaned into her, his mouth searching hers, tasting. Low in her abdomen, Nia burned for him. She'd ne'er burned for another.

Nia lifted one hand to Cyric's neck, then found his hair with her fingers. Long, wild, with a single narrow braid, she threaded her fingers through it. When Cyric's tongue touched hers, she gasped, so powerful the touch. Cyric groaned, and lifted a hand to Nia's jaw.

She instantly jumped back.

Both were out of breath.

Then, before either could react, a hissing sound streaked downwards from the pit's opening above. Cyric yelled in another language and pushed Nia against the wall. Then, the small cave filled with angered voices, heavy thumps and swords being drawn.

Nia couldna see a thing, but she verra well knew what was happening. The guardsmen had discovered her and were here to take her away.

Out of the inky darkness a hand viciously clamped over Nia's mouth, and another yanked her hard around the waist. In the next second she was being lifted straight up. Her mind reeled and silently shouted, *Cyric! Please!*

Nia could barely see a thing as she and the guardsman holding her tightly cleared the opening. The moon was nothin' more than a sliver in the sky, and it caused more shadow than light. She was shoved to the ground as the battle ensued, that idiot of a guard firing arrows into the pit! So fearful for Cyric, her brain was a scrambled mess as she searched blindly on the forest floor for a weapon. Finding a heavy branch, she smacked the guardsman so hard his helm flew off. He fell to the wood floor with a curse and a grunt.

The sound that next came from the cave below chilled Nia clear to the bone. First, 'twas the screams of the guardsmen. Next, the pained roar of . . . something. *Someone.*

Cyric?

In the hazy moonlight, a guardsman's body flew from the hole as though launched by a medieval catapult. His limp and bloodied self landed no' too far away, and 'twas just enough light for Nia to see his mangled flesh. Two more bodies followed, and then, with another loud roar, a creature exploded through the hole, earth and roots and rock spraying about. Without thinking, Nia knew what it was. *Who* it was. Feral, and nigh unto unrecognizable as a man, yet she knew.

"Cyric!" she called. "Cyric, please! Run!"

The beast turned, faced her and stilled. The guardsmen were dead – that much Nia knew.

"There will be more to come," she warned, stepping closer. "You have to flee!"

With a blood-curdling roar, Cyric jumped towards her. In the shadows Nia could see a hulking form, long, wild hair, claws and a face covered in animal-like fur. Fangs jutted like tusks, and still, she showed no fear.

For admittedly, only to herself, she'd fallen in love with Cyric of the Wood.

"Run!" she hollered. "Go, now!" With a fist, she pounded his chest. Sobs shook her and escaped her throat. How she hated to cry. "Please," she said, softer. "I can't bear to see you hurt."

Again, Cyric lurched. His face, so animal-like, stared at her intently with human eyes that shone in the moonlight. He searched her face, so it seemed, and it was only then that Nia remembered her own disfigurement. She turned and quickly covered her face with her hands.

The empty night was filled with Cyric's harsh breathing, and now Nia's stifled sobs. Even as a beast, she didna wish for him to see her hideousness. But, she knew he had. Shame filled her and, for the first time since encountering Cyric, fear as well.

Fear of the disgust she'd seen in so many others eyes – including her verra own da's.

A shout broke the silence, followed by the shrill whistle of an arrow.

With a deafening roar, Cyric charged the guard and killed him. Then, he turned back to Nia, scooped her up and threw her over his shoulder and ran. With each step he grew faster, and the weight of his clawed hand pressed against the backs of Nia's legs to hold her steady as they forged into the shadowy wood of Killarney.

Nia could do little more than hold on.

Nia knew not how long they ran through the wood; exhaustion had overtaken her and she'd fallen asleep against the beastly back of Cyric. She lay still now, alone, on something soft, and without opening her eyes she listened to a strange sound. It was one she'd dreamed of hearing one day. Could it be?

With a long pull of air, she tasted the salt of the sea on her tongue. Slowly, she opened her eyes, sat up and looked about. She lay on a soft bed of thick furs in what once had been a grand castle. Hollow windows allowed the fierce breeze to blow in, and lichen covered the walls of the roofless stone shell that probably housed a hundred different memories. Standing, she moved to the window. Outside, green grass covered a rocky hill, whilst the sea's waves crashed against the sheer cliffs of the castle's dais. She gasped as she took in the view. A gust of wind pushed the cloak from her head, tossing her hair back. She closed her eyes and inhaled again, revelling in the feel of the sea breeze against her skin. A shrill scream sounded and she cracked open her eyes to watch a gull dive and screech.

"Nia."

Nia turned before she thought, and the moment her eyes met Cyric's, she hastily turned away and covered her face with her hands. "Please," she begged. "Please, leave me." She didna want him to look upon her marred skin, ever again. 'Twas bad enough he'd done so in his other form. Both Cyric and the Berserker were one and the same; they'd looked upon her with the same pair of eyes and the same memory. They'd seen. Cyric had seen. And it shamed her fiercely. Uncontrolled quivers began inside her, and no matter what she did, or how many deep breaths she took, they wouldna cease. Angered, Nia swore.

A light chuckle sounded behind her.

"Nia, turn round."

Nia shook her head. "I willna, so leave me." She pulled the cowl of her cloak closer about her face.

Then, a pair of strong hands gripped her shoulders, and Cyric's deep voice washed over her. "You've ne'er seen the sea?" he asked gently.

Nia wouldna answer. What was he about? He'd seen her face, and still he tormented her? He acted as though he wasna affected by her fire-marred skin. No man wasna affected by it. No' even her own father.

"Nia, look at me."

Finally, she'd had enough. All the resentment and anger of being shunned the whole of her life emerged. Nia turned then, and flung her cowl off her head. Bravely, she met his gaze with her own. "There! Are you happy now?"

A slow smile started on his beautiful mouth. "I am indeed."

Nia blinked. Only then did she take in the features of Cyric of the Wood. For a moment, she nearly forgot the anguish he was causing her by looking at her face, so overcome was she by his. Her gaze searched his features. She'd never been more intrigued in her entire life.

Standing well over six feet, Cyric was bare to the waist. Broad shoulders cut into a muscular chest, narrowing into a rock-hard abdomen. His skin was flawless – where you could actually see skin at all. Intricately etched black markings covered his body and sinewy arms – even up the left side of his jaw and face. To some, 'twould be menacing. Frightening. A beast. To Nia, he was—

"Beautiful," Cyric said, barely above a whisper. "My God, Nia." He moved closer and stared directly into her eyes, searching. "How could you think yourself otherwise?"

Nia, still mesmerized by the ancient Pict warrior before her, continued her perusal, ignoring him completely. Cyric's hair was as black as the markings burned into his flesh, and hung wild and tousled nearly to his waist. The front was braided into two long strands and hung on either side of his temples. She even noted how the markings crept up into part of Cyric's lip. How she remembered those lips tasting hers . . .

A slight grin lifted one corner of Cyric's mouth.

Still, Nia ignored.

Green eyes. Cyric of the Wood had the smokiest green eyes she'd e'er seen on a man, with long, black lashes and perfect black brows. She could do little more than stare at his all-too perfect features.

Again, the corners of his mouth lifted. Nia noticed for the first time a deep dimple in either cheek. God Almighty, no' only was he mythical, he was bloody beautiful.

That awarded Nia with a deep-throated laugh.

Even his teeth were straight and white. And those lips?

Heat flooded Nia's face. She knew the fool listened inside her brain. She didna care. She wasna finished yet.

Slowly, Nia walked around Cyric, inspecting each and every inch of his exposed skin. The markings fascinated her. Ancient markings started at his chest and wound around his abdomen, his back and spine, and disappeared below his waistline. Down the length of his muscular arms and on to his hands – even down each long finger.

Nia couldna imagine the pain he'd endured to receive such intricate markings.

She thought him to be the most beautiful creature she'd ever laid eyes upon.

"Are you quite finished yet, madam?"

Nia, surprised at the ease she felt in Cyric's presence, faced him. She tilted her chin. "Aye. And now you see why I didna wish for you to neither see nor touch my face."

"I wish to now," he said, those green eyes burning into hers.

"Drink your fill," Nia said, a bite to her words even she could hear. She held her gaze to his, and Cyric did exactly that.

She watched his green gaze slowly move over her face before he lifted a hand to her cheek. Inwardly, Nia flinched, but she wasna going to shirk his inspection. He'd saved her life. If he wanted to see the horror of her scars for himself, she'd let him. Then, she'd leave.

Cyric's eyes flashed as he firmly but gently grasped her chin. "Do you think so little of me, Nia of Clare?" Slowly, he released her, and let the back of his knuckles drag slowly over the very skin marred by the fire that took her mother's life. His eyes softened, and when they moved to her lips, turned even smokier. "You've no right to judge me by others, Nia," he said quietly. His thumb grazed her lower lip, and his eyes followed the motion, seemingly fascinated by it.

Then, he cupped her face on either side with both of his hands, tilted her head just so, and lowered his mouth to hers.

She allowed it.

His lips were a whisper away from touching hers when he stilled. "You are the most beautiful woman I've ever seen," he said, his lips brushing hers softly with each word. "The way you look at me – you didna fear the beast." He brushed his lips over hers. "I've waited for you my whole life, Nia of Clare." He pulled back and searched her eyes. "I think you were meant to be mine." He kissed her again, his thumbs brushing the puckered skin on her face. "Ne'er has any mortal been able to tame the Beast, but you did. I knew who you were last night," he said. "And you feared me not. You were so verra brave."

Nia was lost in his touch and his words. Ne'er had she been looked upon with such love. "My da deemed me unworthy of a husband because of my face," she said. "I was being sent to the abbey to live a life worshiping God, alone." She cocked her head. "Why have so many men before you seen my face and thought me ugly, yet you find me beautiful?"

Cyric's gaze stared down at her, and the sincerity Nia saw in the green depths rocked her to the core.

"Fools, for one," he began, and lowered his head once more. He brushed a light, teasing kiss across her lips. He leaned back, just far enough so his eyes weren't crossed at being so close. "And I've seen inside your head," he said proudly. "What's in there has a powerful beauty, as well." He cocked his head and stared directly at her scars. For once, she didna cringe. "When was the last time you saw your face, Nia?"

Nia had to think – quite difficult whilst being held in the arms of a half-naked marked man, centuries old. Then, she laughed. "I don't recall."

Cyric smiled. "Come. Let me show you something." He tugged her hand and pulled her away from the window. Then, he suddenly stopped, wrapped his arms around her and pulled her close, lowered his head, and covered her mouth with his. Everywhere his hands touched, her skin burned, and Nia slid her hands over his marked skin to clasp her fingers behind his neck. He moved her slowly until her back was against the aged wall, and they kissed until breathless.

Finally, Cyric pulled back and rested his forehead against hers. "Come," he said. He pulled her out of the ruined room, down a stone corridor, then down a narrow flight of steps. "Careful," he warned, leading the way.

Nia smiled at that. Cyric could turn into a bloodthirsty, frothing-at-the-mouth fanged beast that could rip a man in two, and he was telling her to be careful of the stone steps.

Finally, they reached the bottom. The roof of the castle was mostly gone, with wooden beams and sky exposed overhead. Cyric guided her to a wall where an old knight's shield hung askew. He reached up, grabbed it and, with the tail of Nia's cloak, polished it. He stared into it, grinned, and turned it around and held it up.

"See for yourself."

Nia stared into Cyric's mischievous eyes, then slowly let her gaze settle on the polished metal. Although no' a perfect mirror by any means, she could certainly see her reflection.

Nia blinked and drew closer. She felt her mouth slide open in surprise, and she lifted a hand to her marred cheek.

Rather, the cheek that was once marred. Now, 'twas just a bit pinkish and ever so slightly puckered.

'Twasna nearly as bad as it used to be.

Then, Cyric's image edged into the shield as he looked on

with her. "Beautiful," he whispered and, for once in her life, Nia felt it to be true.

He then set the shield down and walked Nia to what once was a massive landing overlooking the sea. He pulled her close and tucked her head beneath his chin. "You and I make quite a pair," he said, holding her tightly. "I dunna ever want to let you go." He lifted her chin, forcing Nia to meet his gaze. "Will you stay wi' me? I canna offer much, other than warmth, food and safety—"

"Aye," Nia said, joy filling her soul. "I never dreamed of finding someone who loved me as much as I loved them."

A wide smile stretched across Cyric's breathtaking face. Nia noticed how it curled one tip of the black Pict marking in his lip. "You love me, then? Beast and all?"

Nia wrapped her arms about Cyric's waist. "I do love you, Cyric, Beast of Killarney Wood." She raised on tiptoe and pulled his head down to her. She kissed him. "I'll love you forever."

Cyric embraced her tightly, then kissed her back with just as much fierceness as she. "I love you too, Nia of the Wood."

With a deep laugh that reverberated off the walls and cliffs of the sea, Cyric scooped Nia up and kissed her some more.

Beyond the Veil

Patricia Rice

Connacht Region, Ireland – 161 AD

One

A blast of wind and hail burst from the roiling black clouds, battering bodies crumpled in a sea of red. Rain lashed at the valley and the grassy mound rising above the fallen warriors, as if to wash away the stench of death. But the carrion crows already gathered.

Mortally wounded and bleeding profusely, one soldier determinedly staggered up the greensward, away from the battle scene. Caught sideways by a fierce gust of hail and rain, he sagged to one knee. But his will was mightier than the storm. With gasping breath, he dug his fingers into a boulder and hauled his big body up again. A cut across his cheekbone bled freely down his square jaw and into his long, wet hair, staining it a deeper shade of auburn.

The great sword slung across his back dripped with the blood of his enemies, but Finn mac Connell knew, in the end, they had killed him. Others like him, warriors all, the kind of which legends are made, lay slaughtered in the valley below. The battle had been won, but at a high cost.

Finn lurched on to a rocky path, his gaze fixed on the wooden fort at the top of the hill, where he'd left his wife. The women and children had fled with the cattle to the woods and hills when the battle arrived at their doorstep. But Niamh had been in childbed.

He had fought furiously to protect his home so he might return to the woman who owned his heart, and the child she was about to bear.

He prayed to all the gods that she was safe. In response, the gale blew so wildly, Finn stumbled backwards, but he fought for his balance and pushed onwards. The gnarled Druid Oak sheltered him momentarily, allowing him to fill his lungs, giving him the strength to continue, although the gash in his side was deep, and he'd lost more blood than any normal man could survive.

No smoke curled from the chimney. She would be freezing in this blustery damp air. He would start a fire for her before he left – because he knew he was not long for this world. But Niamh must live. And his child. Without them, he had no home to defend, and brave men had died for nought.

Using his sword to hold himself upright the last few steps, Finn pushed open the crude plank door of his home.

At the sight within, his roar of rage and agony surpassed the thunder, bringing him to his knees at last.

Niamh, his beautiful black-haired Niamh, lay in a bed of blood, her usually rosy cheeks now as pale and still as the winter snows. Her once flashing eyes stared lifelessly at the ceiling. Her warm smile would never greet anyone again.

The warrior crossed his arms on the timber bed and buried his face against them. He was not a man who wept, but his heart howled like an infant—

Like an infant. His head shot up, causing his long hair to swipe the tattered shoulders of his tunic. The cry was real! Alive. Bellowing with hunger and rage – the cry of a warrior's son.

Pressing his hand to Niamh's cold forehead, he blessed her, kissed her cheek and closed her eyes.

With his last fading breath and hope, he lifted the cover concealing his son. Niamh had wrapped him in swaddling clothes and kept him warm for as long as she'd had life in her body, sacrificing her fading strength to save their child.

Hugging the howling babe to his chest, the newly widowed

warrior wept, and prayed, "Aoibhinn, please, save my son, take him to your bosom, care for him as your own so that I may follow my heart."

"And lose the finest warrior that ever walked this land?" a harsh voice asked from the doorway. "I think not, Fionn mac Connell. If you wish to save the child, you must do so yourself. Stand like a man and come with me."

He had no choice. Much as he'd rather die beside his beloved Niamh, he could not let his son, Niamh's flesh and blood, die here cold and alone. With the last of his strength, Fionn stood, huddling the now quiet babe.

The wraith in the doorway gestured impatiently.

Accepting that he left the mortal world for the one beyond, Fionn followed the cloaked figure in grey out of the door he'd just entered – into a world that looked like his own but wasn't.

The wind and hail that had rattled the walls miraculously vanished – to reveal a sun shining in a sky of brilliant blue. Flowers danced in the valley where blood had moistened the trampled earth. The Druid Oak stood young and healthy, shading the richly garbed fae on their fine horses, awaiting his arrival.

The wound in Fionn's side had already begun to heal. He knew he had to pay a price for this peace, but for his son – for Niamh's son – he would forfeit whatever they demanded.

On the other side of the Veil, in the real world, a high keening shrieked over the roar of thunder.

Connacht Region, Ireland – 1161 AD

Anya O'Brion listened to the keening of the *bean sí* and shivered. She feared, in another few minutes, the wraith would have reason to wail again. The fine tapestries, rich panelling and precious gold adorning the high-ceilinged chamber could not stop Death.

Tears sliding down her cheeks, Anya sat on the bed beside her sister-in-law, holding Maeve's frail, cold hand. The keening could be dismissed as the wind on a blustery night such as this, but Anya knew it was not. The *bean sí* always recognized the death of an O'Brion, and the stillborn child in the cradle was the last of them, except for Anya herself.

The priest called the *sídhe* "fallen angels", but Anya had been born with the caul, and had seen the Other World before she'd breathed her first breath. She would not call the fae ones by any name but "Good Neighbours". She did not worship their ancient gods of the earth, but she respected their ways.

She knew her family thought her soft in the head for believing in the old tales, so she'd learned not to speak of what she saw. Instead, she had trained to become the tough, decisive ruler required of a king's daughter. That did not stop her from hearing the *bean sí*'s cry and feeling the hairs rise on the back of her neck as the spirits walked.

Maeve whispered incoherently and attempted to squeeze Anya's hand. The rising wind rattled at the windows. Murmuring a prayer, Breeda, both maid and midwife, shook her head sadly while removing sheets soiled by birthing.

Outside the richly panelled door of this tower room, guards waited, guards who would report to the household with great joy if an heir was born to their recently murdered king, Anya's brother.

If Maeve did not bear a son, those same guards would lay down their swords and swear fealty to a man Anya despised with all her heart and soul. The man whose consort she would become once the heir was reported stillborn, and she became the last remaining O'Brion to defend her family's keep.

"Sleep, Maeve," Anya said soothingly, shoving aside her own fears to reassure the dying Queen. "You have done well. You've borne a son and heir. You have done your duty. Rest easy."

Not quite a lie. Heaven would surely not deny her for easing a dying woman's heart. Feverish, Maeve still fretted at the sheets.

For her father's people, Anya was prepared to stand steadfast and do her duty, but her soul would surely wither within her, piece by little piece, once she was wedded to the Beast who had killed so many of her family. As he had killed her father and brother.

The tears slid off her cheek to fall on the simple tunic she'd worn to aid in the birthing. Turning away from Maeve, Anya gazed helplessly at the still, cold form, swathed in white linen, in the cradle at her feet. Even in death, a king's heir would not lie naked. The boy had dark hair, like his mother. Born early, he'd been too frail to breathe so much as a single breath. Her nephew, the king-who-was-meant-to-be, had passed from the womb directly to heaven.

As she wept over the dead infant, the air over the cradle began to shiver with translucent blues and reds.

Recognizing that ethereal shimmer, Anya pressed the back of her hand to her mouth, hiding her gasp. She had not seen this so close since childhood, when others had laughed at her foolish visions. She was no longer a child, but still, she was aware when the fae pierced the Veil between this world and the next. She knew when the faerie court went riding.

To her knowledge, they had never before entered the castle.

Muttering and shaking out fresh linen, the midwife had her back to the bed. Only Anya could see the cradle rock. Transfixed, she watched the shimmer form a fog that hid the child within. Surely, a dead child could not move? Her heart raced, and she feared to stir.

The mist parted, and a man appeared. Biting her tongue to keep from crying out, she studied the apparition standing tall, straight and strong. Hair the dark red of drying blood fell to his shoulders. A scar marred his harsh jaw. No smile softened his expression, but as he leaned over the cradle and rocked it, the streak of a single tear glistened, as if he wept for the dead King.

Standing again, he caught her eye, nodded and vanished.

In the cradle, the new King whimpered hungrily.

Anya froze, until the midwife swung around at the sound. She breathed again that she was not imagining what she had seen. Or heard.

Seeing the cradle rock, Breeda cried out to all the blessed

saints and hurried across the room, her gnarled hands wrapped in her apron, her face lit with disbelief.

"It is a miracle, Breeda," Anya whispered. Terrified her anguish had led her to visions of what she wanted, and not what *was*, Anya leaned over to touch the crying child. The *live* child. She could feel his warmth and solidity. Tufts of dark hair crowned his delicate skull, just as she'd noticed earlier. She unwrapped his perfect limbs, and strong feet kicked at his covers. A tiny fist popped deliberately into a rosebud mouth.

But even though his limbs had been hidden, Anya knew this was not the puny infant that had been delivered dead a few minutes ago. This one was healthy and strong.

Committing the first lie of her new life, Anya placed the changeling against the Queen's breast. "Your son, Maeve, your beautiful son."

The Queen died with a smile of peace upon her pale lips.

And the *bean sí* wailed again.

Two

Fionn stood outside the stone bailey wall of the grand castle that had been built on the hill where his timber fort had once stood. With the passage of time in the Other World, he'd buried the melancholy of losing all he knew and loved. But now, he had to let his son go – to mature in the human world where he belonged. He grieved mightily at the loss of his boy.

Below him, he could see that the Druid Oak was gone, no doubt reduced to ash for a winter fire as people forgot the old ways. The greensward had worn to a barren hill of rock beneath the passage of so many horses and carts – prosperity took its toll. At the foot of the hill, a ditch had been half completed – a fine defence once it was finished and filled with water. Aobinnhe had been kind in choosing a time when his son could return to his rightful position.

He could leave now. Should leave. He was no longer chieftain here. He was from the past, a time forgotten. He had watched from the safety of the Other World as battles were fought and won, new gods were worshipped, new families ruled. Time did not change the dimension he inhabited. He was the same now as he had been then, but the human world had moved on.

But he still possessed a warrior's fierce heart, and a warrior protected his own. Fionn had heard the *bean sí*'s cry, seen the worried face of the lass inside as she sat beside her dying queen. All was not well here.

The lass had not been frightened when he'd appeared. Fionn smiled for the first time in a long, long time. He wanted a woman of courage to care for his son, a woman who might understand that the old ways had passed but the gods lived still beyond the Veil.

Aware of the pounding of the distant sea and the rising dawn, Fionn called his horse from the Other World and waited for the sounds of jubilation and mourning to ring inside the castle.

His duty to his son was not yet done.

"Your Highness," the elderly steward said, interrupting the prayers in the Queen's chamber.

The steward had come from the formal courts of France and could not be convinced that the Irish did not bow to titles. He lost his bearings and grew confused unless he was "my lording" or "your highnessing" someone, and Anya had grown accustomed to his ways. She looked up from rocking her nephew, no longer annoyed with the man. How could anyone be annoyed while holding the future in her arms?

"Yes, François, what is it?"

"There's a knight outside, says he's been sent by the High King to serve the new O'Brion. His mantle is lined with fur, and the fibula must be pure gold! Shall I bring him here?" The last was asked dubiously since the upper chamber was filled with keening women.

Honouring a knight of the High King would be Anya's first duty as the new King's guardian. She had to play the part of ruler well or lose the respect she must command until the child could lead on his own. A daunting task for a gentle woman who would feed on dreams if allowed, but one to which she'd been raised.

"I will meet him in the hall, of course. Summon Garvan, if you will, and any of the other knights with him. Have the kitchen provide suitable fare for a man who has travelled far. I will be down shortly."

Anya's Norman mother had introduced many of the French ways to the O'Brion stronghold, but Conn the High King was pure Irish warrior. His men would not be gallant knights. Calling for scented water and her richest tunic and mantle, Anya pondered whether or not she should accept this "gift" of service. Did Conn mean for his knight to rule the O'Brions in the absence of a male O'Brion leader? If so, did she dare turn him away?

The maids wrapped silver ribbons in her long, blonde hair and one fastened the triple spiral gold fibula to her blue wool mantle. Anya owned nothing so fine as fur but would not have worn animals on her back anyway. Even her shoes were of matted felt and not leather. Her kingly brother had laughed at her odd ways, but her mother had seen the caul when Anya was born and accepted that her daughter was more attached to the natural world than most.

"Jewellery, please," she told the maids eagerly arranging the red and gold striped train of her best gown. She might eschew fur, but her people produced the finest linens in the world.

"The queen's jewellery?" one maid asked hesitantly.

"It was my mother's," Anya agreed. "Let us impress the High Court with our elegance so they do not think us weak barbarians."

By the time she'd been fastened into torque and bracelets of gold delicately wrought to fit slender throat and limbs, Anya was anxious to meet the knight sent to honour her nephew. Anxious – and afraid.

She bent to kiss the infant nursing at the breast of a wet nurse. None would believe her tale of the child's birth even should she relate it, so she had not spoken of what she'd seen. Straightening her mantle, she proceeded down the four flights of stairs to the castle's great hall. Conscious that this would be her first appearance as the O'Brion leader, she held her head high and her shoulders straight, determined to make her ancestors proud.

Surely the whole army had turned out to meet the newcomer! The hall was packed with men milling about, pounding each other on the back, elbowing each other to silence as she entered. Her father and brother would have been right there with them, pounding and shouting.

She swallowed hard as the room silenced. Breeda held the train of her striped gown from the flagstone floor. No rushes rotted under the toes of the O'Brion ladies these days. The silence continued as Anya climbed to the dais where her father, and later, her brother, had sat at the head table. Two ornately carved, high-backed chairs faced the hall, with the enormous hearth at their backs.

Garvan, as her brother's best friend and chief warrior, dropped to one knee and held his blade across his chest, declaring his fealty to the O'Brions, if not necessarily to her. Behind him, all the other men did the same. Except one.

Taller than any other man in the hall, wider of shoulder, an auburn-haired stranger in fur-lined mantle stood in the shadows of the hearth, watching her as if she were some new form of animal, not quite cat or dog. Anya wished she'd worn her hair up so she might look older and more commanding, but she'd been in a hurry – to meet this disrespectful oaf?

Instead of wearing his sword belted at his side, she could see he wore his weapon hung over his back like an uncivilized churl, despite all his finery. And his clothing was very grand, indeed, although not as fine as the form that wore it.

Realizing she stared, Anya settled into Maeve's slightly smaller chair and beckoned the newcomer to approach the dais. She spoke three languages. She hoped he spoke at least one of them.

He stepped from the shadows of the hearth into the light of the candlelit iron chandelier and made his bow, not quite so courtly a one as Garvan's, but fair enough. When he straightened, the light fell full on his face, and Anya inhaled with shock.

His jaw was scarred in the same manner as the vision she'd seen last night over the cradle. His stature was as broad and tall as she remembered. What meant this? Was he a ghost? Or a portent?

She had the urge to reach out and touch him, to test his reality, but that would cause others to wonder if she'd lost her mind. Her grip tightened on the gilded chair arms. She wore a short sword in her girdle, and her father's spear leaned against his chair. Her dream world clashed with reality. She was trained to face threats with weapon in hand, but she had *seen* this man weep for the child.

Deciding she did not act from a position of strength, she waited silently, as taught, learning all she could before showing her hand.

"Your name?" she asked in the language of her father's Irish ancestors.

The handsome stranger hesitated at her question, as if considering how much truth to offer. Then bowing his head with respect, he replied, "Finn mac Connell, my lady."

He spoke the old language and used the old name of *mac Connell*, son of Connell. Connells were once legendary gods and kings to whom the O'Brions had sworn fealty. These days, simmering enmity separated their descendants.

"I see," she said coolly, although her thoughts raced ahead of her to dire situations that might require that the King place an enemy in her father's stronghold. Or did the stranger lie? "Did His Majesty send a message with you?"

Again, the hesitation, as if he pondered every word before speaking it. She did not trust a man who could not speak from the heart. And she could not trust a man who had appeared in a vision, like one of the elusive, ever mischievous, Good Neighbours.

"His Majesty wishes to show his friendship for the new King of the O'Brions, and to offer his protection. I am at your service, my lady," he finally replied with bold authority.

In this, she believed him. The vision had watched over the babe with tenderness. For all she knew, the next king of the O'Brions was fae born, since he was most certainly not Maeve's. It did not matter. The child was all that stood between her clan and destruction. He needed all the protection she could summon.

She must see the boy christened immediately.

"Garvan." She turned to the captain of her small army. "Have we a place for the King's man?"

Garvan stepped forwards eagerly. Before he could say *aye*, the stranger had placed himself between Anya and her knight quicker than she could think.

She wrapped her fingers around the dirk in her belt and regarded his broad back. Did he think her so helpless that she could not stop him? Or did showing her his back mean he trusted her?

"My place is to serve the boy," Finn declared firmly. "I will guard him with my life, but I will not guard him from the bottom of a mountain of stones. My place is beside him."

Garvan's hand went to his sword hilt. Finn merely crossed his massive arms and stood like the mountain of stones he scorned. There would be violence if Anya did not interfere. Did she side with her brother's friend or a stranger?

Garvan's men had not been able to protect her father or her brother. What chance did an infant have in their care? She had no reason not trust the vision who had wept over an infant. Yet.

"Pax," Anya said softly, rising from her chair. "We have a funeral and a christening for which to prepare. If the High King sees fit to send his man here, let the mac Connell take his place on the landing. For now, the babe stays with his wet nurse in the women's quarters, with me."

Calling for the priest, she swept past the roomful of towering soldiers, aware that the largest of them all followed her to the stairwell.

The haughty wench hadn't even introduced herself, Finn recalled in amusement, watching the O'Brion princess carry his son down a chapel aisle to the waiting priest. He'd learned her name, of course, but name and title were unimportant in comparison to the woman who wore them. Before he left, he needed to know she could defend and care for the boy.

Anya O'Brion's temerity alone ought to terrify half the men in the land. She'd stood at the head of a hall full of armed soldiers and commanded respect like a warrior queen, instead of a petite princess. Standing to one side of the altar so he might observe all who entered, Finn hid his grin. Even the goddess Brigid must approve of a woman who could slay grown men with her flashing eyes.

In his time, he'd left worship to the women. That men now commanded the sacred waters and prayed to male gods did not bother him. What bothered him was the tension he sensed in the chapel as Princess Anya kneeled before the priest, holding his son. They doubted her ability to lead them or protect their king – against what enemy?

Was this the price the Old Ones commanded for providing his son the home he deserved – knowing the boy must fight for his place? The Others did not speak plainly but left the consequences of Finn's actions on his shoulders. He supposed they would smite him dead if he did not obey, but as far as Finn was concerned, he was already dead. He'd died with Niamh.

He glanced at the colourful glass in the chapel windows and wished it gone so he could see outside. How could a man protect his kin if he could not see all the land around him?

Hearing the thunder of hooves, he stepped from the shadows of the altar to stand directly behind the Princess, his sword and his knife crossed over his chest in warning.

The audience gasped at his warlike action, but in the next instant, others heard what he had. The men pushed for the exit, heading for the ramparts, Finn hoped.

"I christen thee Ardal Patrick Connor O'Brion, in the name of the Father, the Son, and the Holy Ghost," the priest intoned, blithely ignoring the departing soldiers.

Finn did not recognize the name *Patrick*, but Ardal was a fine old name, and *Connor* was fitting for the son of a king. *Conn* was the origin of his own name. The Princess had chosen well. Now that the naming was done . . .

Finn grabbed the lady's arm and hauled her from the floor. "Upstairs, now," he ordered.

Holding the babe, she could not reach for her knife, although he saw murder in her glare. She had eyes the colour of emeralds and hair of the finest flax. And a glower that would pierce stone walls. "Release me," she whispered harshly.

"After I'm seeing you up the stairs, where no man can go without dying on my blade." With determination, he rushed her down the aisle.

Rather than submit to the indignity of struggling with him, she hurried ahead as if fleeing the chapel were her idea. She shielded the boy with her heavy mantle as she walked, so Finn approved.

"They fly the Connolly flag," a guard called from his post in the tower.

The slender woman under Finn's hand jerked to a halt, forcing Finn to stumble rather than fall over her.

"I will not run from the Beast," she announced. "Breeda, take Patrick to our chamber." She placed the protesting bundle of flailing limbs into the hands of her gnarled old maid.

Finn scowled, unprepared for the two to separate. Did he follow his son or stay with the woman? Narrowing his eyes, he watched as the servant carried his son to safety, while the foolish Princess swung to meet some foe called the Beast.

"Are you run mad, woman?" he muttered. "Let the men do battle. Your place is with the boy."

Her look of scorn would have melted iron. "*Your* place is with the King. Mine is to slaughter the man who has taken my family. I may start with that part of him that makes him male." She drew a deadly dirk from her girdle and hid it between the folds of her mantle and tunic.

Finn winced as he caught her meaning. "And wouldn't it help to be seeing what the man wants before emasculating him?" he asked dryly.

"I know what he wants, and he cannot have it. Emasculating is exactly what he deserves," she said with satisfaction.

Finn could not resist a challenge like that. He'd have to stay with the mad Princess to see how this game was played. Planting himself in front of the tapestry concealing the stairs, sword in hand, he watched over the Princess Anya as she assumed her chair on the dais.

Three

Well trained, the castle knights formed a phalanx around Anya as the visitors hailed the sentry on the wall.

"Order them to allow Connolly and one of his men in, no more," she commanded. The moat hadn't been completed, so there was no way to prevent riders reaching the walls. But horses couldn't fit through the narrow aperture through which the sentries allowed visitors.

The men who strode in wore mail and helmets and strutted like peacocks. They were big men, without question, but Anya had known them all her life. They had small minds and only two thoughts in them – her, and the lands she now guarded for her nephew.

"You have come all this way to express your condolences?" she asked dryly. "Would you not have done better to bring your mother and sister so we might console together?"

Dubh Connolly removed his helmet to uncover thick black curls interspersed with grey. "I regret the passing of Queen Maeve," he said gruffly. "How fares the child?"

"Very well," Anya said sweetly, blessing the saints and the Others and all responsible for the child upstairs. She did not glance behind her at the giant guarding her hall, but for now, her blessing encompassed him as well. "Patrick shall be a fine, strong king someday."

"But not this day," Dubh stated bluntly. "And not for many years to come. Your father meant us to wed so that his lands and people would have a strong hand to guide them. I have come to claim my bride."

Anya fingered the dirk in her skirts and imagined all the ways she could use it. But her choices were no longer her own. She had her father's people to consider. For now, she must deny personal satisfaction. "It is grateful I am to so fine a man for his offer, but my father is dead. He is dead at the hand of your men, as is my brother. I do not think their wishes would be the same today as they may have been in the past."

"It was fair battle, Anya," Dubh declared. "We disagreed over boundaries. There would be no such disagreement between us. Marriage will bind our lands in one, and your nephew will be guarded well."

"My nephew will be guarded better if he is nowhere near a man who kills me and mine!" Unable to hold her temper at his crass assumption that she was as stupid as he, Anya stood and grabbed her father's great spear from its post.

Dubh did not look deterred. "You have no choice. You cannot lead your men to war against me."

He was right. Every man in here knew he was right. They knew her as a dreamy child who spoke of Other Worlds and cried at bloodshed. She knew that did not make her weak, but that was hard to prove to men who only respected war.

Her hand tightened on the spear, desiring nothing so much in this world as to use it. And start a fight she couldn't win.

The men around her dropped their hands to their sword hilts, and tension mounted.

"I can," a deep voice declared – not loudly but with enough menace to turn every head.

In surprise, Anya loosened her grip on the spear as the High King's man stepped forward, towering even over Dubh and his captain. Finn wore no mail, but he held with ease a sword broader than any in here. A weapon like that was meant to decapitate in one fell stroke.

He had said he was here to guard Patrick. Anya was fairly certain the High King would not approve of war between his chieftains as a means of protection. What price must she pay for his loyalty to her and not Conn?

Dubh Connolly clutched the sword hilt at his hip and studied her champion. "What man is this?" he asked suspiciously. "He is none of your father's."

"The High King sent him," she said proudly. "He is a mac Connell. You might be thinking twice if you believe I must bow to your wishes." The spear was heavy. Anya knew how to wield words better than weapons, but she understood the art of drama. She held the spear straight, with the point in the air, not threatening but warning.

"Conn said none of this to me." A stubborn man, Dubh didn't take the hint. "The High King desires our lands to be united. I think you have taken a viper into your nest."

She would have been as suspicious as Dubh had she not seen the vision of the man with the tearstain on his rugged jaw. She prayed she was not victim of wishful thinking and let Finn speak for himself.

"No man bearing our forefathers' name would threaten a woman," Finn said in that deep baritone which commanded without bluster. "No man who calls himself a man would need to. There are far better ways of persuading women, and ashamed I am that a man of my name would not know them."

May the saints preserve them, but he'd just thrown the gauntlet in the face of the clan chieftain as if he were High King himself! As thrilled as her woman's heart might be at Finn's bold declaration, Anya knew if she did not control this scene now, her men would be bowing to Finn.

"Garvan, I think you may escort Dubh to the door. He will no doubt be wishing to ask his women how they would like to be treated. I bid you good day, sir, and thank your family for their concern for our queen. The priest will hold prayers for her soul on the morrow."

She did not offer to break bread with Dubh or his men. She would have to poison them if she did so. Anya watched as her troop formed to escort the enemy from her doors. Her knights were good men. She did not wish to lose them to battle. That was the reason women did not win wars.

With a sigh, she set down her spear to confront her new

warrior. "What in all the heavens did you think you were about? 'There are better ways of persuading women'," she mimicked. "Are you after having the bastard court me?"

"It seemed one solution," he replied without apology. "I like to think a Connolly would be an honourable man, and joining your lands rather than fighting over them is good for all."

"Including the High King," she said with disgust, understanding his ploy now. "I should have known not to trust any Conn or Connell. You may leave now, Finn of the Connells. I will fight my own battles, thank you."

She pushed past him to the stairway, weeping inside, where none could tell. She did not possess a warrior's heart. But it seemed she must develop one.

Not known for his obedience, Finn claimed his place on the landing between his son's chamber and the great hall below and pondered his predicament. Resting his shoulders against the stone wall, he pinched the bridge of his nose and muttered, "Aoibhinn, how much time have I here?"

A grey mist swirled above the stairs. "As you are mortal here, not long," she answered dryly. "Warriors do not live long lives, especially when they antagonize their neighbours. Have you not learned that by now?"

"A man does not let worms stand up and speak for him, or he is not a man," he retaliated.

"Then use them to catch salmon." The mist evaporated.

Finn would dip Dubh in the nearest river and let the salmon chew his toes if he thought that would work, but goddesses did not speak in literal terms. He had not lived as long as he had without learning a few lessons, though. The lady – and his son – needed him.

He also knew he didn't wish to see a lady as courageous as the Princess be beaten into submission by a brutal cur like Connolly. The other chieftain was a handsome man, one some ladies might prefer. Finn had had to offer her the choice, but he hadn't enjoyed it. Glad he was that she was smart enough to spit in her suitor's face. But it would not do.

He stalked up the stairs and rapped at the top door. The old woman, Breeda, answered. He did not give her time to dismiss him but seeing over her shoulder, stepped forwards, forcing the maid back.

"We must speak," he announced. "Come with me."

The beautiful, golden-haired Princess raised shapely eyebrows but did not set aside her embroidery. "Breeda, call Garvan. I believe we have bats in the rafters."

The women tittered, and Finn resisted growling and flinging the fool woman over his shoulder. He would have done so with Niamh, but his wife would have grabbed his buttocks and tormented him until he lay her down and took her in the grass. The haughty Princess would more likely stab him in the back.

So, he was not king of all he saw here. He did not possess pretty words any more than a pretty face. But he had not come this far to lose his son to a sweet smile and a sour attitude. "I have an urgent message you must hear. It is better spoken privately."

"I am armed," she warned, rising from her chair. Instead of immediately following him, she stopped to cover the infant in his cradle. "I learned to kill a man when I was only six. I do not fear using a blade."

She lied. Anyone with half an eye could tell the gentle Princess might poison a man with words, but never gut one with steel. A good ruler should have no need to shed blood. She had the makings of an excellent queen.

"I do not wear armour," he told her. "If you wish to kill me, you can. But for now, I am all that stands between you and a wolf hungry for power."

"And wealth," she conceded, taking up her mantle. "Come, I have need of herbs from the garden."

Finn had forgotten the rich, musky scent of mortal women and the heat that pooled in his loins at the brush of soft skin against his callused palm. He'd been living in a perfect world of perfumed air, a timeless world without need or desire. Until now, he hadn't missed the human impulse to reproduce, to make his surroundings better, to create new out of old. He wasn't certain he wished to return to those driving urges again.

Except escorting the exquisite Princess Anya to the kitchen garden reminded him of how much he'd lost when he'd left his humanity behind.

"Do you believe in heaven?" she asked, lifting a reed basket and carrying it to the herb bed. "The priest says Maeve and my brother are watching over their babe from the clouds."

"I am no priest, but yes, I believe Others watch over us," he said honestly. "That does not mean they can help us if you think the ghost of your brother will slay your enemies for you."

She granted him a scowl and crouched down to clip her herbs. "Your urgent message?"

Lost in the sharp scents of herbs and earth and woman, Finn had forgotten what he'd intended to say. The sun here was not the warm, golden light of the Other Side, but he enjoyed the brisk bite of the wind against his skin, recalling the days of flesh and blood – and what he could do with them. "You must catch salmon with bait," he told her, recovering his rattled wits.

"I don't eat salmon," she informed him. "I do not eat the creatures of the field or sea. They have a right to live as much as I do."

It was his turn to scowl. "And such fasting allows you to see things that you have no right to see. You *saw* me the other night when you should not have. Why do you not accuse me of being a demon?"

"If you are a demon, then I must accept that Patrick is one, too, and that I will not. If mortals see you, then you are real and as human as I. It is only the Others, the ones I glimpse through the Veil who are not human. Do they urge me to eat salmon?" she asked with curiosity.

"No, they bait me as they bait you," he growled. "But they must approve of you if they have brought Patrick here."

She nodded serenely as if they spoke of what meal they would have that evening and not the mysteries of the universe. "Thank you for being honest and not telling me I am imagining what I see. The priest would say that I speak with angels, or he would be forced to call me a heretic, but I know it is arrogance to believe we know everything. I certainly don't know what you mean about salmon and bait."

He crouched to help her with the basket, and an arrow hissed past his head, into the earth beneath the keep's wall. Before she could so much as cry out, Finn flattened the Princess beneath him and rolled with her under the shelter of a garden bench. He could feel her heart thumping wildly, in tandem with his. He had not come here to die so ignobly.

The arrow had come from the bailey. Finn scanned the ramparts, noting scurrying figures but no archer.

"I can't breathe," the Princess said from under him. "If we're being attacked, I need to reach my knife."

Beneath him, she felt soft, warm, and curved in all the right places. Finn longed to forget archers and lose himself in her flesh. Lifting his weight on both elbows, he let his hips press against hers. Dodging death raised his appreciation of life. "I see no more archers. You may have a traitor among your sentries. And if you cannot reach your knife like this, then you are very badly trained."

"You would teach me better?" Her fair features expressed more curiosity than fear.

"I would, after I throttle the traitor." He rolled off her. "You are the bait. Choose your salmon and wiggle."

Not wishing for further argument while someone wished to kill him, Finn flung the baffling woman over his shoulder, picked up her basket and carried both into the safety of the keep.

Four

Choose her salmon and wiggle, Anya mused that evening, sitting at the head table, picking at her mushrooms and carrots while the others feasted on fish brought up from the sea. What a strange thing for a man to say, but then, Finn was not really a man, or was he?

He'd certainly felt as solid as any man. If she'd questioned his faeness before, she certainly could not after being shoved from the chapel, rolled under a bench, and carried over a brawny shoulder. Finn mac Connell was all muscled man.

She darted a look to the warrior apparently enjoying his meal. He'd smelled like a man when she'd been lying under him. He'd felt so alive, she could have sworn he'd been aroused. And she'd been too stupefied by her unexpected desire that she'd hardly understood that he could have died out there.

The meal was quieter than usual. While mead flowed freely and the feast was fit for a king, they'd hung one of their own this day – the first death of the battle ahead. The traitor had been caught and tried and justice done swiftly, as it must be. The archer had been kin of Connolly's.

"There will be war, won't there?" the late Queen's lady-in-waiting asked from the seat at Anya's right. Cailleagh had been lady to Anya's mother as well as Maeve. She wore the black of mourning for the many lives lost this past decade.

There would be no war if Anya married Dubh and gave him all the wealth he lacked. His lands were rocky and not suited for farming. He fought viciously for every field of fertile ground he could claim. She understood how he thought and why. But his thinking was of the past. These days, they must fight the enemies that threatened from outside, not each other.

"There is always war," Anya agreed. "It is choosing the right war that matters."

If she married Dubh . . . She would have to kill him before he killed Patrick. She had been trained to defend herself, but she had never killed, for self-defence or any reason.

Her gaze strayed to the big man apparently enjoying the feast. He was of Faerie but not one of them. He was much too solid, too real. Surely, if he could enter the Other World, he had gifts far stronger than her own. He had protected her with his life, *as he would protect Patrick.*

She knew now what she must do, even though it broke her heart. She stood. Few noticed or cared. She quietly departed for the stairwell. Finn followed, as she'd known he would. Even though he'd been as lost in feasting and drinking as the others, he halted, for her. And for the infant.

She left him at his post on the landing and entered her chamber where the maids entertained a wide-awake babe. A beautiful babe, one she would claim as her own, if she could. Smiling as if she hadn't a care in the world, she took the child king into her arms and cuddled him. He swung his little fist as if to touch and explore her. She already adored him with all her heart and soul, and tears filled her eyes as she carried him from the chamber, down the stairs.

Without questioning, Finn followed in her footsteps, outside to the secluded garden where she'd told her brother he could not build because the Good Neighbours rode through this place. A hidden door allowed them to pass through the wall unhampered. Her brother had laughed and called it a Faery gate, but she had felt the appreciation of their unreal Neighbours and known that the passage had been the right thing to do. The Others had inhabited this land well before mortals.

When they were alone in the moonlight, Anya turned and held the child out to Finn. It took all the strength in her to do so. "Take him where he will be safe, until he is full grown."

As usual, he did not do as told but studied her with wariness. "A babe needs a woman to care for him. I cannot."

"Salmon eat bait. If I am to be swallowed whole, then I cannot guarantee the child's safety. I would rather die than lose him that way." Tears sprang to her eyes, tears she hadn't allowed herself to shed since she'd known the mantle of responsibility would fall on her frail shoulders. "I thank you for offering me this chance to escape my fate, but I see now that I was being selfish."

"The child is mine," he said resolutely. "I wish him to grow strong and true and take the place that is his birthright. He cannot do that from a place of weakness."

"Yours?" Surprised, she gazed into the babe's wide dark eyes, seeking a resemblance, but the warrior was hard and stern and the babe had yet to develop such character. Patrick gurgled and sucked his fist. And she loved him. Weeping, she offered the babe again. "I cannot protect him from Dubh. He is ruthless and single-minded. You must see that. If anyone must be sacrificed, it is I, not the child."

At her words, Finn stared as if she had suddenly developed a halo and wings. He brushed her cheek with his knuckles and stared into her eyes. "Niamh?" he asked in a disbelieving whisper. "Have the Others brought me to you? I swear, no other would sacrifice herself for our son."

Memories settled on Anya like a soft mantle, warming her heart and thoughts as she turned them inwards. "No one has called me that since . . ." She tried to recall. "I had a nurse once, a nurse who took me to see our Good Neighbours riding. *They* called me Niamh." She looked at him oddly. "You know me?"

"From another time and place." Finn stroked her face boldly, tenderly, testing the quality of her hair and skin but studying her eyes. "You do not look the same, but your heart . . . your heart is mine."

Anya did not understand his words so well as his expression. Heart thudding at her daring, she stepped forwards, stood on her toes, and tested a kiss against his chiselled lips. And to her amazement, they softened.

"My bait, no others," he whispered against her mouth, pulling her against his chest, with the child gently crushed between them. "You will wiggle only for me."

The intoxicating liquor of his kiss prevented her from laughing at his odd idea of courtship words. Before she fell too far under his magic spell, she pushed away. "How?" she asked, unable to form full phrases while her head spun, for it did seem they were meant for each other. She could feel it in that place that recognized what lay beyond this world.

"They knew," he said obliquely. "They knew I merely survived with them. That to live, I must make things better, and their world is too perfect for an imperfect mortal. They knew this world needs me more than theirs, and they brought me to you. Mortality is a price I willingly pay."

"You can stay?" she asked, holding her breath in fear,

widening her eyes as she studied the rugged, broad-minded man who held her and looked upon her as if she were the answer to his prayers. How could any woman resist such a man?

"I can," he said with certainty. "Together, we will buy Dubh's lands and put his tenants to work so that we all might grow wealthy together. So someday, Patrick may inherit peace."

"Yes," she sighed happily, as the babe gurgled in delight. "Yes, and we will be good neighbours to everyone, even to those we cannot always see. Where have you been all my life?"

With a roar of joy, Finn lifted her and the babe in his mighty arms and swung them around in the moonlight. "I've been here, with you, inside your heart all these years!"

Beneath the spreading oak by the hidden gate, an invisible, elegant troop of riders nodded approval at the joyous couple – before turning their mounts and galloping into the mist rising from the sea.

Shifter Made

Jennifer Ashley

One

Baile Ícín (near Dingle), Ciarraí, Ireland – 1400

"Smith."

Niall knew without looking up from his anvil that the woman who addressed him was Fae, or Sidhe as the villagers called them. He could smell her, a bright, sticky-sweet stench that humans found irresistible.

He kept his head bent over his task – mending a cooking crane for a village woman was far more important than speaking to a Fae. Besides, his name wasn't Smith, and if she couldn't call him by his real name he saw no need to answer.

"Shifter, I command you," she said.

Niall continued hammering. Wind poured through the open doors, carrying the scent of brine, fish and clean air, which still could not cover the stench of Fae.

"*Shifter.*"

"This forge is filled with iron, lass," Niall cut her off. "And Shifters don't obey Fae any more. Did you not hear that news 150 years ago?"

"I have a spell that keeps my anathema of iron at bay. For a time. Long enough to deal with you."

Niall finally looked up, curiosity winning over animosity. A tall woman in flowing silk stood on his threshold, her body haloed by the setting sun. Her pale hair hung to her knees in a score of thin braids, and she had the dark eyes and slender, pointed ears common to her kind. She was beautiful in an ethereal way – but then all Fae were beautiful, the evil bastards.

The wind boiling up from the sea cliffs cut through the doorway, and she shivered. Niall raised his brows; he'd never caught a Fae doing a thing so normal as shiver.

He thrust the end of the crane into the fire, sending up sparks. "Come in out of the weather, girl. You'll be freezing in those flimsy clothes."

"My name is Alanna, and I'm hardly a girl."

She had to be if she responded to Niall's condescension, or at least naive. Fae lived so long and never changed much once they were fully grown that it was difficult to tell what age they were. She could be twenty-five or four hundred and fifty.

Alanna stepped all the way into the forge, darting nervous glances at the iron – the anvil, his tools, the piece of crane he was mending. "I've been sent to give you a commission."

"You were *sent* were you? Poor lass. You must have offended someone high up to be handed the thankless task of entering the mortal world to speak to a Shifter."

Her cheeks coloured but her tone remained haughty. "I've come to ask you to forge a sword. I believe you were once a sword maker of some repute."

"In days gone by. Now I'm a humble blacksmith, making practical things for villagers here and on the Great Island."

"Nonetheless, I am certain you retained your skill. The sword is to have a blade three feet in length, made of silver. The hilt is to be of bronze."

Niall drew the crane from the fire, set it on his anvil, and quickly hammered the glowing end into shape. "No," he said.

"What?"

He enunciated each word. "No, I will not make such a damn fool weapon for you."

Alanna regarded him slack-jawed, a very un-Fae-like expression. Fae were cold beings, barely bringing themselves to speak civilly to non-Fae. Fae had once bred Shifters to hunt and fight for them, and they regarded Shifters as animals, one step below humans.

This woman looked troubled, confused, even embarrassed. "You will do this."

"I will not."

"You must."

Was that panic now? Niall thrust the iron crane back into the fire and got to his feet. The Fae woman stepped back, and Niall fought an evil grin. Niall was big, even for a Shifter. His arms were strong from a lifetime of smithy work, and he'd always been tall. Alanna would come up to his chin if he stood next to her; her slender hands would get lost in his big ones. He could break her like a twig if he chose, and by the fear in her black eyes, she thought he'd choose to.

"Listen to me, lass. Go back to wherever you came from, and tell them that Shifters take orders no more. We are no longer your slaves, or your hunters, or your pets. We are finished." He turned back to pump the bellows, sweat trickling down his bare back. "Besides, silver won't make a decent sword. The metal's too soft."

"Spells have been woven through the metal to make it as strong as steel. You will work it the same as you would any other sword."

"I will, will I? Fae don't use swords in any case – your weapon is the bow. Not to mention the copper knife for gouging out other beings' hearts, usually while they're still beating."

"That is only the priests, and only when we need to make a sacrifice."

"*Sacrifice*, you call it? Seems like it's not much of a sacrifice for you but hard on the one who's losing his heart."

"That's really none of your affair. You need to make the sword for me. What we use it for doesn't concern you."

"You are wrong about that." Niall lifted the crane again, quickly hammered it into its final shape, and thrust it into his cooling barrel. Water and metal met with a hiss, and steam boiled into the air. "Anything I make has a little part of meself in it. I'm not putting that into a sacrificial weapon you'll stick into helpless animals or humans or Shifters who never did any harm to you."

Her brow clouded. "A piece of yourself? Blood or a bit of skin . . .?"

"Not literally, you ignorant woman. I don't christen it with blood, like some Fae priest. I mean I put a bit of my soul in everything I craft. Gods know I wouldn't want Fae touching anything that's come close to my soul."

Her face flamed, and her look was now . . . ashamed? "Shifter, I have to take this sword back with me at first light."

Last light was now streaming through the door, the spring air turning even more frigid. "And where would I be getting time to craft such a thing before morning? Sword-working is a long business, and I have sons to look after. I'm not doing it, lass. Go on home and tell them you couldn't bully the big, mean Shifter."

"Damn you." Alanna clenched her fists, eyes sparkling. "Are all Shifters this bloody stubborn? I thought I could do this without hurting you."

Niall looked her up and down. Fae could work powerful magic, without doubt, but not much in the human world. They'd given up that power to retreat to the safety of their own realm, while Shifters had learned to adapt and remain in the world of humans. Fae still had magic out here – minor spells, glamour and misdirection, not that they didn't use those to lure human beings to their deaths.

"Could you hurt me, lass? In this forge full of iron? I lost my mate ten years ago. That hurt me more than anything in the world ever could. I doubt you could match that pain, no matter how many tiny spells you can throw at me."

"No?" Alanna asked, her voice ringing. "What about if you lost your cubs?"

Niall was across the room and had her pinned against the wall before the echo of her words died, the iron bar he'd just cooled in the water pressed across her pale throat.

Two

The Shifter was stronger than she'd imagined, and the iron against Alanna's skin burned. The spell that her brother had grudgingly let his chief magician chant over her kept the worst at bay, but the bar felt white hot.

Odours of sweat, fire, smoke and metal poured off the Shifter called Niall. He'd scraped his black hair into a tight braid, the style emphasizing his high cheekbones and sharp nose, the touch of Fae ancestry that had never disappeared from Shifters. His hard jaw was studded with dark whiskers, wet with sweat from his labours. The whiskers and sweat made him seem so raw, so animal-like. Fae men were beardless, their skin paper-smooth, and she'd never seen one do anything so gauche as sweat.

Studying the Shifter's stubbled chin kept Alanna from having to look into his eyes. Those eyes had been deep green when she'd entered the forge; now they were nearly white, his pupils slitted like a cat's. He *was* a cat, a predatory cat bred from several species of ancient wildcats, and any second now he'd tear her apart.

And then his two sons would die.

Niall's towering rage held her as firmly as the iron bar. "You touch my cubs, bitch, and you'll be learning what pain truly is."

"If you do as I say, they won't be hurt at all."

"You'll not go near them."

"It's too late for that. They've already been taken. Make the sword, and you'll get them back."

The Shifter roared. His face elongated, and animal lips pulled back from fangs. He didn't shift all the way, but the hand that held the bar sprouted finger-long claws.

At that moment Alanna hated all Shifters and all Fae, especially her brother Kieran, who'd told her that subduing the Shifter would be simple. *They will do anything to protect their whelps. We'll carry them off, and he'll whimper at your feet.*

Niall O'Connell, master sword maker of the old Kingdom of Ciarraí, wasn't whimpering or anywhere near her feet. His fury could tear down the forge and crumble the cliff face into the sea.

"Make the sword." Now Alanna was the one pleading. "Craft the sword, and the little ones go free."

Niall's face shifted back into his human one, but his eyes remained white. "Where are they?"

"They will be released when you complete the sword."

Niall shoved her into the wall. "Damn you, woman, *where are they*?"

"In the realm of Faerie."

The Shifter's pupils returned to human shape, his eye colour darkening to jade as grief filled them. Niall's shoulders slumped, but though his look was one of defeat, the iron never moved from Alanna's throat. "Gone, then," he whispered.

"No," Alanna said quickly. "If you give me the sword, they will be set free. He assured me they would not be harmed."

"Who did? Who is this Fae bastard who's taken my children?"

"My brother. Kieran."

"Kieran . . ."

"Prince Kieran of Donegal."

"There was a Kieran of Donegal in Shifter stories of long ago. A vicious bastard that a pack of Lupines finally hunted and killed. Only decent thing the bloody dogs have ever done."

"My brother is his grandson."

"Which makes you his granddaughter." Niall peered at her. "You don't seem all that pleased to be running this errand for your royal brother. Why did he send you?"

"None of your affair." Enemies saw your compassion as weakness and used that against you, Kieran had told her. Kieran certainly used every advantage over his enemies – and his friends as well.

"Back to that, are you?" Niall asked. "What assurance do I have that you'll not simply kill my boys whether I make the sword for you or not?"

Alanna shifted the tiniest bit, trying to ease the pain of the bar on her throat. "You have my pledge."

He snorted. "And what worth is that to me?"

"My pledge that if your children are harmed, you may take my life. I wasn't just sent as the messenger, Shifter. I was sent to be your hostage."

Even through his pain, his grief, and his gut-wrenching fear, Niall couldn't deny that the Fae woman had courage. He could kill her right now, and she knew it. She offered her life in exchange for his sons with a steady voice, though she obviously knew that a Shifter whose cubs were threatened was more dangerous than an erupting volcano. And even though she'd said she'd been given a protective spell against iron, Niall knew the cold bar hurt her.

Slowly he lifted it from her throat. Alanna rubbed her neck as though it pained her, but the bar had left no mark.

Niall stopped himself having any sympathy. She and her brother had taken his boys, Marcus and Piers, who were ten and twelve as humans counted years.

He looked past her to the darkening night, to the mists gathering on the cliff path, to the Great Island silhouetted by the blood-red sky. "My youngest, Marcus, he likes to fish," he said. "The human way with a pole and hook. Will he be able to fish where he is?"

Alanna shook her head. "The game and the fish in the rivers are for Kieran only."

"My mate died of bringing him in, poor love. She was a beautiful woman, was Caitlin, so tall and strong." Niall looked Alanna up and down. "Nothing like you."

"No, I don't suppose she was."

Shifter women tended to be as tall as the males. They were fast runners, wild in bed, and laughed a lot. Caitlin had laughed all the time.

"Piers, now. He likes to craft things. He'll be a smith like me. He likes to watch the iron get red hot and bend into whatever shape he tells it. He'd love to have watched me make this sword."

Alanna said nothing. Niall knew what he was doing, why he was saying these things. He was letting himself start to grieve.

Deep in his heart, he didn't believe Prince Kieran would ever release his sons. Fae didn't play fair. Niall might be allowed to take Alanna's life in vengeance for his sons' deaths, but it would be an empty vengeance. He would have no one left. No mate, no cubs, no one left in his pride. Niall lived here on the edge of this human village called Baile Ícín, because the other members of his pride and clan had died out. Shifters could marry into other clans, but there weren't as many females as males any more, and other clans were few and far between. The Shifter race was diminishing.

"You'll make the sword then?" Alanna asked, breaking his thoughts.

She didn't have to sound so eager. "I don't have much bloody choice, do I?"

Her eyes softened. "I am sorry."

Sympathy, from a Fae? Had the world gone mad today?

"You will be, lass. If my cubs are hurt in any way, you'll be the first to be very, very sorry. Your brother, now, he'll be even sorrier still. So show me this damned silver and let's be getting on with it."

Three

Forging a sword was a different thing entirely from the usual practical ironworks Niall produced for the humans of the village. Niall never asked Alanna why he'd been chosen for this task, because he already knew.

Once upon a time, Niall O'Connell had been a master sword maker, before Ciarraí had been made an earldom by the bloody English. He'd created beautiful weapons used for deadly purpose in the last Fae–Shifter war. The Shifters had won that war, though Niall knew much of their victory had been due to luck – the Fae had already been losing power in the mortal world, and the Shifters had only made their retreat into the Faerie realms inevitable.

It wasn't often that Shifters from different clans and species worked together, but at that point, Lupine, Feline and Bear had fought side by side. The Fae had conceded defeat and vanished into their realm behind the mists.

Well, *conceded defeat* was too strong a phrase. The Fae had gone, killing, burning and pillaging behind them. Fae didn't care whether their victims were children, breeding mothers, or humans who just happened to be in the wrong place at the wrong time.

Niall still had his sword-making tools kept safely in a chest at the back of the forge. He hadn't touched them in years. He shook his head to himself as he laid out his tongs and hammer, grinding stone and chisel. This sword wouldn't be good, strong steel, but soft silver, which was daft, even if she claimed it was spelled to work like steel. He could craft such a thing, but it would only be good as a trinket.

He briefly considered mixing a bit of iron into the hilt to debilitate any Fae who touched it, but he knew such a trick would make his sons' deaths even more certain. Not that he believed the Fae Prince would let Niall live either, in any case. But Niall would take out the Fae bitch when they came for him. Prince Kieran would watch his sister die before he killed Niall.

Niall glanced at Alanna as he pounded out the bar of metal she'd brought him. She'd found a stool and seated herself on it near the fire. She did look cold, the silly woman, probably not used to the harsh clime of the Irish west coast. The Faerie realms, he'd heard, were warm and soft all the time, which was why she wore flimsy silk robes and let her braids flow. Fae women didn't have to bundle their hair out of the wind.

After a few quick looks at her, he realized that Alanna wasn't staring sightlessly at the forge, or watching him beat the blade. She was studying *him*.

Her gaze roved his bare back and the muscles of his arms, as though she'd never seen a half-clothed man before. She probably hadn't. Fae were cold people, not liking to be touched, preferring robes, jewels and other fussy things to bare skin. They rarely did anything as crude as coupling, bodily seduction being almost as distasteful to them as iron. Shifters, on the other hand, loved breeding and loved children, children being all that more precious because so few survived.

"Are you a virgin, then, lass?" Niall asked her.

Alanna jumped. "What?"

"A virgin. If it doesn't hurt your pristine ears for me to ask it. Are you?"

"No."

Interesting. Fae women didn't lie with males unless they absolutely had to. "You have a lover then? A husband?"

"No." The word was more angry now. "It is none of your affair."

"You like to say that, lass. Did you have a *gasún*?"

"A child? No." Again, the chill anger.

"I'm sorry, love."

"Why?"

"That must have hurt you." When a Shifter woman was childless it was an impossible sorrow to her. As dangerous as breeding was for Shifters, females were happy to risk it to bring in cubs. "I imagine 'tis different for a Fae woman." The Fae were so long-lived they didn't need to bear many children. Fae women who did like children often stole them from humans, rather than bearing their own, raising them to be their doting little slaves.

"It did hurt me."

Niall saw the pain in her eyes. She looked so out of place, sitting in his forge, her strange, elegant robes already soiled from the dust and soot. He never thought he'd feel sorry for a Fae before, but the sadness on her face was real.

"Did your lover not want a child?" Niall asked gently.

"My lover, as you call him, died." Alanna's jaw was fixed, rigid. "We tried to have a child, but I don't know whether it was even possible."

"Fae do breed. I've seen your wee ones." Even crueller than the adults, unfortunately.

"My lover was human."

Surprise stilled Niall's hands. "A human man? Let me guess. A slave?" He couldn't keep the disgust out of his voice.

"He had been captured, yes." She met his look defiantly. "But not by me."

"Oh, that makes it all right then. Whose slave was he? You're royal brother's?"

"Yes. It was a long time ago."

One of her brother's slaves, made into her lover. A typical story of Fae cruelty except for the grief in her eyes. He wasn't imagining that.

He bent over his task again. "How long ago?" he asked.

"One hundred years."

"And you loved this man? Or pretended to?"

Her silence was so flint-hard that Niall raised his head again. She was glaring at him. "Did you love your mate?" she asked in a sharp voice.

"I won't apologize for my question, love. You are the one coercing me into helping the bastard who stole my children. I'll answer yours – yes, I loved her more than my own life."

"My answer is the same."

She met his gaze without flinching. The pain in her dark eyes wasn't false and neither was the loneliness, and Alanna didn't look ashamed of either.

Niall went back to pounding. After a time he asked, "So what happened to this human male so worthy of the love of a Fae woman?"

"My brother killed him."

Niall stopped. "The very brother who sent you here? Why?"

"Because Dubhán dared to touch me."

"The man was your slave, love. He wouldn't have had a choice."

Alanna's face grew cold again. "You see everything through Shifter eyes. Dubhán was my brother's slave, so of course you believe I forced him to service me. I told you, I loved him. I freed him, I fled with him to the human world, and we became lovers. Until my brother found us."

"You sneaked out of the Faerie realms to become lover to a human?" Niall's astonishment and respect for her rose. "You are an amazing and brave lass."

"I was foolish as it turned out. I should have sent him off and not tried to stay with him. Kieran would have forgotten about one slave in time, but he never forgave me for letting a lesser being touch me."

"Which is why he sent you here to become hostage to a Shifter."

"I'm my brother's prisoner and in disgrace. I'm forced to do his bidding."

"Does he not fear that while you're in the human world you'll break away and flee him?"

Alanna shrugged. "I have nowhere to go, and, unlike Shifters, I cannot pass for a human. The spell that lets me resist iron will wear off." She shivered. "And it is so cold here."

Niall rose, fetched the woollen cloak he'd thrown aside when he'd started to work, and draped it over her shoulders. She looked up in surprise, jerking her hand away when his brushed hers.

He'd thought her overly slender when she first walked in, but now he saw that this was a trick of the loose-flowing garments. Her bosom was round and full, her waist nipped in above strong hips. Her face was delicate, a little too pointed for Niall's taste, but her dark eyes drew him in. Her braids outlined her pointed ears, but the ears didn't look as strange and unnatural close up. She was flesh, not cold marble, her skin flushing as she warmed from the fire and the cloak.

"You could pass for human," Niall said as he went back to the forge.

"Unlikely. Look at me."

"I just did." Niall took up the heated bar with his tongs and tapped the rapidly cooling metal. "If you wore your hair loose to hide your ears and dressed in human clothes instead of fancy frippery, no one would look twice." He considered as he flipped the bar. "No, they'd look twice, because you're a beautiful woman, but unless you shouted it, I don't believe they'd realize you were Fae. Most humans don't believe in the Fae any longer, anyway. They pretend to – they avoid the stone circles at night and put out milk to appease the sprites – but deep down, they believe only in hard work, exhaustion, and God, bless them."

"You care for them," Alanna said, sounding surprised. "But you're Shifter."

"If you lived in the human world before, you might have noticed that Shifters are not thick on the ground. We might be stronger and more cunning than humans, we might be able to change into ferocious beasts when we wish to, but we need humans to survive."

She regarded him in curiosity. "Do the humans in this village know you're Shifter?"

Niall shrugged. "They know I'm different, but as I said, they don't much believe in the *other* any more. But they know I'm a good smith and that the villages round about get left in peace now that I live here."

"You're good to them."

"It's survival, love. We each have what the other needs. 'Tis the only way Shifters are going to last."

"The Fae chose to retreat." Alanna said it almost to herself, as though she didn't expect an answer. "We sought the mists of Faerie."

"Aye, that you did."

She fell silent, but Alanna was difficult to ignore as he continued work, and not just because of the distinct Fae smell, which didn't seem so terrible now. Perhaps he was growing used to it.

Niall sensed her presence like a bright light – her beauty, her sorrow, her courage in coming here when she knew she'd likely lose her life. Fae princes could be mean bastards, and the fact that she'd defied this Kieran with the human slave spoke much of her.

Once Niall had the metal thin enough, he heated it again, ready to shape it. As he set the blade on the anvil and took up his hammer, he felt her breath on his shoulder.

"Wait."

"Metal's hot, lass. It won't wait."

"I need to layer in some spells."

His eyes narrowed. "What is this sword for? For ceremony, I know, not fighting, but what sort of ceremony, exactly?"

"I'm not certain myself. Exactly."

Niall's grip tightened on his hammer. "Don't lie to me, lass. If you're putting in the spells, you know what they do."

"I cannot tell you. Please, if you know, then your sons will die."

"I think they'll die anyway, and I think you know that too. Tell me this much – is the sword meant to hurt Shifters?"

Alanna said nothing, but the look in her eyes spoke volumes. He read guilt there, anguish, grief, anger.

Niall shoved the bar from the anvil with a clatter. He sat down on the floor, his hammer falling to his side. "You're asking me to save my sons by forging a weapon against Shifters? What kind of monster are you?"

Alanna sank to her knees beside him, her silks whispering across his skin. "Niall of Baile Ícín, I ask you to please trust me. Make the sword. All will be well."

Niall growled. "Your bastard brother will slaughter my boys the minute he gets this piece of metal in his hands. He knows I'll kill you in retaliation, and then he'll kill me, and laugh about it. That is how things will play out."

Alanna shook her head, her braids touching his bare shoulders. "Not if you trust me. I cannot tell you everything, but you must make the sword the way I have instructed." She put her hand on his shoulder – Fae, who didn't like to touch. "Please, Niall."

"And why should I trust you? Because you once bedded a human? Should I believe you have compassion for the whole world then?"

"Because of a vow I once made. I will never let your children come to harm. I promise."

Fae had a way of enchanting, of charming. Niall knew that, had experienced it first-hand. But Alanna's pleading look was different somehow from the Fae who'd once spelled Shifters to be slaves to them. Fae charmed by being too brightly beautiful, too desirable, stirring a person into a frenzy before they knew what happened. Alanna didn't make Niall feel frenzied or dazzled. He was angry and sick, tired and sad.

When Shifters lost loved ones, they retreated from the rest of the pride or pack to be alone with their grief. A survival instinct, he supposed, because in that gut-ripping sorrow, they had no desire to fight or hunt or even eat. A Shifter might weaken the pack by refusing to fight, and so the he took himself away until the worst passed. Or he died.

Alanna's hand on Niall's shoulder was cool, cutting through his instinct to seek solace. Her fingers were soothing to his roasting skin, and her fragrance no longer seemed cloying, but fresh like mint.

"Please," she said again.

Niall got to his feet and pulled her up with him. "You ask much of me, lass."

"I know."

Alanna's eyes weren't black, as he'd thought, but deep brown with black flecks, her wide pupils making them seem darker. Her hair was like fine threads of white gold, metal so delicate that the merest touch could break it.

Niall stepped away from her, fetched the half-formed blade, and thrust it back into the fire. "And you wager your life on me trusting you?"

"Yes," she said again. "Will you?"

Niall shrugged again, his insides knotting. "Looks as though I'll have to, doesn't it, lass?"

She gave him a smile of pure relief. "Thank you, Niall."

Niall turned back to work, wishing her damned smile didn't warm him so.

Four

Alanna let her hand hover over the red-hot blade Niall laid on the anvil, the metal's heat touching her skin. She murmured the spell, watching the curled Fae runes sear into the metal and disappear.

Niall did not trust her, and she couldn't force him to, but she was relieved he'd at least let her do the spells. Alanna couldn't ask more of him, not without fear that Kieran would discover what she was doing.

Niall beat the sword after the runes faded, as she instructed, then put it back into the fire. Again and again they repeated the pattern – Niall hammering the blade, Alanna chanting her spells.

They worked side by side, shoulders brushing, both sweating from the fire, both breathing hard from their exertion. Spell casting, especially casting spells as powerful and far-reaching as these, took stamina. Alanna soon set aside the cloak and pushed up her long sleeves.

The stench of sweating Shifter didn't seem as bad now. Niall had, well, an *honest* smell, one that came of hard work and caring. He protected the people of this village like he protected his children, a fact Alanna wouldn't tell Kieran. If her brother thought the villagers were important to Niall, Kieran would find some way to use that against him.

When Niall said the sword needed to rest, he shoved it into a barrel of ash, wiped the sweat from his face, and led her from the forge. The dirt track outside hugged the cliffs above the sea, Niall's shop being at the very end of the high street – if the muddy track between the houses could be termed a high street. The western ocean pounded away below them, the moon glowing on the black bulk of the nearby island.

At first Alanna worried that Niall had brought her to the cliffs for some nefarious purpose, but he simply stood looking out over the dark ocean, breathing in the bracing air.

"You know we'll never finish on time," he said. "Blades have to be heated and rested a number of times to make the metal strong, and then I have to grind the blade and make the hilt."

"You'll finish."

"You sound certain."

"The spells I'm using will temper the blade faster than your process by hand," she said. "When we go back, you'll be ready to grind it."

Niall's voice went low. "I'm not ready to go back yet."

He had to be freezing out here without a shirt, the icy wind from the sea whipping his short braid. His eyes were green even in the faint moonlight, hard green, not Shifter white-green.

Alanna didn't flinch when he cupped her neck with his big, rough hand. The touch of others had always sickened her, until she'd met Dubhán. She wondered what sort of strange Fae woman she was that she'd fallen in love with a human man and now didn't mind that a Shifter pulled her into his embrace.

Niall's face was lined with dirt and soot, but by now hers couldn't be much better. His hard body cut the wind, and she melded into his as he scooped her against him and kissed her.

His kiss was harder even than Dubhán's, firm mouth opening hers, his whiskers burning her lips. He tasted raw, of this wild land of Eire, of a bite of ale and of himself.

Niall eased back, and Alanna shivered, not willing to let go his warmth. The wind cut right through her, but she scarcely noticed it.

"This might be our last night, you and I," he said.

"Yes."

Niall kissed her lips, her cheeks, her neck. "You agree that it's our last night? Or are you saying you'll share my bed as I suddenly wish you to?"

"Both."

He cupped her face in his hands. "Be certain, Alanna."

"I am. Very certain."

He nodded once, his eyes darkening. He took her hand and led her behind the forge and into a neat cottage with a garden in front. She saw signs of his family – small boots, scattered tools, half-whittled pieces of wood, animals the boys had been carving when they'd been snatched by Kieran's men.

Niall avoided looking at the carvings as he led Alanna to the loft, where neat pallets had been made up for the night. Niall stripped without word, revealing a body of solid muscle, male beauty sculpted by nature and the ancient Fae. Shifters had been bred to be superior in strength, speed and stamina, and they'd also been made to be beautiful.

He put his hands on his hips, unashamed that his wanting was plain to see. "Are you not getting undressed? I might start to feel ridiculous like this."

Alanna untied the complicated tapes that held her gown to her body and let it fall in one piece. She liked the appreciative way Niall looked at her nakedness, instead of with the loathing or indifference she'd expected. His gaze lingered on her breasts, his eyes dark and soft.

Alanna went to him. He raked his hands through her braids and tilted her head back to kiss her deeply. His hardness pressed her belly. She'd always heard that Shifters were more endowed than humans or even Fae, and she decided that this rumour was true.

Niall's huge, work-worn hand cupped her breast, thumb brushing the tip. He kissed her neck, nipping her a little before he kissed her mouth again.

Alanna had loved Dubhán, and she always would. The fact that loving him had caused his death had haunted her for a century. But this Shifter would never go easily to her brother's men, would never give up without a fight. Niall could have killed her outright when she'd announced Kieran had kidnapped his cubs, but he was giving her the gift of his trust – well, perhaps not his full trust, but at least his hope.

Niall lifted her and set her gently on the pallet. He came down with her, stretching his warm body on top of hers.

"You're such a bit of a thing," he murmured. He closed his hand around her wrist. "See? So fragile."

"I'm stronger than you know."

"I know, lass. You have Fae strength, but I've never seen it packaged in such beauty."

Was he trying to melt her heart? The big, strong Shifter with loneliness and sorrow in his eyes? She suddenly wanted to hold him to her and heal all his hurts.

Niall had something else on his mind besides healing just now. He parted her thighs with a soothing hand and slid himself inside her.

Alanna's eyes widened as he filled her. What a wonder that a huge, barbaric beast of a Shifter could be so gentle.

He stayed gentle as he began the rhythm of lovemaking, his head bowed, his braid sliding across his shoulder. Alanna cupped his hips, urging him with hands and mouth not to be *too* careful with her. Niall groaned as he sped his thrusts, kissing her as she met him stroke for stroke.

Alanna's frenzy began a few seconds before his did. They peaked together, both crying out, both holding hard, kissing and panting, hot breaths tangling. They wound down together, Niall smoothing her hair with a tender hand.

"You see?" Alanna whispered. "I'm perfectly fine."

"That you are, love. And so am I. As you can feel inside of you."

"You mean I've not yet worn you down?"

Niall grinned and licked her upper lip. "Not by a long way, my love. Not by a long way."

He started again, this time more playfully. In spite of knowing that Niall was right, that this might be their only night together, and in spite of her worry about his sons and the choices she'd made before coming here, Alanna pulled him inside her and let herself drown in his loving.

Alanna awoke hours later to see Niall leaving the bed. She lay in the warm nest they'd made, enjoying the view of his buttocks as he bent over to fetch his tunic. Their gazes met when Niall straightened up to slide it on.

His eyes changed to the feral cat within him before returning to dark green. "You're such a beautiful lass." He leaned down to kiss her, his lips warm.

"Where are you going?"

"The sword won't get finished by itself, love. It's not going to be a very good weapon made so hasty."

"My spells will hold it together." The point was for Shifter craftsmanship and Fae magic to join. Alanna wasn't certain what Niall might make of that knowledge, so she kept silent.

Niall descended to the lower floor, and she heard him poke up a fire and clatter crockery. She pulled on her robes and followed him downstairs to find him setting out ale and bread and a hard chunk of cheese.

"I'll do that," she said as he started to slice the bread. "You go to the forge, and I'll bring the breakfast." Niall raised his brows, and she smiled. "I used to make Dubhán breakfast. He was surprised I could do it."

Niall shrugged, set down the knife, and kissed her cheek. She turned her head to meet his kiss with her lips, determined to enjoy this very brief time they had together. Her hand closed around the knife handle, and she gasped.

"Damn," she said. Alanna looked at her fingers, which were creased with light burns. "The spell is wearing off." She sucked on her fingertips.

Niall picked up the knife and quickly cut slices of bread and cheese. "What did you do when you lived in the human world before?"

She took her fingers out of her mouth. "Dubhán found copper and bronze knives for me."

"You need to go back to Faerie."

"When the sword is finished."

They assessed each other again, like enemies who'd learned to respect each other's skills. Niall brushed her hair back from her face and kissed her forehead.

"Eat your breakfast, love, and then we'll finish the sword. Whatever comes, we'll make the best damn sword that ever was."

Alanna didn't reach for the plate. "Let's finish now. I don't need sustenance the same way Shifters and humans do."

"Eat the damn food, woman. You're weak here, and with all this iron about, you'll just get weaker."

"Yes, dear." Alanna sat down, slanting him a demure glance. "Whatever you say, dear."

His eyes narrowed. "Your brother doesn't know what a feisty witch he's harbouring, does he?"

She sent him a grin. "'Tis best that way, do you not think?"

"Vixen." Niall leaned down and kissed her. "To think, when you walked into my forge, I thought you cold and brittle."

"You warmed me, Niall."

"Aye, I wrapped that cloak around you."

"That is not what I meant."

Niall gave her another seductive kiss. "I know."

He grabbed bread and cheese, took a gulp of ale, and banged out of the cottage, sending chill air sweeping through the room. Alanna shivered again, but without the loathing she'd had last night. It was cold in this human place called Baile Ícín, but with Niall to keep her warm, she thought she could weather it.

Five

Whatever else Alanna's magics did, they certainly sped up the forging process. Alanna chanted more spells, and Niall watched runes appear and disappear as he formed the tang, made the hilt, and ground the blade. Alanna closed her eyes for the last spell; sweat stood out on her brow as her musical voice pronounced the words.

The last set of runes faded to be replaced by fine lines that etched themselves all over the sword and hilt. Those lines didn't fade but joined in continuous, interlinked patterns, as though they bound the sword and hilt together.

Niall raised the blade, finding the balance perfect, the edge sharp. If he didn't know better, he'd swear he held a sword of the best, strongest Damascus steel. He made a few sweeps, amazed at what he'd wrought.

No, what *they'd* wrought.

"We make a good sword, you and me," he said. "Now, do you mind telling me what it's for?"

Alanna hugged her chest. "Ceremonial purposes. For my brother."

"Aye, and what kind of ceremonies will he be conducting?"

"I do not want to tell you that."

Niall brought the sword around until the tip was an inch from her throat. Alanna didn't flinch, didn't move, though he saw her draw a breath. "You had better tell me, love."

"If I do, you'll try to kill Kieran, and he'll destroy you. Probably very slowly so that you will beg for death. Please, do not make me watch that."

The anguish in her eyes was real, but Niall shook his head. "Sweeting, he will kill me anyway. I'd rather go out trying to take him with me."

"Niall." Alanna took one step closer, letting the tip of the sword nick her skin. A drop of Fae blood, so dark red it was almost black, welled up from the cut and trickled across her throat. Niall quickly withdrew the sword and wiped the blood away with his thumb.

"I pledged myself as hostage to you," Alanna said. "I made a promise that I would get your sons released. I will fulfil that promise. But to do it, I must again ask you to trust me. Let me take the sword to my brother, let me finish my part of the bargain. Your sons will come home to you today. *Please*."

"You're a daft woman, do you know that? You aren't planning to take this blade and stick it into your brother, are you? Tell me you're not going to try something so stupid."

Alanna shook her head. "It's tempting, but no. He would expect me to do something like that. I imagine his bowmen would shoot me dead the moment I raised the sword."

"Good." Niall set the weapon down and pulled her close. "I'll not have you throwing yourself away on vengeance. 'Tis not worth it."

"You were ready to kill me when I first came here."

"That was instinct. You're Fae, I'm Shifter."

"And now?"

Niall smoothed her hair, loving the satin feel of it. Even sleep-tousled and sooty, Alanna was beautiful. "Now I'm thinking you've made me feel something I've not felt in a very long time. Can a Shifter love a Fae?"

"I don't know. This Fae once loved a human. And she is falling in love with you."

He smiled and cupped her cheek. "So what do we do about it?"

"Let me finish my task. Then if I am still alive, I will return to you."

Niall saw it then, her certainty she wouldn't live through whatever her brother had in mind. She knew she might have to sacrifice her life to save his children.

Niall drew her close. He vowed to himself, then and there, to protect her. He'd make himself trust her, whatever she was planning, because Alanna knew how to get his cubs free and he didn't. But he wouldn't let her pay with her life. Niall would protect her like a Shifter would his mate – damn it, she *was* his mate now.

If they survived this, he'd seek another clan leader and beg him to complete the bond, under the sun and the moon, in the eyes of the Goddess. His own clan leader was long dead, which meant that Niall was, in fact, a clan leader – of the very small clan of himself and his sons, he thought with a grin. But he couldn't mate bond himself.

One thing at a time.

"I'm not letting you go, yet," Niall said softly. He kissed her lips. "Not quite yet."

Alanna pulled him into a deeper kiss. Niall took the sword with him as he led her to the cottage and made love to her again in the light of the rising sun.

When Niall awoke in the bed an hour later, Alanna was gone. Entirely gone – he didn't catch her scent in the cottage at all. Her silken robes were no longer hanging on the peg next to his crude tunic, and the sword he'd laid next to the bed had vanished.

Niall rose, naked, and shifted into his Fae-cat form.

Several thousand years before, the Fae had taken the best of every wildcat in existence and bred the Fae-cat, larger and stronger than any natural beast. Fae-cats had the strength of lions, the ferocity of tigers, the speed of cheetahs, the stealth of panthers. Niall bounded down from the loft and out into the dense fog that had rolled in from the sea.

Alanna wasn't in the forge. He picked up her scent on the path that led to the gently sloping mountain above the village, towards the circle of standing stones even the most sceptical of the villagers liked to avoid. Mists rolled between the stones when Niall reached them. The mists smelled all wrong; instead of salt and fish like the heavy fog over the village, these mists exuded an acrid smell overlaid with the sharp scent of mint.

An entrance to Faerie. Niall regarded it with foreboding before he realized that Alanna's scent was quickly fading. His sons were in there, and now Alanna. Without further thought, Niall leaped into the mists between two of the stones and heard something snick closed behind him.

Six

Alanna found her brother hunting, but this wasn't unusual. Kieran spent most of his time hunting, or rather, having his men chase animals towards him so that he could shoot them.

Kieran was every inch a Fae prince as he stood in the fog-soaked clearing wearing a white kid tunic, soft boots and fur-trimmed cloak, with his white-blond hair held back by a diamond diadem. Two men at arms flanked him: one carrying his bow, the other, his quiver of arrows.

As Alanna approached, Kieran took the bow and nocked an arrow, sighting into the woods opposite her. In a few seconds a wolf charged out of the fog, streaking for the heavy undergrowth on Alanna's side of the clearing. The wolf was larger than most, its blue-white eyes intelligent.

The wolf saw Alanna and veered at the last minute. Kieran's arrow, which had left the bow, bounced off a boulder where the wolf had been a second before.

Kieran shoved his bow back at his armsman and growled. "Damn you, Alanna. I've been tracking that wolf all night."

"Have you?" More likely his trackers had found the wolf for him. "That wasn't a natural wolf," she said. "It was a Fae-wolf. A Shifter."

"Bloody animal. Any Shifter in my realm is fair game."

That was true. Any Shifter who ventured here had to be crazy, which meant the Lupine had probably been captured or lured in somehow. She didn't know enough to tell whether it were male or female, and she wondered if Kieran had stolen *its* cubs too. She hoped it found its way back to the standing stones and out.

Kieran's hungry gaze went to the sword, the Lupine forgotten, and he snapped his fingers. Alanna walked to him, handing over the sword with a little curtsy.

"Lovely." Kieran hefted the blade, testing its balance. "This is perfect."

"What are you going to use it for?" Alanna asked him.

"Simple, dear sister. To defeat Shifters."

Niall had accused Alanna of knowing what Kieran's spells were for, and she did, but she didn't understand exactly what Kieran meant to do with them.

"Defeat them?" she asked. "It's not a good weapon for killing, the Shifter said. Not sturdy enough, even with the spells."

Kieran kept his gaze on the etched blade. "You know that I am named for our grandfather, who was killed by a horde of Lupine Shifters. Demons in animal skins. With this sword, I shall avenge him."

"How?" Alanna asked. "The Shifters who killed him died long ago. Shifters are short-lived, you know; they last only three or four centuries at most."

Kieran gave her a pitying look. "You are simplistic, my sister. I don't need to find the descendants, I have the Shifters themselves. I have their bones."

He waved his hand and mists lifted from the other side of the clearing. Low mounds, a dozen of them, lay side by side, overgrown with green.

Alanna's eyes widened. "Where are those?"

"My loyal men tracked down the graves of each of the Lupines who slaughtered our grandfather. I had their remains brought here and reburied. I've been collecting them for a long time."

"Why?"

"For this day." Kieran raised the sword again. "Did you not understand the spells I gave you? You are a fine mage, my dear, and the only one who wasn't afraid to go to the human world. Surely you will have worked it out."

Alanna nodded. "You wanted to make a soul-stealer."

"Ah, so you have not lost every bit of your intelligence after all. No, I cannot kill the Shifters who murdered our grandfather. But, if I capture their souls and make them do my bidding, they will be miserable for eternity."

Alanna studied the mounds, which looked vulnerable and sad. "But the Shifters have been dead so long. Their souls will be gone – won't they?"

"Not these Shifters. Our grandfather cursed them as he died."

"Cursed them?"

Kieran gave her a disparaging look. "You are ignorant, Alanna. He cursed their souls to cleave to their dead bones. No going to the happy Summerland to chase rabbits for these Shifters."

Alanna hid her revulsion. Even Fae had souls that dissolved when they reached the end of their long lives. The Fae then drifted, content, free of the constraints of the body, which also dissolved. To tie a soul to a cold, dark grave seemed to her the height of barbarity.

"Aren't they miserable already?"

"Perhaps, perhaps not. But if *I* have their souls, they will become aware of their suffering. I will make certain of it."

Alanna shrugged, pretending not to care. She had to make Kieran think she sided with him until the very last minute.

"Well, whatever you intend do with the dogs' souls, the sword maker kept his end of the bargain, to my surprise. I will take his sons back to the human world."

Kieran gave her another disgusted look. "I don't bargain with Shifters." He snapped his fingers. "You. Bring the Shifter's get."

Two attendants disappeared and returned holding the squirming Fae-cat cubs. The cubs were wrapped in nets, both attendants cursing as they dropped the bundles to the ground.

One of the attendants put his hands on his hips, panting. "They refuse to shift back to human form."

Alanna knelt next to the net-wrapped cubs, keeping herself out of reach of their flailing claws. "Your father sends his love," she whispered so the attendants wouldn't hear. "He says to tell you he's proud of you."

Both small cats eyed her in suspicion, but they quieted.

Kieran strode to them. "Let us test the blade on them, shall we?"

Alanna rose quickly. "You said it wasn't a killing blade."

"No, but it will likely do some damage; they are small, and I imagine their souls will be . . . cute."

Alanna tried to grab Kieran's arm, but before she could, a huge Fae-cat tore through the clearing and leaped at him.

Niall . . .

He'd followed her. Alanna watched in panic as the men-at-arms and attendants fought him off. Kieran would kill Niall for certain.

Niall fought hard, but there were ten Fae to one Shifter and, after a few minutes of struggle, Niall was overwhelmed. The men-at-arms bound him in another net, and Niall went insane, fighting and clawing the ropes, foam and blood flecking his mouth.

Kieran approached Niall, rage on his face. "I'll test the blade on its maker instead."

Alanna clenched her hands in fear, but Niall raged and fought so hard through the net that Kieran couldn't get near him. The men-at-arms advised their prince to abandon the attempt.

"Tell him to shift back," Kieran shouted at Alanna. "He shifts back or I kill his cubs."

"Why would he listen to me?" Alanna folded her arms. "I'm Fae. He was foul as foul can be the whole time. I hope you're happy. Shifters disgust me."

Niall roared, the sound filling the clearing. His children fought and yowled, encouraged by their father's wrath.

"Fine," Kieran said. "I'll shoot the bastard, instead. Good target practice."

Alanna touched his arm, trying to make her tone cool. "Why don't you show the Shifter smith what the sword was made for?"

Kieran stopped, then a feral smile creased his face. "Sister, you will make a fine Fae yet. Watch, Shifter. Let me show you how I can reach into the past and hurt your kind in the present."

The Prince walked to the closest mound, flicking back his cloak. He lifted the sword and drove it point down straight through the mound.

Light flashed up the length of the sword, and a shower of dirt shot from the grave. In the midst, a swirl of smoke changed into the misty shape of a Fae-wolf. Kieran laughed. He went to the next mound, and the next, releasing the essences of the Lupines, who floated insubstantially over the places where their bones had been buried.

Kieran flourished the sword, its silver blade flashing. "Behold the souls of those who slew my grandfather." He turned to them, and opened his arms. "You will surrender to me, and do what I bid. You will kill the Shifter Feline and his cubs."

The figures whirled around him. Alanna held her breath, fingers at her mouth. This was not what she'd expected to happen. She'd changed the spells so that the wolves would disperse, their souls free for all eternity, not bound. Instead they lingered, like wolves gathering around prey.

Prey . . .

"Kieran!" Alanna shouted. "Drop the sword. Run!"

Kieran ignored her. He swept the sword blade through the ghostlike creatures. "Obey, wraiths. Now you are mine."

The wolves circled him, their eyes glowing yellow through the mist. As one, they attacked. Kieran cried out as the pack swept down on him in wild glee, and then he began to scream.

Niall shifted to human form, watching in amazement as the insubstantial wolves ripped into Kieran. They were mist and smoke – they shouldn't be able to touch him – and yet the wolves rapidly tore the Prince apart. His pristine white cloak turned scarlet, and his men-at-arms and attendants fled.

The sword flew from Kieran's hand, as though it propelled itself, and landed at Niall's feet. Kieran screamed again. His bloody body turned in on itself and crumpled to dust.

The wolves padded in a circle around the Prince's remains, then they lifted their heads and howled. It was a faint whisper of a howl, eerie and hollow, but it held a note of triumph.

The wolves shifted into a dozen men with broad shoulders and flowing hair, with the light blue eyes common to Lupines. They gave Niall and Alanna a collective look of acknowledgment, shifted back into wolves, and vanished. Wisps of smoke spun high into the sky and faded away.

Alanna caught up the sword, sliced swiftly through the net binding Niall, and helped him out of it. She moved to cut the ropes binding Piers and Marcus. Both cubs shifted into boys, running to Niall and throwing their arms around him. Tears streamed down Niall's face as he knelt and gathered them in.

He looked over their heads at Alanna, who clenched the sword, her dark eyes wild. "Alanna, what happened? What did you do?"

Alanna was shaking, but she lifted her chin. "Kieran commanded me to make a soul-stealer, but I spelled the sword to be a soul *releaser*. Instead of binding the souls of those Shifters, driving it through their remains set them free." She drew a breath, looking white and sick. "That's all I meant to do. I did not realize the Shifters would decide to take their vengeance – I did not know they *could*."

As horrifying as Kieran's death had been Niall couldn't be unhappy that the cruel Fae who'd abducted his children and would have murdered them was gone. "If they hadn't, the Prince would have killed all of us."

"Me, certainly," Alanna said. "I hoped that while he attacked me, you and your cubs could get away."

Niall shot to his feet. "That was your excellent plan? For me to run away while you *died*? 'Tis not what Shifters do for mates, lass."

"It's done, Niall. You must leave now. If they find you here, they will hold you responsible. Kieran's cousin, his heir, had no love for him, but the Fae might demand he make an example of you."

"And what is to say they won't come after me into the human world?"

"Because most Fae had no love for Kieran, either." Alanna smiled. "I doubt any of them will be willing to risk entering the human world again to hunt down a Shifter to avenge his name."

"You cannot stay here, either, lass. They'll blame you too."

Alanna gave him a thoughtful look. "Perhaps, if you exchanged your steel knives for bronze ones, I could better serve you breakfast?"

Niall's heart thumped fast and hard. He reached for her, pulled her into the circle of his family. "Love, you saved my boys, and me. You will stay with me as long as you damn well please."

"Could you bring yourself to love a Fae?" she whispered.

"If that Fae was you, I think I could."

Alanna pulled away and held the sword out to him. "This belongs to you."

Niall closed his hand around the hilt. The sword felt right in his hand, as though he'd made it for himself to wield. "A soul-releaser?"

"I spelled it so that when a Shifter's soul is in peril of being bound to its body or to another's will, this sword will release it in peace. The Lupine souls that had been cursed to linger at their graves have at last gone to the Summerland."

Niall studied the lines that ran down the blade and the hilt. "Why did you do this? Why help Shifters? You're Fae."

"You speak in ignorance, Niall. Most of the Fae are noble people. Some like Kieran, or our grandfather, or the ones who made and enslaved the Shifters in the first place, were cruel – even we consider them cruel. Fae have long lives, and we now live remote from the human world, which makes us view things differently. Kieran's plan was that of a child pulling wings from a fly. I could not let him succeed."

The boys were looking at the sword too, with the bright gazes of lads fascinated by a pretty weapon. Niall saw long days ahead explaining to them why they couldn't touch it.

"Why didn't you tell me, lass?" he asked. "When we made the sword together, why didn't you tell me what you were doing?"

"Because when I walked into your forge, I knew you hated Fae. Why should you help me? You are Shifter. And to be honest, I simply didn't think you'd believe me."

"And you'd have been right, love. I wouldn't have." Niall's heart squeezed as he thought of the danger she'd walked into, taking the sword to the Fae realm and knowing her brother would discover what she'd done. "But you should have told me this morning what you intended."

"I *intended* to have your children back to you before you woke. I never thought you'd be daft enough to follow me to Faerie."

"Daft, am I?" Niall tilted her face to his. "I am, to love a Fae. Now let's be going, before your brother's keepers return for us."

They went, through the mists and the standing stones, back to the freezing wind from the wild sea, the light dancing on the waves and the green of the Great Isle across the strait. The wind tossed Alanna's hair, which streamed like gold.

They returned to the cottage, where Piers and Marcus ate ravenously and regaled them with their adventures with the enthusiasm of boys no longer afraid. Niall hung the sword point downwards on the wall, the blade gleaming softly.

"Keep it well," Alanna said from his kitchen table. "And wield it well."

"There are so many Shifters," Niall replied. "I can't be everywhere in the world waiting to see if a Shifter is in danger of losing his soul."

"Then you will make more. We will forge enough swords so that every Shifter clan will have one, and then your work will be done. You aren't the best Shifter sword maker alive for nothing."

"I'm so glad you believe in me, love."

Alanna rose from the table, stepped into his arms and kissed his lips. Piers and Marcus snickered.

"We'll do it together," Alanna said. "Every piece, every hammer stroke, we'll forge them together."

"Sounds like bliss, it does. Or a lot of bloody work."

"But worth it?"

"Aye, lass." Niall sank into her warmth, took her mouth in a long kiss, ignoring his sons' gleeful laughter. Laughter meant love, and he'd take it. "'Twill be well worth it."

Daughter of the Sea

Kathleen Givens

Western Shore, Ancient Ireland – 375 AD

When they were children, Muirin and Conlan, they played together, chasing through the forest, swimming in the crystal waters of the sea that formed the western edge of her father's lands, climbing over the rocks that jutted out into the water and protected the hidden beach beneath her home. They roamed the nearby hills, explored every cave, and climbed every tree. Together. And never tired of each other's company.

Her hair was dark. "Ebony" he called it. His was fair, the colour of oats at harvest time. "Golden," she said, letting the silken strands slide through her fingers. His eyes were green, the colour of the leaves of the sacred oak tree. Hers were the blue of the deep sea and as full of mystery. He was of the earth, she told him. She was of the water, he would say.

She was a princess, the beloved only daughter of the King of the western shore. He was the son of a woodcutter who served her father. As the years passed they became aware of the differences in their lives, but disregarded them.

When they were grown, they pledged their troth by moonlight. On a summer night, beneath the spreading limbs of the ancient oak tree that crowned the cliff above the sea, with only wild creatures as witness, they agreed to marry. And kissed, a deep, sweet kiss that held the promise of passion to come. Then again, and again, parting to look into each other's eyes and talk of the future. They swore to be together forever. And perhaps they would have been. Had her father not remarried.

The new Queen was much younger than her husband and wanted to change almost everything about his life. She changed his home, telling the King it was for the better when she removed everything that had ever belonged to Muirin's mother. She sent most of those who had faithfully served the King for decades away, some without the coin they had earned, and replaced them with her own people. She pushed him to negotiate for more lands with nearby kings, suggesting that he threaten war, which he had never waged. She sent him to talk to the High King, instructing him to demand more territory, more power. When he travelled, she turned her attention to his daughter.

Her stepmother was horrified when she learned of the freedom Muirin had been given. Even more horrified when she discovered Muirin's friendship with Conlan. "Daughter of the sea" her stepmother would call her derisively, for Muirin loved to spend her time near the water. As her stepmother exerted more and more influence over her life, Muirin sought refuge there more often.

She was no longer allowed to roam as she pleased. She could not leap atop her horse and ride headlong along the strand. She was to walk her horse sedately on the roads, riding palfrey instead of astride. She had always been a good student, read several languages, and wrote a fine hand, but now her schooling was increased, another language to learn, another passage to copy for the Queen.

Her hours were filled, but she did nothing with them. When her father travelled, Muirin was asked to attend her stepmother each day, to sit at the side of the room while the Queen spoke to the King's people, dispensing harsh rulings and unfair verdicts, telling the people that Muirin was in agreement with her decisions, and that there would be no recourse. Muirin would shake her head to let them know she did not agree at all, but she could not change the Queen's edicts.

Her only escape was in the early evening, when the Queen

would receive her friends and dismiss Muirin with a wave of her hand. Muirin would rush to the sea then, to sit and pray for her father's quick return.

Most evenings Conlan would find her there, perched on a rock high above the waves, her knees pulled up against her chest, her arms wrapped around her legs, staring over the water with a forlorn expression. He would tease her, make funny faces, or tell her absurd stories until he got her to smile again.

Until one day.

That evening, when he saw her wiping away the tears on her cheeks, he watched her for a moment, his heart full of love for her, and sorrow for her sorrow. He knew what she would tell him. He'd heard it in the village. Her father was not visiting the High King. He was searching for a husband for Muirin.

It was Muirin's stepmother who was behind it, of course. Few doubted that it was the older woman's jealously that had prompted the suggestion, for Muirin had blossomed into a rare beauty. The King had left some time ago without revealing his purpose, off to visit all the other kingdoms in the west of Ireland. He would travel from Donegal to Dingle, from Sligo to Kinsale, searching for a man who would be the perfect match for his daughter.

Her husband must be tall, Conlan had heard. And strong. A warrior, a hero the likes of which no one had seen since the days of Cuchulainn. And handsome – a man who would give Muirin daughters as beautiful as she. He must come from a royal family, and have great wealth, for the King wanted his daughter to be protected and have the finest of things.

Conlan feared he would lose Muirin to another, and his heart was sore. He was not a prince. He had no riches to share. He thought of all he might do to win her, the things he might say to convince her father to let them marry as they had planned. He could not change his heritage, could not change his father from a woodcutter to a king, but Conlan was already tall. And strong. And a fine warrior, for had he not defeated every challenger at the King's last gathering? He could work hard to acquire coin. He was most willing to do so every day of his life if it meant that Muirin would share those years with him.

She turned to see him then, holding out her arms, and he ran to pull her into his embrace.

"Oh, Conlan!" she cried. "They mean to tear us apart!"

"I know, I know," he said, wrapping his arms tighter around her. "I could not bear to see you with another. I would rather lie under the ground than lose you."

"Do not say such a thing!" she said, looking up into his eyes. "Never say such a thing, my love. I could not bear it if anything happened to you. There is only one thing we can do."

"Anything, Muirin! I will do anything you ask."

"Marry me. This night. Here, under the very oak where we pledged our troth. Then make love to me, again and again. If I am already wed, I cannot marry another."

He smoothed back the hair from her face. "I am not a prince. I have no wealth, only my own hands to earn our way. I cannot give you what your father wants you to have."

"My father wants me to be happy, I know he does. It is only her doing that has him off looking for a husband for me. The man I want is here, before me. Please, Conlan! We are promised to each other. Do not tell me now that you regret that!"

"Never." He kissed her forehead. Then her cheek, then her mouth, showing her with his kisses how full of love for her his heart was.

She pulled back from him with a brilliant smile. "Then go now, love. Meet me this night, when the moon will be full. And we will become one."

"And face the future together."

She nodded, her face radiant. "And face the future together."

They parted then, throwing looks at each other over their shoulders as they walked away, he to his father's small whitewashed cottage, she to her father's shining castle on the hill.

She told only one person: her nurse. Who told only one

person: the cook. Who told only one person: the groom. Who told the Queen.

The hours until moonrise passed slowly for Muirin, but pass they did. She attended her stepmother at the evening meal, careful not to say anything that would arouse the older woman's suspicions. When, soon after the meal, Muirin claimed to be weary and said she would find her bed, her stepmother gave her a smile and wished her a good night. Muirin hid her surprise at her stepmother's warm tone and willingness to let her go, but was pleased to make her escape so easily.

She was at the door when her stepmother called to her. "Your father has written to me," she said. "He has met with the King of the north, who has agreed to marry you to his only son. The contract is being signed as we speak."

Muirin nodded, hiding her horror at this news, but ever more determined to wed Conlan that very night. She brushed her hair until it shone, then bundled its length into a fine net caught at the nape of her neck. She had chosen her clothing carefully, a gown of sea blue silk, a froth of white lace, like the crest of a wave. She wore the golden necklace her mother had given her, a dolphin hanging from the golden links. She took one last look at herself in her mirror, pinched her cheeks to make them rosy, then threw her finest mantle – a cape made of swan feathers – over her shoulders, and hurried from her room.

She left the castle easily, finding the postern gate left open and no guard there to question her. She reached the cliff above the sea just as the moon was reaching its zenith. Conlan was already there under the mighty oak, his tall form in shadow.

He was not alone. The Queen stood nearby, draped in a long dark cloak, her face pale. In her hand was a switch, which she tapped against her leg as Muirin slowed her steps, then joined them.

"Muirin," her stepmother said, her voice smooth and emotionless, "what mean you by stealing from the castle in the dark of the night?"

"It is not dark, madam. The moon has lit my way."

"Have you come to swim?"

"No, madam. I have come but to enjoy the moonlight on the sea."

"Liar! You have come to steal away with the woodcutter's son!"

"No, madam, we do not plan to leave!"

"You would stay here then, with him? Your father is even now finding you a husband, you ungrateful girl!"

"I want no husband but Conlan."

"You mean to defy me? You?" She raised her switch as though to strike Muirin.

"No!" Conlan shouted, rushing forwards from the dark, his arm outstretched.

Before he could reach her, the stepmother whirled to face him. "You would strike me, son of the earth?"

"Do not harm her!" he roared.

"She must be punished!"

"You will not harm her!" Conlan raised his arm.

"Then let it be you who suffers." Muirin's stepmother raised the switch and pointed it at him, her voice rising into the air. "I call upon thee, forces of darkness, to give me strength. Strike him down, he who would harm your priestess, he who would defy me!"

There was a strike of lightning from a sky that had been clear a moment before, a great swirl of wind that brought the sudden smell of sulphur.

"Strike him down, oh forces of darkness!" the stepmother called again, raising her arms high, her cloak spreading behind her like wings. "Make him pay for daring to defy me! Root him to the ground!"

Lightning split the sky again, and a roar of wind blew leaves and branches and dirt into the air. Muirin put her hands over her eyes. There was a clap of thunder so loud that it deafened her. And then silence.

She looked up, but saw only darkness. The moonlight was gone, the sky a black dome above her. Nothing seemed to move, nothing to even breathe. And then, dimly, the sound of the sea came to her, a soft murmur.

"Conlan?" she whispered, reaching for him.

Her hands found only air and she stepped forwards in the dark, then again, reaching for him. "Conlan?" Again there was only silence, and she grew fearful. "Are you hurt? Conlan, speak to me!"

Her hands found the trunk of the giant oak, and she stretched her arms around its width, laying her head on its bark.

"Conlan?" There was only silence.

Muirin spent the remainder of the night under the tree, waking at dawn, surprised that she had slept at all. Night was receding and while the light was still dim, it was enough for her to see that it was not the ancient oak under which she had slept, but a much younger tree, a slender oak tree with leaves the colour of Conlan's eyes. And there, a handful of paces away, the ancient oak.

She stared at both trees. Two. For all the years of her life, there had only been one tree here on this cliff. She jumped to her feet, staring at the two trees.

"Muirin." The voice was soft, feminine.

Muirin whirled around to find the owner of the voice. The cliff was empty but for her and the two trees. Far below her, in the cobalt water of the western sea, three dolphins swam in spirals, and above her, perched in the highest branches of the ancient oak, three ravens watched.

"No," said the voice. "It is not they who speak to you, child."

"Who are you?" Muirin asked in a small voice.

"I am here, child, in the wind, in the air. You cannot see me, but I am with you."

"Mother?"

There was the sound of soft laughter. "No, although I knew her as well. A fine woman who did not deserve to die so young. Nor did you deserve to lose her, or your father to fall under the spell of the enchantress you call your stepmother."

Muirin turned to look all around her. "It is true. But I cannot see you."

"Do you wish to?"

"Oh, yes, please!"

More soft laughter followed, then a small glowing ball appeared in the air before Muirin, slowly enlarging until it was the size of a dainty person. Within the glow was the most beautiful woman Muirin had ever seen. Her hair was golden, her skin soft and supple, her gown of gossamer. She smiled, her eyes lighting with humour. "Is this better, child?"

Muirin stared in awe at the lovely woman. "You are one of the fair folk, come from the Otherworld!"

The creature smiled again. "It is true. I am of the *aes sídhe*, come from Tír na nóg."

"I have nothing to offer you!"

"I have not come to ask for an offering, Muirin, but to aid you in your plight. We are the People of Peace, and this night your stepmother has disrupted our peace. It is she who has done this, who has cast a spell over Conlan and transformed him. She has rooted him in the ground."

Muirin whirled to look at the slender oak tree. "It is true, then? I had hoped it was but a terrible dream."

"It is true. Conlan is no more."

Muirin clasped her hand over her mouth with a moan, then threw her arms around the tree. "Conlan! Oh my love! I should never have defied her! Conlan!" She whirled back to the woman of the fair folk. "Is it forever? Can it be undone?"

"There is one way by which he can be returned to human form, Muirin. But it is very dangerous."

"I don't care about danger! I will do anything that would bring Conlan back to me!"

"It will require great courage, child."

"I will find courage enough to do whatever is required."

"And great physical strength."

"I will find the strength I need!"

"And you must outwit a terrible foe."

"I will find a way to do that! Please tell me what I must do!"

"You must go to the land of the merrow and the mermen. To Tir fo Thoinn, the Land Beneath the Waves."

Muirin thought of all she had heard of the Land Beneath the Waves, the home of the beautiful merrows – the mermaids who sometimes took human form and lived among men. And of the mermen, said to be hideously ugly creatures covered with scales, having the features of pigs and long, pointed teeth.

"The merrow are sometimes hostile, Muirin. You could be in danger."

"How can I go there? How will I breathe?"

The woman looked up at the ravens. "They will aid you."

"What must I do there?" Muirin asked.

"In the Land Beneath the Waves there are mermen who hold the souls of drowned sailors in cages, called soul cages. You must free three of them."

Muirin nodded. "I will do it. Anything to free Conlan from the enchantment."

"There is more you must do."

"Please tell me!"

"In the Land Beneath the Waves there is a castle in which a lovely princess lives. An enchantment has removed all colour from her life, and only a clever human can restore it."

"I will do it! But how?"

"You will have to discover that."

"I will! Anything to free Conlan."

"There is still more, Muirin."

Muirin began to grow afraid. "Tell me, please."

"There is an ogre who has terrorized three merrow sisters. You must kill him."

"But how?"

"You will have to discover that. Are you willing?"

Muirin swallowed, but nodded. "Anything to save the man I love."

"If you are successful, you will return home to find Conlan restored, your stepmother banished beneath the waves and your father freed from her spell."

"Yes! But how . . .?" Muirin clasped her hands before her as the *sídhe*'s glow began to fade. "Oh, do not leave me yet! I don't know enough! Where should I go?"

The woman, already transparent, looked down at the dolphins again. She continued to fade. "The dolphins will aid you. Safe journey, child. Courage!"

And then Muirin was alone again. She stared around her, seeing the lonely cliff, empty but for her and the two oak trees. She looked at the slender oak and lifted her chin.

"I will free you, Conlan!" she cried.

For a long moment, Muirin could not move. She stood where she was, her hands clasped before her, looking out over the sea. She was afraid. Then she walked to the slender oak and threw her arms around its trunk.

"I cannot live without you, my love. I will not live without you." She placed her lips against its bark. "Conlan, if I do not return, I will find you in the afterlife. I will always love you. Always. Stay strong, my love."

And then she left, walking slowly down the path that led from the cliff to the sea. In the water below her, the three dolphins still swam in spirals. She looked up at a harsh cry above her, to see the three ravens spinning overhead. They swooped past her, circling something at the far end of the beach. One lifted it, and with the others flanking it, flew towards her as she reached the shingle, then lay it before her on the rocks.

It was a small red cap made of feathers. A *cohuleen druith*, she realized, recognizing it as the magical cap that enabled the merrows to swim through the ocean. Muirin had heard that if a mermaid lost this cap, she also lost her ability to return beneath the waves. Muirin looked around her now, half-expecting to see the merrow here, but there was no beautiful woman walking on the beach.

"I will but borrow this," she said aloud, in case the merrow might be able to hear her. "I will return it to you, I swear it. Or die in the trying."

She shivered at the echo of her own words, but lifted the red cap and examined it. It weighed almost nothing, was craftily constructed of fine red feathers and what looked like silver thread. She turned it in her hands, looking out to sea.

Could she do it? Plunge into the waves and trust this delicate garment cap to keep her alive? Conlan, she thought, and put the cap on her head. The ravens circled her, their cries sounding like encouragement now. She smiled then walked towards the water.

But there she hesitated, looking at the waves crashing on the beach. How many times had she swum through these crystal waters with Conlan, laughing at the waves as they broke over her? She had no choice. If she did not go, Conlan would never return to her, and how could she live without him? If she perished in the trying, at least she could die without shame.

Daughter of the sea, her stepmother had called her. She was about to be just that, a daughter of Lir, the king of the ocean. She stepped forward, watching the water lick at her shoes. Another step and her skirts were wet. Another and she was in to her waist.

She plunged into the froth when the wave came, expecting to be tumbled, then come out the other side and gasp for air. Instead, she sank under the surface, no longer feeling the damp, her body strangely lightweight. She opened her eyes, expecting them to sting from the salt water, but instead she could see clearly the three dolphins that now swam before her, their heads bobbing at her at though inviting her to join them.

She moved her arms and glided through the water with little effort, realizing that she could breathe as well here as on land. She almost laughed. It was real, the merrow magic was real! But hard on the heels of her amusement came a wave of fear. Somehow she had to find the Land Beneath the Waves, then learn how to do the tasks that would eventually save Conlan. She took a deep breath, and followed the dolphins.

She had no idea of how long she swam, or how far. There were times when she swam alone, others when the dolphins would offer her a fin to hold, and glide her through the water at a speed she could never have matched on her own. Times when she could see the sunlight on the surface, others when all around her was darkness.

Creatures passed her and the dolphins: small fish that darted out of the way; large fish, with fins that looked like sails, that paused to watch them go by; sharks that circled as if wondering if she could be snatched away from her guides; whales that filled the water with their strange songs.

And then Muirin could see it, the Land Beneath the Waves, stretching far into the distance, a walled kingdom of spires and towers, large structures covered with oyster shells. An entire city, with streets and bridges plainly visible. And full of merrows and mermen.

As they neared the undersea kingdom, her fear returned. How would she be able to gain entrance through those enormous gates? And once in, what would she do? How would she know where to find the soul cages, the princess whose castle was without colour, or the three mermaids terrified by an ogre?

How foolish she had been to think for a moment that she could do this! She was trembling by the time they reached the massive gates, sure she would be discovered as an imposter. But she need not have worried, for the gates opened of their own accord, and she and the dolphins glided through with none to stop them.

They paused in a large square surrounded by tall buildings, unnoticed by the beautiful mermaids who swam by. Muirin watched as the gates closed silently behind her, then turned back to discover that two of the dolphins had disappeared. The third seemed to be waiting for her. She pulled her feather cape close, gathered her courage, and followed it.

The dolphin led her across the square and into a wide street lined with what appeared to be shops and houses, and filled with every sort of transport: sea horses pulling magnificent coaches; mighty water horses, which would have terrified her at home; sea serpents pulling huge barges on which mermaids lay, reclining on fanciful couches, combing their long tresses with combs made of seashells.

Muirin was so fascinated by all she saw that she soon lost track of their path, and hardly noticed when they turned into a narrower street, then a still narrower lane. And stopped before a door made of seaweed. The dolphin rapped on the door with its nose, and glided back, leaving Muirin to face the repulsive creature that opened the door.

She drew back in horror from the pig-faced merman. He did not have skin, but was covered in scales. He looked her up and down, then smiled, revealing long pointed teeth.

"Daughter of Lir," he said in a pleasant tone, opening the door wide. "Welcome. I have been expecting you!"

She stepped inside his home, not knowing what she would encounter. The room was large, furnished as one might expect a human home would be. But there, in the corner, stacked high, were a dozen wicker cages like those used for catching lobsters. Most were empty, but four were not. An octopus stared at her mournfully from a cage in the centre row, and above it, in the top three cages, well above her reach, tiny shimmering male faces looked down at her. *The soul cages.*

She had heard the tales of mermen who caused storms, then captured the souls of the drowned sailors, but had considered them too fanciful to be real. But here they were, imprisoned souls, and she must somehow discover how to free them.

"Well," the merman said, offering her a driftwood bench to sit upon while he leaned against the hearth. "How was your journey, daughter of Lir? Not too arduous, I'm hoping?"

She shook her head cautiously. "Not at all," she answered, looking at him out of the side of her eyes. He truly was the ugliest creature she'd ever seen.

"Good, good," he said, offering her a shell full of brandy. "For your troubles in bringing it to me."

She took the shell and sipped at the brandy, trying to think of what she had that he might desire. She could not part with the red cap, for she had promised to return it to the merrow who had left it on the strand. With what else, then, could she bargain?

She had the golden necklace with the dolphin pendant that her mother had given her all those years ago, but one look at his neck let her know it would never fit him. Perhaps he would like to give it to one of the mermaids? She had her clothing, the net around her hair, but what would her want with those? And her cape, made of the finest swan feathers.

That was it! *Daughter of Lir*, he had called her. Lir, the king of the sea. Whose children had been turned into swans by their jealous stepmother.

She slid the cape off her shoulders and casually laid it beside her on the driftwood bench. He watched her movements with a smile. Would he eat her? she wondered. Those long teeth were terrifying. How strange that the female of the species was so lovely and the male so hideous. Small wonder, then, that mermaids sought human mates.

He bent to slide a hand with webbed fingers across the feathers. "As soft as I have heard! Is it true, then, that the cape will allow me to walk as a man in your world?"

"I cannot tell you," she said, keeping her words truthful.

He gave her a merry smile. "Ah, a bargainer, are you? Very well then, how many do you think this is worth?"

"All of them," she said, hoping that he spoke of the imprisoned souls.

"What, all three? Never!"

"And the octopus as well," she said quietly, as a sudden thought occurred to her.

"Why? It is only a play toy for me," he said sullenly. "I like to watch it change colour."

"And the octopus as well," she said again.

He gave a *harrumph*. They were silent then, sipping their brandy. Muirin checked the distance to the door. She would trade her cape for the souls, but not her life. Still, was this not the very reason she'd come, to do these tasks and free Conlan?

"Two?" he asked, leaning to stroke the feathers again.

She shook her head and moved as though she were about to stand.

"It's all three you're wanting, then, is it?" he asked, his tone resigned.

She nodded slowly. "And the octopus."

He stared into the distance. They did not speak. The only sound was the music that floated in from the lane, a mournful tune that threatened to make her mood sink. His gaze shifted to the cape of swan feathers.

He nodded to himself as though he'd come to a decision, then turned those small eyes upon her. "Very well," he said, crossing the room to the cages. "All three it is. And the octopus as well. I can get another in a moment. You drive a hard bargain, daughter of Lir."

She stood, leaving the cape on the bench, and moved towards the door. He held the cages out to her. She took them, surprised to find that they were quite heavy.

"Careful not to free the souls before you reach the surface, or they'll sink back to the bottom and I'll capture them again," he said, his tone merry once more. He threw the cape a glance. "I shall try it at once!"

"I should like to be home before you do," she said.

He nodded as he threw the door open wide. "Then I will wait a day, shall I? Your day, not ours, for ours are quite different."

She nodded and passed through the doorway. "Thank you," she said.

"No, thank you, daughter of Lir. This is a day I will long remember."

"I should think it will be," she said, stepping into the lane.

"Regards to your father," he called as he shut the door.

Muirin had hoped that the dolphin would still be there, but the lane was very empty.

"One task accomplished," she said.

She blew her breath out in a long sigh, hefted the cages, and hurried back towards the wide street. She had no idea where she should go next and she stood at the side of the street as she decided what to do, watching the colourful travellers pass before her, each more astonishing than the last.

Except for one. The Princess, pale and with colourless hair, dressed in a misty gown, rode in an grey open coach pulled by sea horses so pale that Muirin could almost see through them.

And there, on the other side of the street, two dolphins swam forwards to follow the coach. They nodded to her and made room between them for her and the cages.

Muirin smiled. This then was the Princess the woman of the fair folk had told her of, the one to whose life she must restore colour. She bent low over the cage that held the octopus, keeping her voice very low.

"I would like to free you, Sir octopus, but I have a favour to ask in return."

"Ask away," the octopus growled. "I am going nowhere but where you take me."

"That will no longer be the case if you grant me my favour."

"Tell me what it is and I will determine if it is possible."

He listened silently while Muirin told him what she needed. At the end of her explanation, he nodded. "A simple matter, daughter of man. I make my own colour."

"But can you share it?" she asked.

"Why else have I so many arms? Take me there."

And so Muirin and the dolphins, and the octopus, and the souls in the soul cages, all followed the Princess back to her castle, which seemed to be made of glass, for it had no colour at all. Nor did anything within the castle. The plantings in the garden were not green. The apples on the trees were not red, nor the roses on their bushes. The birds in the trees were neither blue nor brown. The coal in her fire was transparent.

"You see my dreadful state," the Princess said, wringing her hands. "I would so love to live in a colourful world again, but only a human can break my enchantment. Can you help me, daughter of man?"

"I will try," Muirin said, "with the help of my brother octopus."

The Princess looked at the octopus and frowned. "Your brother?"

"All creatures are brothers and sisters in this world, Princess. No, he is not human, but he will produce the colour and I will apply it, and together we will endeavour to break the enchantment placed on you and your home."

The Princess nodded, watching at first with a sceptical expression, which changed to joy as Muirin and the octopus coated everything with the colour it required. Coal was returned to black, the roses to red and the trees to a fine green that made Muirin sigh with longing for her Conlan.

The Princess' thanks were effusive, and she offered many gifts to Muirin to show her gratitude. Muirin would take nothing until the Princess held out a magic sword.

"It will only harm evil creatures," she told Muirin. "Never one with a good heart."

Muirin took the sword and let the now three dolphins lead her back to the large square, the Princess' praises still ringing in her ears.

At the side of the square, Muirin opened the cage door wide and told the octopus he was free to go. The octopus, with that strange sidewards motion he used, slithered from the cage. He paused for a moment to thank her, then changed colour and blended in with the building behind him so well that after a moment Muirin could not tell where the octopus left off and the building began.

"Two tasks accomplished," she said.

Muirin blew her breath out in a long sigh, hefted the three remaining cages, and hurried away. She had no idea where she should go next, but she had an idea where she might be needed.

She slowed her pace as she neared the lane where the merman lived, careful to look around her in case he had not waited to try the cape of swan feathers, for she was quite sure the only thing it would do would be to keep him warm.

She hurried past his lane, following the sound of the mournful music she had heard at his house. The music grew louder with every step she took, and it was not difficult to discover the house from which it came.

It was the saddest music she had ever heard, played on more than one instrument, the notes floating with sorrow then plunging to the depths of despair, taking her mood with it. How anyone could play such sadness and still live was beyond her.

She soon found out, for the door was flung wide and in the lovely room revealed were three beautiful merrows, the mermaid sisters of whom the sidhe had told her. There was no sign of the ogre. But, Muirin realized, he must have opened the door, might even now be hiding behind it, waiting for her to enter, for the three merrows were chained to the wall and to their instruments – a lute, a lyre and a trilling whistle. One of the mermaids nodded her head at the door and Muirin knew she had guessed correctly.

She threw a glance over her shoulder to see the three dolphins waiting far down the street, and the three souls in their soul cages watching her with mournful expressions. She put her foot on the threshold, scuffing it as though she had entered, then watched as the ogre leaped out.

He grabbed at the air, his visage so horrible that she stepped back in fright at first, then lifted the magical sword the Princess had given her and, with one mighty blow, severed his head from his body. A fish swam from his body and into his head. She stared at it in surprise, then with horror as the ogre calmly picked up his head, reattached it to his body and glared at her.

"You must capture his soul, then destroy it," one of the merrows said.

"How am I to do that?" Muirin asked, raising her sword to strike him again.

"It will take the form of a fish," the second merrow told her.

"You must catch it and release it in the air, before he will be truly dead," the third merrow said.

The ogre rushed at her and, with another mighty swing, Muirin again severed his head from his body. This time, when the fish swam from his body, she whipped the net that held her hair from her head and tossed it over the fish.

At once the music stopped, then turned lively. The room was suddenly full of merrows and merman – ugly as they were, they were still less ugly than the ogre – who quickly removed the chains from the merrows and set them free. Muirin stepped back from their thanks and out into the street once more.

"Three tasks accomplished," she said. "Almost."

She looked at the fish still writhing in her net, blew her breath out in a long sigh, hefted the cages, and hurried back towards the large square.

"We are going home," she told the souls. "When I reach the surface, I will set you free so you may join your bodies. Your imprisonment will seem but a dream."

But how was she to get there? The dolphins were nowhere in sight and she had no idea of how to reach Ireland from this distant land. She thought of Conlan, of all she had accomplished. To now find herself at a loss was too much to bear, and she wept bitter tears for several moments.

Feeling quite bereft, she grasped the necklace her mother had given her. At once the three dolphins appeared before her.

"You had only to beckon us," one told her.

"We will take you home now," a second said.

Still carrying the cages and the net holding the fish, she followed the third dolphin to the massive gates of the Land Beneath the Waves, which, as they had done before, opened of their own accord. She swam through, turning to watch the gates close silently behind her.

It was a simple matter then.

She had no idea of how long she swam, or how far. There were times when she swam alone, others when the dolphins would offer her a fin to hold, and glide her through the water at a speed she could never have matched on her own. Times when she could see the sunlight on the surface, others when all around her was darkness.

Creatures passed her and the dolphins: small fish that darted out of the way; large fish, with fins that looked like sails, that paused to watch them go by; sharks that circled as if wondering if she could be snatched away from her guides; whales that filled the water with their strange songs. But this time she was not afraid. This time all she could think of was her Conlan and whether she had done all she must to free him from the spell.

And then Muirin could see it, the shore of her own beloved Ireland, her own beach. She thanked the dolphins profusely, but they waved her thanks aside with a whip of a flipper, and disappeared back into the depths. She held the net with the fish high in the air above her head. The fish gasped, gulped, then crumbled into nothing. The net, empty now, sagged against her arm.

She struggled out of the water, her skirts sodden and heavy, and finally heaved herself and the three soul cages on to the sand, opening the cage doors with a sigh.

"You are free to go," Muirin told the souls.

Instead of disappearing as she thought they might, they hovered in the air for a moment, their tiny faces wreathed with smiles.

"Your stepmother is no more," they told her. "The enchantment she placed on your beloved died with her." And then they were gone.

Overhead three ravens circled. Muirin jumped to her feet, tore the red cap from her head and placed it on the rocks before her. One raven lifted it and, with the others on either side, flew away from her, then lay the cap reverently at the far end of the beach.

"I thank you," she called, in case the capless merrow was nearby, then hurried up the hill.

There, standing next to the ancient oak tree under which they had pledged themselves, was Conlan, whole, and looking so handsome that she stopped where she was, taking in the very sight of such a fine man.

"Conlan!" she cried.

"At last!" He leaped across the space between them and gathered her into his arms. "You are my very own Muirin, my daughter of the sea," he cried. "The most magnificent woman who has ever lived, more beautiful than any other woman above or below the waves. Say you will be mine for all time."

"Yes," she said. "Yes and yes and yes."

"Then I will tell you my news. When I was an oak tree, my father, the woodcutter, came to visit me. He told me the secret he has kept hidden all these many years. He was not my father. Instead, I was his foster-son. My father is a king in the north, the very king who agreed to marry his only son to your father's only daughter. It was meant to be, this between us. You need not have faced all that you faced to be mine, my dearest love."

"Ah, but I did, Conlan, for by facing all that I faced, I learned much about myself, and that I would risk anything to be with you. It was meant to be, this between us, my dearest love."

Muirin raised her mouth to be claimed by his.

They were married that very evening, by moonlight, under the spreading limbs of the ancient oak tree. Her father beamed at her when she took her vows, and told her later, with a wide smile, that her stepmother had disappeared at the very moment that Muirin had released the souls.

Muirin and Conlan danced until dawn, and every year, on the anniversary of the day they were wed, they came to the ancient oak and danced under its limbs, remembering the days of their youth and all that had happened.

The Warrior

Jenna Maclaine

One

Castle Tara
Connemara, Ireland – 1260

They had come to kill him. At his invitation they had come, hundreds of them, across seas and continents, until they filled the courtyard of his great castle. They had come to vanquish the arrogant bastard who dared to claim sovereignty over the vampire nation. His summons had appealed to their pride, their vanity, their curiosity: an open challenge that whoever could defeat him in single combat would unite the world's vampires under the authority of one High King.

The warrior braced his hands on the cold grey stone of the parapet wall and listened with satisfaction to the murmuring voices below. When they had embarked on this journey they had been certain that the challenger would be easily dispatched, but now that confidence was beginning to waver, for Castle Tara was unlike anything they had seen before. It was a palace straight out of Faerie, built for beauty and not defence. There was nothing like it this side of the Veil. Indeed, the whole structure often slipped in and out of Faerie in order to keep itself hidden from human eyes.

The vampires below truly had no understanding of what they were walking into. One complained bitterly of the cramped quarters that surely awaited them, for no castle could comfortably house this many people. The warrior smiled. Even now the stewards were showing his guests to their chambers and he had no doubt that they would all find their quarters more than satisfactory. The castle was almost a living thing, expanding and contracting, changing as *she* saw fit. He watched the vampires below gaze covetously at what was his, each of them imagining what it would be like to live in such a place, each of them imagining they would be the one to defeat him. It was truly a pity they would all go home disappointed.

The warrior tensed at the sound of wings beating against the cool night air. A moment later a black raven swooped down, landing on the wall to his right. And a moment after that the bird seamlessly transformed itself into a beautiful young woman. He nearly growled in frustration at the sight of her . . . and at the reaction his body always had to her presence. How he wished he could look at her and feel nothing, but after a millennium he'd finally given up on that ever happening. For some reason she stirred his blood as no woman ever had, or ever would.

She smiled seductively and lounged on her precarious perch, propped up on one elbow with her long, lean body stretched out before him. Her hair looked as black as sin under the night sky but he knew that by candlelight it shone with the subtle, iridescent purple and green of a raven's wing. Her face was angular and strong, her lips full and sensual. Even though he tried not to, he couldn't help imagining those lips doing things to his body, wicked things that he didn't even have a name for. Her gown (if you could call such a thing a gown) clung to her curves like shadows, the black fabric so sheer that he could see her white skin beneath it. She wore the damned thing just because she knew it drove him mad.

"I told you they would come," she said smugly, nodding to the throng below. "And you said they would not."

He snorted derisively. "I have no doubt that a goddess' whispered commands in their ears as they slept had something to do with it."

"I can be very persuasive," she purred.

He scowled at her smiling face. "I know that all too well," he said harshly. "You were quite convincing when you struck the deal that damned me for eternity. Tell me, Morrígan, did you feel the slightest bit of guilt when you had me killed?"

Two

She swiftly sat up from her reclining position, her black eyes boring into him with an intensity that made him take a step back. "Do not pretend that I was some she-wolf taking down an innocent lamb, Cullen. I gave you everything you asked of me and before this week is out I will make you a king!"

"And I will keep my end of the bargain," he assured her. "I will lead your vampires, Morrígan. But I will never forgive you."

"I do not require your forgiveness, nor do I seek it." She slid off the parapet wall and stalked towards him. "By the gods, for such a big, strong man you certainly have become adept at whining like a wee girl." Trailing her long, glossy black fingernails across the rise of his chest, she looked into his dark eyes. "One would think that 1,000 years would have cooled your temper, Cullen."

He grasped her wrist and pulled her hand from his body. "Then one would be mistaken, for I will always hate you, Morrígan."

The words stung, and she looked away. At least they were the truth. She would rather have that than the pretty lies he'd told her when he was human. He had turned the head of a goddess with his beautiful body and his honeyed words. He had made her love him and she would never forgive herself for that weakness. Well, she certainly wouldn't allow him see that weakness now.

She let all emotion drain from her face before she once again raised her eyes to his. Even her skin seemed to pale further, until she was every inch the cold, heartless goddess of legend.

And he flinched. A look something akin to guilt crossed his face before he pulled his gaze from hers.

Satisfied, she took a step away from him. "I believe I will retire to my chambers," she informed him coldly.

He released her wrist and gave her a low, mocking bow. "It is your castle," he conceded.

Morrígan arched one black brow at him. "Yes, it is."

Three

From her window in the north tower Morrígan watched Cullen pace. She imagined she could hear him cursing her name. Turning away, she walked to her bed, the bed she and Cullen had lain in countless times over the centuries. She ran her fingers across the lush fur blankets and the sheets made of Faerie silk. Perhaps he would come to her tonight, despite his anger. Whatever his feelings might be, Morrígan knew he craved her body and her blood. And she had long ago convinced herself that that was enough.

By Danu, she thought, how did something that had started out so well go so horribly wrong?

Morrígan knew that most of the blame rested on her. She was wilful and arrogant and jealous – aye, all that and more. But she was also able to see the past in a way he could not. A thousand years was a trifling thing to her, but Cullen was young yet. The years passed more slowly for him. He had had centuries to proudly recall his accomplishments and forget his failures, to dwell on his virtues and bury his faults. She could hardly blame him for that – it was what humans did – but she remembered his mortal life very clearly, as if it had happened a month ago instead of a millennium. Perhaps she *had* tricked him but, truthfully, all she had done was set the bait. Cullen had sprung the trap himself.

But she did not expect him to remember it that way, for was it not easier to cast her as the villain than to be forced to admit to himself that greed and pride had been the downfall of the great Cúchulainn?

Four

The castle of King Conchobar of Ulster
In the twilight of the Old Religion

It was dark and the castle was quiet, or at least as quiet as castles ever were. Morrígan strode through the halls of Conchobar's stronghold with little regard to stealth. She was the Great Phantom Queen, the shadows themselves bent to her will, and she would not be seen by human eyes unless she wished it so.

When she found his door, she paused. He was the key to all her future plans and she must get this right. She had been waiting so long for him. Smoothing the crimson fabric of her cloak, she scoffed at her nerves. Anxiety was such a human emotion. If she couldn't accomplish this simple task then she deserved to be devoured by the Demon Horde. Human males were so malleable, after all. One could lead them anywhere by their phallus or their sword arm. And Morrígan intended to use whatever means necessary to get what she wanted. Silently, she pushed open the door and slipped inside.

He was sitting with his back to her, waist deep in a hip bath in front of the fire. That surprised her, for humans (and men in particular) seemed to have little concern for cleanliness. She had not made a sound, but he sensed her. In one fluid movement he grabbed the sword from the table next to him and stood, spinning around to face her. The look of surprise on his face almost matched her own.

By the Goddess, he was lovely. He was young, no longer a boy but barely a man. The muscles of his body were lean and firm. She preferred a heavier build on a man, but that would come with age. Already his face was perfection – cheekbones that could rival her own; a strong, square jaw; and lips that any woman would long to kiss. His hair, which fell just past his shoulders, fascinated her. Black at the roots, it then changed to brown and again to a coppery blond. It was his eyes that held her though. They were the dark green of a Faerie forest with flecks of golden sunlight. The emotions behind them ranged from shock to suspicion as they frankly assessed her.

"Lay down your sword, Cullen. I mean you no harm."

His body relaxed (well, parts of it anyway) and he lowered the blade. "You have the wrong room, my lady. There is no one here by that name."

She smiled and strolled further into his chamber, taking note of the sparse furnishings – a bed, a table and chair, and little else. She would have thought King Conchobar's nephew would have more lavish quarters.

"I have not mistaken my destination," she replied. "Your parents call you Sétanta. The people call you Cúchulainn. May I not have my own name for you?"

For a moment he was drawn in by her sweet smile, then his eyes narrowed. "Who are you?" he demanded. "You are not from Ulster."

"Are you so certain?" she asked, cocking her head to one side.

"I think I would remember crossing paths with the most beautiful woman I've ever seen. You aren't one of Conchobar's subjects."

"No, I am not," Morrígan agreed, pleased with his compliment.

"Are you one of Queen Medb's spies, then?"

"I am not your enemy," she assured him. "In fact, I have every reason to believe that you and I will become firm allies."

Impatiently he stepped from the tub and raised his sword. "That is not an answer. I ask you again, lady. Who are you?"

"I am Morrígan, goddess of war. I hear your prayers before every battle, Cullen, and tonight I am here to answer them."

He stared at her for a moment and then threw back his head and laughed. Irritated, Morrígan raised her arm and Cullen's sword was ripped from his grasp, flying through the air and into her outstretched hand.

"Any sorceress could do that," Cullen scoffed.

Morrígan arched one black brow at him. "Perhaps," she conceded. "But could anyone other than a goddess do this?"

She moved, faster than his eyes could track her, and before he could react her body was pressed against his. Her hands were suddenly on either side of his face and Cullen grasped her hips to steady them both. She looked into his eyes.

"Hold on," she said, a moment before the room went black and the floor disappeared from under his feet.

The sensation that followed was not a pleasant one. It felt as though his body was being turned inside out and Cullen gritted his teeth at the pain. Blessedly, it only lasted a moment and then his feet were on solid ground again. Morrígan released him and he fell to his knees, unable to get his bearings and stay upright.

"What did you do?" he gasped.

"I have brought you across the Veil," she said proudly. "Welcome to Faerie, Cullen."

Five

When he opened his eyes Cullen found himself in a world he did not recognize. He knelt before Morrígan in the centre of a small meadow surrounded by lush, green trees. A full moon rode high in the sky, gilding everything with its silver light. Nearby, a doe and her fawn, startled by the intrusion, rushed for the protective cover of the tree line. But none of this convinced him that he truly was in Faerie. What *did* was the fact that everything, from the stars in the sky to the grass under his feet, *sparkled*. He had never seen anything like it and he knew he never would again.

"Goddess," he whispered reverently, bowing his head in supplication, "I beg your forgiveness."

Morrígan placed her hand under his chin and tipped his face up so that she could look into those beautiful green eyes.

"Cullen, we cannot dally here. Time moves differently in Faerie so we must seal our bargain quickly."

"Bargain?" he asked, confused.

Morrígan cocked her head to one side. "Tell me, what is the one thing that you want most in the world? If you could shape your future any way it pleased you, what would you wish for?"

Cullen was silent for a moment, but it was not indecision that made him pause, it was the fear of actually putting into words what his heart most longed for. Finally, he said, "I would be the greatest warrior Eire has ever seen."

Morrígan knelt in front of him, cupping his face in her hands. "Men will fear you, women will want you, and no army will be able to stand against you," she promised fiercely. "In 1,000, nay, 2,000 years bards will still tell tales of the epic battles of the great Cúchulainn. I can give you all that and more, and I require only one thing in return."

His eyes lit up at the prospect of attaining such glory. "Anything," he whispered.

"When your mortal life has ended and I come to claim you in death, instead of going to the Summerlands you must pledge your afterlife to my service. In return for that you will be young and strong forever, Cullen. And I will make you the king of an army the likes of which no man has ever led. Will you strike this bargain with me?"

"I will gladly, my goddess," he answered earnestly.

Morrígan ran her fingers down the sides of his neck, over his shoulders, and across the firm muscles of his chest. She looked up into his eyes and smiled seductively as she slid the cloak from her body, the red cloth pooling like blood on the grass. He stared down at the pale perfection of her naked body.

"Then let us seal this covenant, my young warrior. By flesh and blood I will bind us," she said, her lips a mere breath away from his. "Come, Cullen. Let me give you everything you have ever desired."

He pulled her against him, claiming her mouth in a scorching kiss that would change them both, irrevocably and eternally.

Six

Morrígan laid her head on Cullen's chest, surprisingly sated. She rarely took a human to her bed; she found them generally uninspiring, but Cullen was different. What he lacked in experience, he certainly made up for in enthusiasm. Morrígan smiled, thinking of all the wondrous things she would teach him in the coming years.

"Why me?" he asked softly, pulling her mind back from its wicked imaginings.

"I have seen you fight," she replied. "There is no grace in your skill nor beauty in your movements. You simply overpower your opponents – hard and rough and dirty."

Cullen stiffened, believing her comment to be a criticism. "What need have I of grace when I have victory?" he asked arrogantly.

Morrígan laughed and propped her chin on his chest, looking up at him with a smile. "That is exactly why I chose you, Cullen. You intrigue me. Besides," she said as she raked her fingernails back and forth across his skin, "I like it hard and rough and dirty."

In one swift movement he rolled her over, pinning her to the ground beneath him. The look on his face held none of the virtues she had just mentioned though. The expression in his eyes was so tender that she swallowed the naughty comment she was about to make and waited for him to speak.

"You are so beautiful it almost hurts to look at you," he said, running his fingers through her raven hair. "I never want to stop touching you. Will we have this . . . forever, Morrígan?"

A surge of panic went through her at his question. She was not the sort of woman to put any man and the word "forever" together in the same sentence. The closest thing she had to "forever" was her annual mating with Dagda, which ended the winter season and brought spring to her people. And if she had a choice, which she didn't, she wouldn't even have that relationship. She did her duty though, always, and she rarely had a choice in any of it. But now, with this man, she did. She had chosen him and suddenly, surprisingly, the thought of forever did not tie her stomach up in knots. Her mind wasn't racing to find a reason to rebuff his offer. Instead it was racing in an entirely different direction – imagining hours, days, centuries, spent in his arms and his company.

"Yes," she replied. "We will have this forever."

Seven

How Morrígan wished those words had been true. They did have several wonderful years together, happy and carefree years, before the taint of anger and betrayal touched them.

Before each battle Morrígan would come to him. They would spend hours making love, Cullen eager to learn everything she could teach him. Afterwards, while he slept, Morrígan would drag one sharp, black fingernail across her wrist and spill a few drops of her precious blood into his mouth. Her blood made him strong and she made him fearless. He went into each battle, accepted each challenge, with the knowledge that he could not be killed. Because she would not allow it.

Morrígan fulfilled her end of their bargain with enthusiasm. The name of Cúchulainn became feared and revered throughout the Celtic world. He was a walking legend. He was everything she had promised, and more.

As for herself, Morrígan found the time she spent with him to be the most pleasurable moments of her entire existence. With him she was not a goddess of war, she was not a harbinger of death, she was simply the woman he loved. And love her he did, with wild abandon. When he slid the clothes from her body, all her cares, all her worries, went with them and for those brief hours time stood still.

But it wasn't only their physical relationship that she enjoyed. Often she would take him into Faerie for an hour or two and they would spar in the meadow, the great warrior against the goddess of war. Sometimes she would even let him win. And after they laid down their swords they talked of the great battles of the past, battles that she had seen and that he was eager to learn from. It was his companionship that Morrígan valued above all else. Friends were not a luxury one often found in the pantheon.

It was perfect, perhaps too perfect to last. Every war has a turning point and Morrígan clearly remembered theirs – that one moment when you realize that nothing will ever be the same again.

Cullen had just returned from the festival of Imbolc when Morrígan came to him unexpectedly. There was no impending battle, no pressing reason that he needed the strength her blood provided. She simply wanted to see him, wanted to erase from her mind the memory of Dagda's hands on her as they performed the ritual that would usher in the spring. Unfortunately, she could not as easily erase the evidence of the event from her body.

Cullen was trailing kisses up the inside of her thigh when he noticed the bruises. He paused and then slowly sat up, reaching one hand out to tentatively touch her skin. He laid his palm on her thigh, his fingertips covering each of the five purple marks.

"Who has touched you?" he whispered harshly.

She sat up, noticing for the first time the bruises Dagda's hands had made upon her thighs. Morrígan was immortal but Dagda was a king among the gods. She could not immediately heal the damage he inflicted, as she could any other wound.

"Dagda is a beast," she said, her disgust evident in her voice. "Let's not think of him, my love. In fact, I was rather hoping you would help me forget."

Morrígan reached for him but Cullen pulled away, staring at her in horror. She would remember the expression on his face for all eternity. It was the moment when everything changed.

"You let him make love to you?" he asked incredulously.

"Well, I would hardly call it making love," she replied. "And it isn't as though I had any say in the matter. It is my duty and it must be done. Surely you know that, Cullen."

He shook his head. "I just thought of it as a legend, a story like so many others. I never thought . . ." His words grew softer but his eyes grew harder as he regarded her. "I never thought that you would betray our love."

Morrígan leaped from the bed. "I have done nothing of the sort!" she snapped, her temper rising. "I am a goddess, Cullen, and you cannot hold me to the same morals as your simpering human women. The rituals must be performed. Would you rather I hadn't done it? Would you rather live in eternal winter until every man, woman and child in Eire dies of starvation because the crops cannot grow? That is the price of my fidelity, Cullen. Would you pay it to serve nothing more than your vanity?"

He looked away, having no answer to such a question.

"I thought not," she said coldly. "I do what I must, Cullen. It does not touch what you and I have. If you throw away what we have because you cannot accept that, then you are a fool."

She waited for him to say something, anything, but he did not. Feeling as though he had driven the Sword of Nuada through her heart, she vanished in a blinding flash of light.

Eight

After that Cullen began taking human lovers. Morrígan told herself that was how it should be. After all, she would have him for eternity. It would be selfish of her to deny him the experience of a human life and all that it entailed. But no matter how she rationalized it, it still hurt. She still went to him; she had to. He needed her blood to fulfil their bargain and she would not allow all her plans to be ruined because she had been foolish enough to lose her heart to a human.

Sometimes she came to him at night while he slept, giving him her blood without ever waking him. And sometimes she came to him as she had before, simply because she missed the feel of his hands on her skin. He never again mentioned Dagda and she steadfastly refused to acknowledge the presence of any other woman in his life. They would make love and then spend hours afterwards, talking and laughing. In time it was almost as it had been before. Almost.

Things had changed between them and Morrígan could not pretend otherwise. It was as though all that resentment and doubt was a black cloud hovering just outside, pushing at the door, looking for any crack it could use to seep back in. And then one night Cullen opened the door and the black cloud rushed in, engulfing them both.

She was lying in his arms, content and happy, when he suddenly announced, "I'm getting married, Morrígan."

She went very still, a coldness washing over her. "Is this your idea of vengeance?" she asked calmly.

"Of course not," he replied, genuinely shocked. "Why would you say such a thing?"

Morrígan sat up and looked down at him. "What else am I to think, Cullen?"

"That I want children," he said. "Legitimate children to bear my name. The men I lead, every day I watch them teach their sons to shoot a bow or wield a sword. I want to hold a child of mine in my arms, Morrígan. Emer can give me that. She's a good woman."

"Then I wish you the best," Morrígan said harshly and pushed away from him.

Cullen grabbed her wrist. "She's a good woman, but she isn't you. No one will ever replace you in my heart, Morrígan. This doesn't touch what we have, were those not your words?"

"That was different," she snapped, jerking her hand from his grasp.

"How is this any different than you lying with Dagda?" he demanded. "It is a means to an end, is it not?"

"The difference is that I do not willingly choose to be with him. You have a choice." She laughed harshly as she slid her cloak on. "Think what you like of me, Cullen, but you, with your wife and your string of harlots, have betrayed me far worse than I ever did you." She turned and looked down at him with cold disdain. "Goodbye, Cullen, you will not see me again until it is time for you to fulfil your end of our bargain."

Before he could reply Morrígan was back in Faerie, as far away from him as she could get. And even there she could hear him calling her name. Furious, she stomped through her castle, breaking anything that had the misfortune of being near to hand. When the novelty of that wore off she became tempted to cross the Veil again. A good war would be a perfect outlet for her anger. Queen Medb of Connacht was always good for a slaughter or two.

Morrígan sighed and sank down at the foot of the grand staircase. It was her own fault for believing in him. Was anything he'd ever said to her true? Or was it simply a means to an end, as he'd put it? Keep the goddess happy and she'll give you anything you want.

Morrígan put her head in her hands. Getting involved with a human had been a grave mistake. It wasn't jealousy she felt for his future bride, or for any of the women he'd lain with. She was a goddess and no mortal female would ever threaten her vanity. No, what she felt was a deep sense of resentment that, by the very fact that they walked with him in the human world, they would always have a piece of him that she could not touch. That was the price the gods paid for dallying with mortals.

But he would not be mortal forever. He would still be with her when these humans were nothing more than dust and bone. She should swallow her pride and forgive him. She could afford to be magnanimous.

Morrígan, however, was a war goddess and a generous nature had never been one of her virtues.

Nine

Over the following years Morrígan became quite adept at avoiding Cullen. He still called to her on occasion but she resolutely ignored his summons. When he had need of her blood she would enter the castle disguised as a servant and slip it into his goblet, leaving quickly before she succumbed to the urge to eviscerate Emer on sight. Indeed, Morrígan had not set eyes on Cullen in years, not until the night she discovered that Queen Medb had convinced the sons of Calatin – dark mages the lot of them – to forge a mystical spear capable of killing Cúchulainn. He could not ride against Medb's army, for Morrígan wasn't certain she had the power to save him from such a weapon.

She found him alone in the stables, preparing his chariot for the coming battle. The sight of him made her steps falter and her heart race. His body, once lean and rangy, had filled out into a solidly muscled frame her fingers itched to touch. The boyish beauty of his face now held a rugged masculinity that was breathtaking to behold. If she could have created the perfect man, she could not have done better than the one standing before her.

Walk away, her conscience told her. *Find another warrior, for this one will only bring you pain.*

She could release him from their bargain. She could choose another to lead her army, someone for whom she had no tender feelings. She could do things differently the next time. She could . . . not. He was hers and she would never let him go.

"Cullen," she said softly.

He was crouched down, one hand braced on the wheel of his chariot, inspecting the axle. She saw his body stiffen and his knuckles turn white. Slowly he stood and, almost reluctantly, he turned his gaze to her. She walked forwards, watching him watch her. She could see the desire in his eyes and for a moment she could not remember what could have been important enough to drive them apart.

He had a bit of straw in his hair and she reached up to pull it free. Before she could touch him, his hand clamped around her wrist and his expression grew cold and hard. She sighed. *That* she remembered all too well.

"Why are you here, Morrígan?" he demanded.

"It is time," she replied simply.

"Time for what?"

"For you to fulfil your end of our bargain."

He stared at her blankly for a moment, not comprehending her words. And then a look of understanding crossed his face, followed closely by fear and anger.

"How dare you?" he railed. "How dared you abandon me and then come here and tell me this? You promised—"

"I promised to make you into the greatest warrior not only of *your* time but of *any* time. And in return you promised yourself to me at the end of your life. You never asked when the end would come, Cullen."

"That is unfair, Morrígan," he accused. "How could I have expected it would be when I was merely thirty-five?"

She looked closely at him. "Thirty-five? Truly? You look so much younger."

It must be the immortal blood in his veins, she thought. Interesting.

"What has that to do with anything?" he snapped, dragging her thoughts back to the issue at hand.

"It has everything to do with everything," Morrígan replied. "I need a warrior in his prime, Cullen. If you were to live to be a wizened old man, you would be of no use to me. I do not have the power to turn back time."

"I would be young again when I enter the Summerlands," he pointed out.

"Yes, but once you are there I can never bring you back to the human world. I must take you quickly between your death and the afterlife, Cullen. I must turn you into something dead but living, something more than human but not yet a god, something that will confuse the magic that pulls a soul into the Summerlands. It is the only way for you to remain here."

He scowled at her. "You would make me a monster."

"No, Cullen. I will make you into something glorious," Morrígan said vehemently. "I will give you a portion of my godhood, a small bit of my power. I will make you young and strong and beautiful forever, just as I promised. But it must happen soon. I did not mean to spring this on you so suddenly, Cullen. When I saw you . . . well, the years sometimes pass more quickly than I expect them to. I will give you time to say your goodbyes and get your affairs in order, but you must fulfil your promise by Samhain."

He looked at her and Morrígan could hardly bear the resentment shining in his eyes. This was not how she had imagined it all those years ago. She had been so certain that, when the time came, he would love her enough to come with her willingly.

"You said you did not come here to take me. Then why are you here?" he asked.

"I came to warn you not to ride out against Medb's army tomorrow. The sons of Calatin, whom you slayed, have finally sought their vengeance. They have used the darkest of magics to forge an enchanted spear. If you are pierced by it, it will kill you, Cullen. I will gladly grant you more time, but I cannot save you if you go into battle tomorrow."

He threw back his head and laughed. "I am Cúchulainn. I do not need a woman to save me."

Morrígan narrowed her eyes. "You arrogant bastard. You are only alive because I wish it! If it weren't for me you would be nothing more than a common soldier. I made you everything you are and I can take it away just as easily."

"Then do your worst, Morrígan," he said fiercely, "for I will not run from this battle or any other."

Morrígan sighed. She had set out to create a great warrior and she had succeeded. Unfortunately, he also had the ego of one. Well, on the morrow he would learn not to believe all the stories the bards told of him. He was not immortal. Yet.

Ten

The following morning, Emer – and indeed every man, woman, and child Cullen encountered on his way from his chamber to the stables – begged him not to ride against Queen Medb's army. Obviously Morrígan had been whispering portents of doom in their ears as they slept. His irritation turned to fury when his horse, his faithful Liath who had pulled his chariot in countless battles, would not allow Cullen to harness him.

"Damn her," Cullen cursed. "Is not even a man's horse sacred?"

He was in a fine rage by the time he finally got Liath harnessed and drove out to join Conchobar's army. That is, until he reached the river. What he saw there tempered his anger with fear. It was a sight every warrior dreaded – the Washer at the Ford. The old woman was said to appear to soldiers who were meant to die in battle. The doomed would see her washing their armour in the river . . . and today she was washing his.

"I know I told you to do your worst, Morrígan," Cullen called out. "But this is simply petty. It's worse than causing Emer to be barren."

The crone transformed herself into the beautiful goddess he knew. "I did nothing of the sort," she assured him. "Not that I couldn't, but I didn't. And I am not being petty. I am the Washer at the Ford. This is my duty as a death deity."

Cullen snorted in disbelief and drove his chariot through the shallow water to the opposite shore, never looking back.

Morrígan had to admit to herself that she *was* being a little petty. Perhaps she had gone too far, but the man needed a lesson in humility before she made him immortal. But she didn't realize it would be so hard for her to watch. Taking the form of a raven Morrígan circled the battlefield, flying high over Medb and Conchobar's armies. She was a war goddess and normally she enjoyed watching two worthy hosts clash on the field of honour. This once, though, she took no joy in it, for today she would have to see Cullen die.

She spied him, driving his chariot deep into the heart of Medb's army. The first spear flew through the air and its aim was true; it would strike him. Before she realized what she was doing, Morrígan reacted on instinct, using her power to shift the trajectory of the spear away from Cullen. Instead of hitting him, it pierced Liath's chest, causing the big horse to stumble and fall.

"Oh damn," Morrígan cursed, "Cullen loved that beast."

Above the din of the battle she could hear Cullen's roar of outrage. It was followed swiftly by a cry of pain as the second spear pierced his side. Morrígan had been a death deity through time immemorial but letting that spear hit its mark was the hardest thing she had ever done. She watched helplessly as Cullen drew the weapon from his body and fell from the chariot.

An eerie silence descended over the battlefield as both armies watched the great warrior struggle to his feet. With one hand over his wound Cullen stumbled forwards, cutting one of the reins from the harness of his dying horse. The soldiers watched as he slowly and painfully made his way to the edge of the field. Once there he fell against a standing stone, blood pouring from his side to pool at his feet. With single-minded determination he took the rein and lashed himself to the stone.

"I am Cúchulainn," he shouted, "and I will not die on the ground. I will take my last breath standing, as a warrior should."

A cheer of pride went up from Conchobar's men but they could not reach Cullen, trapped as they were on the other side of Medb's army. Morrígan flew down, landing lightly on his shoulder. She rested her raven's head on his cheek to let him know she was there.

"I'm an arrogant ass," he whispered, the pain now slurring his words. "But I am now yours, if you'll still have me."

Cullen fell unconscious and Morrígan watched as the warrior Lugaid and his men approached. Lugaid had been the one to throw the spears that mortally wounded Cullen and his horse. Morrígan assumed that the gathering crowd of soldiers meant to pay tribute to the defeat of a worthy adversary, but instead Lugaid raised his sword.

"The head of Cúchulainn is mine!" he announced.

As his blade swung towards her lover's neck, Morrígan revealed her true form. Her mighty sword took Lugaid's hand off at the wrist before he could complete his gruesome task. Amid his screams of pain Morrígan smiled, taking grim pleasure in her vengeance.

"Cúchulainn is mine," she hissed to the cowards. "You are not worthy of him."

Then the goddess wrapped one arm around her warrior and they both disappeared.

Eleven

Morrígan brought Cullen across the Veil to her great castle of Tara. Gently, she removed his clothes and armour and laid him on her bed. He had lost so much blood that his heart was barely beating. It was time. Quickly she raked one fingernail across her wrist, slicing deeply.

"Cullen, listen to me," she said. "You must drink."

He opened his mouth and Morrígan's blood spilled across his lips. Before he could turn away in disgust she forced her wrist between his lips.

"You must take my blood into your body, Cullen," she repeated urgently. "It is the only way you can live. Please, stay with me."

He drank and, when he could hold no more, he slept. For three days he lay cold and pale as a corpse in her bed. Morrígan had never attempted such a transformation before and she stayed by his side, hoping that she would not lose him to the Summerlands forever. On the third night he took a gasping breath and sat up, blinking at her in surprise and confusion.

"Liath?" he asked groggily.

Morrígan threw back her head and laughed. Only a man would return from the dead and ask for his horse!

"Liath is here, in my stables," Morrígan informed him. "I had to beg a favour of my cousin Epona in order to save him. It is not a debt I look forward to repaying."

"Thank you," he said grimly.

Morrígan's heart fell. She had hoped that things would be different once he was at Tara with her. At the very least she hadn't expected him to behave like . . . well, like she had killed his favourite horse and allowed him to be slain, not by a stronger foe but by the deceitful use of sorcery. Morrígan rose from the bed and walked to the window. But that was exactly what she had done. She supposed his lack of enthusiasm for her company should not surprise her.

"My heart does not beat," he said.

"No," she replied absently. "It does not."

"You should have let me go to the Summerlands."

"Perhaps I should have," she agreed. "But I could not."

He was quiet for a moment and then he shook his head

and asked, "Why, Morrígan? You do not love me. If you did, you would have come to me when I called you, when I needed you, over the years. What purpose does all this serve?"

Morrígan turned. "You never asked me that, you know, when we first struck our bargain all those years ago."

Cullen snorted. "I was young. All I could think of was the glory to be found in battle . . . and you. But I am asking now."

Morrígan nodded. "Faerie is not the only world that exists beyond the mortal realm," she explained. "It is simply the one where the Veil is the thinnest. There are others, dark places filled with things far more terrifying than the gods or the sidhe. We call them the Demon Horde. Occasionally, the Horde attempts to break through the barrier between worlds. As of yet they cannot physically cross the Veil, but their evil can. The Horde has sent plague, famine, disasters of nature – all in an effort to weaken us. The pantheon believes that any death caused by their influence makes the Horde stronger, and that one day they will become powerful enough to cross the Veil. If they do, it will be the end of us all, Cullen. The inhabitants of Faerie are not strong enough to defeat them and the humans will be nothing more than lambs to the slaughter."

He looked at her dubiously. "I am good, Morrígan, but I am not that good. What is it you expect me to do?"

"You are now a creature unique in this world, Cullen. I expect you to make more like you. And they will make more and so on until I have an army of darkness at my disposal. Perhaps then we can defeat the Horde when they come."

Cullen nodded. "All right," he said gravely. "I will do it, not for you, but for all those innocents who will die if I don't."

Morrígan's gaze raked across his naked chest. She licked her lips, feeling a tiny thrill as he shifted his legs to hide his body's response to her.

"No," she agreed, "not for me. I have never been innocent."

Twelve

Castle Tara
Connemara, Ireland – 1260

Cullen leaned back against the wall and let out a ragged breath. Unable to stop himself, he glanced up at the north tower and watched as candlelight illuminated its windows. As surely as he knew the sun would rise in the morning, he knew that before this night had passed he would climb the stairs to her room. It was as inevitable as the tide.

Cullen was a liar and he knew it. But then again, so was she. He loved her and she loved him. It had always been and would always be. But too much distrust and betrayal had passed between them for either to ever utter those tender words again. And perhaps that was for the best. He was a soldier who had made a name for himself on the battlefields of Eire. She was a death deity, a goddess of war. What did such as they know of love?

In the years after his death he had firmly believed that he'd been no more than a means to an end for her – the perfect warrior to beget her legion of vampires, the perfect king to lead her dark army. But time has a way of breaking down even the thickest walls and time was something he'd had plenty of. Finally, he had seen the truth. It was in her eyes when she thought he wasn't watching her, in her touch when the passion of their lovemaking overcame her. *She had chosen him.* She was as old as time and yet she had bargained with a young man for his soul. She had sworn him to a covenant whose ramifications a beardless youth could not possibly have understood. He could not help but hate her for that. But on those rare occasions when he was brutally honest with himself, he had to admit that he could not help but love her for it as well. She had tricked him, coerced him, seduced him. Of all the men who had ever been, or would ever be, under her dominion, she had chosen *him.*

He closed his eyes, trying to drown out the sound of

hundreds of vampires tromping through his castle. This was not the afterlife he had imagined when he'd been human. It was not what the bards had promised every warrior would enjoy when his last battle was fought. Cullen opened his eyes and looked once again at the tower. No, Morrígan had cheated him of that. But then again, would he really have wanted an afterlife without her in it?

He smiled a wicked little smile and left the parapet, moving swiftly through the castle to the north tower. Climbing the stairs with determined strides, he didn't even bother to knock at her door. Morrígan was standing in front of the window, staring down at the spot he had recently vacated. At his entrance, she turned and he felt a twinge of guilt at the sadness in her eyes.

"If you've come here to fight with me you can turn around and walk right back out of that door," she snapped.

He closed the door and leaned against it, folding his arms across his chest. "But we are warriors, Morrígan. Fighting is what we do."

She rolled her eyes. "Don't you think you'll get enough of that in the days to come?" she asked.

Cullen shrugged. "There are a couple of them who might give me trouble," he replied as he pushed away from the door and crossed the room. "But I have never drunk from a human. The blood of the great goddess Morrígan runs undiluted in my veins. Not a one of them has a chance of defeating me. Now," he said, reaching out and wrapping one lock of her black hair around his finger, "about the fighting . . ."

"I don't feel like it tonight," she said petulantly.

"Really?" he murmured, sliding his other hand over her hip. "What do you feel like?"

He pulled her against him and felt the shudder roll through her body. With a word or two whispered in her ear he could bring her to climax without ever taking off her dress. And he loved her for that.

Cullen stifled a grin as he watched her jaw clench.

Morrígan turned her black eyes up to his. "What do I

feel? I am a harbinger of death," she said coldly. "I don't feel anything."

"Liar," Cullen whispered as he claimed her mouth, sliding his tongue inside as he pulled her hips against his.

They were almost the same height and a perfect fit. He knew the moment her icy reserve melted for him. She let out a ragged moan, a familiarly frantic sound that usually preceded the tearing of clothing. With a growl of triumph he swept her into his arms and carried her to the bed. Breaking the kiss, he looked down into her beautiful face. She was flush with desire – for him. Always for him, only for him. For over one thousand years they had made love and war, and they would do so for the next thousand years.

Cullen cupped her face with one battle-scarred hand. "I hate you," he whispered tenderly.

His goddess smiled up at him. "I hate you, too."

"Aye," her warrior laughed, "but you will always love me."

Eternal Strife

Dara England

Conmaicne Rein, Ireland – 800 AD

Sinead shivered in the early morning cold, tugging her shawl more tightly around her shoulders as she peered into the gloomy grey world ahead. Her breath hung in pale clouds on the air and mingled with the wispy mists rolling in off the water. Here along the lakeshore the earth was soggy and made wet sucking noises each time she pulled a booted foot free of the clinging mud.

Heart pounding, she held on tightly to the clay pitcher in her hands and searched for the resolve that had seemed so strong when she set out. She thought of her mother lying ill and alone in the draughty little cottage she had left behind. That was enough to bolster her determination.

It didn't matter that Mother would have forbidden this desperate act had she been aware of the plan her daughter had in mind to save her. All that mattered was that Sinead was finally taking action.

Courage temporarily renewed, she walked with confidence, stepping free of the cover of the overhanging willow branches and wading through the waist-high grasses leading down to the edge of the waters. She refused to think of what might be crouching, slithering or lurking among the weeds, as she knelt to peer into the murky depths below.

Tiny minnows darted away from her shadow. The light was still too dim for her face to look back at her from the mirrored surface but she knew what she would have seen if it had: a thin young girl of eighteen, with hip-length hair as dark as the feathers of the raven. Somewhere amid that mass of wild, unruly hair would be a plain face, unremarkable but for its pale, tightly drawn features. Her wide green eyes – her most predominant feature – were doubtless large with apprehension at the moment. Yes, perhaps it was as well she couldn't see.

Reluctantly, she inched further forwards until her toes were near the water and her skirts dragged in the filthy mud, so that she could scoop the pitcher into the deeper water.

She moved gingerly, making certain nothing save the pitcher touched the waters. All knew the folk of the lake guarded their watery home jealously and hated to be disturbed. Moreover, they could move as swiftly and silently as the fog; in one breath a man or woman might think themselves alone, in the next they appeared from nowhere to drag an unsuspecting victim down, screaming, into the icy depths of the lake.

Sinead flinched at the thought.

Her pitcher came up filled with cloudy, brown water carrying the stench of the lake. Twigs and bits of decaying leaves floated in the water so that the liquid looked more likely to sicken the person who drank from it than heal them. Nevertheless, a tea made with the special waters of the lake combined with the petals of the joyflower, which grew in the near meadow, and a little fever-wort from the nearby forest, was famed for its healing powers.

Certainly Sinead had tried everything else. Her new-found confidence about as substantial as the shifting fog swirling around her, she hugged her brimming pitcher to her breast and began backing away from the water's edge.

An instant later, she collided with something solid and damp at her back. With a startled shriek, she dropped the pitcher, its precious contents spilling out across the ground.

She had no thought to spare for it.

Whirling, she found herself confronted with a vision from a nightmare – a creature of scale and fin, yet standing upright on human-shaped legs. One of the lake folk.

Sinead trembled, too terrified even to flee as the creature looked down on her. Its form was vaguely akin to that of a woman but not even the quickest of glances could have mistaken this creature for a human being. Long slitted gills ran up either side of her neck, a broad, pale fin covered the length of her spine, and iridescent scales dotted her skin. Intertwined with her fair hair were long strands of green lake weed, which clung damply from the crown of her head down to her waist.

It was her eyes that most horrified Sinead: two orbs of water, clear and colourless, without any hint of feeling or life.

Sinead might have stood forever, paralysed by fright, had she not suddenly become aware of that dreaded icy touch. The lake woman had stretched out a long hand to clasp clammy fingers tightly around Sinead's wrist.

"Come . . . come . . ." The liquid whisper that poured forth from her lips was not a voice, but rather a thin, trickling sound like the dribble of water running downhill.

"Come . . . come with us . . ." Others took up the chanted command and Sinead abruptly became aware of other lake folk creeping in from the water's banks to surround her.

She bit back a squeal as one crept in and wound its slender fingers through her loose hair.

"Join us, join us," the lake folk chanted.

Sinead, cringing, slapped their hands away and tried to back away from the water's edge. She knew it was a futile gesture; few were those who escaped once they had felt the icy grip of these otherworldly beings and looked into their cold, watery eyes.

"No! Leave me alone," she cried. "I don't want to go with you!"

But even as she spoke the words she knew it was no use. Wasn't this what was said always to happen to those unwary enough to allow themselves to be taken captive by the lake folk? They were dragged down into the icy depths never to return; whether their fate was to drown or become one of the folk themselves no one knew.

Sinead did not want to suffer the horror of either fate.

As if reading her thoughts, the first lake woman spoke. "You have taken that which is ours," she hissed, her voice at once as soft as lapping water and as firm as a roaring sea. "Those who partake of the magic, belong to the magic. It is the law of the Sídhe and we abide by it."

Sinead attempted to stumble backwards but found herself hemmed in on every side. The shelter of the willow trees might as well have been miles away.

Desperately, she tried to reason with the folk.

"Please, you don't understand. I didn't mean to offend the Sídhe – or you – but I *have* to take the water. My mother is very ill; the healing properties of the lake could save her. I must have the water and I must return alive to nurse my mother back to health. There is no one else to look after her any more, no one but me to sit with her. She lies awake every night, you see, burning with fever and struggling for every breath. There . . . there is no one else."

She could think of nothing more to add to the plea. As simply as this, her whole life had been boiled down to a few sentences, yet what a load of burden and responsibility those few words carried. Truly, there was no one else.

She might have claimed she had a lover she couldn't bear to leave behind. But she hadn't. She might say she had small children who depended upon her or friends who would miss her. But the truth was, she had none of those either.

At her impassioned plea, the lake woman's eyes had grown even more opaque. "Your mother is not our concern. If you want the water, you must pay the price. It is the law of the Sídhe," she repeated. "We must obey."

Sinead didn't allow herself to despair yet. A terrible inspiration dawning on her, she summoned what courage she could. *I have to do this. I am Mother's only hope.*

Aloud she said, "Very well. I will pay whatever price you set and willingly. Only let me return to my mother first. Let me brew the needed potion and feed her, so that she may recover. Afterwards, if you still want me . . . I am yours." She had to choke out those final words, so great was the sense of doom that accompanied them.

She did not know what she expected from the lake folk, or why they should care for her bargain when they could easily drag her off right then with or without her permission.

She could only feel surprise and then a vague sense of the inevitable as she watched them hesitate – given pause by her brave offer.

Can it be they harbour something akin to human feeling or pity?

The lake woman's face remained as chill and expressionless as ever but Sinead imagined she could see a foaming turmoil within her eyes.

From behind, one of the other creatures whispered, "It is best if she succumbs willingly."

The lake woman seemed to agree. After a moment of studying Sinead, she said simply, "The bargain is struck. You have until the rising of the morrow's sun before the magic will come for you. Until then, take what you need and go."

As simply as that, she faded away – she and the others disappearing into the mist.

If the grey fog near the lake had held one sort of terror for Sinead, her next destination held an altogether different kind of danger. Certainly the peaceful meadow stretched out before her *looked* safe enough. There was none of the marshy land or the wispy tendrils of mist to speak of gloom and danger.

But Sinead was well familiar with the tales. She knew of the more alluring danger that the beautiful meadow before her possessed: the temptations of the Fae. The local tales were tangled and confused. Who could trust them? But on one point they all agreed. To enter into the chosen realm of the Fae was madness.

And yet, as she had done at the lake, Sinead focused her thoughts on the price of failure and the reward of victory as she forced herself to tread through the tall grasses in search of the bright little blossoms of the joyflower.

The flower was not difficult to find; the meadow was

abundant with them and their bright colour combined with their sweet, heady scent led her to a thick patch all too quickly. Sinead gathered the yellow blossoms by the handful, stuffing them into a woollen pouch hanging from her belt. Then, relieved at finishing so quickly, she began to depart.

How still it was here. How peaceful. The sun had now risen to its place in the sky, illuminating the meadow with warm rays of gold. A soft breeze stirred wisps of Sinead's unbound hair against her bared neck and cheek. Her arms were now feeling heavy from the weight of the pitcher of water carried on one hip. *Whatever had possessed her to fetch the water first rather than last?*

If she had not been strongly aware of the need to remain alert how easy it would be to stop right where she stood, to lie down and rest amid the meadow grass and wildflowers, to gaze up at the drifting clouds in the cheery blue sky overhead.

She shook away the temptation as soon as she became aware it had entered her head. She had come here with a mission. She had accomplished her purpose as swiftly as possible and must be on her way.

With thoughts such as these, so caught up did she become in the need to be alert towards what lay to her left and right that she forgot to look where her feet tread . . . Until the moment she realized she was no longer walking amid waist-deep grass. She trod instead on a circular path of well-worn earth, a heavily beaten ring in the centre of an otherwise grassy field.

A faery ring.

Horrified, she froze where she stood, her sudden, clumsy halt causing a small amount of water to splash out over the side of the pitcher and dampen her skirt. She scarcely noticed.

How could she have been so careless? The very thing she had set out to avoid was now surrounding her. There was no spot in the earth filled with more powerful magic than a faery ring.

Moistening her lips with her tongue, she clutched the pitcher more firmly to her side and tiptoed backwards – making her way to the edge of the ring. She almost thought she had made it, almost dared to hope her trespass had escaped their notice.

But such was not her fortune.

"Who is this, brother? Who is this that has come to dance with us?"

Sinead flinched at the light, musical voice coming from beyond her shoulder. Heart heavy with dread, she forced herself to turn and meet the fearfully charming sight.

A pair of Fae folk stood a short distance away, perusing her as though she were some unfamiliar object, some curious, foreign bird or flower that had suddenly appeared where it did not belong.

They were male and female, the pair of Fae, and a very handsome sight they might have been to the unknowledgable eye. Youthful and attractively featured, they were similar enough to have been twins – save that one was a young man, the other a girl. Their clothing was all of gold and silk, their hair as yellow as freshly churned butter. Their very skin seemed to shimmer and sparkle under the light of the sun, as though gold dust powdered them from head to toe. Sinead did not doubt that it did.

"I cannot tell you her name, sister, for it has not yet been given to me." The young male's voice was as tinkling and beautiful as that of the girl. He arched one fair eyebrow at Sinead. "Tell me, maiden, what is your name and why do you come here to steal away our secrets?"

Sinead thought she detected a hint of mockery in those tawny eyes and her back stiffened. "I do not come here for your secrets but for your joyflower. My mother is gravely ill and a potion containing your joyflower may save her."

He appeared not to have heard that last. "Our joyflower? Why, that is even worse, is it not, sister? We would not have one fewer sweet blossom in this meadow than that we already have."

Despite her fright, Sinead found herself staring the pair of them down combatively. "That's the most nonsensical thing I've ever heard," she said sharply. "This field is drowning with wildflowers and a few less cannot make any difference to you at all and might help me a great deal."

His response was quick. "Ah, but suppose it is not our wish to help anybody but ourselves? Therein lies the trouble. For

Fae folk, as you must know, care very little for others and very much for themselves."

Sinead wearied of this verbal battle. "What is it you want from me?" she asked resignedly.

"How tiresome these ordinary folk are, are they not?" he addressed himself to his companion. "Have we not already stated our purpose? Is it not clear to anyone with eyes and ears what the Fae folk want, what we enjoy above all else?"

His sister rushed forwards. "Pay no mind to my brother, little one; he is simply in love with his own wit. He means no harm by it."

When the words were spoken in that lilting, musical voice Sinead found that she could almost believe them. *Almost.*

"Never mind the false kindness. Simply tell me what it is you ask – or rather what you demand, for I've no doubt it will soon enough come down to that."

The golden brow knit and the rosebud shaped lips puckered into a pout. "You see, brother? You see how you have offended her? And now she will never come willingly to the dance."

Her companion glowered. "What matters it whether she is willing or not? She has entered the ring. She is in our power."

Sinead swallowed, for she knew his words were nothing but truth, whether he intended malice or not – and obviously he did.

"I don't understand," she answered, feigning ignorance to buy herself more time. "What is this about a dance?"

"How simple-minded you mortals are." The male sneered at her. "Do not pretend ignorance. There can be no man, woman or child alive who does not know of the faery dance, the endless, eternal dance of bliss in which we pause only during the light of day to gain new partners."

"Of which you are now one," his sister cut in. As she spoke, she shifted oddly, as if to cover something with her skirts.

Sinead's attention was drawn downwards where, for the first time, she noticed an appalling sight. The feet of the Fae were bare despite their other finery. And what feet they were! Battered and bloody, bruised and swollen, they were the feet of immortal beings who spent every night of their lives dancing heedlessly, madly away under the light of the moon, no more able to stop themselves than the ant could stop its toil or the seasons could cease their turning.

"Your feet," Sinead gasped, with mingled sympathy and horror.

The male seemed annoyed that she had noticed the single flaw to their otherwise beautiful persons. "Never mind that, it is nothing." His tone was dismissive. "The pain is scarcely felt when one becomes caught up in the rapture of the dance."

"That is so," his sister agreed.

Sinead's eyes widened. "You are mad. Both of you."

The male simply smiled; the female nodded pleasantly. "But, of course."

Sinead shuddered. "I . . . I think I'd better be going now."

"But you cannot," the female answered. "Once a mortal has entered the ring it is physically impossible for them to depart, unless we will it."

"Let me guess. The law of the Sídhe?"

"Exactly so," answered the male.

Sinead sighed. "I've told you my mother needs me – she needs this joyflower. What will it take for you to agree to let me take it to her?"

"There is nothing that can be given in exchange for a human life. I'm sure you will agree," answered the male faery coyly.

For the first time that day Sinead felt the backs of her eyes prickle with tears – not tears of fear, but of dismay and frustration. *To have come so far only to be defeated by a witless pair such as this!*

It was in this moment of utter despair that an idea came to her mind. "Suppose we made a bargain?" she offered. "Suppose I swore to return at dawn tomorrow? Would you allow me this one last night to return to my home? After all, what could possibly be gained by keeping me now against my will? I can promise you I'd never cease to hate you for it and I should not dance well for you at all. It would be an eternity of strife."

The faeries exchanged looks. Then the female shrugged. "I see no reason why we should not let you go for awhile yet. If you swear to return to us of your own free will, we will grant you this last half-day and night of freedom. We will even grant you the joyflower to carry away."

Her brother looked disgruntled, Sinead noted, but he too gave his assent.

"At dawn on the morrow," the female said, "the magic will come for you."

Regretfully, Sinead agreed.

Scarcely had she escaped this second test when she found herself facing a third. The woods at the edge of the meadow were dark and deep and were rumoured to be guarded by fearsome forest creatures who permitted no human to set foot within their boundaries.

And yet, the fever-wort grew only within the shadows of the wood and, having committed herself this far, Sinead could hardly turn back.

Besides, she comforted herself, she had already sold her life to the lake folk in exchange for the pitcher of water she now carried against her breast and to the Fae folk in exchange for the joyflower in her belt pouch. What did it matter, in the end, whether it was the lake folk, the Fae, or the dreadful creatures of the forest who eventually claimed her? Oddly enough, the thought emboldened her.

With a good deal more resolve now than she had possessed earlier in the morning, Sinead entered the shadows of the wood.

She travelled far, all the way into the heart of the forest, before she at last found a shady little clearing beside a babbling brook, where the fever-wort grew in profusion. Here she gathered as much of the plant as she needed and, tucking it into the little pouch dangling from her belt, set off on her way again.

Relieved at having completed her goal so easily and having met with no interference from the frightful wood creatures, she was eager to leave the forest behind her and to be soon at her mother's side once more.

Unfortunately, that was not to be. She quickly discovered that she had journeyed so far into the shadowy wood that she could no longer recall the way back out.

Picking her way along the path that looked most familiar, she at length found herself back once more in the exact same shady clearing she had so recently left. In fact, no matter which direction she left this spot in, she continued to return always to the same place. What is this? she asked herself. What mischievous magic is at work here? Am I doomed forever to wonder this gloomy wood?

It was as she again came face to face with the babbling brook after her third attempt to leave the clearing that Sinead first began to sense she was not alone, and perhaps had not been alone this entire time. A tingling feeling tickled its way down her spine; she could feel unseen eyes upon her.

Spinning slowly, searching for her watcher, her eyes abruptly collided with an unexpected figure. It was as if it simply appeared from nowhere. One moment there had been nothing but a beam of sunshine slanting down through the treetops to fall across a rotting stump. In the next instant *he* appeared.

He was a great stag of the forest. His graceful body was lithe and muscled beneath his copper-hued hide; massive, spreading antlers towered above his head . . . And yet he was more than that.

What should have been the neck of the stag, widened rather than narrowed, merging into the form of a man's waist and upper torso. Fine, reddish-hued fur ran up to a broad chest, above which soared bare, muscular shoulders and a head as human as that of any young man she had ever seen . . . Well, perhaps not quite human. Certainly there were features distinctly human in that face, but there were also traits that could only have come from the stag. His nose was long and narrow, his high chin and cheekbones were dusted with fine hair of the same hue as the deer hide further down his body.

Even the longish hair of his head was a deep, rich red to match his hide. His mouth was wide and pink and possessed of a more generous pair of lips than would seem natural on most people.

But just as with the lake folk, it was this creature's eyes that made her reassess her impression of its humanity. Those dark, pupil-less eyes were as beastly as the rest of his face was manly. Sinead could read in them no sign of human emotion or intelligence.

There was no more time for gawking. A sudden stirring of the hairs along the back of her neck warned her of still more hidden observers. Daring to look away from the stag-man for an instant, she stole a glance over one shoulder.

The motion was met with a fluttering and a scurrying of movement among the branches of the near trees along the boulders edging the brook. Sinead caught only the vague impressions of an owl with the face of a child ducking back among the fallen leaves of an oak and a raccoon with human-appearing hands and feet scuttling behind a fallen log.

She shuddered, imagining how many more equally strange creatures still lurked in the shadows.

"You needn't fear; we mean you no harm – though neither will we aid you."

Despite having noted his human-like mouth, Sinead was nonetheless startled when the stag spoke in the voice of an ordinary man. Swallowing, she tried to slow the wild thudding of her heart. Unnerved as she was at being addressed by a half-stag, half-man, a tiny part of her mind was beginning to accept such odd things as being somehow natural on a day as strange as this one.

The steadiness of her voice came as a surprise. "I'm glad to hear you mean me no ill, great stag, as I face a mission of great importance and it's imperative that I carry it out with haste. You see, my mother is gravely ill and I mean to brew her a healing potion. I have already collected the needed fever-wort and was just on my way home when, as you probably saw for yourself, I discovered myself somehow turned about and lost.

It's the oddest thing but no matter which path I chose I found myself drawn again to this same clearing."

Even as she spoke, she took the opportunity to study the stag-man further and quickly found herself blushing. It was a ridiculous thought to have at such a moment, but she suddenly realized she had never seen a man with his upper body bared before. She was not certain she was seeing one now.

Luckily, he followed her words and not her foolish thoughts.

"There is nothing strange in your losing yourself here," he said, once more surprising her by his casual tone. He sounded much like any handsome young farmer she might have conversed with in the local village. "The Sídhe of these woods guard the forest by means of an ancient spell, denying not entrance but exit to any foolish or desperate enough to tread this ground."

Sinead frowned at the implied insult. "By 'foolish' I suppose you mean me?"

He agreed. "From the moment you stepped into the forest shadows you have doomed yourself to suffer the same fate as those before you – to wander eternally the twisted pathways of the wood."

"As you do," Sinead ventured with sudden understanding. "Were you and these others once human beings like me?"

The stag-man seemed to consider. "Perhaps," he answered at last. "It is hard to recall a past so distant. For me it has been very long since I walked with human feet upon the earth."

Sinead found that difficult to believe, for his face appeared only a few years older than her own. But perhaps that was a part of the Sídhe spell – perhaps ones such as he did not age or aged more slowly than most.

She realized he was looking pointedly downwards at her small feet, encased in shabby boots, and peeking from beneath the edge of her skirt's ragged hem.

"For you, walking among men and women will soon become a dim memory as well. You will come to accept the wood as your home and to guard it as jealously as we."

"Never. I would spend my life fighting against the spell. It would be an eternal strife."

"You will find soon enough that there is little to fear and nothing to fight, just as you do not now despise your humanity or find it a fate to be striven against. You simply are what you are." Even as he spoke, he turned away.

"Wait!" Sinead cried after him. "Don't go, please; I need your help. I cannot live in this terrible forest forever." At his expression she hastily amended, "I mean, certain as I am that it is a lovely place to call home, I am needed elsewhere. My mother, remember? She has no one but me to look after her."

The stag-man shrugged a powerful shoulder. Sinead could not help admiring how it flexed the long muscles of his back.

He said, "If that is the case then I am sorry for you both, but there is nothing I can do. Only those who have already succumbed fully to the forest magic are capable of escaping its spell, and by then they have lost the desire to do so."

"By succumbing to the magic . . . ?"

"I mean those who have taken on the beastly forms such as those you see around you. Those who have become as we."

A tiny flame of hope flickered to life within Sinead's heart. "Then you, who have already taken your beastly form, know your way past this horrible ensnaring spell that has twisted the path at my feet and made me a prisoner to the wood?"

"We know the proper path out of the forest," he admitted. "It is visible to us who are no longer spellbound."

"Show me the way," Sinead demanded boldly.

The stag-man stared at her with imperturbable eyes. "Why should I do that? It is too late for me. I have given up the human existence. Why should I aid another in escaping the fate that is mine?"

Sinead's temper stirred to life. *How had she ever found him attractive? Heavens, he was a . . . a beast.* Her voice rose in mingled anger and desperation. "It is *because* you could not escape when you still possessed the will that you should help me! Because you were once the prisoner that I am now. Only remember what it was like to possess human compassion, human love and, if you still have any drop of human emotion within you, aid me in returning home to care for my mother."

Something flickered briefly in the stag-man's dark eyes.

She dared to hope her argument had moved him.

"Very well." The declaration was sudden; she had the impression that even he was startled by it. "I will grant your request, but only in half." His lips twisted in an attempt at a human smile that was both ghastly and vaguely appealing. "We do everything by halves here, as you see."

Sinead was too uneasy about her circumstances and too shaken by the sudden and strange pull she felt towards this half-human, half-animal creature to spare patience for his odd bit of humour. Her heart, which had leaped a little at his first words, sank as the last sunk in. "What do you mean you will grant only half?"

The stag-man's tone hardened. "I offer you a bargain. I and the others will grant you safe passage through the forest and will lead you out of this spell-wrought snare, but only on the condition that you must return to this place tomorrow morning. Take the fever-wort to your mother and make your healing potion. Tend her through the night but, at the dawn of the morrow, the magic will call you to us again."

Sinead knew in her heart nothing she could say would persuade him to change his mind. He had been generous in his way. Unexpectedly, she found herself admiring what humanity was left in him. She no longer thought of him as a horrifying creature. There was something unusually graceful and somehow *right* in the blend of animal and man before her. What would it be like to be transformed as he – to lead a half-woman, half-beast existence?

She shook her head, it was not a possibility she was comfortable entertaining. All the same, she found herself speaking words of agreement. As easily as that, the dread bargain was sealed.

She shuddered as the reality of that sank in and tried to comfort herself. *At least out of all of this, I may yet save Mother.*

Back at home in the little cottage nestled at the foot of the hills,

Sinead brewed up a strong tea over the hearth, using the lake water, the joyflower and the fever-wort herb.

Her mother was scarcely conscious and it was with difficulty that Sinead managed to trickle a portion of the tea into her mouth.

Then she crawled into a pallet of straw on the floor and fell asleep wondering if all she had donc would be enough. *What if she had bargained away her life to the creatures of the lake, meadow and wood for nothing?*

She awoke early to find her mother's fever-induced sleep had gone in the night, to be replaced by the deeper slumber of true rest. She had passed the point of crisis and was on the mend. Sinead rejoiced at the healthy pink glow in the formerly pale cheeks and was relieved on pressing a palm to the lined forehead to find it cool to the touch, the fever fading like the last stars of the night.

Fading stars. Sinead recalled the awful events of the day before, the rash promises she had made. She wondered which magic would come and claim her first – that of the lake folk, the Fae of the meadow or the half-beast creatures of the wood.

Reluctantly, fearfully, she stepped out of the cottage and into the grey light of early morning. There was a chill in the air. The grass under her feet was still heavy with dew and on the horizon a faint tint of rose lightened the sky.

How like yesterday it all seemed! Almost she could believe she had simply dreamed the events of the previous morning and afternoon. Almost she could *wish* she had.

It was just as the tip of the bright sun appeared over the far treetops that Sinead became aware of the magics. She could not be sure which of them she first sensed.

A great rushing sound, like the roar of a river overflowing its bank, came sweeping down over the hills from the north. It seemed to carry on it the call of the lake folk: a multitude of watery echoes flooding her way.

Instantaneously, another sort of magic began to well up from the opposite direction. This magic was visible to her eyes as a bright ray of sunlight, a shining, golden stream gleaming over the hilltop and flashing down towards the cottage in the valley. Sinead could almost hear the laughter of the faeries riding on the sunbeam, could almost smell the overpowering scent of meadow flowers and hear the drumming tread of delicate feet pounding out a steady, endless dance of mirth and madness.

And finally, at that very moment, a third magic came pouring towards her from the western hills. This magic took the form, not of a sight or an audible call to her ears, but of a silent urging, a pulsing of the earth beneath her, an insistent tugging of the wind, on which was borne the scent of moss-covered bark, rotting leaves and fertile earth. Sinead had but to close her eyes and she could envision the peaceful clearing with the babbling brook, the soothing shade of the overhead canopy and the strangely compassionate half-stag awaiting her coming. Oddly, the scene was no longer a dreaded or troubling one.

Onwards all three streams of magic travelled down the hills, racing towards her – competing, Sinead imagined, to see which would claim her from the other, for clearly she could not belong to the water, the meadow *and* the wood.

She could do no more than stand motionless and wait to discover her fate. Running would have been fruitless. Dashing into the frail little cottage? What good could that do? No, she summoned her courage and waited, waited.

They were all but simultaneous, the magics, as they slammed into her. It was impossible to guess which had reached her first. Caught up in the heart of the roaring whirlwind of the clashing powers of lake, meadow and forest, Sinead was knocked to her knees.

The gale whipped her hair into her face, showering her in a hail of forest leaves, of forest sights and scents.

She sensed invisible torrents of water beating at her, tossing her helplessly about like a twig in a stream.

The brightness of the sunlight was blinding, burning, scorching through her.

With angry fury the three magics fought over her, until Sinead thought surely when they were done there would be no scraps of her left for any to have. *Perhaps that was their intention?*

And then suddenly . . . The storm abated. As swiftly as they had descended upon her the three magics now abandoned their fight. The torrent of lake voices seeped away, back into the northern hills. The bright beams of sunlight faded back to the dull grey of early morning. The powerful gale of forest magic died down to a whisper of a breeze, then swirled away back over the hills to the wood beyond.

At last Sinead was left alone.

Exhausted after the ordeal, it seemed to require a great amount of effort for her to pull herself upright. Yet when she stood and looked down it was to discover herself still very much a living human being. There were no scales or gills, no delicate feet worn frail and bloody with endless dancing, no antlers or fur. She had not been transformed into anything mad or grotesque but remained simply . . . herself – which suddenly seemed like a very plain thing to be.

Why did none of them take me? I don't understand.

And then, she did. *It is left to be mine. My choice.* Since none of the magics could prevail they had struck a compromise, had left their victim to choose the manner of her doom.

Yet oddly enough, it hardly felt like any doom at all. Not any more. Her decision was all too easily made.

As she made her way lightly up the hill path towards her destination, she looked ahead to her new life in a different, exciting home. She even found herself envisioning a particular figure awaiting her and felt an unexpected thrill of anticipation.

Over the passing years, the poor widow living in the little cottage at the foot of the hills found her life markedly improved. Once she had been an impoverished woman. Her health had been poor. She and her only child had dressed shabbily and often gone hungry.

All of that changed the morning she awoke to find her poor young daughter had disappeared, stolen away for ever by some cruel fate.

And yet . . . life suddenly became so much easier once her beloved Sinead was gone. Little piles of food suddenly began appearing on her doorstep at odd hours. Heaps of berries and dry twigs for her fire were often found nearby, left by an invisible hand. Fever-wort was a frequent gift from the widow's mysterious visitors; great bunches of the stuff decorated her windows and grew along the edges of the cottage.

And sometimes . . . sometimes when she rose in the early hours of the morning she would step outside to find two beautiful deer grazing on the dew-soaked grass at the edge of her garden – a mighty stag and a graceful doe. Strangely, from a distance there was something almost . . . *human* about the pair.

Quicksilver

Cindy Holby

Ireland – 545

Conn Daithi ignored the mist that swirled around him and kept on riding. Even though he was well seasoned in the art of war, he knew his sword and shield would not be of much help for him against the undead spirits that hid in the shadows of the fog. 'Twas Samhain and the air around him swirled as the veil between his world and the next threatened to split apart. Those who lingered at the edge were anxious to show their displeasure at the prospect of Christianity coming to their kingdom even though the stones of the abbey at Sligo were only recently placed.

The mountains of Ben Bulbin were long behind him. He made for Imleach Iseal on the coast. He had seen the festival bonfires earlier but they had long since disappeared into the mist. Niul tossed his head as if to shed the water that dampened his dark-as-night coat and Conn placed a reassuring hand against the stallion's neck. They were both weary of travel and of the ceaseless battles that raged across the Isle. Conn wanted nothing more than to escape the demands put upon him by the highest bidder for his sword arm yet he was forever trapped by the sea. He'd lost too many brothers, too many friends and too much time to war. Mayhap here, in this small fishing village, he could find a boat that would take him and Niul away from this place. Mayhap then, he would find some peace.

Conn could smell the sea and he took deep gulping breaths, hoping it would cleanse his lungs of the scents of death. He trusted Niul and gave the horse his head as they picked their way among the boulders that lined the slope between field and shore. As they moved downwards, the mist cleared somewhat, revealing thin lines of clouds that partially shadowed the full moon. Even though the air was chill, his skin felt moist beneath his leather jerkin and linen *chainse*, as if it were the middle of summer instead of the end of the harvest season. Stranger still, jagged flashes of light danced across the sky even though there was no sign of rain. Conn saw the outline of a tower in the distance.

Túr Rí. The tower was old and legends surrounded it. It was built by the Fomorian king, Conan, who then slaughtered the workers when the task was done. Wars had been raged and the Nemedians had defeated them, but it was said that the Fomorians were once more in possession of the island. There was also talk of a mighty warrior called Balor who could kill just by staring at his opponent with the one eye centred in his forehead. Conn put more trust in his sword than in whispered legends. If someone could kill him with a look he would have been dead long ago.

Niul snorted and jerked against the reins as they reached the packed sand that rolled into the sea. The wind strengthened and swirled about him, tossing his cloak in tandem with the thick mane of Niul. A shiver ran down his spine, a warrior's intuition that he always obeyed. Conn urged Niul into a quick gait and his eyes ran over the sand to see if there were, indeed, a threat.

He saw something rolling in the waves. Niul danced sideways as Conn urged him onwards. He drew his sword from its sheath and held it easily in one hand while he grasped Niul's reins with the other. A wave crashed on to the shore and with it came a body. Conn leaped over Niul's neck and landed in the sand on the balls of his feet with his sword held before him.

The clouds suddenly parted from the moon and cast light down upon the beach as the waves carried the body back out.

Conn waded into the surf and grabbed an arm. As he dragged the victim to shore, he realized that the body was that of a woman. She was completely nude except for her long pale hair, which was the same colour as the moonlight. It tangled about her hips and thighs like seaweed.

Conn buried his sword, point down, into the sand and knelt beside her. He leaned in close to hear her heart beat. She was tall and thin with small breasts and narrow hips but he paid no mind to her form beyond wanting to know if she was alive or dead. A gasping breath gurgled in her throat, which gave him hope. Conn pulled her up by the shoulders and bent her over his arm before giving her back a sound thump. She gagged and coughed and then spewed forth water from the sea.

"There, lass," he said. "'Twill be better once it is gone."

She nodded as she clung to his arm. Her back was to him, revealing a long knobby spine and the definition of her ribs. It was obvious she had not eaten for a good long while. Amidst the tangle of her hair he saw a symbol etched into her shoulder. He pushed her hair aside and examined a double blue triangle formed by three curving lines. He traced it with his fingertip.

She wiped her mouth with the back of her hand and glanced quickly over her shoulder. He caught the flash of her quicksilver eyes and saw the tips of her ears jutting though her hair. In the next moment he was flat on his back, lying in the sand, and the point of his sword was at his throat.

"Sidh." He watched her warily. The Sidh were known for moving quicker than men and being deceptively strong despite their slim and willowy builds. It was the first time he'd ever met one face to face. "Until now, I did not think ye truly existed."

"As ye know what I am, then ye also know that I owe you an allegiance. Ye have saved my life." She knelt before him in the sand with the sword now safely pointed down. "I am Aine. What do you desire?" She kept her head bowed, but her quicksilver eyes looked up at him alluringly and he felt the familiar tightening in his groin. It had been a long time since he enjoyed a woman. A longer time since he'd fallen into a trap. She appeared so regal, alike to a queen, even though her position was submissive and she was clothed in naught but her hair. She stayed her place, waiting for his answer.

"I want my sword back," Conn said and was amused to see a flare of anger light her pale eyes. He held out his hand to help her up as he took his sword from her grip with the other. She put a hand to her head as she stood, looked at him with bewilderment in her quicksilver eyes, and then fainted into his arms.

Aine watched the man through slitted eyes as he placed more driftwood upon the fire. She had fainted. Too long without food or rest had weakened her, just when she needed to be strong. She'd escaped from Tor Inis, had a weapon and a horse at her disposal, along with a strong man that she could enslave, and instead she'd fallen into his arms like a youngling who drank too much mead.

He was handsome in the way of human men. Broader than the Sidh. Nearly as tall. Darker, and definitely more dangerous. His answer to her offering alone was enough to show his intelligence. He also showed kindness – she now wore his linen *chainse* and was wrapped in his cloak. What would a man such as this want?

"Are you hungry?" he asked. He knew she was no longer asleep. She would have to be very careful around this man.

Aine sat up. He had caught a fish and cooked it while she slept. Normally the smell would have awakened her. She must be weaker than she thought. "Once more I am indebted to you," she said as he handed her part of the fish.

He settled back against his saddle and watched her with his dark eyes. His hair was a midnight black, with the straight ends brushing across his wide shoulders. He wore a leather jerkin, which opened against a broad chest and showed long arms bulging with muscle. His nose was proud and straight except for a bump at the top where it had been broken. His strong jaw showed only a day's growth of beard and a scar marred his left cheek from the corner of his eye to the curve of his chin. Everything about him bespoke a warrior, from the casual closeness of his weapons to the steady perusal of his gaze. He was sizing her up and trying to decide if she would be a friend or foe. His kindness to her could be perceived as a weakness by some. Aine decided to see it as a sign of a sharp mind. Men who overestimated their worth and underestimated hers had suffered greatly for their mistakes. Would he do the same?

"Where do you come from?" he asked.

"By birth or as of late?"

"Of late." He dipped his head to the sea behind her. "How came you to be on this shore?"

"I was held captive on Tor Inis." Aine licked the last of the fish from her fingertips. "By Balor and his minions."

He gazed out at the isle and the lightning that slashed across the sky. She knew Balor would soon find her escaped from the tower. She must be gone from this place before the tide moved out and the passage between his isle and this shore was opened. Yet she could not leave until this man released her. She had traded one form of captivity for another.

"You escaped?"

"I threw myself into the sea from the tower," she said. "It was my hope to escape. Or die."

"'Tis the way of most things in this world." He sounded weary and bitter. There were more questions he could ask her, should ask her, yet he did not. Most men would. But then again, most men would have taken advantage of her weakness by now, and then regretted it when they realized her true power.

The fire popped and crackled as a piece of the driftwood split and fell into the coals. The flames shot higher and turned his face into shadows and light as if it were carved of stone. If she were to return to her home world, then she must do it soon, ere the chance would be lost for another year. Not that a year was much to her in this world. Still she had been too long gone and longed to see her people again.

"What is your name?"

"Conn Daithi."

Daithi. An old and proud name. As old as Ireland. "Who do you fight for Conn Daithi?"

"I fight for myself." His eyes were steady upon her, challenging her to say otherwise.

A roar broke the peace of the night and drifted across the water from the isle behind them. "'Tis a good thing then," she said. "As soon enough you will do battle."

Conn heard the war cry as it rolled across the waves. Aine spoke of Balor as her captor. Balor who was a myth, just as the Sidh were a myth. Yet a Sidh sat across from him at the fire. If the Sidh existed then Balor must also. It was the way of things.

He should have left her in the water. Left her to drown. He would be in the village by now, drinking fine mead and eyeing a wench to help pass the long hours of the night. But alas, he did not, so he picked up his sword and walked to the water's edge.

"Is what they say of him true?"

"'Tis so," she replied.

How did one fight a man who could kill with a look? Conn glanced over his shoulder. She had come to join him, wearing nothing but his *chainse.* The wind whipped the tail of it across her body, along with her hair. Her pale locks swirled around her as if caught up in a whirlwind. She studied him once more with her quicksilver eyes, taking his measure. For some strange reason he did not want her to find him lacking. Conn flipped his sword around in his hands to loosen his muscles and relax his stance.

"He will come across the passage when the tide reveals it." Her voice was steady and calm. "There is still time for you to go on your way."

Her words were like a punch to his gut. "Do ye think me a coward?" Why did he care what she thought?

She kept her eyes on the tower. "Nay, I think this is not your battle to fight."

Conn studied her profile. Her features were pleasant and without defect. Indeed they were most pleasing, yet he preferred his women to be buxom and curved. Still there was something about her. Something that called out to his soul.

Something that he had not felt in a very long time. A thing that he thought long gone and lost in the blood of the many battles he had fought. "What does he want with you?"

She shrugged. "What does any man want with a Sidh woman?"

It was long said that if a man could capture a woman of the Sidh then that man would have his heart's desire. There were also stories of men who had attempted to capture a Sidh woman and suffered greatly from the curses the women put upon them. Some had lost their ears, some their eyes, some their sons and daughters, and some their very souls. Who was Balor that he would not suffer thusly?

Conn studied her closely. "If I go what will become of you?"

"He will take me once more to the tower and use me as hostage against my kinsmen. He thinks to have our treasures. He thinks that they are tangible things that he can place in a chest and lock away. He is a fool as most men of your world are."

"Ye do not have a great opinion of the men of this world," he observed.

"The men of your world seek to use me for their own end. And yet here ye stand, one who could have used me dearly in my weakness and chose not too."

"I am not a raper of women, nor am I a thief. I only take what is due me. My wages, some food, and most nights a dry place to pass the time. I earn my way honestly in all things."

"Ye have honour." She did not question it nor did she seem surprised by it as her earlier words would have led him to believe.

"'Tis all I have to keep me company." He was bitter and his words betrayed his weakness. "'Tis Samhain. Can ye not go back to your world?"

"He holds my key on a chain about his neck. Without it I cannot return."

"I will take you with me."

"He will follow me. If we go to the village he will tear it and the people within it apart to have me. No one around me is safe."

He knew it to be true. He'd seen men and women of power do the same. Was it not the reason he sought peace? He was tired of the senseless killing over the whims of others, especially those who wore the crowns. Was it not the purpose of the kings and queens to care for the people? At least this woman of the Sidh showed compassion for those who were innocent. She would not bring death and destruction to any village.

She spoke without conceit. She knew her value to Balor who thought she was the way to great treasures. Yet she said there were none. Mayhap Balor did not realize that the woman in herself was the treasure, or could be with tender care.

The wind shifted, a sure sign of the retreating tide. How long until the way was cleared? Long enough for him to think on his life and his mistakes. The woman, Aine, must have cast a spell on him ere he would have left long ago. It was his only reasoning for why he still stood with the surf lapping at his boots while he looked at the lightning that streaked about the tower. Yet she had urged him to go before Balor came on shore. There was something inside him that protested the thought of leaving her to the beast.

"How dost one fight someone who can kill you with a look?"

She gazed at him, her quicksilver eyes once more taking his measure. She tilted her head to the side and smiled. "There is a way but it would mean ye would have to put your trust in me. Do you think ye can do so, Conn Daithi?"

Trust her? He trusted no one. The only thing he had faith in was his horse, his sword and the arm that wielded it.

"Have ye charmed me?" He could not think of a time when she could have unless it was when he first saw her face. Conn closed his eyes as if to look inside his mind for the chains that linked him to her. She shook her head. He was in full control of his senses.

"'Tis your honour that bids you stay, naught else," she said as if she could read his thoughts. "Ye can not leave a woman to fend for herself, even though ye know that I am Sidh. Why is that?"

Her quicksilver eyes searched his face, daring him to let her inside his thoughts. He would not allow it so he turned away from her and once more looked to the isle although he did not see it. What he did see was a horrible memory.

He could still see their bodies and feel the flames. His mother and his two sisters, brutalized before they were thrown into the fire to die. Because there was no man there to defend them. How could this Sidh woman know such things about him, about his past? How could he put such thoughts into words? The memories were too horrible, too near.

"Could you fend for yourself?" He growled the words, doubtful of her answer.

"Would my answer change yours? If I told you that I may wield a sword as easily as a man would ye leave me to my fate? If my reply was that I am at his mercy would ye give up your life in an attempt to save mine?" She stood at the edge of the surf with her hair flying about her. She turned her quicksilver eyes upon him. "I will not answer yea or nay so that ye may not cry out that I tricked you."

"If I am dead what will it matter?"

She pulled back the hair that tossed across her face and held it there so that her gaze was unfettered. "It will matter to me."

There were more things he should ask her. There were things he should know about the enemy that would come. He should not trust her yet she said he must to survive the coming battle. All these thoughts he pushed from his head. Instead he put his arm about her waist and pulled her to him. She felt as light as the night air, yet solid in her strength, like the blade he bore in his other hand. He cared naught for that at the moment. If he were to die, then he would know in the next few moments what he was to die for.

She offered him no resistance. She stared at him with her quicksilver eyes as her hair flew about their bodies as if to wrap them into a cocoon. A slight smile twisted her lips. She moved as he did, each turning their head towards a kiss. He was gentle at first, testing her and she complied. He moved his hand up to her head and wrapped his sword arm around her back, pulling her fully against him. Her arms twined about his neck and the kiss turned from gentle question to answering need.

Another battle cry from Balor met his ears but he ignored it. His time to fight would come soon enough. For Conn there was nothing else but this instant, with this woman.

Aine well knew his intent. It was always the intent of men to possess her. Yet this man, at this time, was different. He did not want her for her powers or because he thought she was the key to a great treasure. He just wanted her for her. Because he was alone and about to face death and he wanted to know that life was worth the living. He wanted her because he was a man and she was a woman. It was the most basic of needs that blurred the lines between human and Fae.

Aine decided not to think on it. She decided just to feel. His lips moved against hers, his tongue probed her mouth and she let him in. She felt the pressure of his sword hilt in the small of her back and his shaft rubbing against her belly. She ground her hips against his and he growled, low in his throat. He picked her up without breaking the kiss and carried her to the cloak she'd left lying by the fire.

Conn buried his sword, blade first into the sand. He stood over her, tall and wide of shoulder, narrow of waist and hip. His dark hair shadowed his face as he looked down at her with the firelight reflecting in his eyes. Behind him the lightning flashed across the sky and Balor once more screamed his horrible cry. His muscular thighs flexed as he knelt before her. She rose up to meet him and he lifted the hem of his tunic to pull it over her head.

Her body was not a mystery to him. He had seen her before when he pulled her from the surf, had even placed his chainse upon her body after taking it from his own. Still he looked at her, his eyes sweeping her from head to toe as she once more lay back on the blanket in the sand.

He took off his jerkin and set it aside to expose his deeply muscular chest and the deep clefts of his stomach. She was not surprised when he left his gauntlets and chausses in place. He would not be caught unready should any happen upon them. His eyes covered her, ravaged her until he lay down beside her and gathered her into his arms. She was prepared for him to conquer her in the way that most warriors would. She was not ready for the gentle and tender possession of his arms about her, nor the way his lips softly touched hers.

He kept his eyes open while he kissed her and she saw that they were a deep shade of blue, like the sea on a stormy day. It was strange, gazing into his eyes. She could not have stopped, or closed her own, as they seemed to hold her captive while his arms gave her opportunity to escape, if she desired it.

She did not. She desired more. More of him, more of his kisses, more of his hands roaming her back and side, yet aching with need as he cupped her breast and rubbed his thumb over the peak of her nipple. She gasped against his mouth and arched into his palm while her hips moved closer against him and begged him for more. He shut his eyes, finally, as if falling into a dream, and slowly trailed kisses down her neck. His hair brushed against her skin, guiding the way for his mouth, until she thought she would combust with need. His lips touched her breast and drove her body to a greater desire.

Was she wrong about him? Was he more than a man? More than a mortal? For surely no mortal could send her into this boiling cauldron of want. This was something she'd never felt before and all she could do was wrap her hands in his hair, close her eyes and hold on.

His hand trailed over her stomach and her muscles clenched at his touch as anticipation filled her. He splayed his big hand into the hollow of it, the width of his fingers spread wide enough to cover her from side to side. She spread her legs, willing him and wanting him to touch her, there, in that place that brought the dancing of stars across the sky. His thumb dipped into her folds and she sighed deeply and hooked her leg around his hip.

He watched her. She opened her eyes to see his eyes on her. A quick smile flitted across his face as he looked at her and she wondered, briefly, what it would be like to see him laugh. Then he dipped his fingers inside of her and all thoughts fled her mind save one: *I want him* . . .

Her hips rose to meet his hand.

"Aine," he said and took his hand away. She reached for him. His hands were at his waist, removing his chausses and she helped him, slipping them down and freeing him.

The gentleness left him then. He pulled back and pushed inside her, until he was buried and his pelvis ground against her. She wrapped her legs around his waist and raked her nails down his back and held on. He kissed her again, desperately. He pulled her lower lip into his teeth. She rocked against him, with him. He released her lip and buried his head into her neck. Her eyes were open and she saw the sky, clear now, and the stars like pinpricks in the heavens above. She kept her eyes on them until they began to swirl and she knew if she reached up her hand, she could touch them. She gathered a handful, wrapped her arms around Conn's waist and held on as the brilliance of the stars blinded her.

Aine's fingers gently traced a pattern on the small of his back as Conn lay atop her and gathered his strength. The base of his spine tingled where she touched him. He understood now why men lost their souls in pursuit of a Sidh woman. He'd never experienced a release such as the one just past. He felt blinded from it, as if he'd looked directly at the sun. It was strange, the feeling of disquiet, mixed with something he could only call contentment. If only he could stay in her arms for the rest of the night, nay, for the rest of his life.

Balor's battle cry, drifting once more across the water, reminded him that he could not. Without a word, he rose, adjusted his chausses, and handed his chainse to Aine before he went to his stallion. Niul lowered his head and Conn leaned his brow against it in silent communication with the one who had been his dearest companion.

He heard her movement behind him, felt her silent footsteps in the sand. She touched the small of his back once more. "How long have you had this mark?" Her question surprised him. Conn glanced over his shoulder and saw that she had wrapped his cloak about her body. The wind held a bite to it. He should build up the fire while he had the chance.

"Of what mark do you speak?" he asked. "Is it a scar?" He knew of none in that location. He had several, however, all souvenirs of his many battles, but none in the small of his back.

"Nay." She traced it once more with her fingers. "'Tis like mine," she said and dipped her shoulder to show him the blue interlocking lines upon her back.

Conn's hand went to his back. "I have no mark," he said.

"Ye do." Her eyes did not lie, yet it had to be so. He would know if he had a mark. He twisted around in an attempt to see for himself of what she spoke but his body would not bend to suit his desire.

Aine grabbed his hand. "Stop," she said. "I will show you." Conn jerked away from her. This talk of strange marks upon his skin was too much. He should not have made love to her. It was her way of entrapping him.

Yet, you were captivated by her before you made love to her. Your decision was made of your own free will. Was it not so?

"What spell have you placed upon me?" He wrinkled his brow, once more going over the moments since they met to recall if she had conjured something that he might have missed.

Aine smiled and touched the scar upon his cheek with her fingertip. "It is you who have placed a spell on me." She pushed his hair away from his face and behind his ear. "I will show you the mark. Ye must allow it. Ye will see 'tis the only way to defeat Balor." Aine placed her hand against his temple and stood beside him, facing in the opposite direction. "Ye will see what I see," she said. "Close your eyes and it will be done."

I have nothing to lose. I am already a dead man. Conn closed his eyes.

"Use my eyes to see." Her voice held a caress that dispelled the incongruity of her words. He took a deep breath and released it.

He saw Niul, even though his back was to the horse. Niul tossed his head up and down and pawed at the sand. The line of his sight moved and Conn saw dark hair that tossed in the wind and his profile, facing the fire and the sea with his eyes closed. *How can this be?* He was seeing with her eyes. What else could it be? Her hand left his face, yet he could still see with her eyes. Her fingers trailed down his shoulder and back as her eyes followed the trail. He saw the scar below his shoulder blade from one of his first battles. Her eyes moved lower and – there – he saw the mark. She traced it with her fingers. Two sets of blue interlocking lines that looped at the corners and formed a triangle. Just like the mark on her shoulder. It closed into his vision and he realized she had bent so that it was at eye level. Then it faded from view and he felt her lips gently touch him with a kiss at the place where the mark had formed.

The mark and his vision of it were beyond his comprehension at the moment.

"It was not chance that brought us together this night at this place."

He opened his eyes to find her standing before him. "Nor was it chance that placed the mark upon me." He took her hands into his and turned them so they were palms up. They were ghostly white against the bronze of his skin. Delicate, as if he held a bird in his grasp. "Ye did this."

Her eyes were steady upon him. "Believe me when I say I do not know how this happened, I just know that it has." Her hands folded over his.

There were more important things to consider at the moment. "Whatever the cause there is naught to be done now. I am as trapped by this as you are." He could not blame her for anything that had happened, or would happen, when it was his own honour that demanded he stay. The decision was made when he went into the surf to save her. He would not go back on it now.

Conn went to Niul. "Niul will take you, should things go badly." His words were optimistic at best. He had no chance of winning a fight against a warrior who could kill with a look. He could only hope that he would die with honour, and take Balor with him, or wound him enough that Aine could get away. Conn saddled Niul as she watched.

"Let me be your eyes," she said when he was finished preparing Niul. "It can work. You have seen that it will."

"You would have me fight without honour by using your gifts?"

"I would have you balance the field. Balor certainly will not hesitate to use his gift against you. His gift that is endowed by evil and darkness. Let us fight evil and darkness with goodness and light." Aine grabbed his arm. "I would not have you die needlessly."

"I would hope not to die at all." Conn looked at the sea, fallen back now, as the tide was nearly at its lowest point. He walked to the line where wet sand met dry and looked at the tower. The lightning was gone and the moon played a game of hide and seek with the clouds. A long time had passed since Balor's last cry. He would come, and soon. "Could it be that easy?" he asked Aine who had once more joined him.

"Mayhap easier than you think," she said. "Ye must simply trust in me."

"Trust is not something simply given. Once upon a time I believed in it as I believed in the goodness of man and kings. I have since learned that the only thing worth believing in is your own true worth."

"I believe in you. You have just shared your soul with me by this fire and I know it to be good. Indeed ye now wear the mark of my people, a blessing not lightly given. I have been honest with you in all things, not an easy task for me as my experience with man is not one I treasure." She implored him once more. "Let me give you this."

The clouds moved on and the light of the moon shone down upon them. Conn gazed into her quicksilver eyes and saw nothing to give him pause. They shone with emotion and his heart felt strange within his chest. He lifted a hand to her cheek and she moved it against his palm.

"I will trust you," he said. Before his words were done Balor's war cry joined them. He had come.

* * *

Aine stood by the fire with Niul's reins in her hand. Conn stood a body length away before her. Both of them faced north and Balor who would soon be upon them. Conn wore a strip of linen, torn from his chainse, across his eyes and held his broadsword and shield in his capable hands.

Niul tossed his head and Conn jerked involuntarily in their direction. Aine calmed the horse with a touch and kept her eyes to the north. She sensed Balor in much the same manner the horse did.

Finally, from the shadows, he strode forth. He stood a head taller than Conn, completely bald, and with the one large blue eye in the middle of his forehead. The rest of his face was like that of a man, with a large nose and wide mouth with thick stumps of teeth. His chest was bare and his arms bore wide bands of bronze. He wore leather leggings tied with cross-garters, and low boots. One hand bore a sword and the other a mace. Balor walked directly to where Conn stood, thumped his broad chest with the hilt of his sword and roared.

"Trust in me," Aine said. Her eyes focused on the chain about Balor's neck. Upon it was her keystone that would take her back to her world. She must lay claim to it while the portal was open.

Conn spun his sword in his hands and widened his stance. Aine saw his head move, slightly, up and down, in agreement. He trusted her. She would not fail him.

It was as if he looked through a long deep tunnel. Mayhap it was because of her proximity. She was not as close as before when she showed him the mark. She must stay back to give him room to fight.

As Balor appeared from the darkness and stalked to where he stood, Conn was suddenly glad for the blindfold. Every instinct he possessed had screamed against it when Aine tore the strip from his chainse and placed it over his eyes. He knew now that she was right and he would not have been able to stop himself from staring at the one strange eye in Balor's forehead.

He would be dead before he had a chance to strike a blow at his enemy.

If the eye is his tool to killing then is the eye the sure way to kill him? Conn knew in his heart it was so. To kill Balor he must stab him in the eye. An eye that was a good head taller than he was, he realized, when Balor stopped before him, thumped his chest and roared.

"Trust in me." He heard the words in his mind and nodded his head in response. He gripped his sword. He was ready.

Balor came at him in a rush. The giant's frustration at Conn's blindfold was obvious. Conn realized his perspective on Balor was a little off when he had to bend backwards to block an attack with the mace. He pushed up with his shield and swung his sword at Balor's legs.

Aine must have realized the problem because his perspective suddenly changed. She had moved closer. He must be careful not to bring her into the battle. He could not become tangled with her, or, worse, let Balor grab her once more as a hostage.

He felt the satisfying drag of his sword as it nicked Balor's leg. The giant roared once more in frustration and danced back and away from his thrust. Conn stood upright again and pressed his attack, leading with his shield and following with his sword. Balor's reactions were slower but his reach was greater. While Conn barely brushed at the giant, he had to duck to avoid Balor's swinging mace and thrusting sword that threatened to take his head off if either connected. Still he drove the giant back and knew by his vision that Aine followed.

But they were moving away from the firelight and her vision was dimming with the darkness that surrounded them. Aine was to his right, which meant she could not see what was coming to his left. He could only hope that his warrior's instinct would lead him and his shield would do the job of protecting his side. One blow finally staggered him. Balor had come at him with his mace swinging from the side and it buried itself in the shield. As Balor tried to pull the mace free he pulled Conn's arm with him so as to leave Conn's torso exposed. Conn had no choice but to release his hold on his shield while he ducked and rolled beneath the thrust of Balor's sword. He realized he'd come to his feet on the opposite side of Balor when all he could see was the giant's back and himself beyond.

Balor swung his mace outwards, trying to free the shield. Conn knew Aine was running towards him. Still he must take advantage of Balor's distraction. He gripped his sword with both hands and raised it over his head with the point facing straight out. As he brought the full force of his strength into the downwards motion, he felt the impact of metal against the bone of his thigh. Conn's scream was one of pain, anger and frustration but he kept his grip. The loss of his balance pushed him against Balor and his sword went straight into his eye and pierced through his skull. Balor went to his knees and Conn fell to the side, dragging himself away. He ripped the blindfold from his face and turned in time to see the giant tumble face forwards into the sand, braced up by the hilt of his sword.

Aine rushed to his side. "We must get you away," she said.

"Not without my sword," Conn gasped. His entire side throbbed and blood gushed from the wound in his thigh

"They will come," she said. "Make haste."

He knew not of what she spoke. Yet the urgency in her voice caused a shiver to run down his spine. Aine helped him up and he threw an arm over her shoulder for support. They staggered the few steps to Balor's body. Conn watched as she hurriedly snatched a chain from about the monster's neck then stood back. Conn grasped his sword and struggled to pull it free.

"Come." Her face relayed her fear as her eyes searched the darkness behind him. Conn sheathed his bloody sword. She wrapped her arm around his side and once more they staggered away, leaving a trail of blood behind them.

Conn felt a shiver run down his spine that had nothing to do with the wound in his hip as he dropped to the ground beside the fire. Aine's hands were frantic as she tore his chainse into strips. "We must be away," she said.

Conn grabbed her hand as she attempted to staunch the blood of his wound. "What comes? What else is there that I must fight?"

"You cannot fight against these warriors," she said. She jerked her head and stared out at the beach where Balor's body lay. Conn kept his hand on his sword as his eyes searched the beach for a threat. Aine was terrified of something else. By her actions he knew she was much more frightened of this unknown quantity than she had been of Balor. The fog swirled once more over the water and came their way, closing in on them with menace. What came with it?

"We do not have much time." She went back to her work, her hands quick yet shaking as she padded the wound and wrapped a strip about his thigh. She helped Conn to his feet once more and grabbed Niul's reins.

He heard it then: the sounds of many feet marching against the sand; the steady drip, drip of water; Aine's gasp as she quickly slipped the chain she'd taken from Balor's body over her neck and held the stone linked to it in her hand.

"What is your desire?" She turned her quicksilver eyes upon him and he saw her fear.

Conn squinted his eyes shut and shook his head at her question. Her voice seemed so very far away. He'd lost a lot of blood. It was hard for him to stand. When he opened his eyes he saw hands, reaching towards them with flesh falling from grasping, bony fingers. He shook his head once more. Aine stepped to him, stood before him, and looked into his eyes.

"What is your desire?"

There was one thing he wanted more than anything. It was the thing that brought him to this shore on this night. "I desire peace."

Aine smiled at him. "Then you shall have it." She wrapped her hand around the stone and said three words that were foreign to his ears. A bright light burst forth from her hand and blinded him. He felt himself falling.

There is peace in death . . .

Aine smiled as the portal opened and welcomed her to her home world. Niul danced a bit as she urged him forth, but her hands on the reins were sure even though the burden in her arms was heavy. Conn let out a sigh against her face as they passed through the gate. He was unconscious from his wound, and from the passage. She could not wait to see the laughter on his face when he awakened to find himself in the land of the Fae, where he would find peace.

The Feast of Beauty

Helen Scott Taylor

County Cork, Ireland

One

Surprisingly, wrap-around sunglasses looked rather good with a top hat, but Kate wasn't so sure about bare feet and board shorts with a tailcoat. The combination made the man look only half-dressed. But he was so mouth-wateringly gorgeous she decided the fewer clothes he wore the better.

He stood on the front steps of Knock House and raised his arms to attract attention. The gesture was unnecessary. Every woman in the vicinity was already staring at him, along with most of the men.

"Welcome to my domain, my friends. I'm Esras Mac Lir, descendant of the sea god Lir, and Fairy King of County Cork and the Celtic Sea."

Incredulous silence fell over the crowd, broken only by the birds twittering in the roses covering the front of the Georgian mansion, and the distant rumble of waves breaking against the rocky headland on which the house stood.

"I'm delighted to welcome London's Barthurst Productions into my domain. They're going to film an episode of their award-winning travel show *Claudia's Magic Carpet* at my Midsummer Feast of Beauty. I can assure you that tomorrow's feast will be a magical experience for everyone."

Peter Hurst, the producer and Kate's boss, leaned closer to Kate and whispered, "You sure this guy isn't a retired rock star? He's got that touch of megalomania that usually goes with too much money and a lifetime of sex, booze and drugs."

"As far as I know he's just a wealthy eccentric with an interest in Irish mythology. He sounded fairly normal on the phone when I set up the shoot," she replied. Although she'd have booked him to film at the Feast of Beauty no matter how weird he'd sounded. She had her own reasons for wanting to visit this part of Ireland.

"If the Barthurst TV people would like to come forward, my right-hand man Faelan will show you to your rooms." Esras then doffed his dove-grey top hat and bowed with an elegant sweep of his arm. He sported just-got-out-of-bed hair, as though a woman had been clutching it in the throes of passion. The spiky strands were light brown, but as he moved, his hair gleamed with unusual silver highlights.

Peter started forwards while Kate hung back, checking her clipboard for the long list of jobs that she as production assistant had to complete before the shoot the following morning. She had at least two hours of typing to do, what with Claudia's script changes and the shot cards. And it was vital she found time this evening to go down to the little village of Knocknapog half a mile away.

Her grandmother had been born in the village and had lived there until she'd married and moved to England. Kate cradled the teardrop pearl pendant her grandmother had left her, rubbing her thumb over the smooth pink surface. Grandma's last wish had been that Kate should bring the pearl back here. The trouble was, Kate had no idea what she was supposed to do with it now she had arrived.

Two

By the time Kate got round to going to find her room, the only other member of the production company who hadn't been settled was the *star*, Claudia Ravelle. She'd arrived late in a luxury limousine, which hadn't been budgeted for.

Kate mounted the front steps of Knock House a few yards

behind Claudia. The clicking of Claudia's stiletto heels came to an abrupt halt. "Wow," she murmured under her breath. Kate stopped and glanced around, silently echoing the sentiment. She didn't know which way to look first. The floor was an intricate mosaic of tiny blue, green, turquoise and white tiles in a pattern of froth-tipped waves. The walls glowed with a detailed mural of some fantastical palace beneath the sea. White horses pulled a gold coach bearing a smiling crowned man, while multi-coloured fish and sea creatures frolicked around him.

Claudia gave a moan of appreciation. Kate tore her eyes from the artwork to follow the other woman's gaze. The object of Claudia's desire leaned against a wall wearing board shorts, his long golden hair trailing over muscular shoulders.

"Is that Esras?" Claudia whispered.

"Him? No. That's Faelan, I think." Kate could hardly believe she had missed such a gorgeous man earlier. She must have been too focused on Esras to notice anyone else.

As they approached Faelan, he stepped forwards. "May I show you to your rooms, ladies?"

Claudia paused in front of the guy and ran a long hot-pink fingernail across his chest. "I'd like to meet Esras first, big boy," she simpered. Kate winced with embarrassment.

With a nod, Faelan opened a door for them. "*King* Esras is in here."

"Maybe I'll see you later, Faelan," Claudia said in a breathy voice.

Although Kate had a lot of work to do, her curiosity got the better of her, and she followed Claudia into the room. The seascape painted on the ceiling was impressive, but it was the huge gold throne set with mother-of-pearl and sparkling green gems that made her mouth drop open – and the man sitting in it.

Gone were the top hat, sunglasses and jacket. Esras now wore only the board shorts and a loose green shirt with half the buttons undone, revealing tantalizing flashes of his smooth sculpted chest. Now she was closer, she could see that his skin was sun-kissed gold and his eyes an impossible glittering green. He was lean and muscular with a sheen of silver-gold hair dusting his forearms and legs. Rainbows danced along a string of flat mother-of-pearl beads around his neck.

Esras rose and came to meet them. His gaze passed straight over Claudia to settle on Kate. "You must be—"

"Claudia Ravelle," Claudia said, stepping in front of Kate. "I present the travel show." She swept back her hair seductively. "You might remember me from the hit series *Murder Me with Magic*."

"Of course. Delighted," Esras said with a brief frown that came and went so fast Kate wondered if she'd imagined it. He bowed then signalled to Faelan. "I'm sure you must be tired, Claudia. Faelan will show you to your room."

Claudia smiled a bemused smile. She slipped her arm through Faelan's and was swept out of the door without realizing she'd been summarily dismissed.

The clicking of Claudia's heels and her occasional throaty laugh faded into the distance. Esras angled his head. For long moments, he stared at Kate with those incredible green eyes as though he could see right into her mind and into her soul.

Her hand wrapped around her grandma's pearl and it seemed to pulse inside her fist. It was almost as if the pearl had come to life.

"You're Kate Sullivan, aren't you? We spoke on the phone." A slow smile spread across his face like the sun rising on a new world. She blinked. For a moment, it looked as though flickering rainbows danced around him.

"How did you recognize me before you heard my voice?" she asked.

His smile widened and he flicked up his eyebrows in a wouldn't-you-like-to-know expression. "Let me show you to your room." He went to the door and held out a hand to her. After an awkward pause, she slipped her fingers into his because it seemed rude not to.

She stopped at the bottom of the stairs, disoriented by the surroundings, wondering at the significance of his holding her hand. He obviously had an unconventional attitude to intimacy. Was it possible he expected to jump straight into bed with her? Heat blossomed low in Kate's belly and her skin felt too tight. She cleared her throat. "What about my bag?"

"That's already been taken to your room." He gave her an amused smile. "Don't worry. I'm not going to eat you, Kate."

"Oh." She bit her lip.

He tightened his grip on her hand and tugged her up the grand staircase in the centre of the entrance hall.

When they reached the top of the stairs, Esras led her along a wide corridor, threw open a door, then released her hand and stood back for her to enter.

The huge bedroom had a pearly sheen to the white walls, while the bedding, upholstery and carpet were all marine shades of green and blue. A king-size bed with a white and gold headboard dominated the space, the rest of the furniture continuing the white and gold theme. She was pleased the room contained a desk that she could turn into a workstation. She preferred not to share the production team's mobile office. It always became a pigsty within hours of arriving on location.

As promised, her battered suitcase and bag sat on the bed.

"Bathroom's over there." Esras pointed at a door on the far side of the room.

She rested her hand on her laptop bag. "Thank you. This is . . . luxurious." Kate gazed around knowing she would have little time to enjoy the comfort. She waited for Esras to leave so she could get on with her work.

When he didn't move, she glanced back at him. His gaze was fixed on her pearl pendant, a curious expression on his face. "What brought you home, Kate?"

She stared at him, taken aback for a moment. "Home? Did you know my grandma? Do you know something about the pendant?"

His knowing gaze returned to her face. "Don't you?"

She shook her head slowly. "I didn't know my grandmother was born in Knocknapog until six months ago when she died and left me her pendant." She cupped the gleaming pink teardrop in her palm. "I thought it was just jewellery. But there's something strange about the pearl. I feel . . . antsy when I take it off, but it doesn't feel quite right to be wearing it either."

"That's because the pearl wasn't made for you. You should have your own, Kate." He opened the door and held his hand out to her again. "Come with me and I'll show you what it is."

She hesitated a moment, but she'd come here for just this reason, to find out more about the pearl. He led her back down the stairs, then along an inner hallway to an older part of the house. He stopped outside a low wooden door and snapped back the three bolts securing it. An unearthly glow seeped into the darkened hall as he pulled the door wide. She followed him down a narrow winding stairway, the only light a luminous glow from the shells embedded in the walls.

After a little while, he paused and turned. "Do you need a rest? It's quite a drop, two hundred steps."

At her headshake, he moved on. The rushing of water sounded in the distance. As they descended farther, the noise grew louder and a cool breeze carried the scent of the sea up the stairwell.

"I've always loved the sea," Kate said, almost to herself.

Esras turned and flashed her a smile. "Of course. You're one of Lir's people."

Even as a little frisson of excitement passed through her, she shook her head. Esras had introduced himself as a descendant of the sea god Lir. Now he was trying to involve her in his delusion. *But if she thought that, why did she instinctively trust him?*

They emerged into an underground cavern lit only by the same luminous glow as the steps. The sea hissed in and out of an opening in the rocks. They had descended from the top of the cliff, where the manor house stood, to sea level and must now be inside a cave under the cliff.

She followed him along a tunnel leading deeper into the rock and they came out in a small grotto. Above the murmur of the sea, she heard a swishing, sucking sound. They stopped at a circular opening in the rock floor. Water swirled inside the hole, flickers of light and dark dancing in its depths. "The Whirlpool of Lir," Esras whispered.

The pearl resting on Kate's chest lifted towards the well, tugging at the chain around her neck. "Ahh!" She grasped it and hung on as it tried to jump from her hand.

"Don't be frightened." He put an arm around her waist, pulling her against his side. Her skin hummed with his nearness and she leaned into him, enjoying the thrill of touching him even while her heart pounded with uncertainty.

"Give me Lir's favour." Esras held out a hand.

"My grandmother's pearl? What are you going to do with it?"

"Trust me." He leaned closer and stroked the back of his fingers across her cheek. She breathed in the scents of salt, sea and fresh air from his skin, combined with a musky masculine fragrance. She stared at him, mesmerized, and her worries drifted away.

She unfastened the chain from her neck and placed it in his palm. He then removed the pearl from the chain. Before she realized what he was going to do, he dropped the pearl into the swirling waters.

"No!" Kate put a hand over her mouth, staring into the water. She turned her shocked gaze on Esras. "What have you done? Grandma left that to me."

"She wanted you to bring her pearl back here," he said gently.

"I know, but—"

"She wanted Lir's favour returned to him."

Kate stared into the water, tears pricking her eyes. The one memento she'd had of her grandmother was lost forever.

"Kate." Esras stroked some hair that had escaped from her ponytail back behind her ear. "She wanted you to have your own favour from Lir . . . from me."

Esras crouched and scooped a handful of the surging water into his palm. Instead of leaking between his fingers, the water formed a ball. He shaped it, scraping away blobs of water as though they were jelly. When only a small tear-shaped piece of water remained, he stroked it, chanting under his breath. Rainbows danced around him, glowed on the mother-of-pearl at his neck, glittered in the heart of the water droplet in his palm.

Eventually, the colours faded and the cavern was once again lit only by the luminous glow from the walls. Esras held up a pink-tinged pearl teardrop and then threaded it back on her chain. "This one will feel right because I made the favour for you. Wear it by your heart and you will never be far from me – or the sea."

Kate let him refasten the chain around her neck and rubbed her fingers across the pearl. Tingles danced up her hand, spread across her skin, setting her nerves on fire until she longed to feel the soothing cool stroke of the sea over her body.

"How did you make this from water?" she asked.

"Pearls are always shaped by the sea, Kate."

She stared down at the pearl, her mind churning with conflicting emotions. She prided herself on being practical and down-to-earth. The things Esras said and did clashed with everything she believed, yet she couldn't deny what she'd seen with her own eyes – could she?

His fingertips slid beneath her chin and lifted her face so she couldn't avoid meeting the bottomless green of his eyes.

"I'm your King, Kate. You belong with me."

Three

Kate spent a terrible night tossing and turning, unable to sleep. The image of Esras with rainbows dancing around him plagued her mind. By morning, she had convinced herself that the rainbow light had simply been reflections from his mother-of-pearl necklace and his making the pearl had been a trick. He obviously hadn't thrown her grandmother's pearl in the water at all. He'd hidden it. Then by sleight of hand, he'd made her believe he'd created another one.

If he was loony enough to believe he was descended from a sea god, he was likely to be the type of man who'd pretend to have magical powers.

And like a complete idiot, she'd allowed herself to be sucked into his fantasy world. After working in television for two years, she should know better than to believe everything she saw.

Kate joined her colleagues and sat at one of the plastic tables by the catering van with her styrofoam cup of tea and an egg and bacon breakfast roll. She breathed the sea air, marvelling at the fantastic view of white-topped waves on the green Celtic Sea. From the rocky headland where Knock House stood, the land sloped down to the village of Knocknapog: a small harbour surrounded by a scatter of slate-roofed cottages with bobbing fishing boats riding the waves in the bay.

On the lawn in front of Knock House, Esras' people and some of the villagers had started to erect stalls and tents for the Midsummer Feast.

As if her thinking of Esras had summoned him, he stepped out of the house, rested his hands on his hips, and surveyed the feast-day preparations. "Grand. You're all doing a fine job," he shouted to the workers. He had on his dove-grey tailcoat minus the top hat, this time with Hawaiian-pattern board shorts. His gaze found her and a smile kicked up the corners of his mouth. Kate's stomach did a hot flip as she remembered his hard muscular arm around her waist, pulling her against his side. She quickly looked away and tried to pretend she hadn't noticed him.

As he sauntered over to her, the pearl started to pulse against her chest. She ignored it, telling herself it was probably just vibrating with her racing heart.

"How are you doing this fine morning? Did you sleep well, my love?" His term of endearment caused a few raised eyebrows among the production team who were breakfasting with her. Kate's instinct was to tell him that she wasn't *his love*, but if she protested too much it would only confirm everyone's lascivious suspicions.

"I slept well, thank you," she replied. "The room's very comfortable."

"Wonderful." Esras rubbed his hands together and glanced around at her colleagues. "I'm expecting you all to dress up for the Feast of Beauty. I have traditional costumes for you to choose from."

"Ohh," Claudia said, slipping on sunglasses as she joined them. "Did I hear something about costumes? What fun. I adore dressing up." She put an arm through Esras' as she accepted a cup of tea from Peter. "When can we see the clothes, Esras darling?"

"Right now if you like." Esras turned towards the house, taking Claudia with him. The female members of the production team followed eagerly, while the two cameramen climbed wearily to their feet and trudged behind.

Kate had no intention of dressing up. If she did, she might end up on camera, and she hated herself on film. Although she didn't want to see the costumes, the sight of Claudia hanging eagerly on Esras' arm annoyed her. She stuffed the last of her roll in her mouth and washed it down with a gulp of tea, then followed the rest of her colleagues inside.

Everyone had trailed through to the back of the house to a room full of costumes. Each outfit was carefully covered and hanging on a metal rail. What kind of man had a storage room full of costumes in his house for goodness sake? Surely that proved he was weird.

Peter looked puzzled, while the cameramen grabbed the first things that came to hand and retreated quickly. Claudia and the other women *oohed* and *ahhed* over sparkly dresses while Kate watched from the doorway.

Esras came to her and caught hold of her hand. "I have the perfect dress for you. It's the same sapphire blue as your eyes."

She stood her ground when he tried to pull her into the room. "I grew out of playing dress-up years ago."

The corners of his mouth dipped sadly although his eyes continued to sparkle with mirth. "All work and no play makes Kate a dull girl."

His words hit a nerve. "Then I guess I'm dull," she snapped and yanked her hand away from him. How would a wealthy eccentric like Esras understand that normal people didn't get anywhere in life by wasting time playing dress-up and fantasizing about magic?

Work hard and you'll get your reward in heaven, her mother had always said. And Kate wasn't getting any work done watching Claudia fawn over stupid dresses.

Kate stomped back outside, found her clipboard, and started ticking off the jobs she had completed.

Three hours later, all her colleagues and Esras' people were in costume and set to go. Esras walked regally down the four steps from his front door garbed in a gleaming silver and emerald cape over a pearly grey suit. Despite the theatrical costume, he still managed to look damn sexy. He wore a gold crown on his head decorated with mother-of-pearl and huge sparkling green gems. The stones looked like emeralds, but couldn't be; otherwise, the thing would be locked up in a vault. Esras' people had carried out his throne, and it was set upon a dais beside a smaller throne decorated with tiny pink and yellow shells.

"OK, people, are we all ready?" the director shouted. Kate glanced down at her schedule, pleased that they were starting on time despite the fact that most of the team had had to change clothes.

Dressed in an elaborate off-the-shoulder gown of silver and gold with a scattering of tiny crystals across the bodice, Claudia introduced the episode before the crew filmed Esras taking his throne.

"And now, we'll witness the highlight of the festivities here today. King Esras will choose his Feast of Beauty queen," Claudia said in her silky on-camera voice. She turned to Esras expectantly, obviously keen to be called up to sit beside him. A tense silence fell over Esras' people and the watching crowd of villagers. Kate had assumed Esras would select Claudia. She had even pencilled Claudia's name in at this point on her schedule. Still, she couldn't deny a niggle of . . . what? Disappointment? Jealousy?

Esras remained silent for so long that people began to shift restlessly and the director muttered his annoyance. Kate stared at her clipboard, bracing herself to hear Esras call Claudia to be his Feast of Beauty Queen. Finally she looked up at him. His eyes were fixed on her, a hint of a smile on his lips. She seemed to fall into the green depths. A strange tingle that felt like bubbly water raced across her skin. The faint hum of voices and the noise of the feast day faded until all she could hear was the gentle hiss of the sea.

"Why are you ignoring me, Kate? You knew I'd choose you." Esras' words whispered on the wind.

Kate stared at him wide eyed. "I didn't . . ."

"Kate is my queen," Esras announced, and she snapped out of her trance with a jolt. Everyone was looking at her, some smiling, others with raised eyebrows, Claudia with daggers flashing from her eyes.

"You bitch," Claudia grated under her breath.

"You can't have Kate," Peter said, striding forwards. "She's not dressed up. It's much better if Claudia's your queen. It doesn't really matter who you have, does it? It's just pretend."

Esras leaned back and crossed his arms. The temperature dropped. Tendrils of sea mist crawled over the cliff into the garden and drifted between the stalls like wraiths bringing a damp salty taste to the air.

After a long awkward silence, Peter heaved a resigned sigh. "Go and put on a damn dress, Kate. And hurry up."

Kate hesitated in an agony of indecision. She didn't want to be filmed, yet she could barely contain the shivers of pleasure running through her. *Esras wanted her to be his queen.* Of course, she wouldn't have minded if he'd chosen Claudia. After all, this was partly being staged for the television show.

"Kate," Peter said in a warning tone. "I'm getting old here."

"I didn't choose a dress," she said weakly.

"Look on your bed," Esras said, his eyes gleaming with amusement.

Taking the stairs two at a time, Kate ran up to her room with Claudia's make-up artist Tina on her heels.

On her bed, she found a beautiful deep-blue dress with a

satin bodice decorated with a sparkling beading design and overlaid with tulle draping. "Oh, yes," Tina said. "The man has got an eye for colour. This will go perfectly with your dark hair and blue eyes."

After stripping off her jeans and T-shirt, Kate stood obediently while Tina fastened her into the dress. She squeaked in protest when Tina undid her bra and pulled the straps off her arms. "I can't go out there bra-less." Her mother would never be able to hold her head up in church again if her friends saw the show.

"The dress has spaghetti straps." Tina held up Kate's tatty bra with a pointed look.

With a sigh of acceptance, Kate plopped down in front of the dressing table. She watched in the mirror while Tina brushed her long dark hair and quickly applied make-up. Her teardrop pearl gleamed in the reflection, tempting her to think of Esras.

When Kate stood up for inspection, Tina raised her eyebrows. "You look pretty good when you make an effort. You have the most amazing pearly skin. Watch your back, though. Claudia's going to be as mad as hell with you for stealing her thunder."

Holding up the hem of her dress, Kate raced down the stairs and out the front door. The chatter outside hushed, making her pause. Everyone stared at her. One of the cameramen gave her a thumbs-up, and Peter smiled. "OK," the director said, "keep it steady. You're not running to catch a bus."

As if in a dream, Kate listened to the instructions she normally heard from the other side of the camera. On her cue, she started walking towards Esras. He rose from his throne and held out a hand to her. Her heart thundered as his fingers slid around hers and he steadied her as she stepped on to the dais. A group of Esras' people surrounded the throne. The beautiful women shone in brightly coloured dresses while most of the men wore grey or white. Faelan produced a small gold circlet decorated with tiny blue shells, and Esras placed it upon her head. His fingers lingered against her hair, stroking the strands back from her eyes.

"There you are now," Esras whispered. "Doesn't that feel right, my love." His fingers brushed her shoulders and then trailed down her arms before curling around her hands.

The cameras and the people watching faded away as Kate gazed up into the emerald depths of his eyes. Faelan started to chant in a language she didn't recognize, while the rest of Esras' people joined in with occasional words.

Kate couldn't take her gaze from Esras' face. She had thought he was not much older than she was, but she had been wrong. His green eyes held a depth of knowledge that belied his youthful appearance. Even as warmth swirled through her body at the thought of touching his golden skin, a brush of warning slid down her spine. He touched a deep part of her that she'd pushed to the back of her mind and locked away, the fanciful part of her that adored her grandmother and made her mother angry.

Faelan stopped speaking and stepped aside. Esras pressed his lips to hers in a quick chaste kiss for the cameras, which was over before Kate had a chance to enjoy it, and then handed her into the smaller shell-clad throne.

Facing the onlookers, Faelan announced, "King Esras Mac Lir, rightful heir of the sea god Lir, has chosen his queen. All hail the Sea-Fairy King and Queen."

While Esras' people and the villagers cheered, Kate watched her colleagues working. Her cheeks flushed to think she would be the star of this episode of the series. She prayed her mother would be proud of her performance and not embarrassed by it.

Claudia strode forward and thrust a microphone under Faelan's nose. "I suppose the King chooses a different queen every year," she said, casting Kate a malicious glance. "Presumably it just depends on who happens to be *available* and *willing*."

Faelan frowned at her before glancing at Esras for permission to answer. "No. When the King pledges himself to his queen, he does so for life."

Four

Faelan's words took a few seconds to sink into Kate's brain. She blinked at him, opened her mouth to speak, and then closed it again. Surely she'd misheard. When Faelan stepped away to be interviewed by Claudia, Kate turned to Esras. "I'm confused. Don't you choose a different queen at each Midsummer's Feast?"

The hint of mischief that usually sparkled in his eyes faded to be replaced by a deadly serious gleam that sent flashes of warning through her. "No, Kate. I usually preside over the festivities alone."

She shook her head. "Then why choose a queen this year?"

"Because *you* came. I told you last night: you belong with me."

Conflicting emotions ricocheted around inside her, stealing her breath. "But that ceremony . . . it wasn't . . ." She swallowed so hard her throat hurt.

"The Union of Opposites ceremony bound us as one," he said.

Kate jumped up, her legs trembling, plucked off her delicate gold crown and tossed it down on to the throne. When Esras reached for her hand, she snatched it away. "This doesn't have any standing in law. I can leave whenever I want."

Kate had expected a clever reply to her angry tirade; instead, tiny lines formed between Esras' eyebrows as if he were puzzled. "But you accepted my invitation to be queen."

"I didn't know you were serious!"

Suddenly she realized the crowd had fallen silent. A quick glance around confirmed her fear that everyone was watching them – and even worse, the camera was still rolling. Heat flooded her cheeks, part anger, part embarrassment. When her mother saw Kate's *starring role* on television, she was going to have a coronary.

"Come inside. I'm not discussing this in public." Kate stepped off the dais gingerly, wary of her unsteady legs, and tried to keep her expression calm as she headed for the front door of Knock House.

The crowd stepped aside to let her pass. Most of Esras' people eyed her with confusion, a few with disappointment. The villagers looked curious while her production-crew colleagues positively gloated over the unexpected conflict that added spice to the show.

As soon as she and Esras were inside with the door closed, she rounded on him. "What in hell's name do you think you're playing at? This is a performance; we're pretending."

He opened his mouth but she didn't give him a chance to answer. "We've only known each other for a few hours. I can't imagine why you thought there was anything serious between us."

"Calm down, Kate."

"Don't try to tell me it's got anything to do with the pearl you made. You might be able to fool most people with your magic tricks. I'm not so easily suckered."

Esras set his crown on a table, then unfastened his cloak and draped it over a chair before turning back to stare at her. His assessing gaze probed her. "Why are you so angry, Kate?"

She threw up her hands in exasperation. "First you pretended to throw Grandma's pearl down a well. Then you conned me into believing you'd made another one *especially* for me. Now you've got me to dress up and go through some freaky ceremony, and you're trying to tell me to take it seriously. You're nuts!"

"Why are you frightened of following your heart?"

Kate pressed her fingers to her temples. "I *am* following my heart. Working in television *is* my dream. I'm a damn good production assistant."

"Do you enjoy your job?" Esras asked in an annoyingly reasonable tone of voice.

Who did the man think he was? A psychiatrist? "Of course I do," she snapped back.

Esras stepped closer to her, bringing with him the salty fresh-air scent of the sea. "Does your work bring you pleasure? Does your work make you feel more alive than you've ever felt before?"

"Don't be ridiculous. Everyone knows working in television is tough to start with. The rewards come later." And there was no way she could give up her dream job. Not when her parents had subsidized her by letting her live at home until she moved up the career ladder far enough to support herself.

"I only invited Barthurst Productions here because of you, Kate."

"What?" She blinked at him.

"The first time I spoke to you on the phone, I heard the music of the sea in your voice and knew who you were."

He stepped closer and raised a hand. His fingertips brushed the teardrop pearl hanging in the valley between her breasts. Tendrils of heat shivered across her skin.

"You're one of the Rainbow People descended directly from King Manannan Mac Lir and Queen Fand." He kneeled at her feet and pressed a kiss to her hand. "You have more right to rule the people of Lir than I do, my love."

Five

Kate's anger dissolved at the note of sincerity in Esras' voice. However crazy she thought him, he obviously believed everything he'd told her. Her head wanted to be mad, her heart had softened the moment he knelt and kissed her hand.

She sighed. "Oh, Esras, can't you see this isn't going to work? I have a job. I'm leaving with the Barthurst people tomorrow."

He climbed to his feet again. She didn't resist when he eased her closer and enfolded her in his arms. She pressed her cheek to the hard plain of his chest, breathing his enticing male fragrance while listening to the steady beat of his heart. When his lips touched her temple, she closed her eyes, not wanting to admit that she could easily get used to this.

"Kate, why don't you want to accept who you are? Your grandmother must have told you something about her life in Ireland."

Happy memories of Grandma swam inside Kate's head like a shoal of sparkly fish. She remembered sitting at her grandmother's feet when she was a little girl. While her mother worked, her grandmother had cared for her. The old woman had spun such magical tales of fairies and leprechauns and people who lived in a city beneath the sea – the Rainbow People.

Kate's breath trembled as memories she had denied and tried to forget flooded back. She remembered ribbons of coloured light flowing around Grandma as she spoke. How the old woman would capture the light in her hands and mould dolphins and seahorses out of the rainbows.

Then one day her mother had come home early and caught the end of a story. There had been screaming, shouting, and tears. And no more stories. Ireland had become a taboo subject.

That's when she'd been sent to the convent school, and the endless chores and lectures about hard work had started. She could hear her mother's favourite advice: *Forget your grandmother's fanciful ideas. Work hard and you'll get your reward in heaven.*

"You must have had an inkling that there was something here for you, or you wouldn't have come," Esras whispered.

"I came to find out about the pearl." Had she also hoped to recapture the sense of magic from Grandma's stories?

Esras' fingers stroked circles on her back, managing to both soothe and stimulate in equal measure. "Do you trust me, Kate?"

Her head said no because her mother would disapprove of Esras and everything he stood for. But even as the word "no" formed in her mind, from a level deeper than mind where instinct ruled the word "yes" rose to her lips.

He withdrew slightly and cupped her face in his hands, staring down into her eyes. "If you trust me, *really* trust me, to keep you safe, I'll give you unquestionable proof of who you are." He leaned down and brushed his lips lightly across hers.

A shock passed through her out of all proportion to the chaste kiss. The tight, hot ball of yearning in her stomach expanded, making it hard to breathe. She'd had boyfriends before, but she'd never felt this immediate, overwhelming need to touch and be touched.

"Kate," he prompted. "Do you want proof of who you are?"

She sucked in a breath, held it a moment before she had the control to speak. "Yes," she whispered. "Show me."

Six

Esras took Kate down the spiral stairs to the sea cave beneath Knock House again. She didn't ask him how he intended to prove that she belonged to a race of sea fairies. Just asking such a question validated the crazy idea.

In the cave, Kate inhaled the salty sea air and paused to enjoy the rhythmic swish as the water hissed through the opening that led out to the vastness of the Celtic Sea.

She glanced around but saw nothing other than the undulating water and the rocky shelves and nooks in the cave wall that she'd seen the first time they came down. "Where is this evidence?"

"Patience, my love," he said with a smile. "We need to get in the water."

"What? Swim?" Kate stared into the shadowy green depths. As a child, she'd adored swimming in the sea. After years of living in London, she'd almost forgotten the pleasure of sand beneath her toes and the power of the sea moving around her body.

Kate looked down at the silky blue dress, which was the most impractical garment she'd ever worn and certainly unsuitable to swim in. "I haven't got a bathing suit."

"You don't need one. Just take off your dress."

Kate's eyebrows shot up. He must have noticed she wasn't wearing a bra. "If you think I'm skinny-dipping with you, you've got another think coming."

His eyes slid down her body, lingering on her barely covered breasts; he gave a wry grin. "Can't blame a guy for trying."

After shedding his grey jacket, he unbuttoned his silky shirt before pulling it off, leaving himself bare-chested. He held out the shirt. "Put this on. It's not ideal to wear for swimming, but it's better than a long dress."

He turned his back. Kate quickly slipped out of her dress and draped it over a rock, before donning the shirt. At least she was wearing panties that could pass for bikini bottoms.

Esras turned back and scanned her from head to foot appreciatively. Then he flicked open the button on his trousers and began to undress himself. A burst of shocking hot need arrowed through Kate. She should turn around while he undressed, but she couldn't take her eyes off him as he slid the grey trousers down his thighs and stepped out of them. His underwear was plain white cotton. She stared for so long that by the time she managed to tear her gaze away her cheeks were flaming.

Crouching, he scooped water over his head. Her eyes tracked the drips that trickled from his hair to his chest and snaked down his golden skin over the ridges and dips of his muscular torso to soak into his underwear.

When she looked back at his face, his eyes sparkled and his lips curved in a wicked smile.

"You tease," she accused.

He gave her a satisfied male grin and held out his hand.

She hesitated. "We can't be long. The director will go ballistic if we don't go back soon."

Esras shrugged. "There's plenty going on at the feast for him to film." He held out his fingers. "Hold on to my hand until I tell you it's safe to let go."

"But if we're only going swimming . . ."

Esras' smile dropped away. The serious intensity she'd seen in his eyes earlier returned. "Trust me, my love. Hold my hand."

"What are we going to do?"

"All I can promise you is that you'll enjoy it." Clasping her hand firmly, he stepped into the water. Kate followed, the first shock of cold quickly passing as she went deeper.

They swam towards the cave opening, Esras pulling her while she swam one-handed. Sunlight glinted off the ripples as they emerged from the shadows. The Celtic Sea spread out in front of them for as far as they could see.

He pulled her closer, treading water. "Now, we go down."

She looked down through the water at the rays of sunlight painting wavering green-gold streaks across his body. He moved behind her and slid an arm around her waist, holding her loosely against his chest. She filled her lungs and they ducked beneath the surface.

He angled them down, swimming surprisingly fast out to sea. She scanned the area, expecting to see whatever it was he wanted to show her before they had to return to the surface. Fish slid among fluttering fronds of kelp and seaweed, while even down here rays of sun pierced the water with golden warmth.

Her lungs started to burn and panic quivered in her muscles. Esras was still descending. They were so deep now, she wasn't sure she could hold her breath long enough to reach the surface again. She should have told him that she was out of practice. She hadn't been swimming for years. She struggled in his grasp, but his arm only tightened around her waist. She tried to turn, see his face, signal her distress, but he kept going down so fast that the momentum prevented her from escaping his grip.

When she was certain she couldn't hold her breath a moment longer his voice slid into her mind. "Relax and stop fighting it, my love. Trust me."

The last air leaked from her lungs in a shower of tiny bubbles that raced away to the surface. In that moment, a strange calm came over her. She stopped struggling and closed her eyes. The water skimmed her breasts and legs, Esras' warm chest pressed tightly to her back, his hard muscles rippling against her as he swam. She became aware of his heart beating, sure and steady.

Water filled her mouth and nose. She waited . . . not for pain and death, because she knew they wouldn't come.

"Breathe." Esras' voice whispered into her head, soft as a caress. And she obeyed him.

Strength and energy flooded into her with the water. Her nerves tingled, blood surged. She heard sounds she hadn't noticed before, squeaks and clicks and deep rumbles and booms that echoed through the water.

She tried to turn to smile at him but he held her tight.

"We're going to ride a current. Be ready."

Ahead the water plunged and churned, dragging at the seaweed and scattering debris like a storm. She tensed as they approached; then they were sucked into it, being tossed and buffeted by the current, moving so fast Kate couldn't see anything but foaming water.

Esras wrapped his other arm around her, hugging her tightly to his body. She felt as though she was white-water rafting without the raft.

"When I tell you to, swim hard," he said inside her head. "Now."

Kate kicked and pulled with her arms for all she was worth. Esras' muscles flexed against her back as he swam with one arm, holding her with the other. After they broke away from the turmoil, the sudden peace of the still water came as a relief. He loosed his arms, releasing her, and let her float beside him. For the first time since they'd dived, she saw him. Her breath caught in her lungs. Everything about him had become more beautiful beneath the water. His hair gleamed with a patina of silver, his skin glowed pale gold and his green eyes shone like starlight through emeralds.

"You're gorgeous, Kate," he said.

She'd been so entranced with Esras, it hadn't occurred to her that *she* might look different. The buttons on the silk shirt she was wearing had come unfastened, but she hardly registered that her breasts were bare. She was mesmerized by the subtle play of colours across her opalescent skin.

Esras gathered a handful of her long hair and held it in front of her face so she saw the gleaming polished ebony strands. He stroked his fingertips across her cheek, traced her jaw. "I wish you could see your eyes as well. They put sapphires to shame," he said.

His fingers trailed down her neck and along her collarbone, drifting lower to the swell of her breasts.

Kate wanted to tell Esras how luscious he looked, but she didn't know how to speak underwater. Instead, she reached out and slid her palms over his shoulders and chest, revelling in the solid strength of his muscles.

His arms closed around her. He drew her closer and kissed her forehead and her cheeks. Then his mouth covered hers. His lips were firm and cool, but his tongue was hot in contrast to the cool seawater as she opened her mouth and he deepened the kiss.

Too soon, Esras pulled away. "You're so distracting. You nearly made me forget why I brought you here."

Kate raised her eyebrows and pointed at herself. Hadn't he wanted to prove to her that she was different? He'd certainly done that. Whatever decisions she made about her life when they returned to the air, she would never be the same person again.

"Try to speak to me. Focus on your pearl as you think what you want to say," he said.

She put her fingers on the teardrop pearl against her chest and concentrated. "Hello, sexy."

He laughed, a rumble in the water as well as the sound in her head. "Hello, gorgeous. You learn fast."

He kissed the tip of her nose, his fingers grazing tantalizingly low across her belly. He stilled, staring into her eyes. A hot needy tension thrummed between them. "I really want to take you back to my bed, but before we leave I must show you your heritage."

Seven

They swam side by side until they reached the edge of a cliff beneath the sea. Esras stopped and released Kate's hand. "We're going deeper now, so I need to make some lanterns." He cupped his hands together as if modelling clay, then spread his palms to release a glowing ball. It floated beside them while he made four more in the same way.

Esras took her hand, guiding her down vertically. The lanterns floated on ahead to light their way. Instead of the water getting colder as they went deeper, it became warmer. Finally, Esras stopped and pointed down at the valley floor.

All Kate saw was the seabed below them. She frowned at him.

"Touch your pearl, Kate."

She wrapped her fingers around her pearl and a veil lifted before her eyes. In the valley below, a city of glowing white houses appeared. She pulled her hand from his and swam on. Her heart thudded with excitement. This must be the underwater city from Grandma's stories.

Multicoloured mosaic floors gleamed, while bright murals decorated the walls – similar to the decorations inside Knock House.

But where were the people?

Kate reached the seabed and floated down between the buildings to street level. From higher up, she'd seen only colours and shapes. Down here, she noticed the buildings were falling down, the mosaic floors fractured. Heaps of sand and shells lay in the corners of empty rooms. Seaweed and sea creatures had moved in, growing between the rocks of the tumbledown walls and the cracks in the tiles.

It was deserted.

Her heart contracted painfully and her eyes pricked with tears that were lost in the sea. These had been her people. She knew it as surely as she knew the sun rose every morning and went down at night.

Esras floated down at her side, an eddy of sand swirling about him.

"What's happened to them?" she cried.

He touched her shoulder and gave a sad smile. "Manannan's Kingdom was wiped out millennia ago by the Irish Tuatha Dé Danann. This ancient ruin has only survived because it's still protected by the powerful magic of the sea god. The people of the rainbow are light through water; they spread peace and love. But the Tuatha Dé Danann walk a dark path, imposing their will with the sword.

"We were no match for them. Most of the survivors were scattered to the four winds and, like you, their descendants have no idea who they are. Only a few of us still live together in our tiny demesne in County Cork."

Bereft and confused, Kate turned into Esras' arms and rested her cheek against his chest. She felt as though she had found her people only to lose them again immediately. She relived the misery she'd felt as a child at being denied the magic of her grandmother's stories. Why had her mother been so violently opposed to her finding out about her people? They must be her mother's people as well.

Esras stroked her hair back from her face. "There's something I want you to see."

He took her into a massive building that resembled a Greek temple, except each of the supporting columns was a sculpture of a man and woman entwined in each other's arms. "We do not worship a god, we worship couples as the Union of Opposites."

He stopped and let her find her feet before taking her in his arms. "The ceremony that joined us at the Feast of Beauty was the ancient Union of Opposites. In the eyes of the Rainbow People we're now man and wife."

Kate tried to remember why she'd been so angry with him over the ceremony but couldn't. Being with Esras now felt like the most natural thing in the world. "What do you normally do to celebrate the Union of Opposites?" she asked.

A smile spread over his face, his eyes glittering. "Make love."

Anticipation quivered through her. She slipped her arms around his neck, moulding her body to his, wanting to forget her melancholy. "Let's celebrate."

Esras cupped the back of her head, then leaned down and kissed her. The unusual sensation of the salty water mingling with their lips and tongues drove her wild. The overwhelming need to possess and be possessed beat in every cell of her body like an elemental force. The tumultuous sea ran through her veins, urging her to be wild and unrestrained.

She pushed the silk shirt off her shoulders and it floated away. His hands cupped her breasts, stroking and teasing. She traced the shape of his muscles with her fingers, sliding her hand down the ridges of his abs. He made a needy sound as her fingers slid further.

Esras pushed off his underwear and soon her panties floated away as well. "We usually make love topside," he said. "It's easier. But I can't wait. Clamp you legs around me."

He gripped her thighs and pressed himself against her sensitive flesh, drawing groans from them both. She clung to him with her arms and legs, digging her heels into his buttocks as he thrust inside her. When they were as intimately linked as it was possible for a male and female to be, they stilled in unspoken assent. They floated together just above the soft sand in the temple beneath the towering statues of ancient lovers.

She had never felt such a sense of peace in the middle of overwhelming desire. Did this mean she was in love?

His fingers gripped her buttocks, then he started to move inside her, slowly, sensuously. His lips traced her throat and shoulder before teasing her nipples.

The water held them in its embrace, playing over her skin like silky fingers as the pleasure built inside her. Waves of sensation flowed through her body. They floated to the ground and her back landed on the soft sand. His green eyes burned with the intensity of his need. Kate touched his finely carved lips, felt the hot touch of his tongue on her fingers. Ecstasy burst through her, sweeping her away from reality to a place of pure sensation.

They clung together as the flutters of pleasure faded, their heart rates steadied, and their bodies settled in sated lethargy. Kate unhooked her legs from around Esras' hips; she felt relaxed and dreamy. Esras started to drift away from her. He held out a hand for her to lace her fingers with his. He closed his eyes and they glided together, letting the water take them where it would.

When Kate recovered from her pleasure-soaked haze enough to open her eyes, Esras appeared to be asleep. With his hand still linked to hers, he floated above her. His lean muscular body glowed with a subtle gold light while his hair shimmered in a silver cloud around his head. A tremor passed through her, ending deep in her belly where it gathered in a tense knot. She wanted him again so badly she ached. But mixed in with the need was a hint of caution.

He was incredibly beautiful and desirable. From what she knew of him, he was also kind and generous and he had a mischievous streak. Was it possible she'd fallen in love with him after only knowing him for twenty-four hours?

Whatever she felt for him he'd only chosen her to become his queen because of her heritage, not because he loved her. A little chill passed through her. Suddenly she yearned to feel the sun on her skin.

Esras had proved to her that she was one of Lir's Rainbow People. She hadn't decided yet if that meant she had an obligation to them. But she was sure of one thing: it didn't matter whether she was human, or even Queen of the Rainbow People; she was not going to stay with Esras unless he actually loved her.

Eight

So much had changed for Kate while she'd been underwater. She felt as though she'd been away from Knock House for half a lifetime, not mere hours. Yet when they returned, the Feast of Beauty was still in full swing. A bonfire roared in a fire pit and the smell of roasting meat drifted on the air.

Kate had changed into her jeans and a T-shirt when she and Esras got back. He had gone to speak with his people while Kate stood near the production company's mobile office, watching the revellers celebrate. Gus the cameraman roved among the crowd, filming interesting people and events to include in the show.

Peter the producer huffed up the hill towards her looking harried with his glasses on top of his head. "What the hell happened to you? I needed you to go with Gus to log his shots and answer questions people might have."

"Sorry," she mumbled. Kate had always worried that if she did something to displease Peter she might jeopardize her reputation for reliability. She had been so determined to make her career in television that she'd worked relentlessly for a pittance and hardly received a thank you from Barthurst Productions. Her mother had told her that the early starts and late nights were character building. Now she felt as if her employers had taken advantage of her.

Esras sauntered towards her, a sexy smile on his face as his eyes caressed her. His hair once again looked brown with silver highlights and his skin just lightly tanned. Every nerve in her body fizzed with awareness at the sight of him. He stepped behind her, wrapped his arms around her waist as he had while they were underwater, and pressed his mouth to her ear. "You are the most gorgeous woman I have ever seen."

His words enfolded her heart like silky ribbons. Closing her eyes, she revelled in the feel of his strong arms around her and the sun-warmed seaside smell of his skin. He feathered tiny kisses down her neck and nipped gently at her shoulder. She had only kissed him underwater, and she wanted to taste him in the air. She turned in his arms and looped hers around his neck.

His lips met hers and she lost herself in the heat of his mouth as their tongues tangled. Finally, she broke the kiss and he grinned at her. "I can't wait until the feast ends so I can take you up to my bed."

There was no doubt that he wanted her to stay, but she ached to know how he really felt about her. He often called her *my love*, but did he love her or was that simply a casual endearment?

Peter scowled at them. "It's obvious what you've been up to for the last few hours when you should have been working. You're as bad as Claudia."

Kate blushed. She'd been so focused on Esras that she'd forgotten where she was. But she hadn't done anything wrong. And she certainly did not sleep with half the men who were guests on the show like Claudia did – and Peter knew that. He was just being a jerk.

"I'm quitting, Peter."

"What?" His mouth dropped open.

She gave a faint smile. "I'm sure you'll find another slave who wants to work in television."

As Peter stomped away to tell the director, Esras pulled her back into his arms. "Don't feel bad. You had to give up your job if you're going to stay with me," he whispered.

She stared up into his face. "Why, Esras? Why should I stay?"

Shock flashed in his eyes. "We're destined to be together. Otherwise I wouldn't have made love to you in the temple."

A little shiver of relief passed through her but she couldn't shake the niggling doubt in the back of her mind. "By destined do you just mean we suit each other really well, or is it something more?"

A frown creased Esras' forehead before he managed to hide it. An answering bolt of concern shot through Kate.

"I'd better tell you the full story." He glanced at the noisy crowd surrounding them. "Let's go somewhere quieter."

He led her around the side of the house to a lush private garden. They followed a narrow winding path between the riotous fragrant shrubs and came to a circular pool containing a beautiful fountain in the shape of a dolphin shooting water from its mouth. Esras pulled her down beside him on a stone bench hidden in an alcove overlooking the pool.

"What did your grandmother tell you about the Rainbow People?"

Kate stared at the cascading droplets pattering into the water, the sound soothing her jumpy nerves. "Fairy stories really." She shrugged. "The last time she spoke to me about the kingdom beneath the sea was when I was five. Then my mother banned the stories. She virtually banned me from seeing Grandma as well."

Esras pulled her hand on to his thigh and ran a finger lightly across her palm, tracing the lines. "The woman you knew as your grandmother was older than you think. She was really your great-great-great-grandmother."

Kate's breath hissed in.

"I knew her as Aine. She was once our queen."

"Grandma?"

"In 1865 she fell in love with a human and had to follow her heart to England. Before she left, she read the future in Lir's whirlpool and foretold that one of her female descendants was my destined bride. She made me king so that when you came to me you could take your rightful place as queen."

The blood rushed out of Kate's head, making her ears hum. *How old did that make him?* She tried to do the maths in her head, but her brain refused to work. She pulled her hand from his grasp and jumped to her feet.

"Kate, my love."

"Just give me a moment." She moved away from him and ended up by the pool. She stared at the bobbing pink water lilies, trying to calm her swirling thoughts so she could make sense of what he'd said. The memory of his mind-shattering kisses and the feel of his sculpted muscular body made it impossible to believe he wasn't young. She glanced over her shoulder at him to make sure she wasn't losing her mind. "You don't look more than thirty."

Esras grinned wryly. "I'll be 219 on 11 August. People of Lir live for centuries. That means you will as well."

Kate turned on unsteady legs and collapsed on to the edge of the pool. *Centuries?* "What happened to Grandma's other female descendants? Are they here?"

Esras rose and came towards her. "You're the first of Aine's female line to take after her. The others took after her human husband."

Kate's breath stilled in her lungs as the truth hit her. "Mum?"

"She isn't one of us," he said softly.

Kate rocked back. *Not one of us.* That explained so much that had happened over the years: the way Mum had cut her off from Grandma, her antipathy to Ireland, her fear of the sea. She must have been frightened of losing Kate and maybe a little resentful that the gene, or whatever it was that defined the Rainbow People, had passed her by.

Esras went down on his knees before her and reached for her hands. When he touched her she quivered inside, half of her wanting to fall into his arms, the other half still struggling to come to terms with his revelation that she would live for hundreds of years.

"I've waited a long time for you. If your mother hadn't hidden you from me, I'd have claimed you when you were eighteen." Esras leaned closer, resting his cheek against hers. His lips brushed her ear. "I love you, Kate."

Pleasure blossomed in her chest. His fingers stroked the inside of her wrists and trailed up her forearms to find the sensitive skin inside her elbows. A tingle of need raced across her skin.

"Do you think you'll grow to love me?" he asked.

Whether her relationship with Esras was destined or not, she could no more resist him than she could hold back the tide. "I do love you." She pressed her lips against his neck.

He gave a little sigh as his arms encircled her, pulling her on to his lap. His lips found her mouth, his kisses gentle at first, but soon becoming more demanding. After long minutes, he pulled back and whispered, "Together we'll search for our lost people. The People of Lir will become strong again now I have you."

"Can we talk about that later?" Kate pulled his face down again and kissed him. When he sucked in a breath, she smiled. "Do you think anyone will miss us if we don't go back to the feast?"

Compeer

Roberta Gellis

Cruachan, Connacht, Ancient Ireland – before 800 BC

Medb was not happy. When her father, Eochaid Fiedleach, Ard Rí of all Eriu, asked her if she was willing to go in marriage to Conchobar of Ulster, she had considered and then agreed. She was young, no more than fourteen summers having passed since her birth, but Eochaid Fiedleach knew better than to give orders to Medb. Nonetheless she was a dutiful daughter who loved her father; she knew Eochaid Fiedleach had been the cause of loss to Conchobar and that providing a wife to Conchobar was part of the repayment of that loss.

As further repayment of the debt, Eochaid had also given Ulster to Conchobar to rule; thus the Ard Rí retained power over Conchobar. And as daughter of the Ard Rí, Medb was her husband's equal in status; when married she would be Banríon of Ulster.

But the union began to go sour from the very beginning. Medb and her escort had ridden into the dark to arrive the sooner in Ulster. They came into the Great Hall through the easternmost of the seven doors after the eating but while the men were still drinking. Silence grew as Medb walked down the aisle from the door, past the sleeping couches and past the drinking benches, to the high seat.

Medb welcomed the growing silence. She was aware of her red hair and white skin, of her eyes, green as the finest emeralds, of the muscles that rippled in her bare arms. She always intended to be fit to rule. She was well trained with sword and knife, and as well trained to run and fight as to law and logic. She walked tall as a man and proud; she expected to be admired . . . and she was not thrilled with Conchobar's greeting.

The Rí of Ulster looked her up and down and said, "Scrawny. One would think Eochaid would have sent something riper for a wife."

Before Conchobar spoke, Medb had started to bend her head in proper greeting to a husband richer than herself, but she jerked upright at his words and replied, loud and clear, "I am the eldest of the Ard Rí's daughters, and we will see how I fill out the role allotted to me."

Conchobar only laughed but added, "The flash in those eyes holds promise, though."

Medb thought him a fool to laugh at her warning, but she held her tongue. Her goods were not the equal of his, so he ruled the household. And he was many years her senior. If he thought her a child, he might be careless until he knew her better. She might have spoken again, but a movement among the men seated on the drinking benches caught her eye.

The cause of the disturbance could have been called scrawny too; he had the unfinished look of a boy growing into a man, but none of the men challenged him. Medb saw the bones held great promise, and the skin was dark and smooth. His hair was black, which stood out among the lighter browns and reds and golds in the room; his eyes, from where she stood, also looked black. And the eyes were fixed on her, not with curiosity or amusement like most of the others of Conchobar's liegemen. The expression in them . . . was hunger.

Not yet, Medb thought, and was surprised. She had to swallow a laugh. To look at another man before her husband's seed was set in her belly and acknowledged was the ultimate in stupidity. Medb was never stupid. Nonetheless, she was just a trifle regretful. Something about the young man who stared at her with such avidity attracted her interest.

She turned away to the women who had come to escort her to her quarters, unwilling to meet the gaze of her young admirer but wondering how long it would be before it was safe to speak to him. To her surprise Conchobar came down from the high seat to walk with her. He had not spoken to her again, but several of his men had come from their benches to speak to him. Perhaps they had reminded him that the girl he had offended was the Ard Rí's eldest daughter.

Likely because of the warning of his men, Conchobar decided not to wait for Medb to ripen further, as he had promised her father. He broached her that very night.

That also did not please Medb – not the broaching; despite the pain, which she discounted, she enjoyed the broaching thoroughly. Seeing Conchobar reduced to a gasping, shuddering jelly taught her a valuable lesson. She saw what a woman could do to a man. She guessed at once how the act of love could be heightened to reduce a man and bind him. What angered Medb was that Conchobar had broken his promise to her father. In her eyes by breaking a promise Conchobar had smirched his honour.

Over the following weeks, she had no complaint about his diligence in his marital duties, although she suspected he still did not find her to his taste. "Rack of bones," Medb heard once under his breath. She held the memory tight. And across the width of the hall on many nights her gaze met that of the black-eyed youth, who licked his lips as if he would eat her with good appetite.

Medb could have taken a bite or two of him herself, but she had not even enquired as to the dark boy's name. Her will was far stronger than her lust. Fortunately she did not have long to wait. Within the second moon of the bedding, Medb got with child. She found that a source of satisfaction when she told her husband two moons later, and Conchobar was very pleased. He announced it to the whole household when they gathered for dinner . . . and took a new woman to his bed when the torches failed that very night.

Fool, Medb thought, as she had thought more than once before, but she made no protest even when the women of the dun cast pitying glances at her. She sat in her high seat beside her husband when he gave justice to his people and listened, and at each meal she ate and drank and spoke to him with good humour. Until one day when she had been watching the dark-eyed lad break a horse and came a little late to the table at dinner time. She found Conchobar's current bedmate sitting beside him in her chair.

"There is a stool at the end of the table," Conchobar said, and at the long tables set up in the hall for dinner some of the men looked up and chuckled at a wife being shown her place.

Medb smiled and kept on her way as if there were no one else at the table. Conchobar looked down into his ale horn, dismissing her. When she reached her chair, she seized the well-rounded, full-breasted woman by the back of her neck and the front of her gown, lifted her out of the chair, and dropped her off the dais down to the ground.

"I am the Ard Rí's eldest daughter and Banríon of Ulster." Medb's voice rose above the shriek of the fallen woman and the gasps of the men seated at the tables, and silence fell on the hall. "I do not care who you take to your bed," she continued, her voice ringing in the silence. "It is no great loss to me. But no one save I sits in the Banríon's chair beside you while I am your wife."

Conchobar had been so shocked by Medb's action and the shriek his bedmate uttered when she hit the floor that he had not moved. Now he sprang to his feet and lifted his hand to strike Medb, only to feel a very sharp pain as a knife dug into his belly just below his navel.

"If you hit me, I will rip you open as I fall," Medb murmured, smiling more broadly. "And then I will go home to my father with your seed in my belly. And Eochaid Fiedleach will appoint a new Rí to Ulster, not of your blood."

Half the men in the hall had risen from the tables at the sign of physical confrontation. Foremost was the dark boy, until he saw the knife in Medb's hand. Then, eyes glinting red with lust as he stared at her, he laughed aloud, a full, rich sound, deeper but just as ringing as Medb's voice – and the tension was broken.

Conchobar dropped his hand; Medb's eyes fixed for one moment on the boy, took in the long knife half hidden by his tunic and withdrew the knife she held ready to pierce her husband's gut. She raised her eyes briefly to meet Conchobar's glare and, still smiling, calmly stepped around her chair and seated herself. From the women's side, several came forward to help up the sobbing concubine and draw her into their group.

Medb used the knife, still bare in her hand, its tip gleaming slightly red with blood, to cut a tender slice from the roast. She ate it off the tip of the knife and licked the knife blade clean. Conchobar sat down beside her.

"I spare you for what you carry," he said.

Medb nodded, accepting the truce, and continued with her dinner with good appetite.

From the end of one of the tables, where the least important of Conchobar's men sat, Ailill mac Máta watched Medb eating. It was clear enough that she had not been frightened by her husband's threat. Her daring sent a wave of warmth across his groin. That woman was what he wanted.

Her marriage to Conchobar did not trouble him. He knew what Medb would do. She would give Conchobar his son, which would pay her father's debt, and then she would break the marriage and leave, go back to her father's house. Another wave of warmth passed through Ailill's lower body and he drew a quick breath. To have Medb . . .

Ailill had not missed Medb's expression when their glances met. But that kind of having was meaningless. She did not yet take him seriously; however, this was a woman who would grow and ripen, would challenge and reward throughout an entire lifetime. To bond with her for life would require much more than a few hot glances and a few sweet words. She would never again, he thought, come to a joining as a husband's inferior in wealth and he, Ailill smiled grimly, did not intend to be any woman's – even Medb's – rag for wiping up messes.

By the end of dinner he knew what he must do. When the servants came to clear away both the food and the tables,

Ailill slipped into the shadows to wait. He watched with satisfaction as Medb rose to go with a gaggle of women to their quarters. Brave, she was, but not a fool. She would not make herself an easy target while her husband was still raw with her challenge.

He followed the women, swiftly, silently insinuated himself among them, and stepped to her side. His skin tingled with her nearness and when she turned her head and looked at him a tide of lust rose through his belly to his throat. For a moment he could not speak and what he felt looked out of his eyes.

Medb's head tipped to the side; she met his gaze without lowering hers and she smiled slowly.

"My name is Ailill mac Máta," he said through a thick throat. "And I find you the most desirable of women."

Medb's eyebrows rose – it was not the most tactful thing to say when she was surrounded by the women of her husband's court – but before she could speak Ailill shook his head impatiently and laughed.

"I wanted you to know my name and remember me," he went on, speaking more easily, "for I will be gone from Ulster while you carry Conchobar's child. Wherever you go thereafter, I will find you."

"I am not likely to forget you," she said. "But can you just leave without Conchobar's permission?"

"I am no liegeman to Conchobar," Ailill said. "He did not think me worth inviting into his household. I am a hired sword and my time will be ended with the coming of the new moon . . . tomorrow."

They were at the door of Medb's house then. The women who attended her went in, but she could sense them clustering near the door, listening. She grinned at Ailill; she was very tall and their eyes were exactly on a level.

"Goddess watch over you," she said, running the tip of her tongue over her upper lip and then smiling. "I will look forward to seeing you . . . whenever and wherever you find me."

He dipped his head once and was gone. Before it was fully light, he had left the dun, riding the young horse Medb had watched him break, and the first place he turned the horse's head was to Conchobar's pasturage. There he could number and judge Medb's cattle.

She had brought other things to her husband's house: silver cups and plates, gold rings and bracelets, garments and linens skilfully embroidered. Such would be easy to match. Though he made no show of it, Ailill had use of a whole family of Firbolg treasure. It was the cattle that would give him trouble – not obtaining them but moving them from the Firbolg fastness to the pastures of Eriu.

The herds were easy to track and Ailill saw with relief that they were still separate, Medb's and Conchobar's herders not yet friendly enough to allow the cattle to mingle. Nor were they too far apart, as each set of herders feared being blamed for choosing less rich pastureland.

It was easy, too, to know which herd belonged to whom. Medb's herd was smaller and the cattle, Ailill thought, of better quality, but not by much. Eochaid Fiedleach had been careful of what he sent with his daughter.

Ailill spoke to Medb's cowherd and fixed in his mind what he had to match. As he rode slowly southward towards the lands his distant ancestors had so briefly occupied, he considered how many extra beasts he should have in reserve. Too many rather than too few. Medb, Ailill was certain, would give attention to her cattle to make sure her value increased. A few too many in his herd would not be important. He could always sell off or slaughter the extra animals for eating.

As the light faded, Ailill found a good camping place, an ancient, grown-over ledge a third of the way up a long worn-down mountain. There was grass for his horse on the flat area and a trickle of water at the far eastern end. Ailill filled his waterskin, watered his horse and hobbled it, threw the horse blanket on to the ground, extracted cheese, dried fruit and journey-bread from his saddle bags and settled down to eat.

It would not be so easy as simply bringing the cattle, Ailill realized, as he watched the thin sliver of new moon-rise. There were all manner of questions to be answered and problems to be solved before he could drive his herd to wherever Medb's was and propose their mating. Like . . . should he speak to Eochaid Fiedleach first or to Medb? A small shudder ran up and down his body. That was no easy question to answer, and—

The thought cut off as a thin wail drifted up from the base of the hill. Ailill sat more upright. It did not sound like an animal cry. The sound came again and broke off suddenly into a yelp of pain. Ailill surged to his feet and drew his sword from the scabbard that lay on the horse blanket beside him. That was a child crying.

Upright, Ailill could see there was a fire at the base of the hill. One man sat by the fire. Beside him . . . Ailill squinted to make his sight longer and, as if at his will, the fire flared up so he could see there was a stake in the ground and a braided cord tied to it. His eyes followed the line to a small, huddled figure at the end. He leaned forward, listening intently and picked up the muffled sound of weeping.

Now, it was no strange thing that a man should strike his son or his servant for ill behaviour or slacking his duties, but that the child should be leashed like a dog made Ailill uneasy. That a son or servant should be desperate enough to need to be tied on a dark night in the middle of a wilderness hinted at a cruel master.

Ailill looked beyond the fire and saw larger bodies. Another flare of light showed him cattle settling down for the night and a second man fixing a flimsy fence of withy boughs around them.

Perfectly ordinary. Two men driving home or to market some six or eight cows and bringing with them a youngling who had misbehaved. Ailill urged himself to go back to his horse blanket and mind his own business, but another glance showed him that the child was trembling and his ears made out muffled sobs.

Two men. It would not be wise simply to step into their camp and ask why the child was leashed and weeping. Even if the treatment was well-deserved they might resent his interference. And he was dressed like a nobleman. What he had seen in the firelight was rough garments. Would those who beat a child and did not comfort its weeping try to rob a rich lone traveller? Perhaps if he were closer he could judge better what to do.

Ailill moved off well beyond the firelight and descended the hill carefully. He could hear the child more clearly now, softly between sobs praying for help from – from Mother Dana! Tuatha Dé Danann? The child was one of the fair folk, out of a sidhe? It could not belong to these common men.

Now Ailill moved with even greater stealth well wide of the cattle so that they and the man working on the withy fence were between him and the fire. Something slipped. It must have hit one of the cows, which grunted and got to its feet. A second cow stirred and rose, and then a third. When the fourth began to rise, the man cursed and shouted to the one by the fire to bring the child to quiet the cattle.

Ailill, who liked little ones, watched with growing anger as the child was jerked to his feet and dragged towards the cattle. The boy cried out as his arms, which were tied behind his back, were wrenched and the man holding him slapped him hard and then shook him. The leash, fastened around his neck, flapped and his foot caught in it so that he almost fell. The man holding him shook him again.

"Make them lie down again," he ordered, and when the child, who was now sobbing hard, was unable to respond, he struck him once more.

Meanwhile Ailill slipped farther around until he was behind the man who had been making the fence. The fence-maker's attention was all on the child and his abuser.

"Hurry up," he shouted, waving a branch in the face of a cow that was moving towards him.

Ailill grinned, took three steps forwards, and struck him hard on the side of the head with the hilt of his sword. His victim fell like a stone, right in front of the cow, which stopped, turned aside, and passed the withy barrier.

"You fool!" the man holding the boy shouted. "What did you do? Trip on your own feet? Get that animal back."

Ailill did not answer. He saw he could not make his way

directly through the cattle, more of which were beginning to get to their feet. He tried to run around them but some turned away from him and others stepped right into his path. Unfortunately that made him too slow to reach the man holding the child before he realized something had happened to his partner. Fear made him take fright. He jerked the boy closer by the leash around his neck and pulled his knife.

"Go away!" the man shrieked. "Take your accursed cows and go back to your sidhe or I will kill the child."

The stupid peasant did not know how rare a child was among the Tuatha Dé Dunaan, how precious. He thought the Dunaan had come after their cattle as a Milesian would.

"And what do you think will happen to you after you kill him?" Ailill asked in a quiet, pleasant voice more terrifying than bellows of rage. "It will take you years and years and years of screaming and begging to die. If you let him go . . . now – right now – without more harm, I will let you run." As he spoke, Ailill openly came closer, making sure the light of the fire glinted on the blade of his sword. "If you even scratch him with that knife, I will gut you and leave you here to die with the flies breeding in your belly."

Ailill could see a small movement, perhaps the man's hand tightening on his knife. He leaped forwards with a shout, although he knew he could not reach them in time. But the man surprised him. He turned about and threw the boy towards the fire.

The child screamed. Ailill shouted again and twisted his body desperately to divert his path. The boy, catapulted forwards, took two involuntary steps and then tripped on the leash again. He fell face towards the fire. Ailill made another desperate leap and just caught the child, his own feet coming down into the burning wood. Sparks and embers flew, scorching the back of his legs, which gave him impetus enough to leap sideways, carrying the child.

Another desperate twist brought them down to the ground so that the child was on top and not crushed beneath him. Ailill gasped as something snapped in his side, but he thrust the child off him, away from the fire, and leaped to his feet. Running thrust a dagger into his chest with each stride, but only slowed him a trifle and it was no more than thirty or forty strides before he was close enough to strike the fleeing man.

"I said I would let you run, not escape," Ailill snarled and swung his sword.

At the last moment, he turned the weapon so the flat, rather than the sharp edge, struck. If the Sidhe were as enraged as he feared they might be about the mistreatment of their child, Ailill wanted them to have both villains upon whom to slake their anger.

He seized the unconscious man by one foot and began to drag him back to the fire. That did not soothe the pain in his chest but at least he heard the child crooning to the cattle and hoped that meant he would not need to chase the cows.

His first task was to secure the man he had first struck. The cattle thief was just beginning to stir and Ailill coldly hit him again. Leather thongs from the man's own pouch fastened his thumbs together behind his back, as well as his big toes. Aside from that, Ailill let him lie where he was to go and bind the second man the same way.

The cows were bedded down where they had been originally. The child was now silent except for a shuddering sob now and again. Ailill went and squatted down beside him, drawing his knife. The child's eyes went wide. Ailill laughed.

"I only want to cut you loose, little one. I will do you no harm. How do you wish me to call you?" He knew enough of the Danaans not to ask for the child's name.

"Do you want the cows?" the boy asked, obviously trying to keep his voice steady.

"No, indeed," Ailill replied. "I am not such a fool as to wish to keep the cattle of the Tuatha Dé Danann which did not come to me as a gift or an agreed purchase."

He lifted the child, hissing with pain as what he feared was a broken rib stabbed him again, and set him down closer to the fire so he could see to insert the knife and cut the bonds without injuring the little boy.

The child was silent until he was free and then he sighed on a half-sob, and said, "You can call me Bress. What will you do with me?"

"Take you home, of course. And the cows too." Ailill laughed. "That is, if you know the way home. I certainly do not."

The boy began to sob more heavily and Ailill drew him close. He was a little surprised when the child actually climbed into his lap, pressed against him and clung as he wept. By ten, which Ailill judged him to be by his height and the fact that he was alone with the cattle, most boys would be trying to resist being comforted, not clinging like an infant.

The fire had been somewhat scattered when he landed in it and was now dying. Ailill caught up a stick and, holding the child with one arm, shoved the burning wood together as well as he could. There was more wood within his reach and he added about half of that to the fire. After a few moments the flames sprang up. Ailill stroked the boy's hair and he lifted his face. When Ailill saw his companion clearly, he drew a quick breath. The child he was holding could have no more than six or seven summers, although he was as big as a Milesian boy of ten. The Danaan were a tall race.

The sobs had quieted and Ailill asked, "What happened? How did you come to be taken with the cattle?" He thought there might have been a raid or a battle and the child might be a survivor.

"They said I was not big enough to mind the cows." The voice was shrill with childish resentment. "So I called to the cattle and they came and followed me. You see how they lie where I bade them."

Ailill's mouth opened, then closed. He took a deep breath. "You mean you took the cattle yourself? You were not set to watch over them?"

"No one listens to me!" The words were garbled with sobs and sniffs. "I knew a better place to graze them. The grass was thick and tender. So I took them there and they were content. But—"

"But no one knew where you were," Ailill breathed. "And that is why the Danaan are not on the heels of their precious child." He raised his voice, holding Bress' head up with a finger under his chin. "You have been a very naughty boy. Your parents are likely half-mad with worry over you. *Do* you know the way home?"

Bress burst into tears again. "Must we go now? The cows are tired and I am, too."

"No, no." Ailill gave him a rough hug. "We will wait until morning at least. Perhaps your people will come before we leave and I will not need to try to follow your trail back to the sidhe. Now let me see what food those thieves carried so I can feed you, then get their blankets and make up your bed."

"No bed for you?" The boy sounded anxious, as if he feared Ailill would abandon him.

"I have my own. I was camping above, up on the hill . . ." Ailill's voice faded. He had heard the boy crying but then he had seen the fire. Those thieves were idiots, lighting a fire that the Danaan would see. He shook his head, and said to Bress, "And I must fetch my horse too."

By the time he had fed the child and settled him to sleep, retrieved his horse and his supplies, Ailill was finding it hard to breathe past the pain in his side. He sank down beside the fire, which was dying again, and wondered whether he could force himself to gather more firewood. Surely the Danaan must now be close, even if they had not known just when the boy was lost or from where he had been taken. Would they need the light of the fire to find this camp?

Ailill really did not want to follow the track of the cattle back to the sidhe. He did not want to move at all. If Bress' people came, he could give them the boy and the cows and lie up for a few days while his rib set. He closed his eyes.

He was to get no peace, however. His long silence had seemingly convinced the thieves that he had gone to sleep. Now he heard one of the men cursing softly and moving about, doubtless trying to free his thumbs. Ailill jerked upright and yelped as it seemed as if a knife stabbed his side. Gritting his teeth, he levered himself to his feet more carefully. No matter the pain, he had better bind his prisoners more securely.

And suddenly the small clearing was full of men, half with drawn swords and the other half with drawn bows. And every nocked arrow was aimed at him. Ailill raised his empty hands.

"I am not the man who took your child," he said. "Those who did lie bound. The child is here, asleep."

"I am not asleep," Bress called, sitting up. "And what this man says is true."

There was a high, musical cry, and a woman came running from behind the men to catch the child into her arms and kiss him. The men lowered their swords and relaxed the tension of the bowstrings somewhat. Holding his side, Ailill let himself sink to the ground. One of the men lifted the hand not holding his sword and gestured. Lights formed bright, misty balls in the air and the clearing was as bright as day.

Ailill swallowed a shriek of terror. A thin sound worked its way up his throat, but both the cattle thieves screamed their fear aloud and covered his small exclamation. A babble of sound came from those around the boy, the woman asking questions of the child to discover if he had been hurt, was hungry, was cold, was thirsty. The men were not so sympathetic and mixed scolding with many questions.

Eventually the tall man who had gestured the witch-lights into being came and crouched down beside Ailill, who swallowed the heart that seemed to be trying to climb up his throat and into his mouth. He did his best to straighten himself.

"How did you come to notice the child and the cattle?" the man asked.

"I heard the child crying. At first I did nothing, believing that a cattle drover had punished his son or his apprentice, but then I heard the little one begging Mother Dana for help . . ."

"So you saved him, knowing he was Danaan."

"Yes."

"How?"

Ailill started to laugh and then gasped, his hand against his painful ribs. "It was easy because the pair that took him were such fools." He described how he had overcome the thieves, ending, "Perhaps they had never heard of the Tuatha Dé Dunaan. But even so, imagine stealing cattle and then lighting a campfire as if no one would pursue."

"You know it was not the cattle we pursued," the tall man said. "What do you want for protecting our child?"

Ailill glanced sidelong at the lights floating above the men's heads, lighting the whole area. He took a breath, wincing and holding his side, but he described his desire for Medb.

The tall man shook his head. "I cannot interfere with a Milesian marriage or—"

"Gods, no!" Ailill exclaimed. "If Medb should learn you had anything to do with freeing her from Conchobar, she would kill me. No, that is her business and she will manage it. But I must come to her with goods exactly the equal of what she has and to do that I must gather my goods and hold them in this area until she is ready to be bound to me. Only I have no one I can trust to hold my wealth for me until Medb is ready."

"And you would trust me, who you have never met before, whose name you do not even know, to hold your goods?"

Ailill laughed and glanced up at the magical lights. "What I will gather will be riches for me but little above dross for you. I have seen your cattle. I see the clothing you wear to chase thieves through the woods. The torc around your neck would buy a kingdom. And no, I do not want any of it. Medb could not match any gift you gave me and all such wealth would do is wake envy and desire in my equals."

For the first time the man crouched beside Ailill smiled. "A wise man, and scarcely a man yet. Very well, I will hold your wealth for you although to do that I must give you the key to my sidhe. That I cannot give without recompense; my gratitude for your rescue of our child is not enough."

"What recompense can such as I give a being who can light up the night?"

"We are strong, but few. If you Milesians gathered together enough force, you could drown us in numbers. My recompense is that you never seek a quarrel with the Tuatha Dé Dunaan for any reason at all. If you are attacked, you may defend yourself but you may not follow to gain a victory, even from your attacker."

Ailill was silent, considering. If the Danaan should attack and he drove them away, he could still lose men and property and if he could not continue the fight, he would not be able to seize compensation. And then he thought that he had never heard of the Danaan attacking anyone who had not first injured them. Most of them did not live in places where they came in contact with ordinary people. A few did live in the world but . . . And then he bit his lip to keep from smiling. He would not need to worry about losses. Medb would retrieve whatever he lost for him.

He had forgotten his ribs, started to draw a deep breath of relief, began to cough, and groaned. Nonetheless he managed to say, "I will swear to that recompense." And as the words left his mouth, an odd tingle took hold in his chest. "You have laid a *geis* on me." he gasped.

"So I have," the tall man said calmly. "It will do you no harm, unless you violate your oath. And even then, it will warn you first by what you now feel. Otherwise you will never know you carry the *geis*." He smiled again and his eyes looked kind and the odd tingle disappeared from Ailill's chest. "My name is Bodb," he added, offering with his name his trust, "and if you will take no other gift, at least let us see to your injury."

To that Ailill agreed with some relief, for the pain in his side was sapping his strength, but he did not expect to fall suddenly asleep and to wake sitting on his horse in bright daylight in a place he had never seen before. Their party seemed to be emerging from a dense wood that, to his right, opened into a wide valley of grass. In the distance, Ailill could see more cattle, like those with the boy, and a small herd of horses.

To his left was a hill broken by a shallow cave. Ailill could see the bare, unworked rock at the back of the cave because it was illuminated by sunlight.

"Dismount now," Bodb said, coming to Ailill's side and offering an arm to help. "How do you wish to be called while you are healing with us?"

Ailill laughed aloud and was instantly aware his rib was still painful, if not as excruciatingly painful as it had been. And when he tried to draw breath, he was also aware that his chest had been bound. He took Bodb's arm and slid to the ground. One of the men who had been in the clearing when the Danaan found him came and took his horse, murmuring that the animal would be cared for. Ailill nodded thanks.

"My name is Ailill mac Máta," he said, "my true name since you already have a hand on my heart. And I have also been called Ailill Dubd, Black Ailill, for obvious reasons."

"Come with me," Bobd said, offering his arm as an aid when Ailill swayed.

They were headed directly into the cave. Ailill hesitated, expecting Bodb to slow down lest in a step or two they walk right into the back wall of the cavern. But when they came under the cave roof, a sharp pang and a sense like a blow on the back of his neck made Ailill cry out and close his eyes in protest.

He had a moment of bitter shame and rage for allowing himself to be charmed and betrayed, but when his eyes opened an instant later he saw not bare rock nor more Tuatha Dé Danaan to make him a prisoner, but a broad corridor, lit with the same witch-lights that had lit the campsite of the cattle thieves.

Bodb tightened his grip on Ailill's arm as he swayed again. The corridor was alive with beauty, with such pictures that the walls seemed to open into successive scenes of Eriu: in a moonlit glade couples of Danaan danced; in a sunlit valley the golden cattle of the Danaan grazed; sharp, bare cliffs rose from a landlocked harbour where fishing boats furled or raised painted sails; fields were tended by women with skirts kilted above their knees, who looked, laughing, over their shoulders.

Farther down the corridor a metalsmith worked, the flames of his forge seeming to leap out of the painted image. Danaans sat before looms on which the half-formed weavings were of superlative beauty, a minstrel, lap-harp on his knee, sang to a spellbound audience. Only one part of life did not appear;

there were no images of war. No Danaan attired in precious armour swung a shining sword; no Danaan rushed upon another with upraised axe.

Ailill was surprised. It was true that most of the few Danaan he had come across had been minstrels or bards, but the others had served as men-at-arms in the households he knew and they were superb fighters. It seemed that despite their proficiency in arms they did not honour the art of war. Before he could ask about that oddity, the corridor opened out into a huge room. A fire burned in the centre on a polished marble hearth without smoke, although heat waves distorted the air above the leaping flames.

Such flames . . . red and orange and yellow, yes, but among them and around them were glints of green and lavender, blue and silver. And they seemed to sway and leap and dance to the sound of such music as Ailill had never heard.

Beyond the fire was a dais on which was a high chair cast, it seemed, of silver. Lower than the chair were stools, three grouped together. From one a silver-haired Danaan stood, abruptly cutting off the music of his harp with a hand flat on the strings.

"Lord," he called, "what of the child?"

A crowd of Danaan rose from the benches that circled the fire and turned to look at them.

"In by a lesser gate with his mother," Bobd said, laughing. "He was unrepentant enough, proud of how the cattle obeyed him, so that I would not further flatter his vanity by having you all petting him and telling him how glad you are to have him again." Then the laughter was gone. "That little devil went right out of the *lios* into the unprotected land where no one thought to look for him at first. We were near two days behind and might have lost him, except for our guest here."

The bard or minstrel frowned. "A hard-used guest," he said uncertainly.

"Not by us," Bodb said, smiling. "This is Ailill mac Máta, who was injured in wresting our ill-behaved babe from the two villains who had seized him."

A murmur passed through the watching crowd, and two men and a woman began to work their way around the benches to come to where Bobd and Ailill stood. Bobd continued to speak.

"If not for Ailill Dubd's injury, which I think we must heal before we return him to the world, I would say we had wasted our effort in following the boy's trail. Ailill was intending to bring the child back to us." The smile on his lips disappeared. "The thieves he delivered to us bound, and bound they will remain, to labour in the depths of the sidhe without sight of sun or moon until they die."

The woman had reached them, and she stretched a hand to touch Ailill's side very gently. She shook her head. "And if you would hold your tongue for a moment or two," she said severely to Bodb, "we could make a start on the curing. First do something useful. Call for a litter."

Those words were the last thing Ailill remembered clearly. Because of his sense of wonder at what he had been seeing and hearing, Ailill had been fighting the intense pain in his side and a growing weakness. He remembered fingers gently prying his hand from Bobd's arm, to which he had been clinging with increasing need. Then he was lying down and seeing with amazement above him a clear blue sky with white clouds and a bright sun.

Ailill closed his eyes. He knew they were underground. He remembered entering the shallow cave, feeling a pain in his head and neck, and then seeing the long corridor form. When he opened his eyes again the sunlit sky was gone and he was lying in an ordinary chamber with a whitewashed ceiling. Beside the bed was an open window that looked out on a corner of the forest and a patch of meadow. Ailill raised a hand and touched cold stone.

The woman from the large hall bent over him, smiling. "It is only an image. You are still in the sidhe."

Ailill blinked and nodded, understanding. He shifted slightly. The sheet above him was incredibly smooth and the blanket was light and warm, but . . . He shifted again.

The woman shook her head. "I am sorry the bed is so hard but your ribs will hurt less if you move in your sleep. Now—" she put an arm behind him and raised him up; Ailill was amazed at her strength because she was so slender and looked frail "—drink this and you will soon bcgin to feel much better."

It was true enough. The pain in his side disappeared almost completely, but Ailill continued to be weak and very sleepy. By what seemed to him the next day, however, he was able to sit up with only the faintest ache in his side. And the day after that, Bodb came and helped him walk around the sidhe. Ailill was surprised at how feeble he felt although by now the pain was completely gone. He could bend and twist without a twinge. Bodb said he was longer healing than a Danaan would be and suggested that he exercise a bit before he left the safety of the sidhe.

Ailill was in no hurry. Medb had five more months to carry the child and he doubted she would leave Conchobar before her babe had survived the illnesses of childhood. He thanked Bodb for the invitation and sought out those who would be willing to spar with him and teach him.

A week passed. Ailill was thrilled by what the Danaan were willing to show him. His sword work, which had been good, was now superlative. They gave him a bow – he needed time to master its pull without strain. A month passed, and then another. He rode out with a hunting troop and took a boar without help, other than from the dogs, and when he looked at his arms and legs he realized they had lost any hint of boy. He was all man now. Another month passed and another. Ailill bethought him of what he still needed to do to match Medb's wealth and he told Bodb he would need to leave soon.

A week later, his horse was readied and saddlebags generously filled with travel supplies, his bedroll tied atop. Ailill once again thanked Bodb for his kindness and hospitality and asked, "When I have gathered what I need, how will I find the sidhe?"

Bodb smiled. "Only desire to find it, and you will be drawn."

* * *

Now and again during her pregnancy Medb thought of the dark-haired boy and wondered what had happened to him. With her belly full and the child within acknowledged, Medb tasted this man and that – circumspectly, as she did not wish to annoy Conchobar further. But there were none among Conchobar's liegemen or among the visitors who came that were much to her taste and she thought again of Ailill mac Máta and the red hunger in his eyes.

However, as her time drew near, Medb began to think of what she would do about the child. Less than ever did she intend to stay in Ulster and she did not want to be tied to suckling a babe. She would need a wet nurse.

She looked at the women who were also with child and due a little ahead of her. Among them, Ethne of the High Hills seemed suited. She was neither unkind nor too tender-hearted; it did a child no good, especially not the child of a king, to be too much indulged. One fault Ethne had was that she was too fond of her husband; she might get with child again too soon. Medb considered whether there was a way to have the man sent away on a long mission but, most conveniently, he went on a raid . . . and died.

The shock of grief brought on the woman's labour and she delivered a boy child a few weeks early. Medb thought Ethne might have died of grief herself, except for the child who held her to the world. He lived, but was frail. Medb went to Ethne and asked if she would suckle her child also. Ethne's breasts ran with milk and her own boy took little.

"Why not?" Ethne said.

Medb made her bargain but she also saw Ethne's eyes were dark with fear as she looked at her own child. If he died she would have nothing. She would cleave to Medb's young one.

"You will have the keeping of him," Medb assured her. "I will be busy with other things."

She was within days of her time. She had been doing women's easy tasks for a few weeks, carding and spinning wool, for she was heavy and awkward, but now she took up her sword practice again and went to run down game in the forest. It was no surprise to anyone when her labour pains started. Nor was it much of a surprise when her bearing was quick and easy and a big, strong man-child howled on her belly.

The women sent to Conchobar as soon as Medb was clean, and he came and looked at his son. "What will you name him?" Medb asked.

Conchobar scowled, but his expression softened when his eyes rested on the child. "Name him Glaisne," he said, and turned and left the house. Medb watched him go. That he had named the boy was important and during the months of their silent, wary truce she had discovered some worth in Conchobar. He ruled his people well. She had learned much sitting beside him as Banríon of Ulster.

Ethne had attended the delivery and when Conchobar was gone she took up the child and cleaned him and wrapped him. Glaisne took the breast she offered and suckled hard.

"I will watch over him," Ethne said, and Medb turned on her side and slept.

In a week, Medb was well recovered. After that she was seldom in the house. She was giving all her attention to her weapons practice and her herd, which had diminished under the care of Conchobar's herdsmen. Seeking widely in the pasturage, she found three calves – with the red and white markings of her cows – separated from their mothers. For a moment she fingered the knife on her belt, but then dropped her hand and instead sent her youngest lover to Tara to bring back servants bound only to her.

Medb would not abide treachery. Three things she required of a husband: that he be without fear, meanness or jealousy. Conchobar was brave enough and he took no revenge on the men she now and again took to her bed. But it is mean to steal from a wife's herd to keep her subservient. He had taken her cattle; she would take his son as soon as he was weaned. But when she returned to her house at the time when usually she was at weapons practice, she found Conchobar bent over the child's cradle.

Knife in hand, Medb stepped silently towards her husband. To harm his own son just because she was Glaisne's mother . . .

But now, close enough, she heard Conchobar's soft murmur of praise, of love. What held him bent over the cradle with a hand outstretched was no desire to do harm but the tight grip of baby fingers on his thumb.

So Medb waited warily, and the men she had bound to her by lust and by admiration and by the judicious giving of rings and armlets watched her back and helped her avoid strange accidents. She waited a whole year longer, until Glaisne had teeth in his mouth and toddled among the men, already reaching for their bright attractions, their swords, their knives.

She waited until she saw Conchobar teaching the boy with more patience than she suspected he had. Then in the autumn of the year when Conchobar rode out hunting she called the men who answered to her, gathered up her possessions – the silver plates and cups, the gold armbands and neck torcs, the embroidered linens and fur-trimmed wool mantles – and bade her herdsmen drive her cattle south, to Tara.

Eochaid Feidleach was not overjoyed to see her, but he was in contention with Tinni mac Conri, Rí of Connacht, and when Medb offered to lead the men who had come with her in Eochaid's support he agreed. She did so well that when Tinni was driven out, Eochaid gave Connacht and the dun at Cruachan into Medb's hands.

For almost a month Medb watched from the walls for a dark-haired, dark-eyed warrior with just her equal of goods. When he did not come, she laughed at herself for being a fool and wondered instead what it would be like to utterly rule her husband. So she welcomed Tinni back into Cruachan and into her bed, making sure he got no child upon her.

That was no success. Although Tinni raised no challenge to her, she learned that her father had not put the man out for nothing. He was useless in the defence of the lands and people of Connacht against any active threat, and he was not honest; he stole, an armband here a neck torc there, to buy warriors. Medb only learned that after he was gone, but it taught her that a husband without possessions was no better than a husband richer than she.

She was rid of Tinni without much effort though. It so happened that Eochaid Dála had conceived a hot desire for her during the war against Tinni and he came and challenged Tinni for his place. Medb made no protest, although she did not yet know Tinni had robbed her; she had no distaste for Eochaid and was pleased to take him to her bed and share with him the rule of Connacht.

Yet she still took care not to conceive although she knew she would need an heir for Connacht. She did not know for what she was waiting until, in the spring of the fifth year since she had come to be Conchobar's wife, she came to the central of the seven doors of Cruachan to welcome a visitor – and her gaze met the hot eyes of Ailill mac Máta.

"You are a little late in coming to find me," Medb said, Eochaid standing behind her and staring at the black hair and black eyes of her guest.

Ailill bowed his head. "I will tell you why, Medb of Cruachan, but not now when it would seem I was excusing myself for not holding to my word. When you have cause to trust me better I will tell you. Now I will offer my services in what capacity you wish to use me."

She looked him over as she would a horse offered for sale, except that she did not examine his teeth. There was no need for that; they shone white and strong in his dark face when he smiled. But scrawny was not a word that fitted him now – as even Conchobar would have admitted the phrase no longer suited Medb either. Ailill's limbs were thick with corded muscle, his chest deep and strong, and his shoulders were three axe-handles wide.

"Conchobar has not forgiven me for leaving him and taking with me my possessions," Medb said. "Though they do not wear his plaids, raiders come from Ulster to steal my cattle and harass my farmers. I have need of fighting men to protect my land."

Ailill bowed his head again. "As you order, Rí."

Behind her, Medb heard Eochain Dála mutter discontent. Although she did not turn, his grumblings did not please her. Eochaid seemed to think that because they were bedmates he had a lock on her body, which was pure foolishness. Her body was hers to seek pleasure with but more important, it was goods with which she won loyalty and paid for debts and favours, just as were the rings on her fingers or the armlets she wore. Any man who wished to be her husband needed to be free of jealousy as well as brave and generous.

But she did not pay Ailill with that coin, and although he ate her with his eyes whenever they came together, he gave no sign of asking for that favour.

Within a month she noticed the men of the dun tended to look towards Ailill rather than Eochaid whenever an action was planned. And over that time she had noticed that the men who served with Ailill came back from their protective forays in better spirits and with fewer injuries. Before the second month of Ailill's return was ended, a deputation came to her to ask that she make Ailill chief of her warband.

This Medb did gladly, lifting a thick torc of gold from her neck and leaning forward to place it around Ailill's. He did not look at the gold symbol of power as she offered it; he looked at her bare throat and at the swell of her breasts and he wiped sweat from his upper lip when he bent his head to receive the symbol of his new authority.

Eochaid was not pleased and he whispered to Medb that Ailill and the men he had brought with him out of Erna exaggerated their successes against the raiders from Ulster. He told of secret arrangements between Ailill and Conchobar's troops that they cease raiding now and when he was seated on the throne beside Medb he would give them her cattle as if they had been won as prizes of war.

Only the men bound to Medb herself did not confirm Eochaid's warnings and so Medb met the glance of the dark eyes, saw the pink tongue touch the lips in the swarthy face and shook her head at Eochaid Dála.

"No," she said, laughing. "Cattle are not the pay Ailill mac Máta desires of me. I will not outlaw him on your word. My own men say he is a leader with whom they are content."

Others came to her also, a few she suspected were in Eochaid's pay, but she would listen to none of them and her gaze locked more and more often on that of Ailill when he sat just below her on the drinking benches. They laughed at the same jests, and Eochaid's expression grew blacker and blacker.

Eochaid and Ailill did not ride together and did not know each other's strength. Ailill, obedient to Medb's warning of trouble from Conchobar, rode north and east towards Ulster; Eochaid rode mostly south and west to guard against those of Casil. The Casili had no grudge against Medb but they saw no harm in picking up a cow for slaughter that had not come from their herds, or a pig or a pretty farmer's daughter. Medb rode with a smaller escort, less to fight, although she gave a good account of herself when necessary, than to look over all the lands and the people.

Although Eochaid did his duty well enough, Medb thought less of him as a ruler. He spent too much time trying to rid Connacht of Ailill and too little judging crops and grazing lands. Half the women in the dun threw themselves at Ailill and he welcomed every one with good-humoured indifference, but the hunger in his eyes did not lessen a jot when he looked at Medb. As important, neither women nor that hunger took his attention from the crops and the pasturage or made him a less wise judge of his men and the people.

Unable to turn Medb against her favourite, Eochaid set traps for Ailill, which he avoided and commented on with amusement, enraging Eochaid further. Moreover, Medb was not amused and denied Eochaid her bed until, she said, he should understand that who she slept with was at her discretion alone.

Eochaid then saw that if Ailill died by attack or accident, Medb would blame him. So Eochaid set an open challenge on Ailill. With this, Medb did not meddle; nor did she show any preference when she came to watch the fight.

It did not last long. In a hundred heartbeats Eochaid knew himself to be outmatched. Whereupon he made a fatal error. He desired to mark Ailill before he yielded and launched a fiery attack. Ailill did not match it with defence but with an attack of his own.

Eochaid had his desire; his sword bit lightly on Ailill's left shoulder, but his extended weapon opened a path. This Ailill leaped upon – his sword struck down. Eochaid was cloven from where his neck met his shoulder down to his breastbone. The jugular was sliced clean through. Blood burst in a fountain over Ailill's sword and arm, even over his face as he drew his sword out of the wound and the body fell towards him.

"You killed him!" Medb had arrived so quickly that she too was spattered with blood and her eyes were round with shock. "He was not a bad man, just not enough for me. Did you need to kill him?"

"Yes." Ailill's breath was still coming hard and his own blood trickled down his left arm. "He called you wife. I will suffer no other man to call you wife."

"If I take you in marriage, you think you will be the only man ever to lie in my bed?"

Ailill laughed. "Mother Dana forbid. I know you may drop a favour here and there for curiosity or to pay a debt or tie a cord around a man's heart. That will cause me no pain so long as I know I give you pleasure also."

Medb stepped back, away from the body that lay on the ground. She glanced down, made a gesture to summon Eochaid's men to take him up and fit him for burial. Then she looked back at Ailill.

"How would I know that? Your eyes promise, but you have never sought to fulfil that promise. You seek to share the rule of Connacht. Agreed you have saved me much loss in protecting my lands, but if I share what is mine with you, we will both be poor."

"No!" Lifting his hand in protest, Ailill very nearly spitted Medb on the bared sword he was still holding.

He gasped and pulled the hem of his tunic out to wipe the weapon so he could sheathe it. Medb had hopped aside from the motion of the sword, with practised reaction to the weapon's movement. She did not even look at it as she spoke.

"But I have resolved never to take another husband who had nothing of his own."

"Most rightly," Ailill agreed, smiling. "I will go tomorrow to fetch my own property and we can match what we have."

Medb stared at him for a long moment. "I will not wait another five years for you to make good your word to me."

Ailill laughed heartily. "No, indeed, I promise you I will not step even one foot inside the sidhe." He started away.

"Inside a sidhe?" Medb echoed to his back. "Is this what you promised to explain to me when you first came?"

He turned back towards her, leaned forwards suddenly and put his mouth to hers, not trying to embrace or hold her to him. His lips were firm but soft, not dry but not wet with spittle either. And then, just as she was about to embrace him, he drew back.

"I must go and have this shoulder bound up before I lose too much blood."

She saw then that a fine sheen of sweat glistened on his face and remembered that the lips that touched her had been cool; his skin was pale and greyish and he was unsteady.

"Go then," she said quickly. "Go and have your wound bound. You can tell me about the sidhe tomorrow."

But he was gone before dawn the next day. Medb said several words that delicately raised ladies did not know. He had taken about half the men he brought from Erna with him. Medb questioned the men he had left, but they knew nothing of where Ailill was going. They had come to him with his possessions after he had come from the sidhe . . . if that was from where he had come.

So Medb cursed Ailill to unease and sleeplessness and went with some of her own people to Tara. Her father was sorry to hear what had happened to Eochaid Dála, who had supported him in several wars. He asked whether Ailill was likely to be as useful and all Medb could say was that he would be even more useful . . . if he had not disappeared again. Eochaid

Feidleach shook his head at her and told her she should not be so careless with her men – one dead and another missing. Medb ground her teeth and set out for Cruachan to guard the lands Eochaid and Ailill had watched.

But when she came to the dun, Ailill was there, his cattle in the pasture, his goods spread out on the trestle tables where the people of the dun sat down to eat. There was no lack in the goods, in the silver cups and the horns wound with gold wire in their gold stands, in the platters and the linens and the close-woven cloth. He laughed at her rage over his departure and she stamped on his foot so that he howled and hopped about holding it in his hand. And then they fell into each other's arms, both laughing, and called witnesses to count over what was hers and what was his.

It was a very close thing, very close indeed, except . . . The bull with Ailill's herd was far superior to that in Medb's. Both were silent as the witnesses gave their judgment and they looked into each other's eyes. An icy chill ran down Medb's spine. A bull would bring disaster to her. Still . . .

"I promised myself that I would not take a husband to whom I would be subservient," Medb said.

"I desire you for my wife far more than I desire to rule you," Ailill said, "but the law is the law. All I can offer is to geld the bull—"

The chill struck Medb again. "No!" she cried. "It would be an evil thing to spoil so fine a bull."

Ailill nodded. "You are too clever to destroy something of value. And think, Medb, you have a dozen yearling bulls that are already better than their sire. Take me for a year while those yearlings grow into their full power on my oath not to use my authority."

Medb thought. It would not be so easy to rid herself of Ailill as of her previous husbands, but the hunger in his eyes roused her as no other man's gaze ever had. She held out her hand and he clasped it, and so they were wed before the people of the dun.

Medb ordered a great feast to mark the occasion, taking care that exactly so many steers and sheep and pigs came from Ailill's goods as came from her own. But they themselves did not attend the revels for long. When the serious drinking got underway, Medb and Ailill slipped out of the hall to her house, where Ailill's hunger was slaked at last, and then slaked again, and still again so that Medb knew no satisfaction would still it for long.

In the morning, they still lay together, sated, yet Medb was eager to start the day to see how well Ailill would keep his promise not to try to rule her. When she started to rise, however, he held her back and she laughed.

"You still desire me so much?"

"Yes."

"You think me the most beautiful woman you have ever seen?"

Now Ailill burst out laughing. "No, indeed I do not."

"You are at least honest," Medb snapped.

The laughter died and he said, solemnly, "With you, Medb, always."

Ailill held out a hand and Medb put hers into it. Ailill smiled at her. "With others . . . I am honest as is most profitable. But those beautiful women – they were from the sidhe. The beauty of the women of the sidhe is unmatched and they are free with their favours. Only . . . they had nothing else – and I do not mean goods and cattle. They do not care, not for me, not for their own men. And the men are the same. Sometimes kind but always careless, especially of us mortals."

He told her then about rescuing the sidhe child and that he thought he stayed there no more than five or six months. "When I left, I thought I would be coming to seek you soon after you left Emain Macha. I had no idea I had been five years with the sidhe, and none of them ever thought to tell me that time runs differently in their *lios* – slower."

That was a weight off Medb's mind; there had always been a doubt in her about Ailill's constancy, whether he might disappear again. So she tightened her grip on the hand she held as he told her how careful he had been when he went to gather up what Bodb held for him, so as not to get caught in the time trap.

"That was well done," she said. "You have made a good friend in Bodb."

She made to rise again. This time – a little to her regret – he did not hold her back, but also rose from the bed. When they were dressed though, he stopped her from leaving at the door.

"Wait here," he said. "I have a morning gift for you."

Medb burst into laughter. "I was scarcely a virgin when we came together, my love. My morning gift—" Her bright eyes darkened with remembered hurt; Conchobar had given her nothing.

"—was not paid," Ailill said. "I could do nothing then. But you will have it now and it will content you for all past injury."

Which left Medb blinking and wondering as Ailill left. A very short time later the door was flung open again and Ailill stood at the side, holding the halter of . . . a bull. It was red and white as were Medb's cattle but it was every bit as fine a beast as the black and white bull that Ailill owned.

"Your morning gift," Ailill said. "Now we are equal."

Medb's eyes widened with understanding. She would go her way; Ailill would go his, but they would always be together.

"*Compeer*," she breathed. "Partner."

On Inishmore

Ciar Cullen

Inishmore, Aran Islands, Ireland – 1890

Maeve wrapped her shawl tightly around her shoulders against the howling wind, biting back laughter as the new master of Kildooney House made his way up the path. Green as moss, he was, from the ferry crossing. How did the Americans make the crossing when they couldn't stand the few miles from Rossaveal?

He was soaked, was Brian Fitzgerald, late of Boston. Maeve had known his father, and his father's father, and no doubt a few ancestors before them she'd since forgotten. All drawn to Inishmore, searching, longing for meaning in their life, a phantom that never materialized, or perhaps a love that was under their noses all along. A welling of her own longing filled her but she brushed it aside, not willing to open a wound she no longer cared to stitch close. The pain of that mending wasn't worth the risk.

Fitzgerald took the few steps to the porch and stopped short at the sight of Maeve. She could practically read his mind. He'd expected a housekeeper, but not one of Maeve's advanced years and ugly countenance. He took a deep breath and pulled off his bowler, shaking water in a near stream from the rim.

"Mrs MacGearailt? I am Brian Fitzgerald."

"That much is obvious, lad. Welcome to Kildooney House. Welcome to Inishmore."

He nodded his thanks and stood in awkward silence, as if

he needed further permission to enter. He didn't. He owned Kildooney since the recent death of his father.

"It might be best if you come in out of the rain. You need a hot meal, dry clothes and a good night's sleep. All will look better in the morning. Except for me." She winked and Brian Fitzgerald laughed in embarrassment.

"I am very pleased to finally meet you." He seemed sincere.

Maeve peeked in at him as he warmed his feet near the fire, half asleep with exhaustion. The young woman enchanted within the crone stirred restlessly at his fine figure, long legs stretched out, broad shoulders wrapped in a blanket of her own making, silky auburn hair brushing his once-starched collar. No, she reprimanded herself, do not imagine he is the one who will lift this enchantment.

He was the first of the Fitzgerald men to travel without a manservant, and Maeve wondered idly how long he would stay in the rambling mansion with the quiet bearing down on him and the luxuries of Boston an ocean away. The young woman in her surfaced again momentarily, wondering too what life alone under the same roof would bring. No doubt disappointment. She would put that dream in a box and lock it with a key, throw the key into Galway Bay.

"You must let me help, Mrs MacGearailt." Brian bit back a testy tone, anxious to make headway on his writing. She dropped an enormous basket of laundry near his desk.

Maeve MacGearailt was the toughest, most stubborn woman he'd ever had the fortune, or misfortune as the case may be, to encounter. Maeve looked to be a thousand years old, give or take a few centuries. How she carried pails of water with her crooked back and withered limbs confounded him. Her body looked like one of the aged scrubby trees dotting the landscape, grown twisted and knotty against a cruel climate.

She rose in the morning before him, tidied up the mess he left in his study, cooked a hearty breakfast, and scrubbed the floor or washed the curtains by the time he brushed sleep from his eyes. He'd grown accustomed to her haggish appearance – at least it no longer startled him. Although the first sight of her, standing in the doorway of the mansion, with lightning and wind as a haunting backdrop, had nearly sent him to his knees in prayer against an Irish curse.

"How far along are you now, Mr Fitzgerald?" She folded clothes in his study, a habit that irritated the hell out of him.

Further by thousands of words if you would leave me be, he thought. "Please, let us stop this formality. Call me Brian."

"I am Maeve."

Brian frowned, feeling a bit guilty he'd never even asked about her given name, never asked her a thing about her life. How did she come to be alone at Kildooney House? Did she have family or friends? She never spoke of anything but his comfort, listening to him rant away about the difficulties of penning his grand novel. The barristers had always seen to the house, and no doubt to the pittance Maeve earned keeping the place standing.

At times in the last few months, he'd questioned the wisdom of selling the *Boston Daily Traveler*, the newspaper that had brought wealth and esteem to the family. At twenty-four, he'd yearned for a different life. Without a compass, he'd latched on to the first intriguing notion introduced at the reading of his father's last will and testament.

He owned a mansion in Ireland. Brian glanced at Maeve, her tattered dress and shawl blending with the tattered furnishings of Kildooney House. A mansion in Ireland had a different meaning, no doubt.

Still, it was lovely and wild and quiet on Inishmore. No social obligations pulled him away, no insipid young ladies sent unsolicited notes and invitations. There was only a warm house, a bluff overlooking a wild bay, a town four kilometre's walk away with nothing but a pub, a smithy and a few poor shops, and Maeve.

To Brian, Maeve embodied all he knew of Ireland. As far from the ton of Boston as a person could be, Maeve was ugly, evidently poor and filled with a mixture of what seemed like fortitude and longing. She tugged at his heart, and he wondered why. No doubt just melancholy for his own mother and grandmother, long since crossed.

"Well, Brian, it seems you're in need of a *Leannán* Sidhe, but do take care should you meet her."

"Please, Maeve, no young women. I've had my fill, begging your pardon for mentioning it. I came for quiet."

Maeve cackled out a laugh so hearty she collapsed on to the couch hugging her stomach. "You don't know of the Aos Sí? The faery folk? The Gentry?"

Brian rested his head on his typewriter. He'd been warned that to open the door to an Irish story could mean the waste of hours of precious time. He turned and glanced at Maeve, still red in the face from laughing. How could he be rude to her?

"Go ahead; tell me about the wee faeries."

"Wee? Ah, I see. Little brownies and such, is that it?" Maeve rose and brushed at her apron, which no amount of straightening would ever make crisp, and tucked her parchment white hair under her kerchief.

"I meant no offence! Do tell me." Brian bit back a curse, knowing that he had to mend this rift lest guilt haunt him the rest of the day. The novel would have to wait. It seemed it always had to wait.

"If you truly insist?" Maeve sat again, and folded her hands reverently.

"I do insist." Brian pulled the paper from his typewriter to show his willingness to listen, and lit his pipe.

"You are a writer, an artist, is that not so?"

A subtle smile pulled at her lips and Brian saw the joke. "As you well know, I have yet to write a thing of any import. I take that is an example of the famous Irish sense of humour."

"That is why you must find your Leannán Sidhe!" She clapped her hands as if she'd made the cleverest announcement. "Your muse, Brian. A Leannán Sidhe is a lovely young woman, one of the Gentry. She imbues artists with intense creativity, and from her, they rise to the summit of their abilities. But one must take care, for your muse may also torture your spirit, so alluring is her form and well . . . ways, shall we say?"

"I'm finding that writing is torture enough, without throwing a Lea—?"

"Leannán Sidhe . . ."

"Without complicating matters with one of those."

"Ah, all matters are already complicated, whether you wish for them or not."

Brian wondered if Maeve had ever been lovely, had ever inspired a young man to great heights. And as he looked into her twinkling eyes, a fine shimmering mist arose between them. Beyond the veil of mist, sat a young Maeve, a much younger Maeve. The most beautiful girl Brian had seen or imagined. He shook his head and the illusion lifted as quickly as it came. I have the imagination of an artist, he thought. If I only had the talent to match.

"Well, Maeve, if you ever run into one of the Gentry, I will gladly accept any help they are willing to bestow. For I am now one month behind in my work. I may as well have stayed in Boston. No doubt I will return there as a failure. At least, I now wish I'd not told my friends that I would return a novelist."

Maeve cheated every morning, as she had for hundreds of years. While the master of the house slept, she assumed her youthful form to perform the most arduous tasks. Technically, as a Corrigan, she could assume either of her personas at will, as long as she gave them equal time. Long ago, she'd found it easier to drift through the years as a crone. The bones ached, the muscles were weak, and there was no joy in glancing into the mirror, but men left her alone. Because no man cared about an old crone.

This is exactly what was required to break the spell of her kind. A man needed to love the crone as much as the beauty. She'd learned after much heartbreak, more than once, nay, more than a dozen times, that beauty was the only prize men cherished. Wasn't this the curse of womankind, faery or human?

A youthful body made easy work of scrubbing a floor or

pulling weeds from the garden, though. Brian Fitzpatrick was blessedly a sound sleeper. Poor fellow, she mused, wondering if he'd ever finish his book. He'd made good progress in the last few weeks, but he cursed when he didn't think she heard. She'd found many pages of discarded would-be brilliance balled up under his desk or surrounding the ash can.

She tried to leave him alone, truly she did, but her mixed nature betrayed her at times. She'd knit an Aran sweater for him while sitting on the couch near his desk, eyeing his handsome profile, knowing that she drove him to near insanity with her clacking bone needles. At times she almost wished he'd speak his mind, tell her to leave the room, or worse, send her packing. Then she would reveal herself to his great amazement and shame, she fantasized.

No, Brian Fitzgerald was genteel and mannered, although without airs. He was not the sort to insult an old lady. He seemed to have come to enjoy their evening pipes by the fire nearly as much as she. Once, a bit in his cups after a particularly gruelling day of staring at a blank page, he'd pulled her in for a benign hug. Maeve had forced herself to stay the crone, while her spirit craved to cleave to his warm embrace as a young beauty.

Ah, just one kiss before he left for Boston, she fantasized as she pushed the basket of clean wet clothes on to her hip and set to the lines for hanging in the salt breeze. What would it hurt? One touch of that dark handsome cheek, one rake of her hand through his silken hair, one—

"Hello."

Maeve jumped with a squeal and turned on her bare foot to see Brian, a bit sleepy, pushing a hand through his hair. His eyes widened as he took her in, and Maeve, for the first time in hundreds of years, fell mute.

"I'm sorry to have frightened you. I haven't . . ." Brian went mute as well, and ran his gaze up and down her, sending coils of excitement and fear through her veins. He took a few hesitant strides and extended his hand.

"I'm Brian Fitzgerald, from Boston."

Think, Maeve, for the love of the Goddess, think.

"Yes, of course you are!" She pinned his shirt to the line and ignored his extended hand. "Just getting this done. I'll be out of your way presently."

"That's my washing."

"Is it now? Oh my, well, no need for you to see this. Back in the house with you. I'm sure you'll want some tea and bacon, and Maeve will have that for you shortly."

"Where is Maeve?"

"I mean, she'll have that for you when she returns from Kilronan. That's where she is, Kilronan."

"How did she get to town? She said nothing of it to me. Please do not say that my dear Maeve walked all that way."

"Yes, she did. She does so quite often."

"I must take the horse and cart to retrieve her then. She is not fit for that. Why did you let her go?"

"No! She did get a ride, now that I recall. I am so silly today, you must forgive me." *Maeve, Maeve, you are doing quite poorly here. Pull your knickers on straight and catch your breath.*

She turned and faced Brian, feeling the heat rush to her cheeks. He'd think her a simpleton, and he'd be right to do so. "I am Fiona, Maeve's granddaughter, come from Kilronan to help."

"Ah, then I'm very pleased to meet you, Fiona." Indeed he was, eyeing her with the lust that emanated from every man she encountered. He caught himself and straightened up, all but slapping himself in the face to stop gaping.

"So there is nothing wrong with Maeve? She has not called you here because the work is too arduous? I wondered about her family, but she never mentioned a granddaughter."

Maeve started at his tone, a bit reprimanding. "I do help when I can."

"I am very glad to hear it. I thought perhaps to hire a man to do the heavy work. It pains me to see her at her chores. I would just as well have her here as a guest. I would not insult her, but she is quite old. And I do believe she is the worst cook on the island." He laughed lightly as Maeve's blood started to boil.

"The worst cook, you said? On the island?"

"Perhaps the worst in Ireland. The woman can burn water, truth be told."

Maeve bit at her bottom lip and narrowed her eyes, holding back a curse that would turn the bastard into a hare.

"Listen, you ungrateful, good for nothing *American*, with your fancy ways and tastes. My grandmother is a fine cook, a fine cook indeed. Imagine, calling Maeve MacGearailt a poor cook. Why don't you push her to the ground and kick her? Do you know what it is to say such a thing about a MacGearailt? *Go n-ithe an cat thú is go n-ithe an diabhal an cat.*"

Brian had backed up several steps and was dangerously close to falling into a bramble. "What?"

"I said, may you be eaten by a cat that is eaten by the devil!"

"I'm very sorry, I had no idea . . ." He held up a hand to ward off her ire and tripped into the hedgerow.

Maeve saw her chance and made a break for it, picking up her skirts and running for all she was worth to the path leading to the beach. He'd follow her, she was sure, so she ducked behind a tree and cast a light shadow spell to remain hidden.

"Miss Fiona?" His call was but a whisper, and Maeve regretted lashing out at him so, at least a little. "Miss Fiona, where are you? I'm very sorry. I love your grandmother, and never meant an insult."

I love your grandmother. Oh, if that were only true, Maeve thought.

He searched the beach, every room of the house, every foot of the grounds. Fiona had disappeared as suddenly as she'd materialized. Her impression on him, however, lingered.

Why was it that the most beautiful woman in the world had the temper of a crazed dog? Who would have guessed that one could become so irate over a comment about cooking? Surely the granddaughter knew that Maeve burned everything? And why hadn't she come even once in the four months he'd been at Kildooney? Was she so busy in Kilronan, or did she care so little for her grandmère?

And if she was such a shrew, why did she burn in Brian's mind and body like he'd been branded for eternity by the mere sight of her? What a beauty, with long straight dark hair and bright blue eyes – Maeve's eyes, for sure, but without the film of the years clouding them. Her pale skin and wide curves figured heavily in his fantasies of kissing her and hovering an inch over her ready, loving and naked body.

Well, with Fiona gone, Maeve was the priority, for sure. He hitched the jaunting cart to old Eamon and headed for Kilronan, intent on finding his aged friend and, with any luck, becoming friends with the younger MacGearailt.

The road to Kilronan took him past tiny estates, so small they seemed fit only for the faery folk Maeve loved to speak of. He wound his way down to the sea, looking for Maeve and taking in the grey vista of the port and bay that would one day start his journey back to Boston. Without a novel in hand, at least one worth reading.

The best source of information in any Irish community, even in America, is the local pub, so that's where he hitched Eamon. When his eyes adjusted to the low light and his nose to the strong odours, Brian settled on the oldest patron he could find – the most likely source of information. He was nearly as wizened as Maeve and, for all Brian knew, could have been her brother, so interrelated were these Aran folk.

Brian removed his hat and indicated the stool next to the man. "Do you speak English?"

"When I like."

Brian bit back a groan and didn't bother sitting. "I don't suppose that this might be one of those times?"

"Depends on what you want with me, Brian Fitzgerald of Boston, Massachusetts."

Lord, of course. There wouldn't be a soul in Kilronan who didn't know his identity and his business, and probably his hat size as well.

Brian put a coin on the bar and motioned to the keep to bring another round to the stranger.

"I'm looking for Maeve MacGearailt, and her granddaughter, Fiona. Have you seen either?"

"Fiona?" The man turned to face Brian and narrowed his eyes. "There is no Fiona of Maeve's blood, you fool. Daft, are you? Looking for the Tuatha Dé Danann?"

Brian stared blankly, wondering frantically how to avoid another long tale.

"The Gentry, lad. You don't look for them; they find you. Now be off with your Fiona and Maeve. Find one and find both. You'll be in Boston before Samhain, for sure, with Maeve's boot print on your arse."

Brian picked up his coin and turned on his heel, hearing the stranger mutter "*Imeacht gan teacht ort*" behind him.

"I certainly won't come back," Brian called over his shoulder. He'd not found poor Maeve or irate Fiona, and had only a thirsty horse and a fierce headache for his trouble. Perhaps it was time to think about going home. They were all crazy, superstitious and ill-tempered, these island natives. Still, the whole ride home, the vision of Fiona danced in his head, and started an enchanted spiralling journey into his chest.

Maeve pulled her shawl over her head as she walked the grey strand, thinking of Brian, as she did most waking moments. For four months she'd endured the torture of his closeness. Torture because it was not close enough. He was a good man, and a good man deserved the truth, but she was not free to give the truth to him. Within weeks, he would tire of his would-be sanctuary, tire of his hag of a housekeeper, and sail away forever.

Didn't she deserve his touch, a bit of closeness, a kiss, an embrace? Could she stand, just one more time, to enjoy the attention of a man without falling in love with him?

Too late, she thought, wiping a tear from her cheek. Unrequited love was her fate, the fate of all the women of her kind, for all eternity. And indeed, she did love Brian.

Maeve fretted with a tangle in her hair as she walked, wishing now she had not left a note for him. For as sure as day would turn to night an hour hence, Brian Fitzgerald would be happy to have a beauty under his roof instead of a hag. But he would not stay; he would not love her.

Be strong, Maeve, she chastised herself, and made her way up the path towards Kildooney House. Enjoy this time you have. You may not see the likes of this man for a long time.

He sat on the steps and rose as she approached the house. "Miss Fiona! I've looked for you. I'm very sorry to have angered you."

Maeve smiled at his blush. "Was I angry? I cannot recall." She winked and his blush deepened.

"I am forgiven? I saw Maeve's note saying that she must visit her sister in Galway for a week. I had no idea she had a sister!"

"Aye, a twin sister."

"Imagine, two of them! I have been the worst friend to her. Thinking only of myself and my petty cares."

"You are the master of the house, Mr Fitzgerald. Your cares are ours."

"I do not need care, Miss Fiona. I can take care of myself, and you can return to Kilronan if you like." Maeve saw it pained him to suggest it, and wondered what manner of man turned away a beautiful young woman ready to serve him.

"No, I promised Maeve I would look after you. Especially your meals." Maeve winked again and this time, Brian laughed fully. What a sight, she thought, as his handsome face came to life. I'll have him for a time, and Goddess willing, it will be sweet enough to help me swallow this bitter pill of fate.

"I will eat what you put before me, without a word. Please, will you let me do any heavy work? I am tired of watching Irish women work their fingers to the bone on my account."

"We shall see." Maeve swept by Brian into the house, letting him catch a whiff of her magical scent to set the wheels in motion. He'd be on her in an instant.

To her amazement, Brian strode into his study, lit his pipe, and settled in at his desk. She stood and watched from the doorway as he threaded a new sheet of paper into his machine, cracked his knuckles, and starting tapping away.

Maeve ran to the great room and scurried before the full-length mirror, terrified she'd morphed permanently into an ogre. The exquisite image she'd seen for centuries stared back at her in concern. She'd flirted, and he'd sat down to work. Well, that would not do at all! Maeve hadn't imagined that Brian had undressed her with his eyes, that he'd had to pick his tongue off the earth at the first sight of her.

Perhaps the isolation had finally taken its toll? Had he gone mad?

Maeve hurried to the kitchen to brew a kettle of tea, tapping her foot as she waited for the water to churn. When she entered the study, Brian did not look up, but continued tapping away.

"Excuse me, Brian. Tea is on."

He looked up, confusion etched on his face. "Tea?"

"Certainly Maeve brought you tea while you worked?" Maeve poured and sat on the couch near his desk, not waiting for an invitation to join him.

"Yes, sorry. I say, my brain has sprung a leak on to the page! Oh, I wish Maeve were here to tell. She'd be so happy for me. I have you to thank." He smiled and Maeve's heart lurched in her chest.

"Me?"

"Yes, I believe you may be the muse she warned me about! An exquisite beauty who would bring me to my highest level of creativity."

"Do you mean a Leannán Sidhe?"

"That's it exactly! Now, I don't believe all of Maeve's tales, but she did warn me to take care should such a beauty appear. As soon as I sat down, the words came pouring from my fingertips. I fancy they're good words."

Maeve covered her mouth with her hand. The man thought her a threat?

"I'm no muse, Brian. Just a pretty face. You can't honestly believe that I could torture you into a terrible lovelorn state?"

"Oh, I believe you could wear down a holy man. Your beauty has inspired me to write a tale of unrequited love." He sipped at his tea and smiled sincerely.

"For the love of . . ." You imbecile, she wanted to scream. "Must it be unrequited? Couldn't it be more . . . requited? Returned? Consummated?"

His eyes widened and he rattled his cup on its saucer. "Miss Fiona, I . . . I can barely imagine . . . well, I can imagine . . . I could not dream of . . . could I?"

"I'm not speaking of hopes and dreams, Mr Fitzgerald. They do very little on a cool fall Aran evening to warm the body."

Maeve bit at her lip, shocked a bit at herself for her open offer. For the first time in aeons, she waited anxiously for a man's acceptance as her young beautiful self. The crone in her was quite used to rejection.

Brian stood, took off his spectacles, and ran his hand through his hair. Maeve could practically hear the wheels grinding inside his head, could cut the silence with a knife. He held her gaze and sent her blood racing.

He didn't make a move, or sound, or even, it seemed, did he breathe. Perhaps he was shy, perhaps he was a lover of men, perhaps . . . he could actually refuse her. Shame and hurt clutched at Maeve's heart and she turned to flee. With a strong grip on her elbow and a firm arm around her waist, Brian turned her around and held her still. He smelled of fresh air and sweet pipe tobacco. His burning lustful gaze at her bosom belied the gentle smile pulling at his full lips.

"So, Fiona, you have caught me in a terrible lie."

"Have I now?"

"I do not care about the cost of your allure, my muse." He leaned in and brushed his lips gently against hers, setting her skin tingling.

"I am not a muse, Brian."

"Still, you are enchanting. I care only what Maeve will think of me."

"She would think you quite the horse's ass to refuse her granddaughter." Maeve could stand it no longer, and reached her hands around Brian's neck, pulling him down for a real kiss. It may as well have been her first kiss, for how it turned her bones to jam and her heart racing in her chest.

Brian's moans of pleasure drummed through her body as he slashed his tongue against hers and pulled at her lips. He brought his hands down her back and cupped her flesh, none too lightly. The shy would-be novelist was on fire, white-hot and growing more scorching by the second. He fisted her hair and pulled to expose her neck to kisses and nibbles that sent Maeve's knees wobbling. He whispered her name, his breath hot in her ear.

"Fiona, I would have you, but only with Maeve's permission to court you. I love the woman and will not dishonour her. No matter the cost to my sanity." He squirmed and adjusted his trousers, then pulled back.

Maeve could barely breathe. He must be teasing. *Maeve's permission.* She wanted to scream. You have Maeve's permission, you idiot!

"Well, isn't this a bloody fine twist on enchantment!" She ran from the room, scurried to her bedroom, and locked the door behind her. He did not even follow.

Brian stared at the blank page, wondering if he should get up, go to the cliff, and throw himself into Galway Bay. For he certainly didn't deserve to go on in this state. Fiona hadn't thrown herself at him, she'd instead shrunk herself down to the size of a pin and poked at every fibre of his body. Relentlessly. Was this the torture Maeve warned him about? The burning he'd never felt in his life. So complete was her hold on him, his blood ran hot each time he heard movement in the house.

She'd avoided him completely, for two days. Breakfast – undercooked – would be waiting upon his awakening. Tea manifested as if by magic when he returned to his study. He'd wandered the halls, only to see her shadow disappear around a corner.

Now his lust turned to obsession. Now he simply wanted to see her, to speak with her, to learn about her. Why could she not sit in his study and knit as her grandmother had? Could they not go for a stroll on the beach? Did she now find him odious?

The Irish were all insane, but those on Inishmore took first prize. Or, perhaps, as the old salt in the pub had warned him, Maeve, Fiona and Kildooney House were enchanted, and he would not leave the island with his own sanity.

Fiona took his breath away when she suddenly swept into his study with a note in hand, which she slapped on his desk with fervour.

"There, Brian Fitzgerald. There is your permission. You may court me should you find me worthy."

He stared at the envelope and then back at Fiona. She crossed her arms over her lovely breasts and tapped her foot in annoyance. Brian tentatively opened the envelope and read the note: "Mr Fitzgerald, once again I am sorry that I left suddenly. My sister is doing better. I will return shortly. You may court (or do as you like with) young Fiona. Signed, Maeve MacGearailt."

What a thing! "Do as you like with." That didn't sound like Maeve, but here was her note, in the same hand as the one she'd previously left him. His hand practically shook as he placed the note on the desk and stared at Fiona.

"I know what I want, Brian, so do not look at me so. There is no shame in it. You have your permission. I can be your love or your maid. The decision is yours."

"As I like your kisses more than your cooking . . ." He held up his hand as she narrowed her eyes to fiery ice-blue daggers. "That was a joke, Fiona. How did Maeve get a note to me in two days from Galway? You have been here the whole time."

"Have not." Fiona flushed and pushed her toes at the carpet, eyes downcast.

"Have too."

"Maeve is now on Inishmore, visiting another sister in town before returning."

"How many sisters does Maeve have? Oh, never mind I asked." Brian thought of the large families in Boston and realized he must sound silly to Fiona. She must already think him the oddity – only child, parentless, aspiring novelist. What did such a woman want with such an uninteresting man?

"How rich do you think I am, Fiona?"

She slapped him. She slapped the smile off his face, and then did it again.

He grabbed her hand to stop a third slap.

"You are the devil himself. You insult my cooking . . . my grandmother's cooking and my cooking, you insult my kisses by turning away, and now I'm a *drùth*? As if I care a whit about your money. I can conjure money from the air and call gold from the sea to wash on to the shore. I can make the skies rain silver and milk emeralds from a cow."

Her cheeks blazed scarlet and her chest rose and fell quickly with her fury. Brian looked into her eyes and saw she spoke the truth. She could do those things, and more. Icy fingers crawled up and down his spine, and electricity coursed into the hand that clutched her wrist.

"Is that why I fell in love with you the moment I saw you? Because you cast a spell on me?"

"Stupid *guraiceach*. I could have cast any spell . . ." She dropped her hand to her side and Brian let go of her wrist. Her eyes softened and she wiped her lips. "Did you say something about love?"

Brian nodded, wondering if she'd slap him again. "It makes no sense, but despite how much I seem to anger you, I feel as if I've known you for quite a while."

"For quite a while?"

"And that underneath that beauty and temper is a wise, strong woman."

"A wise woman?"

"And strong."

Fiona's mouth pulled to the side and a frown creased her brow as she considered his words. Brian's heart raced as he waited for her to say something, anything, to indicate what she thought of him. He'd offered love to an enchantress, to the most beautiful enchantress ever born, if indeed they were born and didn't spring from the earth full grown. She would think him an idiot. In fact, she was now looking at him as if he were quite the oaf.

"Would it be best if I return to Boston, Fiona? I would understand. I know not how it became so complicated once Maeve left . . ." Maeve. How could he leave her as well, and without a word of thanks or care? He would find her in Kilronan.

"Because of my very nature, Brian, I am forbidden to tell you why it is so, but I love you too, not as a stranger."

The world spun beneath Brian's feet. No, life did not bring such things to him so easily. Was this part of her enchantment? Again, he gazed into her eyes, searching for the truth, and found it. She loved him.

Enchantment be damned, he thought as he rose from the desk and swept Fiona off her feet. She moaned in pleasure as he kissed her and fumbled up the winding stairs to his bedroom. He plopped her on the bed and her surprise turned to mischief as she wiggled a long finger for him to join her.

What then, Maeve? she asked herself. What happens when you must give the crone equal time, when Brian finds you missing, begins to ask questions, becomes obsessive, grows suspicious and angry? No, put it away, she thought. Take this for yourself.

For a few hours, Brian kissed and caressed away all thought. He stripped her bare with torturous slowness, showering every inch of her skin with his hot kisses and tongue. She returned the favour, again and again, adoring the feel of his strong embrace, the wonderful feel of his skin against hers, the cries of pleasure as she took him into her mouth, into her body. They fell into one another's secret lives, limbs and burning bodies enmeshed as if they would always be one. Brian was not timid, not awkward, not silly or vain. He was the man of Maeve's dreams.

They lay in a close embrace, hours later, listening to the wind howl in suggestion of a terrible storm to come. Rain pelted the glass, and the candle flickered with the draught that tore through the old rafters.

Brian caressed Maeve's hair and kissed her forehead. "Tell me this isn't the only day I'll have you like this. Tell me this is the first of many."

"The first of some, for certain."

He tilted her chin so their gazes met. "How can I make it go on forever?"

Ah, so there it was. The question she craved and feared, that stabbed at her heart. She turned away, lest he see the answer.

A terrible pounding at the front door startled them from their embrace. They both sat up and Maeve scrambled into her dress.

"Oh, let them knock," Brian said, pulling her back down.

"It will take only a moment."

He sighed and pulled on his trousers, followed her down the staircase and stood behind her as she unbolted the front door. A young man, soaked from the rain, stepped in and fretted with his cap.

"Why, Padraig, what brings you from town?"

"I do not know you, miss. I was hoping Maeve was about?" He looked past her at Brian, and his eyes widened.

Brian stepped forward. "Come in, lad. Maeve is in Kilronan."

Maeve stepped in front of Brian. "Oh, I think she went back to Galway. She will be a while."

"Then it's true!" Padraig troubled more with his cap and looked to Brian. "Sir, I am sorry to be the one to say so, but the ferry has floundered in the storm."

Maeve's heart raced. She would surely know someone on that ferry.

"The fishermen have recovered most aboard, and they are well, or will be. But one old lady . . . who looked like Maeve MacGearailt . . ."

"What!" Brian pulled his sweater from the coat rack and slipped on his boots while Maeve and Padraig stared.

"I must go. Fiona, you stay here, out of harm's way."

"It's not her, Brian." Maeve pulled at Brian's sleeve and snapped at Padraig to leave.

"It could be her. They named her, Fiona. And you said she was crossing to Galway or back from Galway, which was it?"

"Do not go, Brian, I beg you. The fishermen are putting themselves at great risk to search, and I cannot lose you."

"Ah, sweet girl. I will be fine. But we must find your grandmother. Please, God, let it not be her. Let no one be hurt." He made the sign of the cross and pushed Fiona firmly aside.

"If you love me, you will not go."

Brian hesitated, then took her hand and kissed it. "I do love you, and I will still go. What kind of man would I be if I stayed to please one woman when another I love is in danger? I love Maeve too, Fiona. I trust that you understand that."

"No, please. She is an old lady, it is her time."

"How could you say such a thing? You cannot mean it. You are trying to trick me. Fiona, I could not live with myself. Please, sit and wait. I will return, I promise."

"You love her as much as you love me?" Maeve cried openly, so frustrated at the ridiculous, needless risk her beloved was taking.

"Yes, I do. Differently, of course."

Maeve nodded and gave up, turned her back on Brian and wept as he rushed out the door. So, she might lose him to the sea, and needlessly. "Goddess, protect him."

A sudden thought brought her to her feet. If she showed Brian and the rest that Maeve was alive and well, they would call off the search! She closed her eyes and chanted to bring on the change.

And waited.

It must be her anxiety, she thought. *Come on with it!* This time, she added a prayer to the chant and ran to the mirror.

"Oh!" Maeve fell to her knees and wept like a babe. The crone and maiden were joined, forever. The power lifted, the curse broken, all by the love of one man.

Brian returned, soaked, happy to have helped to rescue ancient Mrs O'Connell from the sea. Well, truth be told, he'd been fairly useless, only helping to clear onlookers as the fishermen carried the old lady to safety. Maeve was indeed safe with her sister or sisters, as all aboard the ferry were now accounted for.

"Fiona!" He called out, running from room to room when she didn't answer.

He found her sitting in his study, knitting the sweater that Maeve had begun for him, needles clacking. She smiled up at him.

"It was not Maeve! All are safe. Your grandmother is not harmed."

"I know, Brian."

"Who told you?" He sat in his chair, dripping on to the floor.

"Why don't you put a page in that machine of yours? I have a story to tell you."

The Morrígan's Daughter

Susan Krinard

Ancient Ireland

According to the Leabhar Gabhála Éireann – The Book of Conquests – *Éire has had many rulers. The first were the Fomóiri, cruel brutes and savages who knew nothing of plough and oxen and metal. Then came the Partholónians, descendants of Noah, who fought the Fomóiri and won, only to be wiped out by a terrible plague and buried on the Plain of Elta. The third race who sought to rule Éire were the people of Nemed, kin to the Partholónians. Nemed, like his forerunners, defeated the Fomóiri, but in the end the Nemedians were destroyed in a mighty flood. The fourth race were the Fir Bolg, who held Ireland for thirty-seven years before the coming of the Tuatha Dé Danann.*

But when the People of the Goddess Danu came from the north with their arts of magic and won the right to rule Éire in the First Battle of Maige Tuired, they would have no peace. When their king, Nuada, was forced to give up his crown, the half-Fomórian Bres held the people under his tyrannical rule for seven long years. Only when Nuada was restored to his throne was Bres compelled to flee, and urged the evil chief Balor to raise an army against the Tuatha Dé Danann. So came the Second Battle of Maige Tuired, won by the People only when Lugh Lámhfhada put out Balor's evil eye and turned the tide.

Many are the tales of bravery and loyalty and betrayal during that great battle and what came after. Many are the heroes who fought and died for freedom. But there is one story that has never been told . . .

Séanat pushed aside the low-hanging branches and entered the clearing. The Fomóir she had been pursuing was nowhere in sight. He, like the other survivors of his evil race, had fled the battle in terror and humiliation, defeated at last and for all time.

At first the Fomóiri had fought bravely, in their way, until they had brought their chief Balor with his evil eye to strike down the King Nuada. Then the Morrígan had lent her powers to that of Lugh, Nuada's champion, who put out Balor's eye. The battle had broken.

But the stragglers remained, and it was the duty and pleasure of every warrior of the Tuatha Dé Danann to pursue and destroy them. Every warrior including the Daughters of the Morrígan, whose ferocity matched that of any man among the followers of Lugh of the Long Arm.

Lifting her bloodied sword, Séanat took a cautious step. A great oak spread its arms over the clearing like a Druid giving his blessing to those who would fight and die. There was a peace here, and Séanat felt the killing lust drain from her body.

Surely no Fomóir could have remained in such a place for long. *This* place belonged to the People of Danu, to the magic that had made the land strong.

The weight of Séanat's armour began to sit heavily upon her, and she looked again at the oak with its broad tangle of roots and the thick cushion of last year's fallen leaves that made a bed for anyone who should wish for rest.

You must not, she told herself. It was not her privilege to rest when any Fomóir roamed free upon this island. Let them be driven into the sea from whence they had come long ages past. Let Lir swallow them and never give them up again.

But it was difficult now to feel the rage that had carried her through the battle and made her forget the wounds on her legs and the dirt on her face. The oak stirred in a gentle wind, brown and yellow leaves sighing as they floated gently to the earth.

Only a little while. Just long enough to regain her strength and her resolve. The enemy she pursued might get away, but it would only be for a little while. She would find him, or another like him, and go on until nightfall called an end to the hunt.

Wearily she made her way to the oak, touched its rough bark with a chant of thanks, and laid herself down. The cushion of leaves accepted her like the arms of the lover she had never had. The root that served as her pillow seemed to soften under her head. Even her armour lost its hardness. She laid down her sword with a sigh, and the sound let loose a fresh fall of leaves that settled over her in a blanket of warmth and contentment.

She didn't know how long she slept. It might have been the faint crack of a twig, or no more than the rustle of a single leaf that woke her. But Séanat opened her eyes, and there was a man in the clearing, no more than a dozen steps away.

Her sword was already in her hand as she leaped up, prepared to slash and stab. The man didn't move. He stood completely still, his own sword pointed towards the earth, dressed in the armour of the Fomóiri.

But his face was not hideous or twisted with evil, nor was his body misshapen. He was broad of shoulder and comely like the disgraced King Bres, who carried the blood of both the Fomóiri and the Tuatha Dé Danann in his veins. Like Lugh, born of Ethlinn, Balor's daughter. His hair was like smoke to Séanat's flame.

Still he was of the enemy. Séanat lunged towards him, her sword reaching his throat before he could raise his own.

"Prepare to die, Fomóir," she cried.

His eyes, blue as the sea, met hers. "Kill me, then," he said, his accent so light that she might never have noticed it had he worn the armour of the People.

Her hand twitched, and her sword drew a thin line of blood from his neck. "Do you seek death?"

He smiled with a great sadness that tore at her heart. "I do, for I have no people and no place." He lifted his chin. "Finish it, warrior."

If it had not been for the old oak and the magic of its peace, she might have severed his head then and there. But her fingers trembled and the sword went slack in her hand.

"Who are you?" she demanded.

"I am called Aodhan," he said in his soft, low voice. "I fought with the Fomóiri."

"You are no Fomóir!"

"Am I not?" He gestured at his armour with its sigils of writhing wyrms and ravening wolves. "Will it help if I fight you now, woman of the Tuatha Dé?"

She backed away. "I will fight you, and win!"

He shook his head, stirring the black forelock that curled over his brow. "You will win," he said. He dropped his sword and spread his arms. "Come."

Séanat's heart danced a wild jig in her chest. "Coward," she hissed.

"Yes," he said.

Moving clumsily as a newborn calf, she stumbled backwards until she came up against the oak's massive trunk. Light filtered through the branches to lie across Aodhan's head and shoulders like a crown of fire.

"I am a traitor," he said, "a traitor to both my peoples."

"Both?" Oh, she had known it, known from the beginning . . .

"You asked who I am," he said. "But that I do not know. I was raised by Fomóiri to be Fomóir. But my heart has told me—" He shook his head again. "It matters not. I fought beside those who gave me food and shelter and cared for me in times of illness. I would die with them."

Oh, how simple it would be to give him his wish rather than pay heed to the pity that weakened her. Bes had been half-Tuatha Dé, though in the end he had chosen his Fomóir father's people. Lugh had chosen the opposite. This warrior, like them, was half light and half darkness.

But he had made his choice.

Séanat raised her sword again. Aodhan closed his eyes.

She dropped the sword with a wretched cry. She could not do it. He was unarmed, a pig for the slaughter. She was a warrior, not an executioner.

And he was comely. So very comely. The light was there,

shining in his eyes, almost eclipsed by the shadow of his pain and sorrow.

When he moved, she had no time to think how easily she had been tricked. In an instant he had her sword in his hand. The blade glittered in the waning light.

She laughed inwardly. She'd been a fool. And soon she would be a dead fool.

Séanat stood very straight, raised her head, and lifted her arms. *Morrígan, Great Queen, be with me. Let me die with honour.*

The blow never came. She heard a grunt of pain, and the sound of a body falling to the ground. Aodhan lay curled like a newborn babe around the hilt of the sword he had plunged deep into his chest.

Séanat dropped to her knees beside him. His blood was already soaking into the soil, painting the brown leaves with crimson. She didn't dare pull the sword free, for that would surely end his life. He must die slowly, his life leaking away, with only an enemy to witness his passing.

There were songs for the dying – taught, it was said, to the People by the Goddess Danu herself before the coming to Inis Fáil. Never had such a song been sung by one of the Tuatha Dé for a Fomóir. But Séanat laid her hands upon Aodhan's shoulders and began the lament, her voice rising and curling among the heavy branches above her head. One tear came, and then another – no shame, for the emotions of the Tuatha Dé ran high, in battle and in sorrow.

"Why do you weep, child?"

Séanat opened her eyes. The scent of flowers filled her nostrils, and the oak's leaves murmured as the great tree bowed to the one who had come.

"My lady," Séanat whispered. Bluebells and primroses had sprung up where the lady trod, covering her bare feet and clinging to her robes like the finest embroidery. No shadow fell over Séanat as Brighid came to stand beside her.

"He is dying, lady," Séanat said. "Though I know not why I should mourn."

Brighid sighed, and a dozen tiny birds settled on her

shoulders. "I have mourned," she said. "Mourned because there is no peace, and my son is dead."

Sickened by her stupid mistake, Séanat bowed, her braided locks brushing Brighid's feet. She knew the great loss the lady had suffered in this battle, the sacrifices she had made in the name of peace. She had married Bres when he had become King of the Tuatha Dé, hoping that the union would bring the two warring peoples together at last.

But Bres had enslaved his subjects, making a mockery of Brighid's hopes. He was deposed and sent into exile. Their son, Ruadán, had become a spy for the Fomóiri and had met his death in the camp of the Tuatha Dé. Brighid's keening had been heard the length and breadth of Inis Fáil.

"Forgive me, lady," Séanat said.

Brighid's tears fell on a scattering of acorns, and new trees sprang from their hearts. "My son was misled," she said. "He was destroyed by his father's lust for power. But he was not evil." She knelt, laying her hand on Aodhan's arm. "This one, too, was misled."

Séanat's breast swelled with hope. "Is he Tuatha Dé, lady?"

The lady gave no answer. She bent her head over Aodhan as the last breaths shuddered out of his mouth. "Do you wish him healed, *a nighean ruadh*?"

Yes. Oh, yes. "He is the enemy . . ."

"Is he?" Brighid stroked Aodhan's damp hair. "I see only a boy driven to his death." She touched Séanat's hand. "It is your choice, warrior. But know that if you choose yes, you are bound to him forever."

Forever. The Tuatha Dé lived long. Séanat had always known she might die in battle, but such battles must be fewer now. She might live many years yet to come.

"I accept," she breathed. "Let him be healed, lady."

One touch was all it took. One touch of the lady's fingertips upon the torn flesh under the armour and cloth beneath. One moment, and the sword slipped from Aodhan's chest. A spurt of blood followed, stanched with another touch of Brighid's white finger. Aodhan groaned, and his muscles went slack.

But he was not dead. He was sleeping, the rest of one who has fought every battle and staggers back to the *ráth* to lick his wounds. In his face was an innocence Séanat had almost forgotten.

"You must stay with him," Brighid said, rising. "He will have no defence until he wakes." She brushed Séanat's forehead with the back of her slender hand. "Remember, he is yours now. All that he is will be within your keeping."

She turned and walked away, her white form dissolving into the gloom of dusk. Séanat stared after her until there was no more light to see. She removed her cloak and gently spread it over Aodhan. The night would be cold; Samhain was done, and the season was turning. Wolves crept in these woods, silent and yellow-eyed, creatures of Badb and her grim sisters.

I have betrayed my queen, Séanat thought, shivering as she drew her knees tight to her chest. The Morrígan would never forgive her for such mercy shown an enemy. Had not the Morrígan summoned all the Druids and magicians to defeat the Fomóiri? Had she not foreseen victory? Had she not predicted the very end of the world?

The other Daughters would not understand. But Séanat had made *her* choice. She must return to the royal camp and tell Lugh what she had done. If he sent her into exile . . .

It was a warrior's place to accept her fate.

Her skin puckered as the warmth left the earth. Brighid's flowers withered, and the birds scattered for shelter. Séanat lay down beside Aodhan and pulled the cloak over her shoulder so that it covered them both. His breath stirred the hair at the nape of her neck.

"All that he is will be within your keeping."

The Dagda grant he was worth it.

Aodhan woke with a start. The air was crisp on his face, but his body was as hot as the fire that shaped the sword.

She lay beside him, the warrior with her mane of red hair and dimpled chin and wide, wild eyes. She had curled into him, her hands tucked under her breasts, her legs drawn up as if she meant to keep one last barrier between them. A barrier besides the sword that rested in the narrow space between his body and hers.

Releasing his breath, Aodhan touched her hair. He had seen such hair many times before among the Tuatha Dé. But hers was brighter, shot with gold, spitting sparks when he touched it.

He didn't even know her name.

Not even when he felt his chest to find unscarred flesh did she wake. Only when he began to rise did she come to wakefulness and spring to her feet.

Aodhan raised his hands to show them empty. "Lady," he said softly, "how is it that I am still alive?"

The tension left her body. She bent to pick up her sword and flung it into the brambles. "No thanks to yourself." She brushed the leaves from her breeches and ran her fingers through her hair to untangle the strands that had come loose from their braids. "You won't be trying that again."

Struck by sudden weakness, Aodhan sat on the hump of the mighty oak's root. "I remember nothing," he said, "after the blade touched my heart."

"'Tis no surprise," she said. Her brow furrowed. "Are you well?"

He didn't laugh, though the temptation was great. "You have taken my honour from me."

Hands on hips, the warrior looked him over with disgust. "Your honour? You said yourself you had none to lose."

And he did not. Unless he could win it back again. Perhaps now that was possible. "How did you heal me?" he asked.

"'Twas not myself who did it." She walked towards the oak, keeping her distance from him, and sat on another root. "'Twas the Lady Brighid herself."

Aodhan started. It was not that Brighid, royal daughter of the Dagda, wise woman and healer, could not work such magic. It was that she chose to do so. She was of the Tuatha Dé.

Yet she had lost a son at the hand of one of her own people, a half-Fomóir son whose loyalty had lain with his father. In his despair, Aodhan had confessed to the girl that he had questioned his own blood and heritage. And so he had, more than ever during the battle, even to questioning his own loyalty.

That had shamed him beyond bearing. He had wished for the warrior to end his shame. But she had spared him, and Brighid had brought him back to life.

"Did you ask for the lady's help?" he asked the girl.

She jerked up her chin. "Why should I?"

Aodhan got up, testing his strength, and crossed the space between them in three steps.

This time she did not rise to face him but remained where she was, her back against the rough trunk, and looked up at him with all the pride and defiance of a captive warrior.

To whom was she captive? Not to him, who owed her and her lady his life.

To something else, then. Something that lay within her heart. Something he might use if he chose.

Aodhan knelt before her. "I cannot thank you," he said, "but it is a debt I must repay. What would you have of me?"

Her eyes, as green as the forest in spring, met his. Fear was what he saw in them . . . not the fear of battle or death, but of something far more deadly.

"You must do as I say," she said. "You must make no further attempt to take your own life." She swallowed. "And you must give yourself into my keeping."

Even though he had begun to guess at what lay behind her fear, her words struck him like the magical spear that had slain Ruadán in the camp of the Tuatha Dé. He knew now that the girl had paid a price for his healing, and she loathed that price even as she accepted it.

"Why?" he asked.

She looked away. She knew the answer but would never speak it. He was still her enemy. She could not trust him, though she was bound to hold his welfare even above her own. Bound to keep and protect him, even from himself.

"What is the name of the one I must obey?" he asked.

Her voice was so low that he could barely hear. "I am Séanat," she said.

"'Eagle'," he said. "And so you are, lady."

Séanat laughed and shook her head. "Eaglet, more like," she said, "fallen to earth before it learns to fly."

Slowly Aodhan reached out to touch her hair. She flinched. He gentled her as he would gentle a fine steed, stroking the heavy tresses as a butterfly strokes the blossom.

"You are brave," he said, "and fair. Too good for the likes of myself. But I will follow you, lady, and do your will."

Séanat trembled. Her breath came fast. Aodhan felt the first flush of desire, for she was no warrior now, but a woman, yearning for that she did not want to accept.

Had it not been for the whisper of the trees and the lingering scent of flowers, they might have stood apart again. But the memory of death was too near, and life would have its due. Aodhan cupped her face in his hands, wiping away a crust of dirt from her cheek with his thumb. He drew her towards him, and when his lips touched hers they opened and drew him in.

Séanat was as fierce in love as she was in battle. She would not give way even when he pulled her to her knees and embraced her with all his body, chest and hip and thigh. It was she who bore him down to the earth, she who straddled him and unlaced the hardened leather of his cuirass, casting it aside. Only when she sought to remove his tunic was she forced to let him join in, and then it was an easy thing to strip her of her armour and shirt and breeches until he and Séanat lay naked together.

Her body was a glorious thing, lean and muscular yet blessed with the delight of sweetly curved breasts and thighs made to rock a man to blissful release. Her skin was scarred and yet as soft as lambskin where no blade had touched it, fair and freckled and exquisitely responsive to his caresses.

When he would have rolled her on to her back, she resisted with the growl of a she-wolf and mounted him. She hesitated, looked again into his eyes, and impaled herself on him, gasping in astonishment and pleasure.

Aodhan understood the gift she had given him. She had

never taken a man into herself before, yet she kept nothing back, holding him and then releasing him again with a fervour that matched his own. He raised himself up to take her brown, peaked nipple into his mouth, and she flung back her head, her loosened hair cascading over her shoulders and sweeping the earth.

Glorious it was when she cried out, bucking as the pleasure took her and carried her into realms of light and joy. Aodhan followed before his heart could beat again, and for the first time since his earliest youth he knew how it felt to be whole.

He tried to keep Séanat with him after it was finished, but she was having none of it. She lifted herself and swung away without a lover's endearment. She walked across the clearing, snatching up her forgotten cloak as she passed by.

Aodhan meant to stay where he was, as stubborn as she, unwilling to admit to more than a fleeting pleasure. He should be shamed by his need, as she was.

But he rose, shook the leaves from his body, and went after her. She stood facing the forest where it grew dark with secrets, where any man might hide forever.

"*A chuisle*," he said.

She stiffened. "Don't be calling me such things."

"Would you have me curse you, *a chroí*?" He moved so near that he could feel the warmth of her skin. "What would you have me call you?"

"Nothing but my name."

She shifted, and the cloak slid from her shoulders. He caught it and laid it over her, drawing it close around her neck. "Look at me, Séanat."

"Leave me in peace!"

"How can I do such a thing when you have said I must give myself into your keeping?"

She turned about, despair in her eyes. "Dress yourself," she said, "but leave your armour behind. We go to the High King."

It was exactly what Aodhan had hoped. He nodded and returned to his discarded clothing, careful not to let Séanat see that he was pleased . . . not only to be alive, not only to have enjoyed her, but to know he would soon have his honour back again.

All the camp was rejoicing. Warriors sang of their exploits and drank sweet mead and ale until they staggered and fell into fits of laughter; women grinned as they filled bowls with great ladlefuls of stew; horses stomped and whinnied, pigs squealed and banners snapped in the sharp, bitter air.

Séanat would have given everything she had to join her sisters where they sat around a fire with the other warriors, singing songs of victory in high, sweet voices. The spears she carried over her shoulders, Goibhniu's finest; the sword she had won with her own skill when she was barely more than a child; her armour and her finely wrought golden helm – all these, and more, she would have surrendered to change what had happened the night before.

But there was no going back. No undoing what had been done, no leaving Aodhan to his death.

The terrible thing was that she knew she could never have done aught but save him, not even had the Morrígan herself appeared to forbid it.

Forgive me.

"Where are we going?" Aodhan asked softly at her shoulder.

"Hold your tongue," she whispered. "It is not for you to speak, but to be humble and silent."

She thought she heard him laugh, but the sound was quickly gone. Here he was surrounded by those who would cheerfully have killed him had they met him on the battlefield or found him alone afterwards. There were doubtless many who would still be glad to spit him on the end of a sword. Ruadán's betrayal had not been forgotten.

But they would not do so as long as she vouched for him and staked her honour upon his behaviour.

"Séanat!"

Niamh, her black hair flying loose behind her, ran up to Séanat with a cry of relief and joy. She embraced Séanat with her strong arms, kissed her cheeks and stood back, laughing.

"We thought you dead!" she said.

"*You* thought her dead, Niamh," Ríona drawled, coming up behind her. "I always knew she would return."

Niamh made a face and embraced Séanat again. "How many did you slay?" she asked breathlessly. "I killed ten, and I would have slain four more if only—"

"Don't believe her," Ríona said, crossing her arms across her chest. "She always—" She broke off, looking over Séanat's shoulder. "What's this?"

Both women stared at Aodhan. He bowed and stood quietly under their inspection.

"I am looking for the Ard Rí," Séanat said quickly.

But Ríona was not to be distracted. "I do not know you, stranger," she said to Aodhan. "From which *fine* do you come?"

"Do you forget the laws of hospitality?" Séanat snapped. "He is my guest."

There was nothing Ríona could say to that. She frowned and pulled Niamh aside.

"Lugh is in his tent," Ríona said.

"Very well," Séanat said.

As she began to walk away, Aodhan at her heels, she heard Niamh's whisper. "She is not herself. What can be wrong? Who *is* he?"

They can feel it, Séanat thought. They know he is not of the Tuatha Dé.

And indeed it seemed as if every man and woman they passed – cooks and smiths over their fires, warriors and pages, healers and poets – turned to look as she made her way to the great tent in the centre of the camp. Still, no one stopped her, nor spoke except to welcome her back. Perhaps it was only her imagination that their eyes followed her when she stopped before the warriors who guarded the new High King.

"Cathal," she said, nodding to the larger man. "Fearghus. Will you ask the Ard Rí if Séanat of the Daughters of the Morrígan may speak with him?"

"Our king rests," Cathal said. He looked at Aodhan. "Is this an urgent matter?"

Urgent? She might go to one of Lugh's lieutenants and report what she had done. She might hope that Brighid would soon return from her mourning to speak for her. But it was Lugh to whom she must appeal, Lugh who had slain his own Fomóiri grandfather to save the Tuatha Dé.

"I ask to see him," she said.

The warrior turned, drew back the tent's flap and went inside. Séanat heard low voices, and then Cathal came out again.

"The Ard Rí will see you," he said gruffly, with another long look at Aodhan.

Séanat unslung the spears from over her shoulder and removed her sword and dagger, leaving them with Fearghus as custom dictated. Cathal nodded, and Séanat lifted the flap.

Lugh sat on a stool padded thickly with sheepskin, deep in conversation with his uncle Goibhniu, the powerful smith of the Tuatha Dé. Both men looked up as Séanat and Aodhan entered.

"Séanat," Lugh said. His golden hair was as bright as ever, his eyes as blue, but his forehead was streaked with blood and the cuirass he still wore was slashed and dented. "What do you ask of me?"

His weariness shamed her. "My lord," she said, hesitating. "I ask a hearing."

"For what purpose?" Goibhniu said. He looked, narrow-eyed, at Aodhan. "Who is this boy?"

"My lords," Séanat said, "he is Aodhan. I have brought him under my protection."

"Your protection?" Goibhniu said. "Why should he need—"

Lugh raised his hand, and the smith fell silent. There was a coldness in the High King's face that chilled Séanat's blood. "I see why," he said. "Come forwards, Aodhan."

Aodhan obeyed and bowed deeply. "My Lord King."

"Your king is dead."

Straightening, Aodhan met Lugh's eyes without fear. "Many I knew are dead, or driven into the sea."

"Fomóiri," Goibhniu growled. He began to rise, but once again Lugh stopped him.

"Why is he here?" Lugh asked. "Why have you brought an enemy among us?"

Séanat would not tell him of Brighid's challenge. She would not lay any responsibility upon the lady when it had been *her* choice and no one else's.

"I came upon him in the forest," she said. "He fought fairly and with honour. I spared him."

"And brought him here?" Goibhniu demanded. "Have you so soon forgotten Ruadán?"

"I have not forgotten, my lord. But the Fomóiri are no longer a threat to us. They will not return. And Aodhan . . ." She took a deep breath. "It may be he is like the Ard Rí, as much of the Tuatha Dé as the Fomóiri."

Lugh rose. "Is this your claim, Aodhan?" he asked.

"I do not know, my lord," Aodhan said. "I was fostered to Fomóiri. I was raised as one, and fought for them. For this I make no apology."

Goibhniu growled again. "You must not permit this serpent in our midst, nephew," he said.

Séanat held her breath. Lugh was staring at her again, weighing, judging. She had offered her hospitality to Aodhan, which could not be withdrawn. He had three choices: to kill Aodhan, compelling her to defend him unto death, even against the whole of the Tuatha Dé; to exile them both; or to accept her word of honour that Aodhan would do no harm. She would not have blamed him if he had chosen the easiest way: exile.

But he sighed and shook his head. "I do not understand you, Séanat," he said. "It is not like the Daughters to show mercy in battle. If you have lost your taste for fighting . . ."

"Never, my lord!"

He searched her face again. "If our enemies still had the means and will to fight, I would not be lenient. But my judgment is this: he is yours, and whatever he does is on your head. You will face *his* punishment should he flout our hospitality."

It was the very best Séanat could have expected. She bowed low, avoiding Goibhniu's piercing stare, and took Aodhan's arm. He paused, gave a bow of his own, and followed her out of the tent.

"My thanks, Séanat," he said.

She continued towards the Daughters' tents without stopping. "You may not share our quarters," she said. "My sisters will not accept you easily. You may sleep by the fire outside, with the hounds."

"Am I your hound, Séanat? Am I permitted to go freely about the camp if I wear your collar?"

His quiet mockery stung worse than any wound. "I have no use for collars. Your honour binds you, as mine does myself. I will see that you have blankets and food and ale."

"But not your company?"

She gritted her teeth and didn't answer. She pointed out the fire to him, where a pair of Daughters, Brónach and Úna, were warming their hands and talking quietly.

"This is Aodhan," she said without preamble. "He is my guest. I offer him the hospitality of our fire and a share of our food."

The Daughters exchanged glances, but neither challenged her words. Séanat nodded to Aodhan, went on to the tent and gathered up her blankets. By the time she brought them back to the fireside, Aodhan was seated and the Daughters were walking away, casting sharp glances over their shoulders.

"It seems they care no more for my company than you," he said.

Séanat grunted. "They spend little time with men."

"Are you forbidden to take lovers then?"

Her skin grew hot. "Not forbidden. It is easier when . . ." *Show no weakness.* "You are not my lover, but my guest."

"Will you tell them what you told the Ard Rí?"

Never had Séanat had cause to lie to her sisters. But she *had* lied to Lugh when she'd said Aodhan had fought with honour. He had not fought at all.

But to tell them that he was Fomóir, in every way that mattered . . .

"Let them think what they will," she said harshly. "Stay here. I will bring meat."

He stayed, and afterwards she spent a little time sitting and eating with him to show that he was, indeed, her guest and not to be troubled. She knew how easily rumours flew around any war camp, and she wanted his position secure before the questions came.

They came soon enough. Séanat had just sought her blankets in the tent she shared with Ríona, Niamh and Brónach when the three warriors burst in.

"It's true, then?" Ríona demanded. "He's Fomóir?"

Casting off the blankets, Séanat sat up and pushed her hair out of her eyes. "He is," she said wearily.

"Here!" Brónach exclaimed. "In the very camp of the High King!"

Séanat got to her feet. She could tell them he was almost certainly half Tuatha Dé, but she was too angry.

"You speak of the Ard Rí," she said. "I have seen him. He has granted me the life of this warrior, whatever he may be."

Ríona glared, her arms tight across her chest. "You've gone mad, sister! Send him away! He will bring only sorrow!"

Brónach muttered agreement. Niamh moved her hands as if to soothe the anger that bubbled like a cauldron near overflowing.

"Séanat is no fool," she said softly. "There must be good reason."

"Is there?" Ríona asked. Her eyes narrowed. "You have a smell about you, sister. The smell of a lover."

Niamh gasped. Brónach sneered.

"His lover, are you?" she said. "Can you stoop so low, Séanat? A *Fomóir* . . ."

"Thus did Brighid take Bres the Beautiful, and Cian take Ethlinn," Niamh said, "to bring peace—"

"Which never came!" Ríona said. "And there is no need for conciliation when the Fomóiri have been driven from Inis Fáil!"

"There is even more need," Niamh said, "and our king has given his blessing." She approached Séanat with a gentleness that Séanat could hardly bear. "You have your reasons, Séanat, even if only your heart knows them. I will stand beside you."

A look of pain crossed Ríona's face. Brónach continued to sneer. Séanat pushed past them, walked out of the tent and went straight to the fire.

Aodhan was sitting almost where she had left him, knees drawn up and hands dangling between them. He was so intent on the fire that he didn't hear Séanat until she was almost on top of him.

"Get up," she commanded.

He rose slowly, watching her face warily. Séanat heard the others come up behind her. She seized Aodhan by the shoulders and kissed him as hard as she could, feeling the shock of his surprise and then the eager response. She pushed him away and spun to face the others.

"Does that satisfy you, Ríona?" she asked. She stared at Brónach. "Now you truly have reason to despise me."

Pale with anger, Brónach stalked away. Ríona lingered, glanced at Niamh, and followed with a heavy tread.

Aodhan stood unmoving, his body tense with anger. Niamh would not meet Séanat's eyes.

"I will stand with you," she said. "But it would be wise not to provoke—"

"I'll provoke whom I choose," Séanat snapped.

With a gentle shake of her head, Niamh went into the tent.

"Did you find that amusing?" Aodhan said behind her.

"I found it necessary."

"To prove myself your property?"

"You are not my—" She broke off as Aodhan's hands settled on her shoulders, stroked down, came to rest on her hips. She could feel the heat of him through her thin sleeping shift.

"Prove it," he murmured. "Where can we go to be alone?"

Her belly ached with desire, but she knew better than to give in. "Go to sleep," she said.

⋆ ⋆ ⋆

Aodhan didn't sleep. He was angry and lustful and bewildered all at once, thinking of Séanat in the tent, of her breasts and thighs and firm lips and green eyes. He thought more than once about creeping into the tent, finding her sleeping place and lying down beside her. He could begin his lovemaking before she woke, and then there would be no protests. He would make her beg for his caresses.

But she wasn't alone in the tent, and he had more important things to think on. He had come to Lugh's camp for a reason, and his purpose had yet to be fulfilled.

You will betray her, he thought. He would destroy Séanat as surely as if he'd slashed her throat with the sharpest bronze, for she would lose her people and possibly her life. Exile was the best she could hope for.

That would be nothing to the loss of her honour.

Aodhan hardened his mind. He had set his course when he had survived the blade in his heart. No mercy, no pity. Just as *they* had shown no mercy to his people.

He waited until the most of the fires around the camp had burned down to coals and the Tuatha Dé had fallen into drunken, exhausted slumber. If there were sentries, he could see none. These fine folk were arrogant in victory, even with a Fomóir in their midst.

Still, he moved with great care, working his way little by little across the camp. Lugh's tent rose up in the flare of guttering torches, but the warrior guards were slumped over their spears, snoring as loudly as the rest.

Silently, he entered the tent. Lugh of the Long Arm lay on his pallet, a cloak of woven gold and wolf's fur draped over his body. Goibhniu rested on a similar pallet near the tent's entrance. He mumbled and rolled over as Aodhan passed, oblivious to the danger.

Because Lugh had taken Séanat at her word.

Aodhan hesitated. Séanat's kiss burned on his lips. He shook off the memory and crossed to the spears that rested on the wall.

Goibhniu's spears: magical weapons forged by Inis Fáil's

greatest smith, one of which Lugh had used to slay Balor. One of which had slain Ruadán, son of Bres and Brighid, when he had come to the camp and tried to kill Goibhniu to save his father's people from destruction.

Tears came to Aodhan's eyes. Ruadán had had no choice. Nor did he. Aodhan grasped one of the spears, weighed its perfect balance in his hand. One blow would be enough. If he killed Goibhniu, his foster-brother would be avenged. But to slay Lugh, the greatest of the Tuatha Dé, the golden king . . .

He raised the spear over Lugh, took aim. And stopped. Sweat slicked his palm.

"I will follow you, lady, and do your will." Those had been his words to Séanat before they had lain together, binding body to body and soul to soul.

The spear sank in his hand as if it were forged of the heaviest stone. He backed away from Lugh, from Goibhniu, and out of the tent.

The point of a sword pricked his back.

"Traitor," Séanat snarled under her breath. "Faithless cur!"

Aodhan raised his hands. Once he had been prepared to let her take his life because he had failed to die with his people. He had failed them again.

He had failed *her.*

He dropped the spear. Séanat kicked it away. The blade rose to lie against his neck. In a moment his head would fly from his body, and at last the agony would end.

"Did you . . ." Séanat choked and caught her breath. "Did you kill them?"

All he need say was "aye". The lie would not come to his lips. "No," he said.

"Why?" she asked. The blade nicked his skin, and he felt the blood flow. "*Why?*"

He turned, careless of the pain. "Because of you, *a chroí.*"

She stepped back, her face turned away, and moaned. The sleeping guards sprang up, dazed and wild. Instantly they were on Aodhan.

"Stop!" Séanat cried. "He did nothing!"

Lugh emerged from the tent. "What goes on?" he demanded.

Goibhniu came out behind him. His eyes found Aodhan's. "You!" He brought up the spear he clenched in one fist. "Filth of a Fomóir!"

Like a stoat upon a mouse, Séanat leaped at Aodhan and dragged him away, her arm around his chest.

"You will not touch him!" she growled. "I saw him come out of the tent with a spear in his hand. Had he wanted you dead, you would not be breathing now!" She turned to Lugh. "My lord, has he done you harm?"

The High King's expression was grim. "None. But you were honour-bound to keep him, and you have failed."

"She hasn't failed," Aodhan said. "It was because of her that I took no vengeance for the death of my kin and my foster-brother."

Others had come to hear Aodhan's words, and they murmured in consternation and anger. "What brother?" Ríona said, her sisters around her.

Aodhan met Goibhniu's furious stare. "Ruadán," he said, "son of Bres."

The gathering crowd grew quiet. Séanat was as rigid as one of the great standing stones that rose on the banks of the River Bóinne.

"And this is what you brought to us!" Brónach said. "Another who spits on the hospitality of the Tuatha Dé! I say they both must die!"

A swell of argument rose up, shouts of agreement and mutterings of dismay.

Lugh raised his hand. "Aodhan has come armed and unasked into a place of peace. But I have suffered no injury, nor has my uncle." At the sounds of protest he raised his hand again, and the light from his face silenced every voice with its glory. "In this," he said, "I cannot judge, for all Tuatha Dé must be affected. Let every warrior and chieftain meet in council to decide the fate of this man and this woman."

Séanat released Aodhan and bowed her head. "I surrender to the will of the People. I ask only one boon—"

A great, black host of crows appeared in the sky, deafening the camp with their guttural cries. Around and around they flew, descending like a whirlwind, spinning closer and closer to each other until they formed a single black shape that came to earth as lightly as foam on the shore.

"There will be no boon," a harsh voice said. Long-nailed hands pushed the dark hood back from hair equally dark, and a woman's face appeared, beautiful and cold and deadly.

"There will be no mercy for one who has betrayed her oath," the Morrígan said. The crowd broke before her long stride, and the Daughters dropped to their knees. It was to Séanat she went, her cloak billowing and hissing around her.

Aodhan moved to stand between her and Séanat. "I know you, Raven of Battle," he said. "If it is blood you want, take mine."

The Morrígan laughed. "I will have yours, Fomóir. Never doubt it. But this woman has betrayed her oaths to me. No mercy on the field of battle. Death before surrender." She swept up to Lugh. "Ard Rí, you have no authority over those sworn to me. You would not have won the battle without me, and now I demand payment. Give her up and let her face the price of her betrayal."

Lugh's gaze moved slowly to Séanat. "She has the right of it," he said heavily. "When you gave your oath, you put your fate into the hands of your lady. I can do nothing."

Aodhan started towards Lugh. Crossed spears snapped up in his path. He turned back to face the Morrígan and fell to his knees. "Her weakness is my doing," he said. "Let her be exiled, Slayer of Kings, but spare her."

"Let *him* be spared," Séanat said, pushing Aodhan aside. "The fault is in me. The weakness was always mine."

The Morrígan's laughter flew skyward, and shrieking crows emerged whole from her black garments. "Is it true?" she asked. "Do you care for this creature, Séanat? Are you bitch to his cur?"

"I am nothing," Séanat said. "Rend me with the beaks of your birds and the teeth of your wolves, but let him live."

Still laughing, the Morrígan raised her arms. An invisible blow struck Séanat to her knees. Aodhan lunged towards her, but Lugh's warriors held him back.

His gaze met Séanat's, and all the fierce rage Aodhan felt, all the hatred for his enemies, dissolved into acceptance.

And something more. He broke free, knelt beside Séanat and took her in his arms.

"Know that I love you, Séanat," he whispered. "When our blood mingles in death, there will be true peace at last."

She looked into his eyes and smiled. "I am not afraid."

"Not even of dishonour?"

Her fingers brushed his cheek. "No longer, *a chuisle*. You are my honour." She pressed her lips to his. "I love—"

Strong arms jerked her to her feet and seized Aodhan. The Daughters dragged them after the Morrígan, Ríona's face without expression, Niamh weeping.

"You shall end at the hands of your sisters," the Morrígan said, "hacked to pieces and left for my crows. But first you shall watch your lover die."

She nodded, and the Daughters hurled Aodhan to the ground. They stretched his arms and legs across the earth and crouched to bind him with their hands. The Morrígan's cloak exploded into a flurry of wings and red eyes. The crows descended upon Aodhan, claws rending, beaks stabbing. Séanat cried out, fighting Ríona and Niamh like a madwoman.

Aodhan raised his bloody face and met her eyes. It was enough to dull the pain. It was almost as if the beaks and claws could no longer touch him.

"*Enough*."

The new voice was as soft as the Morrígan's was harsh. All Aodhan could see of the lady's form was her feet, shod in cloth embroidered with leaping deer and forest flowers. All at once the crows scattered, circled, and dived again to be enfolded within the Morrígan's cloak.

"Brighid," the Morrígan said, anger and surprise mingled in the word. "This is none of your affair."

"Is it not?" The lady knelt beside Aodhan and touched his blood-smeared hair. Warmth reached into him, soothing his hurts like a balm.

"What did you do to bring the people's wrath upon your head?" she asked him.

"It was *I* who brought it," Séanat said, wresting free of Niamh and Ríona. "I failed to keep him as I promised."

The lady met Séanat's gaze. "Do you regret your vow to me?"

"She had no right to make any vows!" the Morrígan hissed. "She was sworn to me!"

"You are wrong," Brighid said. She swept her hand over Aodhan's back, and all his wounds were healed. "There is a bond greater than that between warriors."

Lugh came to stand over her. "Your interference is not welcome, Brighid," he said.

"But it is necessary, Lugh mac Ethlinn . . . unless you would be a kin-slayer."

No one spoke for a terrible moment. Séanat held her breath. The Morrígan's cloak rustled and spat. Lugh's frown was like an eclipse of the sun.

"Speak your meaning, lady," he said.

Brighid rose and spread her arms to embrace the assembly. "All know the tale of Lugh Lámhfhada's father, Cian, son of Dian Cécht, who sought Ethlinn, daughter of Balor, in the crystal tower on Oileán Thúr Rí. There he got three sons upon her. Two were said to be drowned by Balor in a whirlpool. Only Lugh survived."

There were mutters of agreement. All knew the story of Lugh's birth, his fosterage with Tailtiu, daughter of the chief of the Fir Bolg, and how he came to join the Tuatha Dé when he reached manhood and won his place among his father's people.

"But there is one thing you have not heard," Brighid said. "One other child of Ethlinn survived, to be fostered by Ochtriallach, son of Indech, king of the Fomóiri. His name was Aodhan."

"Still more our enemy!" someone shouted.

Brighid's beautiful face turned towards the voice. "His foster-brother and companion in battle was Ruadán, my son. His father was Cian." She looked at Lugh. "He is your brother, Ard Rí."

Séanat's legs nearly gave out beneath her, and only Niamh and Ríona kept her on her feet. Goibhniu thrust the tip of his spear into the ground with such force that the earth shook with the blow. The Morrígan's eyes burned with rage. Aodhan, coming to his knees, stared at Brighid in wonder.

Lugh's face filled with sorrow. "Is it so?" he asked. He offered his hand to Aodhan. "If you are my brother, it is no fault of yours that you never knew your kin."

"I knew them," Aodhan said, rising without touching Lugh's hand. "As you never knew your true mother, King of the Tuatha Dé. With the Fomóir, with my foster-brother, I would gladly have died." He looked at Séanat and smiled, driving the last despair from her heart. "Because of her, I found cause to live." He knelt again at Brighid's feet. "I once promised to do Séanat's will. I broke my oath. I will gladly pay my debt in any way you choose, but Séanat is blameless."

Even from a distance Séanat could feel the power of Brighid's healing love. "We are none of us without blame," she said, "but there must come an end to feud and vengeance. In your blood, in Lugh's, lies the hope of reconciliation." She turned to Aodhan. "Your people are not gone so long as you live." She held out her hand to Séanat. "Come, child."

The Morrígan stepped between them. "You will regret your intrusion, Brighid. A time will come when such weakness will bring about the downfall of the Tuatha Dé. 'Summer without blossoms, cattle without milk, every man a betrayer, every son a reaver.'"

Eyes met, bright and dark. "Nothing is forever," Brighid said. "All things come to an end . . . all but one. As long as that one thing exists, there is hope."

She stepped around the Morrígan, took Séanat's hand, and offered the other to Aodhan. He rose, and Brighid placed his hand in Séanat's. "As long as you live, may you be as one."

With a screech of fury, the Morrígan spread her arms wide. Her body flew apart in an eruption of black feathers and rasping croaks as the crows burst forth and spun into the sky.

"Will the world end as she prophesied?" Aodhan asked.

"Not yet." Brighid bowed to Lugh, smiled on the assembly, and walked away.

Séanat leaned her head against Aodhan's. "Is it over?" she whispered.

"Embrace me, brother," Lugh said, coming to join them. "Let the bloodshed end here. Let there be peace."

And so there was. In time, Séanat gave birth to a girl-child, whom she and Aodhan named Brighid in honour of the lady who had saved them. The Tuatha Dé Dunaan ruled Éire for many years more, until the coming of the Milesians with their iron weapons and new kind of magic.

But that is another story.

Tara's Find

Nadia Williams

She shouldn't be here.

Tara McGinty pushed an errant strand of hair from her face. Around her, tendrils of early-morning mist rested on the damp heather coat of the field they were excavating. The light green of a copse of ash trees to the north of the archaeological dig contrasted with the backdrop of the darker slopes of the round-topped Mourne mountains in the distance. An army of dark clouds loomed on the West horizon, emphasizing the fleeting nature of the fragrance of fresh dew in the air. A lone crow's *caw* didn't break the silence as much as accentuate it.

In four hours, the first of the staff would arrive. The smell of coffee would mingle with young voices, students grateful for the summer job, flirting and bantering. With a sudden sense of urgency, Tara ducked under the canopy that protected her demarcated soil squares from rain. She cast a glance at the tent near the entrance to the dig. Thomas, Dr Dullaghan's faithful sidekick, was still asleep. There hadn't been as much as a stir from inside the tent when she'd slipped a note through a small gap in the tent flap:

> *I couldn't sleep, so I started to dig. Call me when you wake up and I'll make both of us tea.*
>
> *Tara*

She'd have been surprised if he wasn't asleep. It was only four in the morning, a chill bite in the air belied the fact that summer was at the height of its power.

Tara opened her knapsack. With deft movements born of hours spent scraping soil away in search of the past, she first took out a small square of canvas and laid it on the ground. On that, she placed a trowel, brush, metal dustpan, measuring tape, folding metre stick, clipboard and her camera. She checked the remaining contents: a flask of tea and a sandwich, in case she got thirsty or peckish before the rest of the staff arrived. These could stay in the pack.

Tara picked up the trowel and stilled. There it was again. That same prickling feeling that often crawled up and down her spine when she met certain people. It wasn't as intense as usual, but the feeling was unmistakably there. She'd felt it from the first day she arrived at the dig, but shrugged it off. It would soon disappear: it always did. This time, however, it had not settled into an almost pleasant buzz, it had become a constant irritation.

She clicked her tongue and stepped into the shallow hole. Dullaghan had decided to let her choose her own square to excavate, with no supervisor peering over her shoulder. "Away from the rest of the dig, so you can have some privacy," he'd said. But she'd sensed something else under his words, a kind of frustration. The man didn't like her, she was sure of it. He'd appointed another worker, who also held a BSc Honours in Archaeology and Geology, to be square supervisor. Tara didn't mind, but Dullaghan had insisted on giving her the option of working alone to "make up for it".

The dirt made a scraping sound as she brushed it into the dustpan. She emptied it into a bucket beside her square to be sifted for possible relics later, and tackled the next layer of soil.

In the end, worried about Dullaghan's attitude to her and feeling miserable at the prospect of being apart from the camaraderie that often developed on a dig, she'd picked her spot to dig at the exact place where the prickling feeling along her spine had been strongest. What a fool. The feeling had driven her to distraction over the last few weeks: invaded her dreams, stolen her sleep.

This morning she'd got fed up with tossing and turning. Sure, midnight had been an all too recent memory in the air, but the long summer day was already chasing darkness from the skies. She'd given in to the sense of urgency and driven to the dig to start working. And now, three full hours before the rest of the crew were due to arrive, she'd unearthed something . . . interesting.

Something round and beige was revealed when she carefully scraped away the next layer of dirt. It was about the size of her thumb. A river pebble, probably, though its mere presence here could tell a story. She brushed away more of the dirt, reached for her measuring tape and noted the pebble's exact position on her clipboard. The temptation to dig just more and more ate at her tired brain, but Tara resisted. She removed another layer of soil with the trowel, leaving the dirt around the pebble for last. Then she took up her brush, excitement rising in her chest.

It was a face, probably a statue or a bust. Although, when she leaned closer, it didn't look right for that. It seemed too real. Measure, note, photograph – with hands shaking from excitement. Should she go and wake Thomas? But no, she wanted to unearth this alone. Tara set to work on the next layer of soil. It was more than just a bust. A body emerged as she carefully removed another layer of the earth that had hidden it. This was no statue. It was human remains.

This time, before she reached for her measuring tape and camera, she set her brush aside and stared at the man she'd uncovered. Something was seriously wrong here. She'd taken every grain of soil from the body herself, there was no indication of recent disturbance. From the settled state of the earth, she'd have guessed he must have been buried for at least 100 years, possibly more. Yet the body looked fresh.

Soil and climatic conditions were not condusive to mummification, yet the corpse had not skeletonized. In any case, it didn't *look* mummified. It looked as if life had animated the man's long limbs and sensitive lips just yesterday. As if he'd open his eyes and lift an arm to scratch his one-week beard any moment now.

Another anomaly puzzled her: though there was no sign of as much as a scrap of clothing on him, a rusted belt buckle had emerged as she'd brushed away the dirt on his stomach. The rest of the belt, and the trousers it had held up, must have disintegrated. That meant a good few years' underground.

Tara peered at his finely sculpted face, more that of someone asleep than long dead. The stillness of early morning hung around her like a shroud. Rain started pattering on the canopy over her head. A deep sense of melancholy overcame her as she stared at the corpse, still half encased in tight-packed soil.

She rose, picked up her camera and took photos of the find from every angle, circling him clockwise, then she retraced her steps to put the camera away again. Tara climbed back into the hole, grateful now that she'd given in to the impulse to excavate two squares side by side. Her man lay diagonally across them.

What had he been like when this body was still filled with life? she wondered as she crouched beside him. The little she could see of his face spoke of a handsome man with fine features. Only his face showed, his head was still encased in soil. What colour was his hair? It was impossible to tell if his dirt-caked chin was covered with dark or light stubble.

His lips were perfect. Not too thick, not too thin. Made for smiling. For kissing. "Come back to life, sweet man, and tell me your story," she whispered. She kissed her fingers and dared to touch them to his mouth.

His lips moved.

At the same moment, a shock of impressions flooded her mind. A feeling of pressure around her ribs, of an overwhelming desire to gasp a deep breath but no space for her chest to expand. She snatched her hand away and scrambled from the hole with a suppressed yelp, falling on her backside.

The chill touch of sloppy mud seeping into her trousers brought her back to reality. What the hell had just happened? She rubbed the needles-and-pins feeling from her fingertips and shook her head as if to dispel her silliness. For long moments she sat in the mud, rain tapping her head as if impatiently demanding she make a decision.

She'd touch him again, that's what she'd do. Show herself there was nothing to it. Tara swallowed away her stupid fear and crawled closer to the corpse, into the shelter of the canopy. She climbed into the hole. Gritting her teeth with determination, she reached out a shaking hand and rested it on the man's forehead.

Suffocating, she was suffocating. Tiny, shallow breaths into a chest gripped tight by something and she couldn't move . . .

When Tara came back to her senses she was frantically digging away at the soil around the corpse's chest. She stopped herself, horrified with her carelessness. She'd flung the earth asunder without a thought to taking careful measurements, or checking for artifacts. God, she'd ploughed her way through dirt she would otherwise have taken days to remove.

Dullaghan was going to kill her.

A small sound drew her attention and she fixed her eyes on the corpse's lips. This time she had no doubt. They'd moved. In fact, his chest rose and fell with small, gasp-like breaths as she watched. There was only one possible conclusion she could come to: she'd gone insane.

So insane, in fact, that the memory of that closed-chest feeling moved her to grasp her trowel once more and carry on digging. She hacked at the soil around the body with total disregard for long-learned principles of practical archaeology. Her only consideration was to free the man from his earthy prison. Anxious glances in the direction of the tent showed no movement, no sign that Thomas had woken and was about to discover her need for a padded cell and men in white coats.

When at last she was sure he could be lifted easily, no longer in the grip of his grave, Tara set her trowel aside and knelt next to him. She leaned forwards, peered intently at his handsome face. He still wore a soil halo, and only once she'd washed him would she be sure of the colour of his hair.

Once she'd washed him? Where on earth were her thoughts going? She swiped a filthy hand over her face, heedless of the streak of dirt she probably left there. The best thing she could do now was to get away as fast as possible. That way she'd have a very, very slim chance of not being blamed for this travesty.

Except, she'd left the note in Thomas' tent. Oh, God, she was so screwed, on so many levels.

And with that realization, Tara crossed a line. She was so far gone, so deep in trouble that nothing she did could make it much worse. Why not explore this experience to the full, so that at least she'd not have unanswered questions eating away at her when she sat in her padded cell?

Quickly, before she could change her mind, she placed her hand firmly on the man's forehead again.

Able to breathe now, grit in my mouth, nose blocked, very cold. Broth. Warm broth.

This time she didn't lose herself in his sensations. Was it because he was no longer panicked, suffocating? She stilled, rubbed her tingling hand. What exactly did that thought tell her? It meant she believed she felt the man's feelings. The corpse's feelings.

Hell. This was no corpse.

Tara's whole body started shaking. Shock. Her mom always swore by sweet, hot tea for calming one down. With nothing to lose, the decision was easy. Tara dug out her flask, poured half a cup of steaming tea and drank it down. Then she poured another half-cup and held it over the man's parted lips.

Drip-drip-drip.

She watched, not sure if she dreaded or desired this supposedly lifeless body to show some reaction. Long moments passed. Then the lips pressed together, his Adam's apple moved.

"Oh. My. God." Tara dripped more tea into his mouth, watched as he swallowed again. And again, and again. At last he'd drunk half a cup of tea, and she couldn't stop smiling. Bugger the dig, bugger Dullaghan. She was taking this man home.

With feverish haste, Tara screwed the lid on the flask, then tossed it into her knapsack with the tools she'd brought along. She peered through the now almost solid veil of pouring rain. There was still no sign of movement from Thomas' tent. That was normal enough. Though it felt to her as if ages had passed, it was still an hour before the normal starting time for the dig. Furthermore, he wouldn't even have to leave his camp bed to realize there would be no digging today because of the rain. Hopefully, he'd take the opportunity to sleep in.

She got to her feet and ran past the tent, pushed open the never-locked gate and hurried to her car. The temporary fence was for keeping animals out – here, in the country, there was little if any chance of human interference with the dig. Once she was seated behind the wheel of her twelve-year-old hatchback, she flung her knapsack on the passenger seat. The engine purred to life at the first try and she drove carefully down the road, to the corner of the fence closest to her man. There was a bend in the winding, crumbly tarred path there, and she parked out of sight of the dig.

Quick as a flash, she opened the hatchback and put the rear seats down. Would he fit? How on earth was she going to carry him there? She'd make a plan, somehow.

It wasn't difficult to undo the loosely twisted wire that kept the two sections of the fence together nearest her man. With more anxious glances towards Thomas' tent, she stole to the former corpse's side. This was it. From here, if she was caught, no explanation could possibly save her. Tara took a deep breath, bent down and scooped up the soil she'd loosened away from his shoulders. She grasped the man under his arms.

She did her best to support his head as she struggle-dragged him through the mud. Her heart did its best to climb out of her throat and abandon the body and mind that had clearly lost all traces of sanity. Fear gave her strength, and the rain-soaked ground helped her slide the man's body ever closer to her car. *God, he was heavy.* They had left a brown trail of mud over the bright green heather once they made it from the churned ground.

Oh-God-oh-God. She was sure that at any moment Thomas would poke his head from the tent, stare straight at her and the game would be up. She was mad, mad to do this. And still she fought to drag her man to her car.

She was exhausted by the time they made it to the little hatchback. The rain had washed away much of the mud from her man's face. She saw him squinting against the sting of the pelting drops, saw him lick his lips. The last traces of doubt that he was very much alive were blown away when he sneezed a gob of mud from his nose, then spat weakly. He opened his eyes for a moment, looked straight into hers.

Tara froze. She was convinced she'd seen those bloodshot eyes somewhere before. They seemed as familiar as her own blue ones. His were light green, like the Mediterranean Sea when the sun caught it just so. From somewhere, bizarrely, relief flooded her heart, as if something that had been missing in her soul had been returned. He smiled, then his eyelids fluttered closed again.

The car. She had to get him into the car. Would he even fit? There was no time to wonder or doubt now. She opened the hatchback, then squatted and took a firm hold of his upper body. His head rested against her breasts. She forgot about the flick of the raindrops, about the danger of discovery, about her tired muscles. For a moment, she just stayed like that, cradling him in her arms.

What was she thinking? She willed her mind back to the pickle they were both in, took a deep breath and lifted with all her might.

Weeks of hard manual labour paid off now. Grunting and straining, Tara managed somehow to struggle backwards into her car, hauling the limp body of the man in with her. One last heave and they both fell backwards into the car. Panting for breath, Tara rested for a few precious moments, hugging him to her soaked body. Was he OK? She could feel him breathing in her arms, a small tremor as if he was starting to shiver. It was the best she could hope for. Once she had him home, she'd be able to take better care of his needs.

Again it took an effort of will to remind herself that she was in deep, deep trouble, and didn't have the luxury of time. She wriggled out from under him, lay him down as best she could and tumbled from the car. She had to bend his knees to get his legs in, but thank heaven he did fit. A picture of herself driving off with his legs dangling from her car, sporting a red flag from one toe, flashed through her imagination. She closed the hatch door, suppressing a hysterical giggle. Her mind wanted to hammer on the absolute lunacy of what she was doing, but she forced her focus back on to practicalities. Enough of her self-preservation instinct remained for her to think of ways she could cover her tracks.

Gusts of wind tugged at her sopping jacket and flung rain in her face as she ran back to the gap in the fence. There was one very, very slim chance of getting away with this. At least for the time being. She slipped into the site, crept to her man's former grave. Each corner of the canopy was fixed to the ground by a guy rope. Tara kept her eyes on the tent as she dropped into the shallow hole. She had no tools with her, but adrenaline and fear helped her use her hands to fill the gaping hole in her dig area with loose soil. That task done as best she could, she glanced at Thomas' tent again.

The flap moved.

She fell flat on her stomach in the hole, her heart in her mouth. Seconds passed like hours. At last she scraped together enough courage to take a peek. Thomas chose that moment to emerge, a poncho draped over his head. He jogged in a half-crouch to the Portaloo, opened its door and slipped inside. Tara ducked down when she saw him turn. She counted to ten, then risked another peek. The door was closed. It was now or never.

She sprang from the hole and raced to the first guy rope, pulled with all her might. The peg stuck for a moment, then yielded reluctantly and slipped from the ground. She dashed to the other one, coaxed it from the ground as well, then half fell back into the hole. Now she needed Thomas to come out of the confounded toilet; he seemed to have moved in there permanently. Minutes dragged by, then the door opened and he emerged. Another gust of wind tugged at the canopy and Tara's breath froze in her chest. If the other leg fell over now, she'd be dead meat. She risked reaching out and grabbing the nearest metal leg of the frame to keep it in place.

Thomas didn't even look her way. He crouch-ran to the mess tent, holding the poncho over his head, unzipped the door flap and stepped inside. Tara ducked down when he turned to zip up the door. She counted to ten again, risked a glance. He was gone.

She clambered from the hole, grasped the leg of the canopy she'd held in place and lifted with all her strength. It was almost a superfluous effort: another gust of wind near tore the canopy from her hands. It toppled over, leaving her man's grave exposed to the deluge. Hopefully, all sign of foul play would be obscured by its wash. The mud trail to the fence would, with a bit of luck, also fall victim to the rain's cleansing touch.

One last hurdle. She had to close the gap in the fence. Tara slipped through and pushed the fence sections back together, found the stiff wires that had kept it together before.

Why now did things have to go wrong? Her hands were too slick to grasp the wires she had to twist. They kept slipping from her fingers. How long before Thomas would turn to the plastic window to stare out over the dig as he drank his tea? His gaze would no doubt be drawn to the toppled gazebo straight away.

She couldn't do it. The wires were simply too slippery. But who would come and inspect the fence this closely? She'd just have to remember to fix the wires next time she came into work. With that promise to herself, Tara turned and ran as fast as she could back to her car.

Her man was still breathing. He was shivering noticeably, and his skin was still as cold to the touch as it had been when she first unearthed him. She wondered what he'd been wearing when he died.

When he died! What an overwhelming thought. *Had* he died? What was his story? Was he even human?

She had nothing to cover him with. Her own clothes were soaked through. Though there was a bite to the air, it wasn't that bad. There had to be more to the man's shivering than cold. She turned the heater on full blast as she sped back home.

When she got the job on the dig, a contract that would last at least six months, Tara had found a two-bedroom detached house half an hour's drive from the site. It would have made sense to share, but with the old place a few kilometres outside an already out-of-the-way little village, the rent was so low she could afford the luxury of keeping it to herself. She now thanked her lucky stars for this happy coincidence. With no curious neighbours around, she could take more time and care unloading the man than she had done loading him.

Whether it was the lack of fear-spiked adrenaline, her already tired state or just the more awkward job of getting the man out of, rather than into, her car, it proved much more difficult. She managed, at last, to heave him into her sitting room and lay him down on the carpet. Exhausted, Tara sank down on to the floor beside him, her back against a stuffed chair. He still shivered, but she simply had to catch her breath before she could try to do anything about that.

It looked, now that the rain had washed some of the dirt away, as if he was blond. His hair, plastered to his skull and streaked with mud, was probably shoulder length. Tara's gaze slid down to his exposed torso. She swallowed. Whatever her mystery man had done in his former life, it must have involved a fair amount of exercise. The muscles of his dirt-mottled chest, covered with skin as pale as milk, were well developed. And lower down . . .

His eyelids flickered, opened. He looked to his left, then to his right and saw her. As if it was a huge effort, he rolled his head to see her better. Tara froze. For long moments, they stared at each other. Then the man mumbled something.

Tara leaned forwards. "I couldn't hear you. Please, speak again." Damn, she hadn't even considered that he might not speak English.

He closed his eyes; she thought he'd fallen asleep again. Then his lips moved, and she had to lean right over him to hear his whisper. "Ye are very beautiful, lass."

Warmth blossomed in her heart. She smiled. "Thank you."

A spasm of shivers shook his body. "Broth. Warm broth."

"Of course." She'd have said *bath, warm bath* would take precedence when you're hypothermal, but she knew little of bringing the dead back to life and would rather go with whatever he said he needed. Broth. Did she still have some of that soup her mother had made in the freezer? It was quite chunky, but if she put it through the blender, it would probably work as well.

Tara first fetched an old sheet from the cupboard in the spare room, which she spread over her man. After that, she took the duvet from the spare bed and covered him with that, too. Shivering herself now in her wet clothes, she stole to her bedroom, whipped off the wet stuff and changed into her bathrobe. Then it was off to the kitchen. Twenty minutes later, she had a steaming saucepan of thin soup ready.

Tara knelt at the man's side. She reached out to touch his cheek, to gently roll his head up so he could drink the broth, but stopped herself. Would she feel his feelings again? He still shivered. She braced herself and put her hand on his cheek.

He was so cold. Bristle and grit rubbed against her palm, but she felt no emotions other than her own. And her own emotions puzzled her. Under the excitement, fear, wonder, anxiety and curiosity, was something like tenderness. Concern. Why *had* she taken this man from the dig? She lived for archaeology, had worked many years to get her degree and the work experience she wanted. Why risk it all?

She stroked the man's cheek. "Hello. Are you awake? Can you hear me?" No reaction. Would he choke if she dripped soup into his mouth while he slept? Yet she had done so with the tea earlier, and he had swallowed automatically. She decided to take the risk.

Drip-drip-drip. She watched anxiously, and yes, he swallowed the soup. Satisfied, Tara fed him some more. The bowl was soon empty, and she noticed his shivers had subsided. What else could she do for him? Would he ever wake up completely, or was this as conscious as he'd get? He was the find of the century, a man who'd come back to life after being buried for who knows how long.

Realization struck her then, and Tara felt herself pale. Yes, she'd made the find of the century, but she would never be able to prove it. Even the photos would not be enough, not considering the claim she'd be making about him. What an idiot she'd been!

Then she let her gaze rest on his muddy face and her regrets faded. She thought of him lying in a laboratory, being poked, prodded, sliced and inspected. No way. Minutes slipped by as Tara stared at him. He was shivering again.

Her phone beeped, and she checked the text message on the screen. No work today. That was to be expected. Had they inspected her squares yet? Was Dullaghan on his way right now, perhaps with the Gardai? Or no, this dig was just across the border, in Northern Ireland – it would be the police accompanying him.

"Lass." Tara started at the sound of the hoarse whisper. The man's eyes were open. "Broth. Warm broth."

This time, when she fed him the soup, he was awake. He kept those light green eyes focused on her face. It was almost embarrassing. She had to look a sight, probably as dirty as he was, and she didn't have the excuse of having been dead and buried for years.

Ye are very beautiful. Tara's cheeks warmed.

When the bowl was empty, he still stared at her. "Thank ye, fair lass."

"Is there anything else I can do for you?"

"Aye. I am very cold."

"I wish I could get you into a hot bath, it would be just the ticket to warm you."

He smiled. "Ye need not drag me into yon bath, lass. I think I can move to it with yer aid."

Tara nodded. "I'll run a bath first, then I'll come help you to it."

She filled the tub with steaming water, added a dash of jasmine-scented bath oil. When she returned to the sitting room, her man was sitting up on the floor, his back against her couch. "What is yer name, lass?" he asked.

"Tara." She smiled, awkward. "And yours?"

"I am Ulick."

"Ah. Pleased to meet you. The bath is ready. Can you stand?"

"Nay, lass, not without yer aid."

How was she going to do this? Ulick made the question superfluous when he struggled to pull himself up on to the couch. She hurried to his side, grasped his arm and helped. He soon slumped on her couch, breathing hard, eyes closed, as if he'd run a mile. She sat down beside him, suppressed the urge to stroke his forehead with her fingers, the even greater urge to stare at his crotch. Minutes passed before he opened his eyes again.

"Ready?" Tara asked.

"Aye."

She slid her hand behind his back, then dragged him with her into a standing position. He leaned heavily on her, and Tara thanked her lucky stars she only had to get him to the bathroom. Step by staggering step they made their way down the short passage. Holding him this close, she could still feel him shivering. Wouldn't it be nice to feel this firm body warm against her?

He crumpled in a heap on to the mat when they made it, one hand grasping the rim of the bath.

Her mobile phone rang.

"Damn. Just wait here." She sprinted down the passage to the sitting room, grabbed the thing just in time. It was Dullaghan. She forced words from a suddenly dry mouth. "Good morning, Doctor D. How are you?"

"I'm grand, thank you. Thomas found your note, but you were nowhere to be seen."

"Yeah, it started raining cats and dogs, so I left. It was still early, I didn't want to wake him up."

"Great. Nothing out of the ordinary happened, did it?"

Oh, God, he knew. "No, nothing. I scraped away another layer before I left, but nothing came up."

"Okay. Well, as long as you're all right."

"I am. Just a bit muddy. I was about to get in the bath." She screwed her eyes shut and bit her lip. That had been a mistake. He'd wonder why she was only going to wash now. "I had to wait for the boiler to heat."

"Mmm. I find a shower usually does it for me. So you found nothing so far?"

"Nothing."

"Well then. Hopefully I'll see you tomorrow. Enjoy your bath."

Tara ended the call, nothing but a nauseous hollow where her stomach used to be. He suspected something was amiss, she was sure. There was nothing she could do about it now, though. She just had to remember to fix those wires at the fence as soon as possible. Right now, she had to focus on Ulick. She plonked the phone on the coffee table, dashed back to the bathroom and froze.

Ulick sat naked on the floor, hanging on to the side of the bath, eyes closed. An unexpected heat flushed her skin. She stared at him for long seconds before she realized what she was doing and quickly closed the door. Damn! This was really awkward. She was sure he'd need help getting in the bath, but . . .

"Lass. Do not be shy, I need yer aid."

Tara tried to swallow away the dryness in her mouth and pushed the door open again. Ulick looked up at her, unashamed. Not that he had anything to be ashamed of. His body was lean, muscles sculpted but not gym-bunny over-perfect.

"A hand, lass." He reached out to her, and Tara stepped closer without hesitation. She helped him up, and he half climbed, half fell into the bath. For long moments, he simply lay in the water, soaking up the heat, eyes closed.

When he lifted his head, she noticed a difference in the movement. It didn't look like a terrible effort any more. "I need to bring word to the King. He is in great danger."

Tara's heart ached. "I hate to break this to you, but whatever message you had to deliver is a little late. Very late, actually."

He rested his head against the bath again, a determined set to his firm lips. "Nay. It is not too late."

"What year do you think it is?" she asked.

"I do not know what year I find myself in now. The year I was last conscious . . . I know not what year that was, either. I had stepped . . ." He closed his eyes and sighed. "How did ye find me?"

"I work on an archaeological dig. You were buried, two feet under the surface."

"And ye knew the resurrection ritual?"

She shook her head. "No. I'm an archaeologist, not a magician. I have no idea how I managed to wake you up."

Ulick opened his eyes, a flash of sharp interest in them. "Ye did not know the ritual, but ye resurrected me?"

Tara nodded. "Aye. I mean, yes. I have no idea how that happened." She braced herself. "Are you human?"

Ulick smiled. "Nay, lass. I am of the old race, the Tuatha Dé Danaan."

She suppressed the urge to snort a laugh. "You're a fairy?"

"Aye. I am of the Fae." He opened his mouth as if to say more, then closed it as if deciding not to. "I must get to the King. He is in grave danger. Will ye take me to him?"

"Ulick." How would she put this? "You've been buried a long time. Whatever king you needed to give a message to is long dead."

"Nay. He lives. He lives and rules. By the grace of Rónán Tiarna an Ama I will not be too late."

She'd break it to him gently, when he was stronger. The last thing she wanted to do was crush the spirit that shone in his eyes. "Do you want some soap? Shampoo?"

He frowned, uncertain. "Pray tell, what is *sham-pooh*?"

It took three baths for Ulick to finally be clean. Tara had a spare toothbrush and Ulick seemed to know what to do with it, though toothpaste was strange to him. Tara threw some clothes on, dirty as she was, and used the time he was in the bath to drive to Newry and buy two pairs of tracksuit pants and three T-shirts she hoped would fit him.

He emerged from the bathroom minutes after she got back,

only a towel wrapped around his waist. Tara forgot to breathe. An unfamiliar tightness gripped her lower belly.

"My clothes?" he asked, sheepish.

"You were buried long enough for your clothes to decay. There was nothing left but a belt buckle."

Tara watched him take in that bit of information. Ulick shrugged, unperturbed. "What do men wear in this time?"

"I put some clothes on the bed in the spare room for you, down the passage there. Right now, I'm quite desperate for a bath myself."

Half an hour later, clean and fresh, Tara padded back into her sitting room on bare feet. Ulick was fully dressed and fast asleep on the couch, but he woke up when she came near. For a moment, Tara was at a loss for words.

Ulick met her stare. "I am very hungry," he said, his voice a near physical touch to her cheek.

"I'll . . . I'll do us both a fry-up."

He smiled as if he knew something she didn't and came to his feet. "Ye do that, lass. I shall aid ye, and ye can tell me of the world that is now."

"First I need to know what year you came from, so I can fill you in on the rest."

"I do not know the year I was in when I died."

How was that possible? She stored the question for later. "Tell me some things you remember, stuff people won't forget in a while."

Ulick followed her to the kitchen. "I was in sister England one month before I journeyed back to Ireland. My quest was to meet one like us, who knew of a plot to overthrow the King. I found this man in Warrington. The enemy could not find us, and shook the ground to kill us both."

Bingo. "There was an earthquake in Warrington in 1750."

"Aye. Men would think of it as that. I escaped with my life, but the enemy and some who serve him were in pursuit. One caught up with me in the fair county of Armagh. By grace of Eireann she was not as strong as her master. I defeated her, but could not heal."

Tara glanced at him. It seemed unreal to hear this now, with him clad in a dark grey T-shirt and black tracksuit pants. They fitted snugly about his hips, over a pair of firm buttocks. "I didn't see any marks on you." And, boy, had she seen a lot of him earlier, when he was still covered in mud, and ice cold.

"Aye. Fae heal in death, but do not regain life unless resurrected by another. My enemy had constricted air around me and broke one of my ribs. It pierced my heart. The bleeding was too much for me to stop."

"Good God." Tara lay rashers of bacon in the pan, added three sausages. From the corner of her eye, she saw Ulick watch her every move. Tara smiled. "All this technology must seem strange to you."

Ulick shook his head. "Not really. In Tir na nóg, people from many different times settle to live. I have seen much like this, and have been told of electricity. There, magic is instilled to work the machines we use to ease life."

"Tell me about it."

He did. As they cooked a huge breakfast together, Ulick described a land where the absence of death by natural means led to a slower pace of life, where command of magic gave rise to different technology which was in many ways similar to modern machines. When they'd finished eating, he gathered the dishes and took them to the sink. "Yer turn. Tell me of what passed in the time I slept in death."

Tara's heart glowed. Beloved history. She filled him in on the broad details. He nodded when she got around to the world wars. "I have heard of these great wars. There is a man in the land beyond time who fought then."

Tara brewed tea, and Ulick listened grimly to the modern history of Ireland. "Aye," he commented when they settled in the sitting room, each with a steaming cup of tea. "Fair Eireann's children bear much sorrow."

"And a lot of time has passed since you died."

Ulick smiled. "Never fear, Tara. I am not too late to pass on my message. The king I speak of is Nuada Airgethlam, Lord of Tir na Nóg, ruler over Tuatha Dé Danaan in all worlds. As long as the Lord of Time gives me grace to enter Tir na nóg when I need to, I will not be too late."

Her heart sank. "So you're going to leave?"

His smile faded. "I must. But not yet. My strength has not fully returned. If I may prevail upon your hospitality . . ."

"Of course." He could prevail upon her hospitality as long as he liked. Tara looked away from him, and gulped her tea. Her phone trilled, and she dashed to the sitting room to answer it. Dullaghan again.

"Tara, sorry to bother you again. There's been some interference with the dig, we suspect it was with your squares. Did you see anything when you were there earlier?"

"No, nothing." She thought fast. "I did pass a van parked at the side of the road when I left."

"And what time was that?"

"Around seven, I think."

A pause. "OK, we'll let you know if we find out anything. See you tomorrow."

She ended the call and put the phone down. Dullaghan had sounded deeply suspicious. Tara chewed her bottom lip as she went back to the kitchen.

They sat at the kitchen table through the rest of the morning and into late afternoon. Ulick drank endless cups of sweet tea, ate everything she offered him. He was quick-witted and an excellent storyteller, fascinating her with tales of Irish gods who often seemed so different to the way they were portrayed in mythology.

He also listened well, getting Tara to tell him every detail she knew of her own family history. "I never knew my grandmother on my father's side. She died in a car accident when my dad was a baby."

"Ah."

Why did that "ah" sound as if he suddenly understood something he'd been wondering about? But Ulick changed the subject to her job and Tara stored her questions at the back of her mind.

That night, for the first time since the dig began, she felt at peace when she lay down in her bed. The events of her extraordinary day swirled like a kaleidoscope in her mind. Was it the excitement? The fatigue? Or perhaps the warmth of knowing Ulick slept on the other side of her bedroom wall? Whatever the reason, she soon fell into a deep sleep that was lined with dreams of the ancient Irish gods from Ulick's tales.

When Tara arrived for work next morning, the blue and white of a police car at the gate dampened the normally jovial atmosphere. With her heart in her throat, she crunched across the gravel at the entrance before stepping on to the pathway of wooden boards that kept the dig from turning into a quagmire. The familiar invisible spider crawled up her spine as she approached the mess tent. This time she wondered if fear was coaxing the prickly feeling over her skin.

"Tara." Dullaghan popped his head out of the admin tent. "Could you come in here, please."

An hour later, Tara emerged from the tent, suppressing a satisfied grin. They'd asked a million questions, but she stuck to the truth: no, she hadn't removed any valuable artifact from the dig. Ulick was no artifact.

"Let me put it this way," the policeman had said. "Did you remove anything valuable from the dig?"

Tara smiled. He was no fool. She shook her head. Ulick was a person, no value could be placed on his life.

The policeman nodded, satisfied. "Thank you, Ms McGinty. You can go."

And go she did, a kind of giddy joy stuck in her throat, making her head feel too full. She'd done it. She'd rescued Ulick and got away with it. He'd be there when she got home, and they'd talk the night away. Tara began scraping soil from a new square, no more than the turf removed so far. Ulick's grave was closed off with red-and-white-striped tape that flapped in the snappy breeze.

The policeman soon stepped from the admin tent wearing a stoic look as Dullaghan argued with him. Silence fell on the dig as everyone tried to hear what their boss was saying. It soon became impossible not to.

"I'm telling you," Dullaghan shouted, "a very important artifact was removed from this site!"

The policeman kept his face impassive. "As soon as you bring us proof, doctor, we shall do everything in our power to recover what might have been stolen. Until then, my hands are tied." From his tone of voice Tara guessed he had no burning desire to untie them, either.

When the patrol car disappeared around the bend, Dullaghan stormed back to the admin tent. Tara glanced up just in time to catch a venomous look he cast her way. She shrugged and kept scraping.

"You mean to tell me," Tara said that night at her kitchen table, "that there are hundreds – perhaps even thousands – of faeries living among normal people?"

"Aye." Ulick had spent the day sleeping and eating, and looked somehow more real, more *there*, than he had that morning. She didn't mind that she'd have to go shopping for food again tomorrow. "When our race realized the age of Men was dawning, we withdrew from this land. We call it the Leaving. Some chose to live in Tir na nóg, the land beyond time. Others chose the hidden world, where twilight reigns all hours. Yet others chose to hide among men. Each choice carries its burden both of sorrows and of joys."

"But Fae are immortal. How do they hide that, if they live with ordinary humans?"

"We can allow our bodies to age as those of humans would. At the time it would be considered normal for them to die, these faeries slip into the hidden world and allow their bodies to renew. They then re-enter the world of men and start a new life."

"Can they have children?"

"Aye, and many take human mates. The sons and daughters sometimes inherit the Fae nature, sometimes not. Sometimes their nature skips a generation, and grandchildren inherit. That is common. But unless someone tells this child or grandchild what they are, they will age and die as they believe they should."

"That seems sad. A waste."

"Aye." Ulick looked straight at her, his green eyes clear and kind. "It is."

And whether it was the steady stare or the husky rasp in his voice as he spoke, Tara found herself leaning forwards over the small table, and Ulick did the same. He rested his hands on hers, stroked her thumbs with his own. She wanted his firm lips on her mouth, so very much.

But as if he reminded himself of something, Ulick pulled back. She felt the moment shatter and drift away. They carried on speaking as if nothing had happened. Between them, invisible yet impossible to ignore, *something* grew stronger as the night waned.

Tara turned her car's engine off and slumped in the seat. She sighed. On one hand, her life had turned into something wonderful since Ulick had entered it two weeks ago. Nightly talks trailed into the small hours. He could do magic – real magic! – and amused her with what she suspected he considered to be simple tricks. He kept the house clean, cooked delicious meals and, when she had time off, they went for long walks. She'd taken him to town, to the cinema, and he was fascinated with modern life.

Things couldn't be better. She was madly in love, it was useless to deny it. She was also certain Ulick felt the same.

But every time they got physically close, every time things went quiet between them and she could almost hear his heart beat in her ears, Ulick shied away. She even caught a groan of frustration now and then. Tara understood why he didn't want to take their relationship further. Though neither of them brought up his determination to still convey his message to Nuada Airgethlam, it sat between them like some warty chaperone.

He knew he would have to leave soon. And Tara ached at the thought of the inevitable. His quest had killed him once already. Who was to say it wouldn't kill him again? And what if no one ever found his grave this time?

What if she never saw him again?

She grabbed the four bottles of wine she'd bought on the way home and went inside. The fragrance of roasting lamb met her at the door, with Ulick right behind it. He'd learned how to use modern razors, and his chin was smooth. He'd also insisted she try her hand at hairdressing. She refused to cut too much off, instead leaving his hair in a short bob. It was enough: his hair was naturally curly, and framed his strong face so he looked like a surfer. Except for the lack of a tan, of course, but on Ulick the milky skin looked right.

Would wine have the same effect on Fae as it had on humans? She was about to find out.

She and Ulick talked as always, but this time over wine. "I have not had wine for a good long while," he said when he refilled his glass the first time. "I had better take care, or I might make a fool of myself."

Tara waved a careless hand. "You're among friends." They clinked glasses, drank, and talked some more. Ulick drank slowly, he didn't get drunk, but she sensed a definite relaxation about him that she hadn't seen before.

And as the night wore on, the silences between them grew. They weren't empty spaces, bereft of words. Instead they were overflows of unspoken understanding.

He laid his hand on hers. Tara smiled, savoured its warmth. Ulick stared at the table, as if scared to face her. When he lifted his gaze, it held an edge of recklessness, as if he'd made up his mind: about what, she could only guess. Her heart answered the plea she saw in his eyes. They rose from their seats simultaneously, leaned over the small table.

There were no preliminaries, no tentative explorations. Ulick played his tongue over her lips and she opened for him willingly. He plunged it deep into her mouth with a shocking suddenness. A warm weakness spread from her belly through the muscles of her pelvis, into her upper thighs. Her nipples peaked into a pair of sensitive crowns under her bra.

Ulick steered her away from the table, drew her close to him. She gave her hands and fingers free rein to explore every plane and curve of his body as she had so longed to do, welcomed the sensation of his touch to her skin. As if he couldn't get her close enough, he put his hands under her buttocks and lifted her from the floor to straddle his hips.

Oh, boy, did he want her badly. Her own desire flamed to fever pitch at the realization.

"Bedroom," she whispered as he spread his kisses down her neck. He walked her down the passage without answering.

Later, when they lay entangled in the aftermath of the explosion between them, she placed her hand on his abdomen and asked the question that had been in the back of her mind since that first night.

"Ulick. Why, when I told you about my grandmother's death, did you say 'ah'?"

He chuckled. "What would ye have had me say?"

"There was meaning in that 'ah', Ulick. I heard it."

For a moment, she thought he'd fallen asleep. Then he pulled her closer, laid her head on his chest. His voice was a comforting rumble against her ear. "Why did ye choose to dig where ye found me? Was it chance, or did some matter guide yer decision?"

Tara hesitated. "Well . . . All my life, I've often felt this curious prickly feeling along my spine when I meet certain people. It usually goes away after a minute or so." She felt silly for confessing this eccentricity, but the feeling was like chaff in the wind. This was a faerie she spoke to, after all. "When I arrived at the dig, I felt this prickle all the time. Non-stop. It got really irritating after a while. The dig supervisor told me to choose my own square to excavate. I don't think he likes me very much."

Ulick stroked her hair. "Continue, please."

"I wandered around the edge of the dig and, because I felt miserable already, I chose the spot where the prickly feeling was worst."

He sighed, shifted his body, but when she wanted to move away, worried she made him uncomfortable, he stopped her. "Lass, I do not know how to give ye this news gently. Ye are Fae, Tara."

She suppressed a laugh. "No, I'm not."

"Aye, ye are. We can sense thc presence of another of our kind. Ye felt me there."

"No. It's not possible." Half of Tara wanted to roll off Ulick, go for a walk to process this strange claim of his. The other half wanted to snuggle closer to him, where she felt safe.

He moved his hand down to her back, stroked fingertips over her shoulder blades. "It is possible, sweet Tara. The feeling ye described, ye would have felt it when near yer own."

"But . . ."

"Most likely, yer grandma would have told ye of yer nature, had she lived. But if we die in the world of man, we can only resurrect if a stranger wakes us again. Our kin must walk away. The only other way is for the body to be taken to Tir na nóg, where resurrection is an easier task. But to enter Tir na nóg, ye have to be gifted with time magic. Not all are."

"So . . . you think I'm a faerie, like you?"

"Aye." He pulled the duvet up over them. "And, Tara . . ."

"Yes?"

"Moments before I was killed, I had implored Mother Eireann to lead me to one of my kind who had the gift of time magic."

Tara blinked. "So?"

Ulick didn't answer.

And then he didn't need to. She sat up beside him. "What? Me? Now I know you must be joking."

"Nay, lass. I do not jest."

Tara laughed. Ulick put an arm behind his head, watched her with a quiet smile. "Ye set my soul on fire when you laugh like that."

Her giggle subsided. Ulick reached out and pulled her down on top of him. Tara felt blindly for the lamp switch. She found it. Velvet darkness poured into the room.

* * *

"So what do I do?"

They were on the couch in the sitting room, windblown from their walk. The smell of fresh heather and yesterday's rain clung to their skins, their hair. Three days had passed since they became lovers, and their hunger for each other burned day and night.

"Let go of yer thoughts first." Ulick got up and drew the blinds to shut out the bright realness of the sun. "Close yer eyes, if ye must, but empty yer head. Then think of Tir na nóg." He sat back down beside her.

"But surely the Tir na nóg I'll think of will be the wrong one? It will be the image I've formed of it in my mind from the stories I've heard and read, not the place as it actually *is*."

"Tir na nóg is in the heart of all Fae, Tara. Ye know it here." Ulick rested his hand on her chest. "Try." He shifted away from her and gave her an encouraging smile. "I think it might be easier for ye than ye think, because ye're a scholar. Yer mind is disciplined already."

She'd try, for his sake. In truth, she was still sceptical about his claims. Her? A faerie? Come on.

Yet at the same time, she couldn't just dismiss what he'd said. It made sense. Yes, she would try unlocking the time magic he was convinced she carried in her soul. She'd really try.

Tara closed her eyes and imagined herself sitting in an empty, white space. Her breathing slowed. Every time a thought tried to muscle its way in from the outside, she focused harder on the white space. Just white, nothing else.

When she felt empty and relaxed, Tara allowed a single name to join her in her space. *Tir na nóg. Mythical land beyond time, home of the Irish gods.*

Nothing happened. She shook her head regretfully, and opened her eyes. "I'm sorry, Ulick, I . . ."

The sentence died on her tongue. For a mere moment, she saw something like a hole in front of her, obliterating the furniture and wall behind it. Inside was a sense of absolute nothingness, as if everything stopped inside this darkness.

And then it was gone.

Tara turned to Ulick, her mouth opening and closing, but no sound coming from her throat. He grinned at her like a proud teacher. "I was right. Yer mind is disciplined already. Ye have strong time magic in ye, Tara. Ye opened a door to the space between time and time, the passage to Tir na nóg."

"I . . . I . . ."

She felt it herself even as alertness sprang into his eyes and his lips pressed into a thin line. That familiar prickle, a spider wearing football spikes crawling up her spine. A shadow passed over the drawn blind.

Tap-tap-tap!

Tara rose automatically to open the door, but Ulick pulled her back. "We need to know who it is first. Remember, the knowledge I carry can yet harm those who work to undermine the King. They will be looking for me."

"More than 250 years on?"

"Aye. Ye do not understand, Tara, time means something different when you have eternity."

Her caller knocked again. "Helloooo! Tara? Are you home?"

"Oh." Tara smiled. "It's just Dr Dullaghan, the dig supervisor. My boss, actually." She turned to Ulick and the blood froze in her veins. He had turned deathly pale. His body adopted a deep, dangerous stillness in every line. Like a leopard, cornered, which turns itself into a statue to make full use of its camouflage, but at the same time tenses to fight.

"Tara," he said, his voice low, as Dullaghan knocked again. "The man ye think of as yer leader is not what he seems."

"Tara? Hello? I know you're home, pet." The familiar Irish way of using endearments for all and sundry sounded wrong on Dullaghan's tongue. "Open the door, Tara."

"He is a powerful faerie, who works to gather enough power to kill Nuada Airgethlam and take his throne. Our King has learned over millennia to rule with wisdom and grace. War has been eradicated from Tir na nóg, the land beyond time. The hidden world has always been treacherous, but for several hundred years now it has worn peace as its preferred outfit."

"Tara, I know you're in there. Open the door." Every patch of false friendliness Dullaghan had first plaited into his voice was now gone. He hammered at the door, making the knocker rattle.

"Taking away the man who keeps the balance, who knows the diplomacy to preserve this peace, will trigger wars that will reverberate in this land, and cost the lives of countless faerie." He glanced at her, a plea in his eyes. "I cannot let this happen. I must stand against him."

Ulick sprang to his feet and Tara followed suit. "Open an entrance into time for us, Tara," he said, his voice still low. He stepped in front of her, between her and the front door. "Do it. It's our only chance."

"Can't we—"

The end of her sentence was swallowed in a massive crash. Her front door splintered into a thousand pieces. Tara flinched, braced herself for the shower of debris that would hit her, but nothing did.

Ulick had lifted his hands to chest level. The air in front of him seemed *different*, as if it was somehow separate from the rest of the air in the room. Debris bounced away in front of him as if from a shield.

As if he'd solidified the air.

Dullaghan strode into her ruined sitting room as if he owned the place. He rested contemptuous eyes on Ulick, sighed and clicked his tongue. "There you are. Do you have any idea how much trouble I've had to take to find you?"

"Aye. I guessed. Ye became a man of history, an excuse to dig where ye felt other Fae resting, looking for me."

Dullaghan clapped his hands slowly. "Bravo. Ten points for logic. And I would have found you sooner if Tara hadn't been there to muddle my senses. Now, I'll not ask if you want to go easy. I know the answer to that already. Never one for making things simple if they could be complicated, Ulick."

He wasn't even paying attention to her, as if she was completely inconsequential.

"Tara," said Ulick.

She snapped out of her shock, grasped his waist with shaking hands, rested her forehead against the hard muscles of his back. Comforting, yes, but how in hell could anyone stand against someone who oozed menace and chill cruelty like Dullaghan did? How had he ever managed to hide the monster he truly was?

"Tara," Ulick said again, his voice low and calm, helping her focus.

Dullaghan misunderstood. "Oh. Tara? We can negotiate there. I am willing to give you my word to let her go, if you will give yours in return to yield to me without making things difficult."

"Nay. I will promise no such thing."

Focus, focus, focus, but how could she call into mind the empty white space when her brain screamed with fear?

"Then she will die with you," Dullaghan said. Tara didn't look, just heard the creak and crash from above. She felt a *whoomp* around her, her ears blocked, and she heard Ulick grunt. She had to risk a glimpse.

There was little to see. There was empty space around them, but if she reached out, she could touch a mass of broken timber, pieces of ceiling, shards of glass and lumps of brick wall. Light filtered through the mass, but faded fast. Dullaghan was breaking the house up around them, piling all the debris on their heads.

Ulick groaned. "Any day now, lass," he said, teeth clenched. He was holding a pocket of air rigid around them. Tara watched his arms start to shake, the light disappearing.

They were going to be crushed. She had to find a way to make that entrance. Silence. Emptiness. White space. *Please, white space, come on!*

Something flashed in her mind, a memory of the emptiness she'd seen briefly in the hole she'd called with her mind. Not quite emptiness, though. Empty, but very, very full. Tara grabbed Ulick around the waist. His air-shield crumbled, and tons of debris tumbled down into the space where, moments before, they had stood.

"Wonderful." He kissed her. "Wonderful." Another kiss. "Clever woman." Three more kisses accentuated his words, then the playful elation at their narrow escape turned serious. His kisses deepened, her arms wound tighter around him.

Ulick lifted her from the ground and twirled her around, laughing. "Thanks be to mother Eireann, I found ye. She is nothing if not complicated, our wee island's soul. Why just take me to a wielder of time magic, if she could find my soulmate at the same time?"

Had he said soulmate? But Tara was too overwhelmed to savour the term. Right now, she wanted to take in the sea of forest around her, the blue-green giant pine trees that undulated to a rim of mountains in the very far distance. Snow lay heavy on the boughs, twinkled in what looked like early morning sun. They stood on the round top of a hill that alone bore no trees, only grass on its gently sloping flanks. Tara thanked her lucky stars that she still wore hiking boots with thick socks.

Ulick turned and scanned the world around them. He gasped, then started laughing.

"What?" Tara asked.

"Do ye see those footprints, lass?"

She couldn't exactly miss them. A lone line in the virgin snow, they snaked up the side of the hill and ended abruptly a few steps from where they stood. Another line of prints seemed less churned, the snow less disturbed.

"Those are my footprints," Ulick said.

"What?"

"I ran here before I left Tir na nóg. I was very tired by then. And I know it was me, because in that tree yon, I left my lunch. See? The red sack. I was walking in the woods when I overheard the man ye call Dullaghan meeting with another. A servant in the King's castle. The man I met in Warrington had discovered their plot, though he knew not who was involved. I turned and ran for the gate to Tir na nóg."

Tara frowned. "Not for the King?"

He shook his head. "They were between me and the castle, and I felt power roll off this enemy in waves. I would not have stayed alive much longer, had I tried to reach the King. Instead I aimed to reach the one who knew of their doings. Each of us knew half of their plan: he the details but not the mastermind, myself the names but not the plan. I thought if both of us knew all, we stood a better chance of getting word to King Nuada."

"You mean to tell me that here, it's no more than hours since you left? Yet you lived through more than 250 years while you were gone?"

Ulick grabbed her hand. "Aye. And in the here and now I must make all speed to the castle."

Tara glanced over her shoulder as she hurried after him, fear clutching her throat. "What about Dullaghan? Won't he just step through that empty place to Tir na nóg right after us?"

"He will indeed. And there the Lord of Time will let him through into Tir na nóg when he feels it is best."

"When is he likely to feel it is best?" Tara let go of Ulick's hand to run better. He snatched the lunch bag from the tree as they passed, and settled into an easy trot. He grabbed Tara's wrist to slow her down. "It's a long way to go, lass. Pace yerself." He remembered her question. "The god of time is a good friend of the King. I judge he will feel it is best for the enemy to step into this land with not enough time for him to catch us, but enough time to tempt him into trying."

"And then?" A stitch grew in Tara's side, but at this pace, she felt she could go on for hours.

"And then prepared men will meet the man ye call Dullaghan, with his fiendish accomplice trussed and ready for judgment. Not men caught unawares, with a cancer in their midst they do not know of."

Tara jogged beside him in silence for a while. "And then?" she ventured.

Ulick glanced at her. "And then we explore this land together. Or Eireann. Whatever ye wish. As long as we can do it together."

"Sounds like a plan." She grinned at him, and ran a little faster.

The Skrying Glass

Penelope Neri

The Village of Glenkilly, southeast Ireland – 853

Prologue

"Siobhan! It's your turn! Come!"

"I don't want to. I'm frightened!"

"Frightened, *mo muirnin*? There's nothing to be frightened of! What could go wrong on your lucky day? 'Tis but a mirror, after all," her mother soothed, stroking Siobhan's tangle of black curls.

"Aye, a mirror that shows the future where my face should be, Mother! I'm thinking 'tis better not to know what lies ahead," she added with a wisdom that belied her years.

"Oh, very well then. Ask it a question instead. What would you see?" Deirdre thought for a few seconds. "I know! Bade it show us your wedding day!" She smiled. "And your future husband. Wouldn't that be fun?"

Knowing her mother would not give up until she took part in her fortune-telling games, Siobhan rolled her eyes and sighed. "Very well, Mother."

Taking her seat, Siobhan gazed deeply into the skrying glass. Her lovely face was grave, her expression intent, her brow furrowed.

The large oval looking glass was framed in silver. The precious metal had been exquisitely cast with crescent and full moons, stars, and all the constellations of the heavens, including the sign of Scorpio; the lucky star under which Siobhan had been born twelve years ago that very day. However, the polished silver oval that should have reflected her face was instead as black as a raven's wing.

At first, Siobhan saw nothing in its inky depths, although she stared, unblinking, for what seemed an eternity.

She was about to give up when her mother motioned her to try again.

"You must ask it your question aloud, daughter. Bid the glass reveal your future husband on your wedding day!"

Siobhan nodded. "Very well. Show me, mirror!" she commanded. "Show me my husband on our wedding day!"

She stared into the mirror's ebony depths. Did the future even hold a husband for her? she wondered. Perhaps not. Perhaps she was destined to die a young and tragic death, like one of the martyred Christian saints the monks at the monastery had told her about?

But then, a grey mist began to boil and gather within the mirror's dark depths, like billowing smoke.

Little by little, the silvery fog cleared, revealing a tableau of figures and an unfamiliar place.

Her mother's watching maids gasped.

Siobhan saw three tall men in the looking glass. They stood around a low couch on which sprawled a fourth man. He was bare-chested, deathly pale and very still. Siobhan could not make out his features, but his terrible battle wounds were plain to see.

The gorge rose up her throat. It was all she could do to keep from retching.

"A Druid healer has been summoned, *min jarl*," murmured one of the men. "He will be here before sunset."

"Too late for this brave warrior," said a second man. "He is already dead. By Odin, three of our finest fell like trees before his sword! He will feast in Valhalla this night!"

The little tableau began to blur and dissolve. The three men slowly disappeared. The fourth image – that of the dead man – lingered for a heartbeat more, then he too, vanished.

Blackness returned to the looking glass.

Siobhan jumped to her feet. Horror and sorrow contorted her lovely face. "No!" she cried. "No! It cannot be!"

"Siobhan! What is it? *Mo muirnin*, sweetheart! What did you see?" Deirdre cried. "Was it your bridegroom? Tell me!"

Siobhan did not answer. Rather, she fled her mother's bower.

The Lady Deirdre and her serving women stared after her, wondering what great tragedy the skrying glass had foretold for their chieftain's daughter.

It was on that day, the day of her twelfth birthday, that Siobhan vowed she would never wed.

The looking glass had shown her that she was cursed. She'd surely become a widow before she was ever a bride.

One

Never, in all her eighteen summers, had Siobhan seen a man more handsome than this one. The look of him made her heart beat so wildly 'twas a wonder it did not soar from her breast like a frightened bird.

For the first time since her twelfth birthday, Siobhan wondered what it might be like to take a husband.

Her companion gasped. "Oh, mistress, will ye look at that one!"

"Shush, Aislinn! He'll hear you!" her mistress hissed. "Besides, I'm not blind, girl! I see him well enough!"

From their perch in the ancient oak, where they had climbed when they heard the hunters coming, Siobhan and Aislinn held their breaths as the man and his party – hounds, horses and all – halted directly beneath them.

Clad in tunics and tartan mantles, and shod with boots of fur, the hunters blended well with the forest greenery. The ornate buckles and shoulder pins of Irish red gold that fastened their cloaks said these were the sons of chieftains.

". . . Nay, that's where you're wrong, Finn. I have heard old Diarmaid boasts but the one treasure," a man with wild red hair, bushy brows and a merry grin was saying.

"Aye? And what is it?" asked the handsome fellow. He was

smiling, his teeth white and even against a wind-browned face and curling black hair. His deep blue eyes twinkled. "A hundred head of cattle? A magnificent red bull? Or is it fine torcs and gold wristbands the old miser's hoarding?"

"You're not even close, Colm. Old Diarmaid's daughter is his treasure. A lovely maid she is, too, they say. It is said the Lady Siobhan's beauty could make the stones weep."

"Weep, is it? Ha! I've yet to meet a maid whose beauty made me weep. Mind you, I've met many an ugly one that had me sobbing into my beer!" His companions laughed. "Enough of your blarney, Fergus. Hand over a bit o' that mutton, and leave the maids to me. I'm the one who's wanting a bride, after all!"

Siobhan's cheeks burned.

"Did you hear that? They were talking about you, mistress!" Aislinn squeaked. "Why, the cheeky devils!"

"Aye," Siobhan agreed, annoyed. She disliked being discussed by a band of rogues like this as if she was no more than a joint of beef. She was more than her looks, after all. Why, she was better educated than most men in Eire, thanks to the Christian monks at St Kieran's monastery. The holy fathers had not quite persuaded her to become a Christian, but they had taught her Latin, and how to illuminate their Christian manuscripts with coloured inks and pens. She could sew, weave and play her harp. She excelled at chess, and could dance, hunt, ride horses, and run her father's household. Even better, she had another skill: a supernatural power that even her father knew nothing about. She had the ability to shape-shift to any form she chose, a magical power she'd inherited from her mother's bloodline. Such things were best not spoken of, however, for they came not from this world, but the Other.

She scowled, scrunching her face up so that furrows appeared in her brow. She had a mind to show this Lord whatever-his-name-was that she was more than a pretty face! Aye, and so she would!

"Wait here until they leave," she told her servant crisply, "then take the baskets home. I shall see you anon."

The baskets were filled with the medicinal herbs and plants they had gathered for Siobhan's healing potions.

"Why? What are you going to do, my lady?" Aislinn asked, suspicious. She was familiar with her mistress' unusual talent. She also knew that Siobhan's changing spells rarely worked exactly as her mistress intended.

"Nothing that you need to know about," Siobhan came back pertly. "Now, hush."

She closed her green eyes and began to chant the spell: "Fleet of foot, / Yet white as snow / Let this hind / Escape the bow. / By the magic / In my blood / Change me!"

The leaves ceased their whispering.

The air grew very still, as if the forest was holding its breath.

Aislinn held her breath, too.

Within a heartbeat, there was a faint tinkling sound, like fairy laughter, or the silvery chiming of tiny bells.

The fine hairs rose on the back of Aislinn's neck as light began to stream from Siobhan's fingertips in a shimmering aura. Siobhan beckoned the light to come to her.

The aura slowly expanded, until it limned Siobhan from her head to her toes.

In another heartbeat, Siobhan dissolved into the sunshine that dappled the leaves, and was gone! The branch beside Aislinn was empty.

Aislinn cursed under her breath, and made the horned sign against evil for protection. Unlike her pagan mistress, she had been properly baptized by a Christian priest.

Almost immediately, Aislinn saw a delicate white doe appear across the forest clearing. She held her breath. It was Siobhan in magical form.

The doe took an elegant step or two, emerging from between two leafy green thickets. Its dainty white head was lifted to the wind. Its velvety nose twitched. Catching the hunters' scent, the doe turned, and was gone with a parting flirt of her tail.

"Whoa! Did you see that? A fine white doe, it was!" exclaimed Fergus. He took up his bow, swung his quiver of arrows over his shoulder and looped his hunting horn over his belt. "The little beauty's mine."

"Not so fast, cousin. You took the stag, remember? This one's mine," Colm said firmly. "Eat! Drink! I'll see you later, at old Diarmaid's hall."

"Take your time, Colm," Fergus said generously. "By the time you get there, I'll be betrothed to his lovely daughter, not you. Fifty head of cattle, cousin! That's all he's after askin'. Why, by all accounts, the Lady Siobhan would be cheap at five times such a bride price! Imagine the sons she'll give me!"

Still perched in the boughs of the oak tree, Aislinn groaned. She did not want to be nearby when Siobhan found out that her father was marrying her off for fifty cows.

Two

The doe was swifter than Colm expected. She ran like the very wind, nipping and tucking in and out of bushes, springing and turning this way and that, soaring over hollows and ridges, darting between firs and oaks, ashes and birches until Colm was dizzy. He began to doubt he'd ever overtake her.

Why, it was as if the fleeing hind was a mythical creature. A magical doe that could escape a mortal hunter's pursuit.

Pausing to catch his breath, Colm leaned up against a tree to nock an arrow against his bowstring before he raced on. The challenge to overtake the doe drew him onwards, not the thought of the kill: the tantalizing flag of the doe's white scut, its small twinkling hooves. The little beast tested his hunter's skills!

The doe fairly flew before him now, leaping over the tussocks of thick turf, a white streak that nimbly leaped over rocks and deep drifts of russet and gold leaves. It was as if she fled a snarling pack of hounds, instead of a lone and badly winded hunter.

After a half-league at such a pace, he found himself short of breath, weary and wishing for his horse – or even his favourite wolfhounds – to help run the doe to ground.

He was thirsty too, his throat as parched and dry as a bit of old leather. Although it was a crisp autumn day, with the chill bite of winter on the wind, sweat rolled down his back. More seeped into his deerskin boots.

And then, just when he was about to give up, he tripped over a gnarled tree root that snaked across his path and went flying.

With a startled grunt, he landed heavily on his belly. The bow flew from his grip. The arrow sang through the air towards the doe.

With bated breath, he watched its flight; heard the animal's shrill scream of pain, abruptly cut short.

The white doe plunged between some gorse bushes and vanished – but not before Colm had seen the bright splash of blood that stained its right front leg.

He set his jaw, his expression hard but resigned. He had injured the pretty doe. It was now his responsibility to put her out of her misery. No creature would suffer a slow agonizing death for his misdeeds, intentional or otherwise.

He got to his feet. He drew his dagger from the scabbard at his waist and thrust his way into the gorse bushes in pursuit of the hind – only to trip flat on his face a second time.

He landed across a young woman, hidden in the bushes.

A young woman who was, moreover, the loveliest maid he had ever seen. Her dark-lashed eyes were as green as shamrocks, and her skin was clotted cream.

But at the moment, those shamrock eyes were consigning him to the devil.

"Well, now! And who might you be?" Colm exclaimed, pushing himself up on to his elbows, to look down at her.

She had long curling black hair, and lips like wild strawberries. A mouth made for a man's kisses.

His body stirred appreciatively.

"Who am I? I might ask you the same question, sir," she shot back, "since you're poaching in my father's forest! Get off me, ye great lummox!" She thrust her palms full force against his chest. She tried, in vain, to slam one or both of her knees into his groin.

He propped himself up, on his elbows, keenly aware that his body was far from indifferent to her charms, despite her efforts to geld him.

"Forgive me. I mean you no harm, my lady. Be still!"

"Just as you meant that poor creature no harm, I suppose?" she said caustically, sitting up and glowering at him. "I pity those you *do* intend harm, sir!"

He scowled, shooting her a dark look. "I did not intend to shoot the doe, my lady. But I shall find her, and put her out of her misery, my word on it. No living thing shall suffer needlessly by my hand."

"I'm touched, sir. But you should have thought of that before you released your arrow! The doe fled in that direction," she told him through gritted teeth, waving a hand towards the west. "Poor wee creature."

"I shall go after her straight way," he murmured. Sheathing his dagger, he retrieved his bow from the grass. He hesitated. "If your father owns this forest, then you must be the Lady Siobhan, aye?"

She said nothing.

"Shall I see you tonight at Glenkilly keep?"

She smiled sweetly. "Not if I see you first."

He grinned. "Ye don't mean that, Siobhan, my darlin'. You'll seek me out. All the maids love me," he boasted with a roguish wink.

"Not this maid!" Siobhan gritted, uncomfortably shifting position. She grimaced. "Now, then. Weren't you going after that poor doe when you flattened me like an oatcake?"

"I was, aye. I am," he amended. His eyes twinkled. His smile was merry.

He was laughing at her, the brute!

His grin, his eyes, the very size of him, with those broad shoulders and those muscular horseman's legs, made her feel weak. Vulnerable. Excited.

"Then be on your way, my lord—?"

"Colm," he supplied, starting off in the direction she'd indicated. He looked back at her, over his shoulder, adding,

"I am Colm mac Connor of Colmskeep, County Waterford. Nephew to the High King – and the man you're going to marry, *mo muirnin*!"

Three

"Shall I comb your hair for you, my lady?" Aislinn offered later that same evening.

The sooner her mistress was dressed and gone to join her father and their many guests at table, the sooner Aislinn could get away to join her own friends – the other serving girls – in gossip and flirting with the stable boys and the grooms.

"Aye. Please do," Siobhan said thankfully. Her right arm ached. She had dreaded the thought of combing out her own hair. It was so long and thick.

Surprised by her unusually gracious tone, Aislinn took up a comb and began ridding her mistress' hair of tangles, one curly lock at a time. She was surprised to find pieces of leaves and even a strand of moss caught within the inky mane.

With all the tangles gone, Aislinn pinned Siobhan's hair back behind her ears, with carved ivory combs set with amethysts and pearls. The jewels caught the rushlights and sparkled prettily, a lovely foil for the rich amethyst kirtle she was wearing.

It was her mistress' finest garment. The long, fitted sleeves ended in deep points at the wrists, but left her creamy shoulders bare. A girdle of tablet-braided silver and purple silk spanned her slender hips, its free ends finished with tassels.

Looking over Siobhan's shoulder at her mistress' beautiful reflection in the mirror, Aislinn smiled.

"'Tis lovely you're looking this even', mistress," she said with a sly half-smile on her dimpled face. "Might our special visitors have anything to do with that?"

"Special visitors? I don't know what you're talking about," Siobhan lied. "My father told me there would be guests at supper tonight, so I dressed in my finest. I always try to look my best when we have guests at Glenkilly."

"Aah. Lord Diarmaid didn't tell you, then?"

"Didn't tell me what?"

"That these guests are special – suitors for your hand? Didn't he tell ye he'd named a bride price for ye, mistress? Fifty head of cattle, he's asked for. Fifty! Oh, my lady, aren't you excited? The daughter of the High King of Eire could command no higher price from a suitor! Everyone says lords and princes have come from all over Eire t' make offers for your hand, my lady. Aye, and mayhap from foreign parts, too."

"My father did what?" Siobhan echoed in a faint whisper. The colour had drained from her face.

"He offered . . . he offered your hand in marriage, for a bride price of fifty cows, my lady. Everyone says that—"

"I don't care what everyone says! Everyone says I should box your ears, but that doesn't mean I shall, does it?" Siobhan snapped, but her voice broke. "Or that I won't! Oh, be off with you, you wretched girl! Leave me be."

Seeing her mistress' shock, the pain and tears that sprang into her green eyes, Aislinn felt a sharp twinge of remorse.

She should not have told Siobhan in such a cruel blunt way about the bride price Lord Diarmaid had offered. She'd known Siobhan knew nothing of her father's plans, but had taken spiteful pleasure in telling her anyway. Still, what was done was done. It could not be unsaid.

"Forgive me, Lady Siobhan," she said with one last flick of her comb. "Truly, I did not mean to cause you any— Oh! My poor lady, you're hurt!" Aislinn exclaimed suddenly, apologies forgotten. "Whatever have ye done to yourself?"

Blood was trickling down the pale curve of her mistress' right shoulder. Finding a linen kerchief, Aislinn dabbed at the red angry wound. It was long, but not very deep, just as if an arrow had creased it.

An arrow?

"Blessed Saint Patrick! The hunter, he shot you, didn't he, my lady? When you shifted shape?"

Siobhan nodded glumly. "He did, aye. Oh, Aislinn, when his arrow creased my shoulder, the pain broke the spell! It was agony! Is it still bleeding?" She bit her lip as she craned her neck to look over her shoulder, trying to see the wound for herself. It stung like fire.

"Not any more. Be still, my lady, or it will start up again. Did he— Did the hunter say anything to you?"

"Who?"

"You know very well who, mistress! The handsome one! Colm mac Connor!"

"Oh. Him. Yes, yes, he did. Alas, for all his fine looks, he's a . . . a coarse unmannered lout! A clumsy lummox. Aye, and I told him so, right to his face!"

"Aaah. So you liked him," Aislinn said with another of her infuriating smiles. "Did ye not?"

"Aye, I did, damn his black heart," Siobhan admitted with a ferocious scowl. But there was a certain look in her green eyes, for all that. "He's a handsome devil, sure he is."

"Aaaah," Aislinn pronounced again, looking even more pleased. "And what did he say to you, mistress, that has you so riled up? Will ye tell your Aislinn, hmm?" Cook and the other serving wenches would be open-mouthed when they heard about this turn of events. As the harbinger of such juicy gossip, she would be the centre of attention!

"He said that— He said that he was the man I was going to—"

"—aye, aye, going to what?"

"—to marry!"

"To marry? Did he now, the bold wretch! The rogue!"

Aislinn's spirits soared. She had heard much of County Waterford, which lay to the south of Glenkilly at the mouth of a bay. She would love to live near such a bustling port. It would be exciting, what with all the ships, the comings and goings, the trading, the merchants, and such. Who knew? She might be wed herself, if Siobhan were to wed the nephew of the High King.

"And would you accept his suit, my lady?" she asked eagerly. "Do you think you could love him?" She held her breath as she awaited Siobhan's answer.

"I think I could, aye," her mistress confessed tearfully. Her lower lip wobbled.

"Then why do ye look so glum? It will be wonderful, if this Lord Colm makes an offer for your hand, will it not?"

"He can't! I could never marry him, no matter how much I might love him!"

"Why ever not? You said yourself that you could come to love him, given time?" Aislinn said, thoroughly confused. She saw her dreams of a fine husband and a Waterford cottage sliding out of reach.

"Exactly. And I can never marry him because I might come to love him!"

"My poor love." The serving wench pressed her palm to Siobhan's brow. "The wound has given you a fever, that's why your wits are so addled. You're making no sense, my poor lady!"

"Nothing has addled my wits. 'Tis the curse put upon me! Don't you remember what the skrying mirror foretold on my twelfth birthday? That my husband would die on our wedding day! Don't ye see, Aislinn? If I marry Colm mac Connor, he's as good as dead!"

That evening, in the hall of Glenkilly, Lord Diarmaid told the gathering that he had chosen a husband for the Lady Siobhan from among the many suitors who had flocked to his hall. Her prospective husbands had come from as near as County Waterford, and as far away as Gaul and Britain.

The gathering held its breath. The future bride felt sick to her belly as she awaited her father's announcement.

"My beautiful Siobhan received more than a hundred offers for her hand. One hundred of the finest men! After – but only after – much thought, I have chosen the young man she shall wed from among them. Her husband shall be—"

An expectant hush fell over the gathering. All eyes were fixed on the Lord of Glenkilly. The only sounds were that of the spit, squeaking as it turned, roasting the juicy side of beef that would soon be carved for the celebration feast.

Siobhan peeked nervously under her lashes at the motley assortment of men ranged along wooden benches pulled up to the long trestle tables.

There was a fat fellow who'd come all the way from Gaul sitting across from her. He had a swarthy complexion, and a huge hairy mole on his chin that rose every time he smiled at her, which was often. She frowned. She wouldn't be too upset if he were to be chosen. After all, she would only be his bride for a day, at most.

Or perhaps the one with the long beaky nose and only a few wisps of hair left upon his shiny pate would be a better choice? The less attractive, the better. She was not as likely to love a man she did not find attractive, as she was if she married a man with hair as black as jet, eyes of sparkling blue and a smile that would lighten the darkest room better than any rushlight . . .

She caught herself in mid-thought.

What sort of wretch was she, to think such low and unworthy thoughts? How could she calmly sit there and choose a husband solely by his lack of appeal, because if he was unattractive, she would not be overly distressed if he were to . . . to well, to die?

"—She shall marry Colm mac Connor, Lord of Colmskeep!" Lord Diarmaid finally declared.

Her heart sank.

The old man was weeping with joy as he raised his drinking cup in a toast. "Good health, and a long and happy marriage to you both, my children. Aye, and a fertile marriage, too! Give your father a dozen grandbabies to dandle on his knee, Siobhan, Colm, my son! I only wish my Deirdre had lived to see this happy day." His eyes filled with tears.

Siobhan and Colm drank deeply from the loving cup, then stood and clasped hands as they received her father's blessing, and the cheering and good wishes of their guests, who lined up to congratulate them.

The feasting followed, the serving maids and lads moving between the tables, delivering great portions of juicy beef and wheels of soda bread served upon trenchers, along with venison and roasted capons, duck, fresh salmon taken from the river just that morning, and cheeses.

Colm fed titbits of the choicest meats to Siobhan from his own trencher, spearing the juicy morsels on his own eating knife, and popping them into her mouth, as was the custom among sweethearts.

He laughed when, shuddering, she refused a piece of beef that was still raw and bloody, turning her face away from it and grimacing in disgust.

"Do you not like this juicy morsel, my dove?"

"Uggh, no. I do not, my lord. I prefer my meat well roasted and unbloodied. Why, I would sooner eat a worm, or a snail than half-cooked meats! The blood turns my belly."

Her finicky complaints seemed to amuse him. "Very well. When we are wed, I shall tell our cook that his new mistress wants her worms and snails well cooked."

She blushed at his teasing. "Please do, my lord."

After the feasting, the fiddlers and pipers took over. The evening was given up to the wild joyous music of pipes and flutes, drums and whistles; to dancing, drinking and storytelling.

The evening was growing late when Siobhan took up her harp, Lamenter, to play for her betrothed. Seated upon a carved stool, she was beautiful in her purple kirtle, like a bard at the court of an Irish king. The firelight, and the light of the torches and sconces, reflected in her midnight hair and shamrock eyes.

She chose to play a love song for Colm; a haunting song that matched her mood. Her rippling chords told of two lovers who had been kept from marrying by their respective families, but later died of sorrow. In remembrance of the pair, the families planted two willows near a sacred pool, some distance apart. But within days, the two trees had grown into an arch, entwined in death as they had yearned to be in life.

There was hardly a dry eye in the hall when her last chord trembled into silence. Tears were flowing freely down Siobhan's cheeks, glistening in the fire's flickering golden light.

Colm watched her, listened to her, and was spellbound. He was already in love with his bewitching future bride. In truth, in but a day, she had ensorcelled him with her beauty, her fiery spirit, and a certain fey quality about her that drew him like a lodestone.

It was well into the evening, and the rushlights were burning low when Siobhan, yawning and still a little dazed by her unexpected betrothal, bade everyone a good night. Rising from her chair, she staggered off to bed.

Colm caught her by the upper arm as she passed the shadowed nook where he lay in wait for her.

She gasped in surprise as he pressed her back against the wall.

"Well, now. I'll have a proper goodnight kiss before you're off to your bed, my love," he murmured. "After your ballad, sure, I need something sweet to bring a smile t' my lips. And what could be sweeter than your kisses?"

He kissed her throat, her ears, her bared shoulders, frowning when she winced and drew away. "What is it? Do my kisses repulse you?"

"They do not, sir." Far from it.

"Then what? Did I hurt you?"

She shook her head. "Please, it's nothing really – just a small scratch on my shoulder. I was out gathering herbs this morning. I must have got caught on a branch"

"Aah. I see it. Aye, it's a deep one. Here. Let me kiss it," he whispered. His voice was husky as he pressed his lips to the wound unwittingly made by his arrow.

"Better?"

"Much better, my lord," she said softly.

Their eyes met, green to blue. They both knew it was not the arrow wound of which they spoke. The air between them was suddenly charged, as if a lightning storm was crackling in the air.

"Siobhan," he said thickly. "Darlin'. You've bewitched me. I shall go mad with wanting you. We must set a date for our wedding. It cannot come soon enough for me."

"Nor me," she agreed, arching against the warm hard curve of his body.

His kisses had ignited a bonfire in her belly. His gentle touch made her shiver with pleasure. Her weary head rested upon his shoulder like a lovely flower, drooping on its stem. She wanted nothing more than to spend the night in his arms. To be his bride.

"Hmm. Your skin tastes like honey, *mo muirnin*. I crave your sweetness. What say you to the last day of the old year? Can ye wait that long?"

It was on the tip of her tongue to tell him nay, she would marry him that very day, if that were what he wished. But she caught herself in the nick of time, and pulled free of his arms.

"Samhain Eve? But . . . that's only a week away!" Only a week to love him, when they should have had a lifetime? She could not bear it. But to marry him was to condemn him, and so she dare not name a day.

"A long week it will be, too, until I have ye in my bed. So? What say you to Samhain Eve, my dove?" he persisted.

"Then you . . . er . . . you have agreed to my lord father's other conditions?" she asked hesitantly, her mind racing for a way out.

He laughed. His blue eyes sparkled wickedly in the rushlight. "I have. He's an old rogue, but I like him well! Fifty fine red cattle he asked for, and fifty he shall get. They'll be delivered to Glenkilly before the first snows. I'm adding a score of sheep and a fine black bull to sweeten the deal, just so the old divil can't change his mind about having me for a son-on-law. He was overjoyed, to say the least. Judging by the amount o' whiskey he was drinking, he'll be overjoyed for some time."

Colm planted an ardent kiss on Siobhan's mouth that she felt down to her toenails. She could not think straight when he kissed her like that. If he let go of her, she thought she might slither down the wall into a warm gooey puddle at his feet.

"Is that the condition you meant, love?" he added.

"Nooo. I . . . I meant the other condition. The condition that tests your . . . your true feelings for me. And your courage, of course. Courage is very important in a husband."

"It is?" His dark brows rose. "And what test might that be? Diarmaid said nothing about tests."

He was frowning as he looked down at her. He had one palm planted against the wall, beside her head. The other cupped her chin as he tilted her lovely face up to his. She wouldn't meet his eyes, he noticed. What did the wee minx have to hide? "Siobhan? What test?" he repeated.

On his lips, even her name sounded sweeter than when others said it. "*Shivonne*," he murmured. "Tell me!"

"It's not much of a test, not really. Not for a . . . a skilled hunter like you. A huge wolf they've named Airgead has been killing the shepherds' late lambs. They are terrified of it. It is twice as big as a wolfhound, according to those who've seen it. You must find the wolf and bring back its pelt, to prove that you've slain the brute."

"And after?" His eyes searched her face. His gaze was intent, his expression stern.

Siobhan swallowed. Her betrothed was a little intimidating, if truth were told. Despite those laughing blue eyes, that disarming grin, he would not be a good man to cross, she sensed, nor one to lie to.

"Siobhan?" he repeated. "What then?"

"And then, I shall name a date for our wedding," she promised.

Again, she would not meet his eyes.

He hooked his finger under her chin and turned her face smartly upwards, forcing her shamrock eyes to meet his. "Do you swear it, my love?"

She crossed the fingers of both hands so that her lie wouldn't count as a sin. "I swear."

She had not been baptized a Christian but there was no sense in taking chances.

He nodded. "Good enough, my lady. I shall leave at dawn on the morrow."

And with that, Colm gathered her into his arms and kissed her witless.

Four

The following morn dawned fine and clear. The sun shone, and everywhere was green and vibrant. It seemed impossible that winter would soon be hard upon them.

Siobhan ordered food to be prepared for her suitor's journey. Dried venison, oatcakes, skins of wine and mead. She watched as the provisions were loaded on to the pack ponies.

Colm's hounds – great shaggy wolfhounds that wore spiked leather collars – milled excitedly about the courtyard, yelping and fighting their handlers' restraint.

The horses, saddled and fresh after a good night's rest and a few handfuls of grain, were tossing their heads so that bits and bridles jingled.

Finally, Colm's huge black horse, Dibh, was led out by its groom. Its master, looking the worse for wear after a night spent out-drinking her father, strode from the hall.

He swung himself easily into the Spanish saddle of fine red leather, then saluted Siobhan and her father.

The old chieftain seemed confused.

"Why are ye leaving so soon, my boy?" the old man demanded, scowling up at Colm through rheumy bloodshot eyes. "You promised me a game of chess, don't you recall?"

"You had best ask that question of your daughter, my lord father," Colm said, casting Siobhan a pointed look. "I'll be back for you soon, Siobhan," he murmured, leaning low in the saddle to lift her hand to his lips. "And when I return, ye'll be mine in every way. My word on it."

"I shall be here, my lord. Hurry back to me, for I cannot wait to be your bride!" It was true, at least in part. She could not wait to see him again.

Aislinn fanned herself with her hand as her mistress' suitor, his kinsmen and his servants rode forth from Glenkilly keep, hooves clattering against the cobbles.

"Oh, the way he looked at you, my lady. Why, he fairly gobbled you up with his eyes. I thought I should swoon!"

"I don't think 'gobbling' was quite what he had in mind," Siobhan murmured, her own hand flying nervously to her throat. A wicked half-smile played about her lips. Imagining what her betrothed was thinking left her almost as breathless as his kisses.

"What was it your man said last night?" Lord Diarmaid frowned. "Something about a giant wolf. What wolf did he mean, Siobhan? And what late lambs was he talking about? Is the poor lad tetched in the head, then?"

"It is nothing to worry about, Father. Truly. I've taken care of it. Go and rest, now, dear man. You look tired," she urged, shepherding him back inside to the comfort of his carved chair and the fireside.

If truth be told, she was still vexed with her father. He had not told her that he had set her bride price, nor that he was accepting offers for her hand. Instead, she had been the very last to know of his plans for her.

Still, it was possible the old fellow had forgotten the arrangements he'd made, just as he'd forgotten to tell her about them. Lately, he forgot a great many things, including that her mother was dead. He would spend ages wandering the keep, looking for her, calling her name.

"Rest, ye say? But, I just got up," the old fellow grumbled in protest. "Did I not, Siobhan?" Nowadays, he could never be sure.

After the old man had been settled comfortably before the hearth with his drinking cup – the hollowed skull of one of his enemies, polished and set with precious jewels – in one fist, and a wineskin within easy reach of the other, Aislinn drew Siobhan aside.

"What are you going to do when Lord Colm returns, my lady? You'll have to marry him then. You won't be able to keep putting him off. He won't let you, not that one." Aislinn would love to see her mistress given her comeuppance by Colm mac Connor.

"No," said Siobhan with a rueful smile. The back of her hand still tingled from his farewell kiss. She shivered. "He won't."

"Then whatever shall ye do?"

"I don't know." Siobhan sighed. "I suppose I must cross that bridge when I come to it."

Siobhan fretted and worried about Colm mac Connor for the next three days. She could not sleep a wink for thinking of him! And with every passing moment, she came to love him just a little bit more, although she had known him only a short while.

She had heard it was possible to fall in love with a man at first sight, but had not believed it – until now. Now, she thought it was quite possible, quite possible indeed.

She dreamed of Colm, too, when she finally fell into a fitful sleep. Dreamed of how it had felt to lie beneath him in the forest, his weight heavy on her. Of the taste of his mouth, and the scent of his skin. Aye, and she burned for him, ached for him, as she lay in her bed, alone.

She pretended the soft fur of her coverlet was his passionate embrace, its heavy weight his powerful arms enfolding her. And she wept with longing.

By the fourth day, she was sick with worry. Had she sent Colm to his death? Would he be attacked by a giant wolf that had not been seen on her father's lands for at least a half-decade or more? Would he and his party be set upon by murdering brigands, or attacked by a ferocious wild boar? Would they all be killed because of this wild goose – *wild wolf* – chase she'd invented?

"It is no use! I cannot just sit here and wait, Aislinn!" she wailed. "I am grown ill with worry for my dearest lord. I must see with my own eyes that he is well."

"Hmph. Ye should have thought of that before you sent him away, I'm thinking," the serving wench muttered.

"What? What was that?" Siobhan demanded, sharply yanking one of Aislinn's tawny braids. "Tell me, or I'll pinch you!"

"Ouch! Nothing, my lady. Nothing. I was just humming a jig. The one Lord Colm's cousin, Finn, played at your betrothal, remember?" But then she saw what Siobhan was up to. "Oh, no, mistress! You're not going to do it again?"

But she was.

"On wings of white / Pray, let me fly!" Siobhan chanted softly, her green eyes gleaming in the rushlight. "Mistress of / The azure sky! / By the magic / In my blood / Change me!" As it did whenever Siobhan cast her shape-shifting spells, the air grew very still. It was as if the bower was holding its breath.

Aislinn held her breath, too.

The fire on the hearthstone ceased snapping and crackling.

The shadows on the walls leaped up, became dragons, giants, wizards and other monstrous creatures.

Aislinn heard tinkling in the distance, like fairy laughter, or the chiming of tiny bells. Sounds that came from the Otherworld.

The fine hairs rose on the back of her neck as light streamed from Siobhan's fingertips. Eyes closed now, like a priestess of the Moon, lost in a trance, Siobhan beckoned the light to come to her, to surround her.

And it came.

The golden aura slowly expanded, until it limned Siobhan from head to toe.

A second later, she melted into the deep shadows and was gone!

Straightway, Aislinn heard a fierce whirring of wings. Something heavy – something alive – landed on Aislinn's shoulder. She screamed, and tried to bat it off her with her fists.

"Stop!" she heard Siobhan's sharp command in her head. "Stop, Aislinn, else I'll change you into a mouse and eat you!"

Aislinn stopped flailing, although the snowy hawk's sharp talons dug painfully into her flesh.

She had no fondness for birds. Nor did she like the way this one perched on her shoulder, peering at her right eyeball with its own beady ones as if selecting a tasty morsel for its supper.

Aislinn jerked her head to one side, as far from the hawk's beak as she could get. "As you will, my lady. Oh, there's a bloody mark upon your . . . your wing!"

"Enough! Carry me outside where I may fly free!"

The sun was setting in the west when Aislinn went out into the courtyard, carrying the heavy white hawk on her wrist.

"You must tell everyone I am sick with heartache that my lord has gone. Tell them I have taken to my bed," Siobhan instructed, "and cannot be comforted."

"How long will you be gone?" Aislinn wondered aloud, imagining the merry times she could have with her friends while her mistress was away.

"As long as it takes. And while I'm gone, you can busy yourself sorting and hanging the herbs we gathered. Take the acorns to the mill for grinding into flour. Oh, and spread fresh rushes in my bower, too. Now, what was that about a red mark on my wing?"

"Nothing, my lady. Will there be anything else, my lady?" Aislinn asked, tight-lipped. There was a rebellious edge to her tone.

"No. I don't think so. Just do whatever needs doing. And there's to be no gossiping and silliness with those wretched serving wenches while I'm gone!"

Beady golden eyes looking down her cruel curved beak, Siobhan gave her servant a fierce glare.

With those parting words, the white hawk rose up on her talons and spread her snowy wings. She flapped, beating the air, nearly putting out Aislinn's eye as she lifted off from the girl's wrist.

Up, up, up, Siobhan climbed, a shrill cry of *peeeeeewhit! peeeeeewhit!* bursting from her hawk's throat as she soared.

She rose higher and higher into the streaming orange, red and charcoal sunset until it seemed her snowy feathers were gilded by fire.

"Fare thee well and good riddance, my lady!" Aislinn muttered. She rudely stuck out her tongue. "Pray, take your time. Don't hurry back on my account!"

Five

Siobhan passed the night in a round stone tower. It rose from a grassy headland that faced seaward. The tall conical tower, called St Kieran's Tower by the local people, was her favourite place. She went there whenever she wanted to be alone.

Monks had built the tower over a hundred years ago to keep out the Viking invaders who came to steal their religious treasures. To date, it had served them well. Glenkilly had not been sacked, razed or robbed.

Ousting a startled barn owl, Siobhan took up her perch with her head tucked under her wing. Exhausted, she quickly fell asleep, only to dream of mice and voles and rabbits.

She awoke as the sun was rising, lighting a shimmering trough of silver across the glassy grey of St George's Channel.

Spreading her wings, she soared up into the pearly pink-and-lemon washed dawn, wheeled once over Glenkilly Bay, where the seals and sea otters were playing, and flew north.

Below her, she could see fishermen, already hard at work, mending their nets and patching their coracles despite the early hour and the sharp nip in the air. Then, with a shrill cry, she headed deeper into the mountains, beyond which lay the Viking stronghold of Dublin. It was the direction Colm had taken.

It had been only four days since he rode forth from her father's keep, yet already she ached for the sight of him.

I love him, she thought with a sense of wonder. I truly love him – yet my love will prove his undoing!

Riding the wind, she glided on, wheeling and stooping through the heavens as if she had been born a she-hawk, rather than a mortal woman bound to the earth.

Never had she enjoyed her shape-shifter's powers more than she did in that moment. To soar above land and sea, riding the four winds, with the valleys and mountains an ever-changing tapestry of colours and textures far below was a wondrous gift; one that ordinary mortals were not blessed to enjoy.

The land that was Eire spread out beneath her in green and unending beauty.

To the east, dense forests of oaks and firs clustered between gently rounded mountains and beautiful little valleys, like Glenkilly. Tiny villages of wattle and daub, or cottages of dark grey stone thatched with straw were scattered between them, as were larger farmhouses, with the flocks and herds that had survived the autumn cull grazing in the pastures.

Several small monasteries and miniscule churches of grey stone, and ornate stone crosses etched with ancient spiral patterns, showed that the old gods, the pagan gods she followed, such as Lady Moon, and the Tuatha Dé Danaan who lived beneath the ground, were losing their followers, one soul at a time, to the Christian God.

Was her betrothed a pagan or a Christian?

She did not know.

Would he care that she followed the old gods? Or that she possessed powers that came from the Otherworld? Again, she did not know.

Rivers twisted and turned between the stubbled fields like shining ribbons. Lakes gleamed like looking glasses of polished silver. And, bordering it all, to the east, lay St George's Channel.

Once, Siobhan thought she glimpsed dark vessels on the hazy lavender horizon – vessels that looked much like Viking *drakkars*, or dragon ships. Their dreadful serpent prows reared high above the water, screaming defiance at the evil spirits of storm and sea. Their sails of red-and-white striped wadmal splashed a vivid threat across the horizon.

But, when she looked again, the ominous vessels had vanished as if they had dropped off the edge of the world.

She must have imagined them, she decided. Or perhaps what she'd seen had been a small flotilla of merchant vessels, bound for Waterford to the south. After all, it had been many years since the first Vikings had sailed up the east-coast inlets to attack Irish ports, or places with wealthy monasteries, like Glenkilly.

Those early invaders had stayed, married Irish women, or brought their Norse kinswomen over the sea from Denmark and Norway to marry Irish men. Norse and Irish now lived side by side, in peace and harmony.

It was not until the next day that she caught sight of Colm and his two cousins, camped by a lake. Of the remainder of his company – horses, hounds and servants – there was no sign.

She drifted lower and lower, riding upon the air currents, until she found a perch in an oak tree close to Colm's campfire.

From her perch, she eavesdropped as Colm talked with his cousins, Fergus and Finn.

Six

"The beast is twice the size of Bram," Colm was saying. Bram was the shaggy wolfhound that followed him more faithfully than his own shadow. "Or bigger."

"Aye, and 'tis a she-wolf, " Finn said. "I expected Airgead to be a male, from what the shepherds told us."

"A bitch is more deadly," Fergus observed. "This one has a litter of whelps to feed. That snare about her throat makes hunting no easy task. 'Tis why she's killing the late lambs. They are easy prey."

Colm nodded. The three of them had tracked Airgead, an enormous silver wolf, to a farmer's pasture less than a half-league from their camp. The wolf had been crouched over the carcass of a dead lamb, its jaws stained crimson with blood.

Turning to face them, the wolf's baleful yellow eyes had ignited, glowing like embers, challenging the hunters to draw closer at their own risk. Baring her pointed fangs, she snarled deep in her throat.

They had fallen back, allowing Airgead to take the dead lamb in her jaws, and flee unharmed towards the mountains with her prize.

Colm, Fergus and Finn had continued on alone, tracking the huge wolf's paw prints to a cave in the foothills of the Wicklow mountains. Inside were five cubs. To Colm's eyes, they had appeared half-starved.

The hungry whelps had fallen eagerly on the meat their mother provided, growling and yelping as they devoured the lamb's carcass.

Before long, each cub's muzzle was bloodied, each lean belly swollen with food.

When the exhausted mother had dropped down to the cave floor to rest, Colm and Fergus, watching from a nearby thicket, discovered why the wolf, though a giant, was only skin and bones beneath her silver-and-black pelt.

A metal snare was wound so tightly about its throat, the beast could hardly breathe, let alone eat. The silver-and-black fur of its mane had been worn away by constant chafing, which had left its throat constricted and raw. In parts, the metal snare was deeply embedded in the wolf's flesh.

Unable to hunt or eat her fill, the she-wolf was dying a slow painful death.

"In the morning, we will bait our trap, then lie in wait. Before day's end, I'll have Airgead's pelt draped over my saddle, and we'll return to Glenkilly in triumph. And on Samhain Eve, I shall take the lady Siobhan as my bride, as planned," Colm said with relish. "I— whoa!"

All three men reached for their daggers at the furious sound of wings flapping, bushes rustling. Colm sprang to his feet. Dagger in hand, he strode across the clearing.

"Show yourself, rogue, else suffer for it!"

But instead of the outlaw he expected, Colm saw only the white hawk.

It had fallen from its perch in the oak tree, and was flopping clumsily around like a wet hen.

He laughed. Its loud squawks sounded more like a chicken than a hawk. And who had ever heard of a hawk falling from its perch?

Slipping leather jesses from a pouch at his waist, he harnessed the struggling, screeching hawk by the legs before it could escape him, slipped a hood of soft suede over its head to calm it, then set the hawk upon his gauntleted fist.

"Nicely done, cousin! You've got yourself a fine hawk there."

"Aye," Colm agreed, stroking the hawk's snowy breast. He could feel its heart beating frantically beneath his touch. Was the bloody wound on its right wing the reason it had fallen? Was it injured, was that it?

In that instant, he could have sworn he heard a faraway tinkling sound, like that of fairy laughter, or chiming bells.

The fine hairs on the back of his neck stood up.

First, there had been the white doe with the bright splash of blood on its shoulder that he'd chased and lost.

That same evening, his betrothed had complained of a bloody scratch on her right shoulder.

"And now, a hawk, similarly marked on its right wing . . .

You know, Fergus, what this hawk lacks in intelligence," he said loudly, "she makes up for in beauty, does she not? A man could ask no more than that from a wife, eh?" He grinned.

"*Peeewhit!*" the hawk screeched indignantly.

Fergus threw back his head and laughed. "She understood ye, cousin."

"Aye," said Colm thoughtfully. "I think she did. Will you sup, my pretty?" he asked, drawing a strip of raw venison from his pack.

He offered the bloody meat to the hawk.

But instead of tearing eagerly at the deer meat, the hawk recoiled. She chittered and opened her beak wide, as if she was gagging.

"Well, I'll be! Did you ever see a hawk refuse raw meat?" Fergus exclaimed, bushy red brows raised. "Fancy that!"

"A hawk, no. But a dove—?" Colm grinned. "Aye, I did. Perhaps a well-cooked snail or a roasted worm would be more to my lady-hawk's liking?"

"What?"

"Nothing, cousin," Colm said, returning Siobhan to her perch. The hawk's rejection of the bloody meat had confirmed his suspicions. His lovely fey Siobhan was a shape-shifter. The question now was what should he do about it?

"Nothing at all."

Airgead, crouched in a thicket of trees across the forest clearing, threw back her head to scent the chill night air.

She had followed the rich scent of the humans back to their lair. She watched them now with hungry golden eyes, licking her chops as they rolled themselves into blankets about the campfire.

From the forest in the foothills, Airgead could hear her brothers' full-throated chorus to Lady Moon. Their mournful howls echoed through the amethyst dusk.

Soon, moonlight would dapple the forest with coins of white and silver, and Airgead would be invisible. Only then, when the moon was at its highest, would she hunt.

Her babies were hungry.

Seven

Siobhan was dozing in her roost when Airgead came, slipping through the moon-dappled shadows like a wraith.

She could see nothing, thanks to the soft hood over her head that blinded her, but she could hear the stealthy rustling as the she-wolf approached the three men, asleep by the fire.

Frantic to warn them, Siobhan stretched herself to her fullest height and beat her wings as hard and as fast as she could. She screeched a loud, "*Peeeewhit! Peeewhit!*"

Colm heard the frantic hawk as if from a great distance away. Her harsh cries echoed through his dreams.

He awoke as Airgead leaped on him, going for his throat. Her amber eyes were like twin coals, the burning eyes of a demon. Strings of saliva dripped from her jaws.

Colm thrust his forearm into her mouth, forcing her still powerful jaws apart. He flung the wolf over, on to her back, and would have leaped after her if Fergus had not rapped her across the skull with his club.

The beast fell with only a yelp.

Fergus quickly drew his dagger. Crouching down, he grasped the wolf's muzzle, and jerked its head back. He would have slit its throat, had Colm not stopped him.

"Wait! She has done no wrong. It is in her blood, a part of her very nature. If her whelps are to live, then so must she. Remove the snare, then run her off with a brand from the fire. She will not seek out such easy prey when she is healed."

Siobhan gasped, astounded by Colm's compassion.

In that moment, the spell was broken.

"My lady! Where did you come from?" Fergus asked, slack-jawed to see her over Colm's shoulder. He looked astonished. The Lady Siobhan had appeared from nowhere! "And where did the hawk go?"

"Those questions are ones we shall leave for the morrow, cousin," Colm cut in smoothly. "My lady? You must be cold?"

"I am, yes. Just a little."

He removed his tartan mantle, and draped it around Siobhan's shoulders. She was shivering, for the night was chill and her thin white kirtle was no thicker than an under-chemise. She smiled gratefully. "Thank you."

"And hungry, too, I'm thinking?"

She eyed him askance, remembering the bloody venison, and gave a delicate shudder. "Not at all."

He smiled.

"Remember the shepherd's hut we passed yesterday?" Colm asked Fergus. "I will take my lady there, that she may pass the night in comfort. Meet us there at dawn, with the others. I would be back in Glenkilly by sunset tomorrow."

"Dawn it shall be. Goodnight, my lady. Colm."

Fergus continued to stare after them long after they had walked away.

Eight

The shepherd's tumbledown cottage was a poor place of spiders, cobwebs and mice, but better than sleeping outside in the frosty air. Siobhan was glad that it was too dark for her to see much of anything, for mice and spiders might not be her only companions. The only light was the full moon's light that spilled through the ruined walls. The only sound was the solemn hooting of hunting owls, and the rustling of the trees in the night wind.

While Colm lit a fire of twigs, she took his mantle and spread it across the dirt floor, before kneeling on it.

The fire started, Colm followed her down to the floor. Finding both her hands in the darkness, he took them in his own. He drew her cold hands to his lips, kissed each one, then drew her against his chest and cradled her in his arms. His body warmed her.

"Love me," she whispered. "Take me, my lord!"

"When we are wed, then shall you be mine, and not before. Sleep, my sweet."

"Colm? Do you know . . . what I am? What I can do?" Perhaps she could use her gift to frighten him off, make him think twice about marrying her. He would be safe then.

"I think I do, aye."

"And you still want me for your bride?"

"More than anything. It is in your blood, this magic you have, this power. It is your nature, a part of who you are. To love you is to love all of you. And I do."

Hearing his simple declaration of love, tears filled her eyes. "There is something else I must tell you, my love."

"You need not tell me any—"

"No, no, I must. You see, when I was a little girl, my mother bade me ask a skrying glass to show me my future husband on our wedding day. The man I saw reflected in the glass was dead," she finished, her voice catching. "And that man was you. I could not bear to lose you! But if I name a date for our wedding, you will die on that day, I know it! I am cursed."

"'Tis but superstition, and that is all it is, my love," he murmured, stroking her hair. "We shall be wed on Samhain Eve, and there's an end to it. Sleep now."

"But my lord—"

"Sleep."

Long after Colm had fallen asleep, Siobhan lay awake, staring at the tiny glimmer of light given off by the smoky fire.

Her head cradled on his chest, she listened to the steady beat of his heart beneath her ear, wanting more than anything to believe he was right.

The skrying glass was a toy for telling fortunes, something superstitious young girls played with and giggled over then just as soon forgot, was it not?

But if that were so, then why could she not put it out of her mind?

Why this terrible dread in her heart?

They had almost reached Glenkilly when some of Colm's kinsmen met them, coming in the other direction.

"What do you here, Liam?" Colm demanded as a stocky fair-haired man reined in his horse alongside his own.

"Viking ships have been spotted in the channel, sir. We believe they are bound for Waterford and Colmskeep. We came straightway to warn you. An attack is imminent."

"I must leave at once," Colm told Siobhan urgently, lifting her down from Dibh's back. "My servants will see you safely home to Glenkilly. Finn, stay with my lady. Defend her with your life, if needs be."

"I will, cousin. God be with you and with Colmskeep!"

"Keep me in your heart, Siobhan, my love, as I will keep you in mine. Until I return—" With one last lingering kiss, Colm took his leave.

A moment later, he was gone

Nine

Two days came and went. Two long days in which Siobhan heard nothing from Colm, although some travellers on their way to Dublin in the north reported heavy fighting to the south, in the area of Colmskeep.

And then, on the third day, the thing she had dreaded finally came to pass.

Fergus clattered into the keep yard on a lathered horse. He appeared bruised and dishevelled as he toppled to the ground.

She ordered the servants to bring him into the hall. Her hands trembled as she hurried to meet him. Her belly churned in fear. The very first words from his mouth did nothing to still her dread and terror.

"I bear grave news, my lady. In truth, I would sooner suffer torture, than tell it." Fergus appeared exhausted and close to dropping as he bowed before her. There were tears in his eyes, trails in the dirt and smoke that blackened his face.

"Tell me anyway, good Fergus. I would hear it from your lips, and no other's," she whispered. Her face was ashen, her green eyes dull with fear. She could hear the thud of her heart in her ears, like the slow beating of a drum.

"After we left you on the Glenkilly road, we rode south, my lady. By the time we reached Waterford, the Vikings had already sailed up the inlet to Colmskeep. There were thirty-five men to each *drakkar*, six dragon ships in all, by my count. They outnumbered us two to one. The Norsemen were armed to the teeth as they waded ashore. Swords. Two-headed axes. Daggers. Clubs. You name it," he said bitterly. "The berserkers came first, whirling their swords over their heads as they do. They were screaming curses, calling on their pagan gods to bring them victory. 'Odiiin!' those barbarians roared. 'By Thor's mighty hammer!'" Fergus shuddered. "Their war cries still echo in my head. 'Twas enough to make even the bravest man tremble in fear – but not your lord, my lady. Not our Colm!

"Colm was like a . . . a bear – a lion – swinging his sword to left and to right, and calling upon the One God to help him. While lesser men ran, he pushed forwards into the heat of the battle.

"One by one, they fell like cornstalks before Colm's sword. He carved a path through their numbers until only three of the Norse devils remained. Olaf the Red was one. Sven the Widow

Maker was another. Lief Snorrison was the third. One by one, Colm sent them to dine with the Valkyries in Valhallah!"

He stopped, overcome by the memory, unable to go on. Exhaustion ringed his eyes with dark shadows. His cheeks were hollowed and gaunt.

Siobhan feared he would collapse before he had told her what she must know.

"Bring wine – nay, nay, bring whiskey! Quickly! Here, Fergus. Drink. Drink it down, cousin," Siobhan urged when the cup was brought. She pressed her hands over his and gazed earnestly into his eyes. "Is he truly dead? You must tell me everything! Is he truly lost to me, Fergus? Would I not feel it in my heart, somehow, were he gone from me for ever?"

The fiery "water of life" restored Fergus somewhat. He drew a deep breath before he carried on. "Forgive me, my lady, but your lord is dead. We were cheering him on from across the inlet when a berserker hurled his sword into the air like a spear. It hurtled towards Colm, spinning end over end. Its jewelled hilt flashed in the sunlight. The blade pierced my cousin's side. A great gout of blood poured from his mouth. I heard him call your name as he fell, my lady, and then he moved no more. We could only watch, helpless, as those godless heathens carried his body away," he ended bitterly.

"Blessed Lady, no!" she whispered. "No, no . . ."

"The Vikings called him a hero, my lady. They admired his warrior's skills, you see. His courage. That he was an enemy lord meant nothing to them. They said their *skalds* – storytellers – sang Colm mac Connor's praises about their campfires that night, for all that he is Irish. He died a hero's death, my lady. He is – was – a man to be proud of."

Siobhan swallowed over the choking knot of tears in her throat. If she gave way to her grief, she would not be able to go on. "And what became of his . . . his body?" she whispered. "Where did they take him?"

A great shudder ran through Fergus. He hung his head. "We heard Colm mac Connor was to be given a hero's funeral. One fit for a Viking prince, my lady."

"Then you could not find my lord's body?"

"No, my lady." Fergus hung his head in shame.

After Fergus had left, Siobhan sat and stared into the fire. She felt numb. She felt neither sorrow, nor rage. She felt nothing.

Colm is dead, she kept telling herself, over and over. Just as the skrying glass had foretold. Fergus had seen Colm take a mortal blow, had seen him fall.

But though she believed Fergus, and knew he would never lie to her, she loved Colm, loved him with all her heart: she would not, could not, believe that she would never see him, touch him, hold him, again.

Surely she would be able to weep, if he was truly gone? Surely she would know, in her heart, if he were no longer of this world?

"What am I to do, Aislinn? What?" she whispered. "How shall I bear this?"

Aislinn's heart went out to her mistress. She was close to tears herself. "Oh, my lady," she murmured, putting her arms around Siobhan's shoulders. "Don't despair. If your lord was truly dead, you would know it." She hesitated. "There is . . . There is a way you could learn the truth."

"There is? What is it?"

"The skrying glass, mistress."

"No! Never again! That wretched glass has caused trouble enough!"

"But it could tell you what has befallen your Lord Colm!" Aislinn pleaded. "'Tis the only way."

"I've not seen that wretched glass since before my mother died. I have no idea where it went."

Her twelfth birthday was the last time Siobhan had seen it.

"It is in the carved chest, my lady. The Lady Deirdre's chest. I saw it only a few days ago."

"Oh?"

Aislinn reddened but for once made no excuses. "It is wrapped in black cloth. Hidden at the bottom of the chest."

"Very well," Siobhan said, deciding. "Bring it to me, Aislinn. And be quick!"

With every passing moment, her fear and uncertainty were mounting, spiralling out of control. Her heart said Colm was not dead; that the mirror had been wrong those many years ago. But Fergus had believed otherwise. He had been inconsolable, certain that he had seen his cousin struck a mortal blow. What harm could it do to consult the looking glass? Besides, what more had she to lose?

Knowing something, anything, was surely better than this endless torture?

Refusing Aislinn's offers of help, she carried the skrying glass to St Kieran's Tower. There, she propped it against the tower wall.

Standing before the ebony glass with its frame of tarnished silver, she drew a deep breath and demanded to be shown her husband on this, their wedding day.

'Twas the eve of Samhain.

A night when the impossible seemed possible.

At first, smoke boiled and gathered in the black glass, swirling and billowing.

When, little by little, the smoke cleared, she saw Glenkilly Bay reflected in the mirror. The sunset sky was streaked with red, gold, orange. Coming night darkened the edges of the western sky like a great pall of black smoke.

And, from out of that glorious sunset sailed a Viking funeral ship, listing like a wounded swan as it sailed into the bay.

Atop the cliffs and headlands, the Samhain bonfires had already been lit; beacons to guide the funeral ship to shore on this All Hallows Eve; a night when both pagans and Christians believed the dead returned to earth.

A sob caught in her throat as Siobhan turned from the glass to look out of the window – and saw the same scene as that reflected in the glass.

She sped down the tower steps, then climbed the ladder to the ground, ten feet below. She missed her footing in her haste and fell the last two feet, but was up and running towards the shore without missing a step.

It had come to pass, just as the skrying glass had foretold so many years ago. This had been her doing, hers alone. She had no one else to blame! She had known what the terrible cost of loving Colm would be from the very start.

By yielding to his wishes, by naming their wedding day, she had also named the day of his death. She was as responsible for it as the berserker who had slain him.

Onwards came the terrible *drakkar*, sailing onwards with its pall of smoke. A funeral barge fit for a fallen hero; one that showed the high esteem in which even Colm's enemies had held him.

The Vikings had honoured Colm mac Connor with a funeral given to only their bravest warriors; a blazing ship to carry him to the feasting halls of Valhallah.

A few small flames yet licked at the serpentine prow as the dragon ship was drawn closer to shore by the incoming tide.

Against all odds, Colm had come home to her.

She stared at the vessel, willing it to come deeper into the bay, hoping it would become stranded on the rocky shore so that she might see with her own eyes that Fergus was right, that her beloved was truly dead and gone, lost to her for eternity.

But as she gazed out to sea, tears streaming down her pale cheeks, willing the vessel to come closer, she saw the impossible: a movement where no movement should be.

The rays of the setting sun had reflected off a golden wristband as the dead man raised his arm.

A wild sob of joy tore from Siobhan's throat.

He was not dead.

She had seen him move!

And as long as there was yet life inside him, there was also hope . . .

"A water creature / Shall I be," she whispered. "Swimming in / The restless sea / By the magic / In my blood / Change me!"

As always, whenever she shifted shape, the air grew very still. The cries of the gulls ceased. The harsh caws of the crows that hung in the trees – black omen birds, harbingers of death – fell eerily silent. Even the sound of the waves breaking against the shore was stilled as light began to pour from Siobhan's fingertips.

She beckoned the light, bidding it engulf her, bidding it surround her in its magical golden aura.

"Change me! Change me!" she pleaded urgently.

All at once, Siobhan, the woman, was no more. In her place was now a silkie, a creature half seal, half woman.

She slid off the rocks and dived into the shallows as sleekly as any mermaid, streaking through the lapping waves of the bay towards the dragon ship.

"Follow me!" she called to the fishermen mending their nets. "My lord lives! All of you, help me!"

The fishermen rubbed bleary eyes, unsure of what they were seeing. The light was fading. The rays of the setting sun dazzled their eyes. Was it a sleek brown silkie that begged their help? A magical silkie with the voice of their chieftain's daughter, the Lady Siobhan? Or Siobhan herself?

Quickly, carrying their coracles on their backs, they hurried down to the bay, where they set the small round crafts into the water.

Straightway, they began rowing towards the smouldering *drakkar*, and its precious cargo.

As they lifted Colm from the vessel into one of the coracles, Siobhan closed her eyes. She offered a heartfelt prayer of thanks to the gods, both Christian and pagan, that Colm had been returned to her alive.

All that remained now was to summon her healing arts and all the spells and simples in her stores to see that he remained that way.

Siobhan sent a fisherman for a cart to bring Colm home to Glenkilly.

He opened his eyes to find her hovering over him. There were tears in her green eyes, more rolling down her cheeks. He had never seen a sight more beautiful than her face. He smiled and whispered, "Summon a priest, Siobhan, my darling."

"Why, my lord? Not for the . . . the Last Rites?"

"No, my silly love. To hear our wedding vows! Did I not tell ye we should be wed on Samhain Eve? Aye, and so we shall. I shall put an end to your wretched curse, woman, once and for all – before it puts an end to me!"

Siobhan and Colm mac Connor were wed in a Christian ceremony in the chapel of St Kieran's Church before midnight that Samhain Eve. The bride wore a gold kirtle. A harvest wreath of wheat, and red and golden leaves crowned her black hair.

That night, as Colm slept a deep and healing sleep, his bride celebrated their union in another, secret ceremony, deep in the woods; a ceremony that had its roots in pagan times. She also gave thanks for her husband's life in a second ceremony that was nobody's business but her own.

Magic was, after all, a part of her nature, a part of who she was. Siobhan mac Connor – shape-shifter.

The Houndmaster

Sandra Newgent

Hollylough, County Meath, Ireland – 1422

One

Branna Mordah understood little of weddings, but knew she wanted one like Mama's.

Her mother knelt before the altar in the little stone chapel. Tiarna, the only name Branna had ever called the man on his knees beside Mama, recited the priest's words in a deep, comforting voice. "I, Gavin, take thee, Aideen, to my wedded wife, to have and to hold from this day forward, till death do us part, if the holy church will ordain it: And thereto I plight thee my troth."

Branna turned her attention from the priest's droning words to the beautiful window above the altar. Decorated with pieces of coloured glass, the moonlight streamed through the window, spilling green, gold and red on to the stone floor. A familiar object formed the centre of the design. The image resembled a tree, yet it was unlike any she had seen in the forest.

The priest's movements recaptured Branna's attention. He held an item in his wrinkled hand, but it was hidden beneath a white cloth embroidered with a tall cup.

The priest lifted the cloth.

Branna gasped. "'Tis wondrous, Mama."

The brilliant gold cup bore green stones and mysterious etchings, giving Branna reason to look again at the window.

"The wee one should be abed. She has no business here."

Shaking his head, the priest filled the chalice with deep, red wine.

"I am not wee. I am five." Branna held up the correct number of fingers as proof.

"She is my one child." Mama's voice held a slight pleading tone. "Hush now, Branna. 'Tis time to drink from the chalice."

"The little one stays, Father." Tiarna's voice was calm and the old man held his tongue.

With a wave of Tiarna's hand the priest continued with his final prayer and blessing. He placed the cup in Mama's two hands. She turned, faced Tiarna and took a sip, her blue eyes meeting his above the gilded rim.

"'Tis my heart's desire."

Mama looked beautiful. Her dark hair fell over her shoulders in gentle waves, haloed by the circlet of white flowers Branna had tied all by herself. Her mother passed the chalice to Tiarna and he sipped from the cup.

The blessed quiet was pierced by a chorus of high-pitched howls. Branna grabbed her mother's skirt when three white hounds crashed through the double doors and galloped down the isle towards the priest.

Mama bent down and whispered, her voice calm, "Hide, my sweet, under the bord's sacred cloth." Mama pushed her towards the table, and then stepped off the dais. Branna saw Mama take the chalice and Tiarna's proffered hand. He raised Mama's hand to his lips, kissing her fingers. Then they turned, standing shoulder to shoulder to confront the terrible dogs.

Branna faced the altar, but her feet would not obey Mama's command. She could only stare at the table covered by crossed white cloths embroidered with the same tree as in the windows. Tears stung her eyes. She wanted Mama.

Tiarna scooped her up, kissed the top of her head and pushed her under the table. "Do not come out till the dogs leave, Little Raven."

Branna crouched under the heavy table. From a gap between the cloths, she saw the frenzy of the battle. The priest chanted words Branna did not understand. He stood before Mama and Tiarna, drawing a cross in the air. For a moment, the dogs hushed. Then, the hound with the reddest eyes leaped upon the old man, ripping at his throat. Branna had seen Tiarna's hounds tear apart a hind in the same manner. The dogs turned next to Tiarna and Mama.

Mama stepped forwards and raised the chalice. Wine sloshed over the lip and down her arm. She stood ready to strike down the lead dog. Tiarna swept her behind him.

Terrified, Branna squeezed her eyes shut, determined to make the bad dogs disappear. The screams died quickly and all was quiet again. Branna felt hot, tinny air upon her face. She slowly opened her eyes straight into the blazing red orbs of a dog. The hound panted in her face, its breath heavy with the scent of the battle, his white fur flecked with blood and wine.

He growled low in his throat, and Branna crawled further under the table. With a last threatening snarl, the dog captured the chalice in his jaws, and led the other Hounds of Hell out of the chapel and into the night.

Branna ventured from beneath the table. Tiarna and the priest were sprawled in the aisle, not moving. Branna crawled to her mother who lay still at the base of the dais. The white flower crown had broken, its blossoms scattered about her mother's body. Branna touched her beautiful mother's face, which was torn and bloodied. Mama's lifeless eyes were locked on Tiarna.

Branna screamed, the sound echoing in the empty chapel.

Branna swallowed the scream that threatened to escape her lips. She rode past a snagging tree, its bare branches sticking out like fingers twisted by age. The nearly full moonlight shimmered off its bark, turning it silver. A light breeze shook its limbs, as if warning her away. She shivered and wrapped her heavy, fur-trimmed cloak closer. She squeezed Molly's ribs urging her on. The terrifying images of the past still left her quaking, but it would not dissuade her from her task. She must find the emerald chalice.

Branna's memory of the man her mother had loved was small. She did not know his full name, only had called him "Tiarna", the Gaelic name for lord. Two things she knew for certain – he had made her mother sing and he'd saved her from certain death. No matter what Aunt Meeda whispered amongst her friends, Branna knew Tiarna had been good.

Her life after that night had changed. She'd been whisked away and taken to her uncle's modest house to live, but had never felt welcomed by his family. Her raven-dark hair and blue eyes, different from their red and hazel, had not helped.

Molly picked her way over an ill-repaired, stone packhorse bridge, its rough surface interspersed with timber planks. She stopped the mare on the other side and looked across the rocky field towards the imposing Norman castle upon the hill.

Castle Hollylough.

Aunt Meeda had warned her to never travel to this land, as it was evil, but Branna could no longer abide her wishes. She would face down evil if necessary. She had to find the magic chalice and bring her mother back.

Dismounting, Branna removed the small spade from her leather pack. She led her horse across the field, carefully stepping over a low hedge, moving closer to the standing stones. Outside the ring, she dropped Molly's reins to let her graze on the last of summer's sweet grass.

Branna entered the circle, striding to the large dolmen in the centre. This is where Grandmama had said the chalice might be buried, inside the portal tomb. Branna couldn't have attempted this without Grandmama's assistance.

Her mother's mother had been Branna's only friend and confidante after Mama died. She had oftentimes been the shield between her and Aunt Meeda, who'd never been warm to her. Branna not only wanted to find the chalice for herself, but for Grandmama, who was becoming frailer every day.

Branna stepped beneath the huge angled capstone, supported by other upended boulders. Looking around the perimeter, she estimated the centre of the tomb and pushed her spade into the earth, marking the spot.

Sweeping the hood of her cloak from her head, Branna tied a loose knot in her hair. She knelt and easily scraped away the upper layer of hardened topsoil, hitting solid rock with the next thrust of her shovel.

On her hands and knees, Branna grabbed the rock nearest the surface and wiggled it to and fro, moving it enough for her to grab. Sweat beaded her forehead as she threw the rock aside and began working the next one.

A soft snort and whinny sounded from the field. "Patience, Molly. The ground is harder than I expected. I've only made a small hole."

She cleared away more dirt with the spade before hitting additional rocks. Branna attacked those with as much strength as possible, not caring if she tore fingernails or suffered cuts and scrapes. The dirt and pain would pale if she could see her mother again.

Molly whinnied again, this time louder and of a different timbre. Branna straightened and looked over her shoulder. Molly stood still, her ears pricked forwards. Branna scanned the field. Had a shadow moved near the thicket of trees in the distance? The hair rose on her neck and arms. She squinted, forcing her eyes to pierce the darkness. Her heart pounded in silence for several minutes, but nothing stirred.

Branna hummed the tune her mother used to sing when she was scared. Her intuition told her to leave, but she wasn't about to relinquish her quest. The song's words spilled from her lips in time with her work. Scrape using the spade, wiggle the rock, wrest it out of the ground and throw it aside. It could have been minutes or hours she worked making small, but determined progress.

"I see you dig your own grave."

Branna whirled. She lost her balance and sprawled at the feet of a large, white stallion. Through strands of her tousled hair, she stared at the imposing man upon the great steed.

Wrapped in a dark cloak, the moonlight creating shadows across his face, he wielded a great broadsword. He vaulted from his mount and brought the point of his sword to her throat.

Her heart thumped wildly. Just as sure as Aunt Meeda had warned, she looked straight into the face of evil.

Two

Devlin gripped the weapon tightly, his anger building. "Who dares to dig a hole on my property?"

He couldn't keep the venom from his voice. "State your business."

The intruder brushed aside long, wavy hair exposing a delicate face. Devlin realized his thief was a woman. He instantly withdrew his sword, but didn't yet sheath it.

When his horse Ailbay had scented someone unfamiliar, Devlin expected to find sheep thieves or wolves, but a woman singing and digging in the dirt? Never.

She stood, brushing soil from her skirts. "'Tis my concern and not yours."

Devlin lifted his brows at the edge of impatience in her tone. Her feathers were ruffled, were they? The moonlight offered a taste of her light eyes and high cheekbones. Her voice, strong, confident and with a hint of tantalizing sweetness, poured over him like thick Irish cream. Her other features would wait for better light.

He rubbed a hand over his face, irritated at her intrusion. He was already on edge. "I'm Devlin, Lord MacKenna, Master of Hollylough. Every rock holds my interest."

"Then your land holds an object of mine."

Devlin sensed movement in the shadows behind her. His hounds had spread out in the darkness. Waiting. Watching.

"What here would be of interest to a common grave robber?"

Her quick intake of breath told him he'd hit a sensitive mark.

"Nay. 'Tis nothing common I seek."

A high-pitched howl split the quiet. The dogs grew bolder, circling closer. The woman heard it and bolted towards him, coming dangerously close to the blade of his sword.

Devlin sheathed it with a snap. "Witless goose, do you wish to die by my sword?"

She stepped back. "Nay. I've no wish to die by sword or by dogs."

"The hounds are restless. You'll be safe with me." He offered her his arm.

"Nay. I'm not leaving till I find what I seek."

He felt his ire rise at the battle of wills. If she told him nay once more, Devlin would be tempted to leave her.

He glanced towards the trees, then to the sky. His response was curt. "You'll be fortunate to escape with your life. Come, the moonlight has disappeared and a storm threatens."

She pointed to a horse in the distance and worried her bottom lip. "I'll follow on Molly. I'll not leave her to the dogs."

Her horse stomped nervously outside the stone circle. Devlin understood her uneasiness. He had yet to take his vows, not for another night. He wasn't sure he could control them should they attack.

"Nay. She is too distant. I'll grab her reins as we pass. Get on Ailbay."

The woman approached his white steed with caution. Giving her no more space to disagree, Devlin reached down and grasped her about the waist. He easily lifted her to the neck of his horse, her legs positioned to the side. Then he settled back into the saddle and brought her back against him. He crossed his arms around her waist to keep her seated safely and grabbed the reins.

Devlin spurred Ailbay forward, his horse easily taking the extra burden over the stone wall, and galloped towards the protection of Hollylough.

Devlin leaned over to grab Molly's reins.

The woman blocked his arm. "Nay."

She put her fingers to her mouth and whistled loudly. Molly raised her head and fell in step behind Ailbay. Devlin nodded his head, impressed.

"My lady, your horse is well trained, as if she'd follow you to the ends of the earth."

"Aye, she would."

With each stretch of Ailbay's stride, his arms clasped the woman's ribcage, her warmth infusing his upper body. She felt trim, but muscular, not so delicate that she'd break at the slightest stumble.

Her rose scent reached his nostrils and dared him further. He'd been a long time without a woman to warm his bed and blood. This comely one aroused his interest as well as his manhood.

Devlin knew he was restless. He had grown to manhood knowing this day would come. His family's bloodline was cursed. Written long ago, all the children were destined to become Hellhounds. He was the Chosen One; the one selected to master the hounds that guarded their supernatural treasures. This rite would occur on the day of his twenty-fifth year, on the morrow. He'd become one of them.

His attention strayed to the woman who relaxed against him, snuggling deeper into his chest as she adjusted to Ailbay's motion. With her buttocks nestled between his thighs, he realized she fitted well enough in his arms, better than most. She might prove to be the distraction he needed this night.

Once past the gatehouse and inside the curtain walls, he slowed Ailbay and angled him towards the stables in the lower bailey. He reined in and slid off the horse, handing both horses to his waiting groom. Devlin ruffled the boy's hair.

"Finn, I know 'tis late and your mother wishes you to be abed. The horses have worked hard tonight. Give them extra oats and curry them well. I shall make sure tomorrow you have a lighter load."

Devlin reached to assist the woman down.

She put her hands on his shoulders and winced, pulling her hands away as her feet touched the ground. Devlin snatched one hand and saw her roughened, bleeding fingers.

He gently touched her abraded palm. Before his groom left the yard he called, "Finn, bring me the healing salve." He waited for the lad to hand him the paste, then took her arm and led her towards his keep.

Branna pulled back. Lord MacKenna, with his fierce, dark eyes regarded her critically. She prayed he couldn't know how badly her hands shook. "I . . . I should return home, my lord."

Branna didn't wish to be with him a moment longer than necessary. She had no idea why she couldn't breathe.

He shook his head. "Not this night." The stony stillness of his expression gentled when he gave her a half-smile. It changed his face, softened it, adding a touch of vulnerability.

"I will escort you home on the morrow. For now you are under my protection."

They entered the great square keep from a steep set of stone stairs and a thick wooden door. They climbed more stairs at the corner, spiralling upwards past several floors to the top, where he opened another heavy door and they entered the upper solar. "This is my private chamber. In here you will be safe."

Safe from whom? Him?

He strode to a sideboard against the far wall. While he searched for something, Branna looked about the room, soft light from several candelabras illuminating the darkest corners.

The primary item of furniture dominating the room was a great bed with a heavy wooden frame overlaid with quilts, a thick fur coverlet and pillows. The bed was curtained; its linen draperies pulled back and tied to the bedposts with leather straps. An arched fireplace took over one wall, soot blackening the protective hood of stone. Several chests and a hanging tapestry graced the opposite side of the room.

"Remove your cloak."

Branna complied, even though the room was damp. She laid it over a nearby slatted chair.

Devlin came back to her with the pot of salve and a cloth. He dipped his fingers into the paste and took her right hand.

With surprising gentleness, he rubbed the waxy paste into the palm of her hand, covering the cuts and abrasions.

"Your name?"

"'Tis Lady Branna Mordah."

"Pray tell me, my lady, what was of such significance tonight that you would risk your life?"

She glanced at his face. His eyes met hers, as dark and shiny as wet slate.

"I seek an heirloom of my mother's which was stolen when she died."

"And you think 'tis buried here? You are surely mistaken."

The salve had been well worked into her skin, but he continued to massage her hand, sending delicious tingles up her arm and down to her toes, making her even more nervous.

"Your one hand will need a dressing. 'Tis the most damaged."

"What is this ointment? It has the scent of flowers."

"'Tis calendula salve, made from the leaves of marigolds and lavender. 'Tis used upon the horses."

Did his horses receive such wonderful rub-downs? She wanted to be covered with the fragrant salve. Branna shook her head before those thoughts went further.

As he wrapped her right hand with a cloth, Branna shifted her eyes to the decorative windows. Moonlight spilled through, glinting off the pieces of coloured glass, highlighting the central tree design. Branna gasped and pulled her hand away.

"Your windows. I've seen that design."

"Nay, 'tis impossible. It was created for Hollylough Castle years ago. My home is so named for the holly trees in the thicket by the lough's edge. There are no windows like it."

Her heart thumped wildly. But Branna had seen them long ago. She gripped Devlin's arm. "Do you have a chapel with those same windows?"

"Aye, of course."

"Take me there."

"Tomorrow. The windows are most beautiful with the coming sun."

"No. Now." Branna touched his arm, feeling his steely muscles beneath the tunic sleeve. "Please, I mean you no trouble, but I must see the chapel tonight." Branna hated the desperation in her tone, but couldn't be refused.

He searched her eyes and smoothed a lock of hair from her face. He carefully took her hand. "I'll take you."

In the outer ward, the wind gusted, blowing dirt and straw about. Branna was sorry to have left behind her cloak. Devlin led her to a stone building adjacent to the great hall. He opened the double wooden doors and stepped aside.

Branna walked towards the altar. "The first time I walked down this aisle, I touched all the wooden benches along the way."

Branna knew Devlin listened behind her.

"We were to be a family. Mama looked beautiful in a yellow wedding gown with her dark hair free about her shoulders. She wore a crown of white flowers I made for her."

Branna had reached the front of the chapel and looked up at the window, her mind far back in time. "I remember the stained glass with the tree at its centre, the curled branches and red berries. So beautiful. So perfect."

Branna shuddered as she ran her hands over the altar. "Until the dogs came. Tiarna helped hide me under this bord and I was safe."

Branna turned to Devlin. Tears ran down her cheeks. "The dogs killed them. Tore at them and stole my mother's emerald chalice; took her life." She tightened her jaw. "I want them back."

Three

Devlin drew Branna to him. He wrapped her in his arms, drawing comfort as well as giving it. He breathed into her hair, "God's blood. That was your mother."

She raised her head and looked at him askance. "My mother was here that night, in your chapel, as was I. You must know what happened?"

"I know very little. Only that the hounds killed my father by accident that night. I was twelve and squiring at a neighbouring estate. I was summoned home for the funeral, but only told the dogs were driven crazy and had wrongly attacked him."

"Tiarna was your father? Why did you not find me?"

"I knew nothing of you. By the time I arrived home, it was days later. You were long gone and my household was ruled by my uncle. I could not legally return and take over as master until I had reached my majority."

"'Twas the chalice the dogs were after." Branna buried her face into his chest.

Devlin didn't know what to believe. There was more to his father's death than he'd been told. His uncle had only said that he was to take on the leadership role after his father had died.

"You were looking for the emerald chalice at the tomb."

Branna nodded against his shoulder.

Devlin frowned. "How can this chalice bring your mother back? She's been dead nearly fifteen years."

She stepped out of his arms and her blue eyes brightened. "The chalice is magic. It can bring my mother back from the dead. 'Tis my heart's desire."

Devlin had never heard of such a cup. "How did your family come by this magic chalice?"

"My ancestor Liam once saved a gnome from the jaws of a serpent. The gnome was very grateful and, since gnomes are known for excellent metalwork, as a reward, the chalice was given to Liam, with the instruction that drinking from it would bring forth his heart's desire."

Why had he never been told of their parents' marriage or the chalice? He'd have to ask his uncle for an explanation to determine the truth of her words.

"Your mother died long ago. Why have you waited until now to get her back?"

"You can drink from the chalice only once in a lifetime." She dropped her head. "I waited till I knew my heart's desire."

He slipped a finger beneath her chin. "What convinced you?"

"My uncle's family is to marry me off, as I am past my prime, but no one has offered. Everyone is afraid."

"Afraid of what?"

"Of me. My aunt has spread lies about me, saying I was the evil one who called the dogs, killing my own mother. She is jealous and hateful. I could not endure the shame."

He held her a few more moments, rubbing her back, worried by her chilled skin.

"We must leave. The storm worsens." In truth, he needed to leave this place of painful memories.

Fear came into her eyes, darkening them to a deepwater blue. “Will the dogs be waiting for us?”

Devlin kissed the tear stains on her cheeks. “I’ll protect you, my lady.”

The wind howled and rain lashed Branna’s face as Devlin took her hand and they stepped outside the chapel. Even with his promise, Branna’s eyes darted around the bailey, waiting for the dogs to attack. Every sound heightened her fear, pulling at her memories.

In the safety of Lord MacKenna’s chamber, a blazing fire snapped in the fireplace, beating back the chilled dampness and her panic. Branna was surprised his servants were still up at this late hour. She stood by the warmth of the fireplace and rubbed her wet arms.

“You should remove your wet clothing.” Lord MacKenna held out to her an armful of fabrics. “You ought to find something warmer in here.”

Branna took the proffered garments. “Thank you. I *am* chilled.”

“There is a wardrobe behind that tapestry.” Devlin pointed to a thick wool carpet hanging from the wooden rafters dyed vibrant colours.

Hidden behind the tapestry, Branna slipped out of her damp, low riding boots. She unclipped her brooch and slipped out of her loose-sleeved surcoat, wet almost through. She touched the deep blue wool of her long-sleeved gown and discovered it was almost as wet and radiated an unpleasant odour. It too had to go. She sat on the wooden bench and peeled off her hose.

Finally, Branna stood only in her long linen chemise, exposed to the draughts. Branna rummaged through the garments and chose one of Lord Connal’s linen shirts. The neckband and the wristbands were embroidered in colour and design to match the windows of the castle. She slipped it over her head and smoothed the material down, admiring its quality. She breathed in Devlin’s scent of wood smoke, sweat and horses, which clung to his shirt. She liked the earthy, very masculine aroma.

Taking a deep breath, Branna stepped out from behind the tapestry. She instantly felt Lord MacKenna's eyes on her, but snapped her head around when she heard the door to the chamber close.

"My steward has brought an evening repast. Come and eat. You must be famished."

Lord MacKenna was seated at a small table beside the bed. Branna approached the table set with trays of food, two bread trenchers and a pair of glass goblets.

One tray was piled high with cheese, almonds, figs, dates and raisins. The other tray held a selection of meats and fish: venison, chicken and haddock. Her mouth watered.

"Aye, 'tis been many hours since I've eaten."

Devlin indicated the empty chair and from a flagon poured a pale yellow liquid into the two glasses.

"Sit."

Branna nodded and gratefully took the seat. She sampled a few of the selections and gulped a swallow of the sweetened wine. It burned going down and she coughed. It wasn't watered as she'd expected.

Once she caught her breath, she asked, "Your mother, what was she like?"

Devlin studied her a moment. She met his eyes without apology. "She was like sunshine lighting all the corners of the castle. We'd take long summer walks in the sweet fields and sometimes pick berries in the wood. Then she was gone."

He shrugged his shoulders and she felt him take an emotional step back.

"I remember my father was bereft. Shortly after her death I was sent away, earlier than the other children had been. I was never certain if my father loved me or if I was too much a reminder of her. That is why I was surprised to learn of his new marriage."

"Your mother sounds very much like my mother." Branna swallowed hard over the sudden lump of sadness in her throat.

"Since I was so young, my grandmama has told me stories of my mother and her childhood. I'd like to find the chalice before she passes on to the heavens."

"I too have an uncle who took me in and gave me reason to go on," Devlin said softly. "I doubt you remember anything of your father?"

"Nay. He died when I was only two years. My mother told me he was a good provider, but I don't believe she was content."

"My father, do you have memories of him?" Devlin's tone was tentative, the question carefully asked. It touched a place in her heart.

Branna smiled and gripped his hand that lay on the table. She wanted to pull him into her arms, as he'd done for her, and soothe him.

"Many times he spoke to us of his son with great love and pride. He welcomed the day you would return. He wished for us to meet and have in this castle a great family." A mixture of tenderness and longing hit Branna. "He was a good man. He used to call me 'Little Raven' for my dark hair." She whispered, "He saved my life that night."

Devlin abruptly pulled his hand away. He cleared his throat and rose. "Please excuse me while I change into dry clothing."

She watched him stalk towards the wardrobe, not sure if he was upset at her or his father . . . or both.

Within the wardrobe, Devlin sank to the bench feeling the weight of his heritage. Bitter agony rose to his throat. He didn't want to be Houndmaster. He liked being a knight and living at Hollylough, especially now that he knew his father had loved him. Yet this curse was part of him, who he was. He had no other choice.

Devlin removed his damp clothes and dressed in a fresh tunic and hose. His uncle Hugh, the current Houndmaster, believed it to be a great honour and had prepared him well over the years. Devlin's true wish was to live out his years in relative peace at Hollylough.

Devlin came from behind the tapestry. In the far corner, Branna stood at the stone sill of an arched window. She reached to touch the crimson rabbit atop a board game drawn with a cross.

Devlin's grip on her wrist stopped her.

"I . . . ah . . . I only wished to brush off the dirt. 'Tis evident no one has played in many years."

"This was my father's game. We played after evening meals. I've not played since his death."

Branna caressed his hand still fastened upon her wrist.

"Forgive me, my lord. I meant no disrespect to Tiarna. I loved him as if he were my own father. Would you be willing to play in his memory?"

Devlin felt like he'd been punched in the gut. He hadn't been able to play the game for nearly fifteen years, yet this slip of a woman offered him a reason to put it to rights.

Her fingers continued to caress up his arm, her touch sending ripples of sensation through his body. "I'll teach you what I know of the game."

Emotions warred through Devlin, his battle instincts stirring. He *would not* grow close to her. His destiny lay with the Hellhounds. Only he had not expected such comfort on his last night as a mortal man.

Lady Branna had given him a wondrous gift – the truth about his father. Devlin had spent too many years blaming himself for driving his father away. His uncle always at his side, insisting Devlin's father could not bear to look upon the son who reminded him of the beloved wife who died bringing Devlin into the world. He would deal with his uncle soon.

He released her wrist and picked up the board. "Be cautious of what you ask, my lady. We shall play. But understand there is a cost for winning and losing. Let us sit by the fire."

He set the board on the carpet and grabbed two pillows from the bed, tossing them next to the game. He waited until she'd taken position on the other pillow.

"Since you're so taken with the hare, 'tis yours to play. I'll play the fifteen hounds. Place your hare in the middle of the board. I'll place my hounds along one side of the board, like so." Devlin arranged his pieces in a line.

"The point of the game is for you to capture as many of my hounds as possible before they can surround the hare so it is trapped and cannot move. The hounds and harc can move to any empty space, including a diagonal move. The hare can jump over the hounds, capturing them. The hounds cannot jump. Are you ready?"

"Yes," Branna said. "Before we start, I wish to make a wager."

Devlin raised his brows. "A wager? I am intrigued. What should we wager?"

"If I am victorious, you will help find the chalice."

"You think I know under which rock it lies?" Devlin watched her toy with a wooden hound.

"You are master of Hollylough, every rock is of concern to you." Branna laughed and then turned serious. "My aunt insists your family is evil."

"Mayhap your aunt is right."

"I do not believe you are evil nor was your father. I do believe there is much more to you than you say."

An explosion of hunger and need fired inside him. She might be in more danger than she realized. "Is this your heart's desire?"

"Aye."

She hesitated and then asked, "What is *your* heart's desire?"

Devlin felt himself pulled to reveal more than was wise. This little minx could easily set upon his heart with her quick mind and innocent words.

Devlin kept his face neutral and his words vague. "I imagine 'tis the same as yours, to right the wrong cast upon us." Then he asked, "If you fail to win, what have you to lose?"

"I have not much to give."

The beat of forbidden desire, strong, thick and unrelenting hammered within. She had more than she knew.

"If I win, I shall require a melody from your sweet lips."

"A song?"

"Aye, a song of your choosing. You have a melodious voice and I wish to hear it. Do you accept?"

"Aye, I'll accept those terms as a wager."

Devlin remembered the soft caress of her hand and the taste of her tears. "It's traditional to hallmark such a wager with a clasping of hands."

Branna stretched her arm out to him. Devlin took her small hand in his, and squeezed lightly. When she would have pulled back, he held fast.

A primal force inside him demanded more. Giving in to the need, he pulled her to him, until she leaned into his arms, bracing her other hand on his chest.

Anticipation thickened the air in his lungs. He whispered, "I'm not a traditional man. I wish to mark *our* wager with a kiss."

Devlin released her hand and cupped his palm around the nape of her neck, drawing her face to his. Slowly, lazily, never breaking eye contact, he lowered his mouth and captured her lips. He wasn't prepared for the sweet taste of her, silky and warm. Instead of pulling away like he'd planned, he wanted more and teased her mouth with his tongue, gaining entrance.

The soft sound of her sigh whispered through him with her need and hunger. Starving, he stroked deeper into her open mouth.

Her touch on his chest burned into him and he had to steel himself not to ravish her, no matter how badly he wanted her. That would not accomplish his goal.

Sanity returned slowly and Devlin reluctantly released her lips. He eased her limp body off his and took a deep breath.

"*Now* I'm ready to play."

Branna stared at him with aroused, heavy-lidded eyes. "Play?"

Devlin chuckled, pleased she was as affected by the kiss as he. "Yes, *muirnin*. We were about to play a game of Hounds and Hare."

They played the game until the fire burned low, casting shadows and radiant warmth throughout the room. Each move Devlin made with his hounds was sufficiently countered by a deft move by Branna's hare. She expertly played the game, capturing more than enough of his hounds.

"I believe, my lord, I have captured numerous hounds so they can no longer trap my hare. Hence I win."

Devlin was pleased with her prowess. "So it would seem. On the morrow, before I return you home, we will search for your chalice."

Branna yawned, her eyelids drooping. "I do not wish to appear rude, but 'tis sleep I now need."

"I wasn't expecting guests this night. I have no other chambers readied. Please slumber comfortably in my bed and I shall take up residence by the fire."

She sat on the enormous bed, the sight of her there pleasing him. "Thank you for your kindness. My aunt was wrong. You are not the evil incarnate."

Devlin knew otherwise. "Sweet dreams, *muirnin.*"

Branna blew out the candle by the bedside and untied the bed curtains, allowing them to drape around the bed, cocooning her in privacy. Not wanting to soil Devlin's shirt, she slipped out of its comfort and folded it neatly, then placed it at the foot of the bed. She slipped between the coolness of the sheets in only her chemise. Although Lord MacKenna had shown her every courtesy, she couldn't be too careful with her modesty.

Branna brushed a finger over her lips. Except for that kiss. His kiss had been neither courteous nor modest, but had fired in her wonderful sensations she'd never before experienced. Enough so that she wanted more.

Four

Devlin awoke to red embers glowing in the fire, and silence. Only it was not silence that had woken him. He listened intently, his hand on his sword. Soft whimpers came from his bed. *Branna.*

He rose naked from the floor and padded to her side, throwing the bedclothes about his shoulders. She thrashed beneath the fur covering. He felt her forehead, worried she may have caught cold in the rain. Her skin was damp, yet not feverish. A gasp escaped her lips.

Branna bolted upright and screamed, the sound chilling in the predawn dark. Devlin dropped the scrunched coverlet in his hand and grabbed her shoulders.

"Wake up, *muirnin*. 'Tis a bad dream. You're safe."

"The dogs!"

She thrashed, trying to get out of the bed, her eyes wide and hair wild about her face. Devlin shook her but couldn't wake her from the clawing tentacles of the nightmare.

In desperation, he pulled her to his chest and held her tight.

"Shush, Little Raven." He stroked her hair and crooned into her ear, drawing out the night terrors. "The dogs are gone. They can't hurt you here."

She relaxed, some of the tension leaving her body. He sat on the bed and pulled her closer, on to his lap.

"They're coming for me. I must hide."

Devlin couldn't speak. Her warm breath on his bare chest sent shivers through him. He realized the bedclothes had fallen from his shoulders. Her chemise had been pulled low, exposing one pert breast.

"I can't die like my mother."

Devlin found his voice, a ragged whisper. "I won't let you die."

He ached to kiss her but he shouldn't get involved. She was too dangerous, too innocent. He had no future to give her. Tomorrow he would rule the Hellhounds. A pit of hopelessness opened in his stomach. He had to send her away.

Devlin eased back.

"Don't leave. Hold me. I need you. Don't you want me?"

Devlin almost choked hearing those words. He'd felt protective of her since they'd first met. Yet his feelings for her were more complex. He admired her strength. She brought light to his darkest hollows.

"Aye, I want you."

"Love me. I need this. I need you."

Devlin saw her clear blue eyes, free of the nightmare. Hope flared within him. "You understand what you're asking? I will not seduce you."

"I know. You are a good, caring man. Even if it's just this night, I want you."

"You are certain?"

She breathed, "Aye."

Devlin crushed his mouth to hers, their tongues entwining as Branna opened to him. He'd never tasted anything sweeter than the honey of her mouth. Devlin hungrily deepened the kiss and followed her down as he laid her back on the bed.

Branna plunged her hands in his hair, stroking through the dark, silky mass, keeping him close. She almost groaned when his mouth left hers, but moaned with pleasure as he planted wet kisses along her neck and shoulder, suckling gently at the hollow of her neck.

His lips moved downwards across her shoulder and collarbone to the top of her breast that had popped out of her chemise. She angled her body towards him, begging him, the tingling anticipation almost unbearable.

His tongue moved lower, clamping around her nipple, his tongue striking and swirling the taut peak. Sexual excitement curled in her stomach, pooling moisture between her legs. Slipping her arms around his magnificent back, Branna stroked his hard muscles, from neck to buttocks.

Branna's chemise had ridden high and was bunched around her thighs. Devlin slipped his hands beneath the folds, caressing her bare thighs. Her belly fluttered as his palms slid up her soft skin and over her ribs. He closed his eyes and savoured the exquisite feel of her.

He raised her up and pulled the chemise over her head, exposing all of her. He planted light kisses to her cheek, tracing its curve.

"I won't hurt you. Do you trust me?"

Branna reached up and smoothed his chest, feeling the rapid beat of his heart. "I trust you."

⋆ ⋆ ⋆

Devlin awoke, his body curved around Branna, her head resting on his shoulder. He held her close, revelling in the feel of her. He felt warm and more content than he could ever remember.

Although his body was tight with need, Devlin slipped out from beneath Branna without waking her. He walked naked in the frigid early-morning air to the washbasin and sluiced cold water over his skin, washing away the night's passions.

Branna. She'd made him feel like he could have a future on earth. She was the one person who knew him. She'd touched his heart. He would love to have more of her. A lifetime would suit him.

Knowing it was impossible, he donned his drawers, a green tunic, surcoat and a mantle lined with fur, without the help of his chamberlain. He fastened the mantle at his neck with a brooch. He pulled out his sword. He needed a sparring match to numb his mind to what he had to do. A life with Branna could not be.

Devlin had his own destiny to fulfil. His life had been mapped and he'd trained for this moment.

He paused to admire Branna, lying warm and soft, nestled into the bedding, her hair spilling dark on the pillow. Devlin turned and closed the door on the sleeping woman and his heart.

Devlin slid over the bench and sat beside the large, behemoth of a man at the long wooden table within the great hall. Uncle Hugh slapped him on the back. "'Tis almost midday, my boy. What has detained you?"

Devlin preferred not to mention Branna. "Only the mundane duties of this castle."

"Those will soon not be yours to bear."

Devlin chose to say nothing. He grabbed a plate of food and nibbled from it. "My father. How did he die?"

Uncle Hugh looked at him in surprise. "We've already discussed this, years ago."

"I know, but humour me and speak it again."

"The night before he took his rites, he was accidentally attacked by the hounds. No one knows why."

"He didn't wish to marry?"

"Marry? Where would you have heard this?"

"Here and about."

"Well, there was a woman who captured his eye."

Devlin glared at him. "What happened?"

Hugh sighed. "They were in the chapel with the priest when the dogs burst through. She didn't wish to die and pushed your father towards the dogs, hoping they would be occupied, allowing her to escape with her life. Unfortunately, this was not her destiny and she perished as well."

"Why did you not tell me this before?"

"I thought to protect you from the hurt of knowing your father was betrayed by a woman he loved. I didn't want you to be misguided and make the same mistake."

Devlin smiled, trusting his uncle's words. Branna had been young. Her grandmama had obviously filled her head with false information. Such a magic chalice surely didn't exist.

He pushed away from the table. "No need to worry, Uncle. I know who I am and will accept my responsibilities."

Devlin left the hall to seek his knights knowing his father had given up everything, including his life, for the sake of a woman, a woman who'd betrayed him. He would not repeat the mistakes of his father.

Five

Branna stirred in the deep comfort of the bed, the sound of male laughter and clashing steel interrupting her dreams of dark eyes and a warm mouth. No longer afraid of the nightmares, Branna opened her eyes to beams of sunlight streaming through the slats in the shutters.

Her discarded clothes from the night before lay neatly folded over a chair, now dry. Her chemise lay with them on top. Branna smiled. Today, Devlin would take her to find her chalice.

With the air still cool, Branna wrapped the fur around her bare shoulders and padded to the window. She opened one shutter to the bailey below. She picked Devlin out most certainly as he sparred with his knights. He looked resplendent in a dark-green tunic, covering light chainmail, his immense sword in one hand and his shield in the other. Branna watched with pride as he exuded confidence and evaded his student's powerful thrust. His exact timing and light footwork gave him the edge over his larger opponent.

As if he could feel her eyes on him, Devlin paused and glanced up. Branna quickly hid behind the shutter, not comfortable with him knowing she watched. Her feelings were too raw and uncertain. He'd said they'd have just one night, but Branna had to convince him they could have more.

She gathered her clothes and within the wardrobe found the washbasin and a clean linen towel. She cleansed herself, patting lightly between her legs at the unfamiliar sore feeling. Branna dressed quickly and managed to find her way through the keep to the bailey below. As she passed through the kitchen, she grabbed some bread – she was starving! She didn't want to enter the great hall without Devlin, unsure if he wanted her presence known.

Arriving at the upper bailey, Branna's heart sank. The knights still practised archery and fencing, and there was a group of children playing horseshoes, but Devlin had disappeared. He probably had to meet with his steward and bailiff, or attend to other important duties. Her desires were minor compared to his responsibilities.

She turned around, intent on returning to Devlin's chamber. Then she saw him. He stood across the bailey near the hall. He held the reins of Ailbay and Molly.

Branna slowly walked towards him and he moved to her.

Devlin handed her Molly's reins. "I thought to take a ride about the lough before we search for your chalice. Would you join me, Branna?"

Branna's heart leaped. "Aye, my lord."

"My given name is Devlin. I wish for you to use it."

Devlin took her by the waist and lifted her on to the edge of the saddle. Branna raised her skirt, swung her left leg over the horn and sat astride. Devlin mounted Ailbay and she followed him through the outer ward to the gatehouse. Once they'd cleared the portcullis, Devlin spurred his horse to a gallop and Branna followed close behind. They raced over the high rolling hills, a tapestry of subtle shades of green: darker under the blackberry bushes, lighter as sunlight dappled through the sycamore trees.

Branna loved this land and its wild ruggedness tugged at her heart. She would hate to leave this beautiful place and return to the dour confines of her uncle's house.

Devlin stopped on a high bluff overlooking the calm, blue waters. "Lough Ceo is oftentimes in fog. We are in luck this day as the view is clear."

He dismounted and approached Molly, reaching for her. Branna leaned forwards, but as she slid into his outstretched arms, her skirt caught on the pommel of the saddle. Branna's feet never touched the ground and she fell against Devlin, grabbing him around the neck.

Devlin stumbled back, but gained purchase before they both tumbled to the ground.

"I am ever so sorry, my lord." She couldn't keep the amusement from her voice.

"I am not." He held her tightly and sealed his lips over hers, taking possession of her mouth. The first hungry swipe of his tongue took her breath away. She dug her hands into his hair, pulling his head closer.

Growling soft and low in his throat, he dragged his mouth away. His tongue rimmed her bruised lips. "Maybe 'tis best we find the chalice."

He reached up and unhooked her arms from around his neck. There was unmistakable regret in his tone. Yet, she felt he held something important from her, something that lurked in his eyes that he couldn't hide. Perhaps after they found the chalice she could speak to him of a future.

"Aye, 'tis best."

* * *

Devlin approached the tomb where Branna had scraped the earth the night before, her shovel on the ground where she'd dropped it. He hopped from Ailbay's back and walked the central tomb, studying the boulders. He knew the dogs and their fears. They wouldn't have buried the chalice under the dolmen itself. It was a sacred place. They would have buried it outside the tomb, beneath the lowest end of the capstone, pointing downwards.

"I believe you were digging in the wrong place. You should find your chalice buried at the end point of this rock."

He grabbed the shovel and began digging, making great headway in a short span of time. He easily removed and tossed away rock after rock. Within only a few minutes, he'd made a large, wide hole. Now on his knees, Devlin dug with his hands, capturing dirt in his cupped palms and throwing it aside.

The sunlight gleamed off a shiny object. Devlin's heart thumped in his chest. He carefully removed more dirt, exposing the sides of a metal cup. Branna hovered beside him, her sky-blue eyes briefly meeting his.

Devlin hesitated. "Would you like the honour of removing it from its grave?"

"Nay, my lord." She laughed, a silvery rush of pleasure. "As you've stated, 'tis on your property."

Devlin smiled at her, then reached in and lifted the chalice out of the hole, brushing away the last vestige of dirt and dust. He held it high, admiring the graceful curves of the hammered gold cup. Engraved panels of filigree decorated the lower portion. Emerald stones gleamed around the edge of the upper band and lower girdle.

As he lowered it for Branna to hold, he felt a foreboding, a darkness descend upon his soul. He became cold, even as the sun warmed him. Evil thoughts consumed his mind. Why should he give it to her? Its magic had destroyed his family. He had to get rid of it.

Branna dropped her raised hands as Devlin's face became distant and cold. His eyes were fixed on her but they looked very far away. He scared her.

"Devlin, what is wrong?"

He said nothing, but stared through her as if she didn't exist.

Branna touched his arm. "Give me the chalice."

His eyes grew luminous, glowing like red orbs in his now ashen face. She'd seen those eyes before . . . on the dogs.

He gripped her wrist, exerting hurtful pressure until she let go.

"Nay. You shall never touch this cup. Tonight I become Lord of the Underworld, ruler of all that is evil. The chalice is dangerous to us and will be destroyed."

Branna gasped, horrified at his words. "Devlin, something is wrong. The chalice is hurting you."

He forcefully shoved her away and Branna stumbled backwards.

She ran back at him. "Drop it. I beg of you to release it."

Devlin withdrew a short dagger from his belt and wielded it at her threateningly. "Leave me and never return."

Branna gasped and stopped, tears tumbling down her cheeks. "You can't mean that."

He took a menacing step towards her. "Would you challenge me and lose your life?"

Pain ripped through Branna's heart, almost doubling her over. This couldn't be happening.

She'd lost her chalice. She'd lost Devlin.

With little choice, Branna gathered Molly's reins. Branna's tears made it difficult for her to mount her horse, but somehow she managed to crawl upon its back. After a last look at Devlin's stone cold face, Branna dug her heels into Molly's flank.

With an aching heart and empty arms, she rode as if the Hounds of Hell had given chase, away from Castle Hollylough and the love of her life.

Branna dropped Molly's reins and lay across her neck. Molly slowed her pace, sensing Branna's distress, but Branna didn't care. She buried her face into Molly's silky mane and cried, huge heart-wrenching sobs. Devlin didn't want her.

She was barely aware when Molly stopped in front of her uncle's two-storey house. However, she noticed a flurry of activity seemed to have gripped the household, as all manner of people scurried about.

Wiping her face, Branna slid off Molly. She had to go on with her life and would have to force herself not to yearn for what she could never have. She woodenly stabled Molly and entered through the back door of her uncle's house, hoping to get to her room without detection.

"Branna!"

She cringed and stopped, but didn't turn around. Aunt Meeda.

"Where have you been all day? We are expecting a guest for supper. More than a guest and a normal supper, I'd say. We have found someone to take you in marriage, so 'tis a celebration with . . ."

The roaring in Branna's ears cut through the remainder of her aunt's words.

"Branna . . . Branna, are you listening? You are to be married tomorrow."

Her aunt grabbed her arm and spun her around. Her gasp and hardened eyes were enough to snap Branna's remaining threads of hope of ever seeing Devlin again. "You are filthy! Go wash at once. I'll not see this marriage contract destroyed by your unseemly hoyden ways. You will act a lady until you leave this house as a married woman. Do you understand?"

Branna knew her aunt expected a positive response and so nodded her assent. Her aunt released her arm and Branna fled to her room. She closed the door behind her and crossed to her washbasin.

Branna picked up her small mirror. She *was* a mess. Her eyes were red and puffy and tears had stained her cheeks. Her hair hadn't been brushed and her gown was dusty and torn.

She took a deep breath. If this was to be her life and her wedding celebration, then she would wear the colour her mother had worn on the night she was to be married, the night she'd died. It was the only way Branna knew to bring her mother close. She donned her yellow gown, made from patterned silk. It had long gathered sleeves trimmed with fur cuffs and a wide fur collar. She wrapped her best cloak about her shoulders and fastened it with her favourite silver brooch, a gift from Grandmama.

Branna left her room quietly and went in search of her grandmama, regularly found in the spinning room. She knocked lightly on the door and entered the room. Her grandmama sat at the side of the great spinning wheel, teasing the yarn into beautiful cloth. Branna stood without speaking, watching her grandmama's fingers work their magic.

"Something on your mind, child?"

Branna took a deep breath. "Aunt Meeda has informed me of my marriage on the morrow."

"I have also heard this. Are you not pleased?"

"I . . . ah . . . I cannot say as I have not met him."

"This matters to you?"

"Aye. You have told me many times my mother loved the man she was to marry. I hoped to someday have the same."

Her grandmama looked at her with sharp eyes. Branna couldn't keep a flush from creeping up to her face.

"You have met someone who interests you." It was a statement and not a question.

"Aye, but it can not be." Branna changed the subject quickly. "Tell me more of the magic chalice. Can it make someone evil if that is in your heart?"

Grandmama resumed weaving. "Nay. It does not have such power."

"It must. As Lord MacKenna held the chalice, I viewed a great evil take over his soul."

Grandmama grabbed her arm. "You have seen the chalice?"

"Aye." Branna cast her eyes to the floor. "But I lost it to Lord MacKenna, the man who helped me find it."

"This man is your heart's desire?"

Branna whispered, "Aye."

"My child, the chalice has not the power to change what's in one's heart, but it can pass on lingering energy from the one who held it last. This might sway someone who has both good and evil in his heart."

Branna raised her head and stared at her grandmama. "The dogs, they touched it last." Hope flare within Branna. "You believe their evil was transferred and 'twas not truly him?"

"'Tis possible. Do you wish to know?"

"Aye."

"Then you must trust your heart as did your mother."

"Thank you." Branna hugged and kissed her grandmama.

She ran from the spinning room and out to the stable. She pulled Molly from her stall and set her to saddle and bridle. A dirk lying across a table caught her attention. *The dogs.*

Branna grabbed it before mounting. If she had to kill them to save Devlin, so be it.

She knew without doubt that Devlin would never harm her.

Six

Devlin stood within the old stone circle, just outside the portal tomb. The full moon illuminated the three cloaked and hooded men by his side.

He shifted on his feet, transferring the chalice to his other hand. Devlin was anxious to begin his new duties, to rule the Underworld. Yet, he couldn't shake the feeling that something was amiss. It was nothing he could lay a finger upon, but a hollow feeling persisted in his gut, similar to when his father had died.

Could his feelings of disquiet be due to his ill treatment of Branna? Devlin grew more uncomfortable. She hadn't deserved his anger. Yet, he'd felt compelled to hurt her. He still could not understand why. Branna had only brought him comfort, lightness and ultimately . . . ecstasy. He could still smell and taste her skin after making love to her.

No woman had made him feel as whole or complete as Branna. Why was she not by his side? He knew the answer. His destiny lay in the Underworld and hers was in the light. His life was set and to bring Branna into it would cost her her life. He had to do this alone.

Devlin shook his head, dispelling his unease. Nothing would interfere with this transition. Devlin's grip on the chalice hardened. It was now his duty to be sure this magic never reached mortal hands again. It was his heart's desire, wasn't it?

The thumping of hooves reached his ears. He turned and saw a woman on horseback. He knew who it was by her silhouette.

Branna.

The cloaked men around him transformed into sleek, powerful, white hounds. His uncle and the dogs moved as one to take up offensive positions.

Devlin raised his hand, stilling them. "I shall handle this."

He stepped a short distance from the circle, headed for Branna. "Halt. You must leave at once."

"Not until I get what I want." She slid from the horse and walked towards him.

"You have no more business here. Return to your family and forget this."

She didn't stop. "Nay."

Devlin drew his sword and held it stiffly before him. She stumbled when the moonlight struck it, glinting off its broad edge, but continued walking until she reached its sharp tip.

Devlin search her face, agonizing over his next words, barely moving for fear he'd nick her throat. "Please . . . don't come closer. I've no wish to harm you."

I wish to take you in my arms, but it would be your death.

She swallowed and whispered, "Nay."

A chuckle almost escaped. He remembered their first meet had gone this way. "You must give up the chalice. It is lost to you."

"'Tis not the chalice I seek."

"What then?" Devlin words were ragged, not sure he could bear her closeness.

"'Tis you."

"Nay, *I'm* lost." The words slipped out painfully from

between his tightly clenched teeth. "My uncle told me of your mother's betrayal. She pushed my father into the jaws of the dogs. You must understand, she had to die. "

"Nay! Your uncle has lied to you. My mother took your father's hand, prepared to fight beside him. But your father pushed her back to protect her. I was there. I saw it. My mother loved your father, as I love you."

Confusion and anger ripped through Devlin. "You saw them fight together?"

"Aye."

Devlin knew she did not lie.

Branna eased forwards until the tip of his sword pressed the base of her throat. "You are not evil. The evil you feel is from the dogs, as they last touched the chalice before it was buried. I believe you want to be released from this burden. I believe you want *me*."

Devlin's knees buckled as she leaned into the point. The sword pricked her skin, drawing a bead of blood. She closed her eyes. "You won't hurt me. I trust you."

The sight of crimson against her smooth white skin, skin he'd kissed and stroked, made him ill.

Aghast, he sank to his knees, sick and shaken. His sword dropped, the blade falling to the ground beside him. "Nay, I cannot harm you. I love you."

The dogs growled menacingly behind him. He felt their presence closing in.

Devlin set his jaw. The idea seeded in him earlier had now taken root in his soul. He'd gain *his* heart's desire – revenge against his uncle. He would not allow this evil to continue; it would stop with him. Even if it meant losing himself to the Underworld . . . and losing Branna.

Devlin stood, thrust the chalice into Branna's hands and retrieved his sword. "Go. The chalice is yours. This is my fight."

Branna shook her head. She pulled a small dirk from the folds of her skirt and grabbed his hand. "Nay. I will fight by your side. Together, we will defeat this evil."

The dogs moved and encircled them, three to their two. Branna stood back to back with Devlin, each of them keeping the dogs within sight.

When Branna came close to the tomb, she threw the chalice within, praying its sacredness would protect it.

While she was distracted, the dogs attacked. Devlin whirled, pushing her against the tall rock. Branna stifled a scream as two hounds simultaneously launched at him. With a wide swipe of his sword, he scraped the first dog in the chest, splaying open a wound.

The blade continued its deadly path cleanly connecting with the neck of the other dog, beheading it. Both dogs fell to the earth. The headless dog was instantly sucked underground. The first dog lay panting hard, gravely injured. Its breaths slowed and stopped, then it was pulled below.

The third dog growled low in his throat. Branna gasped and moved out from behind Devlin. By its eyes, she recognized him as the lead dog, the one who'd panted in her face when she was a child. He snarled and bent low, jumping not at Devlin, but at her.

"Branna, no!"

Devlin brought his sword around, the blade awkwardly twisted away from its target. As she saw the dog flying towards her, Devlin threw his body in front of her and the dog's jaws clamped down mere inches from her face. Devlin and the hound fell, snarling and grappling, a tangle of limbs. The dog gained the top, standing on Devlin's chest, his hand and wrist in its jaws.

Branna gripped the dirk hard and threw herself at its back, stabbing it in the neck. It yelped and fell off Devlin, rolling on the ground, injured but not dead. Devlin quickly gained his feet and stabbed it in the chest. It too went still and disappeared under the earth.

"How very touching."

Branna was yanked by her hair and pulled against the chest of Devlin's uncle, his sword to her throat. This blade she knew could end her life.

Devlin gained his feet, his heart thumping as once again a blade rested at Branna's throat.

"Release her. This is our fight, not hers."

"I'm the better swordsman, especially with you injured." He nodded to Devlin's bleeding hand. Devlin held his sword strong and true, even as his bloodied arm throbbed. He didn't care about the pain. He'd bear it to save Branna.

"Would you like to lose an arm to prove it?"

"Would you betray me as did your father?" His uncle's voice turned soft, pleading. "She is of the same evil seed as her mother. She'll destroy you. We must kill her, destroy the chalice and continue with our heart's desire – the ceremony that will make you a ruler."

Devlin had his heart's desire in Branna. "I want the truth. Why did my father die?"

"It was an unfortunate miscalculation. Your father was besotted by that woman. He'd already sipped from the chalice and betrayed us. I couldn't allow the marriage. I called to the dogs."

"*You* called the dogs?"

"Aye. She was evil. Your father couldn't see the wisdom of her death. He was weak, not like you who are strong."

"What was of such great consequence you would sacrifice your own blood, your brother?"

"I was supposed to lead the Underworld, not the dogs. I made a bargain with the Lord of the Underworld, the most powerful of rulers. Yet there is always a sacrifice. The cost of my heart's desire was my brother . . . and now you."

"That is why you groomed me? To replace your brother, so you could have power?"

His uncle's expression turned cold. "You shan't judge me." He glanced at the moon. "We waste time." He pulled Branna by her hair towards the tomb. "Give me the chalice."

Branna exchanged glances with Devlin. She reached in and retrieved it.

Once she had it in her possession, his uncle grabbed the

chalice and pushed Branna away. "This is mine. I have to make it right." He backed up and tripped on one of the discarded rocks from the previous night. He lost his balance and stumbled into the portal tomb.

His eyes turned into glowing red orbs like the dogs. His feet began sliding under the earth. "What's happening? No, no this can't be right. I gave you my brother. I'll deliver my nephew to you. Don't do . . . this . . . to me."

A loud roaring filled Devlin's ears and, within seconds, his uncle disappeared under the earth in a puff of smoke. The chalice bounced unharmed on the charred surface.

Branna lay where she'd fallen, exhausted by the ordeal but relieved. Devlin strode to the burned earth beneath the dolmen. He picked up the chalice and kicked the empty ground. With a shake of his head, he walked to her and offered her his hand.

"'Tis once again we find ourselves here."

Branna gave him her hand and allowed him to pull her into his arms. "Aye, yet this time I'm not afraid."

Devlin kissed the wounds on her neck, his warm lips soothing, removing the sting. "You were afraid of me?"

"Quaking in my boots, my lord. You have a most powerful sword."

Devlin said, "And now what do you feel?"

"I feel the evil has been captured as surely as the hounds, save one."

He smiled broadly. "Aye. Enough so the triumphant hound wishes to marry the hare."

He held out the chalice. "Would you give up your quest to see your mother reborn? Will you have me?"

Branna placed her hand over his, moonlight glittering off the chalice's green emeralds.

"Aye, I'll have you."

Branna knelt beside Devlin at the altar of the little stone chapel. Sunlight streamed through the stained glass windows, projecting the tree and colours on the stone floor. Branna's freshly cleaned yellow gown flowed about her ankles. A garland of white flowers had been woven in her dark hair and streamed down her back.

"I, Devlin, take thee, Branna, to my wedded wife, to have and to hold from this day forward, till death do us part, if the holy church will ordain it: and thereto I plight thee my troth."

The priest handed Branna the golden chalice, embedded with brilliant emeralds. She took a sip, her eyes meeting Devlin's over its gilded rim. She passed the chalice to him. He took a sip and then held the cup high.

Branna placed her hand over his, both their hands wrapped around the chalice's centre.

They said in unison, their voices blending as strong as their love: "'Tis my heart's desire."

The Seventh Sister

Sue-Ellen Welfonder

The Beginning

Howth Village, Ireland – twelve years ago

Maggie Gleason, American tourist, self-declared adventurist and soon-to-be college student, stepped off the bus from Dublin and straight into her dreams. At last, she was following the path of her ancestors. She glanced about, her pulse quickening. Shivers of excitement raced through her. She wanted to lift her arms and twirl in a circle. Instead she stood still and simply absorbed. Without doubt, she'd never experienced a moment more thrilling.

Dublin was wonderful, but busy. This was the Ireland she'd come to see.

The little quay was everything she'd imagined. Colourful fishing boats bobbed in the harbour. The curving stone pier looked just like the photos she'd seen. And the neat line of cottages and pubs stretching along the waterfront couldn't be more perfect.

Howth was magic.

It was a living postcard, full of charm and quaintness.

Even the weather gods greeted her kindly. Low grey clouds made a picturesque backdrop and the light wind off the sea let the waves dance cheerily. Maggie pressed a hand to her breast and walked over to the sea wall, enchanted. She took a deep breath, savouring the cool, damp air. It was so different from the stifling heat and mugginess of summer back home in Philadelphia.

Everything around her felt so welcoming and special.

So Irish.

Maggie smiled, the Gael in her filling her soul and making her pulse race with a giddy sense of recognition. Tingling happiness rippled through her, even warming her toes. Suddenly she wasn't a tourist standing on the quay, here because she'd seen a few yellowed pictures of Howth in her grandmother's old photo albums.

She was someone who belonged.

Above her, a seagull wheeled and cried before settling on to the swaying mast of a yacht. The bird angled its head and peered down at her, looking on as a wave smacked the jetty, dousing her with a mist of spray.

Laughing delightedly, Maggie swiped the moisture from her cheek, secretly deciding that Ireland had kissed her. Sweet, too, would be a few kisses from the tall, dark-haired young man working on one of the boats in the harbour. The boat – a sturdy, blue-hulled craft called *Morna* – was moored only a stone's throw from where she stood, but the cute Irishman didn't appear to notice her.

Which was fine as it gave her a better chance to admire his deeply cut dimples and how his black shoulder-length hair whipped in the wind. The way he wore his faded jeans, Aran sweater and thick work boots wasn't too shabby either. When he glanced up at the rolling clouds and she caught a glimpse of his sky-blue eyes, she really wished he'd kiss her.

He made her breath catch.

From nowhere, or perhaps from her heart, her grandmother's words flashed across her mind. "Someday you'll see, Maggie girl. The glory of Ireland isn't just the green of our hills and the blue of the sea. Nor is it all those soft, misty days. Or the way the light shimmers, polishing the sky until you'd swear you're looking at the world through a swirl of finest gossamer silk. That's part of it, true. But the real magic is inside us." Here,

Granny Gleason would lean forwards, clutching the arms of her rocker. "It's the music in our voices and the fullness of our hearts. The way we can move forward when we must, yet still keep our traditions alive."

Maggie blinked and swallowed, half-sure her long-dead grandmother had just stood beside her, whispering the words in her ear.

Now she knew the truth of them.

She also knew the dishy Irishman on the boat was looking at her.

Maggie's heart slammed against her ribs. The Irishman grinned. His blue gaze locked on hers and the pleasure in his eyes made the ground tilt beneath her feet. Heat swept her, tingly and delicious. She touched a hand to her cheek, feeling the warmth of her blush.

It was then that a large black and white dog bolted past her, almost knocking her down as he made a sailing leap into the *Morna*. The Irishman bent to scratch the dog's ears as the collie leaned into him, his plumed tail wagging in enthusiastic greeting.

Maggie stared, embarrassment scalding her. She wished she could disappear.

The Irishman hadn't been flirting with her.

He'd been watching his dog's running approach.

And she'd had no business making moony eyes at a local cutie who was surely tired of being gawked at by love-struck American tourists.

Certain she must be glowing a thousand shades of red, she wheeled about, nearly colliding with a tiny, stoop-backed old woman.

"Oh, I'm sorry!" Maggie reached to steady her. But there was no need. The woman beamed, her lined face wreathing in a smile.

"An American, are you?" The woman's eyes twinkled even more. "But it's home you are now, eh?"

"Home? I . . ." Maggie blinked. Something about the woman seemed otherworldly. Yet she looked solid enough and her smile was full of warmth. And if her clothes were a bit old-fashioned, her small black boots were tied with sassy red plaid laces that were definitely modern. She also sported a glittery shamrock on her jacket.

"I just got here yesterday." Maggie tried again. "Well, to Dublin. I flew in from Frankfurt. And I'm tired." She paused as the wind kicked up, tossing her hair. "This is the last stop on my grand tour of Europe before I head back to Philadelphia and start college. And, yes, Ireland does feel like home." She didn't feel silly saying so. It was true. "I've never been here before, but my grandmother came from Cork."

"Ah! Sure and I had the right of it!" The woman nodded, seeming pleased. "There's the look of Ireland about you, there is." Her gaze flickered to Maggie's coppery-bright hair. "I once had tresses so fine myself. Back in the day . . . But it was the wonder on your face that gave you away. It doesn't matter how many oceans a body crosses. Or how many generations lie between, the Celtic heart is always drawn back home." She stepped closer, her tone almost conspiratorial. "That's the magic of Ireland."

"You sound like my grandmother." Maggie's heart squeezed, remembering. "She used to say such things."

The woman bobbed her head again, this time sagely. "You'll not be finding a soul in the land who'll tell you different. It's a truth we all share. But enough of an old woman's prattle." She tapped Maggie's arm with a knotty finger. "What do you think of Howth?"

"It's wonderful." Maggie glanced around, dismayed to see the *Morna* empty. The Irishman and his dog were gone. "I haven't seen much yet." She took a breath, not wanting the woman to see her regret. "The quay, the whitewashed houses and neat little shops, everything, is so perfect."

That was true.

Every corner of Howth beckoned, tempting her.

Although the delicious aroma of fish and chips wafting from a waterfront pub called Flanagan's could tip the scales in the public house's favour.

She was hungry.

A fine half-pint of ale didn't sound bad either.

Just then the sun burst through the clouds to sparkle on the choppy water. The wind filled with the tang of salt air and tar, making a good sip of ale in the cheery warmth of Flanagan's seem even more inviting.

Maggie cast another look at the pub, liking the idea more by the minute.

Flanagan's had atmosphere. Half-barrels of bright red geraniums, daisies and sweet pea flanked the blue-painted door and a curl of pleasant-smelling woodsmoke rose from the pub's squat chimney. Diamond-paned windows lent just the right air of Old World charm and the gold lettering of the pub name added dash.

She found herself smiling, her decision made, when the old woman gripped her arm. "Have you heard tell of the Seven Sisters?" She cocked her head again, her eyes almost eager. "The stone circle up on the hill behind the ruin of Howth Castle?"

"A stone circle?" Maggie tried to remember. "My grandmother came here sometimes when she was a girl, but I don't think she ever mentioned such a place."

"Oh, in her day, folk hereabouts kept such places to themselves." The woman released Maggie's arm and lowered her voice. "If she wasn't local, like as not no one spoke of the Seven Sisters. They'll have feared she might take away some of its magic when she left."

"Magic?" Maggie forgot about fish and chips and a half-pint of ale.

"All ancient places have a touch o' enchantment." The woman spoke as if such things were real. "The Seven Sisters aren't well known because they're hard to find if you don't know where to look for them."

Maggie considered. "I saw a signpost for the castle from the bus window. Can I get to the stone circle from there?" She glanced over her shoulder, along the coast road. "Is there a path?"

"You could take the road to the castle and follow the path up the hill. But—" the woman's face brightened "—if you're good by foot, there's a better way. You'd have to climb a wee track that starts behind yon pub." She indicated Flanagan's. "The path isn't marked, but you'll spot it easy enough."

"You're sure?"

"Look for where the roses tumble over a break in the stone wall behind the pub." The old woman winked. "Once you slip through there, you'll find your way just fine."

"Well . . ." Maggie turned up her jacket collar. The sun had dipped back behind the clouds and the wind suddenly felt much colder. "I would love to—"

"Then away with you and enjoy yourself." The old woman gave her a gentle nudge and then turned away, hurrying across the road and disappearing down a narrow walkway between two thick-walled houses.

For a moment, Maggie wondered why she hadn't heard the tap-tap of the woman's sturdy black boots on the pavement as she'd hobbled away so quickly. But just then a fat raindrop landed on her cheek and – she knew – if she didn't hurry herself, she'd never make it up to the stone circle and back without getting drenched.

A glance at the sea confirmed what she'd guessed: a storm was definitely brewing.

She only had two weeks in Ireland.

And all her Gleason ancestors would turn in their graves if they saw her let a tiny bit of Irish wind and rain keep her from climbing a hill. So she crossed the road and nipped behind Flanagan's. She saw the gap in the wall right away. Dusky pink roses spilled over the stones, marking the spot. The path stretched beyond, leaf-strewn and muddy.

And so exciting in its possibilities that Maggie's skin tingled.

But she'd only gone a short way, climbing hard and steadily, before her sense of adventure dimmed. This couldn't be the right path. Although she could catch glimpses of the sea, she couldn't see anything of the harbour. Yet she had to be right above the village.

Even more disquieting, each step was taking her deeper into a tangle of gigantic rhododendrons. Huge, dark and with oddly twisted trunks and branches, they towered over the path, forming a canopy. She felt as if she'd entered some weird primordial forest. Drifts of damp, gauzy mist even floated about, turning the wood into a place she could easily imagine inhabited by faeries, trolls and other such creatures she didn't want to consider.

Of a stone circle – or even the end of the path – there was no sign.

Maggie shoved a hand through her hair.

She had to be lost.

The wind picked up, whistling ominously and tossing the rhododendron's strange, shining branches. Maggie took a deep breath of the damp, woodsy air. She tried not to worry. She didn't really think a wart-nosed troll was going to jump out of the bushes at her. And her chances of being waylaid by an axe-murderer were slim.

This was Ireland, after all.

But the day had darkened and icy raindrops were beginning to splatter the path. Somewhere thunder rumbled. Or maybe it was just the crashing of the sea. Or – and she really hated this possibility – the sound of footsteps charging up the path behind her.

Maggie froze.

Someone *was* coming up the path.

She whipped around, wondering if she could use her rucksack as a weapon, when she recognized the man striding so purposely up the path.

It was him.

The black-haired, blue-eyed cutie from the fishing boat *Morna*.

Maggie's breath caught. Her heart flipped and a thrill shot through her. Thoughts of axe-murderers fled, replaced by the image of a sword-wielding Celtic warrior, fierce and proud, as he stood on a cliff's edge, a wild sky behind him, the wind tossing his hair.

"You!" She could feel her eyes rounding. She noticed other things, too. Like the way the air around her seemed to crackle. And how a wildly exhilarating mix of eagerness, joy and longing spun inside her. She hoped he couldn't hear the hammering of her heart. She also strove to speak in a halfway normal tone. "I saw you at the harbour."

"Aye." He stopped, panting a bit as he leaned forward to brace his hands on his jean-clad thighs. As if he knew how he affected her, he looked up and flashed her the most blinding smile she'd ever seen.

"That would've been myself. Conall Flanagan. You saw me on my uncle's boat, the *Morna*. My dog, Booley, almost knocked you down. I'm sorry for that. He can be a bit rowdy at times." He straightened, his eyes twinkling. "But there was no harm done, was there?

"Though just now—" he stepped aside as Booley cannoned into view, skidding to a halt beside him "—I'm thinking you're lost."

Booley barked as if he agreed.

But they were wrong. She was right where she was meant to be. She could feel it in her soul. This was her place and the rightness of being here was as strong as her attraction to Conall.

Nor was she going to sound looney by telling him so.

"I'm Maggie Gleason, from Philadelphia, and I'm not lost. I wanted to take this path." It was all she could think to say. On the boat, he'd caught her eye. Here, standing so near, he dazzled her.

"So-o-o, Maggie Gleason of America—" he smiled again, dimples winking "—is the old country everything you thought it would be?"

"It's a dream. Like a living fairytale, but—" She bit her lip, not wanting to gush. "How did you know—"

"That you're Irish?" He rubbed his chin, pretending to consider. "Could be the name Gleason. Or maybe that wild tumble of fiery-red hair spilling down your back."

Maggie's pulse quickened. She couldn't think straight. But she *had* heard his name.

"Do you have anything to do with the harbourside pub? Flanagan's?"

Booley barked again, this time swishing his tail.

Conall put a hand on the dog's head, stroking his ears. "My father owns Flanagan's. It's been in the family for generations. I was in the back when I saw you nip through the wall. That's why I came after you. This isn't a tourist path. The way is steep and—"

"I know where I'm going. An old woman gave me directions to the Seven Sisters." Maggie adjusted the strap of her rucksack. "She was local."

Conall lifted a brow. "Any local wanting to do their part for tourism would have sent you to the marked route, down by the castle ruin. This path leads to our family farm and nowhere else."

"I don't understand." Maggie frowned. "The woman seemed so nice. And she did say that the path cut through the stone wall behind the pub."

Conall shrugged. "Aye, well. There is a another way to the Sisters. I can take you there. If—" he glanced at her shoes "—you don't mind pushing through some thorn bushes and getting your feet muddy?"

Maggie dismissed his concern. "I'm already pretty mud-splattered."

"Then watch your step, Maggie Gleason. The ground beneath the rhododendrons is slippery. Getting through the brambles beyond is even trickier." He reached to pull back an armful of dripping branches. "We'll have to hurry if we want to get to the Sisters and back before the storm breaks. If we do get drenched, you can come with me to Flanagan's and I'll give you something to warm you."

"I'd like that." Maggie knew he meant food and likely whiskey.

She wanted his kisses.

But he only curled strong fingers around her wrist, helping her as she ducked beneath the branches. "My band, Two Jigs, is having a session tonight." His free hand touched her shoulder as she passed, guiding her. "I play fiddle and sing. We'll be full to the rafters and there'll be dancing."

"I love to dance. I—" Maggie straightened, her jaw slipping. She'd stepped through the bushes on to the edge of a large field of rolling green, boulder-studded and dotted with sheep. She could see the stone circle in the distance. Her breath caught, everything in her that was Irish crying out in wonder and appreciation.

Beautiful and eerie, the stones stood silent, rising out of a drift of rolling mist. They were taller than she'd expected and looked almost lifelike. Slender, graceful and evenly spaced, they all seemed to be facing the sea and did resemble women.

But something wasn't right.

There were only six stones.

"Did I miss something?" She glanced at Conall. He was still holding her wrist. "I thought they were the *Seven* Sisters?"

"And so they were. Once." He kept his eyes on the stones as he spoke. "I'll tell you about the seventh sister on the way across the field. But be warned—" he was already pulling her forwards "—it's a sad tale."

Maggie scarcely heard him. She wasn't worried about some long-ago tragedy spoiling her day. Conall's warm fingers around her wrist were sending the sweetest shivers all through her. And she was sure that when they reached the stone circle, he would kiss her.

She could feel those kisses coming.

Too bad she didn't sense the heartbreak that would follow them.

One

The Cabbage Rose, near Valley Forge, Pennsylvania

"What's happened?" Darcy Sullivan, owner of the Cabbage Rose, incurable romantic, and Maggie's best friend since college, took a seat at Maggie's window table. She leaned forward, her green eyes concerned. "Did another job interview go wrong? Is your landlord refusing to give you an extension on your rent? If so, I can—"

"There's nothing wrong." Maggie put down the forkful of colcannon she'd been about to pop into her mouth. "It's Sunday and I just felt like—"

"Your favourite comfort food." Darcy eyed the steaming mound of mashed potatoes and cabbage on Maggie's plate. "You're forgetting I know you always order an Irish farmhouse breakfast on Sundays."

Maggie glared at her friend. "I like colcannon."

"And—" Darcy wasn't backing off "—you only ever eat it when you're upset."

"You're wrong. I eat it all the time." Maggie took a bite, belligerent. "I can make it myself, you know. Even if—" she gave a defiant smile "—my own version is never quite as good as yours."

"You ordered a turf-cutter's portion. You never do that unless—"

"Everything is fine."

Darcy snorted. "And I serve bratwurst and sauerkraut."

Maggie was about to dig in to her colcannon again. Instead, she ignored her friend's jibe by glancing out the window. The Cabbage Rose had an idyllic setting and a light autumn mist was rising from the duck pond behind the tea room. Thick woods edged the meadow beyond the pond and some of the leaves were already turning. It was a chilly day and would surely rain before she started the drive back to Philly.

It was the kind of weather that reminded her of Ireland.

"You could move out here, you know." Darcy reached across the table and nudged her elbow, her words proving how perceptive she was. "You in the craziness of a crowded, fast-paced city is as impossible as trying to fit a square peg in a circular hole. You weren't made for—"

"Philly is home." The admission bit deep into Maggie's substance.

Ireland should have been her real home.

And she wasn't about to tell Darcy that although she loved

visiting the Valley Forge area on Sundays, anything else would break her. Lovely and pastoral as the countryside was, it would always pale to her memories of Ireland. And if she couldn't have the real thing . . .

She didn't want a substitute.

But she did need peace.

"Ahhh . . ." Darcy sat back and folded her arms. "You're going to tell me now, aren't you? I can see it coming. It's about a man, isn't it?"

Maggie started, almost knocking over her water glass. "No, it isn't about a man." She could feel the tops of her ears burning on the lie. "It's about Ireland." She opted for a half-truth, knowing that for her Conall Flanagan and Ireland were almost one and the same. "I'm going back to see the Seven Sisters."

"Maggie!" Darcy's eyes widened, her face flushing with pleasure. "That's splendid news. But how are you swinging it? Did you win the lottery?"

"No, it's better." This time Maggie did treat herself to more colcannon. "My sisters and cousins pitched in and are giving me the trip for my thirtieth birthday. They're saying it's payback for all the times I've babysat, painted murals on their walls or stayed with their dogs when they went on vacation."

"Good on them." Darcy looked delighted. "Though, really, your mural work alone is worth a thousand trips to Ireland." She glanced across the tea room to where Maggie's artful hand had turned a plain wall into a whimsical collage of the Emerald Isle. "I've had so many customers say they wished they could jump into your painting."

Maggie followed her friend's gaze, secretly amazed the collage was hers.

It *was* fine work.

Everything that was the quintessence of Ireland was somewhere on the wall. Dapper city dwellers in their Sunday best strolled the streets of turn-of-the-century Dublin, three fiddlers entertained a foot-stomping crowd in a smoke-hazed pub and rosy-cheeked children tumbled with a dog in a daisy-studded meadow. Winding country roads disappeared across rolling green hills and, here and there, gleaming whitewashed cottages caught the eye, their thick walls and thatched roofs enchanting the Cabbage Rose's American clientele with the charm of a long-ago, slower-paced world.

Maggie's heart squeezed, her gaze settling on a particular cottage. A farmhouse, really, it was long and low in the traditional style and she'd painted a faint curl of bluish smoke rising from the chimney. In the garden, laundry could be seen fluttering in the breeze and, just beyond, a sparkling sea glinted, stretching into the distance.

She lived in that distance and it'd been breaking her for twelve long years.

"Too bad none of those customers loved the mural enough to commission their own." Maggie regretted the words as soon she spoke them. It wasn't Darcy's fault she was a starving artist. "I'm sorry, I meant . . ." She tore her gaze from the Flanagan farmhouse and let out a shaky breath, furious that a few strokes of paint on a wall held such power over her. "Sometimes I just wish—"

"I know what you wish, dear heart." Darcy's eyes filled with understanding. "But now, thanks to your wonderful family, you're going back. So tell me—" she nodded and smiled at the server who brought them a pot of tea "—which sisters are you visiting? Are they Gleasons or maybe great-aunts on your mother's side?"

"They're neither." Maggie reached for the teapot and poured them both a cup. "The Seven Sisters are a stone circle. You can see them there—" she twisted around, indicating a section of the mural near the tea room's gift shop "—just above the little harbour and its fishing boats."

Darcy peered across the room, her eyes narrowing on the silvery stones, rising eerily from a swirl of mist. "But there are only six of them. You said—"

"The *Seven* Sisters, I know." Maggie sipped her tea, welcoming its soothing tang. "They're called that because there once were seven sisters. Now—"

"I feel a tall tale coming." Darcy reached for her own teacup, her lips twitching. "I just don't understand why you've never mentioned it before, seeing as you painted the stone circle on my wall."

"There is a legend, yes." The words caught in Maggie's throat. Even now, it was so hard to speak of the place. "But it's very sad and—"

"All good Irish legends are sad."

"This one is different." Maggie felt the skin on her nape prickle, then a stab of deep longing inside her. "I think this story is real because I've been there and have felt the power of those stones. The circle shimmers in the air, I swear. And once you've stood there . . ." She bit her lip, pausing. Heat was swelling in her chest, clamping around her ribs like a vice. It was the yearning, she knew. And just now, it was sweeping her so fiercely she could hardly breathe.

"I have to go back, Darcy." She curled her fingers around her teacup, feeling the cold grit of ancient stone instead of the delicacy of tea-warmed porcelain. "We both know I'm obsessed with Ireland. But my life is here, whether I like that or not. I need to undo whatever spell those Sisters cast on me. I'm turning thirty. It's time to move on."

"So who were the Sisters?" Darcy was watching her over the rim of her teacup.

"They were the seven daughters of a lesser Irish king who lived in the days when the Vikings first began raiding Ireland." Maggie closed her eyes, returning in her mind to that distant, windswept cliff. "Though some legends claim the Sisters are even older than that, going back to a hoary time perhaps even before the coming of the fabled Tuatha Dé Danann.

"The King loved all his daughters, but there was one he favoured above the others. She was the youngest and also the sweetest. Men in all the land vied for her hand, but her father would see her wed to none but the great champion he loved like a son – for the young warrior had once saved the king's life in battle."

Maggie peered at her friend, not surprised to see Darcy scoot her chair closer. "Many of the other kings and their sons were disappointed by the King's choice, but everyone understood, for the valiant warrior had a good and noble heart. He was also said to have been so handsome that even the stars in heaven envied his beauty."

"You're making this up." Darcy refreshed Maggie's tea. "But it's a lovely tale."

"It is. And I'm telling you the legend exactly as it was told to me."

"And who would it be who told you. Hmm?"

"Someone who lives near the stones." The truth slipped out before Maggie could catch herself. "Someone I met on my college trip to Ireland."

"Would that someone be a man?" Darcy twinkled at her.

Maggie stirred milk into her tea, ignoring the grin spreading across her friend's face. "It was a man, yes. Ireland is full of them, you know. And they're all born storytellers. They enjoy sharing their tales with visitors. They—" Maggie glanced at the window, sure she'd caught a movement out of the corner of her eye. But nothing stirred except the mist curling above the smooth surface of the duck pond. "You've sidetracked me." She turned back to Darcy. "Do you want to hear the rest of the legend or not?"

"Of course, I do."

Maggie took a deep breath, fighting the urge to look out the window again. "Well," she began, remembering, "the wedding day approached and the King ordered preparations made for a grand feasting the likes of which had never been seen in his small but mighty kingdom. The bride thought her heart would burst with happiness. She'd always feared she'd be made to wed a king or prince whose land would be far from her father's and she loved her home dearly and dreaded having to leave. She'd also fallen deeply in love with the young champion who was to be her husband. But as often happens when life seems so good, the young girl's happiness was about shatter."

"Her champion dies." Darcy made the words a statement.

"And she pines away until she's an embittered old woman, mourning her lost love forever."

"That's close, but not quite how it was."

"Then what *did* happen?"

Maggie slid a glance at the window again, unable to help herself. Nothing sinister or faelike lurked in the drifting mist. But there was an elderly woman down by the pond. She moved slowly along the water's edge, feeding the ducks from a brown paper bag. She didn't look Maggie's way, but something about her sent a chill down Maggie's spine.

"Hey!" Darcy poked her arm. "I'm waiting. How does the story end?"

Maggie reached for her teacup, needing a bracing sip. "According to the legend, sea raiders landed on the eve of the wedding. The King and his men and all their guests were taken by surprise, the raiders storming into the hall in the middle of the celebrations. Many of the King's men and his friends were slain, including the valiant young warrior. But the bards claim he fought ferociously, once again saving the King's life, this time through the giving of his own.

"Of the girl's fate, nothing can be told. She was seized by the attackers and carried away from Ireland in one of their war galleys. No one ever saw her again."

"Damn, that's sad." A frown creased Darcy's brow. "Now I know why I read so many romance novels. You're always guaranteed a happy ending. Wait—" she looked at Maggie sharply, the furrow on her forehead deepening "—you still haven't told me why the stone circle is called the Seven Sisters."

"Ah, but I have." Maggie glanced across the room to her painted likeness of the stones. "The King's daughter is the seventh sister. The stones are named in her honour and in memory of the six sisters who never forgot her. In fact, it's said that they spent so much time standing on the cliff, looking out to the western sea and grieving for her, that their sorrow turned them to stone."

"So that's why there are only six stones?"

"That's how I heard the tale."

"Well, I'll never walk into the gift shop now without glancing at those stones on the wall and feeling a shiver." Darcy stood, smoothing her frilled white apron. "Now, dear heart, I'd better get back into my kitchen. I'll have someone bring you more colcannon—" she snatched Maggie's unfinished portion off the table "—you've let this turn cold."

Maggie watched her stride away, expertly manoeuvring a path through the crowded, linen-draped tables to the back of the tea room. Any other time, Maggie would have smiled. She loved her friend and was proud of her success. The Cabbage Rose was one of those irresistibly cosy places, bursting with character and charm. There wasn't a corner that didn't delight the eye of those who appreciated the appeal of quaintness. It was a rare day that Maggie visited without the tea room's magic banishing her cares.

Unfortunately, this wasn't one of those times.

It'd been a mistake to tell Darcy about the Seven Sisters. Doing so had only set loose a cascade of painful memories. And even Darcy's delicious colcannon and her perfectly brewed Irish breakfast tea wasn't enough to get Maggie's mind off the part of the tale she'd kept to herself.

Like how she'd lost her heart to a black-haired, blue-eyed Irishman on her long-ago trip to Ireland and how they'd spent her last night on Irish soil making love on the cold, damp grass in the centre of the Seven Sisters.

Then, as now, it was raining, she remembered, as she stepped out of the Cabbage Rose. She paused beneath the tea room's covered back porch, debating whether she should make a run for her car or wait until the deluge lessened. Not that rain ever really bothered her.

Actually, she loved it.

But something was niggling at her.

And whatever it was lifted the fine hairs on her nape and filled her with an odd reluctance to move or even think about anything else until she could pinpoint what was making her all shivery.

Frustrated, she stared out into the rain. The mist was thicker now and drifted across the meadow in great, billowing curtains so that she could barely see the trees on the far side of the duck pond.

She focused on the dark, rain-pitted water, trying to concentrate.

Her heart gave a lurch. "Oh, God!" She raised trembling hands to her face, pressing them hard against her cheeks. *It can't be*. The words froze on her tongue, denial holding them there.

But she'd seen what she'd seen, even if it had taken her till now to remember.

There *was* something odd about the old woman feeding ducks by the pond.

She'd worn small black boots with red plaid laces.

Two

Howth village, Ireland: Flanagan's on the Waterfront

Conall Flanagan was in trouble.

His Celtic blood smelled it as soon as he'd spotted the wizened old woman sitting in a darkened corner, sipping a glass of whiskey. The woman wasn't local, yet she also wasn't a tourist. From the looks of her, she could have been every Irishman's grandmother. Or, judging by the old-fashioned black clothes she wore, perhaps even every Irishman's great-great-great-grandmother.

Although her red plaid boot laces were a little trendy.

But it wasn't her outlandish appearance that bothered Conall. It was his certainty that he hadn't noticed her enter the pub. He was also sure he hadn't poured her whiskey.

Something wasn't right. He could feel it in his bones, with or without a strange old lady sipping a drink he hadn't served her and who apparently favoured red plaid bootlaces.

He *really* knew it when the door of the pub flew open and his life-long friend Morgan Mahoney burst in on a blast of chill, damp air. Conall set down the pint glass he'd been polishing and waited. Morgan yanked off his waterproofs and hung the dripping jacket on a peg by the door. His face was as dark as the cold, rainy night he'd just escaped.

Not that anyone could be blamed for a sour mood when the wind howled like banshees and the seas churned and boiled as if the little harbour had been spell-cast into the devil's own cauldron.

It was wild weather, not fit for man or beast.

But inside Flanagan's, it was cheery and warm. A turf fire glowed in the old stone fireplace, filling the pub's long, narrow main room with the earthy-rich tang of peat. The delicious smell of fried herring wafted from the kitchen, tempting palates. And the heavy black ceiling rafters glistened with age, reminding patrons that this was a place where time and tradition were honoured.

Those who spent their evenings at Flanagan's liked it that way.

This night, several local fiddlers had claimed a corner, their bows flying as they played a lively reel, much to the delight of the appreciative crowd. No one cared how hard the rain beat against the windows or how many bolts of lightning flashed across the sky.

But heads did turn as Morgan elbowed his way to the bar, his scowl worsening with each long-legged stride.

Morgan Mahoney was a man known for his belly-deep laughs and smiles.

Just now he looked ready to murder.

"Gone daft, have you?" He grabbed the edge of the bar and leaned forwards, glaring at Conall. "I'm thinking all those years in the hot Spanish sun fried your brain! Or am I home asleep in my own fine bed just now, having a nightmare? Only dreaming that I heard you—"

"If you mean the farm—" Conall knew at once why his friend was upset "—the rumours are true. I'm putting the old place up for sale and all the land with it. I haven't yet chosen an estate agent, but—"

"You're mad, you are!" Morgan's hazel eyes snapped with

fury. "Flanagan's have held that land for centuries. Longer! And the house . . ." He raised his voice, seemingly unaware that the pub had gone silent. "That farm isn't just where you sleep and eat, laddie. It's where you come from. Your parents will be turning in their graves."

Conall looked at his friend's angry, wind-beaten face – at all the well-loved faces turned his way – and bit back the only answer that would have chased the unspoken accusation from their eyes.

If he didn't put the past behind him, he'd soon be in his own grave.

Regret and the impossible yearning for a woman he hadn't seen in years and couldn't ever call his own, would put him there.

And much as he'd always shared with Morgan Mahoney and the well-meaning locals crowding the pub – Howth was that kind of place – his feelings for Maggie Gleason were his own.

He wasn't going to pour out his heart on this black autumn night. No one needed to know how fiercely he wished he'd never chased his youthful dream to run an Irish tavern on the sun-baked coast of Andalucia. Or that the adventure had cost him so much more than toil, hardship and the eventual shame of admitting failure.

Flanagans kept their troubles to themselves. He wasn't going to be the one to break family tradition.

He nodded at the fiddlers, signalling them to take up their tune. They did, and his patrons returned to their *craic*. The noise level in the busy, smoke-hazed pub quickly reached its usual level.

Only Morgan refused to pretend nothing was amiss. He set a fisted hand on the bar counter, ignoring the pint Conall set before him. "What about your brother and your sisters? They'll never agree—"

"Do you think they care?" That they didn't, twisted Conall's innards. But that sorrow, too, he kept to himself. "You know my brother moved to Australia decades ago." He reached for the perfectly good pint Morgan wasn't touching and took a healthy swig. "Two of my sisters married Scots and are now in Glasgow. And Kate—" his heart squeezed when he thought of his youngest sister who, in his view, worked way too hard "—has her hands full with her own family, up in Donegal. You know they run a farm three times the size of our old home place. They take in guests, too."

Conall's aging collie, Booley, padded out of the kitchen then and came to stand beside him. The dog pressed his black and white bulk against Conall's legs and swished his tail. He looked up hopefully, expecting Conall to tear open a packet of bar crisps and give him a few. They were Booley's favourite treats.

But Conall simply reached down and rubbed the disappointed dog's ears.

He'd give Booley a big bowl of minced beef later. He'd even crumble a handful of crisps on top of the mince. But first he needed to deflect Morgan's prying and steer the nosy bastard from a topic that left Conall feeling like he'd been cut off at the knees.

"Is that all you have to say?" Morgan proved his stubbornness. "Kate's busy and the others are scattered to the winds?"

"If you'd hear the truth—" Conall continued to stroke Booley's head "—my siblings don't have the right to object. I bought them out years ago, when I was still in Almeria and Fiddlesticks was doing well. They might not be happy about my decision, but—"

"It still isn't right." Somehow Morgan had come around behind the bar. "You can't sell ground that is sacred. What about the Seven Sisters?"

Conall flinched. The name sent images whirling across his mind. A wild, dark night full of wind and rain, then a beautiful young girl linking her fingers with his, her eyes shining as she leaned in to kiss him. He remembered how he'd clutched her to him, kissing her frantically even as they'd ripped off their clothes. He'd swept her into his arms and carried her into the centre of the stone circle, rain sluicing down their naked bodies, the wind buffeting them as he lowered her to the cold, wet grass where . . .

Conall scrubbed a hand over his face, forcing the memories to fade. They withdrew slowly, the last one a painful echo of Maggie's words. *I could stay here for ever. In this place, loving you . . .*

It'd been her last night in Ireland.

And he'd known it would break her heart to leave.

But he and his Two Jigs mates had already poured their savings into a cheap, much-in-need-of-repair pub on the beach at Almeria. They'd renamed the tavern Fiddlesticks. And with the arrogance of youth, they were sure the venture would bring them a fortune. British tourists would flock to an authentic Irish pub offering good, reasonably priced bar food, fine spirits and nightly music. Locals would appreciate a change from the tapas bars.

Fiddlesticks had done well, as they'd believed.

Until a thousand other Irish expats had the same idea and business dwindled.

Conall frowned and finished the pint he'd poured for Morgan, downing the remaining ale in one long gulp. It didn't chase away the frustration that was forming a cold hard knot in his gut. Gnawing anger because, he knew, even without Fiddlesticks, he wouldn't have asked Maggie to stay.

She'd been about to start college.

No one in his family had ever achieved a college degree. He could not have been the cause for her to turn her back on such an opportunity. He curled his hand around the empty pint glass, his scowl deepening.

They'd just been too damned young . . .

"Well?" Morgan poked his arm. "Don't think I'm going away until you answer me. What of the Seven Sisters? Would you just abandon them?"

Conall drew a tight breath. "They won't crumble if I can't see them from my bedroom window." He cast an irritated glance at Booley. The old dog hadn't even growled when Morgan had all but punched him.

Looking back to Morgan, he aimed for a light tone. "You're worrying for nothing. Those stones are older than time. They stood long before a Flanagan ever came to these parts and they'll go on standing when someone else's name is scrawled on a land deed."

"Humph." Morgan snorted. "We both know what happens when incomers get their hands on prime land in areas popular with tourists."

Booley whined.

"See?" Morgan flashed a triumphant smile. "Even he knows the way of it."

"He wants crisps."

"And you?" Morgan's hand shot out again, this time gripping Conall's elbow. "What do you want?"

Again, Booley didn't raise a hackle.

"Bloody peace is what I want." Conall jerked free and turned away from them both. "You should know I'll not be selling the place to some greedy developer who'll smother the cliffs beneath a five-star American-style hotel."

He looked out across the pub, waiting for Morgan to argue. Rain still blew past the windows and although the fiddlers were performing a lively rendition of "The Irish Washerwoman", he could hear the thunder of the sea, booming just steps beyond Flanagan's thick, smoke-blackened walls. Lightning still cracked across the heavens and a full white moon was just sailing behind thick, dark clouds.

It was the kind of night Maggie Gleason would have called exhilarating.

Magical.

She'd understood such things.

And he was a fool to grieve for her. They'd shared the same path for only two weeks. Yet those fourteen days had felt like a thousand years. When he'd followed her up the hill and she'd whirled to face him in the rhododendron wood, it wasn't like a first meeting. It was recognition. As if their souls had run together forever and had found each other again at last.

They'd been so perfectly suited.

And he'd let her go.

"A monster-sized resort isn't the only threat." Persistent as always, Morgan appeared at his elbow. "Have you not heard how many big developers use harmless-seeming chaps as buyers these days? They want you to think you're selling to another farmer who'll keep things as they are. Then, lo, some inflated arse in a suit arrives in a sleek black car, waving planning permission and telling you there'll soon be a new community of executive homes covering land you thought would remain empty!"

Conall stiffened. "I won't let that happen."

"You might not be able to prevent it. Unless you give up this fool notion and don't sell."

"My decision is made. I've already started cleaning out the storerooms above the pub. I'll be staying here as soon as I've made the loft habitable." He gazed out across the crowd, not wanting to see his friend's face. "It's not like I'm selling Flanagan's."

"Then what is it? Do you need the money?"

"It has nothing to do with my finances." Under different circumstances, Conall would have laughed. Flanagan's was the best-doing pub in Howth. In the few years since he'd returned from Spain and the Fiddlesticks disaster, he'd earned back his losses threefold.

"I won't be keeping the money." He paused, watching Morgan's surprise. "I'm putting most of it in a college trust for my nieces and nephews. The rest—" he shot a glance at Booley, winding his way through the busy tables, hoping for a cuddle or a treat "—is going to my favourite dog rescue organization."

"Then some woman has influenced you." Morgan's eyes narrowed. "Not that I've seen you with one for years."

"It has nothing to do with a woman." The lie sent heat shooting up the back of Conall's neck. Equally annoying, out of the corner of his eye, he saw Booley sitting beside the old woman in the corner. She was feeding him crisps. "Damnation."

Conall snapped his gaze away. Something about the woman gave him the willies.

"I've got it!" Morgan slapped his forehead. "It's her. The American."

Conall nearly choked. "What American? Howth is full of them."

"You know damned well who I mean." Somehow Morgan knew. "You're selling out because you're going after her, to Pennsylvania. Isn't that where she was from? Her with the hair like a 'cascade of fire' and skin so 'dewy and soft' you swore just the memory of holding her would drive you mad. *Maggie Gleason.*" Morgan grinned, looking pleased.

Conall glowered. "Maggie Gleason was twelve years ago." That, at least, was true. "And I am not going to America. Not for her, not for a holiday, not for any reason. But I will hear how the hell you know about her?"

"Right, well." Morgan examined his knuckles. "Can it be you've forgotten a certain old box carved of bog oak that you kept under your bed? Maybe you should have burned its contents when you went to Spain, knowing your mother would set your sisters to tidying your room after you'd gone. Kate found the box and—" Morgan glanced up, his lips twitching "—it could be your sisters showed me a few love letters you wrote yet never posted."

"You read those letters?" Conall's blood boiled. If he weren't standing behind the bar of his pub, if they were anywhere else, he'd lunge at Morgan and beat him to a pulp. "Those scribblings were my private property. They were locked in a chest beneath—"

"Your sisters took turns with a hairpin until they picked the lock."

Conall shoved a hand through his hair, furious. "Who else saw the letters?"

"Well . . ." Morgan considered. "I'd guess only your sisters and your mother. Your sisters found the box. And your mother caught your sisters going through its contents. She burned the letters, if I recall rightly."

"And where do you come into it?"

"I was just there that day."

"Sure and you were, sweet as you were on my sisters back then." Conall reached beneath the bar and produced one of his best bottles of whiskey. He poured a measure and tossed it back quickly. "Or—" he set the glass on the counter and wiped his mouth "—were you after mooching one of my mother's famous bramble pies?"

"That could've been a reason, too." Morgan shrugged. "It was long ago."

"Damned right, it was."

"So you're not going to America?"

"No." Conall frowned.

"But you're still in love with her." Morgan was eyeing him speculatively. "You wouldn't be so riled if you weren't."

"I forgot her years ago," Conall bluffed, returning the whiskey bottle to its shelf. "And I'm annoyed because I have better things to do on such a busy night than listen to your nonsensical blether."

"Tell me why you never looked her up and I'll leave."

"Because—" Conall's head was going to explode "—I don't believe in poking into the business of people I haven't seen or heard from in years. For all I know, she could be married with a half-dozen children by now."

"And if she weren't?"

"Then she could have come searching for me, don't you think? She's always known where to find me. She could've contacted my parents. Someone could have put her in touch with me, even when I was in Almeria. But—" bitterness rose in Conall's throat "—she never made the effort."

"Some might say you didn't either, my friend." Morgan bent to fetch Conall's bottle of prize whiskey. "I'm thinking you didn't deserve her."

"You're an ass, Mahoney." Conall watched his friend fill a generous glass. "I'm not surprised my sisters wanted nothing to do with you. You're—" Conall snapped his mouth shut, his gaze on the table in the corner.

The old woman was gone.

Her empty whiskey glass still sat there. And Booley sprawled nearby, enjoying the warmth of the hearth fire. A crumpled crisps packet on the table indicated why the dog looked so content.

That was all.

Conall blinked, disbelieving.

Sure, the woman had been odd. But never in all his years as a publican had he been stiffed by a little old lady. There could be no other explanation. If she'd just slipped away to the loo, he would have seen her. Flanagan's *comforts* were down a short hall at the back of the pub.

Frowning, Conall left the bar and strode across the room. He was almost to the deserted table when he spotted something green and glittery winking at him from beside the empty crisps packet.

It was a shamrock brooch.

The pin twinkled at him, its emerald brilliance almost blinding. He stepped closer, intending to put the trinket behind the bar until the old woman returned. But when he reached to pick it up, the brooch vanished in a swirl of green and white sparkles.

Conall froze, staring.

At the hearthside, Booley barked and wagged his tail.

It was then that Conall saw the sweet wrapper. Crinkled and made of shiny green foil, it peered up at him from the exact spot where he'd seen the brooch.

The shamrock pin he'd imagined.

And he'd done so because Morgan – as so often – had annoyed him to the brink of madness.

Pushing the shamrock and his friend from his mind, Conall snatched the wrapper and the empty crisps packet. He also picked up the old woman's empty whiskey glass. She wouldn't be back after all, and good riddance.

But if he'd glanced over his shoulder as he stomped back to the bar, he might just have seen a shimmer of her sitting there still.

She was, of course.

And she was smiling for she knew what he didn't.

Maggie Gleason was on her way.

Three

It was the same.

Maggie stepped from the Dublin bus and took a steadying breath. Howth hadn't changed. If anything, the harbour village appeared even more dear than in her memories. Her calming breaths weren't helping. She was trembling and although she prided herself on not being a woman who burst into tears at the drop of a hat, she had to blink to banish the heat pricking her eyes.

She'd come here to rid herself of old hurts, not to be enchanted anew. Yet as soon as the bus had swept into Howth's curving Harbour Road, she knew she'd been kidding herself.

This was her place.

And, painful or not, being here was a homecoming.

Too bad her reason for visiting concerned more than her passion for Ireland. Even if Howth was still a place of magic, she knew that if she ran into Conall Flanagan, she'd find him much changed.

Likely, he wouldn't even remember her.

Not that she expected to see him.

He might have forgotten her over the years, but she remembered he'd gone to Spain. After so much time, he was probably married to some fiery Andalucian siren who'd seduced him with hot flamenco dances, sangria and torrid sex on a moonlit beach.

Maggie frowned.

She blotted the images from her mind and walked to the sea wall, finding the place she'd stood so long ago. Her pulse jumped when she spotted the *Morna*, looking not a day older, but moored deeper out in the harbour. The fishing boat bobbed on the waves and its hull was still painted blue.

Only this time the *Morna* was empty.

Maggie shivered. She couldn't shake the urge to close her eyes and reopen them, sure that if she did, she'd see Conall on the boat. Everything felt so familiar, as if she hadn't stepped off a bus, but back into the fateful day that had changed her life.

So much was the same. The waters of the harbour tossed and danced, with the waves smacking the sea wall, the larger ones sending up spray. Seabirds wheeled and screamed, some of them swooping low as if to greet her. Fitful autumn sun tried to pierce the clouds and it was colder than summer, but the damp sea air still smelled of salt and tar. Many of the houses and pubs had fires going, the rich, earthy tang of peat smoke adding charm. And – her mouth watered – she also detected a tantalizing trace of fish and chips in the chill wind blowing down the waterfront.

She turned her face into the gusts and breathed deep, appreciative.

How she'd yearned to drink in this heady brew. To her, the scents were an elixir. The essence of Ireland. And to fill her lungs with them again was a privilege. Wishing she could do so every day, she pressed a hand to her heart, savouring each inhale, regretting the exhales.

It also stung that she might not have the nerve to enter Flanagan's. The popular tavern had already blindsided her. She'd caught a quick glimpse of the pub's bright blue door and diamond-paned windows from the bus window. Even the flower tubs had been there. Seeing them, along with the pub's gold-lettered name, had felt like a kick to the ribs.

She wasn't sure it'd be good for her to go Flanagan's.

But she *would* see the Seven Sisters.

They needed exorcising.

Hopefully once she made her peace with them, vanquishing the stones from her heart and her dreams, she'd also be free of Conall Flanagan. Something inside her pinched and twisted, resisting the notion. Her heart thumped hard against her chest, equally anguished.

Maggie set her jaw, determined.

She had to do this.

So she gave the harbour one last, embracing glance and treated herself to another greedy gulp of the tangy air. Then she set off down the waterfront. She walked determinedly away from Flanagan's, grateful that the hill path behind the pub wasn't the only way to reach the stones. She wouldn't make that mistake twice.

This time she was taking the tourist route.

The wind picked up as she walked, the chill gusts tossing her hair and bringing a hint of coming rain. Maggie hunched her shoulders against the cold and quickened her steps along the castle road.

She was not going anywhere near the stone circle in the rain. Even a light drizzle would undo her. Too many hurtful things lurked in Irish rain.

So she walked as fast as she could, hurrying past quiet, thick-walled houses with wood or peat smoke curling from their chimneys and soft, yellow light shining dimly in the windows. She pretended the sight didn't bother her. But it was so hard not to let envy eat her alive each time she glanced at such a window and imagined the cosiness behind the pretty white lace curtains.

In her mind, she saw Conall sitting before the hearth fire, a whiskey glass in his hand and his dog at his feet. She'd be busy in the warm, stone-flagged kitchen, stirring a pot of steaming soup or taking a round of fresh-baked bread from the oven. After they'd eaten, they'd enjoy a late-night stroll around the village. They'd talk about whatever pleased them, occasionally stopping to admire the stars.

Such a life might not be every twenty-first century American woman's dream. But, it sure was hers.

Somewhere a dog barked and she also heard the distant bleating of sheep. If she listened closely, she could still catch the roar of the sea.

It was all so idyllic.

And felt a trillion light years removed from the hectic bustle of Philadelphia and the mad, rushed world waiting for her return. How sad that she'd rather have someone pull out her toenails than board the plane that would carry her away from Ireland.

She swallowed a sigh and threw another glance at the houses lining the road. They were spaced a bit farther apart now, each neat little cottage boasting tidy, well-kept gardens that, she knew, would absolutely burst with flowers in the summer.

"Damn." She felt her chest tighten; the images she'd conjured thrust a spear through her heart.

She was so pathetic.

It was pointless to let such things get to her. Circumstances she couldn't change, dreams she couldn't possibly seize. She lengthened her stride, careful now to keep her gaze on the road.

She could see the ivy-covered shell of Howth Castle up ahead, its half-standing walls and empty, black-staring windows beckoning her. She could spend days exploring the castle's warren of hollowed rooms and long, grass-grown passages. Just now the ruin meant she should soon spot the marker for the Seven Sisters.

Howth Castle would have to wait.

It was time to put the past behind her.

But when she did find the trail sign, her heart started hammering so fiercely that she almost wished she hadn't made the trip.

She was fooling herself. Coming here had only made things worse.

Each step she took up the wide, well-marked tourist path to the stone circle proved her folly. Hot, throbbing pain stabbed her in the side and every indrawn breath was a struggle, each onwards stride an agony. Her insides were on fire and it wasn't because the trail was steep or difficult.

It was because being here again was torture.

And it burned her soul.

"Damn you, Conall Flanagan." She pressed a hand to her hip and soldiered on, her breath ragged and her heart in shreds. It wasn't supposed to be this way.

One, two, three more steps, and then she could feel the

Sisters' presence. The low humming in her ears that she'd only ever experienced here. And the way the air thickened and crackled. It was like walking through a sea of invisible fourth of July sparklers.

She was almost at the top of the hill and thin mist was already twisting through the trees. Wispy blue-grey threads of it rolled across the ground, curling around her ankles, pulling her onwards.

Then the path ended, the woods fell away, and she found herself at the edge of the sheep field she remembered so well. The Seven Sisters loomed before her, shimmering silver as always, close enough to touch.

She was there.

And so was Conall Flanagan.

Maggie froze, staring. He stood near the stone circle and had his back to her. His hair was shorter and his shoulders broader, but she knew it was him. She'd recognize him in the darkness of 1,000 aeons. Just as she'd spent the last twelve years feeling his touch, his kisses, and his lovemaking, even though endless ocean miles had stretched between them.

And seeing him now sent every imaginable emotion whipping through her. Her heart hammered painfully and her knees buckled, making her sway. A wave of dizziness washed over her and, for a moment, she feared she was going to be ill.

For sure, she couldn't breathe.

She pressed her hands hard against her chest, trying to inhale, but each great gulp of cold air that she pulled in felt like ingesting fire.

Conall wasn't alone.

And the woman leaning in so close to him, her hand resting possessively on his arm, was so sophisticated, so stunning and polished, that Maggie hated her on sight. She had glossy black hair, stylishly cut. And she was wearing a sleek leaf-green suit and a cream silk blouse. Maggie couldn't tell, but she knew instinctively that the woman's nails would be perfectly manicured.

Maggie swallowed, feeling nauseous.

Even in New York, she'd rarely seen a creature so elegant.

And she wasn't about to shame herself by butting into their intimate rendezvous.

Shaking, she took a step backwards, but something that felt like a firm hand stopped her. She tried to wheel around, but couldn't.

"There'll be none of that now." An old woman's voice lilted the words. "No running away after all the years of waiting and the long miles you've crossed to be here."

"Wait!" Maggie still couldn't move. "I don't know who you are, but I can't go out there. Conall—"

"Conall has been foolish. But he's a good lad and he needs you." Then the crone gave her a nudge, just as she'd done twelve years before.

Maggie caught a fleeting glimpse of two small black boots with red plaid laces and then she was stumbling forwards, out of the wood and into the open sheep field. She caught herself quickly and whirled about, staring at the path.

The old woman wasn't there.

It didn't matter.

She'd regained her legs and was leaving. But she'd only taken three steps back into the woods when she heard a shout behind her.

"*Maggie!*" The surprise and joy in Conall's voice stopped her.

She turned slowly, because she was afraid to believe what her heart was telling her. Conall was sprinting over to her, his dog hard on his heels. The raven-haired beauty was striding in the opposite direction, away from the Seven Sisters and across the field towards the Flanagan farmhouse.

She looked furious.

Maggie swallowed, sure she knew why.

"You still have Booley." She spoke when Conall was almost upon her. "I'm so glad to see him."

"You're glad to see my dog?" Man and beast skidded to a halt. "After all these years, you're finally here, and you're more interested in Booley than me?"

Booley pranced, clearly approving the sentiment.

"I've always loved dogs." Maggie couldn't believe her voice was so calm. "You know that. Unless—" she couldn't help herself "—you've forgotten such things."

"I haven't forgotten anything, Maggie." He stepped closer, set his hands on her shoulders. "Not one single moment we shared and not an hour since. Hours I've spent missing you and regretting that I let you go. Hours that—"

"And the woman you were with just now?" Dear God, had she really said that? "Does she know about those hours?" she added, unable to stop. "I'm assuming she's your wife. She looked quite angry—"

"She was livid." Conall's lips twitched. "And with good reason, because she's one of Dublin's top estate agents and she just lost the land deal of the century."

Maggie blinked. "She's not your wife?"

"God forbid." Conall slid his hands down her arms, linking their fingers. "She'd sell her own granny's false teeth if it'd put money in her pocket. She was here to persuade me to let her hand-sell my land to someone wanting to build a community of executive homes. I declined the offer." He glanced at the Seven Sisters, then back to her. "You of all people should know I could never love such a woman."

But do you love any woman?

Do you love me?

The words snagged in Maggie's throat. "So—" she braced herself "—you're not married?"

"Would I marry a woman I don't love, Maggie Gleason of America?"

"That's not an answer."

"It is if you're listening with your heart." He raised her hand then and brushed a soft kiss across her knuckles. "Do you really not know what I'm telling you?"

"I . . ." Maggie's voice broke. "It's just . . . damn!" She jerked free, pressing her fingers to her lips.

"You're looking fine, Maggie." He circled his arms around her from behind, leaning down to nuzzle her neck. "You've become a beautiful woman and—" he kissed her hair "—I can tell by your upset, that you're still the wonderful girl I fell in love with all those years ago. I love you still, Maggie." He turned her to face him, used his thumbs to smooth the tears from her cheeks. "I've always loved you. And I'm hoping that your being here means you still care for me?"

Maggie rubbed her eyes, blinking rapidly. She never cried. She *ached*, but she never shed tears. "You know how I feel. I told you back then and nothing has changed. But I didn't come here looking for you. I came to forget you, to make peace with the past and move on with my life. I never expected you to be here." She was so glad that he was! "I thought you were in Spain and—"

"I came back three years ago. But that's a story I'll tell you later. Just now—" he pulled her close and kissed her deeply "—the only thing that matters is that you're here. And this time I'm not letting you go. Unless you think you might get homesick for America?" He looked at her, his eyes twinkling. "You might grow weary of Ireland," he teased, dimples flashing. "All the storytelling and fiddle music, our turf fires and castle ruins. The long cold nights with the wind howling round the—"

Maggie slipped her arms around his neck, stopping him with a kiss. "I'm not going to answer that. But I think you already know how likely it is that— Oh, my God, look!" She jumped back, pointing to the Seven Sisters.

The sky had darkened with heavy black clouds rolling in from the sea and turning day into night. But the stone circle shone brightly, each tall, graceful stone glimmering with an eerie blue light. Thick mist, equally luminous, swirled and eddied everywhere. And the soft humming Maggie had heard earlier now sounded like low singing.

Beautiful female voices raised in a sweet, rhythmic chant.

Most amazing of all, a seventh stone now rose from the middle of the circle. Not quite as tall as the other stones and just a bit more slender, the new stone shone with the most brilliant blue of them all.

It was also translucent.

Maggie stared, her jaw dropping.

Conall reached for her hand, gripping tight.

Booley squeezed between them.

"She's the seventh sister." Conall's gaze was riveted on the glowing stone.

Chills raced down Maggie's spine. Her entire body tingled. "But how—"

"Shhh." He spoke low. "Just watch."

And she did, looking on in wonder as the stones shimmered and sang. The beautiful blue light seemed to come from deep within them, though their edges glittered like sapphires. Maggie was sure sparkles danced between them, connecting the stones like a web of brilliant jewels.

Then the mist whirling around the stone circle spun faster and – Maggie's mouth went dry – the Sisters began to dance. They swayed and rocked, tipping slowly in one direction, and then twirling in another. The humming increased, almost sounding like cries of joy, when suddenly the stones rushed together in a dazzling blaze of white-blue light.

It lasted only seconds. Then they snapped apart, springing back quickly. So fast Maggie wasn't even sure she'd seen them move at all. But she knew they had.

And when the swirling mist settled and slipped back out to sea, she saw that the seventh stone was gone.

She turned to Conall, this time not hiding her tears. "Did we really see that?"

He glanced at her, but kept on stroking Booley's trembling shoulders. "I'm for saying we did."

"The seventh sister, too?"

"Aye." Conall's gaze warmed. "Her most of all."

"You don't sound surprised." Maggie could hardly speak.

Conall shrugged. "I'm Irish."

"And that explains everything?"

"It's as good an answer as any." He tweaked her nose. "Or would you hear what the tale-tellers would say about what we just saw?"

Maggie nodded. "I'm for the tale-tellers."

"Then—" he pulled her to him again "—you might be interested to know there's an important part of the legend that I didn't tell you years ago."

"Oh?" She waited.

"The six remaining sisters weren't the only ones who wept when the raiders stole the Princess across the western sea. There was someone else in the King's household who grieved her loss.

"The story is that she was a wise woman who travelled the land helping those in need where and when she could. Some say she hailed from Scotland, others insist she was Irish. Whoever she was—" he paused to glance at the sea "—she was often an honoured guest in the King's hall and she loved all seven sisters dearly.

"So when she saw that the other sisters' sorrow had turned them to stone, she vowed to use her greatest powers to grant them a reunion with their lost sister."

Maggie rested her head on his shoulder, listening. Each word sent shivers rippling through her and her heart was beating so fast she had to strain to hear above the rush of blood in her ears.

Booley was watching them both, his eyes sharp.

"Maggie Gleason of America, it's said that every seven generations, the seventh sister returns." He paused to smooth her hair, the touch gentle. "And when she does, she and her sisters dance and sing and are able to embrace each other once more. Such is the gift of the old wise woman who loved them like the daughters she never bore."

"But that's so sad!" Maggie could hardly speak for the thickness in her throat. "They were only able to be together for one fleeting instant. Their dance, the embrace, was over in a flash."

"Aye." Conall nodded, looking suspiciously untroubled.

"Doesn't that bother you?"

"Not really." He glanced at the stones, so silent and still now. "I'm Irish, remember."

Maggie dashed at her cheek, not liking his story at all.

"I thought you were Irish, too?" He lifted her chin with a finger, peering deep into her eyes. "Can you not guess why I'm not worried about the Sisters?"

Maggie puffed her hair off her forehead. "I suppose I'm more American than I thought."

"Or you're not thinking hard enough." Conall kissed her softly. "Maybe I should tell you there are some hereabouts who believe only those closely involved with the wise woman's magic can see the seventh sister's return."

"What are you saying?" Maggie's heart skittered.

"Only that once the returning is seen, it can be said that the seventh sister's mortal counterpart has also returned to her beloved homeland. And when she does, she always looks after the others. She tends the stones as if they were living flesh still."

"Oh, God!" Maggie stared at him. "You can't mean . . ."

"Who knows?" His eyes said he did. "But I'll share something else with you. A few nights ago, a very strange old woman came into Flanagan's. She had a touch of the fae about her and she was dressed oddly, even wearing—"

"Small black boots with red plaid laces!"

This time Conall looked surprised. But he caught himself and grinned as quickly. "So you've seen her?"

Maggie nodded. "Yes, several times. On my first trip here, then more recently outside a friend's tea room in Pennsylvania. And today when she kept me from leaving after I saw you with that woman. She pushed me forwards into the sheep field. That's why I stumbled."

"Then I say a thousand blessings on her and may she rest well for another seven generations. Or—" he rocked back on his heels "—will you be keeping the poor woman busy by running home to your America?"

"Oh, no, I'm not going anywhere, Conall Flanagan." Maggie hoped it was true. "At least not until I have to fly back to Philly in fourteen days," she added, needing to hear him say the words.

"Fourteen days?" The glint in his eye told her he was playing along. "That's the same amount of time we had years ago." He stepped close, sweeping her into his arms. "I'm thinking that's not nearly long enough for you to enjoy being in Ireland. Everyone knows—" he began walking towards the low, thick-walled farmhouse that had belonged to his family for centuries "—it takes longer than that to fully appreciate such a pleasure. A lifetime at my side, as my wife and the only woman I've ever loved."

"Conall!" Maggie squirmed against his chest. "Put me down so I can kiss you!"

"But will you be saying yes?" He set her on her feet and stood back, his arms opened wide. "That's what I'm waiting to hear."

"Then yes!" Maggie threw herself at him, her heart almost bursting.

He crushed her to him, kissing her hard and fast. "Then let's go home, Maggie Gleason. We have a lot of catching up to do."

Maggie smiled. "Yes, we do."

She was eager to get started. They'd waited longer than she'd known.

By the Light of My Heart

Pat McDermott

Sligo, Ireland – 1911

The black mare started up the hill too fast. Tom O'Byrne shifted on the wagon seat and tugged the reins to curb her quickened gait. He couldn't blame her for hurrying. Grass and water awaited her. Her weary bones required rest, just as his troubled soul craved the peace of Tobernalt, as sacred a place in the year of Our Lord 1911 as it had been in Ireland's pagan times.

Tom often stopped at the holy well when he returned to Sligo from the north. Each time he did, he met other visitors, but no carts or wagons occupied the clearing on this sunny afternoon. His favourite spot, the one near the entrance, was free. He guided the mare to the dappled shade of the old oak tree and set the brake.

His driving skills had impressed Davy Bookman, the Ballymote merchant who owned the wagon. Small but sturdy, the unadorned vehicle had a flat roof and panelled sides painted slate blue. An overhang above the driver's seat protected Tom from the weather, and he'd given thanks more than once for the shelter. He travelled the roads for miles at a time delivering Bookman's tea to shops all over Ireland.

"A good job for a trusty young buck of twenty-five," the jovial merchant had said. "See a little of the world before the farm ties you down."

Tom's neat leap from the footboard set the bag of coins in his pocket jingling. He'd sold most of the tea this trip. He'd make a fine commission. His sister Kate would grumble and say it wasn't enough to fatten her meagre dowry, but the gold would please his father, for all the good it would do him. The old man would always be tipping his hat to the Anglo-Irish landlord who owned his farm.

So would Tom. For now, he dismissed the gloomy prospect. His thoughts were on the holy well and the chunk of currant bread the innkeeper's wife had given him that morning.

He patted the mare's sleek nose. "Here we are, Mally m'love. Long past time for lunch, but live, horse, and you'll get grass, eh?"

As if she'd understood the old proverb, the horse snorted and shook her head. Tom's soft laughter rippled back at her. "You love this place as much as I do, don't you, girl?"

And why wouldn't she? The sparkling stream flowing down from the well splashed over the rocks on its way to Lough Gill. Fair-weather clouds cast fleeting shadows over the rustling greenery. Such a peaceful, sweet-smelling place, so different from the sorry farm Tom would inherit one day.

Leaving the contented mare to graze near the water, he followed the stream to its lofty source. By sunset he'd be back in Ballymote, sloshing in the muck of his father's farm, tending the stinking cows and pigs until he stank himself.

Today was the first of August. The turf would need cutting, and his arms would ache for a week after cutting it. Then he'd be thatching the neighbours' roofs. He'd learned the craft to bring in more gold for Kate's dowry, and good riddance to her. His sister had a tongue that would cut a hedge. He pitied the man who'd become her husband.

Once Kate married – if anyone would have her – Tom's father would be after him or Dan to bring in a wife to keep house. The O'Byrnes couldn't afford to hire help. But who'd marry the heir of a no-account farm or his fanciful younger brother?

Tom didn't care to ponder the relentless quandary now. He preferred to savour the fragrance of the verdant glade and the warbling of colourful birds flitting from tree to tree. Their constant song declared the woodland safe.

Sligo was a haunted place, and Tobernalt had more than its share of spirits. Tom sensed them all around him. He'd never seen one, despite his grandmother saying he could because he'd been born in the afternoon. On each of his previous stops to the well, he'd only met elderly visitors, mostly women, seeking to cure their ills.

"Maybe today, Gram," he said, missing the kind-hearted woman who'd raised him.

Whomever he met today, he meant to look his best. He'd brushed his coat and trousers before leaving Bundoran that morning, but his hulking six-foot frame seemed to draw the mud from the road to his clothes like an angler's lure drew salmon. A few good pats swept the worst of the splotches away.

After rinsing his hands in the stream, he adjusted his tie and straightened his cap. The mist from Lough Gill had dampened the tweed, but at least his head was dry. When his hair got wet, it curled to a wild black tangle.

He paused near the entrance to the well to touch a square pile of stones that predated Christian times. The locals had named it the Mass rock because it had served as an altar for the saying of secret Masses during penal times, when the English put a price on the heads of the priests. One legend said St Patrick himself had left the imprint of his hand upon the stones.

Tom moved on and gazed about the woods, hoping to catch his first glimpse of a fairy. A lady's bicycle caught his eye instead. Its owner had leaned it against a hazel tree. The old girl would be up at the well, saying her prayers or drinking the water to relieve her aches and pains.

When the crumbling stone wall encircling the well came into view, he saw no one. He approached the sacred spot, circling clockwise as he should, offering a silent prayer of thanks that Tobernalt was his for a little while.

The water gushing from the well's solid sheet of rock dallied briefly in a frothy pool before spilling into the stream. Above the site, a rainbow of torn rags dotted the leafy branches, each strip of cloth representing the supplication of a devout pilgrim.

Doffing his cap, Tom knelt and wet his fingers. The water's icy cold refreshed him. He blessed himself – and then he froze.

Was that a face in the pool beneath him? Fatigue after the long drive from Donegal surely had him seeing things. He squeezed his eyes shut and looked again.

The face still bobbed in the water: a woman's face, heart-shaped and pale in a frame of long wavy hair as dark as his own. Eyes blue and pleading transfixed him, compelled him to stroke her rippling cheek. When he touched the water, she faded away.

"Wait!" he tried to say, but a sudden languor had stiffened his tongue. The birdsong above him changed to the loveliest music he'd ever heard. Wave after wave of a haunting harp melody set his soul awhirl. Faster and faster went the tune. He dropped to the grass and fell asleep.

Lured from his rest by the pungent smell of burning turf, Tom sat up on a strange featherbed, blinking at his surroundings. He found himself in a rustic kitchen awash in the glow of a wide, sooty hearth.

A cauldron hung over squares of steaming sod whose sizzling red edges flared into flames now and then. A crook-backed woman emerged from the shadows and stirred the pot. Her black shawl covered her misshapen shoulders and white-haired head. She turned towards Tom, peering at him through falcon eyes that smouldered like coals in her skeletal face.

He sensed no threat from her. In fact, she reminded him of his grandmother. One quick swing of his legs brought him to his feet. He crossed the room to present himself, reaching to remove his cap on his way, but it wasn't on his head. "God save all here," he said.

"One hundred thousand welcomes to you, Tomás O'Byrne." The woman stirred as she spoke. Her aged voice lilted with mischief and mirth. "You've travelled far this day. You'll travel farther still before you find your rest."

"How do you know me, ma'am? Who are you?"

"I am Sorcha, the Guardian of Tobernalt. All who visit Lough Gill's holy well are known to me."

Tom slanted his head to one side and squinted at her. "In all the times I've stopped at the well, I've never seen the likes of you."

"The door to the Otherworld only opens at certain times. Today is one of them. August first. Lughnasa." She pointed to a rough-hewn table set against the wall. "Go and sit, Tomás O'Byrne. I've prepared a meal for you."

More curious than concerned, Tom complied with her request. A bowl of potatoes and scallions boiled in milk appeared before him, though the hag never moved from the hearth. While she hummed and stirred, he sampled the food. Its earthy flavours compelled him to eat until he'd emptied the bowl. At last he set his spoon down. "Why have you brought me here, ma'am?"

Again, her head turned towards him. "Finvarra, the King of the Fairies, has taken the healer Doreen. You must bring her back."

"I know no woman by that name."

"She chose you to save her."

The young woman's face appeared before Tom as clearly as it had in the water at Tobernalt. Her sad blue eyes beguiled him. He must rescue her, this healer named Doreen. "What would you have me do, ma'am?"

Sorcha smiled and nodded her approval. "Finvarra claims he took the girl to heal an injured knee that keeps him from dancing." Disgust twisted the old woman's face. "The bumptious ass is never short of excuses to steal mortal women. You must go to his summer palace and free Doreen before it's too late. Once she eats his fairy food, she'll forever be his prisoner."

Tom glanced suspiciously at his empty bowl. Had the old crone tricked him?

Her cackle resounded through the murky room. "'Tis true that the King of the Fairies isn't the only one who serves enchanted food to mortals. But Finvarra's food entraps. Mine empowers. Rise up now, Tomás O'Byrne. Find Finvarra's palace. Free the healer and bring her to her true destiny."

Despite the hag's assurance that her supper would magically strengthen him, an inkling of doubt beset Tom. He pushed back his chair and stood. "I thank you for the meal, ma'am, but I don't see how I can challenge the King of the Fairies. His magic is great, and I have no weapons."

Sorcha shuffled towards him holding out her withered fingers. Instinctively, Tom extended his hand towards her.

She dropped a small round lump into his open palm. "This golden bean grew in my garden. If you place it in your mouth in times of danger, you'll become invisible. So will the healer, as long as you touch her. Go forth now, Tomás O'Byrne. Follow the path to the crossroads where the crystal lark sings in the silver oak tree. Take the left road and you'll find the entrance to Finvarra's palace."

Still unconvinced, Tom placed the golden bean in his pocket. He strode to the door, opened it and gazed at the pitch-black night. "I've never seen such darkness. How will I find my way?"

"The moon and stars cannot shine beneath the hills of Ireland. You must find your way by the light of your heart."

Sorcha vanished. So did her house. Sniffing a last trace of turf smoke, Tom scratched his head and wondered what she'd meant.

The anguished face of the healer Doreen appeared in the black fairy night. She fixed a beseeching gaze on him.

"Don't worry, *mavourneen*," he whispered. "I'll find you. I mean to see you smile."

The pebbled path before him glistened.

He heard the lark before he saw it. The glorious trilling led him to wisps of whirling light that grew fatter and brighter, spinning at last into a silver tree. When he reached the glossy trunk, the birdsong ceased. He thought he'd frightened the lark away, but the true reason for its sudden silence quickly became clear.

The sound of horses' hooves boomed in the distance, rumbling towards Tom with the speed of a storm-driven wave. Wary rather than frightened, he slipped behind the tree just as seven white steeds sprang from the darkness, chargers geared for battle by the looks of them. Jewels glittered on their foreheads. Flames shot from their nostrils. The knights atop them might have been human but for the armour and helmets of radiant gold they wore. Broad green mantles snapped behind them, and each held a golden spear.

They cut to a halt at the silver oak, and Tom's lips mouthed a silent curse. Did they know he was there? Had they come to kill him? If so, he'd give them a good fight.

The golden bean, Tomás O'Byrne . . .

Sorcha's voice rustled in his ears like windblown eddies of autumn leaves. He fumbled in his pocket and snatched the golden bean to his mouth.

Nothing happened.

The lead rider walked his steed to the tree and circled the trunk. Tom stood as still as a wound-down clock. Would the horse smell him? Would the horseman hear his pounding heart? Sure he was about to die, he glared defiantly at the knight, but the fairy only raised his arm and galloped off.

His fairy troop raced after him. Tom didn't move until the clatter of thundering hooves faded away. The crystal bird resumed its song, and Tom knew the danger had passed. Still, he ran down the road to the left of the tree as if the devil himself were chasing him.

At last he stopped at a stand of rocks. Gold glittered around a gap in the stones. This must be the Fairy King's palace. Where did the fairies find so much gold? The coins in Tom's pocket, a sum he'd thought a small fortune that morning, seemed a beggar's portion in contrast to the wealth he'd seen so far.

Suspecting he'd soon see more, he entered the cave. A raucous blend of music, laughter and merry female squeals wafted from its depths. Tom crept deeper into the cave and found a marble staircase. Down he went with the golden bean in his mouth.

Soon he came to a torch-lit room. He stepped inside, and the sounds of revelry faded. Three grey-haired women sat at golden spinning wheels spinning golden thread. From their plain attire and listless air, he judged them to be mortals.

He took the bean from his mouth. "God save all here."

The women's hands flew to their faces. The oldest of the three blessed herself. "Mother of God, who are you?"

"I'm Tom O'Byrne of Ballymote. I've come to save a mortal woman called Doreen."

An exchange of desolate looks preceded the women's responses. "Ah, poor thing," said the youngest.

"You must hurry," said the woman neither young nor old.

The oldest spoke again: "I warned her not to taste the fairies' food, but mortals must eat, and she won't hold out long. After one bite, she'll be like us, a prisoner for the rest of her days."

"There's naught you can do for us," said the youngest, "but you can save the healer, Tom O'Byrne."

"I mean to try. Where is she?"

"In the banquet hall." The woman neither young nor old turned and pointed behind her. A door appeared in the wall. "Go quickly, and take great care. The King of the Fairies wields powerful magic."

Tom returned the golden bean to his mouth. As he stepped through the door, the noise of the party resumed. He followed the din to a glittering golden banquet hall. Torches blazed high on the walls. Candles flickered in massive chandeliers. Two narrow bench tables ran the length of the long wide room. A third bench, undoubtedly the head table, ran perpendicular to the other two, forming a three-sided rectangle.

Cloth made of rose petals covered the tables, where men and women, handsome and human in appearance, sat swilling down meat and drink from golden plates and goblets. Tom assumed that the few vacant seats belonged to the fairies dancing near the biggest hearth he'd ever seen.

He knew the King of the Fairies by his elaborate attire and privileged place at the head table. Yellow-haired and clean-shaven, the rogue had a muscle or two beneath his fancy dress. Tom had trounced bigger men, and he thought he'd like to tap his knuckles into Finvarra's face. Yet magic was afoot here. Despite Sorcha's bolstering supper, Tom realized he might never see home again if he challenged the King. Rescuing Doreen must be the priority.

She sat unsmiling beside Finvarra. Her thick dark hair flowed past her shoulders. Her pallid face and haunted eyes melted Tom's heart. He would save her from this place or die trying.

If he could touch her, he'd have a chance. No one saw him tiptoe towards the head table.

The King's handsome face suddenly darkened. "Your healing arts have cured my foot, yet you persist in refusing my generous offer of thanks."

Doreen raised her chin. Her blue eyes blackened with hatred. "When you first brought me here, you said it was your knee that needed curing. Make up your mind. If you really want to thank me, let me go home." Both pride and fear played in her pearly voice.

Finvarra pounded the table. Silence fell over the banquet hall. "You insult us by refusing our food, woman! We'll see how long you last on an empty belly. Lock her away!"

A liveried guard seized Doreen's arm and yanked her from the table. She jerked herself free of him. He flinched at her ferocious glare, and Tom smiled. Standing tall, she turned her back on the scowling King. With the flustered guard at her heels, she stalked from the hall ignoring the muttering crowd that parted to let her pass.

Tom scurried to intercept her. Eyeing her up and down, he understood why Finvarra wanted the well-formed beauty. He wouldn't have her if Tom had his way.

She came right at him and might have walked through him if he hadn't seized her hand. The screams and shouts that erupted around them told him she'd disappeared. They could see each other, but the golden bean kept them from the fairies' sight.

Doreen's black look changed to one of disbelief. She stuttered before she spoke. "You! You came for me!"

Afraid to reply lest he lose or swallow the bean, he raised a finger to his lips and nodded towards the door. Doreen nodded back.

They bolted towards the exit. The crowd stampeded after them. Tom wondered how they knew where he and Doreen were until he realized the flames on the candles were flickering as they passed.

Plates and goblets flew at them. One struck Doreen's arm. She stumbled out of Tom's grasp and fell in an undignified heap.

"There she is!" the fairies screamed.

Tom plucked Doreen from the floor, and a new round of hostile shouts reassured him she'd vanished again. Dragging her with him, he shot from the hall, past the spinning women and up the marble stairs, up and up and out into the night.

If the moon and stars cast no light down here, it seemed the sun did. Or would, when it rose. The sweeping darkness had brightened, and though night would reign a while longer, the pebbled path still glowed in the budding dawn.

Tom and Doreen ran to the silver oak tree. The crystal lark sang in its branches, and Tom knew they were safe, at least for the moment. Still holding Doreen's hand, he plucked the golden bean from his mouth and slipped it into his pocket. They sat on the ground to catch their breath.

What would he tell her? How would they get home? He must try to find Sorcha.

Doreen had no worries, it seemed. With a great fond smile, she twined her arms around his neck and kissed him.

Joy he'd never known filled his soul. He kissed her back, gently at first, then as firmly and deeply as she kissed him. He held her close to his heart so her breasts pressed against his chest. Lost in their kiss and the sweet perfume of her long dark hair, he reeled like a drunken goose. Faster and faster he whirled, until he was falling . . . falling . . .

Stiff and sore from the graceless position in which he'd fallen asleep, Tom struggled to his knees blinking at the well and the woods around it. No one was near. The adventure had been a dream. A pleasant dream, he thought as the fairy world dissolved from his mind like tendrils of smoke. He retrieved his cap and lurched to his feet.

"Are you all right?"

The woman's question came from behind him. Cap in hand, he twisted about, expecting an aged arthritic. The lady who'd spoken stood in the gloom of the woods. A young mother then, come for a cure for her ailing child.

She stepped into a patch of sunlight and asked again: "Are you all right?"

Tom's mouth fell open. The heart-shaped face of the healer Doreen frowned at him from the top of the path. He gawked at her, unable to speak, powerless to offer even a nod.

Wariness sharpened her probing gaze. Tom, in turn, inspected her. She wore her dark hair fashionably twisted up beneath a brown brimmed hat. A lacy neck-to-chin collar gave her a well-heeled look. Her hip-length coat, tailored to her slender waist, covered the top of a long black skirt loose enough to pedal her bicycle.

Yes, he thought. The bicycle. He must have had a glimpse of her, and she found her way into his dream.

She remained where she stood. Did his towering frame frighten her? He set his feet apart and affected a nonchalant air to appear less threatening. "God be with you, ma'am. I'm Tom O'Byrne of Ballymote."

His proper greeting seemed to ease her apprehension. She strolled towards him. "God and Mary be with you, Tom O'Byrne. Dolly Keenan from Tubbercurry."

Dolly. Not Doreen.

Appearing more confident now, she came towards him, brushing bits of dry leaves and grass from her sleeves. The curve of her bosom enticed him. As she drew nearer, he noted the lacy silver work on the buttons of her smart tweed coat. A decent enough coat, he thought, though he'd seen finer garb on women in the cities. Still, her attire outshone the frippery his sister wore.

Dolly Keenan stopped an arm's length away. Butterscotch seemed to melt over Tom. "Tubbercurry isn't far from

Ballymote, but it's a long way from here. Surely you didn't come all that way on your bicycle?"

He couldn't imagine Kate riding a bicycle half that distance. She wouldn't even go into town without a wagon.

Kate left his thoughts altogether when Dolly Keenan raised her chin the way she had at King Finvarra's table. "Indeed I did. It's better than walking, though the ride up tired me out, and that's the gospel truth. I'm after having a bit of a nap in the woods myself."

Maybe she'd ride home with him. It wouldn't hurt to ask. "I'm on my way back down, ma'am. You're welcome to ride with me in my wagon."

A smile that would shame the northern lights broke over her face. "Thank you, Tom. I wouldn't mind a lift as far as the road to Tubber."

Bursting with triumph, he stepped to her side. "Let's get your bicycle, then."

When Dolly Keenan linked her arm through his, Tom set his cap on his head and rejoiced.

They stopped in Collooney to rest the horse, and Tom bought two apples at a shop near the train station. He sat with Dolly on the wagon seat, devouring the apples and chatting about Sligo until they pitched the cores into a nearby barrel.

A handkerchief embroidered with blue and green leaves appeared in her hand. She dabbed at lips he longed to kiss and returned the cloth to her pocket. "Give me a minute, Tom. Since we're at the station, I want to get a timetable."

He feared he'd done something to offend her, that she'd decided to take the train home, but the line ran to Ballymote from here, not to Tubbercurry. Mystified, he sighed. Whatever she'd gone to get, her going had left a hole in his heart.

Soon she returned with her prize: a square white page with rows of tiny print set beneath a troubling title. He wondered why she'd want the times of trains for Queenstown, though of course he didn't ask. It wasn't his business.

He'd been to Queenstown selling tea, but few souls ventured

to the deep Cork port on Ireland's southern shore unless they meant to emigrate. The thought of Dolly Keenan leaving saddened him.

Whether she emigrated or not, he doubted he'd ever see her again. The wagon ride was all they'd have. Familiar with disappointment as any Irishman, he helped her to the wagon seat, intent on enjoying every minute of her company.

A porridge of weather followed them from Collooney. Showers came and went. Blue broke through the clouds in snatches. Gram used to call it a rainbow sky.

"Be on the watch, Tomáseen," she'd say. "Seeing a rainbow brings good luck."

Tom needed no rainbow today. Good luck was already his. Dolly Keenan rode beside him on the compact wagon seat. Their arms and thighs collided as the springs bounced, and she didn't shy away. Nor did she complain about the mist that dampened her cheeks and hair. They gossiped and bantered, talking of nonsense, of favourite foods and ancient legends. She laughed a lot, and so did he.

The mare clip-clopped over a twisting road rutted in some spots, soggy in others. Sheep dotted the knolls and bogs. Cows grazed in square green pastures divided by hawthorn hedges. Now and then an abandoned stone cottage, roofless and overgrown, provided a landmark that told Tom where he was.

The idea that Dolly had ridden this road by herself both impressed and worried him, yet she wouldn't have been alone. Several cyclists passed them. They called out pleasant greetings, as did many foot travellers and the drivers of drays and donkey carts. Tom and Dolly waved cheerfully back.

Before they'd left Tobernalt, she'd shared the cheese and scones in her saddlebag, and he'd split his chunk of currant bread in half. While they'd eaten, he'd spotted the pearl ring on her right hand. He'd carried her bicycle from the woods thinking how she'd surely look down on him once she knew more about him.

She'd peeked inside the wagon when he opened the rear doors. "What've you got in there, Tom?"

"Tea." He'd helped her to the wagon seat. The touch of her fingers thrilled him, and though he knew right well she didn't have to, she leaned on him when she mounted the step. "I travel the counties selling tea."

"Is that where you're coming from now? A sales jaunt?"

"In Donegal and Tyrone, yes." He'd settled beside her and tugged the reins. "Got as far as Strabane. There's trouble up there. At the inn where I stayed, the landlady said I shouldn't go out. Said the local lads were on the prowl for southerners."

The idea still amused him, but furrows had appeared on Dolly's forehead. "My father's spoken of such goings on in the north, but I've never heard of them firsthand. Still and all, you don't look like the sort anyone would be stupid enough to take on." Her cheeks turned crimson, as if she'd said something she shouldn't.

Tom had been delighted she'd said it at all and, thinking of it now, he sat taller on the seat. He guided the horse to the side of the road to let a northbound wagon pass. Once it did, he eased his hold on the reins and continued conversing with Dolly.

She'd recently returned from England, where she'd attended nursing school. She'd lived with her brother Lanigan and his wife.

"Lanigan's a crackerjack carpenter, but he had to go to London to find work. My brother Maneen and sister Badie have emigrated to America. Mac is still in Tubbercurry. He's a teacher, like my mother. Sissie was, too, but she died of consumption two years ago."

Tom recognized the grief in her voice. "I'm sorry. There's a lot of that about."

"Too much. That's one reason why I want to be a nurse. To help. I deliberately failed the teaching exam so I could go to nursing school."

Tom's delighted laughter echoed over the bogs. "It's grand that you could. My father took me out after sixth grade to work the farm and do odd jobs."

"That's not uncommon. Most of my friends ended their

schooling likewise. I'm lucky my parents let me go off at all, with twenty acres to manage. They were disappointed about the nursing. An unsuitable calling for a proper young lady, they said. Wanted me to stay home and teach, like Sissie and Mac. When Mac isn't teaching, he helps my father about the farm. He'll inherit the place some day."

"So will I, though it's little I want it."

"I wondered about that, Tom. A Ballymote lad travelling all over Ireland. When you see other ways to live besides milking cows, it's hard to go back to farming, isn't it?"

Tom tightened his hold on the reins. He didn't want to talk about cows, not now. "Your brothers and sisters have odd names. Nicknames, are they?"

"Yes. Jim is Lanigan, John is Maneen. Michael is Mac, and Annie's called Badie. Kathleen was Sissie."

"Is Dolly a nickname as well?"

"It is. They called me that because I was the youngest. My real name is Doreen."

Hearing the name from his dream stunned Tom, though he recovered quickly. This was Ireland after all. And a fellow got used to such odd occurrences.

Awake or dreaming, he had no business befriending an educated young lady whose father held a good strong farm of twenty Irish acres. "The matchmakers will be hopping about like hungry hens over a girl as pretty as you."

Dolly blushed again. Her lips pressed into a thin straight line, and she shook her head. "Marriage would be the death of nursing for me. I'm thinking of emigrating. To Boston, like Maneen and Badie. That's why I was at the well. Looking for guidance, for something to help me find my way."

The heart turned crosswise in Tom. He might convince her to stay, but how could he blame her for wanting to go? He wanted no part of a life here himself.

Locking his gaze on her sparkling eyes, he released one hand from the reins and dared to squeeze her fingers. "Someone told me once, you must find your way by the light of your heart."

She squeezed back, an agreeable response indeed, and then she smiled again. "That's lovely, Tom. You know, I feel we've met before. At a dance? Or in church, perhaps?"

It seemed she'd forgotten her time with the fairies. Had it really happened at all? Tom's other hand slipped into the pocket that in his dream had held the golden bean. He felt nothing but the hard seam in the cloth.

A dream. It had all been a dream. "Somewhere like that, I suppose. I do get around."

Her heavy sigh seemed to unleash a new round of showers. She leaned back under the overhang. "There'll never be any light in my heart if my parents have their way. Mac says they're going to forbid me to be a nurse. They thought I'd get it out of my system in London, but just the opposite occurred. Studying at the hospital and seeing all those ill and dying folk only made me more determined to help them."

Suddenly jealous of every sick man in the world, Tom released her hand. She might hit him, but he couldn't hold back. "I wouldn't like to see you go so far away, Dolly Keenan. The light in *my* heart has grown brighter since I met you."

Nor could he keep from seizing her and sliding his lips over hers, gently at first, gauging, sensing, expecting an outraged shove. Instead, she kissed him back with a fervour that unlocked a secret door in his soul.

Could he go with her to America?

His cousin had gone to Boston and found work as a train conductor. An aunt named Mary, his father's own sister, had gone to Boston too. She ran a boarding house and made good money, a lot more than Tom made selling tea. With all the skills he had, he could do anything.

Could he leave Ireland and his family forever?

For Dolly Keenan he could, and her eager kisses said she'd have him.

"Good man yourself!" shouted a farmer leading a donkey laden with turf-filled panniers.

Tom backed breathlessly away from Dolly. He licked his lips, savouring the taste of her, entranced by the same perfume he'd smelled in her hair behind the silver oak tree. Dolly in turn looked away to the west, touching her smiling lips as if she couldn't believe he'd kissed her.

Tom picked up the reins and tried to focus on the road. He'd sinned with a girl or two around Ireland, but he sensed no sin here. He loved Dolly, and she loved him, he knew it.

Maybe they wouldn't have to leave. He'd speak to his father, have him send the matchmaker to Mr Keenan, convince the man that Tom O'Byrne could support his daughter well with his tea sales and roof thatching and all his odd jobs.

Still, she'd have to do for his father and brother, mind the chickens, gather the eggs, churn the butter and mend the clothes. Tom would work hard to bring in more gold, enough to hire a local girl to help her.

Maybe her nursing could bring in some extra gold. Sligo had the fever hospital. She could work there, if tending potatoes and cabbage left her any time.

No, he thought. The farm would kill them both. They had to get away.

Yet he couldn't speak the words that would change their lives forever, and perhaps not for the best. They rode on in silence until they reached the crossroads. No silver tree here, no crystal lark.

She insisted she'd be safe enough riding to Tubbercurry from here. He stopped at the roadside and opened the wagon's rear doors. Before he reached in for the bike, she came at him, hugging him, kissing him, deliciously rubbing against him.

He held her close and ground against her, sin be damned. "Dolly. Oh, darlin', what are we to do? I can't marry you. Your father wouldn't have me."

"I'd have you, Tom O'Byrne. We can marry in America."

They could. Others had done so. Tom's heart thumped in his throat. "When are you leaving?"

"I don't know. Soon. Come with me, Tom. Leave the farm for Boston."

Leave the farm . . . The words struck him like an Atlantic gale, knocking down fences, ripping up hedges, tearing down the walls that threatened to imprison him to the end of his days.

Did he really have the neck to leave?

One look at the promise glinting in Dolly's eyes gave him his answer. "I will, *mo chroí*. I'll go anywhere with you."

He caught her in his arms, silencing her delighted squeal with a kiss that reached for her soul. When she finally wobbled from his arms, her crimson cheeks and ragged breath told him he'd succeeded.

"I'll send you a letter," she said when she could speak. She twisted the ring from her finger and pressed it into his hand, apparently unconcerned that he'd nothing to offer in exchange.

Swearing she'd have a ring for every finger one day, he slipped the pearl in his jacket pocket and watched her ride away.

An hour before midnight, the Irish twilight lingered over Ballymote. Hungry, tired and longing for Dolly, Tom trudged home from Davy Bookman's house with his share of the gold snug in his pocket. His satchel contained his few toiletries and washing for Kate. She'd begrudgingly launder his socks and shirts, though he'd look after his trousers himself. She never put the crease in them right.

The homey odours of pipe tobacco and roasting turf greeted him at the door. Subtler aromas of bacon and bread sharpened his hunger. He set his bag on the rough plank table, eyeing the furnishings and holy pictures as if seeing them for the last time.

His father sat by the hearth holding a briar pipe to the mouth concealed in his long white beard. As Tom approached, the old man lowered his pipe and turned his book on his lap. "Thanks be to God, it's himself at last."

Tom always pictured his father's beard red, saw his freckled bald pate with a full head of ginger-red hair. The family and neighbours still called him Red Brendan. "I've only been gone two weeks, Da. How are you keeping?"

"I've often been better and often been worse. And yourself, Tomás Og?"

I've been to the fairies. I'm in love and thinking of going to Boston. "I'd be well enough if I wasn't hungry. Is there bread?" He handed the bag of gold to his father.

"There is, and cabbage and bacon. Kate's just after finishing the mending. She's gone to her room to brush out her hair." Brendan rattled the coins and smiled. He placed the bag on the table beside him, near the tobacco can, and turned his head towards the back room. "Kate! Tom is home. Come out and get him tea, girl."

Tom would have found the food himself, but he'd only earn his sister's wrath for messing things. He glanced at the blue and white delft in the cupboard. Not a piece missing, every plate clean and in its place. She kept house well, he'd give her that.

On the top shelf sat the framed photograph of their mother, Ann. Dark-haired and lovely, she watched over the room with a neutral expression that over the years had turned cross or approving depending on Tom's own behaviour. He barely remembered her. She'd died giving birth to Dan, when Tom had been three years of age.

"You favour her, Tom," old Gram had said.

Kate and Dan had their father's red hair, and Kate had the temper to match. Her entrance from the back room reminded Tom of the fire-breathing stallions at the silver oak tree. He caught himself before he laughed. "Hello, Kate. You're looking lovely tonight."

She tossed her well-combed mane and tied her shawl over her nightdress. "Never mind your trick-acting, Tom O'Byrne. Coming home near midnight and expecting me to drop everything to fix you a meal. I suppose that bag is full of filthy laundry. As if I don't have enough to do."

"It's grand to see you too, Kate."

After Ann passed away, Brendan had sent Kate to live with an aunt. His mother moved in to look after him and the boys, but Kate grew up on a moneyed farm, and she fancied herself a step above the buttermilk. She'd just turned twelve when

Gram passed on, and Brendan had called her home to tend the house and chickens. She'd been doing so for nearly ten years, and she clearly resented every minute of it.

Pots and lids clacked and clanged while she rewarmed the supper and steeped a pot of tea. Wincing with each slam, Tom took the dish she offered at last and thanked her. She retired to her room, and he sat near the fire, setting the plate on his lap, relaying the highlights of his trip between bites, neglecting to mention the well and the fairies and Dolly Keenan from Tubbercurry.

Ever hungry for news, his father puffed his pipe and took it all in before reporting on the farm. Two of the neighbours had stopped by to see if Tom could rethatch their roofs before winter. Dan had started cutting the turf, but he needed Tom's muscle to finish the job.

Brendan pinched some tobacco from the can beside him and replenished the bowl of his pipe. "I don't know what will become of that boy. He won't get muscle by drawing pictures and playing the fiddle. Kate will marry, and you'll have the farm, but I'm thinking Dan may have to emigrate."

Tom held his breath. A chance to escape had presented itself. Looking to keep a steady voice, he exhaled slowly. "Where is Dan? I doubt he's sleeping in the loft with all the racket Kate made."

"He's in town tonight. A Tuesday night, can you believe it? Playing the fiddle at a dance with his friends. Said he'd spend the night at Mick Jordan's. I'll have to speak to him soon. He can go to Boston. Stay with my sister Mary."

Gulping for air, Tom braced himself. He shot out the words before his courage failed. "No, Da. I'll go. Dan can have the farm. He does most of the work now. He'll really buckle down if he knows it will come to him."

Brendan jerked as if nettles had stung him. He set the pipe on its tilted stand and pinned Tom with a piercing glare. "While you were gone, the matchmaker came about Kate. Séamus Hunt in Roscommon will take her, thanks to the gold you've brought in. The Hunts have a strong farm, twenty-five

Irish acres, and she'll have a daily girl in the kitchen. But I can't let her go until you have a wife to do for us."

"Da, please listen."

Brendan disregarded him. "I asked the matchmaker to find a suitable girl for you. It cost me a bottle of good whiskey, but he's turned up three good prospects. We'll choose by the end of the month. You'll have the farm when I'm gone, and your son after you." Pinpricks of ice gleamed in the old man's eyes. "And Dan will go to America."

Fists bunched tight, Tom leaped from his seat. "I've met the girl I want to marry. A girl from Tubbercurry. Can the matchmaker try for her?"

The bald head wagged from side to side. "You wanted to leave Ireland a minute ago. Now you want a girl from Tubber. I'm thinking it's good I'm here to guide you, Tomás Og." Brendan sighed without making a sound. "Who is she?"

Grateful for the kindness that had seeped into his father's tone, Tom reclaimed his seat and explained about Dolly, omitting her thoughts on emigrating. If the old man knew she was thinking of leaving, he'd never approve the marriage.

He rejected Dolly anyway. "No father would give a girl like that to a no-account farm."

"I can always bring in more gold, Da."

"Perhaps, but after I'm gone, you won't be off selling tea. You'll be here all the time, and so would she." Brendan stood easily. "Even if her father agreed, a girl who's been to London would never be happy tending chickens and vegetables. She's seen too much of the world. Like you, Tomás Og. Get her and your lofty ideas out of your head."

It sounded so logical, put like that. The old fella was right. Yet as Tom watched his father lift the ladder from the corner, the memory of Dolly's kisses sparked an indelible yearning in him. He slipped his hand in his jacket pocket and fingered the pearl ring. The light of his heart flickered and dimmed.

His father had obviously dismissed him. The old man set the ladder against the wall by the hearth and snatched the bag of gold from the table. Moving as his age allowed, he climbed the rungs to the rafters, to the secret cache he'd cut from the biggest beam.

Tired and heartsick, Tom sought his bed in the loft.

Over the next week, he cut enough turf for the winter and went to work thatching. He'd just finished Charlie McGowan's roof when the letter from Dolly came. A lad on a bicycle rode past McGowan's vegetable garden late in the afternoon. He stopped by the piles of old thatch and said Miss Keenan had instructed him to give the note to Tom O'Byrne or no one. Watching the boy ride off, Tom strolled to the well as calmly as he could with his knees quaking and his heart skipping beats. He'd nearly despaired of hearing from her again.

Drinking a cup of water gave him a moment to muster his courage. He opened the envelope and stared at the elegant script until the words made sense to his befuddled mind.

> Dearest Tom,
>
> My father has sold me off to a man his own age. I want nothing to do with him. I have enough gold to book us both passage to Boston. The train leaves Ballymote for Queenstown tomorrow morning at nine. I'll wait for you under the clock.
>
> Ever yours,
>
> Dolly

Short, sweet and dangerous as hell. Could he do it?

What of their parents? Was leaving them selfish? Tom didn't think so. Dan could look after their father, and Dolly's brother could take care of her old ones. The matchmaker would find a girl for Dan. Dan would have the farm, and his son after him, God help him. Kate would marry Séamus Hunt and have a new family to terrorize. They'd all be fine.

Tom had little to pack, no more than an extra pair of trousers and a few spare shirts and socks. He wished he didn't have to sneak off, but he'd never have his father's blessing, not now. Maybe never.

So be it. The hospitals in Boston would welcome Dolly's nursing skills, and Tom would find plenty of work, more than enough to send money home.

Yet he needed money now. He wasn't about to let Dolly support him.

He'd earned every coin of gold in the rafters. He had as much right to it as Kate. He wouldn't take it all, just enough for his train ticket and passage, and some respectable clothes and lodging when he reached America. Once he found work, he'd pay it back. He'd say so in the note he'd leave his father.

Giddy with joy and pricked by guilt, he hurried home. His father and Dan were out somewhere, mending a fence, he recalled. They'd had to walk, as Kate had taken the wagon to town for groceries. Feeling like a boy stealing apples from an orchard, he set the ladder against the wall and climbed to the rafters. He counted out twenty pounds, no more. Kate would have plenty for her dowry.

Moving carefully about the loft to keep from waking his brother, Tom gathered his belongings. Just before dawn, he bid Dan a silent farewell and stole downstairs.

In the light of the banked turf fire, Tom kissed his mother's picture and whispered goodbye. Sure she was smiling, he ventured into the starless gloom, finding his way by the light of his heart.

They'd miss him at breakfast. They'd read his note and know what he'd done, but they'd be too late to stop him. By nine o'clock he and Dolly would be on the train to Queenstown.

At ten to nine he jogged into Ballymote station, wrinkling his nose at the fug of tobacco, stale whiskey and acrid coal smoke. He saw the big round clock right away. Dolly waited beneath the black Roman numerals, dressed in the same clothes she'd worn when they'd met at Tobernalt. A satchel similar to his rested by her feet.

"Dolly!"

Her head jerked towards him. Her brilliant smile offered

hope of a blessed new life. Oblivious to the people around them, he dropped his bag beside hers and kissed her.

Her lips trembled before she spoke. "Tom. You came."

"Did you think I wouldn't?"

The welling tears in her eyes suggested she'd had doubts, yet she clasped his hands and smiled. "I knew you'd come, Tom. I bought you a train ticket." She drew two tickets from her pocket to prove it.

He took them from her, and the train whistle blew. "Thank you, darlin'. We'll settle it later. Let's get aboard now."

Halfway up the steps, he turned to see Ballymote one last time – just as his father stormed into the station. Kate hurtled along beside him, her hair a frightful tangle, her face contorted in venomous fury. They must have come in the wagon and raced the poor horse half to death.

Tom swallowed hard. "Hurry, Dolly. Get inside."

Dolly's eyebrows arched in question, but she obeyed. They hurried through several coaches until they reached an empty carriage near the end of the train. Tom stowed their bags on an overhead rack. He and Dolly plopped on to seats facing each other. He pulled out his pocket watch. Five minutes to nine. Not enough time for his father and sister to search the train.

But it was. Kate's shrill shouts spewed from the adjacent car. She was coming quickly towards them, screeching Tom's name, imploring her father to call the guards and have her thieving brother arrested.

Dolly plainly understood the significance of the shrieks. "Oh, Tom! What will we do?"

Throttling Kate came to mind. She'd cause a scene and demand the dowry she thought he'd stolen. He could plead with his father, but the old man would surely side with Kate. He just might call the guards if Tom refused to come home, and they'd take him away in handcuffs.

All hope drained from his heart. Dolly must go without him. Sure he'd never see her again, he reached into his pocket to return her ring to her.

The ring was gone. His fingers encircled the golden bean.

Hurry, Tomás O'Byrne . . .

Stunned, he slipped the bean into his mouth. Dolly's jaw dropped in disbelief, and he knew he'd disappeared. He seized her hand just as Kate blew through the door.

"He's not here either. I'm telling you, Da. Call the guards! The miserable scut has stolen my dowry!"

Brendan marched in behind her. "Silence, girl! I'll not call the guards on my own son." The train whistle blew a second time. The old man brushed a tear from his cheek. "We have to leave the train, Kate. If this is what your brother wants, good luck to him."

Thank you, Da. I'll write often, and send money. And I'll come back to visit you.

With his sputtering daughter stomping behind him, Tom's father left the train. They'd just reached the big round clock when the train whistle blew again. The engine chugged, and Tom took the golden bean from his mouth.

"It wasn't a dream," Dolly whispered. "I remember it all now. You were there, Tom. You saved me from the Fairy King."

"The old woman who guards the well at Tobernalt saved us both, *mo chroí.*"

"What's that thing in your hand?" Dolly gently uncurled his fingers. Her ring lay in his palm. Nothing remained of the golden bean.

The train picked up speed. Tom slid the pearl ring on to Dolly's finger and smiled. One day soon, he'd place a gold ring on her other hand.

Glossary

Ard Rí	High (or Supreme) King.
A chuisle	My pulse.
A nighean ruadh	Red-haired girl.
Aos si(dhe)	The faerie race (*see also* "Sidhe"); singular "*Aes si(dhe)*".
Banshee/*Bean sí*	Female spirit whose screams herald death. Also called a "washer woman", she's often seen washing bloody linens at a stream; woman of the fairy mounds.
Berserker	In Viking lore, a warrior who gained the blood-lust of fighting, and charged into battle so fiercely that nothing or no one could stop him. Some say his form even changed into that of a raving beast.
Bog-oak	Ancient wood found buried in peat bogs.
Chainse	A white long-sleeved undertunic of fine linen worn in the early Middle Age.
Chausses	Armour for the legs, usually made from mail.
Colcannon	Irish traditional dish consisting of mashed potatoes and cabbage.
Cohuleen druith	A red cap made of swan feathers that enables merrows (*see entry*) to swim through the ocean.
Compeer	Partner.
Craic	Gossip/chatter.
Dun	Fort; usually covered a whole hilltop with walls protecting many buildings.
Drùth	Harlot.
Éire/Ériu	Ireland.
Fine	Clan.
Gael	Celtic, Gaelic-speaking ethnic group of Ireland, Scotland and the Isle of Man.
Gardai	The police force of the Republic of Ireland.

Gasún	Child.
Geis	A curse, spell, or incantation.
Guraiceach	A blockhead, oaf.
Imbolc	An ancient Celtic religious festival, celebrated on 1 February to mark the beginning of spring.
Imeacht gan teacht ort	"May you leave without returning".
Irish acre	Unit of measurement historically used in Ireland, slightly larger than a standard acre. One Irish acre equates to 1.62 English acres.
Jig/Reel	Lively Irish/Scottish folk dance. Also refers to the accompanying music.
Leannán Sidhe	Female "faery lover" in Celtic mythology. She seeks out artists and poets, and in return for inspiration, she feeds off their life force.
Lios	Ring fort or enclosure; property belonging to a chieftain or group.
Lir	King of the ocean.
Lughnasa	The Celtic harvest festival named for Lugh, one of the chief gods of the *Tuatha Dé Danaan*.
Màistreàs	Mistress.
Mavourneen	My darling.
Merrow	Mermaid.
Mo chroí/A chroi	My heart.
Nuada Airgethlam	Lord of Tir na Nóg, first king of the Tuatha Dé Danaan.
Og	Irish for young. Tomás Og is "young Tomás".
Ollphéist	Monster.
Pict	An ancient Celtic warrior race.
Publican	Proprietor/Licensee of a public house (pub).
Ráth	A walled enclosure in Irish antiquity.
Sidhe	The people of the *Tuatha Dé Danaan* (*see entry*), aka the Fair Folk; *Daoine Sidhe*; the faerie race (as "sidhe" (lower case) it refers to the mythological underground palaces in which the Sidhe live, aka Fairy Hills); singular "Sidh", a faerie.
Sithen	A fairy mound.
Tiarna an Ama	Lord of time.
Tir fo Thoinn	The Land Beneath the Waves.
Tir na Nóg	The Land of Eternal Youth.
Tuatha Dé Danaan	Mythical Irish race.
Will o' the wisp	The fabled lights of the fey.

Author Biographies

Cat Adams
Cat Adams is the new pen name of USA *Today* bestselling authors C. T. Adams and Cathy Clamp. The *Romantic Times* BOOKreviews Career Achievement Award winning paranormal romance and urban fantasy authors live in Texas and Colorado. Their award-winning "Tales of the Sazi" and "Thrall" series for Tor Books will soon be joined by a new urban fantasy series "The Blood Singer", in 2010.
www.catadams.net

Jennifer Ashley
Jennifer Ashley is the *USA Today* bestselling and RITA-award-winning author of historical romances, paranormal romances and mainstream novels. She also writes award-winning paranormal romances as Allyson James and award-winning historical mysteries as Ashley Gardner. Read more about Shifters and their prides, packs and clans in *Pride Mates*, by Jennifer Ashley, Book 1 of the Shifters Unbound series.
www.jennifersromances.com

Ciar Cullen
Ciar Cullen is the award-winning author of paranormal romances, fantasies and Irish-American short stories.
www.ciarcullen.com

Claire Delacroix

Bestselling author Claire Delacroix has always loved stories, both telling them and hearing them. She sold her first romance novel – set in the medieval period – *The Romance of the Rose* in 1992, and has been happily writing ever since. *The Beauty*, part of her bestselling Bride Quest series, was her first title to land on the *New York Times* Extended List of Bestselling Books. Claire also writes romances as Claire Cross and as Deborah Cooke.

www.delacroix.net

Dara England

The pen name of Carol Green – a writer of fantasy, paranormal romance, and historical fiction – Dara's work has appeared in print and electronic format from such publishers as Lyrical Press, Allegory, Art & Prose, and many more. She lives in a small town in Oklahoma with her husband, two children, and a Yorkshire terrier named Ajax.

www. daraenglandauthor.com

Roberta Gellis

Roberta Gellis has been one of the most successful writers of historical fiction of the last few decades, having published more than forty meticulously researched historical novels since 1965. Most recently, Gellis has been writing historical mystery and historical fantasy. Gellis has been the recipient of many awards, including the Silver and Gold Medal Porgy for historical novels from the *West Coast Review of Books*, the Golden Certificate from Affaire de Coeur, The *Romantic Times* Award for Best Novel in the Medieval Period (several times) and a Lifetime Achievement Award for Historical Fantasy and Romance Writers of America's Lifetime Achievement Award.

www.robertagellis.com

Kathleen Givens

The author of bestselling historical romances set in the British Isles, her books, which range from the thirteenth to the eighteenth centuries, have been translated into six languages. She is currently working on the latest in her Highland Shore series.

www.kathleengivens.com

Cindy Holby

The author of the bestselling Wind series, Cindy Holby also writes award-winning sci fi/romance under the name Colby Hodge.

www.cindyholby.com

Shirley Kennedy

Shirley Kennedy is the author of numerous Regency romances for both Ballantine and Signet.

www.shirleykennedy.com

Susan Krinard

New York Times bestseller Susan Krinard is the author of over twenty paranormal romance and fantasy novels. She makes her home in New Mexico, the "Land of Enchantment", with her husband Serge, their dogs Freya, Nahla and Cagney, and their cats Agatha and Jefferson.

www.susankrinard.com

Jenna Maclaine

Jenna Maclaine is the author of the highly reviewed Cin Craven series, paranormal romances that span the centuries.

www.jennamaclaine.com

Margo Maguire

Margo Maguire is the author of seventeen historical romance novels, published in more than twenty languages. For more Druzai stories, featuring Ana MacLochlainn's hunky cousins, try Margo's Warrior series.

www.margomaguire.com

Pat McDermott

A frequent visitor to Ireland, Pat McDermott is the author of the romantic alternate-Irish history adventure, *A Band of Roses*, and its forthcoming sequel, *Fiery Roses*. Pat, a Boston, Massachusetts-native now lives in New Hampshire, where she is working on her next novel.

www.patmcdermott.net

Cindy Miles

National bestselling author of ghost and paranormal romances set in England, Scotland and Wales. Cindy Miles spins tales of ghostly heroes from the past encountering their soulmate heroines of the present.

www.cindy-miles.com

Penelope Neri

British author Penelope Neri is the bestselling author of more than twenty-five historical romance novels, which feature various time periods and exotic locales. She is best known for her acclaimed Viking trilogy – *Sea Jewel*, *Enchanted* and *The Love Within*.

www.penelopeneri.com

Sandra Newgent

Her first short story appeared in *The Mammoth Book of Time Travel Romance*. She writes paranormal, time travel, romantic adventure and historical romance.

Patricia Rice

New York Times and *USA Today* bestseller Patricia Rice is the author of over forty-five contemporary, historical and paranormal romances, including her popular Mystic Isle series set during the French Revolution.

www.patriciarice.com

Helen Scott Taylor

Winner of the American Title IV contest, Helen Scott Taylor writes contemporary fantasy romance based on Celtic and Norse mythology. The first book in her Magic Knot Fairies series was chosen as a *Booklist* Top Ten Romance for 2009.
www.helenscotttaylor.com

Sue-Ellen Welfonder

USA Today bestselling author of Scottish medieval romances, including her popular MacKenzies of Kintail series, Sue-Ellen also writes Scottish-set paranormals under the pseudonym Allie Mackay.
www.welfonder.com

Nadia Williams

Author of Irish mythology-themed romance and erotic novels. Nadia has had short stories published in well-known fantasy e-zines such as Dragons, Knights & Angels (now Double Edged Publishing). Her novels *The Pebble* and *The Ancient* (under pseudonym Anida Adler) are available online.
www.nadiawilliams.co.uk